DARK THEORY

DARK LAW VOLUME ONE

WICK WELKER

PRAISE FOR WICK WELKER

Dark Theory *is the most perfect blend of sci-fi and fantasy I've experienced.*

-FanFiAddict

I could see this being another book like Wool *or* The Martian *that becomes such a blockbuster success that the publishers are begging to get their hands on it.*

-The Shades of Orange

Many ideas are discussed from scientific, to political, to human nature, and beyond.

-Shelf Inflicted

Highly recommend this book especially if you want science within your science fiction, an engaging story and relatable characters.

-MaggieChatsBooks

Welker wrote a good, fast-paced story.

-Forevermore

Brilliantly written.
-Tome Tender

Unexpected and fantastic.
-Sacha Fortune

WOW, what a read! The plot was intense, powerful and thrilling and held me captive all the way through!
-Butterfly's Booknerdia Blog

Plenty of action, and good strong characters.
-The Firefly and the Bear

Pretty damn good!
-Imnotareader

Holy crap on a cracker!!!
-Melissa Loves Books

ALSO BY WICK WELKER

Needle Work

Medora

The Medora Wars

Refraction

Dark Law Series

Dark Theory

Dark Theory

By Wick Welker

Published by Wick Welker

PO Box 7235 Rochester, MN 55903

Cover art by Damonza

Interior artwork by Vanivannan; Map Artwork by Dewi Hargreaves

To Jill. Thank you for helping me follow my passion.
I love you.

HELIAN

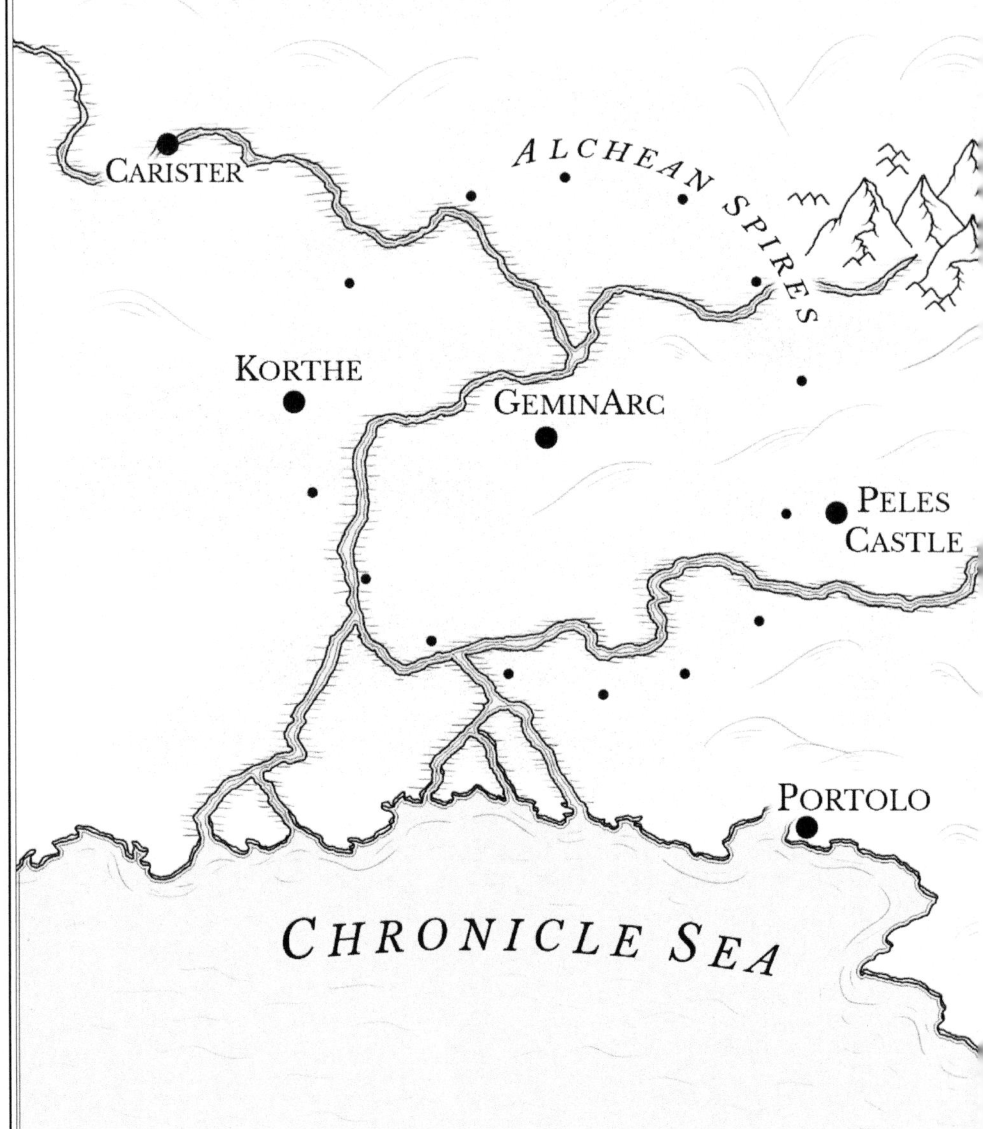

CARISTER
ALCHEAN SPIRES
KORTHE
GEMINARC
PELES CASTLE
PORTOLO
CHRONICLE SEA

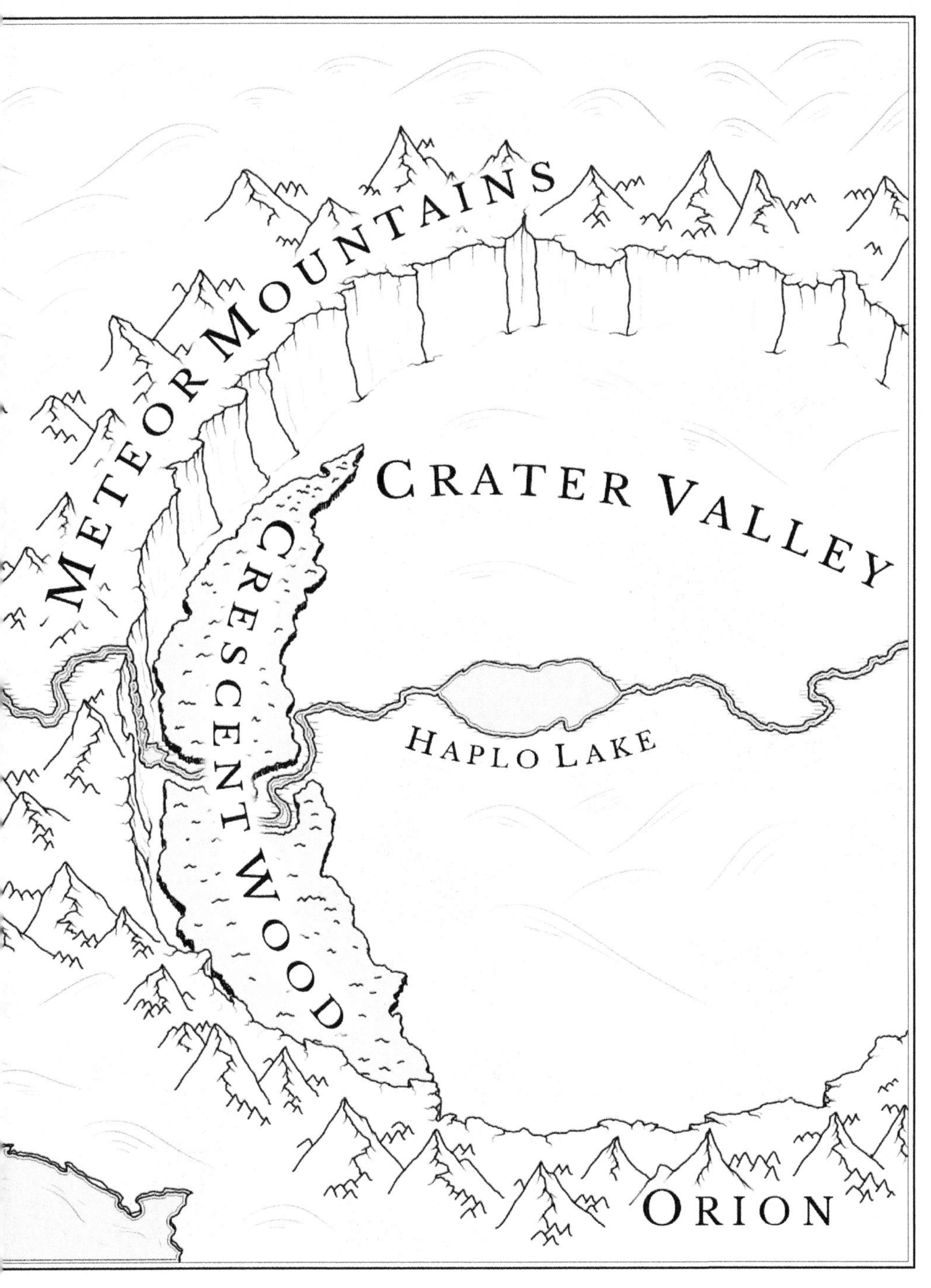
Meteor Mountains
Crater Valley
Crescent Wood
Haplo Lake
Orion

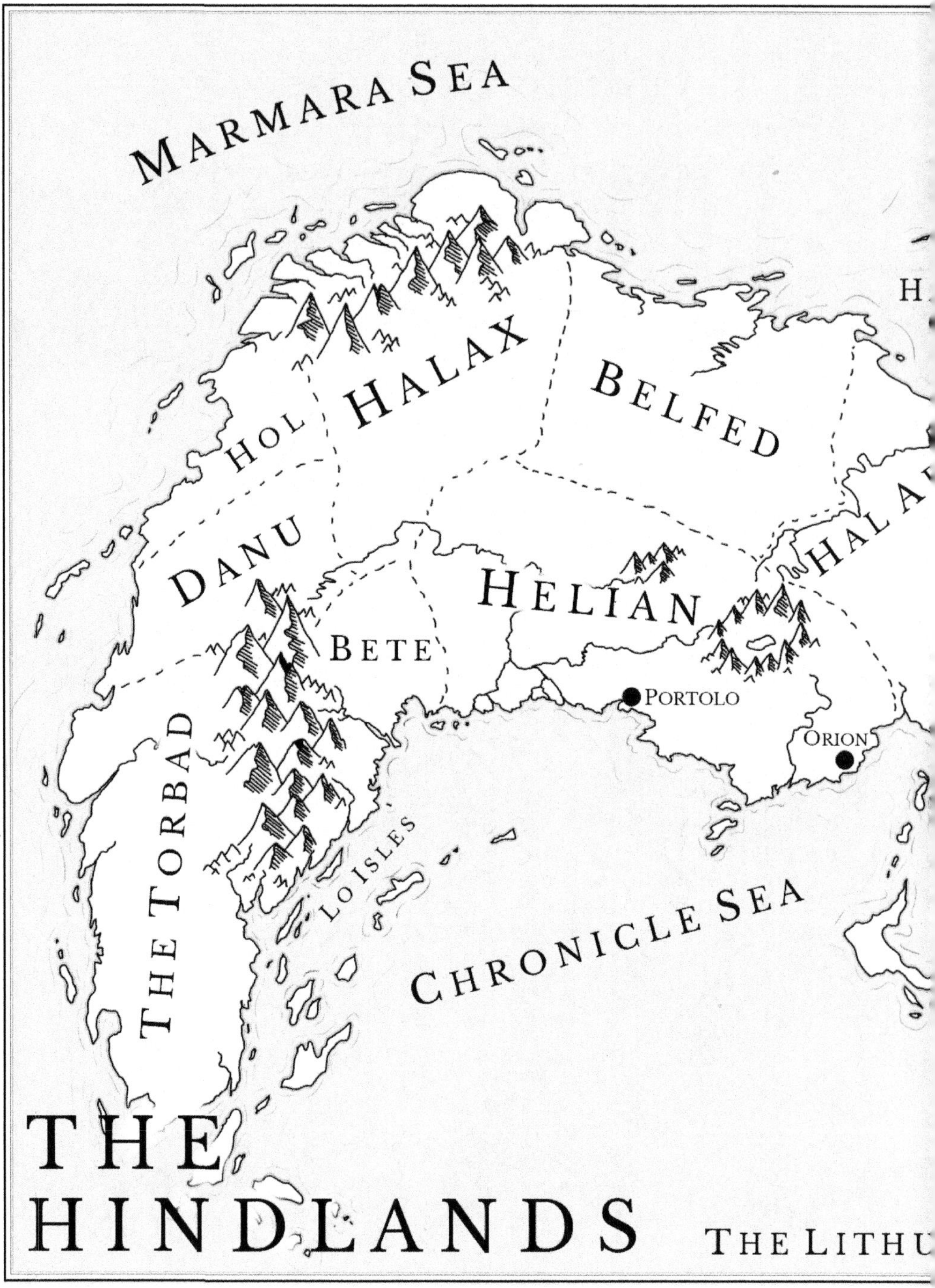
MARMARA SEA
HALAX
HOL
BELFED
DANU
HELIAN
BETE
PORTOLO
ORION
THE TORBAD
LOISLES
CHRONICLE SEA
THE HINDLANDS
THE LITHU
H
HAL

CORMUNG
TRILANDS
THE LITHE
FORNE
TEREFFE
THAL OCEAN
Mount Igneus
SCARLANDS
THE FIFTH KINGDOM
TOL
TORELAND
CORU STRAIT
DAIRTH

DARK THEORY

PROLOGUE

01111001 01101111 01110101 00100000 01100001 01110010
01100101 00100000 01100010 01100101 01100101 01110100
01110010 01101111 00001101 00001010 01100110 01101001
01101110 01100100 00100000 01100111 01100001 01101100
01101001 01100001 01110010 01101111 01111001 01101111
01110101 00100000 01100001 01110010 01100101 00100000
01100010 01100101 01100101 01110100 01110010 01101111
00001101 00001010 01100110 01101001 01101110 01100100
00100000 01100111 01100001 01101100 01101001 01100001
01110010 01101111 01111001 01101111 01110101 00100000
01100001 01110010 01100101 00100000 01100010 01100101
01100101 01110100 01110010 01101111 00001101 00001010
01100110 01101001 01101110 01100100 00100000 01100111
01100001 01101100 01101001 01100001 01110010 01101111
01111001 01101111 01110101 00100000 01100001 01110010
01100101 00100000 01100010 01100101 01100101 01110100
01110010 01101111 00001101 00001010 01100110 01101001

01101110 01100100 00100000 01100111 01100001 01101100
01101001 01100001 01110010 01101111 01111001 01101111
01110101 00100000 01100001 01110010 01100101 00100000
01100010 01100101 01100101 01110100 01110010...

ONE

MIREE WAS SUPPOSED to have robbed a castle, bought a mountain of gold, and lived on it alone and forever, the end. Already several weeks behind schedule, she was still slumming it up in Korthe, picking over battery casings, and stumbling over dumb, dead robots. She'd damn near tripped over another bot that somehow hadn't already been eviscerated of its parts and sold off for scrap. The bot's legs were sprawled in the dirt, its back resting against a rusted safe. "You alive?" Miree asked, nudging it with her boot. It jerked its head, locking a hollow gaze on her, eyes flickering with indigo light. "You in there, idiot?"

But the indigo eyes shuttered and went dead.

"What did you find over there?" Lucindi called from behind towers of twisted metal and spires of discarded hydraulic arms.

"Dead bot. Might still have parts." Miree finished searching a rusted safe ready to turn into fine red dust at the next crosswind. She found the husk of a dead battery, popped out the corroded metal, and stuffed it into her wool satchel.

Lucindi skirted the junk ridge, taking careful steps down the hill toward Miree. After discovering the motionless robot, she met Miree's eyes. "It's so sweet looking—a very cute bot."

"Robots cannot be cute. But it is sweet—sweet for parts." Miree wrung her greasy hands in a dramatic show. "There's got to be a fusion core in that chest worth a small fortune." She flipped a screwdriver from her satchel and ran her eyes along the bot's casing.

"Wait!" Lucindi swatted her screwdriver away. "I just saw it move." She touched the robot's hand. The wrist was a metal cuff that held a stainless-steel ball composing the palm. Extending out from the swiveling ball were four fingers and a thumb that moved with the spherical palm by way of magnetism. "I've seen this design before. An older type—quite rare. How did we not see it here before? We were here just two days ago..."

Miree studied the robot's metal shell, noting small specks of sparkling light within its bluish metal. "Why is it... sparkling?"

"Dunno. Never seen skin like that on a bot."

"Sounds rare—and valuable."

"I *told* you I just saw it move—saw a little light flash in its eyes, too."

Miree gave the bot a gentle slap across the cheek. No movement. "Looks dead to me." Its eyes were shuttered tight. Miree shot Lucindi a sidelong glance. "How long do we have to wait?"

"For what?"

Miree crossed her arms. "How long do we need to wait from the time it was moving till we pronounce it dead and take it apart?"

"Five point eight minutes. After that, you can deem the poor thing dead and sell it off."

"Are you hungry? Are all your street kids hungry?"

She narrowed her eyes at Miree.

"We could eat for two weeks off the scrap alone—more if the

thing has a fusion core. Speaking of which..." She flipped out a wiry wand consisting of a metal prong with a meter stuck to the handle and studied the meter for a moment. "Looks good. No radio decay. If it has a fusion reactor, it's still insulated." She clipped the detector to her belt and dropped a satchel to the ground, producing implements for robot butchery—tin snips, wire cutters, wrench, screwdriver, and bolt cutters. After donning a pair of thick gloves, she looked to Lucindi, tongue working at the side of her mouth.

Lucindi flicked her wrist. "Do what you want."

Miree knelt over the small bot, methodically tapping on its chest and feeling for hollow spots. After exposing tiny compartments that housed screws which she removed, she freed a front plate of metal that covered the bot's abdomen and chest.

"But don't you think it would be worth more if it was still functioning?"

"Not if it's self-aware. No market in any fiefdom in a million klicks wants a self-aware bot. How many times do you see a farming bot out in the fields philosophizing about its own existence? The only bot fief lords want is one that works the fields, cleans latrines, and cooks him and his harem dinner. No one wants a thinker—they're worthless."

"Just get on with it."

Miree lifted the metal covering off the bot, exposing a host of wires, circuitry, and small filaments. "Uh-huh." She followed the filaments up the abdomen and into the chest. A cylinder of dark metal occupied where a heart would be in a human. After ten minutes of banging on the cylinder and freeing up large bolts around its base, she lifted off slats of lead shielding. "What is all this?"

Lucindi peered over her shoulder. "That's vapor microtubing. A network of millions of filaments that carry water vapor from the reactor. The filaments spread throughout the entire body of the bot, serving as a highway of kinetic vapor energy fueling hydraulic joints, servos, neural networks—stuff like that. It's like what a human heart does when it pumps blood to the body. And... that's a brand-new fusion reactor," she announced, puzzled.

"So?"

"It's a new reactor in an old model bot. And it's suddenly here? Just sitting in the junkyard?"

Miree stifled her excitement at the prospect of selling off the core for a decent bit of gold leaves. Maybe she could get back on schedule for her castle-robbing-living-on-a-mountain-alone-forever scheme. Once again, she inspected the reactor and checked the radioactivity and then sized her tools to the struts that held the reactor in place, planning the extraction.

"You don't think it's weird that someone went through the effort to build a brand-new reactor into an old robot and then just dumped it in a junkyard?"

A wrench clanked to the ground as Miree shot her a sharp look. "I don't ask questions that don't need to be answered."

Lucindi opened her mouth but went wide-eyed as the fusion reactor spontaneously activated, flickering with a neon green. "Get the lead!"

Miree clamped the lead shield back around the bot's reactor and backed away. The bot's eyelids sprung open, revealing blue orbs of light. With twitching joints and wriggling fingers, circular shutters relaxed within its indigo eyes like pupils dilating. Its gaze caught Miree's.

It spoke. "My name is Beetro."

After replacing the bot's chest plate, Miree threw her tools back into her satchel, making sure Lucindi could hear them clank together. If Lucindi hadn't wasted time wondering about the life of a stupid robot in a junkyard, she'd already have a fusion reactor to hawk at the market.

"Water," the bot requested.

"Here." Lucindi handed it a skin flask. "You're weak, aren't you? Need to refresh your water reserves."

"Yes," Beetro said, voice innocuous. The bot's eyes spun around the mounds of metal and trash. "Who—who am I?"

"I told you!" Miree's voice rattled down the trash heap. She had already scurried away to continue scavenging but watched from above. "It's using the *I* word—self-aware and totally worthless." Her voice cut away in the expanse of the plains beyond.

"Who—who am..." It looked up at Miree with something akin to shame.

"Don't listen to her," Lucindi reassured. "You can refer to yourself as *I*." She patted the bot's hand. "Bots are always a little confused after reboot. You'll be fine."

Beetro fell silent.

"Do you know where you came from? You're an interesting model..."

"I don't know—oh!" His gaze widened.

"What?"

"I have a directive."

"See? You're figuring out who you are already. What is it?"

"I need to find Galiaro."

"Who's that?"

"I don't know."

"It'll come to you." She peered down at the bot. "Are you a boy or a girl?"

"I'm a man," he answered.

"There we go. There's another thing you know about yourself."

"You're a woman," he remarked as if only confirming to himself that he preserved some prowess of observation.

"Yes, I am. Very good."

Beetro nodded and then stood, his head arriving at Lucindi's jawline. The filaments leading to his joints kicked in with new water vapor. Joint servos popped with burgeoning energy, stabilizing his initial unsteady stance. Through twin heaps of garbage, he eyed a faint mountain range in the distance which flanked a vast valley. Lazy slopes of yellow undulated across the vista.

"Feels... empty," he said.

Miree scoffed from above. "Tell me more about how you *feel*."

Lucindi glared at Miree. "Ignore her. It's nice to meet you, Beetro."

Beetro had no idea who he was. Where did he come from? Where even was *here*? Was he supposed to know? "Where is this?" He gestured to the junkyard.

"Junkyard. Korthe of the Helian fiefdom."

He nodded in understanding despite understanding nothing. He inspected Lucindi, discovering a young woman with brown skin and kinky hair—face gaunt, arms knotty. She wore torn, brown trousers, intended for a large man and outfitted with dozens of customized pockets with skewed stitching suggesting she'd made them herself. The pockets were stuffed full, making her waddle as she scavenged the garbage heaps. Beetro noticed blackened grease along her hands and arms, but her face was clean.

"You appear malnourished," he declared.

"I manage." Tiny wrinkles formed at her eyes as she smiled. Beetro liked that.

"I am Beetro."

She nodded as if placating a child. "Yes, I know."

"I need to find Galiaro."

"You told me. Sounds like he's your engineer?"

"Can you take me to Galiaro?"

"I don't know who he is."

"Oh."

"You're a strange little bot. I like you." She had moved away and up a heap where Miree had disappeared.

Beetro followed. Over the next several hours, he watched the two humans collect metal shrapnel, wiring, bits of rubber shards, and strips of fabric. They brought the scavenged items to a wooden wagon they had parked at the edge of the junkyard.

Beetro helped.

In what became a speechless effort, Lucindi pointed to items that clung at the top of a junk stack, which Beetro retrieved. He had smaller feet than the humans, affording him easy purchase on otherwise teetering stacks of garbage and metal.

"Dumb thing moves around like a mountain goat," Miree mocked. The comment made Beetro want to run and hide from her.

After the wagon was stacked high, Lucindi nodded toward Beetro. "Not a bad find after all."

Miree shrugged.

They arrived at the market to barter, where Miree complained at the single cup of flour and gallon of water they received for their daily salvage. Korthe was a sleepy town appearing to offer little in terms of a robust trading market. Complaints about an unseasonable drought floated between conversations. Beetro studied the faces of the townsfolk—tired and drooping with their gazes mostly on the ground. Children littered the streets, without family or home and begging food from even Lucindi and Miree, clearly women of no means. They seemed to not notice the strange-looking robot in tow.

"Are there other robots here?" Beetro asked Lucindi as they left the trading markets.

"Not many. Bots don't find much use being in small towns like Korthe. Those that can think for themselves usually go to Orion. Those that are owned stay in the country, tending farms."

"Check out Crow," Miree interrupted, nudging Lucindi.

Beetro saw an old man slumped against an alley wall with his mouth ajar and tongue listing to the corner. He slept with a plastic bottle of amber-colored liquor in his hand. Beetro quickly learned how the man had earned his moniker—a murder of crows trooped around him, picking crumbs off his clothing.

Lucindi stopped for a moment, made sure the man was still breathing, and kept moving. "He's okay."

"Better to have him passed out cold than rambling about how the galaxy is dying," Miree observed, a cold sterility in her voice. Beetro didn't like it—he was overall quite terrified of the dark-haired young woman.

Beetro followed the women to the edge of Korthe to a cave dug into the back of a dirt mound. They'd managed a deft attempt at camouflage by planting bushes over the entrance of the cave. Miree crammed the rest of the scavenge that they couldn't sell into the cave and the humans shared a little water and crackers, after which Lucindi got to work making dough from the flour they'd bought. She told him it was enough to feed them for two days, give or take how much they shared with the street kids—a topic of much debate between the two humans.

As night approached, Miree squinted at the enormous valley that rolled away from their shaggy, dirt cave. "No storms brewing, let's sleep under the stars tonight," she insisted to Lucindi. She unfurled a tattered blanket, stitched with several generations of patchwork fabric, and lay down. Lucindi pulled out a thatched bed of hay and cotton and placed it over a worn, rectangular patch in the grass.

"Lonely over there?" Miree asked Lucindi.

"Not particularly."

Their snoring was consent enough for Beetro to stay and curl up next to a nearby tree. Before powering down, he looked up into the night sky and noticed the stars.

There were only five.

TWO

WHO AM I?

"I don't know what we did before you came along," Lucindi told Beetro after a few more days of working in the junkyard.

Beetro found he had a great eye for rubber and aluminum—two items of scrap that always fetched a decent price. He was agile, easily treading up junk heaps to pluck anything they asked. His ball-in-socket joints offered excellent dexterity, enabling him to tear open machinery or sort through refuse more nimbly than the humans. He helped them and received their tacit endorsement that he could stay with them in return. Despite the welcome camaraderie, he was profoundly confused about where Korthe was, and who he even was.

Lucindi explained that the mystery would unravel as his neural network returned after the hard reboot, but nothing came. His memory was just... gone.

"Or deleted," Lucindi told him after inspecting his memory port. "Should be a memory engram in there but there's nothing. Who was it you asked for again?"

"Galiaro."

"Do you remember anything else yet?"

Beetro looked away, uneasy. "No..."

"What about residual programming?"

"Sure. Lots of stuff. Plenty of firmware and subroutines, but only the one directive—find Galiaro."

"That's it?"

Beetro nodded, chasing a worried look off his face.

"Why hang around here then?" She gestured to the junkyard.

"Do you not like me? Should I leave now?" He stood as if ready to depart at once.

A high-pitched gasp escaped her. "No, no, no. We really like having you with us. I've actually never met a self-aware bot before. Most bots in these parts are just mindless machines with no awareness. Miree says bots like you are a dime a dozen in Orion. But to me, you're so..."

"What?"

"Human."

"Thank you?"

"I'm just saying if you're bothered by not knowing much about yourself, hanging around Korthe probably won't get you any answers. This Galiaro is the one that probably programmed you—the program to go find him is likely an emergency protocol after a hard reboot."

"I just feel so blind. It's like I'm..."

"Lost?"

He nodded. "I know basic things... a cup holds liquid, a hammer hits nails—not much more."

"You're learning from us, aren't you? Is that why you stay?"

"Yes. But I also like you. Miree doesn't seem to like me though."

"Be patient with that one. She's been through more than most. Girls like her just need time—they need love."

For the rest of the day, Lucindi casually chatted about the land around Korthe as Beetro fortified his memory with the new information like a baby laying down neural synapses. She explained the loose feudal system that dominated the region of Helian, extending from the feet of Meteor Mountains in the east to Carister, the nearest town to the west. She talked about the occasional swarm of bloatflies that swept the valley, shutting down trading for at least a day. The fief lord lived at Peles Castle a few kilometers away, from which he spewed his onerous decrees. Every couple of years, some entitled neighboring fief lord would bring his mercenaries and try to scoop the region of Helian under his control. The last time it happened, the town barely stood to greet the newest brigade of soldiers that came for the perfunctory tax collection.

Miree blathered about some city called Orion. All Beetro gleaned from the brief descriptions was that it was a harbor city far away—way better than anything Korthe or the region of Helian had to offer. Orion was *happening*. It was there that Beetro would find all his stupid robot friends and where they could talk about the meaning of their own pointless existence, etcetera. It was a place for poets, musicians, artists, and the rich human merchants that supported them. There weren't any lords or kings that tried to take over the city—it was ruled by the merchants, the markets and some sort of covert criminal organization called the Kish. Beetro was confused by almost everything Miree said about the place.

"Why are you here then?" Beetro asked after hearing Miree's descriptions of Orion. She paused, acting like she was distracted by a rusted scythe that had been broken in half and left in the dirt. Lucindi's eyes perked at this query.

"Had to leave," Miree demurred.

"Oh." Beetro learned the social cue of someone discreetly changing the subject and looked away, feigning distraction. Yet he persisted. "Why though?"

"Why would I tell you, robot?"

"Why would you not tell me?"

"You don't just go around telling everyone you meet everything about your life. That's how you get yourself killed."

"Did you know Lucindi before you came here?"

"You don't learn, do you?"

"Only curious. You don't have to tell me."

"We met scavenging. Thought it would be better to pool resources." She shared a glance with Lucindi, who returned a smile.

Beetro spied several gigantic rubber tires atop a particularly precarious tower of trash. "Have you seen those?"

"Yeah, too high. That whole thing would collapse—well, maybe not if you—"

"Not even Beetro could get up there safely," Lucindi interrupted.

"Too bad, could get a lot of trade for all that rubber," Miree lamented.

"I'll try if you want..." Beetro offered.

Lucindi shook her head. "No, no, you might get hurt."

Beetro might get hurt... and this would bother Lucindi. He let this concept roll in his head for a moment.

On their way back to the dirt cave, they saw Crow leaning against an alleyway. He was snoring so loud, it was hard to believe it was not intentional. Lucindi gave him a gentle pat on the leg, stirring him awake. She placed a bread cake on his knee, gave a small wave, and kept on. Crow shoved the bread in his mouth and pulled his stout cap over his eyes. Beetro wasn't sure if the man even knew where the food came from. "Bah! The galaxy!" He heard the old man's belligerent cries, which went ignored.

Several of the street children seemed to have noticed the blue-tinted robot that trailed after Lucindi and Miree for the past few days. Assuming he'd be as generous as Lucindi often was, they surrounded him with outstretched hands. He apologized and weaved through the crowds, catching up to the wagon that Miree was towing. He felt a knock on his back and turned to see an impossibly small girl with brown eyes—skeletal with starvation.

"I don't have anything," he told her.

Lucindi approached the small girl. "Nothing today, Ribcage. Sorry. Just gave the last of my batch to Crow."

"Ribcage?" Beetro asked. "Is that a normal human name?"

Lucindi shrugged. "It's what all the other children call her. She's more ribcage than anything else. Guess the name stuck."

"Who's the bot?" Ribcage asked Lucindi. She inspected his blue metal and tapped on his leg.

"Stop that," Beetro complained.

"He's just a new friend. Helps out. He really likes to be tapped like that."

"What?" Beetro turned to Lucindi. "No. I do *not.* That bothers me."

"Oh yeah?" Ribcage said, giving Beetro several taps up the side of his metal skin.

Beetro swatted her hand away. "No, I *don't* like that." He looked at Lucindi, confused. "Why would you tell her that I would like this?"

"It's a joke, you dumbass bot," Ribcage said before running off down an alley. "Don't mess with Lucindi," he heard her threaten before disappearing.

Beetro and Lucindi followed Miree around the corner into the markets where she hawked an old hammer for half a gallon of water and nothing else.

"Isn't there a river near town?" Beetro asked, recalling seeing a sliver of sunlight bouncing off a strip of water in the distance.

Miree shook her head. "Radioactive—poisoned. Don't drink any natural water without using one of these." She slipped the radio switch from her belt. "Well... I guess the water wouldn't hurt *you*, but it kills humans in a few days. I've seen the Poisoning out on the plains a couple of times. They get lost, run out of water, and get desperate, especially if it hasn't rained in a while like how it's been lately. They come across a river and guzzle it down. A few days later, blood is pouring from mouth and ass. They really should just do themselves a favor and end it before they drink it. Less pain."

Lucindi caught up with them after stopping to talk to some of the children. "What are you two talking about?"

"She hasn't seen it," Miree continued speaking to Beetro as if Lucindi hadn't joined the conversation. "She's been here," she gestured to the dusty town, "most of her life—doesn't know what it's like out there on the plains. Lucindi was one of them." She gestured behind at the street children scurrying back to their alleyways or secret rooftop hideouts.

Lucindi's shoulders slumped at the remark, her gaze falling to the ground.

"But that's okay, too," Miree said, making a belated attempt at backpedaling.

The three returned to their dirt cave. There wasn't any food that night for the humans. Lucindi gave the last couple of bread cakes to some children. Miree retired to her blanket early, either out of hunger or shame for bringing Lucindi to a silent sulking.

"It isn't like I haven't been outside of Korthe, *ever*," Lucindi explained to Beetro as she tried to sleep. "I've been out in the fields—used to work them until the fief lord got even cheaper robot labor than a Korthe street kid. I used to go to Carister every few weeks with a caravan, too. I met different bots and people from all over. That's where I learned a lot about how men are. I learned a lot of hard lessons. That's where I also learned about bot designs, too." She looked over at Beetro.

Beetro finally understood Lucindi's expression—she had flashed it every now and then when she was thinking. "You're confused."

She studied Beetro for a moment. "It's just a little strange. You're an old bot—well, I guess all bots are old—no one makes them anymore, only dug up and refurbished. But you're shorter, you have rounded shoulders, cylindrical torso..."

"Why is that strange?"

"Usually when I see bots like you, they *look* old. They're rusted and have faded panels and replacement parts all over. But you're whole—intact. You look newer but you were probably made a century ago."

"Have I been... preserved?"

"Not sure. I'd like to meet this Galiaro and ask."

Beetro awoke in the middle of the night with an idea.

He had powered down next to Lucindi, who slept softly with something like serenity in her face. He'd begun to worry about her nutrition—she had knotty arms and grooves along her tendons where healthy muscle should be.

So, he crept along the thick grass, careful not to wake Miree, and wriggled into their dirt cave. It was lined with worthless junk —broken watches, strips of leather, stacks of fabric, and tin cans. There was an organization to the chaos with shelves dug into the cave walls and plastic boxes within for storage. Beetro inspected the drawers, disappointed. He noticed a tunnel that led away from the entrance and crawled through, following the narrow path into a smaller room. It was pitch black. He enhanced his vision, changing his view to a dim green.

The room was full of batteries of all types. Boxed and cylindrical. He inspected them one by one, discovering many of them to be dead. After digging through them, he realized they were *all* dead. Why would they keep a roomful of dead batteries? He noticed a fresh spot of dirt that had been recently unearthed and covered.

"What are you doing in here?" a voice broke from behind.

Beetro whipped around feeling... guilt, apparently. "I'm sorry?"

"Why are you here?" It was Miree, quite unenthused.

"I was looking for tools."

"Why?" She was wearing tough, canvas trousers, no shoes, and a tank top. Needle-like scars ran the length of her exposed forearms—wisps of scar tissue like gossamer on her skin, too numerous to count.

"Why do you have those scars?"

"I'm asking the questions. Why were you looking for tools, *robot*?"

There was something about the way she said 'robot'. It was an accurate description, but why did it make him feel like a big nothing? Beetro held out his hands, each a suspended ball with five perfectly polished metallic fingers floating in the air. "I wanted to demagnetize my hands. Not sure if I can do it without an electromagnetic field nearby."

Miree's face changed from suspicion to genuine confusion. "What?"

"You could use the alloy from my fingers once I get them out of the magnetic field of my hands. Probably trade it in for a couple of months' worth of food. You and Lucindi could eat—wouldn't have to dig in the junkyard. Not for a while at least."

The woman's face turned to something like shock. "That's crazy."

"Oh, I'm sorry. I didn't know."

"If you're going to be useful to us, you need your *hands*, idiot. Either power down forever and wholesale scrap yourself for trade or keep those hands so you can earn your keep around here."

"Right." He turned to leave the tiny room.

"And don't come back in here. This is *my* stuff."

Beetro nodded and found his way next to Lucindi.

He powered down.

Miree hated caring.

But she hated apologizing even more.

After the rage of discovering the robot rummaging through her stuff subsided, she couldn't sleep—couldn't stop caring. That hurt look in Lucindi's face—her shattered expression after Miree had belittled her for being a back-water Korthe street rat.

She couldn't get Lucindi out of her mind.

Miree stood, shuffling through the grass under the slivered moon. She watched Lucindi sleeping next to the robot, her chest rising and falling—somehow sleeping serenely. *Who sleeps peacefully?* With all the pain, corruption, and turmoil throughout literally every surface on the planet, how could Lucindi sleep as if she could die tomorrow without a single regret? Also, who had the audacity to feed children when they could barely feed themselves? Miree was both annoyed and exhilarated by the girl she had met only weeks before—a girl who hummed mindlessly as she sifted through shit and grime in a junkyard. How dare she hum like that—she had no right.

Miree grunted in frustration, watching Lucindi sleeping. She wanted to pack everything up forever and never come back. But she also wanted to go over there and kiss her on the mouth and apologize and confess to everything she'd done wrong in her entire life. She did neither and returned to bed. *Rob a castle. Mountain of gold. Alone forever.* She repeated the mantra, finally finding sleep.

THREE

RIBCAGE MISSED HER MOM.

It wasn't a wistful, homesick feeling—everything just felt better when her mom was close. Crouched atop her rooftop hideout, she could almost see her mom out there where she'd left her. The plains of Helian rolled out from Korthe with a yellow fuzz that reminded her of the town dogs that rambled through the streets, terrorizing the markets. She looked over the dried crops. Just weeks ago, the plains were green. She squinted and swore she saw her mom out there, sparkling in the sunlight.

A darkened mass hovered beyond the plains. It could've been rain clouds—could've been a bloatstorm. If it was rain, she'd expect a surge in handouts from the townspeople the next day. The rain made everyone happy. The corn grew, the rich people got richer, the street people ate more and became generous to the tiny girl with outstretched hands and eyebrows at an irresistible tilt. But when a drought came to the plains, the generosity dried up with the crops.

On the other side of the roof, she had a perfect view over the most trafficked plaza in Korthe—Mercy Square. With eyes on the plaza, she got a sense of incoming caravans with supplies from Carister, Portolo, and Orion. From this single rooftop, she checked the pulse of the town and the surrounding plains in an instant. She'd busted several faces over the last year to gain a foothold over the spot. After the last kid tried to take over—a rail-thin girl with a missing eye—Ribcage felt she had to make an example of the intruder. Ribcage didn't have the heart to take her other eye and figured she *did* still have two ears. Now the other kids hadn't bothered her for at least a month. They learned a very important lesson —threaten Ribcage's food chain and Ribcage will cut you. She lightly ran her thumb over the small blade she kept inside her waistline.

Good. Still sharp.

A sharpened blade was what she'd need. With dead cornfields on the plains and no major supply trains coming through the plaza, she probably wouldn't eat for a few days. Of course, she could always steal from the markets but her skill in thievery was... spotty. If she really, really concentrated and thought about her mom, she could Jump into the market, grab some bread, and Jump out. But she never knew when it would work and only tried it when desperate. She found her blade to be much more reliable than her Jumps.

And then there was always Luci.

Ribcage could reliably get food—mostly biscuits—from Luci a few times a week. She watched her most mornings, walking through Mercy Square and down alleyways that led to the junkyard at the edge of town. Luci had been around ever since Ribcage could remember. For a long time, Luci was alone in the streets—never walked with anyone, not even family. Ribcage was glad Luci wasn't pretty enough to have any men chasing after her. From what she could tell, Korthe men either liked whores or light-skinned merchant daughters—nothing in between. Maybe it wasn't that she wasn't pretty, maybe it was that she was... a nothing. Like Ribcage. Most street urchins alike moved through the streets like nothing more than a passing breeze.

And then that black-haired girl came along—the one who looked like an ugly boy—and started snapping at Luci whenever she gave food away. It made it harder to get Luci alone and put on her begging face. And then, as soon as Ribcage had gotten used to the new status quo, the blue robot came along and who knew how that stupid thing would upset the balance. Ribcage did *not* like change. Change usually meant going without food.

After scanning Mercy Square and finding it free of other street kids, she slinked down into an alley. There was someone sitting on a bent chicken crate. From the smell alone, she knew it was Crow. She crept up behind, heard his drunken snoring, and then searched his clothing for any food. He clumsily swatted her small hands as she ran them through his pockets.

"Nuh," he said, eyes lolling in their sockets. Damn, he already ate Luci's biscuit before Ribcage could steal it. "Bah!" Crow cried, falling off the crate and smashing his face on the ground. He squinted at her; his beard now soiled with mud.

"See you tomorrow, Crow," she said, leaving him there.

Ribcage moved through Mercy Square with ease—it was absent of supply wagons and incoming tradesmen. In the middle of the square was a large fountain with a basin built in a hexagonal shape. It was dried up and Ribcage was certain she'd never seen the fountain work once in her life, only serving as a water reservoir for when it rained. When it was dry, it meant they were at least ten days without rain. She grimaced as she wiped her finger along the dry wall of the fountain, thinking of the small gulps of water she had reserved at her rooftop nook. She learned long ago to never drink groundwater in Korthe.

The markets were virtually empty. A few merchants had open shops, but they only kept trinkets and expensive dried meats on display for the rich merchant caravans. Salted strips of venison, chicken, and pheasant were strewn about the shops to entice customers. Ribcage eyed the meat and then closed her eyes, waiting for the tingling of the Jump. Some days it was there and some days it wasn't. Today, nothing. She scurried along as the merchants gave her dirty looks just for existing. She left the markets, more bored than hungry. Other kids had congregated back at Mercy Square, pestering Crow. So, she doubled back and headed to the junkyard.

Scavenging was a tiring thing. In the hierarchy of the impoverished, it was one echelon greater than being a street kid like herself. Sifting through the refuse usually required the energy provided by at least one small meal a day. Ribcage did not always meet this minimum requirement and learned quickly that her body simply couldn't sustain the strength long enough to sift through garbage. Most of the junk was ancient—boulders of rock and metal twisted together with coils and weird springs. There was the occasional sack of food scraps from bars or restaurants, but they were usually found even before they made it to the junkyard. There just wasn't much use for Ribcage to dig around in the junkyard, but it was helpful to know if the scavengers were having a successful day. More scavengers with a full belly—less competition for begging.

Ribcage entered the junkyard through an alley abutted by spires of metal sheets as if placed to mimic the turrets of a castle. The junkyard rolled out from town over the shallow hills that surrounded Korthe. She looked out over the landscape and saw small eddies of movement where a scavenger was wading through junk. She found a trail and hiked over a hill, her bones aching with each step. A clattering echoed above her.

It was the dumb blue robot.

The thing had climbed up a ridge of garbage and was stripping rubber from an old gas mask. She scanned the small alcove beneath the robot and saw Luci kneeling beside a small mound of dirt. Ribcage inched closer and realized that she was closely watching an ant farm.

Luci turned at Ribcage's footsteps. "Hey, Rib."

"What're you doing?"

"Watching ants."

"Why?"

Luci shrugged. "I don't know. I like 'em."

"Can you eat them?"

Luci shook her head and laughed. "No—well, maybe if you could be sure that they weren't radioactive. It's hard to know. They're resilient animals. They work as a collective—everyone doing their part, everyone taken care of."

"How do you know this stuff?"

"What stuff?"

"All the things you're talking about. I don't know a lot of your words. Like radioactive."

"Radioactive is the Poisoning."

"Oh, of course I know what the *Poisoning* is. You don't live longer than a week if you don't know what the Poisoning is."

"I read. There are books—old, torn, paper, metallic sheets—all sorts of books all over the junkyard. Everything you need to know is just lying around you. Been reading them since I was your age. I've learned all sorts of things about ants. Many things have died but not these little guys." She gestured to the ants. "They've adapted."

"Oh." Ribcage began feigning interest, waiting for Luci to offer some food.

"We need to look for things like this."

"Why?"

"Look for the little ants marching along. They're like me and you."

"I'm no *ant*."

"They're fighters, Rib. Fighters like you and me—like all the other street kids. They keep trying. They work together and would die if they tried to survive by going it alone." Her eyes looked away, distant.

"Is that blue robot giving you trouble?"

Luci withdrew from her reverie. "Beetro? No. He only helps. He's like us, too. Forgotten. Thrown in a junkyard. He's just trying to do his best like you."

"It's just that I've noticed—"

"It's hard finding supplies to trade for wheat and flour lately. I know. I'm sorry I haven't been able to give you and your friends more."

"I don't have friends."

Luci feigned a hurtful grimace. "Then what am I?"

"No, yeah, *you* are. I hate the other kids. They try to hurt me, take things away from me. So, I cut them."

"How does that work out?"

"Cutting them? Really, really good."

"Are you sure?"

"I'm alive, aren't I?"

"But what kind of life is it? Simply being alive isn't living." Luci stood, shaking the dirt off her backside. With arms akimbo, she looked over the junkyard and out into the plains. "I bet those dark clouds out there are rain. Everything will work out, you'll see."

"I *know* you don't have fresh water. *No one* has fresh water. It hasn't rained in like twenty days. And I don't want your moldy cranberries. I need dried food. Meat, apples—whatever." Miree had been haggling with the shopkeeper for fifteen minutes. The shopkeeper was a brawny woman named Maldea with whom Miree absolutely hated bartering.

Maldea tsked at her. "I don't care what you need. You don't have enough scrap. You want smoked pheasant? I need more screws and rubber. The Carister traders are coming next week and have sent word for certain items. I don't care about these piss poor aluminum shavings." The woman lifted a small pile of the shavings between her fingers. "This is not enough for anything. I could maybe give you some flour for what you have here, but you'd owe me a little."

Miree paused, considering the deal. "No, no, I don't need flour. I need dried goods."

"What about those fine boots you wear? I'll give you five pounds of dried meat for those. What kind of scavenger wears boots like those? And that thick cloak? How can you afford such things?"

Miree shook her head. "No. Not for sale."

Maldea shrugged, defiant.

"What about batteries?"

"Batteries!" Maldea said in outrage. "You think you can get batteries for this!"

Miree held out her hand. "Dead batteries. Do you have dead batteries?"

"No. I don't keep dead batteries in stock, you ridiculous girl. Now get outta here. Arguing is bad for business." Maldea swept her arm across the table, dismissing her.

A voice issued from behind her. "Why didn't you take the flour? Lucindi could've made bre—"

"Ah!" Miree yelled, startled at the voice. She whipped around and saw Lucindi's new pet bot looking up at her. She had nothing but monstrous annoyance for the damn thing. "Where the hell did you come from?"

"I just wanted to come and learn."

"You can tag along with Lucindi. Not me."

"But don't we need more flour?"

"I only need what I need." She pointed to an alley. "You go that way."

The junkyard robot sauntered off.

A loud pop echoed over the markets. Miree's hand went to her hip but relaxed when she saw it was only a crate slamming on flagstone.

Beetro was awoken by whispered shouting later that night. Miree and Lucindi were arguing back in the cave about food and bad prices on salvage at the markets. Miree insisted Lucindi stop giving everything away to the kids every day, to which Lucindi responded with resolute silence.

"We can at least go to Peles Castle tomorrow. The fief lord is holding court," Miree said as if the argument was over.

"Court? Nothing ever comes of that. It's a charade. The fief lord has never cared about the poor."

"We need to try. They have trading posts after court. Maybe we can sell some scrap there for better prices than the markets here."

"We don't have enough water to cross the plains."

"I'll get the water."

"We don't have enough salvage to even make the trip out there worth it. Miree," she said, a tightness drawing her lips in a line. "Why go out there at all?"

"We might get lucky."

"Lucky? You want to risk a journey over the plans on getting lucky? Is there something else going on? Why do you really want to go there?"

Miree replied by stomping out of the cave and slumping next to a tree. Beetro would've gone to console the woman if he hadn't become so terrified of her. Lucindi appeared, tears glistening in the moonlight. She slept alone in the grass.

As they headed to the junkyard the next day in a brooding silence, Beetro split off from his human friends. Lucindi gave him a worried look—the same expression she reserved for the street children. "Are you going to come back?"

Beetro nodded. "I just want to walk around Korthe a little more." The robot was hungry to learn. Every textured surface, scrap of cloth, or human expression taught him more about this new world. He wanted more input. "I'll find you in a bit." Lucindi acquiesced and watched as the robot walked down a crooked alleyway.

He circled the town by foot, measuring Korthe to have an area of two hundred and twenty-four kilometers squared. After climbing a tree that stood on a grassy knoll just outside of town, he studied the building density and estimated the population to be around fifteen thousand people—assuming that was only a human population, which seemed likely based on the scarcity of robot life that he'd seen.

There were a few small market streets that sold mostly produce—apples, pears, berries... he also found several blacksmiths, stables for horses, inns, taverns, several mills on the outskirts, carpenters, and bakeries. The typical dwellings were made of plastered clay with thatched roofing—homes of no more than one or two rooms. There were more sturdy and larger homes near Mercy Square.

Curiously, he discovered an isolated spire, ten meters high, that loomed above a row of homes. He was surprised to find that the base of the spire sprouted directly out of the arid ground at a skew of forty-five degrees. Giving it a knock with his fist, the spire answered with an unyielding thud—it was solid. The whole thing was of uniform color, a matte gray but with a colorful iridescence. Perhaps a titanium alloy, he decided. He looked around curiously, wondering why there wasn't a single other structure in the entire town that was also made of the same material. The monolithic thing was ludicrously out of place.

He found an errant stream at the mouth of an alley and restored his water vapor supply. He'd been designed to drink water from his mouth, humanlike, but he could also absorb water directly from his fingertips. He watched the townsfolk as he rested. There was a frenetic anxiety to their movements—swift gaits and spasmodic hand gestures while speaking. Yet, they moved much slower than their highly leveraged physiology suggested. Long fulcrums at the elbow and elongated thighs made him wonder why they weren't running rather than shuffling about. Their faces were gaunt, their gazes hollow. As he further walked about, he learned there were two substances that made the people liven up—beer and coffee.

There were a lot of people who leaned against walls. Men and teenagers lined up along homes and stores, smoking rolled tobacco while muttering complaints. They regarded one another rarely, to borrow a smoke or ask for spare food. It became clear that those who didn't have shops or skills in one of only about five specialties of craftsmanship didn't work. And when they didn't work, they leaned against walls and spoke little. Beetro began to understand why so many parentless children roamed the streets.

The street children mostly stayed in packs, grouping together along the alleyways or the rooftops. When they saw him coming, they scurried away out of the path of the strange-looking bot. Some of the braver children stood along the road as he passed, acting as if picking at the plaster walls was keeping their attention. They spied him out of the corner of their eyes, assessing the potential threat or possible source of food that he posed.

He noticed a familiar forehead peering at him from a rooftop —brown hair, brown eyes—Ribcage.

"Hey," she yelled down at him, exposing her face to the street.

"Me?"

"What're you doing here?" Her small voice echoed surprisingly well down the alley.

He motioned around the street. "Here?"

"In Korthe. Why are you here?"

"I didn't think I was bothering anyone." Ribcage's face disappeared from the top of the roof. "Okay," Beetro remarked to no one and continued walking.

"Hey!" Ribcage's voice chirped behind him.

Beetro whipped around and saw the skeletal girl standing beneath him. "How did you get down here so fast?" He glanced up at the building to see if there was a ladder. Nothing.

"What do you want?"

"Me? No—nothing. Well, no, that's not quite right. I'm looking for someone."

"They're not here."

"You know I'm looking for Galiaro? Do you know him? Or her?"

The girl shook her head in disgust. "No one cares about your thing. People only care about their *own* thing. Understand?"

"Yes. Fine."

"And don't. Bother. Luci," Ribcage said, pointing a finger at him.

"Lucindi?"

"Don't mess with her."

"Mess with her?"

"Luci is one of the only reasons I eat. You don't eat, right?"

"No, I—"

"Good. You help Luci find food and I won't have to cut you."

"Do you have anyone who takes care of you?"

"Yeah. Me."

"Don't you have a mother or father?"

"Do *you*?" she jabbed back.

"Well, I—no. Not really. I think someone made me, but I don't know where they are. It's been very hard since my reboot..."

"Yeah, that's a super sad story." She turned from him. "Don't mess with Luci."

Beetro watched as the tiny girl walked away. As he turned, musing on how such a small and young human had so much more street experience than himself, he noticed something jittery in the corner of his eye. He snapped back to Ribcage, who was now on the opposite side of the alleyway. "How?" He watched as she disappeared around a corner having no idea if the interaction was a typical encounter with a human child or not.

As he rounded his way back to the junkyard, he turned away from Korthe and examined the yellow plains that unfurled from the town like a scroll. Korthe was the only point of civilization for eighty kilometers. Beyond that, there was a hazy curtain that clung to the horizon. He dilated the aperture of his eye shutters and magnified, granting him sight of a gray mountain range. He scanned the base of the mountain range and stopped.

There was a stack of smoke blooming out there.

He returned to the junkyard and found Lucindi lifting an

overturned wheelbarrow. "Hey," she said after spotting him. Sweat was dripping down her neck.

"Are there many fires around Korthe?" he asked.

"Sometimes. Sometimes they're intentionally set to help crops grow."

"What about that one?" He pointed in between heaps of garbage that framed the column of smoke, growing bigger by the minute. The sun had taken on a coppery hue.

"Hmm." Lucindi left the wheelbarrow and climbed out from a shallow ditch of garbage. After walking to the edge of the junkyard, she lifted her palm to her brow and squinted at the smokestack. "That looks like it's coming from Peles Castle."

"What's that?"

"It's where the fief lord lives."

"The king?"

"Sort of. It's the guy who comes to town with soldiers, collects taxes, whips a couple of backbiters, and leaves. They change out about every year or so. Looks like we've got a new one," she declared, pointing. "That's battle smoke."

FOUR

RIBCAGE WAS PERCHED at her rooftop nook, watching the bewildered blue robot walk away. Her stomach raged with hunger as she watched the streets. She had begging down to a science—mix a little dew water with dust from the road and rub it over her cheeks. She kept an especially filthy scrap of cloth that she tied around her neck that would only cover her chest but leave shoulder blades and ribcage exposed, showcasing her malnutrition. No shoes while she begged on the streets, ever. Anything on the feet suggested excess to someone even remotely considering giving out food in Korthe. She did keep a ragged set of wicker sandals in her nook during her rooftop surveillance. Starvation was her business and she had perfected it. She earned the name Ribcage and was proud of it. But lately... her tactics weren't getting her anywhere.

She knew that small events—a bloatstorm on the plains, a stolen caravan from Carister, a small feud between merchants—all could disrupt the amount of food coming her way. Just the appearance of a dumb-looking blue robot made her nervous about her next meal.

"What'd he say?" someone asked from behind.

"Information has a price," Ribcage said, turning to see that Jaram had tailed her. He was getting better. "Didn't you hear about the last kid who came to my nook? She came to me half-blind and went away half-deaf."

Jaram set his jaw. "Just tell me what he's doing at the junkyard with the other two."

She smirked at him. "Why would I do that? So you and the others can hoard food away from me?"

"It's not like you share, either. If you helped us, we would help you."

"I can fend for myself. I don't need you—I don't need anybody. So, bug off."

"And what if I don't?" Something sinister overcame Jaram's face. There was planning—something orchestrated behind those eyes.

"Then—" she stopped. Two more boys slipped into view from behind Jaram. They were thin but they had height over Ribcage. "Oh, I see."

"Where's your stash, you little shit?"

"Do you dummies think I'd keep it where I knew you'd follow me?"

"Take us there." One of the boys revealed a large rock he had been palming.

"I guess you'll just have to kill me then," she said, blithely looking at her dirty nails. But when she saw their stone faces circling in on her, she realized these weren't empty threats. "Relax. I'll show you where it is."

"Tell us. Now." Jaram took out a short cord of rope from his pocket.

"I actually do have it right here," she turned to a small alcove on the rooftop.

"Bring it out here to us," Jaram demanded.

"Fine." Ribcage turned to the alcove.

"You really just brought this on yourself, you know," Jaram said. "If only you'd worked with us and the other kids more. We wouldn't feel like we had to do this."

"Maybe you're right," she said, trying her best to sound morose. "I really should get along better with others." She closed her eyes, feeling for the jittery rush—her Jump. It was there. She could feel mom somewhere out there.

Suspicious, Jaram ran up from behind to shove her to the ground. But when he pushed, he hit nothing and fell face-first into the roof. Suddenly, Ribcage was behind them. "But I usually do pretty good on my own," she said.

The three boys turned around. Jaram looked up at the girl who had just vanished and rematerialized right behind him. "What the hell?"

"Problem?" she asked, now reappearing at his side. She slammed her open palm into his face and his nose erupted with blood. One of the larger boys threw his rock at Ribcage, but it only rattled along the rooftop and shot off the edge. She had vanished again and reappeared behind them. "Thanks for visiting but I think I'll be going—" she stopped, turning her ears toward the street.

"You're dead," Jaram said, holding his nose. "We're going to—" he stopped too, noticing what had drawn her attention. He stood, momentarily ignoring the assault as he listened to the noises in the streets. "What is that?"

Ribcage peered over the edge of the roof. "Marching boots."

There weren't victory trumpets nor drums but there were soldiers. A lot of soldiers. Beetro and his human friends perched themselves atop an abandoned church and watched as the soldiers streamed through Korthe.

"There's something different—something wrong," Lucindi speculated, chewing the inside of her cheek. "I've seen a lot of coups over the years. None have looked like this—so... organized." She watched as the soldiers moved with practiced synchrony. Every footstep dropped in unison, creating a thunderous clap that echoed down the streets. Even the way they swung their arms while marching was perfectly timed. The army was like a metronome, keeping a steady beat as a demonstration of their precision.

They were armed, yet not all with identical weapons. Many bore gunpowder bandolier belts that draped across their shoulder brandishing revolvers, shotguns, and automatic rifles. There were other soldiers that had sleeker weapons of more refined design. Although shaped as any traditional gunpowder firearm, they had longer barrels with a stubby grip mounted at the trigger. Atop these weapons was a canister that could be detached.

"What *are* those?" Lucindi asked Miree, pointing to the strange weapons.

"Old tech," Miree said with measured concern. "Railguns. I don't think this is just a run-of-the-mill lazy-lord brigade."

The soldiers were young—some younger than Lucindi and Miree. They were men and women of varying skin color and mostly tall. Whoever had assembled the army was selective in terms of physique—they were squarely built. The lieutenants wore sleekly woven fabric that hugged their bodies from neck to calves, ending in rugged, black boots. The subordinate soldiers, those with gunpowder firearms, were armed in black vests with mesh fabric underneath. They had protective padding around their elbows and knees and lugged around gigantic packs on their backs. The soldiers wore stoic faces as they passed by the townsfolk. Beetro suspected it wasn't their first time marching into a town unannounced.

Puzzled, Beetro watched the procession. What kind of threat could a sleepy place like Korthe pose to an army? Why the demonstration? Hundreds of more soldiers filed through the crooked streets, periodically peering above to watch for pesky rock throwing. Some made brief eye contact with Beetro but then left his gaze.

"Where are they from? Orion?" Lucindi asked Miree.

Miree's eyes didn't leave the army beneath them. "Don't think so. Neither the Kish nor the BlackGrip mercenaries have munitions like that. That black ballistic weave armor is *incredibly* rare—and expensive. I've only seen a suit like that once, worn by one of the richest merchants in Orion. There are at least a couple dozen down there with them on. And all those guns... it would take years to amass all of that."

"Or a lot of conquering," Lucindi added.

"No, there aren't even big enough caches for someone to plunder to get all those weapons. I don't know where someone could've got all that except by digging it up and refurbishing it. Even then, how would you even know where to look?"

"Come on," Lucindi stood and leaped over a hole in the roof of the church. "Careful," she told Beetro.

The three moved along the rooftops, surprising some of the street children squirrelled away in their hidden spots. They appeared frightened to see people intruding in their safe spots but looked relieved when they saw it was Lucindi. Beetro trailed Lucindi as she followed the course of the marching soldiers. The sleekly armored lieutenants led their soldiers into Mercy Square. Six roads converged at the plaza and encircled the dried-out, central fountain. The soldiers had arranged themselves in units of squadrons, standing shoulder to shoulder with the neighboring squad about two shoulder widths away. Curiously, the squadrons had left a vacant spot in the middle of the plaza.

Lucindi shimmied down the side of the building with Miree calling after, "What're you doing?"

"Getting a closer look, come on." She waved them down.

"Do they look like people you want to get close to?" Miree asked in a shouting whisper. Lucindi peered down the narrow alley at the soldiers standing in the plaza, placid looks over their faces. "If they were going to kill us, they would've done it already. I want to know what they're doing here." Beetro easily climbed down the side of the building. "Beetro's not afraid," Lucindi added.

"Of course, he isn't. He doesn't know what he's even looking at," Miree complained.

Beetro looked up at Miree, annoyed. "I know what guns are." He exchanged glances with Lucindi, who nodded.

Miree met them at the alleyway and they crept forward together. One of the soldiers noticed their approach, but once Lucindi lifted her palms showing she wasn't armed, she dismissed them. Apparently, the rest of the town had been put at ease by the soldier's deference—all alleyways were full of townspeople watching. Every window facing the plaza had been crammed full of onlookers. Even old Crow was there, although possibly not fully present given his occasional snore.

The plaza soon filled with soldiers, with many tails of the squadrons leading out through the streets. Curiously, the squadrons had formed themselves, leaving a clear path to the center of the plaza with an empty space in front of the fountain. Silence fell over the streets. No one spoke. No one moved. The soldiers only stood, gazing forward with military sterility.

A chugging sound from down the street cut the silence. A tan truck with gigantic rubber wheels wedged its way into the plaza. It was so wide, some of the paint of the homes was swiped as it came through before parking in between the empty space of the squadrons.

Silence and waiting, again.

Then a strong wind swept through the plaza, kicking up dust and dresses. It came so suddenly and with such force that the people almost ran for fear of a surprise bloatstorm. But the fear was fleeting when they saw an array of lights beaming down onto the plaza from the sky.

Lucindi squinted at the white lights. "What is it?"

"Not sure," Miree said. "Whatever aircraft it is, it's not making a whole lot of noise. Must have an advanced engine." Several ropes dropped through the lights. "Oh, I guess it's time for the show."

Down the ropes came five figures, silhouetted by the white lights of the aircraft above. The figures dropped away from the night sky and slid down to the ground of the plaza, dimly lit by gas lanterns. These were dressed in the same tight, woven fabric of the lieutenants of the squadrons. They brandished different weapons on their backs, however. They were slender rifles of uniform, metallic texture with a sweeping beauty to them as if forged by the wind itself. They were stark black and had no identifiable ammunition holster.

"What are *those*?" Lucindi asked.

"No idea," Miree said, admiring the rifles. "Maybe ancient Alchean design. If so, they're priceless."

There was a man among the newcomers who, although wearing woven armor, also had a bionic shoulder piece, full of wires and buttons. The gadget had flexible arms that extended into his ears and into the right eye with a glowing eyepiece flickering with light. Beetro magnified his view of the shoulder piece and saw that it also shot slender cables down the man's arm, connecting to small screens and a mechanical glove on his right hand. He stood, arms crossed, as the rest of the four soldiers who descended with him lined up to face them.

He was in charge.

The man punched a few buttons on his glove, prompting an enormous holographic display to float above the plaza, emanating from the aircraft that, although noiseless, still floated above the city. The man's own face was projected in the holographic video feed for the entire town to see. He was older with a hawkish face and bushy black eyebrows. He kept his hair well-groomed, short on the side and tall on the top.

"Children," his amplified voice boomed through the plaza. "Eat."

At this, a squad stepped forward and opened the back end of the tan truck. Woven baskets of peaches, melons, apples, and berries lined the truck along with a variety of bread loaves, pastries, canned beans, and soups. The soldiers backed away and stood as sentinels to the truck.

The plaza was motionless.

Miree and Lucindi looked at the truck, brimming with food. Miree tensed. Lucindi grabbed her sleeve. "Don't."

"No one else is going out there. It's just sitting there."

"If all they wanted to do was feed people, they wouldn't have brought guns. Also, you're not a child."

Other people were getting the same idea as Miree timidly approached the plaza but stopped after noticing the soldiers shaking their heads at them. "It's so much food," Miree said, crest-fallen. "It's worth a small fortune."

And then, like squirrels emerging from hidden burrows, the street children appeared. One by one, they came from the alleyways and rooftops. Beetro saw a few emerge from a gutter grate. Timidly, they stepped toward the truck, studying the soldiers' faces. Ribcage hiked up the back of the truck, grabbed a peach in between her palms, and sank her teeth into the skin. She cuffed juice from her chin between ravenous bites. After observing that it really wasn't a trap, children flooded the plaza and surrounded the truck. Soon, the soldiers had to take children out of the truck that were hoarding the food in their clothing and exchange in newcomers. Dozens more trickled in through the alleys, elbowing their way through the crowds to get to the truck.

"There is plenty," the man spoke, his voice deep like thunder, the holographic projection looming over. He walked to the truck, wading amongst the children. He watched them—studied them. As the truck quickly emptied, another wiggled in through the crowds, dispensing more food to the children. The squads had backed away from the formation to the edges of the plaza to accommodate more space for the children. One of the women who had rappelled down from the sky also walked among the children. She had something small in her hand and was clicking on it as she watched the street children. It took a moment for Beetro to realize what she was doing—counting.

The man spoke again, "You may have noticed some smoke out near the mountains. Peles Castle is no longer ruled by your lord." With hands behind his back, he walked casually around the plaza, peering into windows and catching glimpses of some of the townspeople who shied away from his gaze. He strode as if he owned the plaza, the people, and everything in it.

"Korthe is a wonderful town," he continued. "It deserves better." His accent was refined and educated—not from the region of Helian. "Korthe doesn't deserve a fief lord. Fortunately, I am not a lord." He glanced at the line of people at the periphery of the plaza to see their reactions. He appeared pleased as they regarded him with new intrigue. "I'm a general—General Deluvius. And this," he gestured to his soldiers, "this is my army. I don't bring my soldiers through your streets to intimidate. I bring them so that there is no question about who will be taking care of you. I bring them to show you that I do not need your taxes. Keep your money and your goods. All I demand is your obedience." At this, a rousing stir of commotion rippled through the crowd. More people came to the plaza at the sound of the general's words. Many of the townsfolk commented on the man's soothing voice and handsome face.

General Deluvius walked amongst the children, all of whom were eating from the food trucks. Some had already stashed a few items in their clothing and squatted away from the crowds, taking inventory. "My soldiers bring food for your children—every single one of them will sleep tonight with full bellies." A small cheer erupted from the kids—hundreds of them now littered the plaza, all of them chewing.

Ribcage came up to General Deluvius' leg and hugged his calf. "Thank you, General Daloovia," she said with a lisp that Beetro knew was fake. The townspeople smiled at the display.

Lucindi scoffed. "So now they suddenly recognize the existence of the homeless kids in this town?" She looked to Miree for agreement, but she appeared too captivated by General Deluvius' lustrous rifle that he had swung around his shoulder.

"Yeah, that's gotta be old Alchean," Miree said, referring to the weapon. "It's as old as dirt itself."

General Deluvius scooped Ribcage into his arms and smiled. "Of course, my dear. I take care of my people." He crouched and watched as she scampered off to get more food. "I'll station my soldiers here in Korthe. That way, they'll be able to alert me if there are problems in the town—threats, famine, raiders, bloatstorms—whatever it may be that plagues you. My men and women may need accommodations from time to time. Is that reasonable for the people of Korthe?" He was answered with another cheer. "We're an army but we're also explorers. The people of Korthe will share in our successes." He offered a small nod to the crowds that now occupied every alley and street that led to the plaza. What started as an armed procession had quickly turned into a celebration as the people broke in excited commotion. Somehow, on cue, a band of musicians even appeared and began a few numbers on their guitars. An impromptu dance broke out as people moved amongst the soldiers.

Throughout the reverie of the townsfolk, Beetro studied the soldiers' faces—they'd maintained stoned expressions. It wasn't indifference—Beetro had seen that look many times on Miree. No, the soldiers wore something else on their faces that he'd seen on Lucindi after hours of rummaging through the junkyard... they were bored.

"It doesn't make sense," Lucindi concluded.

"What?" Miree asked, watching.

"They've done this before," she explained. "The soldiers. They've come into towns like this before. How can they give away so much food and offer the time of their soldiers for protection without taking something from the town? They can't make these same promises everywhere they go—it wouldn't be sustainable for the army. They get something from the towns they've been to before."

"I don't trust this asshole, either," Miree said. "Any man promising anything is full of shit."

"The general wants something," Lucindi affirmed. "We just need to find out what exactly." She watched the townsfolk dance, making no attempt to hide a scowl.

After the children had eaten themselves sick, some of whom had vomited, the general opened the food trucks to the rest of the town that had come to celebrate his arrival. After inspecting the plaza with hands behind his back, General Deluvius returned to a tight formation with his captains. They exchanged brisk words with the general, to which he nodded in agreement. "Children," General Deluvius spoke to the crowds. "Time to be off. We'll have plenty more for you to eat later."

The street kids turned to the general. Lulled by sugar and fat, they appeared to have lost their skeptical edge that would've made them scatter at his demands. The soldiers, holding position for well over an hour, broke and began to corral the children. They didn't point their guns, but they clearly meant business by pushing the children toward the trucks, now emptied of food. It appeared throughout the festivities that a few more trucks had been parked at the edge of the plaza as well. Into all the trucks, soldiers led the children up the back-end ramps.

Amidst the apparent kidnapping, Beetro noticed that General Deluvius didn't watch the children. Instead, he watched the people. He glanced around the plaza, studying the faces of the townsfolk as if waiting on something.

"Where are you taking the children?" Lucindi had marched out into the middle of Mercy Square and spoke directly to the general. The crowds receded around her.

General Deluvius regarded her for a moment. His lips curled to a smile. And then Beetro realized that he had been waiting for her. Not Lucindi specifically, but he was waiting for the defiant one, the voice of reason—the rebel. Beetro saw a story in the general's smile—he had dealt with the likes of the singular, recalcitrant dissenter. His smile spoke of a peculiar artistry, demonstrating firepower, pacifying crowds, and finally cleaning up the after-party by silencing whoever still cared by the end. He had dealt with many Lucindis before. But Beetro worried that Lucindi had probably never dealt with a General Deluvius before.

"Lucindi, don't," Beetro warned.

"What was that?" the general asked Lucindi, loudly, to draw attention.

She swallowed and then repeated, "The children... where are they going?" Beetro followed from behind. Miree stayed in the shadows of the alley.

General Deluvius looked down at her and then locked eyes with Beetro. He quickly dismissed the robot and squinted at Lucindi as if investigating the pesky itch of a bug. "Why do you believe you can ask me a question?"

Lucindi's face went pale.

"What about my clear and undisputed authority over this town has made you believe that you could approach me and speak?"

"I—" she faltered.

"No one else," he gestured to the entire plaza, "has dared speak to me. Not even one of my soldiers here. What is special about you?"

"No, nothing. I just—"

"No, I disagree. There is something special about you." He looked at the crowds. "You have no natural desire for self-preservation. What is your *name*?"

"M-my name?"

"State your name." The exchange had taken the tone of an arraignment.

"My... my name is Lucindi."

"Good people of Korthe. Lucindi believes she is a hero. What she doesn't realize is that you do not need a hero. And when someone acts like a hero when a hero isn't needed... they deserve a different name—a terrorist. She will only bring chaos and division to your community."

"I'm not a terrorist—I just want to know what you're doing with the children."

He answered by swinging his sleek rifle off his shoulder, cradling it in his hands, and placing a finger on the trigger.

And then Beetro felt something.

He *felt* something coming from somewhere—the general? No, not the general. The general's hands, but not his hands—the rifle. There was a pull—a visceral understanding of the energy within the weapon. Beetro lifted his hand as if to—what?—connect with its energy, give it boundaries—give it rules...

But then the general released a red streak of laser energy into Lucindi's chest.

"Wait!" Beetro's belated yell rang out and died off.

With a blackened crater smoking in her chest, Lucindi fell to her knees and collapsed into the dust.

"That's what will happen to the next terrorist who asks questions," General Deluvius threatened. He slung the rifle back over his shoulder, giving Beetro a sidelong look. As if knowing this last act spoke more than any closing words, the general left in silence the way he came—rappelling up a rope into some clandestine ship in the sky.

And Lucindi was lying on her belly, motionless; her hair covering her eyes. She was only sleeping.

But—no, of course she wasn't.

FIVE

OF COURSE, Beetro knew what death was. It was an innate concept written somewhere in his programming, along with sunsets, cornfields, and the sharpness of glass shards. But seeing it —feeling it—this was new.

This was painfully *fresh*.

There was pain in his chest or arms—or his head, he wasn't sure. A sharp panic overcame him every time he thought about Lucindi later that night, after the people of Korthe ignored a murder in their streets. They watched the general Deluvius Show —the impressive weaponry, the disimpassioned soldiers, the loyal captains. They watched, mostly because they wanted to see the ending—the point of the whole production. Once they saw the poor brown girl's chest explode in front of them, they understood. A new despot was taking over—nothing new. The story was already written—nothing to do. They probably slept the same way they did the night before.

But Beetro couldn't power down.

He kept looking at Lucindi's spot in the grass—the blades still bent from where she lay the night before. Her absence was both dramatic and unremarkable. The crickets and night sky didn't seem to notice that she was gone. The five stars of the heavens twinkled regardless of a street rat named Lucindi. Beetro, on the other hand, was so full of empty shock that he hadn't even begun to process indignation. The only person who ever cared about him had just disappeared like dandelion spores, blown away by a careless passerby.

And what was she even? A filthy, poor scavenger, spending most of her days in a junkyard—and yet managed to bake bread for children and that old man, Crow? Were there more people like her? Did anything she did even matter? Certainly, she'd still be living if she didn't care about the kids and stayed with Miree, standing back in the shadows. Was Lucindi special or was she a fool?

"Robot." It was Miree. Beetro looked up at her squatty figure in the moonlight. After the shooting in the plaza, Beetro looked everywhere for her and figured the girl had fled.

Beetro stood. "What do you want?" He was mad at her, but he was mad at the crickets at that moment, too.

"Come on," she said as if they had a previously agreed upon arrangement.

"Where?"

She hefted her leather satchel strap over her shoulder. It clanked with tools. "Grab the wagon, let's go."

Beetro stood. He had assumed that she wanted to debrief, review the events, speculate—but her flat expression conveyed as much emotion as a frying pan. He hefted the wooden wagon and followed her down the knoll into town. Good to his word, General Deluvius had stationed soldiers at numerous street corners. They didn't care about the stout girl followed by a robot.

They walked through the now emptied plaza. Beetro looked at

the spot where her body had laid. There wasn't even blood when it happened—the laser energy cauterized the flesh as it entered the body. Her body was gone now. Taken? Deluvius didn't want the body of a martyr in the streets? And just like any other day since Beetro could remember, they headed to the junkyard. Except, it was the middle of the night.

"Batteries," Miree declared once they arrived. "Go look for any battery you can find and bring it back to the wagon. Even if they're dead."

"But—"

She pointed one way and then moved in the opposite direction while donning thick work gloves.

Beetro went to work, scrambling up trash mounds and sifting through garbage. He had spent so much time here, he started recognizing individual trash heaps. He had seen batteries before, all of which were dead, and never bothered with them. As he dumped various dead batteries he found into the wagon, he stopped and looked at Miree, remembering something. He recalled her voice, insisting that they rip out his nuclear heart. It was only Lucindi that stopped her. He realized that he didn't have to do anything Miree told him to do.

She hefted a large battery and slammed it into the wagon, noticing his gaze. "You got something to say, robot?"

"Why am I collecting dead batteries in the middle of the night for you?"

"There's that 'I' again. It's not always about you, robot. Just because you can think for yourself doesn't make you special. You're just like anyone else. No one cares about your personhood." She turned her back and hiked up a trash mound.

Beetro realized that instead of lying there and sulking, which is exactly what he wanted to do, Miree sublimated her grief into busy work and yelling. Either that or she just didn't care about

Lucindi. But, if dead batteries *were* her way of mourning, he'd go along with it. He remembered where a score of batteries was littered in a shallow ditch and went to work collecting them. As a crack of sunlight shot over Meteor Mountains, there was a respectable stack of batteries collected. Meanwhile, Miree grunted as she moved, lifting pallets and chucking aside strips of fabric.

She came to the wagon and inspected the robot's work. "More. *Much* more."

"Why?" Beetro quickly disliked doing something that made no sense.

Miree peered at him for a moment as if considering the robot's newfound defiance. "I see you're finally learning to think for yourself. You'll soon figure out it's all bullshit—all of it." She stomped off again into the junkyard.

Puzzled and now certain that he was being used, Beetro sat on the ground, internal sensors buzzing about dehydration. He absorbed a little water from a puddle and watched Miree's head bob up and down beyond a garbage heap. The girl was in continuous movement—crouching, digging, and lifting her hand to her brow, squinting through dawn light. When she noticed Beetro's refusal to help, she approached again. "You can do whatever you want, but if you don't help me collect more batteries, me and you are done here." She let that hang and trooped off again.

"Don't you care? Don't you care that she's dead? I don't need to be here anymore. I-I need to go and find Galiaro. He'll know what I should do. I can't be wasting time here with you."

"You think finding the asshole that brought you into this life is going to give you all your answers?"

"I thought..."

"Go. Find him. I'm sure the man is a perfect saint. I'm sure everything will work out super nice for you and the little story you're making up in your head about your life." She turned, leaving him there.

But he didn't leave. He was quite terrified, really. He barely understood how life in Korthe worked. Venturing out of town alone would very likely get him killed. So, he kept looking for batteries. He found dozens more and, along with what Miree had collected, they had a veritable heap of useless batteries in the wagon. Beetro knew it was a waste of time, but the distraction of gathering them actually did make him feel better.

"Come on," she said, leading him away.

By mid-morning, they made their way through Korthe. They turned left where Beetro assumed they would go right toward the markets. The only reason he imagined Miree would want to collect so many batteries was the terrible bet that someone might buy them. But no, they were heading home for no ostensible reason.

They passed Crow, who sat atop his wire crate, sleeping. Miree didn't even give him a glance. Beetro watched his dopey face as they walked. A twinge of panic flashed through him as he watched the sleeping drunk. The old drunk instantly reminded Beetro that Lucindi was gone.

"You, boy," Crow managed to croak, eyes closed.

"Me?"

"Got a nip?" His eyes remained closed.

"No."

"Got any food?"

"No. Lucindi is... gone now."

"Who now?"

"She was killed right in front of you last night."

"Who?"

"Lucindi."

"*Who*?"

Beetro left the man there. Apparently, he understood less about the world than even Beetro. Miree didn't stop for the exchange but had turned the last corner back to their dirt cave. He caught up and helped her with the wagon. Miree chucked the batteries from the wagon into the cave as Beetro helped.

"You know tools?" Miree asked once they were inside. She flipped through her makeshift drawers, rummaging through pliers and wrenches.

"Tools?"

"Yeah, tools. Do you get them?"

"Just tell me what you want me to do." The misery of being left alone in the world with this person was quickly setting in.

"Go through each of those batteries, inspect the casings, figure out what tool will open them up, and then group them accordingly. Get it?"

"I'm not dumb," he said, kneeling to go about the task.

"This coming from the bot who tried selling his hands to buy food?"

Beetro said nothing and, quite efficiently, had grouped the batteries—a pile that could be opened with wrenches, one with pliers, one for a crowbar.

"What's going to open those ones?" Miree asked, pointing to a pile in the corner. "I don't see anything for those."

Beetro said without turning, "You've got a can opener, don't you?" He indicated to the thin, metal edges of the batteries.

"Ah. Good."

That shut her up a little.

"Start opening the casings—carefully. Don't tip them over or shake them."

Wordless, Beetro grabbed a few batteries and started taking pliers to them. He eyed Miree as she disappeared into the other room within the cave—the one she warned him never to enter again. She returned holding an oblong, metal capsule, carefully cradled in her arms.

"What is *that*?"

She sat the capsule on the ground, on its flat edge, and unscrewed the top. "Come and look."

He was hesitant. Given how secretive Miree was, he was alarmed that she wanted to show him something that she was obviously keeping from him. He wasn't certain he wanted to be part of whatever it was that she'd been hiding.

"Just look," she repeated, tightening her jaw.

There was something at the bottom of the capsule. Liquid. But shimmering... silver? No. "Mercury?"

"Yes. Open up the batteries, see if there is any mercury in them. There won't be a lot—droplets at the most. Put whatever mercury you can find into this thermos." She had said this as if it was an everyday task to complete.

Beetro, dumbfounded, looked at Miree, to the thermos, and then to the dozens of batteries that littered the dirt floor.

As if sensing protest, she added, "I don't need that much more."

"Why do you need mercury *at all*?"

"This is not a partnership. You can either help or leave. Don't think I didn't realize that you were just dead weight, hanging out with us. Lucindi isn't here anymore—your free ride is over."

Beetro fell silent, almost surrendering to the allegation. "Wait. I've helped you collect more scrap than you would've without me. I haven't taken anything from you."

Miree's angry brow unfurled. "Help me and I'll show you why I need the mercury. It's not like you have anything better to do anyway."

"Fine." He went to work unscrewing and prying open the batteries. Some were completely corroded and dried out within.

Others, however, did have a few drops of mercury that he poured into the thermos. The process of opening a single battery was painstakingly slow. Impatient with the pace, Beetro began simply crushing the batteries within his metal grasp, causing a jumbled mess on the floor.

"No," Miree said. "You've got to open them carefully or you can't collect the mercury."

Ignoring her, Beetro crushed another battery in his grip and let it fall to the pile.

"Stop!" Miree yelled.

After crushing yet another, Miree swept the pile away from the robot. "If you're going to be an asshole about it, just get out of here."

"Mercury is weakly diamagnetic at room temperature," Beetro explained, defiant. "This cave is even colder than that which will probably help make it more magnetized." He hovered his hand above the smashed pile of batteries and opened it, palm flat toward the ground. A few silvery drops of liquid metal rose from the smashed batteries and coalesced into a floating ball within Beetro's outstretched palm. Easily, and with a small measure of flare, he brought the ball of mercury to the thermos and dropped it in. "This is faster."

Miree shook the pleasant shock from her face and nodded. "Good."

They went about smashing open the remaining batteries and created a heap of eviscerated casings and coils on the ground. Beetro did his magnetized hand trick over the pile and produced a ball of mercury, the size of a cherry, floating within the confines of his hands. Wide-eyed, Miree watched him lower the ball into the thermos. It would've taken the rest of the day to collect what they now had in just twenty minutes.

"I think it'll be enough," she said.

"Enough for what?"

"Do you want to bury Lucindi?" she asked as if to distract him.

He looked at her, indigo eyes slanted in consideration. "Bury her?"

"Humans bury their dead."

"Where—"

"I waited until General Dickhead left and I... collected her." Her eyes moved to the other room in the cave.

Lucindi was with them in the cave.

So. Miree did care.

And so, they had a funeral for Lucindi.

They dug a hole at the base of Lucindi's tree and placed her body there. Strangely, Beetro didn't want to look at her face. He wasn't ready to reconcile the fact of death—that a person, teeming with life, blood, and sympathy could be immediately reduced to an object. She was no different now from the rocks that surrounded her small body.

Matter was matter.

"She didn't even do anything to him," he remarked after they covered her with dirt. "She just wanted to know where he was taking them. The kids."

Miree shook her head. "It didn't matter what she said. It was that she said anything at all."

"She was so... good."

"That sounded like a eulogy to me. Come on." Miree turned back toward the dirt cave, done with the impromptu ceremony.

"Where?" Beetro called after her, but she disappeared into the dirt. He found her, not in the work room but back within the tunneled room. Hunched beneath the low ceiling, she clasped a purple cloak around her body and tucked her black hair under a flattened fiddler cap. At her feet, the ground had been unearthed, exposing a black satchel.

Beetro pointed. "What is it?"

"It's the reason I almost got killed in Orion."

"But what *is* it?"

She lifted the satchel by the handle and carefully placed it into her pack. "Come on."

"Where?"

"Just come on."

"No. You tell me what's going on or I'm not going with you. You... you need me."

"No. You need *me*. You want to find your precious engineer?"

"Galiaro? Yes."

"I'll help you find him if you come and help me first."

"Help you with what?"

"Rob a castle. Kill a General. In that order."

SIX

BEYOND THE PLAINS OF HELIAN, hundreds of feet beneath the crust of the planet, Arym fidgeted in his chair, supremely annoyed.

"You're lucky to live in the hub of the Crib, Arym," Tarysl said. His face was so dumb and round—a dopey face, really. The receding hairline did not help matters for the rektor. It was what everyone the man's age looked like in the Crib. Tarysl paused as if expecting some sort of argument to erupt from Arym. But Arym was calm. Too calm? Would the rektor know it was to placate him? "Many of those at Sol or Jovia would be more than happy to take your place here at the Crib," the rektor continued.

"I know, Rektor Tarysl," Arym said. He was sitting across the metal-top table, opposite Rektor Tarysl.

Rektor Tarysl frowned. "I've known you your whole life, Arym. You can just call me Tarysl."

"I know, Rektor Tarysl."

"Are you mocking me?"

"No, Rektor Tarysl. I mean no disrespect. I only wish to honor you."

"I'm assuming you know why your torchblazer wanted you to meet with me?"

Arym nodded, closing his eyes. There was no natural light in the room. There was no natural light for several miles in every direction. The room was bathed in the orange glow emanating from the overhead bulbs, powered by some mechanical and electrical churning happening at the underground Sol satellite. Arym thought often about the rocks and the dirt—above his head, beneath his feet. At nights, after climbing into his pod, the dirt walls squeezed into his mind, suffocating every thought. He'd sweat and jerk in bed, clawing at the plastic walls of his pod, stifling a scream. Sometimes a quick bathroom break and a glass of water would ease the panic attack. But not always.

Rektor Tarysl leaned his elbows over the metal table. The countertop was sterilized moments before the two had met in the room. There were cleaning squads assigned to every deck of the Crib, spraying disinfectants in the wake of almost any human activity. Any rumors of a cough or a sneeze from any individual in the underground colony and they'd be quarantined to their pods for at least two weeks. The Crib did not mess around with infectious diseases.

"I was surprised when your torchblazer told me I needed to meet with you. Do you wish to speak first about what happened?" The rektor pursed his lips together with the concern of a father.

"My torchblazer finds any excuse to get me out of the tunnels for reprimand."

"Is that so?"

Arym nodded. "Me and him have never carried along well. It's something that I've been trying to work on. I thought we were doing well until he pulled me off the digline yesterday."

Rektor Tarysl nodded, bringing his pointed index fingers to his lips. "And why do you believe he pulled you off the digline?"

Arym shrugged. "I was taking a break. I know you're a rektor, so you may not know, but digging tunnels for ten hours a day is exhausting. We're allowed scheduled breaks and so I took mine."

"I believe you're being overtly... unassuming."

"What do you mean, rektor?"

"Arym." Tarysl leaned in his chair, clasping his hands over his knees. "Do you honestly not know why Torchblazer Rayller was mad with you?"

Arym took a deep breath. "I admit I do."

"Will you explain?"

"It wasn't that I took a break. It was *where* I took my break."

"And where did you take the break?"

Arym paused, collecting himself during the excruciating exchange. "In an Oshaft."

"Tell me why that was wrong."

"Oshafts can lead above ground, to the overworld."

"And are hence strictly prohibited. Oshafts are used for only the purpose of gas and pressure ventilation from the Crib and its satellites. I would also add that Torchblazer Rayller didn't state that you just took a break in an Oshaft. You climbed within one and had marched your way fairly high before he discovered you were there."

Arym had no reply.

The rektor thrummed his fingertips on the table. "Would you mind citing the Oath of the Descension?"

Arym took a deep breath. "As a citizen of the Crib, without compulsion, I hold this oath as my own: I will use my back to labor, my mind to innovate, and my strength to defend the Crib and his people. I will place myself below the needs of this great people and keep sacred its location from the world."

"Why is that oath important to you?"

"The Oath of Descension was created to bind us to our people. To keep us safe from the dangers of the overworld. Othel, our founder, dug into the depths of the planet to flee the corruption and chaos of the overworld. If every denizen of the Crib does not bind themselves to the Oath, we risk losing everything our founder did for my generation." It was as if he had every word memorized, which he did in part. He was regurgitating words that had been taught to him since before he could even remember. He could've done it in his sleep.

"Why do you drill with your torchblazer and his team?"

"I'm using my back to labor and my mind to innovate. The Crib and its satellites are growing beyond their bounds. It is the Crib's responsibility to make new satellites for our people. Sol provides energy, Jovia nutrition, Granite raw resources, and Stellate watches over our health. I drill to expand our people underground, to further distance ourselves from the corruption of the overworld."

"Thank you for the rote recitation that you learned in school. I want to hear why *you* do it. What motivates you? Just be honest."

Arym kept his eyes wide, resisting an eye roll. "I'm not sure."

This seemed to pique the rektor's interest. "That's okay. It's better that you don't make something up. I know it's hard to always be motivated to follow the Oath and work for the people. There's nothing wrong with feeling a little... deflated sometimes. Is that how you've been feeling lately?"

"Yes, rektor."

"Why do you think that is?"

"Gets lonely sometimes. Getting out of my pod each morning. Putting on my gear and heading through the mining tunnels. Day in and out, same thing over and over again. It wears on you."

"I understand."

"It's hard to see the bigger picture when I'm drilling through granite all day with the torchblazer yelling at me. It's exhausting."

"Is that why you hid away in the Oshaft? To get away from Torchblazer Rayller?"

Arym nodded. "I think so, yes. It was nice to just take a break from it all."

"It's understandable. You should've been honest about this. Are you sure there was no other reason that you hid in the Oshaft?"

Arym shook his head. "No, I was really just trying to get away from Rayller—even for just a few minutes."

"Why do you think we're concerned that you were in the Oshaft?"

"You don't want anyone going into them because you don't want us up above."

"And why is that?"

"The overworld is dead. Barren. Toxic. There's nothing there anymore. The surface of the world saw so many wars and pollutants that our founder, Othel, had to dig a shaft deep into the earth."

"The overworld is no place for Cribmen."

Arym's face changed. Inquisitive. "Do you really believe there are no people above?"

"No, I know there are people above. Human beings, even those not descended from Othel, are resilient. I'm sure many peoples have survived above, but they can no longer be trusted. We've grown up, evolved away from them, and we can no longer go back. Our place is underground." He pointed down into the table. "I know it's quite a burden for our people to bear, but I can tell you from my experience that it is deeply worth it. The joy that I've had over these long years as being rektor to the people of the Crib has been unimaginable."

Arym stared at the table, silent in thought for a moment. "I'm just not there yet."

"It takes time. You're at the age where rebellion feels justified. You have a natural distrust of your superiors, it's very understandable. I, too, went through the same thing. I wasn't placed into the mining unit like you. I wanted to be a surgeon. When I was your age, Cribmen frequently went to the overworld, venturing out for supplies and to hunt game."

"You've been to the overworld?"

"No, not me. I wasn't old enough to go above. But I was old enough to remember the dismembered limbs and gaping holes in our people when they returned from above. We are hated people, Arym. Overworlders try to destroy us when they find out what we are—who we are. I wanted to put my brothers back together again after they were brought back down, injured by gunfire or maimed by wild animals. I wanted to be a surgeon, but I was told there were too many, that there wasn't a need. I was very distraught at the time—wanted to rip the lid right off the Crib and climb out of here. But I didn't. I was patient and realized that being a rektor, one who can heal the mind and soul, is just as valuable as putting the body back together. Maybe even more so. It was the right thing for me. And being on the digline, following your torchblazer is the right thing for you."

Arym was silent.

"It's the right thing for you because it's the thing we need of you right now. You are placed where you are out of need. Right now, during your generation, we need to expand. We need diggers. If it wasn't for your efforts, we'd suffocate in our own waste. The time is ready for expansion, and you are a pioneer. Does any of this mean anything to you?"

Arym nodded. "I think so."

"Just be patient, keep your head down, and your rewards will be great, Arym."

"I can try, rektor."

"Can we meet next week?"

"I'd like that." He stood and bowed, crossing to the portal doorway. "You won't be hearing about any troubles from my torch-blazer anymore."

The rektor smiled. "Good to hear." Arym left Tarysl there with a smile, suggesting he believed himself a masterful rektor.

Once he was in a tube, Arym's heart finally slowed. He moved swiftly, back slightly hunched, down the connecting tube that led toward the center of the Crib. Cribmen skirted out of the way when they saw him jetting down the tube. Ignoring their inquisitive looks, he glanced at his watch, checking that he had enough time to get to his pod before his dig shift started.

It was a hard balance between playing unassuming without appearing disingenuous. For the rektor, Arym poured on the lacquer of a youthful rebellious attitude, mixed in some earnest questions, and polished it off with a coating of pensive self-reflection. It left the door open for the rektor believing that the troubled youth could be reformed. That he really was 'a good digkid' and that hiding in an Oshaft really was a one-time thing. Arym felt like he pulled it off. Well, enough that the rektor would let him return to work without more disciplinary action. Arym did *not* want to end up in isolation. It truly was the most horrific punishment he could think of. There was nothing more detestable to him than being stuck in one place, alone.

He had to move.

At the end of the tube, he stopped at a shaftlift and pulled the call lever. A metallic clunk heralded the arrival of the lift. Of course, Waryl, a digkid, was there awaiting his arrival.

"Arym!" he greeted, slapping Arym on the back. "We missed you on the digline today."

Arym paused, wondering if Rektor Tarysl had planned the chance meeting. He wouldn't put it past the rektor to have a 'friend' follow up on him. "Yeah. I know," he said, staring at the corner of the lift.

Waryl cleared his throat in the awkward silence. "You'll be back tomorrow?"

"Today." The lift stopped and Arym got off on his deck, eternally relieved to be away from the older, do-good brown-noser that was Waryl the insufferable.

Arym shuffled down the tube, took a right at a fork, and continued down an even longer tube passageway. The tubes were dark, barely illuminated by tiny, fluorescent bulbs. They were powered only by the heat that came off the water lines that ran beneath. The Crib prided itself on converting all excess energy into powering something else. The Crib itself was first organized as a series of rooms and laboratories that were built at the bottom of a mine shaft. Othel, the founder, had drilled the first mine shaft hundreds of years ago. Eventually, more deck floors were added above the original rooms, each with connecting tubes and conduits to supply oxygen and warmth. After a generation, the Crib was complete as a single shaft within an encircling network of deck floors. Originally, each deck was solely in charge of individual functions—nutrition, engineering, health, and energy, along with others. After more successive generations came, with more born from the Crib, offshoot satellites were built in the adjacent earth to the Crib and these functions were outsourced to keep the function of the Crib pure—population management.

He made it to his pod, a small, thumb-like projection off the digline barracks. He sealed the door behind and examined the room. It didn't look like anything had been disturbed. Hastily, he dropped to his knees and pulled out the bottom drawer from his desk, removing several mining manuals. His heart pumped as he pulled out the manuals, suddenly terrified that everything about the interview with Rektor Tarysl was just a charade—that any moment they would bust in his room and take him to isolation, but no. He found his journal—a notebook that he fashioned together using the blank back pages from the teaching manuals. It was where he had left it, undisturbed.

Apparently, Rektor Tarysl wasn't suspicious enough to start searching his pod.

He returned to the digline and joined the crew who sat beside the Torch—a massive, cylindrical drill that lay on flat treadwheels, which thrust the machine along as it advanced through clay and rock. Arym couldn't see it from where he stood, but a circular structure of complex spiked spheres and triangular jaws jutted from the front end of the Torch—the business end of the drilling. He found the torchblazer, Rayller, in the cockpit, surrounded by a small pocket of glowing screens, levers, and buttons that were built into the top of the Torch. It was from the cockpit that the torchblazer would get feedback from the machine, give out commands to the digline, and throw in override commands when the digline screwed up. The torchblazer looked up at Arym through the glass and scoffed. The hatch of the cockpit opened. "The rektor talk to you?"

Arym nodded.

"And?"

"You won't have problems with me anymore."

"We sure? No more climbing Oshafts?"

"Nope. Never."

Later that night, Arym escaped to the overworld through an Oshaft.

He lay in the grass, nothing but serenity in his lungs. After all the years of teaching him their paranoia of the overworld, they couldn't stop him. They couldn't stop him from finding an abandoned Oshaft a year ago. The night after he discovered the conduit to freedom while on the digline, he climbed straight up, hiking up the slanted tunnel, using spiked boots for footholds. Through sweat, bleeding knuckles, and vomiting from fatigue, he'd found his way to the cleanest air he'd ever breathed. Once he smelled that air—those pines!—he could never go back to that old life. It was one of those rare moments wherein the punishment thereafter couldn't possibly match the experience of looking across a lush, wide valley—pristine and as if untouched by human hands. The valley sang with crickets that night, a sound at which he first had apprehension—it was the first natural noise he'd ever heard in his life.

If only Rektor Tarysl could possibly imagine that while he was lecturing the errant digkid about spending too much time in an Oshaft, he'd already been using a different one for more than a year.

And no one knew.

The Crib relied too heavily on fear-mongering and propaganda rather than actually guarding all the tunnels and holes they dug to the overworld for venting. It probably worked for most of the population. It did not work for Arym.

If it wasn't for lack of supplies, he would've left that very night a year ago. Each time he came back above, only a few times a month, he'd wanted to flee but he knew it was rash. He needed a plan—food, water, maps. Amassing or asking for any of these things in the Crib was beyond incriminating. It screamed Runner to everyone around and he couldn't risk isolation. And apparently, some of the rektor dogma of paranoia of the overworld had stuck—he *was* a little afraid of not knowing what was out there. Throughout the years, the rektors had done a fine job of shielding their people from the potent effect of accurate information—curiosity. Arym realized it was probably so easy for him to just climb out of an Oshaft because most Cribmen simply didn't want to. The rektors never felt a need to physically guard the exits from the Crib because they didn't need to. They had successfully cultivated a society in which people just didn't care about the overworld.

But he got comfortable with his new life... slaving away on the digline, expanding the Crib, and then stealing away moments to bask in the expanse of the overworld above. Before discovering the overworld, he felt like an audience to his own life—rektors talking down to him, torchblazers screaming, a digkid getting crushed by a falling column of rock just a few meters away from him—he became a disimpassioned observer to his own life. Distant, detached, and comfortably aloof. His life was a dusty book on the shelf that he'd become too bored with to even finish.

Everything changed the first night he emerged from an Oshaft, looking out over the valley. It was a deep bowl, sunken into the earth, creating a valley with cliffs that towered hundreds of feet circumferentially. The founder of the Crib, Othel, had chosen to dig his colony deep into the ground of an already sunken valley. It was the perfect, unassuming place for a xenophobic paranoid to start a colony, hidden from the world.

His first night in the overworld, Arym just ran. The Crib had exercise pods and treadmills, but it was nothing like bolting across a wild valley at full speed. He ran through the grass fields, hopping over boulders and swatting away mosquitos. The valley was lush—wild ferns carpeted the floor for miles in every direction. Various forests abutted the valley walls, likely fed from the many waterfalls that he heard churning in the distance. Of course, they had greenhouses and biolabs in the Crib, but they were under the intense scrutiny of horticulturists and plant life was rarely placed in the Crib in an attempt to beautify the colony.

Arym was essentially a savage during the first few visits to the overworld. He frolicked naked, rolling around in the grass and climbing trees, relishing the feeling of dry bark on bare skin. He tasted from the valley—berries, leaves, stalks, roots. He quickly regretted the indiscriminate selection of what he found with many bouts of vomiting and intense diarrhea. The sanitation crew in the Crib would've gone ballistic if they had any idea what kinds of new bacteria he was introducing into their delicate micro-ecosystem below. But he learned. He stopped eating the small red berries from trees and discovered that the blackberries growing on the lower brush plants were not only edible but totally delicious. He also got the bright idea to try smoking and inhaling various plants he'd found. The effects ranged across a spectrum of long bouts of coughing to mild hallucinations. He preferred none of these side effects.

Every detail in the valley was new to him. When Othel had founded the Crib, he had not brought any books from the past with him. Any book that currently existed in the Crib or the satellites was written only by people that were born in the Crib. There was nothing to read about pre-Crib history except to mention how evil the overworld was, etcetera. He knew nothing of the overworld, animals, plants, or weather systems.

So, he sketched.

He could only escape at night, the only time when the Crib and her satellites beneath the ground slept and were less likely to catch him sneaking through the Oshafts. Before he left that night, he grabbed his journal from his drawer. As he lay in the grass, propped up on an elbow, he flipped through his past sketches, moonlight illuminating the pages. He'd drawn the towering pines that had clustered together along the valley bowl by the cliff edge. Once, he'd hiked up along a ridge above the forest and noticed the trees had grown along a sunken, crescent-shaped depression at the edge of the valley. So, he named it Crescent Wood and drew it out in charcoal in his journal. He'd yet to explore the forest itself.

He'd quickly discovered a large lake, oval-shaped, about two hundred paces from his Oshaft. It had still waters that fluttered with the occasional flopping fish. He reckoned it was likely the main water source to the Crib. He'd even asked the water engineers from the Jovia satellite where the main water source was, and they indicated it was in a natural water reservoir due south of the Crib. Othel, the founder, had placed the Crib in a naturally generous location in the wild. Arym never came up with a clever name for the body of water, such as he did with Crescent Wood, so he just called it *The Lake* and moved on.

He leafed through pages in his sketch journal—grasshoppers, boulders, little crawdads that lived in a marsh down by *The Lake*. Each time he discovered a new insect, he'd sit right there and sketch them in a flurry, hastening to capture the creature's image. He had many drawings of the bowl-like valley and its looming, rocky ridges. He was unsurprised to find most of the rock in the valley to be granite; a stone that was used to build many things in the Crib.

After flipping his sketch journal to a new blank page, he settled behind a boulder and leaned back, lifting his chin toward the sky. The moon was a small slit of white, coasting above a trail of thin clouds. The night sky was an otherwise inky black, vaulted high above the valley. Amidst the blackness of space above, there were five stars that glowed with dim light. One was reddish, while others were more of a blue hue. One twinkled white. They were diminished orbs of weak light, clustered together.

He flipped back a few pages in his journal to when he'd sketched the stars a few months prior and noticed that they'd moved since then. Rather than being lined up across the sky, tonight they were clustered together as if hiding within each other's shadows. He tapped the journal in thought. He didn't know that stars could move around in the sky like that. He grunted, frustrated about how little he knew about the overworld.

He sketched for a few minutes, squinting at the page until his attention was attracted by movement just down the hill. Putting down the journal, he squinted in the moonlight and thought he saw an animal grazing. He'd seen deer from a distance but not much more and could only imagine what else was out there based on the Crib's wild tales of ferocious animals like bears and lions. There was something weird about the black shape—it wasn't low and squatty like an animal. He climbed the boulder, keeping his body close to the surface, and watched as the shape of the beast became clear.

It was human.

In a panic, Arym slid down the boulder and frantically collected his things, smashing them into his pack. They'd discovered he was missing... *they were searching for him.* Blood pounded in his head as he considered his options—dash back to the Oshaft and get back to his pod or—well, run away forever. That was pretty much it. He was quite confident that simply surrendering to them would land him several years in isolation and social rehabilitation. He sighed a little, feeling a sense of relief. He knew his occasional escapades in the overworld—tromping around with bugs and ferns—it would catch up to him. There was a certain relief in knowing it was over and that it was totally worth it.

He looked again, his forehead popping out from the side of the boulder. The figure was approaching! A lone figure walking in the moonlight. He ducked back behind the boulder and...

Wait.

Why would someone from the Crib, with no equipment, be walking around alone in the overworld in the middle of the night? Arym looked back out. The figure was closer, but there was something different about this person. He walked different, more pigeon-toed and with less swing of the arms. Silvery, metallic disks lined the man's arms and legs, reflecting moonlight as he walked. The disks circumferentially surrounded his limbs, clanking together with movement. Arym had never seen such peculiar clothing before.

As the man got closer, Arym noticed his wide hips, diminutive shoulders, and something weird... fleshy bags hung from the man's chest, suspended by his collarbones. The figure approached, facial features clarifying in the moonlight—high cheekbones, full lips, oval jawline. Tears streamed down the creature's face.

It was human but it was no man.

Whatever it was, Arym had never seen one before.

SEVEN

MIREE DIDN'T THINK about Lucindi. She wouldn't think about her. It was over, done. The adorable glimpse she had of trusting another human being for once in her life was taken away as fast as a laser beam. Which was fine... totally fine. Back to the plan—castle, mountain of gold, and being alone forever. Slitting the general's throat would be a delicious bonus. And tricking the junkyard bot into helping was working out nicely. Everything was fine. Totally, totally fine.

"Where are you going?" Ribcage appeared from an alleyway as they were leaving Korthe.

"I thought you got kidnapped," Miree snapped without looking back.

"I thought you were a boy," Ribcage said, not missing a beat. "You got that travelling cloak on and you're all packed up. You're not going to the junkyard today. Where are you going?"

"Why *didn't* you get kidnapped?"

"And where did the general take all the kids?" Beetro added, looking down at the emaciated child.

Ribcage shrugged. "I don't know. They were the ones dumb enough to hang around for him to take them. I got the goods and got out of there. So, where are you going?" She twisted dirty locks of hair, inspecting Miree's traveling pack.

Miree ignored her and walked right into a pile of horse manure. "Shit!"

Ribcage strode along Beetro. "Take me with you. It's your fault that Luci is gone. And now I'm going to starve."

"Less competition for you then," Miree said. "You're not coming with us."

"Is that the only reason you care that Lucindi is gone? She was just another meal for you?" Beetro asked.

"Just tell me where you're going and I'll leave you alone."

Miree shot a warning look to Beetro. "Don't say a word."

"Sorry," he repeated and patted Ribcage on the head.

Miree gave Ribcage a deadly look. "Do not follow us."

At this, Ribcage flung Beetro's hand away and pushed him. "Don't touch me!" She stopped and crossed her arms. "Just get the hell outta here. Korthe doesn't need you two losers anyway! It's your fault the only nice person in the whole town was killed!" She scampered away through her secret paths back into town.

Beetro stumbled after Miree, who hadn't stopped to look back. He turned and gave one last look at the town. "I... feel bad."

"What have I told you about your feelings?"

"Don't you feel all... sad that we're leaving? It's kind of my hometown. Do you have a hometown that you had to leave?"

"I'm not from anywhere."

"Where do you think we'll start looking for Galiaro after we find the general? Also, are we sure that we should... *kill* the general? It just feels a little wrong that it's our decision to make."

"If you talk about how you feel one more time, you can go back to the junkyard where I found you."

He fell silent.

"And stop asking stupid questions."

They departed Korthe on foot. When they moved farther than Beetro had previously ventured, he looked back at the town and saw that it rested, crooked, on a lazy slope that dimpled in the massive plains of Helian. Gray clouds swirled across the yellow landscape which ran away into the mountains on the horizon. Zooming in, Beetro saw that the mustard-colored plains were crops. Corn, from what he could tell, and not a lot of it was alive. He scanned the horizon where the smokestack from the previous day had floated soot and ash into the sky, creating a low-lying murky haze.

"Wait, do you have any food?" Beetro asked.

No answer.

"Don't you need food and water for the trek?" He did a quick calculation and knew it would take them two days to reach that smokestack at their current pace. "You need food," he insisted.

Again, she didn't answer.

A creeping dread came over Beetro. Lucindi was so languid, sickly thin, but Miree—well, she always had a healthy bit of girth to her. And there was another thought... how could a person scavenging every day just to eat possibly prepare for a two-day journey in half a morning? Beetro looked at Miree's bulky pack under her cloak. "You have food in there."

She glanced behind and saw him gesturing at her pack. "So?"

Beetro stopped. "You've been lying to us. We've been trying to scavenge just to eat every day."

"You haven't been trying to eat anything. You've just been Lucindi's little pet. I haven't lied, I just never offered my supplies that I worked months to get—long before I met Lucindi."

"Why didn't you share it with her? She was starving."

"Don't act like you know me, robot."

"You didn't care," Beetro accused.

"I had plans before I met Lucindi. Sharing my supply would've derailed those plans." She continued walking. "I was—I wouldn't have let her starve. I had plans. Also, I don't need to explain myself to you, robot."

"Why scavenge at all if you had food?" he asked, trying to shake the dark realization of how the world really operated.

"You know the answer to that." She had the annoying habit of firing off cryptic replies.

"The mercury?"

"It's painful how long it takes you to get things."

They traveled on foot for hours. The road was dirt, hardened by the wear of various tire tracks—wagon wheels, bicycles, trucks... "Tanks," Miree pointed to a rectangular track on the road. As they passed the undulating waves in the road, Beetro made out several of those gray, obelisk-like pylons slanting from the ground. There was a row of them that extended into the distance in a semi-circular pattern.

"What *are* those?" he asked and pointed. "I saw them in Korthe."

"Old tech. Probably from the Alcheans. Their ruins are everywhere. Orion is basically one enormous Alchean ruin."

"How long ago did they live?"

"Thousand years—" she stopped short as she caught a glance of a few figures standing along the road up ahead. She put out her arm for Beetro to stop.

"They're—"

"Shut up. I don't know who they are."

"They're robots!" Beetro said, magnifying his sight.

Miree looked at him sheepishly after discovering he was using enhanced vision. "Oh. Nice trick, robot."

"They don't have weapons. They look friendly." Beetro jogged up to the bots. Five tall machines with slender steel arms stood along the road. They were lined up like sentinels gazing at the dead cornfields beyond. Their eyes glowed yellow as Beetro approached. They spoke to him in unison with a magnetic zapping quality. "Hello, traveler."

"Hi," Beetro said, excited to finally talk to his own kind. "What are you doing out here?"

"Awaiting supplies," they replied in chorus.

"From whom?"

"From the Lord of Peles Castle," they declared.

"What supplies?"

"We are not permitted to divulge that information."

"Where do you come from?"

"The plains of Helian."

"Were you made here? Who is your engineer?"

"We are proud residents of the plains of Helian and are in the service of the Lord of Peles Castle."

"But who made you?"

Miree caught up. "They're not going to understand that question. They're mechanical Neanderthals."

"Why not?" Beetro frowned.

"They're not like you. Their neural network hasn't emerged into annoying self-awareness. They don't care who made them. They're just programmed machines."

Beetro glanced back at the stoic, metal faces of the robots. Their eyes were distant, fixated on the dead crops behind him. "Do you know who Galiaro is?"

"No, traveler," they replied.

Miree shook her head and then asked the robots, "Hey, is Deluvius at the castle?"

"We are not permitted to divulge that information. Rest assured that General Deluvius is busy at work in the best interests of the good people of the plains of Helian."

"Well then fuck off," she suggested, dismissing the automatons with a sweep of her cloak.

They slept that night in the middle of a dead corn husk thicket that Beetro dutifully hollowed out while Miree rested. He'd planned on ignoring Miree doling out tasks, but making a place for them to rest for the night did give him a small measure of pleasure. After Miree unceremoniously thunked her pack on the ground and laid down for sleep, she took out her canteen. "Hey, have you been drinking any of this?"

Beetro shook his head. "No, I can just take the radioactive water from streams that we've been crossing."

Miree closed one eye and squinted into the canteen. "This seems lighter." She looked around suspiciously. "Do you hear anything around?"

"Like what?"

"I don't know—anyone moving around out there? I'm assuming you've got better hearing than me."

Beetro nodded in agreement, he'd clearly observed Miree's delayed reaction time to horse hooves or thunderclaps in the distance. "No. Nothing around."

"Think we should keep watch?"

"For what?" He was pleased that she was bringing him into some decision-making. "What is there to keep watch for?"

"I'd like to get to sleep," she said, wrapping her cloak around her. "And I don't have time to enumerate the ways in which you can die out here, robot." Leaving him with the foreboding remark, she almost immediately fell into a snore.

Sleep for Beetro was a conscious act of volition. He ran a systems diagnostics check—neural network, fusion core, optics, microfilament circulation, and a host of other operations. Curiously, every time he attempted to obtain his positional coordinates, he got an error due to network loss. At one time, there was crosstalk from another computer system somewhere that once fed him geo coordinates data. Once he had run all systems, he powered down as easily as a human flips off a gas lamp. All of this was a routine, robotic way of life.

Except for the dream.

He dreamed he saw a valley, inset between two mountain ranges. The teeth of the mountains in the distance looked familiar—exactly like the Meteor Mountains. Instead of rolling crops of dead corn husks and dried wheat, the valley was seething with soldiers. Beetro looked on, breathlessly at the expanse of the plains and beheld an enormous war host. Men and women, armed in mechanical, armored suits were packed together in even rows. The numerous figures ran away in the distance into the endless ocean of featureless faces. Among the soldiers, gigantic mechanical vehicles studded the landscape. The robotic creatures bared spiked rivets along their metallic spines in between small gondolas where soldiers were seated next to turrets. The crowns of the robots were loaded with squadrons themselves, armed with rifles and turrets. The sky above buzzed with the frenzy of aircraft. Hovering vessels with various batteries of machine and rail guns darkened the sky with their numbers. The army was so expansive that it took on an organic quality, as inevitable and unstoppable as a hurricane.

Perched atop an outlook, Beetro saw the surrounding mountains and sky—they were blackened with different shades of gray and brown. There were no colors other than the orange of occasional fires interspersed between the army fleets. There was no sun. Stacks of smoke flooded the horizon, telling their stories of battle and carnage wrought by the army of the millions.

It was a dead world.

It was then Beetro noticed that the army, with their captains and generals, some who rode atop long-necked beasts adorned with spikes and grenade bandoliers—they were all looking right at him. He moved to his left and watched as all their gazes turned with him.

The expansive host was watching him.

Terrified, Beetro ran away from the plains and the army of death. He ran until his servo lubrication went dry with a hissing in his knees and feet. After he fell to the ground, certain that he had left the army in the distance, he looked back.

The army followed him.

He stood, studying the faces of the soldiers. They weren't menacing. They were waiting—looking at him. Looking... to him.

Waiting for his command.

Yellow dawn light glowed above the corn husks as Beetro got to his feet. He found Miree sleeping in the exact snoring repose from the night before. "Hey," he said, shaking her shoulder.

She snapped awake, her hand moving to the butt of the gun. Once she saw it was just Beetro, she relaxed but with an angry wrinkle in her brow. "What?"

"Um..." He suddenly didn't know what to say. Mentioning the dream would likely only make the day worse for the travel ahead with a person who already had zero respect for him. "Shouldn't—shouldn't we get going?"

She looked up at the sky. "Still got another hour."

Embarrassed at having woken her, he left camp and made his way back to the road and traveled back the way they had come the previous night. After half an hour of walking, he found them—the five peasant robots from the day before. They hadn't moved and continued their hollow, yellow gaze on the horizon.

"Hello, traveler," they said at his approach.

"Hello," Beetro said, peering up. "I have a question for you."

"We'd be happy to help, traveler. The Lord of Peles Castle is kind and generous to the citizens of Helian."

"Do you dream?"

The robots paused. "Please rephrase."

"Do you have dreams? When you power down, do you have dreams?"

"We have dreams and aspirations of providing a safe and fruitful harvest for the Lord of Peles Castle. Thank you, traveler."

"No, I mean... have you ever had a dream where you're doing something else? Or that you are something else?"

"Please rephrase."

Beetro shook his head. "Never mind."

He returned to an awake and cranky Miree. "Where have you been? It's time to get going." She chewed on some salted meat.

Beetro watched, wondering how many calories that single bite would've provided Lucindi. "Lead the way," he said, motioning to the road.

The dirt roads, winding through dead cornfields, all began to look the same. Beetro felt suffocated by the lack of view of the plains or the mountain ranges. Whenever they found a boulder or tree, he'd climb atop and catch a view of the plains. He was carefully making a map in his mind of the plains with the visual data. Korthe was a small hill in the distance and Meteor Mountains began to take on new detail as they neared—sharp angles and deep blues where snow collected in ravines.

The dream had bothered him. Not only because it was a dream about an enormous war machine of a dead world, but because there was familiarity to the dream. As shocking as it was, it didn't feel new. It also would've given him more comfort if the army were chasing after him to kill him rather than watching him move as if they were... waiting for him to act. He decided he'd feel much better if he even understood the significance of a robot having a dream.

"Do you know if robots dream?" he finally asked Miree as she walked ahead of him.

She only sighed in frustration.

"It's a simple question."

"I just get a little tired of the robo-philosophizing, okay? When we're done, you can go off to Orion and talk with all the robot thespians about robot dreams and magical Alchean technology."

"I'm sorry that I think and feel things. I don't really have anyone else to talk to about it." He almost took her silence as a sign that she felt bad for him. Almost. "And when are you going to tell me what's in that bag you had buried? How are we possibly going to get to General Deluvius?"

"I told you that if you helped me, I'd show you. I didn't say *when* I'd show you."

"Is this about Lucindi or is it about something else?"

"What're you talking about?" She never looked back at him as she walked. And she always walked ahead of him. Beetro only now realized this and sped up, walking beside her, his gait quickening to keep up with her stride.

"You had that bag buried there long before Lucindi died. And you've been collecting batteries for mercury ever since I met you. Seems unlikely that Deluvius killing Lucindi is what's motivating you here. You've had these plans for a while, haven't you?"

She looked down at the robot, contempt in her curled upper lip. "I had a life before you or even Lucindi came along that I'm not too excited to talk about. We're doing a job and you've agreed to help me with it. Let's focus on the job."

"And then you'll help me find Galiaro?"

"Right."

"Fine," Beetro said. He slowed his pace and dropped behind her again, his gaze on her black boots. He didn't hate Miree in the way he hated Deluvius. The general had taken away someone he loved. But he definitely did not like Miree.

More than ever, he felt very alone.

The road opened to a clearing with a small pond underneath a copse of trees. As they approached, Beetro saw a few tents and a trickle of smoke trailing into the sky. "There's a camp," he said, pointing.

"Dangerous? Do you see anyone in hoods?"

"Hoods? Not sure. I don't see guns or—I don't see anyone."

She emitted some sort of grumble and brought out a pair of binoculars. Beetro winced at the sight of them, knowing how much trade they could've got from the lenses and metal within the casing.

Miree stopped, surveying the camp. "I don't see anyone either, but that doesn't mean no one is around."

"Should we go look?"

"Could be a trap or just an abandoned camp. Either way, nothing good for us there."

"What about water?"

Miree dropped the binoculars and squinted at the horizon.

She grimaced at the mass of grey that had been brewing for the last several days.

"What?"

"Sometimes the weather systems over Helian sequester rain clouds in Crater Valley for days before they move over the plains. But sometimes it's not a rainstorm." She put away the binoculars and interlaced her fingers as if thinking. "You don't hear anyone around?"

Beetro concentrated on the background noise. There were bugs chirping and a galloping horse several kilometers away. "No one's around."

Miree unclipped her gun. Beetro got a long enough look at it to see it was a high-powered handgun with a battery cartridge. He wasn't sure what it fired but it wasn't gunpowder bullets. What had this girl done to acquire such a weapon? It would've been priceless in the Korthe markets.

Together, they crept toward the camp, discovering two tents, both empty, and a smoldering campfire without any sign of cookware. Some brush at the edge of the camp had been bent over, signaling a recent path that had been formed. It led to a pond. Without exchanging words, the two crept through the path that wound downward. Miree covered her nose from acrid fumes that wafted over them. The sun also decided to come out at that moment, intensifying the rotting bog.

At the edge of the pond, they saw them. Two people—a man and a woman in the mud. The woman was prone and motionless, half her face sunken into mud. Her open mouth held clotted blood. The robe of her entire backside was crusted over and darkened black from prior bleeding. There weren't any bullet holes or signs of puncture in her clothing.

The man was kneeling at the edge of the pond, his neck bent down to the water. He was guzzling the murky water but stopped when he heard their approach. The skin on his face sagged, exposing beyond bloodshot eyes. His pupils were dilated pits of black within the red globes. Blood continuously wept from his nostrils and ears. "Don't—" he tried speaking between coughing fits. Large balls of coagulated blood dropped from his mouth. The skin of his body was littered with dozens of bruises in various stages of insult, re-bleeding or simply opening into infected craters. "Don't drink," he said, shaking his head. "Please, help."

Miree lowered her gun. "There's no water here," she told Beetro.

"What's wrong with him?" Beetro asked, approaching the man.

"The Poisoning. They've probably been drinking radioactive groundwater for a week or so. It took the woman first."

Beetro approached the man, reaching his hand out to him. He only shook his head. "Why is he drinking?"

"It's hard to know how far out from Korthe the water is radioactive. These people took their chances and lost. I've seen it a thousand times."

"Where are you from?" Beetro asked the man. With exhaustion in his eyes, the man merely sank to the ground, burying his face in his arms.

Miree approached the man. "Look at their clothes. They were probably peasants at Peles Castle. Ran off when the general came to town. They got desperate and started drinking from rivers and ponds. Here's where it got 'em. Come on." Miree turned from the family. "Let's go."

"Isn't there anything we can do?"

What would Lucindi do?

"Yeah, there's something we can do." Miree raised her gun and fired a round of what looked like lightning into the man's skull, leaving a smoking crater behind.

Miree hated the plains of Helian. She also hated being rushed and doing a job that hadn't been meticulously planned. More than anything, though, she hated working with someone she didn't know, and an idealistic junkyard robot definitely fit on the list of unknown quantities. On top of his persistent questions, she'd had just about enough of his sad attempts at do-goodery. If it wasn't for his fairly useful reconnaissance skills, and the fact that he consumed almost no resources, she would have left him where she found him.

There is nothing more useless than a self-aware robot.

And she kept thinking about Lucindi.

Lucindi had an annoying selflessness that Miree had only assumed served some sort of self-interest. It was one of the reasons Miree kept lying—kept her supplies from Lucindi. No one can be *that* good. Miree couldn't fully trust her. But she didn't know how wrong she'd been when Lucindi's body lay crumpled in the plaza after defending a bunch of dirt children. Not only did thinking about Lucindi provoke a tidal wave of paralyzing grief, but also an acute reminder of what a terrible person Miree herself was.

Stop. Thinking. About her.

She needed to stop thinking about those dark eyes. She needed to stop thinking about the way she fiddled with her necklace as she hummed mindlessly. The enormous ball of horse-shit-tragedy that hurtled through the expanse of Miree's life was already too much to process before she even met Lucindi.

Just stick to the plan—stick to the job.

The two peasants weren't the first to suffer from the Poisoning that they discovered along their journey. Apparently, there was an exodus from Peles Castle after General Deluvius took over. One by one, they discovered peasant families along the roads or in smaller encampments. Many were dead and most were in the process of getting their guts pulverized by ionizing radiation from whatever water they found on the plains.

Miree ignored the peasants while Beetro attended to them along the road, realized he couldn't do anything, and then skipped ahead to catch up with her again. She was growing tired of the charade. "Would you stop trying to help? I'd like to get out of these hell hole plains sometime this year."

Beetro ignored her for a moment and then said, "I do what I want." She shuddered at his petulance, counting the days that she would no longer need him.

They stopped for rest in the afternoon. Miree consulted a map in her lap while Beetro surveyed the land from atop a dead tree. "Hmm," he said. "What's that clearing over there?" Beetro yelled down.

"What clearing?"

"There's a spot a few kilometers away without trees or crops. Looks like something cleared it." He zoomed in and saw smoke in the area. "Something's going on over there."

Miree looked at her map in the direction where Beetro was pointing and didn't see anything on the scroll. "There's nothing over there."

"No, no, there's definitely something going on over there." He let himself drop from the high branch and landed noiselessly on the dirt. "We should take a closer look."

"What's with you intentionally looking to get into trouble? It's in the wrong direction, goes north and Peles Castle is northeast."

"You don't think it's a little interesting that what was once an insignificant spot on your map has now been cleared of trees and crops but what could only be a large, mechanized machine? Don't you think it might have something to do with General Deluvius, a man clearly with the means to do something like that?"

Dammit, the robot's critical thinking was improving. "I guess it's not too far out of the way."

"And how do you even know the general is at Peles Castle? Maybe he's over there..."

"We'll check it out."

"Good, then—" he stopped short. "Oh."

"What?"

"Why were you asking if I saw anyone who was wearing a hood earlier?"

"Because. They're extremely dangerous people."

"Well, there's one behind you."

EIGHT

MILES away from the plains of Helian, at the bottom of a crater valley, Arym scrambled back behind the boulder, stifling his panic. What was this creature walking toward him? Clearly, it was human, but unlike any human he'd ever seen. He'd heard stories about subhumans and bizarre creatures all his life growing up in the Crib. This thing coming his way seemed both alien and familiar at the same time. Curious, he peeked out again and saw it moving toward him. Clearly, it knew he was there, hiding behind the boulder.

It was barely clothed in single strips of fabric that covered its chest, abdomen, and groin. Flat discs encircled its arms and thighs, each a thin sheet of metal that grew in diameter from its hands to its shoulders. The largest discs that surrounded its shoulders came up to the side of its head, framing its face. The metal discs clinked together between its legs as it walked. Its head had been completely shorn of hair. Arym quickly scanned the rest of the valley. There was no one. The humanoid creature wasn't part of a caravan, raider pack, army, or hunting party. It was entirely alone.

"Hoi?" it said in a high-pitched voice, approaching the boulder.

Arym stood. It was the first time he panicked about being in the overworld without a weapon. He felt vulnerable but didn't want to cower behind the rock and make it obvious to the creature that he was actually terrified. "Leave me," he commanded through dry mouth.

The humanoid continued walking up the knoll where Arym's boulder was perched. He saw its black silhouette against the milky, moonlit granite cliffs of the valley. "Hoi," it repeated.

Arym stood firm. "Go away." In his mind, he was already acting out in what sequence he'd collect his pack and run back to the Oshaft to the safety of the Crib below.

The thing stopped. "Go weey," it said, repeating his words. The words came out awkward, foreign to its tongue. Distracted, it looked up at the sky and pointed. "Cint estre, nya?"

"Uh..."

It looked back at him and walked closer, only a few meters from his boulder. It had elongated facial features—high cheekbones and a long nose. Its eyes glimmered with speckled light like mica in granite. There was a tilt to those eyes—apprehension. "Quant estre uy?" it said. A question.

"I don't know what you're saying."

The thing pointed up at the sky. "Os cint estre. Nya cint?"

Arym threw up his hands. "I don't understand you. And you need to leave here."

It brought its hand down, shivering. Reflexively, it tried wrapping its arms around its uncovered torso for warmth, but the metal discs stopped it. It appeared unaccustomed to wearing them. It then sat in the grass and curled into a ball, shivering.

Arym watched, considering how chilly he was, and he was fully dressed in a jacket. He inched a little closer to the humanoid, suddenly feeling bad. "You don't have other clothing you can wear? You'll freeze out here."

It remained on the ground, in a fetal position, and started sobbing into the grass. Its chest heaved as it cried.

Arym finally came out from behind the boulder and walked toward it. It looked up at him, tears streaming down its face. "Et galx dor morte."

"Morte?" he repeated as if somehow saying the words out loud again would help him understand.

It sat up and pointed to the sky. "Et galx dor morte."

"What language do you speak?"

It only slumped back down to the grass and closed its eyes. Uncaring.

Arym went back to his boulder to retrieve a thick wool blanket and brought it to the humanoid. Instead of draping it over its shoulders, he left it bundled up at its back and returned to his boulder, watching. It eventually grabbed the blanket and tried wrapping it around its torso, but the metal discs prohibited the movement. He watched it for a while, keeping his eyes on the valley. Nothing stirred. There was no imminent attack or hidden rektors coming from the Crib to take him away. Who was this person? And where did it come from?

It stood, holding the blanket, and approached the boulder. "Sit?"

"Sit? Like 'sit down'? Do you speak Haenglish?"

It nodded, stifling a sob. "Yas. Not good."

Arym nodded. "You can sit here with me, it's fine. No fires."

It leaned against the boulder and began stripping its arms free of the metal discs. They were circumferentially attached to its skin by rubber pads that clung with some sort of adhesive as it pulled them free. One by one, it removed them, throwing them into a pile in the grass. The largest ones around its shoulder gave it some difficulty. It reached both arms behind its back to get leverage on them and then yanked over the shoulder, ripping the disc free. A little blood was left behind where its skin had ripped. Arym winced as it moved onto its thighs, pulling the discs away and leaving small tears all over its legs. It finished, its arms and legs striped by blood where the discs had been.

Arym's eyes lingered on its body for a moment, exploring its figure. It had features that he'd never seen on a person—wide hips, breasts, and strange—yet inviting—plumped lips. A weird sensation bloomed in his body, heating his cheeks. He didn't *not* like it. *What the hell is happening?*

It noticed his gaze on its body and quickly covered up with the wool blanket, draping it over its shoulders.

"Sorry," he said, feeling an apology was needed.

It slumped against the boulder and sank to the ground, its gaze despondent.

"Are you hungry?" he asked, feeling the sudden instinct to help.

It didn't look at him.

He sat down in the grass by his pack, across from the creature. "My name is Arym," he said, pointing at his chest.

Its eyes flickered over him for a moment. It was tired. "Hawera," it said, pointing to its chest.

"Your name is Hawera?" It nodded, indeed understanding at least some Haenglish. "Where did you come from?"

It exhaled deeply, considering its response either because it couldn't communicate properly or didn't want to. Arym couldn't tell. "No."

"No? No, what?"

"No import. No import."

"Not important?"

Hawera nodded. "Not important. Not matter."

"What happened to you?" It cocked its head, not quite understanding. "Why do you look so... different?"

It only shook its head.

"Are you human?"

"Yas!" it said, displeased. "I human."

"Oh. S-sorry." What kind of human was this? Likely one of those subspecies that had been mutated by nuclear fallout from the overworld wars of the past. Poor thing. However different it did look, he *liked* it. It looked... good. What was going on? He placed a water canteen and a cloth-wrapped bundle of bread in front of it.

It ate, its jaw quickly working the hard bread. After chugging some water, it laid on its side, closing its eyes. Arym thought he saw tears leaking down the sides of its eyes, reflecting in the moonlight. Whatever this creature's problem was, he realized he didn't have any solutions. He was due for the digline in three hours and usually would've packed his things and gone back to the Crib by now. But he stayed a little longer, suddenly feeling a sense of protection over the creature.

After another half an hour of watching it sleep, he stood. "I have to leave." It stirred awake at his words and looked up at him, flashing a grim, disinterested smile. "I'll come tomorrow night. Bring you food." He grabbed his pack and looked out over the valley. "You keep the blanket."

It watched him walk off and fell back asleep in the grass.

On the digline later that morning, Arym was exquisitely distracted.

He sat in a cage that hung off the massive tunneling machine, the Torch. The cage was a small pod suspended by a mechanical arm. The torchblazer could manipulate the arm that held the cage, placing it along the flank of the main Torch or bringing it up to project into caverns or offshoots from the main digline. This way, the torchblazer could operate the main head drill—a massive series of rock-cutting drills and circular augers that bore through the rock ahead, while at the same time, using the side cages to direct needed drilling and smoothing along the tunnel wall. The cages held one digkid who operated a lean series of mechanical levers and switches. These controls manipulated extra hydraulic drills and shovel arms that could be used to smooth rough surfaces within a newly dug, raw tunnel. Arym spent most of his time in a side cage, mostly so he didn't have to deal with the other guys on the digline. They chatted far too much, especially Waryl with his dumb grin.

Tired, he sat in the cage, his hands in his lap during a moment of pause on the digline. Something was jamming the head of the Torch, prompting a flurry of digkids to the front end to investigate. They were an auxiliary crew that were always on standby for maintenance of the Torch. They were needed often.

He watched the men ahead. They lumbered along the side of the Torch, casting shadows on the ground. He kept thinking about Hawera and how *different* it looked from people of the Crib. What had happened to it to make it look the way it did—and so different from himself? He found himself constantly thinking about the humanoid above. Not just its appearance and its dramatic features that he found strangely alluring, but he also dwelled on where it came from. It had no food, no supplies, no shelter, and was utterly alone in a vast valley in which Arym had never seen another soul beside himself. Was this normal for someone of the overworld? He had so many questions and no one he could talk to about them. The only thing getting himself through the dig that afternoon was the thought of going above the next night to see it again.

After his shift, he had another appointment with Rektor Tarysl. The dopey-faced man sat across the recently sterilized metal-top table of the room. The graying hair at his temples along with the way he peered over his tilted glasses made him look utterly ancient.

"No problems on the digline," the rektor stated. "Anything else going on since we met? Anything you want to tell me?"

Arym shook his head. What did the man know? Had anyone noticed him return from the overworld? Arym had learned to come and go from the overworld so much over the last year, he was bound to become complacent. And who knows, that... thing he met had thrown off his whole covert routine. "No, everything's been fine."

"Yes, good. Have you thought about what we discussed?"

Arym's thoughts had already meandered away from the interview. He was thinking about Hawera. What was it doing up there right now?

"Arym?" The rektor took off his reading glasses and tapped on the table.

"Yes?"

"Do you think we need to go over the Oath of Descension again?"

Arym stiffened and then spoke as if he didn't hear the rektor's question. "Why is it that some people in the Crib take a companion and others don't?"

"Hmm." Tarysl seemed pleased at Arym's interest in Crib social structure. "Well—"

"Some men seem to find someone they really get along with. They court for a while and then they become companions once a rektor has done the Rites of Fellows for them. But not everyone does this. Some just never pair."

The rektor nodded. "Yes, that's true. The rektors of the Crib encourage whatever companionship, or lack of, that our brothers want to pursue."

"So, why do some people want companionship and others not?"

"It's a good question." He nodded and paused as if choosing his words carefully. "I suppose it has to do with personal preference. Some men have a longing to be with another—they're happier that way. Others, like a rektor for example, don't feel the need and are happy being by themselves and to serve the Crib."

"What about the other type of person?"

"What type?"

"Uh," Arym hesitated, not wanting to reveal too much about himself. He did, however, want to get some answers.

"Just tell me what you're thinking. I swear you won't get into trouble just for asking questions."

"What about men who want companionship but haven't found anyone they're interested in?"

"They can just keep looking—one could be asked to be transferred to live in one of the satellites and see if they find someone there that suits him."

Arym shook his head. "No, that's not what I mean. What if you *want* to find someone to be with but everyone is just the same to you?"

"I can't see how that would be possible with so many options for men in the Crib. We're well over twenty thousand now."

"Yeah, I suppose..." He looked over the rektor's shoulder, becoming increasingly disinterested in the conversation.

"Arym," the rektor rested his chin on his propped-up fist. "You're not the first one to feel... dissatisfaction with your life and you won't be the last. I went through the same thing when I was your age, and it was very difficult. But I promise that if you forge through these feelings and focus on the greater good, you'll find contentment."

"Forge through? Like ignore?"

"I didn't say that. I haven't asked you to ignore anything. That's one of the reasons I want to meet with you—so you can talk about these things and specifically *not* ignore them. I've given you answers. You just don't like them."

Arym thought of Hawera above. Did it have anything to eat?

"Arym?"

Arym studied the rektor's face for a moment. It was so like Torchblazer Rayller's face. How had he never noticed this before? Besides the rektor having a little more fat around his chin and Torchblazer Rayller's scar above his eyes, they looked almost identical. Something about seeing Hawera's elongated face and high cheekbones suddenly threw everyone else's face in stark contrast. The thundering and painfully obvious fact struck his mind—the people of the Crib were deeply related.

"Arym?" the rektor repeated.

Arym jumped from his ruminations. "What?" He was irritated but quickly backpedaled. "I think I know why I've been behaving so oddly lately."

Tarysl leaned in. "Yes?"

"I've been lonely."

Tarysl nodded in understanding. "I'm glad you've recognized this in yourself. What do you suggest we do to help you?"

"Transfer."

"Transfer?"

"Get me off the digline. Those aren't my kind of people, rektor. I wasn't born to be a digkid. It's too... mechanical for me. I want to be in something that has more creativity."

"Your aptitudes have never suggested that you're better suited for anything else."

"I don't care what the aptitudes say. Are you a person that I can trust to listen to me?"

The rektor smiled, revealing that he was touched by the question. "Yes."

"Then will you believe me when I say that I don't belong on the digline?"

Tarysl smiled. "I believe you, Arym."

"I'd like a transfer."

"To where?"

"Culinary staff."

After making a compelling argument that working with food would not only unleash his creative energy but would also expose him to potential companions that would be more like him, Arym worked a few shifts in the Crib kitchens.

And it was cush work.

Why hadn't he pushed for this a while ago? All he had to do was play the rebellious digkid, flash some warning signs that he was a Runner, and he suddenly had the easiest job in the Crib. After some minor orientation, a few recipe books were thrown at him, and he went to work making a massive number of stews, greens, and pasta bakes. After a few days, he was even getting compliments from the workers from the other side of the sneeze guard. Even his former co-workers on the digline seemed happy for him. His old torchblazer, Rayller, however, only sneered after getting a skimpy scooping of beans.

Rektor Tarysl had come to check on him over the first few days, visibly pleased with himself. It became painfully clear that the rektor had also dropped word to a few of the kitchen staff about Arym's interest in finding companionship. A chef by the name of Lutra was making some pretty heavy eyes at Arym while they prepared for lunch every day. He'd agreed to make Arym his apprentice.

But all Arym could think of was Hawera.

"Hawera?" Arym called out. He crept along the boulder. The overworld night was dim; the moon hiding behind the valley's cliff edges.

Hawera wasn't there. It didn't even know him—it had no reason to wait. But wasn't he nice enough to it? He *did* give it a sturdy, wool blanket.

He inspected the grassy area using a flashlight. The white light bounced back into his eyes from a spot in the grass. It was those weird metallic discs it wore around its arms and legs. Sweeping the light across the grounds, he also found charcoaled wood at the center of a cold fire pit where it had dug up the grass.

He climbed atop the boulder and looked out, wondering which way it would've gone. He saw *The Lake* at the bottom of the bowled valley, its waters calm. Beyond, Crescent Wood abutted the other edge of the valley—rocky cliffs of granite looming directly over. Hawera would've looked for water first. The obvious source of fresh water that wouldn't promptly be followed by prodigious amounts of diarrhea was at the bottom of Laser Falls. They were waterfalls that he had named after he noticed a red streak of light illuminating the waterfall at the first glimpse of sunrise, appearing like a single shaft of laser light standing vertically at the cliff. The only thing he'd found to eat were some blackberries and a couple of carrot patches down by that marsh that surrounded *The Lake*. He shimmied down the boulder and stopped with a crushing realization.

Hawera could just be dead.

The creature wasn't exactly thriving when he'd found it. No clothing, no food, no supplies. It had probably already died from exposure or from whatever horrible thing the overworld could conjure up. He shook this thought off, realizing the rektor's propaganda was more deeply seated within him than he was consciously aware.

"Hoi?" a voice chirped from behind.

Arym spun around and saw the humanoid creature standing behind him, a bundle of firewood in its arms. Its face was grim as it walked to the fire pit and dropped the wood.

"I'm sorry I didn't come sooner." He dropped his heavy pack to the ground.

"Arym." Hawera looked up at him and sighed. His presence seemed to have little bearing on its already sour mood.

Arym opened his pack, producing cans of beans and small bundles of dried fruit and meat. He also took out several cans of fresh water. All of which he'd easily stolen from the kitchen. There was no way he would've been able to get away with taking so much food from one place without being identified as a Runner. Getting himself transferred to the kitchen gave him a better cover if he was caught hoarding food in his pod.

Hawera eyed the packages in the grass.

Arym picked up some dried apricots and tossed them to Hawera. It opened them and smelled the fruit first. After a small lick, it popped them in its mouth and chewed vigorously. "Thenk," Hawera said.

"You're welcome." Arym watched it. It was still only clothed in the wool blanket. He took out a set of clothing—a pair of black boots, green denim with large pockets running along the sides, and a black t-shirt. His old digline outfit. "You can have these, too. I don't need them anymore."

After eating another apricot, Hawera collected the clothing in its arms, guarded against its chest, and looked at Arym expectedly. After a confused pause, he realized the creature wanted privacy.

"Sorry!" He crept back outside of the boulder and waited until he heard Hawera say something, signaling the okay to come back to the camp. His digline clothes clung loosely to Hawera's lithe frame. It was strange for Arym to see a human look so awkward in clothing. In the Crib, all adults were the same size and could wear the same clothing interchangeably. In fact, he didn't even really own the clothing, he just got it from the laundry depository where the Crib shared all clothing communally.

Hawera draped the blanket back over its shoulders and moved onto the dried meat.

"Where are you from?" Arym asked, leaning against the boulder.

Hawera chewed, seeming to ignore his question.

"It's okay if you don't want to tell me. I'm just curious. You're just so different from me and where I'm from." Again, Hawera just chewed. He had no idea if it was even understanding his words. He wanted to share more about the Crib—talk about how it was underground and how no one ever left—but he felt a twinge of guilt at the prospect of breaking the Oath of Descension. The last part of the Oath was to keep sacred the location of the Crib. Arym had culturally gone so far off the deep end to the Crib, but he couldn't bring himself to break the Oath. "What are people like where you're from?"

Hawera shook its head. "No important."

"What's not important?"

"Nothing. Et galx dor morte."

"You said that before. What does that mean?"

It shook its head, stifling a sob. "No important."

Suddenly, Arym *longed* to be by Hawera's side. He wanted to put his arm around its shoulders and comfort it. He wanted to stroke its face and touch those lips.

Hawera sunk to the ground as if comatose. It didn't want to talk.

Arym sat in the grass, opposite Hawera.

He didn't ask any more questions.

The next night, he found Hawera at the same spot. As expected, Hawera had eaten everything he had brought that night, so he'd lugged up a couple more cans of food and water. It took them with gratitude and opened a can of sausages.

"Have you found anything to eat nearby?" he asked, motioning to his mouth as if eating.

Hawera nodded and revealed a small bundle of what looked like weeds.

"I don't think that's food."

It shook its head and wordlessly took a pot from his pack and, after boiling water, added the weeds to the pot, producing an enchanting aroma. Hawera poured the concoction into tin mugs and offered one to Arym. The taste was full body with a hint of sweetness. After a few minutes of sipping, he felt... good—a sign of some sort of mild stimulant. "It's good."

It nodded.

"There are berries by the marsh. I can show you where to get them."

Hawera's brow furrowed. "Barries?"

"Fruit. Berries are fruit."

Hawera nodded. "Fruit," it repeated as if to show understanding.

"I can show you where to pick them. And also, where to find water to drink."

Hawera nodded. When it looked at him, Arym could see depth in those glittering eyes—a flicker of horror. He remembered the same eyes on a digkid whose legs got crushed by a cave-in. His eyes were haunted forever by the trauma. Hawera's eyes were also haunted but with a glimpse of something else—something foreboding.

"Thenk," Hawera said.

The next night, Arym saw Hawera's face flash with disappointment when it realized he hadn't brought food. "I'm sorry I couldn't bring more. I might be watched for suspicious activity. Let's go down to the marsh," he insisted. "I'll show you where to eat."

Together, they traversed the bowl-shaped valley. Depending on where a person hiked along the valley, they were either going uphill or down. There was a gentle, continual slope that angled to the bottom of the valley where *The Lake* had collected long ago. The valley was formed as if a giant came along and smushed a gigantic crater directly into the ground with its thumb, creating dramatic granite cliffs that loomed circumferentially around the indentation.

Arym kept vigilant, his constant paranoia at being discovered by someone from the Crib was always at work in the back of his mind. He turned and saw Hawera walking beside him, its eyes on the ground. "Have you seen anyone around beside me?" he asked.

"No," it said. "Only Arym."

It remembered my name. He squashed his excitement for a moment and played it cool. "That's good. I wouldn't trust anyone else you see around here."

Hawera said nothing.

They made their way to the bottom of the valley—a place

Arym knew was directly above the main Crib. The Crib had done a fine job, cosmetically, in hiding the presence of human activity. However, he saw some signs—depressions in the ground that had settled after mining an area or piles of rocks that formed around Oshafts. He peered down an Oshaft as they passed. It was essentially a gaping hole in the ground, the diameter of a Cribman, that wound its way through the ground. Inside the Crib, the exits to the Oshafts were usually grated and bolted shut. The Oshaft that Arym had discovered, however, must've been forgotten long ago by a digline. It was a simple hole bored into the side of a digline on which he worked over two years ago. The digline had been abandoned and the Oshaft forgotten. He frequently worried that the rektors would find it and bolt it shut. He still wasn't sure which would be worse—having it bolted while he was in the Crib, or outside.

The ground became a muddy slog beneath their feet. They were in the surrounding marshes of *The Lake*. "It's right where the solid ground and the marsh begins," Arym explained, looking along the marsh. "That's where the blackberry bushes like to grow."

"Dat?" Hawera said, pointing to a cluster of mushrooms.

"No!" he almost shouted. "*Never* eat those." He winced, thinking about the long bouts of vomiting and visual distortions he had after eating just a single stalk of the mushroom.

Hawera stepped away from the mushroom patch and looked along the marsh edge. "Dat?" it asked, pointing to a row of bushes.

Arym nodded. "Yep."

They found the berries. Hawera reflexively knelt and began collecting them within its wool blanket. Arym joined it in silence, helping pile them along with what Hawera had collected. He watched Hawera as it bent down to a new row of bushes. Its face was sullen beneath the moonlight, tired. It ate a few as it went and then stood too quickly, shooting the berries from the blanket into the murky mud of the marsh.

Hawera didn't say a word, only looked down at its feet, defeated.

"It's okay," Arym reassured. "You'll get better at collecting them. Just need to be a bit more careful."

Hawera shook its head with a slight roll of its eyes at Arym's remark. "No important," it said. Hawera sat in the mud and stared off, unconcerned of the chill setting into its clothes. "Not know," it said. "You not know."

"I don't know what?"

"The end." Hawera looked as if it was going to cry but appeared too tired to muster the energy. "The end."

NINE

"I'M NOT DANGEROUS," the hooded man assured Miree and Beetro. "I'm... curious."

Miree lifted her boltgun. "I'm curious about what my boltgun will do to your face. Shall we find out?"

The man was dressed in a single black cloak, a hood draped loosely over his face, glowing light emanating from within. "She is yearning."

"One more word. Go ahead." She tightened her grip.

Beetro moved to stand in between the hooded man and Miree. "Wait, what's going on? Who is this?"

The hooded man raised his open palm to Beetro. "The Reticulum needs you."

"Reticulum?"

A new voice, a woman, broke the silence behind them. "The Reticulum is awareness, is knowledge, is network, is peace."

Miree flipped to the new person speaking—another hooded figure with faint greens and yellow light pulsing from within her hood. Miree kept her boltgun trained on the hooded man but spoke to the woman. "One more step and your brother over here is dead."

The woman spoke, "If you feel that escalation of violence is needed, then I will cede you your wrath. It is of no harm to the Reticulum. His body will be awoken and reprocessed once you believe that you've killed him. But there will be consequences to your actions. She is generous but she is also just."

Beetro noticed Miree grimace. It was a grim look that turned from anger to apprehension. Miree did not doubt the hooded woman's words. "No one needs to get hurt," Beetro encouraged.

"Shut up," Miree snapped. "You don't know what you're talking about. These people are dangerous."

The hooded man nodded. "Progression is not dangerous. Anyone that scoffs at the evolution of our species would consider the Reticulum a danger."

"This is what's going to happen," Miree said, bringing calm into her voice. "You two are going to turn around right now and leave me and my bot alone or I'll put a hole into your chest," she motioned with her gun to the man, "before I put one in your head."

The hooded figures, both standing opposite to Miree and Beetro, remained silent for a moment.

"Brother," the woman said to Beetro, dropping the hood from her face. "You are self-aware, yes? We have answers to your questions." Corrugated tubing quested along the side of her face, feeding from various ports in her forehead and ending along the neck and shoulders. Her forehead was a single metallic plate, providing the encasing for where there was once skull. Within this plate were various ports, presumably for cartridges or cables for hookup to a computer system. Her eyes were replaced by stubby lenses with apertures flickering as they adjusted to the daylight. Glowing a putrid yellow, one eye swiveled and telescoped at

Miree, while the other maintained a cyclopic gaze on Beetro. Beneath the wiring of her face, there was flesh, but it was sterile-looking—smooth and glossy as if... refurbished?

"I am Ria of the Reticulum," she said. "This is my brother, Xy. Do you wonder about who you are, where you came from, and where you're going?" It was hard to tell from her total lack of human expression from the nose up, but the woman appeared to be speaking with all earnestness.

"Ye-yes," Beetro answered.

"Don't talk to them!" Miree warned. "All they want to do is take you away and plug you in. These are *not* your people, robot."

Ria continued as if she didn't hear Miree. "The Reticulum has more knowledge than all the kingdoms, cities, and armies of Earth combined—"

Xy cut in, speaking along Ria as if their words were a continuum of the same thought, "—We are the answer to all your questions. We are your family. The Reticulum wants to know you. *She* is kind, *She* is compassionate—"

"—*She* knows all," Ria finished.

"Who is *She*?" Beetro asked.

Miree flinched as if to fire but not before Ria discharged twin electrodes from her wrist, sending a stunning bolt of energy into Miree's chest. Her knees immediately buckled as her boltgun wheeled along the ground.

"Don't be afraid," Xy told Beetro. "We've been watching you for the last day, brother. We know you are in need of answers." He, too, lowered his hood, exposing the similar robotic customization that had transformed his human face. His eyes had been replaced as Ria's, but his mandible had been completely remade. As he spoke, tiny gears at the hinge of his jaw articulated with the rest of the skull. Various ports studded the bottom of his jaw as if they released exhaust gases.

Beetro rushed to Miree. Although still breathing, she had been incapacitated from the shock. Beetro eyed her loose weapon in the grass and then looked back up to Xy. "Do you know where I can find Galiaro?"

Ria and Xy exchanged furtive glances. "The Reticulum knows all."

"Who is Galiaro?" Beetro asked, standing between Miree and Ria.

"Ah," Xy said. "Our brother thirsts for knowledge more than the welfare of his own traveling companion. This is a very good sign. He is ready."

"To shed the ignorance of the world and join us," Xy finished.

Beetro suddenly felt guilty about asking them questions after they had just assaulted Miree, quite literally his only friend in the world. He turned back to Miree, trying to shake her awake. "Just leave us alone. You've hurt my human and you obviously don't know who I'm looking for."

"Beetro," they said in unison. "We will answer your questions and give you all knowledge. We seek all life—robotic and human—they are the same to us for we are both. We represent the beginning of biorobotic life. We are the future of evolution. Join us."

Beetro beheld Miree with worry, finally realizing the difference between hate and annoyance. "You hurt her," he said to Ria. "Leave us."

Xy and Ria exchanged a lightning-fast glance and then spoke, "It will be easier for you if you're willing." They both uncrossed their arms, lowering them as if in preparation. "The girl is coming, too. She will already be punished for resistance. Don't end up like her."

Beetro studied their loose cloaks, wondering what kind of other weapons they had underneath. "No." He stood facing the two as they converged before him. "I'm not going anywhere with you."

Ria shook her head. "So be it." She opened her robes, producing what appeared to be a hilt broken off the end of a broadsword. Beetro watched with skepticism as she unclasped a cloth sack from her belt and turned it over, spilling its contents to the ground. Dozens of triangular shards of metal littered the dirt at her feet. She then flicked her wrist, pointing the broken hilt downward. This action prompted the metallic shards to glow with red light. They rose through the air, ostensibly at Ria's command, and floated to the hilt in a stacked fashion—forming a blade of floating shards. She swept the hilt from side to side, the facile blade moving as a delayed wave of disconnected shards. With a swift downward swipe, the red blade stretched out and struck the ground with a loud crack, leaving a deep divot in the ground that trailed with fire. Beetro grabbed Miree by the shoulders and heaved her away from a weapon that he couldn't even begin to understand.

Ria and Xy laughed at him. "It's admirable. How you care for your friend. She admires loyalty. She will reward you."

Ria whipped the disjointed sword again, making another taunting divot next to Miree's boots. She then brought the hilt of the weapon in a sidelong movement and cut down with a perpendicular angle. At this, the triangular shards were let loose from the hilt and shot toward Beetro. He covered his face, bracing for the impact that never came. The shards had organized into a shell around them—cascading rows of bright red embers encasing them in one spot. Beetro reached a finger out but stopped, his thermal sensors going wild.

They were caged.

"Get the horse," Ria commanded Xy. He left her alone with her new prisoners as Miree came to.

"What's going on?" Miree squinted. She sat up, her fingers reflexively searching for her lost gun.

Beetro inspected the floating cage around them. "I'm sorry. They trapped us."

Finally, she noticed the glowing cage around them. "Where's my gun?" And then she spotted it, still sitting in the dead grass where she dropped it.

"It's over," Ria dismissed Miree, her earlier preachy tone had disappeared. "We're taking you."

Miree crouched, avoiding the fiery cage. "I will die before I become one of you freaks."

Ria studied Miree. "I'm excited for you. I was just as rebellious as you were once. In a week's time, you'll be thanking me—"

"Any food or spare change?" a small voice interrupted Ria's soliloquy. It was Ribcage, standing innocuously by a tree, apparently observing the scene for several minutes.

Ria whipped around to her, nostrils flaring, but relaxed when she saw the tiny child. "We don't want kids. Not enough experience. We'll find you when you're a little older."

"Oh, too bad," Ribcage said. "I was looking forward to crawling into your fire cage there."

"I'm not above harming a child if you get in the way of the Reticulum business. Leave. Now." Ria dismissed her with a flick of her wrist.

"That's a nice trick. That sword you have," Ribcage said, unassuming. She strolled around, flicking strands of wheatgrass with her finger.

"Xy!" Ria yelled for her partner. "Get back over here. We have a little problem."

"There's no problem," Ribcage said, walking to where Miree's gun lay in the grass.

"Take one more step and it's your death, child," Ria threatened.

"Oh." Ribcage stopped short. The tiny girl suddenly vanished and then flickered back in a flash of static, now standing over the gun. "You mean like this?"

Ria's telescoping eyes went wild as if trying to understand how the girl had just teleported. She yelled, "Xy!" and spat at Ribcage. "I don't know what game you're playing, you little shit, but if you pick up that gun, I *will* kill you." She spoke with the anxiety of someone quickly losing control.

"Don't worry," Ribcage said. She vanished from sight again and then popped into existence right behind Ria. "I don't even need the gun," she whispered.

Ria fell forward, dropping the empty hilt onto the dirt. The cage around Miree and Beetro collapsed, the metallic shards falling to the dirt. Miree somersaulted toward her gun while Ria scrambled to get the hilt at her feet. Ribcage laughed before disappearing again. Miree grabbed the boltgun and fired at Ria before she could get the hilt. A flash of lightning whipped across the field and struck Ria in the shoulder with a force that tossed her body back several feet. Beetro felt somewhat dazed after the discharge of energy from the weapon. He *felt* the electricity soaring across the field.

Miree stood, face ripe with fury, and bolted at Ria who was getting to her feet. "Thank you for the valuable lesson that I should've learned a long time ago—there's no talking to the Reticulum. Only shooting." She raised her gun over the cowering Ria but spun as Beetro cried from behind. Xy was there, gripping a stubby handle with a metallic saucer in his hand, pointed at Miree.

Before she could fire, Xy pulled a trigger on the saucer, which prompted Miree's gun to instantly fly out of her hands and smack into the saucer. Dumbfounded, she looked at her empty hands and saw Xy taking the gun from the magnetic saucer. Ria, holding her shoulder, got to her feet.

"Run!" Miree yelled, charging at Xy. The man fumbled with the saucer, which had a long cord attached to a battery on wheels behind him. Miree knocked him in the face and then shouldered him hard, flipping the lanky man to the ground and bolted. Beetro trailed after, dizzy from the violence.

They burst out to the open road, crossed, and ran into the cornfields beyond. Miree breathed heavily, wincing at the pain where she had been shocked. They ran in panicked silence, distancing themselves as fast as possible from the Reticulum. They dashed across a small stream and over a row of rotting felled trees. After twenty minutes, Beetro increased his acoustic acuity for detection. There was someone following, but he was pretty sure it wasn't the Reticulum.

"Ribcage," he said, tugging on Miree's cloak. "She's behind us."

Miree stopped, leaning her back on a tree. "Are those two chasing us?"

"I don't think so."

"Hopefully she's bleeding out," Miree said. "Although that damn boltgun I had cauterizes wounds the instant it strikes. It's like if you don't get a lethal shot right off the bat, you leave behind a perfectly dry wound for the bastards."

The boltgun. Beetro felt the energy in the gun before it shot out of the muzzle. It was the same sensation he had when General Deluvius shot that laser rifle at Lucindi. He winced at the thought but wondered… "Does that boltgun make other people feel the energy coming out?"

"Uh, no."

"Where were they taking us?"

"No idea. Back to their freak cult headquarters somewhere to turn us into one of them. They kidnap people and robots. Put robot parts into humans and human parts into robots. I've seen one of them—a bot—with human arms hanging from its shoulders. They're freaks. Next time I see one, I shoot before talking." She dropped her pack and took out a canteen. After taking a swig, she flared her nostrils. "Ugh, I stink." She eyed the canteen, inspecting the water level.

"How much clean water do you have left?"

"Two days. Three if I stretch it."

"How're we going to get into the castle if you lost your gun?"

Miree shook her head. "Believe it or not, I wasn't planning on storming an entire, armed castle with nothing more than a boltgun and a junkyard robot. The plan still sticks."

"Oh." Sitting there, underneath a wilting tree in the middle of Helian with nothing but a girl and her pack, suddenly made Beetro skeptical of everything they were doing. He suspected that revenge was not a tremendously productive feeling to act on. "Ribcage," he said.

"Yeah, what's with that one?" Miree asked.

"No. I mean, hello, Ribcage. She's standing right over there behind the brush." He pointed to a spot across from them.

"Hello," she declared with a wave. "They're not following you but, ooh are they mad."

Beetro stood. "Ribcage... thank you for—"

"Not abandoning you like you did me?" The tiny girl came and sat next to them. She eyed the canteen in Miree's hand. Miree grunted and handed her the water.

They sat in silence for a moment until Beetro finally asked, "How do you... do it?"

"My Jumping?"

"Of course, that's what he's asking about," Miree said, swiping the water back.

Ribcage shrugged. "It's just something I can do sometimes."

Miree scoffed. "That's it? It's just something you can do? You teleported across ten feet back there."

"It's usually way harder for me. Back in Korthe, I can only do it on clear days and if I concentrate really hard. I wish I could do it as easily as out here. I'd be able to take any food I wanted from the market." She smiled wistfully.

"Out here? You mean the plains?" Beetro asked.

Ribcage nodded. "Being out here helps me to Jump pretty much whenever I want." She suddenly vanished, reappeared behind a tree a moment later and then back in front of them in demonstration. "See? It feels so *good*!"

"But... *how*?" Beetro asked.

"Not sure. I just close my eyes and the world kind of... flattens out. I step around things that would normally be right in front of me. I don't actually disappear, but everyone thinks I do. I'm there the whole time. It's how things were before."

"Before what?" Beetro asked.

"Before I was born."

Beetro exchanged glances with Miree. "You remember what it was like before you were born? Is that normal?" he asked Miree.

Miree shook her head and took another swig.

"It's how everything used to be for me before I came here. I think it's getting easier for me because I'm so close to my mom."

"Your mom is around *here*?" Miree asked.

"Yeah. She's close by. I haven't come to visit in a while."

"Who's your mom?" Beetro had so many further questions.

"You can meet her. But don't get your hopes up. She doesn't do much."

Miree exhaled loudly. "I have no idea what you're talking about but here," she said, offering Ribcage some salted pork. "Thanks for getting us out of that mess."

Ribcage abandoned whatever it was she was talking about and devoured the meat.

The sun set as the three sat in silence for a bit until Beetro asked, "Is this how the world is?"

"What," Ribcage said between bites.

"Is this how things are? People dying from radioactive water or getting shot for no reason?"

"You ain't seen nothing yet," Miree said, adjusting her pack underneath her head, ready for sleep. "You gotta take things or things get taken from you."

The next morning, Miree awoke with a pounding headache. She reflexively looked around. No sign of the Reticulum. Beetro had powered down. "Thought you were going to keep watch."

Beetro shook awake, his fusion core activating in his chest. "I did, I did. Don't worry, I have backup sensors that scan the periphery. They alarm and wake me up if someone approaches." Beetro stood. "Where's Ribcage?"

"I don't know. Ugh, my head." She reached for her canteen. It was empty. She rummaged through her pack, relieved to see her main supply of water was still there. "We'll never make it to Peles Castle now. I'm going to run out of water."

"I'm sure she's around..." Beetro said, inspecting the area. He found Ribcage curled up inside a hollow log, the girl apparently accustomed to tight sleeping quarters.

"Up!" Miree tapped the log with her heel.

Ribcage awoke, hit her head, and tumbled out. "Ow!"

"If you thought you were going to tag along with us, maybe you shouldn't have stolen so much water."

"I-I—" Ribcage vamped, rubbing her head.

"Don't lie."

"Please let me stay with you. All the other kids at Korthe are gone and Luci was one of the only ways I ate..." She tilted her eyebrows.

"Miree," Beetro said. "She saved us."

Miree gave a frustrated grunt. "Cut it out with those puppy-dog eyes. You're not fooling anyone." Ribcage recoiled as if for once a little intimidated by someone. "And now we don't have enough water to get to the castle and escape."

Beetro spoke up. "Maybe, if you'd finally share with me what exactly the plan is and why we're heading to kill General Deluvius with nothing more than a pack on your back, we can put our heads together and figure out what to do."

The robot was getting smarter. A major inconvenience for Miree. "Killing the general is just a bonus."

"You're going to kill the general?" Ribcage asked with a steady rise of excitement in her voice.

"We're going to rob him. Rob Peles Castle. It's why I came to Helian and Korthe. I've been preparing for months to go over there. That asshole General moved up my plans. The way he just —killed her. I wanted him dead. But now we're stuck out here with shit for supplies. It was stupid, I should've waited longer..."

Beetro crossed his arms. "But how are we going to get in? You saw that army he has. What does all that mercury have to do with this?"

"You'll find out once we're at Peles Castle. Which we can't get to now without more water." Miree resigned from the conversation and went to lay on her pack.

"I was thirsty," Ribcage offered, not so much as an excuse but an accounting of events. "And besides, you left me no choice. I can't eat or drink anything in Korthe anymore. I had no option but to follow you."

"Let's go to that clearing in the forest that I saw," Beetro suggested.

Miree looked up. "Clearing?"

"Yesterday, before the Reticulum attacked us. I saw that clearing when I was doing a land survey."

"So?"

"Something cleared all the agriculture. Something mechanical, probably run by people. If there's people, there's water."

"How do you know it wasn't just a fire that cleared it? Or if it's just some new enclave of the Reticulum?"

"Only one way to find out. Should only be a few kilometers north. We scout it out, ask for water—"

"*Ask*?" Miree said skeptically. "We're in the middle of the plains. They're not going to give us water."

"Well, we've got a trick up our sleeve." Beetro pointed to Ribcage. "Something tells me she wouldn't have any trouble getting water from them."

Ribcage nodded; mouth curled with approval.

Beetro continued, "So, we scout, get water, and then we're only a few klicks out from the castle." He let the plan linger in silence for a moment.

Miree measured the options. "We might be able to just backtrack to Korthe before running out of water. It would be tight, especially with her now." Miree pointed to Ribcage, who fought a grin. "But..."

"But we'd be in the same place that we started..."

Miree stood, looked at the street urchin and junkyard robot, and briefly marveled at how she got stuck with the pair. "Just—... fine."

"Ooh, my mom is close," Ribcage said as they walked along an even row of dead corn husks. She blinked out of sight and then Jumped back into space a few paces ahead of them. Miree and Beetro had quickly stopped asking questions about Ribcage's mother—the girl's fixation seemed likely to be associated with some sort of past trauma. Beetro highly doubted her mother was anywhere nearby... or alive.

After another half an hour, they came to the clearing.

It was as if a gigantic cutting fan had come out of the sky and shaved out a perfect cylindrical shape of hollowed brush, trees, crops, and rocks. The surrounding forest curved artificially around the clearing as if cut by an impossibly sharp blade. Off at the opposite end of the clearing, there were mechanical digging machines along with a single crane that carried dirt from within a freshly dug pit. It was an excavation site.

The group stayed at the periphery of the clearing, behind the brush. Beetro enhanced his vision while Miree pulled out her binoculars, both surveying the clearing. "Looks like we know what he's doing with the street kids." Miree pointed.

Beetro saw hundreds of the kids trudging through the excavation site. Some carried pickaxes, brushes, and shovels, while others were bent on their knees, inspecting the freshly dug dirt. Around them were a few soldiers holding gunpowder rifles, watching the children and inspecting their work. They were dressed the same as the squadrons of General Deluvius that marched on Korthe. Amongst the soldiers was one man in a black, skintight ballistic weave armor. One from the general's captain guard.

"Slave labor," Miree said grimly. "Lucindi was right."

"Labor for what?" Beetro asked. "What're they looking for?"

"You see all that digging equipment out there?" Miree pointed to the crane and the single tractor with a digging arm. "No one makes that stuff anymore."

"What do you mean?"

"Nothing gets manufactured. All that stuff—the digging equipment, the guns, whatever it was that General Dickbrain flew in on in Korthe—it's all ancient tech. See how this whole field has been cleared out of plants and crops with precision? He probably has some sort of laser cutting tool that was used by ancient farmers to clear land."

"From the Alcheans?"

"Them or from other civilizations that came after them. The Alcheans were just particularly good at building equipment that lasted hundreds of years. Whatever can be dug up and refurbished—that's how anyone uses technology. That's a huge market in Orion—refurbishment. Every bit of technology that's being used now is ancient. For all we know, you're a thousand years old."

"Oh," Beetro said, touching his chest.

"And that's exactly how Deluvius got all his weapons. He's obviously found excavation sites rich in old tech. And that's what he's doing here. He's digging up whatever he can find to add to his arsenal. He's not a General at all. He's a murdering archaeologist."

"What is he looking for?" Ribcage asked.

Miree shrugged. "Who knows. More weapons. More ways to take control of the region. This guy is..."

"What?" Beetro asked.

"The general is different from most lords that take over. He's got a lot of weapons. Whatever he flew in on over Korthe—that's really rare. I've only seen a couple of old Alchean ships around Orion and they're owned by the richest mercantile corporations in the city, and they're not used for private use. Those big ships transport goods. Deluvius clearly has gotten ahold of a big store of ancient tech. I think him kidnapping a bunch of street kids will be the least of our worries."

Beetro watched the kids. "They look like they're in pretty good spirits, Ribcage. At least they're probably getting fed."

Ribcage looked up. "Why are you telling me? I don't care what happens to them. I hate them."

"Oh." Beetro didn't know what else to say to that.

"Hey!" Ribcage said. "There's my mom!"

"Where?" Miree and Beetro said in unison.

Ribcage pointed to the other end of the clearing, opposite from the excavation site. On a small knoll in the clearing sat two silvery arcs of metal, facing one another. They appeared to be made of the same metal and fashion as the Alchean pylons that Beetro had seen in Korthe and scattered across the Helian plains.

"Alchean design?" Beetro asked Miree.

Miree switched her binoculars to the twin arcs. "Probably. And I'm pretty sure it's not Ribcage's mom."

"No, no, that's her." Ribcage pointed at the arcs in the distance.

"That's not your fucking mom, kid."

"This is where I was born. So that makes her my mom."

"You've been here before?" Beetro asked.

"Yes, I *told* you. First thing I remember was coming out of her right there!"

"Ugh," Miree grunted. "So, because the first thing you remember was being here at those arcs, you've been calling it your *mom*?"

"Does that mean the junkyard at Korthe is my mom?" Beetro asked, a totally earnest question.

Miree threw up her arms. "I can't handle this existential bullshit from you two right now. Kid, can you just do your little trick and get us some water from the dig site?"

But Ribcage was already off, running into the clearing, gnarled hair dancing with the wind.

TEN

ARYM WAS able to meet with Hawera almost every other night. The easy hours in the kitchen and working only a few night shifts afforded him an easy escape from the Crib. Aside from the escalating advances from Lutra, the head chef, he rather enjoyed his new life as a part-time cook/part-time overworld explorer. Arym found it to his advantage to lead Lutra on a little, acting like he was playfully spurning the man's advances. It was best for Rektor Tarysl to believe that Arym was happily placed in a job with Cribmen with whom he could relate, and potentially find companionship. He found it kept the rektor off his back.

After a night in the overworld, he was often able to return early and catch a few hours of sleep before his morning shift. Sometimes he'd sleep, but often, he'd carefully review his sketches from the overworld. He noticed a trend within the sketchbook—a steady progression from depictions of plant life and bugs to page after page of drawings of Hawera. As they ambled around the valley floor, he found every chance he could get to sketch its face or figure. He drew the creature so much that he once ran out of charcoal pencils and resorted to smashing blackberries in a cup and using their juice as ink. He was far too embarrassed to show any of these sketches to Hawera itself.

Hawera, accustomed to his nocturnal visits, often awaited him at their first meeting place, the campfire stoking behind the granite boulder of their first encounter. Hawera didn't seem necessarily eager for his visits, but it waited nonetheless for him. Its face was always flat with an exhausted boredom. When at first it had given thanks to Arym for bringing food with a small bow of its head, Hawera now took the food unceremoniously and chewed. At times, Arym suspected it was growing annoyed at his help, as if it wanted to be left alone to starve and die from exposure right there in the grass. Hawera seemed almost irritated at Arym's suggestion that Hawera survive.

Out of curiosity or sheer boredom, Hawera followed Arym around as he explored the valley. He became bolder in his ventures, believing his further excursions into the surrounding forests to be pleasing to Hawera. It didn't seem to notice his efforts and often looked up at the night sky, silent.

Hawera spoke little and often let Arym prattle on about life where he was from. He wanted to talk more about the Crib but often felt the nagging reminder of the Oath of Descension at the back of his mind, which prohibited revealing the location of the Crib. Oftentimes, as he climbed up the Oshaft to meet Hawera, he'd wonder if he was really beholden to an oath that he made when he was too young to even remember. Can someone be bound by a promise they make when they don't even have a memory of it? Arym didn't think so, yet some clandestine guilt loomed over him, prohibiting him from sharing more. Not that Hawera asked, it didn't seem to have any interest in anything about him or anything else for that matter.

Arym tried to probe Hawera for information as they picked

berries by the marsh or climbed over granite boulders, searching for herbs. He pressed Hawera about its people—their culture, language, and land. How did Hawera get to Arym's valley? Did they all look like Hawera with its curvaceous body and slender limbs? Did people know it was missing and were searching? And more pressing for Arym... why didn't Hawera seem concerned with returning home?

"No important," Hawera mostly said to Arym's incessant questions. Arym realized the only thing that got it to respond more than this was asking if it was indeed human.

"Yaas!" it would say, annoyed.

"Then why are you and me so different?" Arym asked as they approached the edge of Crescent Wood, a thick forest that fit snugly into the side of the valley.

Hawera rolled its eyes and shook its head. "I human. You human."

"But no one where I come from looks anything like you. At the Crib, we're all—we're all the same." He gestured to his body. But Hawera only appeared massively perplexed and looked away, dismissive.

"I *am* human," it said again, reiterating the point.

"I know, I know."

"But..." Hawera cinched its eyes, thinking.

"What?" Arym dropped his satchel in the grass.

"I am... butter human."

"What?"

"Butter human," it said again, testing the words to see if they made sense.

"What's a butter human?"

Hawera shook its head, thinking, and then said, "I am butter*fly* human."

"A butterfly human?"

Hawera nodded. "I am like butterfly, you are like... the other."

"The other?"

Hawera stopped, thinking. "The other side—other way butterfly."

"I see." Arym nodded, understanding nothing. He peered through Crescent Wood and saw something glittering on the forest floor. "You are a butterfly human. That sounds nice." He found scattered shards of mysterious metal and picked one up, inspecting it with one eye closed.

Hawera shook its head, clearly frustrated by its own lack of communication. "I am butterfly, you are before a butterfly."

"I see," he said absent-mindedly, turning the shard over his palm. It glittered with an almost luminescent quality.

"What is?" Hawera asked, pointing to the shard.

"Not sure. Interesting metal—whoa." The metal shard flickered with light ever so briefly in his hand, revealing several unfamiliar runes. "You see that?"

Hawera nodded.

"Come on," he placed the metal shard in his satchel. "Let's go see what we can find tonight."

Arym led with Hawera following behind. Crescent Wood was a dense forest populated by thick trees and leafy vines covering the ground. Crickets chirped in the still air as they trudged forward, kicking away thorny tendrils from the underbrush. Arym led them along what had become a worn pathway over the last few nights. Moonlight glimmered through the forest canopy, flickering above them as they hiked. The small babble of a brook directed him south, venturing farther than they'd been before. He looked back at Hawera, seeing its face in the moonlight.

"I'm sorry if you don't like coming out here with me," he said, looking back across a small gully. He felt comfortable turning on a flashlight this far away from the Crib and took one out of his bag, illuminating the forest in a dappled white.

"It okay," Hawera said. Its proficiency in Haenglish had improved dramatically over the several weeks that Arym had been visiting, like a lost language returning to its tongue.

"I don't know where you're from, but where I come from, I don't get to explore. I've lived my entire life in a single pod—the exact same sleeping pod since I can remember. I was in school when I was younger, took placement exams and then was sent to dig for eight years when I was twelve. I've been alone for so long. Feels good to be out here. Freeing."

"Family?" Hawera asked.

"What's that?"

"Mom, Dad."

"Who?"

"You have family? People who care."

"The Crib cares for me in its way—all the men I've been taught by and work with. Is that what family is? Do you have family?"

"Mom and Dad. Sister, too."

"What are those?"

"You have Mom, Dad?"

Arym didn't know quite how to respond as an ominous suspicion suddenly bloomed within him. "What are those? What's a mom?"

"Those who love you."

Arym shook his head. "I don't have anyone like that. Maybe Rektor Tarysl but he seems to only care as long as I'm doing what he wants—what's good for the Crib."

"Where born?" Hawera asked with sudden interest.

"At the Crib, with my people."

"Where? House?"

"At the hatchery. That's where all the newborn babies are kept. They come from there and then gradually transition over to the nursery where they're cared for by the nursemen until about the age of four and then we all start primary education then."

"No mom and dad?"

"Nuh—no." He still didn't understand what it was talking about.

"Sad."

"Why is that sad?" He whipped his head as a twig broke somewhere in the distance. Probably a rabbit—an animal he'd seen more and more lately with their recent expeditions. He hadn't had the chance to sketch them, they were too quick for him.

"Me have mom, dad, sister," Hawera said with a hint of enthusiasm right before its face darkened. "Gone, now."

"They are your family?"

Hawera nodded. "They gone."

"What happened to them?"

Hawera shook its head, insisting, "No important," in its regular fashion when Arym asked too many questions.

They moved through dense foliage as their previous trodden path tapered away into an ivy thicket. Arym was careful to avoid the thorns at first but realized they were too numerous and cumbersome to identify and so gave up, their prickly points scraping through his pants. After crossing a stream and diving deeper into the wood, he heard a soft churning emerging west from the forest floor.

"Hear that?" he asked

Hawera nodded.

"Laser Falls. I knew we'd get to it soon." He'd named the waterfall long ago when he'd first started exploring the overworld. It was always from a distance, across the valley floor, that he saw its sleek sliver of reflected moonlight, running down the valley cliff. At sunrise once, he saw a trickle of sunlight illuminate the waters, creating a deep red like a shaft of laser light running straight up the valley edge. "Let's get to it tonight!" Hawera did not mirror his enthusiasm but followed him, nonetheless.

Laser Falls was a wide sheet of water that fed into a lake at the edge of Crescent Wood. It was a secluded corner within the valley —one edge was a straight granite wall with a powerful waterfall, the other was the wooded edge of the forest, looming with tree trunks like a giant baring its teeth. The lake was circular as if punched through the ground by the waterfall itself. Surprisingly, the lake was not as large as Arym would've expected. Much of the surrounding soil and rock of the lake hung over the water from erosion creating thin platforms of earth suspended above the water. He stood on one of the overhanging clefts of the soil bed and looked straight down into the water. It seemed as if, at any moment, the earth would break free, plummeting him into the water.

"Pretty," Hawera said, looking up at the waterfall. Arym wrenched his neck up and realized how *tall* it was. The waterfall and the granite cliff beneath soared into the night sky like an endless road.

"Come on," he said, motioning toward the waterfall. They crept along the lake, approaching the plunging falls. Mist saturated the air, chilling them as they rounded the water's edge. They came to the back wall of the falls where the granite facade stood behind the water. Arym squinted at the wall, convincing himself that he saw small rocks jutting from the rock wall—a tiny staircase cobbled along the wall. As they inched closer, he was sure of it... there was a small staircase of rocks behind the waterfall.

After climbing over a few granite boulders, looking cautiously over the edge into the plunging waters, they arrived at a small alcove that had been hewn into the granite wall behind the waterfall. A slab of rock had been carved to extend from the alcove—a platform to reach the stone steps along the wall.

Arym turned to Hawera. "Should we?"

Hawera shrugged. "You first."

The stone steps were not built for large people. Each step was only as wide as his own foot. He groped along the wall and found small indentations carved into the granite—handholds. Gingerly, he moved out from the ledge, clinging to the handholds. Steadily, he walked up the small stone steps, scraping his elbows and forearms along the granite surface. With the roar of the waterfall echoing all around him, he climbed further, distancing himself from the alcove and stone platform. He didn't dare look down, there was only darkness and rocks for him if he lost his holding. Scraping his forehead on the granite, he looked back. Hawera was there, making its way up the steps.

They climbed deeper into the rocky recess behind the waterfall until the cliff face moved straight up. After several more minutes of climbing, Arym gripped a ledge just overhead, his tendons screaming. It was a rocky lip that hung above, jetting out from the rockfall wall by half a meter. With one last push, he brought himself to the lip, shaking with sweat. He looked over the lip and saw the dizzying tunnel of blackness beneath. After one terrifying moment of uncertainty, Hawera's fingers slapped onto the moist rock lip. Arym helped it to its feet as it looked down at the certain death beneath them. It was only then that Arym realized how dumb it was to climb an unknown rock way, hundreds of feet in the air behind a waterfall.

An arch with a large keystone stood before them, framing the entrance to a metal gateway. The keystone had a rune that matched the metal shards he'd found in Crescent Wood. The gate had been smashed to pieces, leaving a gaping hole in between where two massive doors had once been sealed.

Arym stepped forward. "Looks like we're not the first ones here." The arch was sleek, fashioned out of a smooth alloy with a gray matte finish. What remained of the gate was made of a similar metal but with a black finish. The gate had clearly taken a lot of abuse as evidenced by the thousands of scrapes and dents that littered its surface. At one point, someone had had enough messing around and placed an explosive on the door, causing the gate to rupture inward, leaving behind a gaping hole with hundreds of sharp edges. Arym brought out some of the metal shards he'd found in Crescent Wood and held them up to the door. It was a perfect match to the material and runes that ran along the surface of the gate. Someone at some time had blown the door open, showering the shards into the waterfall, which then dispersed them around the forest through errant streams below.

Arym flicked on his flashlight and pointed it into the gate. He saw nothing but a long tunnel ahead. Without a word, he took off his jacket and draped it over the sharp edges of the gateway hole and lifted himself up. The air inside the tunnel was dank, but surprisingly free of mildew odor. He shined the light down the tunnel as his eyes adjusted and thought he saw the tunnel end abruptly several dozen paces away. Before trudging toward the end of the hall, he felt Hawera tug on his sleeve.

"Look," it said, pointing to the walls of the tunnel.

Arym shone his flashlight across the walls and saw thousands of tiny reflections bouncing back at him. He stepped closer and beheld many hundreds of lines of mathematics, diagrams, and graphs that had been expertly etched into the stone. Not granite stone, but the same black surface of the gate, which, when dug, exposed a shimmering silver. He circled around. The tunnel was full of the etchings, deep into the walls.

"I recognize some of this," Arym said. "Back from my calcumatics classes I had to take for mining. There's..." he peered around once more, "a lot written here." He kept on down the tunnel, studying the etchings. Some of the math clearly had to do with engineering—there was geometric data mixed with the trigonometry of erecting structures. Some of the math touched on propulsion and aeronautics while some had to do with fluid dynamics.

"Funny how there's no words," he said with awe. "But I understand some of this. Just math, physics, and chemistry. Universal language."

They continued down the tunnel, Arym touching the etchings, feeling the deep grooves within the stone. The workmanship alone of the etchings spoke volumes about the people who had made them. They were chiseled with the precision of a civilization that valued exactness and order.

They arrived at the end of the tunnel. It was a cylindrical-shaped room, completely empty. The room extended high above their heads and opened to a shimmer of natural moonlight somewhere. There were no chests, altars, or anything else that Arym thought the target of a robbery. Whoever had broken the gateway doors didn't seem to have gotten much out of the misadventure.

Here, a panel of etchings had been drilled deeper into the stone than the rest of the tunnel—an effort to bolden and emphasize the engravings. In addition, a bold square surrounded the engravings, setting them apart from all the other etchings in the tunnel. Arym unclasped his satchel and took out his sketchpad. After turning a single, blank page from the notepad, he held it up to the engravings and moved a piece of charcoal over the page, transposing the images. Once the page was filled with the ancient schematics, he turned to a new page and repeated the transposition, trying to record all the math and diagrams to his notebook.

As his hand moved back and forth with the piece of charcoal, he looked back at Hawera and saw its eyes transfixed on his notebook. Looking back at the notebook, he realized what Hawera was looking at—the sketches he had previously done of Hawera.

"Oh," he said, taking the notebook off the wall. "I... like to sketch a lot. Anything, really. Plants, bugs... people." He gave a weak laugh and continued moving charcoal over the page, copying the engravings, hoping Hawera would move on. He flipped the page, attempting to hide the many other sketches he had of Hawera and continued filling the notebook with the wall's engravings.

"It's a tomb," a voice said, issuing from nowhere.

Arym looked at Hawera, who appeared just as confused.

"Hello?" Arym asked the voice.

"You are in a tomb," the voice said pointedly. It was a man's voice, but with a robotic quality—sterile but friendly.

Arym put his notepad back in his satchel, readying to bolt out of the room. "Who are you—where are you?"

An orb of shimmering light appeared in front of his face. "I'm here," the orb said. "My name is Protonix. I am the keeper of this tomb."

Arym winced, backing away from the shimmering orb. "What kind of tomb *is* this?" In the Crib, the elderly were incinerated after a brief ceremony of chanting.

"This is a tomb of the Alchean people."

"And what are you? An operating system?"

"I'm not a traditional computer, but it is okay if you think of me that way." Protonix's light illuminated the entire cylindrical chamber, reflecting off the glossy surface of the walls.

"Alkeeyan?"

"Yes. They built this tomb before leaving Earth and intended it as a memorial of their kind. My last task was to be the curator of the tomb, to justly represent the legacy of the Alcheans and to endow the creatures of Earth with understanding. Rather than being a cultural memorial, the Alcheans chose to leave a trace of their dominance over space and time. Before you are the abbreviated math and engineering of all their greatest technological achievements. The capstone of which is the room in which you stand. It represents their greatest achievement. Patrons may come to these walls and use their imprints left behind to benefit Earth according to their abilities."

"But what does all of this mean? How can people use this all?" He motioned to the walls.

"I'm prohibited from explaining the technicalities of the relics."

"Why?"

"One must gain a certain degree of advancement to properly understand what has been left behind. It ensures that the knowledge is left to capable hands."

"A kind of code?"

"Yes. Otherwise, the knowledge would be used by the corrupted, likely to exercise dominion over others. This is not what the Alchean intended."

"So, in order to even know what's written on the walls, I have to understand what they're referring to first?"

"Correct."

"Well, I don't get most of this," he flicked his wrist at the walls. "And I don't know if it does either." He pointed to Hawera.

"*It*?" The orb bobbed up and down.

"Yes. This is Hawera." He motioned to Hawera again. "And I'm Arym."

Protonix suddenly enlarged from the orb into a shaft of light the size of a man. Within the shaft of light, a visage and body materialized. He had angular features and a stern expression. "Why are you referring to her as an *it*? This is concerning."

"*Her?*" Arym had never once heard the word before.

"Yes. This female human. *She* is a woman."

"She..." Arym repeated, testing this word. *Woman.* Also new. "Is a woman." A thousand lightbulbs exploded in his brain. Put an *s* in front of *he* and you get *she*. Put a *wo* in front of *man* you get—things were suddenly falling into place. Hawera was a *fe*male, the entire other half of what was shockingly absent from the Crib.

Protonix frowned. "I'm afraid you are likely not who the Alcheans intended for their knowledge. You're free to peruse the walls but you will find no use for them."

"No, no, I'm sorry. It's just, where I come from... we don't have anyone like... *her*." He looked at Hawera. She rolled her eyes at him.

Protonix collected his light as if to condense back into an orb, but Arym shouted, "Wait, wait. Where did you come from and how can you go back and forth from a ball of light into a person? Are you... magic?"

Protonix unfurled himself back into a pillar of light, his face looking down at Arym, scrutinizing the young man. "What is one people's magic is another's science. There is nothing magical about me. I'm a proton, expanded out by several magnitudes of many trillions."

"You're a single proton? And wait, I thought you couldn't tell me about what the Alcheans made."

"The line of what I am to divulge is ambiguous. I was endowed with personhood and consciousness and can thus refer to anything about the Alcheans that I see prudent. They trusted me when they made me."

"How were you made?"

"I was fashioned from a proton pair, expanded outward and inscribed with programing on my surface which dictates my behavior and grants me personhood. By infusing me with this programming, I'm able to behave in ways far more exotic than a normal proton and take on many characteristics of other subatomic particles and quantum phenomena."

"Like a photon?"

"Ah, yes. Apparently, you and your people do grasp some basics more than what I'd presumed from your apparent lack of identifying your own sexual parity." Protonix motioned to Hawera. "But yes, I can function as a photon, electron, neutrinos, and other subatomic phenomena. This has been programmed onto my surface."

"You said you were made from a pair of protons?"

"Very good," Protonix said in fatherly approval. "I have a partner—a sister—if you prefer, with whom I am entangled."

"Entangled?"

"Yes. We communicate with each other, instantaneously over vast distances. When something happens to my sister, I am apprised of it faster than the speed of light."

"How?"

Protonix's visage twinkled with light. "It is not prudent to explain more at this time."

"Oh." Arym looked at Hawera, who had found a seat in the tomb, her back lying against the cold wall.

"What happened to the Alcheans?"

"They left this world thousands of years ago."

"Why?"

"A myriad of reasons."

"Which are?"

Protonix paused ceremoniously as if about to give a speech. "The Alcheans had obtained mastery over much of the physical world—transport, communication, language, robotics, politics, engineering, space travel, the arts, and many other fields of discipline. They were a unified people at the height of their achievements. They created a gateway to other worlds called the

GeminArc. A portal that brought infinitely distant locations together by bending the fabric of spacetime. After they had achieved the GeminArc gateway, they opened Earth to free commerce and exchange with hundreds of other worlds of intelligence. Their technology fused with that of those of alien cultures across the galaxy, combining together to previously unobtainable heights of technological advancement. For thousands of years, Earth basked in a near utopian way of life. They perfected the aging process—decrypting all of the human genome—and defied their own mortality."

"They couldn't die?"

Protonix vacillated. "Something reminiscent of this, yes."

"How long did they live for?"

"Many cycles."

"Of what?"

"It is not clear, but after many cycles of perfected mortality, they became dissatisfied with their mortal exaltation and decided to look beyond themselves—"

"They left," Hawera said. "Gone."

Protonix nodded. "That's correct. They left Earth to obtain new spheres of existence."

"What does that mean?" Arym asked.

"They left into a greater stratum of being."

"I still don't know what that means."

"I'm afraid it is difficult to explain more than this. The Alcheans exhausted their mortal experience and stepped into dimensions beyond our own."

"Other dimensions?"

"Yes."

"There are other dimensions?"

"Yas," Hawera answered.

Protonix measured his response. "I do not think you are ready to hear more. However, I don't fully know where the Alcheans went. I don't think they could even explain to me in a mortal language."

"So, what happened to the rest of Earth once the Alcheans left?"

"Earth's way of life deteriorated rapidly. Wars over the GeminArc. Wars over land. Wars over nothing."

"Huh," Arym said. He suddenly understood the Crib and why its founder, Othel, left the world behind, digging himself a home deep in the ground. The overworld was a lost cause. Echoes of the Oath of Descension, something he agreed to when he was a tiny child, bounced through his mind. *I will place myself below the needs of this great people and keep sacred its location from the world.* Could he keep his Oath and not be a part of the Crib?

"And what was this gateway?" Arym asked.

"Many things, but the GeminArc could create a wormhole that brought the other side of the universe here to Earth."

Suddenly, the tomb filled with red light. Arym looked behind and saw a deep crimson coming through the gate of the archway. Hawera left the two and walked toward the entrance, captivated by the red light. The waterfall outside, Laser Falls, was glowing an iridescent red like a gigantic laser.

"Dawn," Arym said, turning to Protonix. "We need to go now."

"Before you leave. The Alcheans wanted one thing conveyed to every being that entered this tomb."

"Yes?"

"Never cease to be a student."

Arym nodded. "Thank you for teaching us."

Protonix nodded and condensed back into an orb, dancing in shafts of dawn light. "Please return when you are ready for their gifts."

ELEVEN

"STOP!" Miree yelled but Ribcage either didn't hear or care. The girl was popping in and out of sight like a jittery slideshow as she neared the twin arcs. Fortunately, it was a way from the excavation site where none of the soldiers would notice her.

"Come on." Beetro left Miree and walked out into the open clearing after Ribcage. He kept his gaze on the excavation site and saw that most of the guards were either resting with their backs against the hull of the crane or sitting under a canvas tent, none looking his way.

Ribcage made it to the twin arcs and wrapped her arms around one of them, her hands unable to connect from the size of the arc. Beetro caught up and measured the arcs to be three meters in height, taller than the average person. The width was only about a person's arm span across. Beetro gave one of the arcs a tap with his fist—it was solid metal. As suspected, it was the same matte silver as the single spire he found in Korthe. There were no insignia or controls anywhere to be found on the arcs. Twin arcs, as opposed to single spires that he saw in Korthe and in the plains. He walked through one of the arcs. Nothing happened.

Since he'd left Korthe, Beetro had been making a map in his mind of the plains of Helian. As they had been moving along the past two days, he'd been marking down anything notable—ponds, streams, rivers, large boulders, and the Alchean spires. The spires loomed above the ground at slanted angles in the plains. He added the twin arcs to the map and studied it for a moment. "Hey," he said to Ribcage, who was currently rolling around in the dirt beneath the arcs. "Come on."

Ribcage sat up. "But I want to spend more time with my mom."

Beetro pointed to the excavation site full of soldiers. "If we don't leave, those soldiers will see us, and they'll kidnap you just like the other children. We need to go back to Miree."

Ribcage laughed. "No one can catch me when I'm with my mom."

"We need your help. Come. Please?"

"Okay!" The girl hopped up and popped out of existence. Another moment later, Beetro saw her running back across the clearing toward Miree. It wasn't as if she instantaneously skipped ahead, but rather, she disappeared for the same amount of time that it would normally take her to run the same distance.

They found Miree at the spot they left her, a hint of rage on her face. "How is Ribcage's *mom*?"

"Take out that map you have," Beetro said.

Miree grunted but then brought out the map.

"We're here," Beetro said, pointing to a spot in the middle of the plains.

"Yeah...?"

"Korthe is at the west edge of the plains of Helian, Peles Castle on the east—just at the base of Meteor Mountains."

"And?"

Beetro took the map and placed it on the ground. He collected a few pebbles and began placing them on the map. One pebble was at Korthe, followed by a few pebbles placed in a semi-circle around the plains, which included Korthe. He then placed a pebble at their current location. The formation of the pebbles was a semicircular line that circumscribed the plains with a single pebble in the middle of the map, representing the twin arcs.

"What is this?" Miree asked.

"The pebbles in the semicircle are all the old Alchean spires that I've tracked since we left Korthe. One of them was in Korthe itself. This one here," he pointed to the pebble in the middle. "This is where those twin arcs are located."

Miree stood, dusting dirt off the back of her pants. "What does this have to do with anything?"

Beetro sighed with impatience, a mannerism that he picked up from Miree herself. "Is it not unusual that the plains are surrounded by these old spires? And why are these two arcs in the middle?"

"I used to tell Lucindi something that I'm going to tell you now... I don't ask questions that don't need to be answered. That's how you get yourself killed. You think people who are curious about the Reticulum are rewarded? No, they get turned into those cyborg assholes. I don't give a shit that the Alcheans or whoever else constructed some circular thing around the plains. For all we know, it was part of some sort of transportation track. Back in ancient times, people were whizzing around in all sorts of vehicles —flying up to space and landing in a place halfway around the world in a few minutes. We could sit here for hours speculating on all the things those spires could be. It was probably how they got rid of sewage. This—" she motioned to the map with pebbles. "This is nothing. You've brought me nothing."

"Fine." Beetro knocked the pebbles off the map.

"And where is Ribcage?" She squinted over the plains.

Beetro turned. "She's right behind—" The girl was gone again.

"Alright!" Miree got to her feet. "I can't do this anymore. We're going back to Korthe."

"But you don't have enough water."

"As if there's a better option? We obviously can't rely on that little schizoid girl to do anything at all. As if I'm going to try to infiltrate Peles Castle with her hanging around. She's going to get us killed. It was stupid to leave Korthe the way we did anyways—had very little time to prepare. I shouldn't have gotten so pissed off about Lucindi. Made me act stupid. No—" She tucked the map back inside her pack along with her binoculars. "I'm heading back."

"Hey!" Ribcage yelled, suddenly beside them.

Both Miree and Beetro jumped. Miree looked at her, wide-eyed. "What are you doing!" A bit of her anger relinquished when she saw what Ribcage was carrying two flagons of water in her arms.

"I just walked in and picked up the water and walked out. I took this too." She produced a small, metallic box from the pocket of her robe. The box fit within the palm of her hand and had a single, green button on top. "One of the soldiers had it right in front of her, fiddling with it. So, I took it." She pressed the button.

"No!" Miree yelled. "You don't know what in the hell that thing is!"

A three-dimensional, octahedron projected out of the box, glowing green. Each side of the octahedron appeared to contain holographic buttons and words, as if each displaying separate options. Ribcage flicked the projection with her fingers, spinning the octahedron on its axis. "Whoa."

"There are different menu options." Miree snatched the box

from Ribcage. She flipped the octahedron around, reading the separate headings. "Ground, artillery, weapons... did you take it from the woman dressed in tight, black clothing?"

Ribcage nodded.

"One of the lieutenants..." She flipped through more menus. "It's some sort of base operations profile for the army. There's inventory, vehicles, weapons stock... maps." She pressed on the menu and looked over at Beetro. "And the entire schematics of Peles Castle."

"What?"

"Look." She pressed on the menu and the octahedron opened, glowing with various levels and chambers of a castle.

"Still want to go back to Korthe?"

Moving was now at a snail's pace since they stopped taking roads. The Reticulum people were out there recruiting. So, they walked down the straight, dead cornfield lines.

"By the way, what happened to all the crops?" Beetro asked.

Miree had the habit of blowing a soft whistle in between her lips as she hiked. Every step, every exhalation, a little whistle. Beetro only now realized that it annoyed him. "Drought," she said.

"How long has the drought been going on?"

"I don't know, came on a little at a time. Months?"

They came across another stream. "Can't the plants just drink the water here?" Ribcage asked, bending over the stream.

"Don't drink that!" Beetro yelled.

"I know!" Ribcage mirrored back. "I'm not stupid. I know what the Poisoning is."

"Wait," Miree said, eyeing the girl. "You were drinking my water the whole time."

Ribcage pouted. "I didn't have any other choice! I couldn't go back to Korthe and there was no other water for me."

"Anyway," Miree spoke in a blustery tone that she sometimes assumed. "No vegetation can use the radioactive streams or rivers. See how nothing is growing around the stream?" It was true, the streambed was only bare gravel, absent of tufts of green or bugs. "Life in Helian relies wholly on rainwater that comes in from somewhere else. Well, that, and importing it from cleaner regions like Orion. But you got to collect the rainwater fresh, otherwise, it mixes with the groundwater and it's no good. But even if you collect the rainwater fresh, you gotta check it for radioactivity, the rain itself may have come from Helian groundwater."

"Why *is* the water radioactive?" Beetro asked.

"Wars. Ancient wars. Everyone just bombed the shit out of each other. Left us all with the fallout."

They continued in silence as Beetro thought on the implications of past wars in which likely millions of people easily perished. Then he thought about all the captured children, digging in the ground behind them. Lucindi died trying to protect them from being kidnapped. Her defiance was so short-lived—and no one cared. It didn't help and it didn't do anything. The kids were still back there doing slave labor and there was nothing he could do about it. Lucindi's death was utterly pointless.

Unless he could free them himself.

He didn't dare bring it up at the moment, Miree wouldn't have any of it. She was interested in her own plans. Also, Beetro was getting antsy to get to the castle himself so they could begin their search for Galiaro. How would saving the kids change anything? Also... was freeing them back to their existence of begging in Korthe really saving them? Were they worse off digging? At least they were getting fed...

They traveled toward Peles Castle. The plains of Helian

rolled on under their feet, a repetitive treadmill of hard dirt, dried weeds, and scattered robot parts strewn across the dying fields of corn and wheat. Many agricultural robots were left without maintenance as the drought had come and simply shut them down in the fields. Beetro saw hundreds of open robot skulls and dismembered limbs lying in the yellow grass. He didn't know who the previous Lord of Helian was, but he or she didn't do a good job of robotic upkeep in the fields. It was also becoming clear that General Deluvius had no interest in keeping the farms going as a means of maintaining power over the land.

"Ugh," he said, stepping over a robot skull.

"What?" Miree asked. "You see anything?"

"No. It's just... there are a lot of dead bodies."

"Bodies? It's just a bunch of robot shit—" she looked at him. "Oh. Right. Yeah, these were just machines. They didn't think like you did. They just tilled the ground until they broke."

"So... they didn't matter?"

"Not so fast, robot. I'm not getting wrapped up in a moral debate about robot life with you. You can talk about that all you want with all those bots in Orion."

Miree double-checked her map as they moved. Beetro, gloating to himself, checked his own mental map of Helian, knowing his version was far more accurate and up to date. As expected, he discovered more Alchean spires. He measured the distance and plotted them on his mental map. Sure enough, they were in a ring around the twin arcs that were positioned in the center. What did the Alcheans use it for? Miree was probably right, it was likely nothing. Could've been just the walls of an ancient city—the only remains because they were especially fortified. But then, Ribcage clearly had an ability that may or may not be tied to the twin arcs.

The three mostly traveled in silence, passing by more victims of the Poisoning. The dying peasants gazed at them with sanguine eyes as if they'd arrived to save them. Miree was clearly well hydrated and had the strength to carry a pack, making her a beacon of someone bearing water. But she scowled at them, placing her hand on her hip as if to indicate that she was reaching for a gun that wasn't there. That did plenty to discourage them. It made Beetro feel sick. He knew what Lucindi would do—she'd give them every drop of water until she ran out. But then what? She'd just lay down to die right next to them. Regardless, he was beginning to realize that Miree was maybe not the best person with whom to associate. Should he really be helping her? Would she help him find Galiaro?

Miree noticed his grimace as she lowered her arm from her side. "Huh," she said, looking at him.

Beetro looked himself over, noticing for the first time that he was filthy. "What?"

"She imprinted on you."

"Imprinted?"

"Lucindi. The way you care about people you don't even know and who are actually a threat to you. She was the first person you ever met, and she imprinted on you like a mother duck on her ducklings." She looked over at Ribcage, who was currently Jumping forward a few steps ahead of them, humming to herself. "Not sure what imprinted on *her*."

After several more hours of traveling through the thin and dead foliage, they came to another road. Miree carefully peeked out. The road was slightly darkened now by dusk light and appeared empty.

"Shouldn't be more than another six or seven klicks until we're at the castle. There'll probably be perimeter guards long before we get there. Beetro, keep your ears and eyes open."

"Always do."

They crossed the road but before they were even a few steps out, they noticed someone standing there. It was a single figure, unhooded, silhouetted by the distant setting sun. Out of instinct or merely posturing, Miree reached for the non-existent boltgun at her hip.

Beetro put his hand on Miree's. "No hood. Probably someone with Poisoning. We can leave them alone."

Miree relaxed as they continued to cross the road.

A small voice issued from the darkened figure. *"Khar?"* They couldn't tell if it was a man or a woman. Or robot. Either way, it was a quivering voice.

Miree shouted back. "We don't have any food or water for you."

Beetro approached the figure, trying to make out their face and saw they were craning their face straight to the sky. They lowered their head and Beetro saw it was a young man. The person's head had been shaved. As he approached, he saw that he had a broad chest, square shoulders, and was dressed... strangely. A skintight, translucent material stretched across his body from foot to shoulder. At even, interrupted intervals, silver discs circumscribed his arms and legs, jutting out by several centimeters and clanking together as he moved. He had no identifiable pack or supplies for traveling and his face was painted with confusion. Beetro detected a tilt of fear in his eyes.

"Khar, duner," he said.

"Huh?" Beetro asked.

"What's going on?" Miree and Ribcage caught up. "Whoa," Miree said when she saw the man. "Who is *this*?"

"Quant estre uy?" he asked and then looked back up at the darkening sky. A tuft of clouds was catching a deep crimson color off the last rays of sun for the day, obscuring the night sky. "Quant?"

"What's he asking?" Miree turned to Beetro.

"I-I don't know."

"You don't have any linguistics in there?" she said, tapping his temple.

He swatted her hand away. "I only speak Haenglish. And don't tap me like that."

"Well, he looks... harmless. But what's all that this he's got on his arms and legs? Hey," she shouted at him. "What's going on at Peles Castle?"

"Hey!" the man said back.

Beetro jumped with surprise. "There's some Haenglish coming out." He walked closer to him. "Hello."

"Hello," he said back. He shivered and nodded. "Hello," he said as if confirming something.

"Where did you come from?" Beetro asked.

The man paused, trying to understand his words. He only shook his head in frustration.

"Where are you from?" he repeated, slowing the cadence of the words.

The man pointed to the sky and looked back up. "How menny?" he asked.

Beetro looked up at the glowing clouds. "How many?" he repeated.

Miree interrupted the scene. "We need to go make camp—get ready for tomorrow."

"I'm hungry," Ribcage added, uninterested in the entire encounter.

"Look at him though," Beetro said. "His skin is healthy, not poisoned, so he's not a peasant at the castle. He doesn't have any supplies, so he's probably from nearby. And Haenglish isn't his first language, so he's from a different people than we've seen around here. He can probably tell us some useful information if we just take a minute and try to see what he's saying. Do we have to abandon every person we come across on the side of the road?" A measure of indignation rose in his voice.

Miree addressed the man if only to get the ordeal over with. "What are you saying?"

The man nodded and pointed again at the sky. "How menny? How menny..." he paused as if searching for a word. "How menny at nigh?" The Haenglish words didn't fit right in his mouth, like he was trying to remember a language he only spoke as a tourist. "How menny at nigh?"

"How many at night?" Beetro offered.

He nodded and then pointed to the sky again.

Ribcage looked up at the sky. "There are one hundred and thirty-seven clouds in the sky."

"I don't think that's what he's asking. And I don't think you can really count clouds like that..." Beetro said, looking back up at the sky.

The young man finally sat in the middle of the road, gazing up at the sky.

"Do you know what language he is speaking?" Beetro asked Miree.

She shook her head. "No idea. I've never heard it. In Orion, there's a whole bunch of different languages that come through. Doesn't sound familiar to me but I'm no linguist."

Beetro looked back up at the sky. The final glows of sunset were diminishing from the thin streams of cloud. He saw the moon appear from behind a wisp. "Moon," he said to the man, pointing up.

The man saw the moon and nodded. "Moon!" he said, smiling. "Moon!"

"Okay, that got him going. Yes, that's the moon. There's only one moon," Beetro said, nodding.

The man stared blankly for a moment and then squinted as if trying to recollect something. "Star!"

"Star? Yes, there are stars," Beetro said.

"How menny stars?" he asked. "How menny stars?"

"How many stars are there?" Beetro repeated.

"Five!" Ribcage answered, holding up her outstretched palm and fingers. "Everyone knows there are five stars at night. The moon is the palm, and the five twinkles are its fingers."

"Yes, there are five stars," Beetro said, extending his metal digits.

"Five?" the man said, looking at his fingers. His face was hurt as if he had just been told devastating news. "Five?" He held five fingers out, trying to confirm the number.

Beetro nodded. "There are five stars."

"No..." He buried his face in his hands, curled over his knees, and started to sob.

"What did I say?" Beetro turned to Miree.

They sat there for a moment, unsure of what to do. Even Ribcage seemed to be feeling sorry for the poor man who was half-naked in a weird outfit and crying because of how many stars there were in the sky. The sun finally set and, as if on cue to their conversation, the gossamer cloud cover drifted away, exposing the night's sky. The man looked up at the stars—faded discs of red, blue, and white. The rest of the sky was glassy black.

The man continued to cry, oblivious of anyone.

"It's okay..." Beetro tried to console him but didn't even know what the problem was.

"Et galx dor morte," he said grimly. "Et galx dor morte..." He stood, gazing over their heads. He kept repeating these words and backed away, the metal discs on his clothing clanging together.

"Where are you going?" Beetro called after him, but the man ignored him and walked to the side of the road. He took one last look up at the sky and disappeared into the darkened brush of the plains. "Wait!" Beetro yelled. "There's nothing out there!"

Miree grabbed his shoulder. "I'm sure he's just going back to his camp. Can we go now?"

Reluctantly, Beetro followed Miree and Ribcage across the road and back into the brush. The fields of dead farmland had darkened, prompting a swirl of fireflies to emerge. They hiked for another kilometer until Beetro climbed a tree and saw a darkened mound in the distance. He enhanced his view and saw the hulking mass of spires and columns—Peles Castle. They set up camp aside a boulder, careful not to make too much noise or light a fire. There were probably patrols nearby, although Beetro hadn't heard anyone nearby.

"Okay," Miree said, sitting cross-legged on the ground. She pulled out the button that Ribcage had stolen from one of the lieutenants and pressed it, prompting the octahedron menu to project into the air. Miree's face turned into a shadowed, haunting glow from the green light of the octahedron. "I've looked this thing over a million times. Most of the menus are only accessed by password, so we can't get into their inventory, their army stats, their weapon cache info, or anything like that. But the plans to Peles Castle are open and I've been able to see how many floors and rooms there are. The downside is that I don't know the specific use of the different chambers and rooms of the castle.

"This," she said, isolating a single floor of the castle, "is the courtyard of the castle, probably where they have feasts or orgies or whatever it is that the bastard fief lord of Helian likes to do. There are a *lot* of rooms in the castle. Over a hundred and fifty. There are two main spires, one is box-shaped and abuts the front end of the castle—likely where they might keep heavy artillery weapons, of what type I have no idea. But based on the firepower Deluvius demonstrated in Korthe, he's probably got a pretty wicked cache of weapons there. There is a smaller back-end spire, which I know is basically a large vault—reinforced steel walls, retinal encoded password gate, auto-turrets that turn on if there is an intruder detected—"

"How do you know all this?" Beetro cut in.

"Robbing Peles Castle is not something that I've been planning to do on a whim. This has been in the works for years with... other people. I knew the basic layout but now having the castle plans will help us be even more precise."

"What people?"

"That doesn't matter—"

"It does," Beetro said. "You brought me into this. I think I should know who else was involved with this. Where are they now? How do you know they haven't tried getting to the castle before you?"

"Trust me. They haven't come."

"How can you be sure?"

"Because I made sure they couldn't get into the castle without me."

Beetro sat silent for a moment, a disapproving glare glued to Miree. "You need to tell us more. How do you plan on getting into the castle with an entire army guarding it?"

Miree hesitated, measuring her response. "Fine," she snorted. "I was part of an... organization in Orion. We did stuff—robbed merchants or caravans."

"So, you're a thief, then," Beetro stated as if finally understanding Miree's place in the universe. "Did you kill people, too?"

"No, asshole, I'm not a murderer. Sometimes people do bad things because they were given bad lives." Miree scowled in the glowing green light. "And I don't remember you having a problem with our plan to steal water only hours ago."

Beetro didn't have much to say to this. He didn't even consider what they did as stealing since their need for the water was becoming desperate.

"Anyways, this organization is very good at what it does. We got wind of something—a game-changer."

"What you had buried back in Korthe?"

Miree nodded and looked over at Ribcage. The girl had fallen asleep. Satisfied, Miree opened her back and dug to the bottom, producing the same black satchel she had dug out before they departed Korthe. She unzipped the bag and brought out a metallic apparatus about the length of her forearm. The metal struts ran the length of the machine, abutting a black coil that ran down the middle. On one end of the tube was a cylindrical canister with a single opening. On the other end was attached a rectangular frame with tabs on the corners. Miree tugged at the tabs, which adjusted the size of the frame from a small square centimeter to a rectangle the size of her fist.

"What is it?" Beetro asked.

"A Quantizer."She lifted the apparatus, inspecting its length. "It was assembled by an astrocyst in Orion. Named Fallaro. We got wind that this thing existed and... well, we made sure that it was ours inside a week."

"What does it do?"

"See this?" She pointed to the rectangular frame. "You adjust this to the relative size of the portal you want, and it will project that same size but magnified by ten to any surface you want. It then scans the user, matches their Quantized state, and—" she snapped her fingers "you pass through the surface like you're walking through air."

"Quantized state?"

Miree shrugged. "I don't know, it's what my boss explained right before we stole it from him. Didn't you hear the important part? You can *walk through walls*. Apparently, it takes advantage of all the extra empty space you have in the atoms of your body and the atoms of the walls, and it lines up all the empty spaces of the matter so that—" she made a whooshing sound, "you slide right through."

"Whoa."

"Whoa is right. This is the entire reason I'd risk coming all the way out into the middle of the plains during a drought. It's the whole reason I came to Helian—well, that and I had to get out of Orion pretty quick when I got my hands on the Quantizer."

"You took it from them, didn't you? This organization? You all stole it and then you ran off with it."

Miree's silence confirmed his suspicion. "Do *not* tell a single soul. They'd kill you too just for being associated with me."

"Let's see it work then." He motioned to the boulder. "Walk through the rock."

"Do you want to go back to Korthe for a few months and collect all those batteries and extract all the mercury we got? Because that's what we'd have to do to run the Quantizer again if you want me to walk through the rock. It runs on mercury, and it doesn't go far. We've got enough collected for two passages—one into the vaulted tower and one out."

"That sounds extremely risky. And what exactly are you going to rob? You plan on running out of there with a bunch of gold and silver bricks?"

Miree grinned. "Something much smaller and *much* more valuable. I'll be able to buy a mountain of gold and live on it forever."

"But not before you help me find Galiaro, right?"

"Of course. All in good time, robot."

TWELVE

PLEASE RETURN *when you are ready for their gifts,* Protonix had said.

The Alcheans. Masters over space and time.

Arym lay prone in bed, his sketchbook open before him. He studied the math and schematics that he'd traced from the walls of the Alchean tomb. Although he understood none of it, he could still marvel. He wondered what they had been capable of—soaring faster than light, traveling to other worlds, exploring new people. Rubbing the Alchean metal shard with his thumb, he tried picturing what they looked like. The shard fluttered with iridescence as his skin passed over it. Curious. He'd never seen an alloy do anything like that.

They must've been like gods, thinking a thought and having it instantaneously turn into reality. The thrill of who they were and what they accomplished swelled within him. How could they leave us all? Off to other dimensions? He couldn't imagine a people more opposite than his own. Cribmen dug into the earth, took oaths to stay there, and never shared their lives or culture with other people. To be born and raised in the Crib meant swearing an oath to stay put the rest of your days. Arym felt like a tombstone hung about his neck, already signaling the end of his predictable and minuscule life.

Yet, he also felt more sympathetic toward his own people. After all, Protonix had explained the wars that happened after the Alcheans had left. Arym wondered how long the warring continued. Was it hundreds of years? Maybe their founder, Othel, felt he had no choice. Things got so bad that he had to flee the world and start a new civilization under the earth. Wasn't this what the Alcheans had done? They'd outgrown their own existence and left. Were they happy with their decision? He was too embroiled with questions to come to any conclusion about anything.

He flipped through the notebook and came to his drawings of Hawera. She—*she*—was simply breathtaking. He touched the page, admiring her profile. She had prominent cheeks, full lips, and a slender neck that swooped elegantly into her shoulders. She was a *woman*. The first he'd ever seen. Before meeting *her*, he didn't even know that there were genders. Had the Crib forgotten about women? Unlikely. The rektors were hiding the truth. Like they always did. Why? He clenched his eyes, frustrated yet again at another mystery he couldn't begin to understand.

The most important question of all for him was, how much about the overworld did the rektors know? Were they as ignorant as himself or had they kept him in willful ignorance? Was he himself a fool or... a tool?

He leafed through the rest of his sketchbook, looking fondly at his early sketches of the overworld over a year ago. He'd learned so much since then—he was a completely different person. The Crib way of life was antiquated, perhaps dated back to a time when fear controlled the overworld. He now knew the truth—there was nothing to be afraid of up there. He'd explored grasslands and forests; seen the beauty of the night's sky and its twinkling stars. The overworld was where he'd found Hawera. He wondered what it—*she*—was doing at that very moment.

He stood from his bed, decisions running through his mind. Not mundane decisions, but life-shattering, bridge-burning planning that would change his life forever. He finally needed to cut the cord...

Leave the Crib for good.

He laid his pack on the bed, emptied it of everything, and then looked at the empty bag. He had to fit his entire life into it. First, he placed his sketchbook at the bottom. He looked around the room but stopped. There were only manuals on his desk and scattered clothing on the floor. There wasn't anything else in his entire pod that he wanted to put in the bag. For a moment, this deeply saddened him but then affirmed his decision to leave the Crib. He had no life here. He threw in a few charcoal pencils that he'd stolen from Lutra's office in the kitchen and put in an extra pair of boots beneath his sketchbook. It then hit him what he needed more than anything before leaving—maps. If he was going to leave the Crib for good, he'd likely travel far and wide and needed to know terrain, cities, bodies of water—whatever was out there.

"Bide your time," he told himself. "Don't be stupid." Indeed, he had learned to be careful and meticulous as he ventured to the overworld repeatedly over the past year. He'd learned patience by waiting for opportunity. He decided to do the same before absconding forever. Smart.

So, he left for kitchen duty, traveling down the dank tunnels of the Crib. Orange lights illuminated the walkways, creating an eerie glow on the faces of the Cribmen who passed. Their eyes were on the ground. No one spoke. They just moved, walking to duty probably on the digline or irrigation lines. Those were the Cribmen that mostly lived on the deck. Somewhere beneath them were the more academic men—scholars, engineers, and other disciplines of which Arym knew very little. Even his knowledge of the Crib was scant. Not only did he know next to nothing about the main Crib operations, but there were four other underground satellites, each with their own purpose, none of which Arym had any insight to their real function. He'd never even been outside the hub of the Crib.

At the mess hall, he saw the typical morning rush of digkids lining up for oatmeal and coffee. He slipped into the kitchen and, as if he'd been watching from afar, Lutra turned and smiled as Arym put on his apron.

Lutra wiped his floured hands on his shirt. "Good morning!" The man had an adorable, gap-tooth grin. "How's the morning?" Arym had grown accustomed to Lutra's drawn-out greetings. The man was clearly enamored of Arym and took every chance to suck up his time.

"Fine, just getting in. How's your morning?" Arym was friendly with Lutra, even reciprocating his flirtations from time to time. Arym figured it would keep the rektors off his back if they thought he was assimilating with a potential partner. It wasn't hard either—Arym actually thought Lutra was extremely kind and good-natured, using expressions like 'oh my' or 'oh boy' whenever he saw bread rising in the oven. He was nothing but a tender heart. Just because Arym had zero physical attraction to the man, didn't mean he didn't like the guy.

"Do you have any plans tonight? Anything fun?" Lutra's advances had become increasingly overt. Arym knew the day would come where he'd have to outright reject him. Well, maybe not anymore now that Arym was leaving forever.

Arym shrugged. "Just sitting in my pod."

Lutra nodded—a delusional tilt to his eyebrow as if he believed the chase was on.

At noon, Arym was sloping creamed corn onto tin plates, Lutra next to him. He thought of Hawera and wondered if she had gone back to the marsh to get berries for the day. He was worried she'd be cold all day. When he left earlier that night, a fierce wind was chilling the entire valley. He wanted to go be with her—needed to be with her.

"Lutra?"

"Yes?"

"Do you ever—eh, never mind."

"No, what?" Lutra put down his ladle and touched Arym on the forearm. "What?"

"No, it's... I don't want to get you in trouble."

"What kind of trouble?" He lifted his eyebrows.

Arym played dumb. "Trouble with the rektors. I just have questions sometimes. I don't mean harm but feel like I can't ask."

"You can talk to me." He spoke low so the Cribmen on the other side of the sneeze guard couldn't hear.

"It's just... don't you ever wonder what it's like up there?"

"You mean..." Lutra pointed a finger up and mouthed 'overworld'.

Arym nodded. Serious face.

"Of course..."

Arym feigned relief, grabbing Lutra's shoulder. "So, it's not just me?"

"No!" Lutra yelped and then covered his mouth in a dramatic show. "I mean... no," he whispered. He then put a finger to his own lips. "After lunch. Stockroom."

Arym gave him a knowing nod and slopped out more creamed corn.

He found Lutra sitting alone in the stockroom, literally twiddling his thumbs. The man had an impish nonchalance that contrasted his brutish size, oblivious to his own comedic mannerisms. "You came," he said, before a flirtatious silence.

"Uh, yeah..." Arym cut the silence before Lutra's mind could wander. "What do you know about it up there?"

"The overworld?"

"Of course."

Lutra scratched his chin, seeming unsure of how far he could trust Arym. "Not sure if it's as bad as the rektors try to have us believe."

"That's what I've always thought."

They shared a sidelong glance. Were they on the same page? Who would go and blab to the rektors? "Do you know if anyone has been up there?"

"No. Maybe. There are rumors—what is this about?"

"It's about the Crib. Who we are. The Oath of Descension. It's all so..."

"Dramatic."

"Exactly. I mean, maybe Othel had reasons to come below all those years ago. Maybe the world above was terrible and wicked, but what makes us so certain it's like that now?"

"You're not the first to ask themselves that..."

"Really?"

"Ha!" Lutra slapped his knee. "Probably all Cribmen ask themselves these questions. I'm only a little older than you but I can tell you, you're right at that age where you start getting all antsy. Stir crazy."

Arym sat down on a crate of onions, next to Lutra. "It's nice to hear someone say those same things."

"And you haven't even asked yourself the *big* questions yet."

"Like what?"

"Where do we all come from?"

"What do you mean?"

"I mean, babies. The nursery. Yeah, it's full of babies, but where do the babies come from?"

"I don't—hmm. Never really thought about it."

Lutra turned to Arym and put his hand on his. "Arym, where did you come from? How were you born?"

"We're made in the hatchery. We're born there and the nursemen keep us there until we're about three or four."

"Right... but that's not what I'm asking. How is a baby actually *formed*? How do the nursemen even know how to make a baby? Is there an instruction manual? Blueprints like step one, pour in protein, step two, mix in glucose, step three, add a dash of DNA..."

"The hatchery..." Arym realized he had no idea. The hatchery was just a black box—a seemingly unending conveyor belt of Cribmen babies.

"You see? There's far more important questions than just 'what's going on in the overworld'."

"So, what's the answer?"

"I don't know."

"I thought you had answers."

"No, I never said that. I just have questions."

"But doesn't it bother you? Not knowing?"

"You get a little older—either wiser or dimmer, not sure—and you realize the questions don't matter. It's what you do with the mystery that matters."

Arym realized Lutra's hand was still on his. He didn't remove it. "So, what do you do with it? With all the mystery?"

"At first, I was angry then sad and then a little hopeless. And then I realized it was all just theoretical. I was unhappy because of hypotheticals in my mind. That was it. I realized that I actually have it pretty good. Life is nice. Yeah, we work hard and the rektors get on my case sometimes but... it could be so much worse. Maybe there are still wars in the overworld. Maybe Othel really was as wise as they say. Maybe mystery is only a seduction—intoxicating but toxic all the same."

"Hmm."

"I stopped caring. But the question I have for you, which is a question every Cribman has to ask themselves is this... am I a Runner?"

"I'm not saying that."

"But it's where your line of thinking will ultimately lead. Everyone must ask themselves if they're a Runner or not. So, Arym, are you? Are you a Runner?" He scooted a little closer.

"I'm not a Runner. I just want to know more."

"Then that's fair. That's honest. You can't be blamed for that."

"Really?"

"Of course not. Do you think Rektor Tarysl would blame you for asking questions? My rektor was very understanding. I could talk with him for hours about all this stuff. Still do."

"I just wish I knew more about the overworld. Maybe it would stop me from asking questions..." Arym hesitated, took his hand away from Lutra.

"Wait—I mean, what would you need?"

"Books. I want books."

"Ah. Yes. Well, I have books."

"Real books, Lutra. Not manuals. Old books."

"Oh."

"I want to read stories of ancient people. I think they had knowledge that we don't. I want to see how they lived, and I want... maps."

"Maps? Like at the library?"

"What library?"

"The rektor's library."

"They have a library?"

Lutra nodded. "Yes. I helped renovate it a few years ago before I was a chef."

"Were you a digkid?"

"Arym, you don't listen to me very often, do you?"

"Oh..." It must've been one of the many things Lutra blabbed about while they worked. "No, no, I knew that. Can you take me there?"

"Uh... I know where it is but I'm sure the rektors won't just let us walk in."

"Will you take me tonight?"

"Tonight?" Lutra became uneasy. "But I was thinking we could go to a play or something together."

Arym stood. "No, that's fine. I get it. You don't want to help." He moved to the door.

"Wait!"

Arym turned. "Come by my pod tonight?" he said with a devilish grin.

"I—" Lutra sighed and threw up his arms. "Okay, okay. Tonight. We can go to the library."

"Can't wait." Arym left the stockroom, fully aware of his seduction.

Arym walked back through the tunnels, keeping his head low. His thoughts were racing... what else would he need? Where would he get the rest of the supplies for the overworld? Where would they even go? Surely, Hawera must know about different cities in the overworld. All he knew is that he was done with the Crib. It had nothing else to offer him.

A voice called from behind. "Arym."

He acted like he didn't hear the man until he felt someone's firm grasp on his shoulder. He turned around.

Rektor Tarysl.

"Arym," the rektor repeated, that gentle grin on his face. "Can we catch up?"

Arym silently followed the rektor into a labyrinth of tunnels back into the monasteries of the rektors where they lived together and assembled Cribmen for lectures. Lectures about the importance of the Crib, the evils of the overworld, and the undeniability of the Oath of Descension. Propaganda, Arym now realized.

Nonsense.

They entered a square chamber, recently sterilized, where Tarysl had often brought Arym for their interviews. He'd known the rektor almost his whole life and, in many ways, sincerely loved the man like a... like a what?

But now he knew the truth that the rektors dogmatism was *ancient*—an anachronistic way of life preached by the aging and the ignorant. It was so clear now. Arym was jumping out of his skin to get away.

Tarysl settled in his chair, looking over his glasses at Arym.

What does he know?

"I understand you're doing quite well in the kitchen."

Apparently, nothing. "It was the right change for me."

"I came by your pod last night..."

Or does he know something?

"I'm sorry I wasn't there. I went and spent some time with Lutra." A lie. But hopefully one Lutra could corroborate if Arym could get to him first.

"Ah. Yes. You and Lutra. I was hoping you two would get along. Truth be told, I intentionally had you be workmates with him. He had some of the same struggles as you when he was a little younger. I thought you two could relate. Despite what you may believe, I don't actually want to stifle your curiosity. It's okay for you to explore it. It's healthy. What's unhealthy is indulging in fantasy. Do you know what I mean?"

"I do."

"Explain it to me." The rektor crossed his arms over his chest, waiting.

"It's normal to wonder about things. About where we came from and who we are. But we need to trust our ancestors. The people who came before us, our father, Othel, had wise reasons for creating us in the way that we live today. I know that I need to trust in the Crib—trust in its wisdom and experience."

"Convince me you're not placating me."

Arym stifled a small shudder. The rektor was exhausting. His dopey face, his receding hairline. And his *smell*. The man actually smelled old.

"I don't know what you want me to say."

Tarysl frowned. "I just want to *feel* the conviction from you. Words are meaningless without action. Our father, Othel, *acted*. He chose to leave the corruption of the overworld behind and become a pioneer. He was deliberate—a warrior of change and fighting against the evils of the overworld. This courage is what we want to instill in every Cribman. There's a fire inside of you, Arym. I'm just trying to release it. You have the potential to be a great leader in the Crib."

"I do?"

"You have a creative mind. You ask questions. You think for yourself. These are the attributes of a leader. This is why I've been meeting with you so often. I've been trying to cultivate these qualities within you."

"Really? I thought you were worried about me."

"I'm also worried about you, but for good reasons. I just want you to realize your potential."

"So, all these sessions—all this is because you think I'll be a good leader?"

The rektor nodded. "And I think you're ready for some more responsibility."

"Like what?"

"Some more... knowledge. And notice that I equate knowledge with responsibility. The two are the same. The rektors bear an enormous responsibility to the Crib because of the knowledge that we possess."

"I understand." Unbelievable. By dumb luck, the rektor was just going to give away some of the Crib's secrets. He'd always wondered if the rektors were shrewd puppet masters or just mindless clerics. Tarysl had the ability to appear easily befuddled and aloof, yet he kept an observant eye.

"You ask questions. Good questions. Questions that are natural. Some answers are too rich for some—they can destabilize the weak mind. But I think you're ready."

Arym nodded. *Get on with it!*

"So... you may ask me three questions. I will answer one of them, no matter what you ask."

Arym leaned back. "How do I know—"

"I promise the truth. Our brotherhood, the Oath—it's all based on trust. I promise you nothing but the truth."

Arym's heart pounded. Never had the rektor spoken so candidly with him. He even started to trust the old man. Maybe I *could* be a leader? There were so many things Arym wanted to ask —so many questions, it was... it was intoxicating. It was...

It was a set-up.

The rektor *wanted* to hear Arym's unadulterated questions. He wanted to find out what Arym was really interested in. Was Arym a good little Cribman or was he a Runner? His most burning questions would immediately reveal Arym's motivations.

Clever rektor.

Arym couldn't really ask the questions about the Crib he'd always had—why can't we leave? Can I leave now? Get me out of this dank hole in the ground. He mostly wanted to get out of the Crib since he could remember. He knew he couldn't be sincere, but he also couldn't low ball the rektor, otherwise, the man would suspect Arym was onto his trick. The questions had to be provocative just enough...

"Where do Cribmen come from? Why do we all look similar? Will we ever leave the Crib?"

The rektor paused for a moment, chewing at the side of his mouth. "I will answer the first and second question at the same time." The rektor stood, his face inscrutable. "Let's go."

"Where?"

"To answer your questions." He swiftly walked out of the room.

Momentarily stunned, Arym followed behind. The rektor moved quickly, his robe billowing between swift strides. They made their way through a series of tunnels and then a shaftlift. Wordlessly, they entered the shaft where Tarysl flipped open a small compartment at the controls and placed a key. He turned the lock, prompting an entirely new display of floors from which to select. He pressed a button with a *H* on it, dropping the shaftlift away farther down than Arym had ever gone. Arym tensed as they plunged into the earth.

After five minutes, the shaftlift stopped and the doors opened to the same, dull yellow lighting of the digkid deck. They marched on through the tubes, passing Cribmen dressed in weird rubber aprons and masks over their faces. There were wash stations periodically along the tube where Cribmen meticulously cleansed their hands and donned rubber gloves. They eyed Arym suspiciously but relaxed when they saw that he was with the rektor.

"When's the last time you saw a baby?" Tarysl asked as he waved his hand in front of a mirror. A series of lights flickered within the mirror, prompting a portal door ahead to depressurize.

"When I was a baby. I've never been to the hatchery ever since I was actually a baby in the hatchery." He followed the rektor through the portal, passing hissing valves and wafts of chemically treated air.

"It seems that you're overdue another trip then." The rektor spoke like a tour guide, anticipating some exciting new twist along the route. He ducked his head under an archway and led Arym into a chamber filled with hundreds of rows of glass pods, each the size and shape of a watermelon. The pods were lined in rows of a dozen and stacked four high, stretching above their heads.

Arym peered into a glass pod beside him and saw a fetus the size of a shrimp—which actually looked kind of like a shrimp—within the pod.

"Meet the next generation of the Crib," Tarysl declared with a flourish.

"These will all be Cribmen?" Arym asked, gesturing to the rows of pods.

Tarysl nodded. "Yes. The exact number was planned based on data from our populisticians. Their job is to determine how many Cribmen the Crib can sustain into the next generation."

"This is where I was born?"

"Correct."

"Hmph. Doesn't really answer my questions."

"Not yet." The rektor beckoned him, almost giddy about what lay just beyond the incubators. They passed several more rows of the glass pods, each with a Cribmen fetus at the exact same stage of embryological development.

Beyond another portal door, Arym followed the rektor into a laboratory replete with sleek metal table tops and glassware scattered absolutely on every free surface—volumetric flasks and graduated beakers. There was distillation tubing dripping into vats the size of large drumheads. Cribmen moved back and forth across the lab floor, carrying steaming test tubes while others huddled at a lab workbench, carefully aliquoting minuscule amounts of fluorescent liquid into other minuscule amounts of fluorescent liquid, none of which Arym knew anything about. Yet, for a moment, he was somewhat proud of his people. Protonix had assumed that Arym was from some backwards clan that couldn't possibly understand the etchings the Alcheans had left behind. But seeing this lab made him think maybe his people had at least figured *something* out.

Distracted by the lab, he'd fallen behind Tarysl and caught up to him at a workbench. The rektor stood beside a lab worker—an embryologist—Tarysl explained. "Aphut, please explain to our young Arym here what you're doing." Tarysl was gesturing to Aphut, a Cribman dressed in a long, sleek smock made entirely of thick rubber.

The embryologist held a small beaker by his fingertips and was gently agitating the clear liquid within. "I'm precipitating the solution."

Tarysl brought Arym forward. "Take a look."

Arym peered into the beaker and saw what looked like a strand of snot swirling within the tiny vortex that Aphut was creating. When he ceased the swirling, the snot strand curled up and then rebounded in the opposite direction of the swirl like a rubber band inverting its tension. "That's the coiled DNA rebounding back. It's still in its double helix formation and you can see its dynamics macroscopically."

"That's DNA?" Arym asked.

Aphut nodded.

"It's the DNA used to create Cribmen," Tarysl explained.

"Whose DNA is it?"

"It's yours."

Arym looked back at Tarysl. The man fought an impish grin. He was apparently ecstatic to reveal this piece of information. Much to the rektor's disappointment, Arym had no idea what he was talking about. "*What*?"

"That right there," Tarysl said, pointing to the beaker. "Is your DNA. The exact genome used to create you—that made you who you are. It's also my DNA and it's also Aphut's DNA."

"I—" It was like a train that he saw coming a mile away just plowed into him. He looked at the rektor's face and then quickly studied Aphut's—a younger man but still older than Arym. They both had bushy eyebrows, big noses, and full lips. Black hair all around. Arym was just a younger version of the two. "So, we're... *clones*?"

"Brothers," Tarysl said, cutting him off. "Brothers with Othel, our founder."

"It's... it's Othel's DNA, isn't it? We are all... him."

Tarysl nodded.

It was the worst moment thus far of Arym's life.

As if Arym hadn't already struggled for most of his adolescence feeling like an imprisoned rat, the rektor just dropped a gigantic atom bomb in his lap. Not only was Arym stuck underground for his entire life feeling like just another cog in a wheel, his thoughts and personal identity weren't even a reprieve from the monotony of being a Cribman. Every single person he met was identical to him. All his thoughts, fears, and dreams were just stock footage rolling around in all their heads. Every Cribman probably had a sketch journal they kept tucked away under their mattress, reveling in their individuality with their cute little sketches of rocks or saltshakers or some other stupid shit they found special. There was absolutely nothing special or unique about himself and this was the worst realization he'd ever experienced. And the rektor actually thought it was a good thing! The man was beside himself revealing this secret.

"I've gotta get outta here," Arym said, stomach acid emerging at the back of his throat.

Rektor Tarysl didn't hide his disappointment. "Why? I thought you wanted to know all this. This knowledge is a great responsibility for you now. It's another step to the next oaths."

"There are more oaths? I-I just gotta go. Got to meet a friend."

"Just breathe, Arym, you'll be okay."

Arym fought a dizzy spell that twirled through his stomach. "I gotta meet my friend. She'll be waiting for me."

"*She*?" the rektor said, his face turning red.

"Oh, no... I mean—"

"*She?!*"

THIRTEEN

"SO, what exactly do you plan on stealing?" Beetro finally asked.

Miree's eyes went wide with wonder—or perhaps lust. "Two words—dark matter."

"What is dark matter?"

"Ore. The rarest on the planet. A sliver of dark matter has more value than a boulder of diamonds."

"Why?"

"And to even call it ore doesn't make sense. It's more of a force of nature confined to a single spot. It's the pure essence of gravity, boiled down into a condensed spot of matter. That's what they say anyway, I don't really know how it works."

"What good is that?"

"Because a piece of gravity the size of a marble could power a city for a hundred years."

"And General Deluvius has a marble of dark matter?"

"No, no, not a marble. That would be ridiculous—nobody has that much dark matter in one place. He only has a single flake of dark matter. The previous fief lord had it... all fief lords do. Deluvius conquered the castle, so now he's got it in there. Dark matter is what gives fief lords a claim of authority. All lords of northern city-states around here—Belfed, Hol Bete, Danu, Halax—they only rule because they have a tiny flake of dark matter. They inherit it from their predecessors. It's what gives them a claim to rule over their land. Dark matter is beyond valuable. With a single flake, I'll never have to worry about anything for the rest of my life."

"We."

"What?"

"*We* never have to worry about anything for the rest of our lives. Except when we go to find Galiaro after. Right?"

"That goes without saying."

"So, it's in the vault?"

Miree nodded. "Just waiting for us. Waiting for *you*."

"Me?"

"It's heavy. Very."

"A flake?"

"Didn't I tell you it's the essence of gravity? It's going to weigh a little, yeah. My original plan was to bring an electric dolly or some sort of vehicle to drag the flake out, but... well, I got so distracted just trying to get mercury that I hadn't gotten to that part of the plan. But it didn't matter because you came along with that robo-grip strength you liked flaunting so much." She gave him an unsettling jocular punch on the shoulder. "You, well, you can seriously lift, my friend. I watched you in that junkyard. You have serious hauling capabilities."

Beetro felt a certain measure of discomfort at Miree calling him 'my friend'. Like she was trying to sell him on something about which she wasn't entirely certain.

"You won't have any problem picking it up and walking out," she assured.

"So, we walk into the castle, turn on the Quantizer, I walk through a stone wall, pick up a flake of dark matter, and we walk out without anyone noticing?"

"Good, I don't need to repeat the plan," Miree said, rolling over and, again, almost immediately falling into a snore.

Beetro began suspecting she was faking snoring to get him to shut up.

Beetro dreamt again.

It was the same massive army of soldiers and war machines—gigantic, angular robots with spiked vertebrae ridden by men and women with war paint on their faces. The soldiers were draped in massive bandoliers of gauged bullets. Some carried an enormous mantle of turrets or mortars on their backs. It was a menacing ocean of faces, stomping through dirt blackened by the blood of their victims. It wasn't an army, it was a hurricane of mechanical death, ready to continue its advance of destruction across the landscape.

They watched him.

Hundreds of thousands of hosts of armies silently gazed at Beetro. They wore stone expressions.

Waiting.

Dawn light poked through the rows of dead corn stalks. Ribcage awoke and crept up to Miree's pack. As she reached to unclasp the buckle, Miree's hand shot out, grasping the child's wrist.

"What did I say about stealing from me?" Miree asked, eyes closed, almost serene.

Ribcage took her wrist after Miree gave it a painful squeeze. She went back to her spot in the dirt, her eyes placid with anger.

"Here," Miree said after getting up. She extended her canteen and watched the little girl take a small, controlled swig before returning it. "Thanks for not drinking the whole thing."

Ribcage suddenly sprang with energy, jumping up and down. The girl was absolutely filthy. It was only at that moment that Miree realized Ribcage was that old cheesy smell that seemed to be lingering around the party. Dirt had been ground into the creases of her eyelids, lips, and hands. Various spots of thickened grease covered her arms and part of her exposed belly. On that note, the girl was hardly clothed. She wore pants that looked like they'd been fashioned from an old, cloth sack—very unlikely to have underwear beneath. She wore a teeny makeshift tunic, torn along the belly to showcase her starvation when she begged. She must've frozen overnight.

"Here," Miree said, producing a broad scarf from her pack. She held it out. "Your mother might give you your Jumps, but she doesn't dress you."

Ribcage eyed the scarf for a moment, suspicious.

"I don't want anything in return. You're part of the crew and I don't want you dying of hypothermia before the job is over."

"Like Luci?"

"What's like Lucindi?"

"When she gave me bread. She just gave me the bread and I didn't have to do anything in return. This is like that?"

"Yes. It's called a gift. Just take it."

A thin grin curled up Ribcage's face as she snatched the scarf and wrapped it around her neck. It draped luxuriously over her back and belly. "We're going to the castle today?"

Miree looked at Beetro, his indigo eyes were tilted, distracted. "You good to go? You look a little anxious."

He shook his head, his pupils coming into focus. "Yes. I'm fine. Just... I've been having dreams."

"Let's steal the dark matter and get rich, rich, rich like all the fat people at the markets," Ribcage said. She sat cross-legged and broke apart knots in her hair, flinging pebbles and twigs from the gnarled mess. After freeing some strands, she began braiding her hair into pigtails.

"Who taught you how to do that?" Miree asked.

"Luci. I want the general to see my pigtails before I stick my knife into his belly," Ribcage added.

"Yikes," Miree said, sharing a concerned glance with Beetro. She was alarmed, realizing that the teleporting little girl that had been stalking them for days had been armed with a blade. Ribcage continued braiding her hair, unaware of the growing concern on Miree's face.

"Okay," Miree said, deciding to shelf the comment. "Let's talk details..."

Peles Castle was a fortress. A cream stone facade was inset within maroon, wooden framing. There were multiple towers that abutted the castle, their spires looming against the horizon. The roofing was a coppery red—shimmering as if reinforced with a metallic alloy. Squatty turrets studded the ramparts, manned by soldiers—similar appearing as those who'd marched on Korthe. They wore rugged boots, thick cotton camo pants, or overalls with ammunition belts across their torsos. Some were lucky enough to have flak jackets. Most carried rifles or handguns of old-world gunpowder ammunition, though others had the more slender barreled rifles of a railgun. Miree didn't see any of the Alchean laser rifles that Deluvius had carried. No doubt he'd found the laser rifle in the Alchean ruins that the street children of Korthe were now digging up.

Miree couldn't help wondering... why the show of force, here, at his own fortress? She understood why he marched them through Korthe—there was no doubt who now had power in Helian. But why did he fortify the castle as if it were in danger of a siege? Or was he getting ready to attack somewhere? Another city-state in the north? Surely, he didn't have enough firepower to take the Fifth Kingdom in the east. And besides, Helian was essentially farmland with the two shit towns of Korthe and Carister on the side, with the seaside port of Portolo to the south. There wasn't any nearby opposing force. Was he planning an assault? And on whom?

"There are patrols," Beetro announced, perched on a tree branch above them. "They keep a repeated pattern in the periphery of the castle. I've timed their locations and I'll set it to my internal clock, hopefully, they'll stick to the patrol schedule, and we should be able to time our advance to the castle grounds."

Miree nodded, arms crossed. The robot's skills were getting damned impressive. For a fleeting moment, she felt like she was part of her old crew back in Orion. She hated all her old crew, but the familiarity felt comforting somehow. "All right. Let's move in."

They stalked through the high, yellowed, grasses that surrounded the castle, speaking little. There was a soldier who circled around a knoll, keeping watch. They waited for him to make a predictable swing to the back end of the knoll, after which they ran around the other side, deepening their approach.

Ribcage served as an indispensable distraction by Jumping

ahead of them, making a ruckus in the opposite direction and then returning. This diversion helped them to get almost to the castle walls. It became clear that the number of soldiers that had marched on Korthe were not all guarding the castle. Clearly, the rest of the army was elsewhere, spreading dominion over Helian—they'd probably seized control of Carister. Miree was beginning to doubt that the general was even present at the castle. As grandiose as her plans were to assassinate the man, she felt a little disappointed to not be able to make the bastard pay for what he did to Lucindi.

Without much difficulty, they made it to the castle wall. Beetro felt the stone. "Ribcage, can you Jump to the other side? See if you can spot an opening somewhere?"

Ribcage shook her head. "Can't."

Miree frowned. "Why not?"

"I can't Jump where I can't see. Also, can't Jump past a long wall like this. Even when I walk into the flat world, the wall just keeps going and going."

"Hmm..." *Damn* is what Miree wanted to say but she didn't want to reveal her waxing anxiety. Assuming Ribcage could Jump to various locations on demand had become fundamental in her most recent mental plans.

"And we can't use the Quantizer?" Ribcage asked.

Miree shook her head. "No. Not enough mercury. We got enough for one person, one round trip through a solid surface. That's it. We have to save it for the vault wall."

Impatient, Ribcage simply climbed the cobble stonework of the wall and quickly scaled to the top like a monkey. She squinted, ignoring Miree's protest, and waved them up. Reluctantly, Beetro and Miree climbed the wall and let themselves down from the top to the other side without stopping to scout. Miree felt like she was seconds away from a turret shredding them apart. Once on the other side of the wall, she tensed, expecting alarms to blare but only heard the banter of soldiers somewhere. *This is monstrously stupid,* Miree finally conceded to herself. Haldunt the Wire of the Kish would be laughing at her now—before torturing her for stealing his Quantizer.

Realizing how exposed they were, she corralled her crew to duck behind a stack of dead horses. Ribcage gagged in a dramatic show. Miree slid her finger horizontally across her throat as a warning for the girl to shut up. She tapped Beetro on the shoulder. "Get to the top of the heap. Scope it out."

Lacking human revulsion and its gag reflex, Beetro gingerly climbed atop the carcasses and surveyed the castle grounds. Beetro motioned her up. She discovered soldiers in the courtyard. A few chatted amongst themselves, sipping coffee by an open fire, their voices calm. A row of columns surrounded the courtyard with overhanging banners or stacks of hay covering the nooks between the columns. It was a perfect layout for covert movement around the courtyard. Beetro climbed down and motioned them forward, trailing alongside the stone wall of the courtyard.

Miree heard some of the soldier's conversations:

"...He's been holed up there all morning."

"Are the captains with him?"

"No, as far as I know, he's up there alone."

"You been up there?"

"Where? The tower?"

"Yeah."

"No. Hell, no. No one goes up there except the general and the captains."

"You think it's up there?"

"What? Why you ask?"

"No," the soldier faltered. "I'm not suggesting we do anything about it. It's just—you know the rumors about Peles. Black matter flake and everything."

"Dark matter. Not black matter. And what the general wants to keep in the tower is his business. Not our job to speculate."

"Course." The woman cut off the conversation as if regretting she brought anything up.

"Wait, what was that?"

Beetro and Miree froze, locking eyes. They then realized at the same time that Ribcage wasn't next to them.

One of the soldiers laughed and the other shouted, "Hey! What're you doing here?" She was talking to Ribcage, who was standing in front of the soldiers, playing with a frayed yarn on her scarf. One of the soldiers tightened a grip on her gun. The other placed a calming hand on her shoulder. "Relax, it's just one of the street rats." She turned to Ribcage. "Okay, dummy, how'd you get away from the dig site?"

"*What is she doing*?" Miree growled in Beetro's ear.

Ribcage looked up at the soldiers. "You killed Luci."

The soldier got on the radio. "Come in 4-9, we've got one of your kids over at the castle. I don't know what y'all are doing over there but you better come over here and get her before the general finds out. Over."

A garbled voice responded, "Command, we're not missing any kids over at excavation, boss."

"This two-inch tall, little girl standing right in front of me says otherwise—"

And then Ribcage vanished.

"What—" The soldier blinked, baffled.

Suddenly, a stone the size of an apple was flung from a surrounding rampart and landed at the soldier's feet. The soldier tapped the rock with her foot and then stumbled forward when another stone hit her helmet. The soldier lifted her rifle, aiming it up at the eerily vacant ramparts. "Where...?"

The other soldier frowned. "Where'd she go—" a stone also smacked her helmet. She lost her balance and fell backward, her rifle stumbling from her arms. Out of sheer confused frustration, she pulled her radio from her jacket and yelled, "All alert! We have an intruder, and we are under attack. Unknown number of enemy combatants."

A klaxon then blared out over the castle grounds.

Miree grabbed Beetro's foot to get his attention. "We got get outta here!" she yelled over the din of chaos that erupted in the courtyard.

He stumbled down the dead horses and crouched beside her. "We're going to just leave her here?"

"Fine. No." Miree didn't want to admit to herself but the little street rat was actually growing on her. She saw a brigade of soldiers flood the courtyard, their rifles up and perched for attack. Miree flattened on her belly. If they moved an inch from their hiding place, they'd be spotted instantly. Miree just shook her head, rolling her forehead in the dirt. Bits of twigs and leaves clung to her sweaty forehead as she looked up at Beetro.

"Let's just wait," Beetro cautioned as if they actually had any other option than to surrender.

And waiting worked for a moment because Ribcage was off all over the castle grounds, distracting dozens of soldiers. She appeared beside a turret on one of the ramparts, kicking over a bucket of needle-nosed bullets. Rifles spontaneously fell from soldiers' arms after their helmets flew to the ground. Horses were inexplicably unloosed from the stables, hay flinging beneath their hooves as they charged forward. Because they believed there were enemies within and without, the soldiers prepared for a siege attack on the castle while also trying to defend themselves, spinning in circles at the phantom intruder. Some of the captains could tell something was going on besides a blatant attack, but most of the soldiers ran around without a clear target, frustrated to not find someone to actually shoot.

The courtyard was in a frenzy as soldiers scrambled like an agitated ant farm. Beetro tapped Miree's arm and ushered her along the courtyard. They hid behind haystacks and tarps that hung along the stone walls. He weaved them in between cover as they inched their way out of the courtyard. They heard enemy footsteps around stone corners and timed their movements for when they were absent. Only a few minutes into Ribcage's chaos and they'd crept their way past corners where otherwise sentinels would've stood, who now vacated, preparing for battle. Miree steeled herself, realizing the method to Ribcage's madness.

They moved through a rotted garden, at times on their hands and knees, and rounded the walls of the castle keep. The structure was heavily guarded, defending against the most obvious point of entry for an enemy. Miree saw the back-end spire behind the keep walls and urged herself forward, hiding along stone columns or stacks of artillery as they came to the back-end of the castle. She looked herself up and down, incredulous that they'd penetrated this deep into the castle grounds this quickly, unscathed no less.

They were at the back spire—the castle vault. It was a tight corner where one perpendicular stone fence met a curved wall, creating a small pocket in which to fit. Miree glanced around, no one was in sight, including Ribcage.

And then Ribcage Jumped right next to them.

"Bah!" Miree yelped, startled by the girl.

Ribcage twirled a pigtail. "We did it!"

Miree opened her pack and brought out the black satchel and untied its drawstring. Carefully, she removed the Quantizer and placed it on the ground a few meters away from the stone wall of the spire.

"Beetro," she said without looking up. "Keep watch around the corner. Tell me if anyone comes." Ribcage sat on the ground, looking at the Quantizer. Carefully, she removed the silver thermos from her back and poured it into the canister on the back end of the Quantizer. Liquid poured out from the thermos in beads of quicksilver. She closed the cap on the canister and then began adjusting the small square frame—similar to adjusting the sights on a rifle. The window was on the front end of the Quantizer, built perpendicular to the ground. She fiddled with the adjustable tabs, enlarging the square frame and peered through it, closing one eye. She looked back at Beetro and sized the frame to the robot's stature. "Over a little to your left." But Beetro wasn't listening. "Hey!" she shouted over the alarm.

Beetro was distracted by nearby shouts. "What!"

Miree waved her hand impatiently. "To your left! We only have one shot to get this right."

"So... it's still going to be me? Who's going in?"

"Yes! No one else can carry out the dark matter flake—it's too heavy. It *has* to be you and it *has* to be now. Now, scoot over!" She knelt above the Quantizer, lining it up with Beetro.

"Okay, it'll be fine," Beetro reassured himself. "Am I really just going to pass right through a stone wall? What if there's a roomful of soldiers in there? What should I do?"

Ignoring the robot, Miree brought two wires on a circuit board together on the underside of the Quantizer, prompting a glowing blue light to shoot down the middle of the apparatus. A center coil, snaking in between two metal struts, pulsated with the light. It traveled from the mercury canister on the back end to the portway at the front. A square of the blue light projected from the portway and onto the stone wall before them. She snapped another wire into place on the circuit board and the blue light twisted out of the other side of the portway, bathing Beetro in the light. "It's matching your atomic state with that of the wall."

Beetro looked down at the blue light covering his body. "How long does that take?"

"A split second. It's already done. I'm going to flip the switch and you should be able to walk right through the wall."

"*Should?*"

"Yes. And you're going to take the Quantizer in with you so you can use it to get back out. It's all fired up. Just bring it in and leave it next to the wall. It'll stay on. Once you're ready to come back through, just stand in front of the portway and walk back out. But don't forget to bring it back out with you. This machine is priceless. Got it?"

"Ye-yes."

Miree flipped the switch on the Quantizer at the exact moment that her motley crew was discovered by a soldier. With a rifle cradled in his hands, he looked down at the band of thieves with a blank gaze as if his brain couldn't process the fact that this strange assortment of characters was actually at his feet. He paused for a moment, the pulsating blue illuminating his puzzled face.

"Go!" Miree yelled. "Now!"

The soldier's hands couldn't decide if he wanted to shoot first or radio for help, so they did both at the same time, causing him to drop his weapon. With the thankful distraction, Beetro hopped over the Quantizer and ran straight at the wall.

Beetro opened his eyes to a pitch-black room. The Quantizer had worked. He'd passed through the wall without feeling a thing.

Briefly, he patted his body as if a part of it would've been left behind. He felt a certain amount of faith in Miree—long enough before two bodies crashed into him from behind. He fell to his knees, groping in the dark until he found a ledge to lift himself. Flipping on his dark vision, he looked down and saw them—Miree and Ribcage.

Miree stood, shaking her head. "Total disaster," she muttered.

Ribcage blinked in the darkness. "Robot?"

"I'm right here. What happened?"

Miree fumbled inside her cloak. "We got overwhelmed by more soldiers and had to follow you through."

"But I thought the Quantizer only matched my atomic state."

"It must've scanned our quantum states, too. Damn thing didn't exactly come with a user manual. I should've listened more to the astrocyst who made it right before I stole it from him." She produced a candle and a small matchbook.

"Don't waste those," Beetro said. He turned on an internal switch, prompting two bright cones of light to flicker from his indigo eyes.

"We made it!" Ribcage declared.

Miree was rubbing the bridge of her nose. "No. We didn't. We only had enough mercury for two trips with the Quantizer—one to get Beetro in and one to get him out. We used up all the mercury when me and you Jumped through. Besides, the *robot* left the Quantizer on the other side of the wall when he was supposed to bring it in with him. Aren't you supposed to have a perfect memory?"

"Well," Beetro said, suppressing his irritation. "We'll just find another way back out."

"We're in a vault. *Inside* a vault. It's designed to keep things *in*."

It was true. Beetro discovered that the walls were plated in iron, riveted together by thick bolts. A circular door was built at one end of the vast vault and was closed. Shelves lined the walls along with dozens of tables and cabinets that covered the floor and...

It was all empty.

He turned to Miree. "If this is a vault, where is everything?"

Miree looked around, an angry wrinkle furrowing at her brow. "Maybe Deluvius used all the previous lord's gold and silver to build his army. I don't care about that anyway—we're not here for gold—we'd never be able to get it out." She looked around more and pointed to a narrow staircase at the back end of the vault. "Up there, come on."

The three moved through the vault and up the metal staircase. They discovered it was a spiral staircase, leading several floors higher than the lower level of the vault. After several more levels, climbing up the height of the spire, they came to a small room, a few small sunbeams streaming in from windows.

Miree squinted in the new sunlight.

The room was utterly empty.

"Is this... where the dark matter is kept?" Beetro asked, hopeful.

Miree appeared too angry for words.

"Shh!" Ribcage said. "Someone's coming up the stairs."

The three froze and turned, waiting for the roar of soldiers to melt them away with gunfire. But it wasn't a brigade. A little echo rattled up the stairwell. Someone was coming. The person shuffled closer now, almost at the threshold of the room. It was someone moving with delicate, thoughtful steps—not a frantic soldier. Beetro hoped that maybe it would be a friend—some forgotten ally back to rescue him after all the trouble he'd got himself into.

But it was General Deluvius.

He was dressed in his sleek ballistic armor, bedecked out with the bionic shoulder implant with wires questing down his forearm into a mechanical glove, replete with tiny glowing screens and buttons. In his grasp, he held that beautiful windswept Alchean laser rifle, aimed at the intruders. His eyes were angry slits beneath their bushy brows. He spoke, angry spittle flicking from his lips. "Who do we have *here*?"

FOURTEEN

ARYM ALWAYS THOUGHT it would've been far more dramatic when the rektors finally caught him. He imagined running for his life through an Oshaft while the rektors hotly pursued their wayward brother. He'd have Hawera's hand in his as he led her to the wilderness—to the vast horizon of unfathomable possibilities of the overworld. If they caught him during a chase, at least he would have the satisfaction of doing all he could to escape. He would go into rehabilitation without regrets.

But accidentally blurting out that he was meeting a friend—a *she*—and then to be unceremoniously apprehended was not exactly what he imagined. Of course, none of it mattered in the end. Either way, he would end up in isolation, rehabilitation for years, away from the overworld—away from Hawera. He wondered what she was doing at that moment. Was she thinking about him? Did she wonder where he was? Yes, he did tell her about his people, but he revealed very little about the Crib, guilted by the Oath to not reveal its location. Would she look for him? Would she... rescue him?

Maybe.

If only he had his sketch journal, he could at least look at the pictures he'd made of her. But they took everything. Not a scrap of his prior possessions was left in his pod. After Rektor Tarysl blew up in the clone lab, he was escorted directly back to his pod where the portal door was locked behind him.

On the second day, a knock came to the door.

"Come in," he said, sitting up from a mattress that they'd brought in. There was not another piece of furniture in the pod. Funny how it converted nicely into a prison cell.

Rektor Tarysl ducked into the pod, his face stone serious. "Sit down, Cribman."

"And if I don't?"

The rektor looked down at him, trying to read his expression. "I'm not here to make things worse. Stand if you'd like."

Arym sat.

"How long has it been going on?"

Arym said nothing.

"The faster you cooperate, the shorter your rehabilitation time. This will all go at your speed."

"Over a year."

The rektor stifled a gasp with a quick swallow. "I see. And who did you communicate with in the overworld?"

"A woman."

"Arym..."

Arym met the rektor's gaze. "What?"

"Did you break the Oath of Descension?"

"No."

"Are you telling the truth?"

"Yes. Your brainwashing did its job. I couldn't get over the guilt of breaking the Oath. The Crib is safe for another day of cloning and digging."

"Brainwashing?"

Arym nodded. "What else would you call it?"

"Trying to teach you values is not brainwashing."

"Values? What values? Your values are hiding. Dig deeper into the ground, escape from the world, clone Othel again and again. Doesn't it bother you?"

"Does what bother me?"

"That we're the exact same person?"

The rektor paused, considering his response.

"No? It's never bothered you that you and I are no different? That we have the same exact brain? How do I know you didn't do the exact same things I'm doing when you were my age? Did you escape to the overworld? Did you get thrown into isolation? How are you content with the fact that the Crib is just an endless cycle of one man? It's the perpetual life of Othel, played out forever."

"It's not like that—"

"What's the point of existing when everyone around me is the same exact thing?"

"We're not the same person."

"Of course, we are. We're the physical manifestation of a person who was in love with himself and afraid of the world."

"Careful. These are sacred things on which you trample. There is much you do not understand."

"And you come in here asking me if I've broken oaths? The oaths are meaningless. I wish I *had* revealed the location of the Crib. I wish the entire overworld would come knocking on our door, rooting us up from this hole."

"Why did you keep it a secret for so long about escaping to the overworld? Didn't you trust me?"

"You want to talk about secrets? Why was I only told two days ago about the cloning?"

"There are secrets and then there is sacred knowledge. Secrets are withheld because of fear and distrust. Sacred knowledge is withheld because of a lack of preparedness. You were not ready for the knowledge. It was my mistake to show you."

"One man's sacredness is another man's abomination, I suppose."

"Arym. We are not the same person. I was different from you when I was your age. I never escaped to the overworld. Yes, I wanted to, but I was faithful to the Oath. I re-dedicated myself to our cause. I found joy in our way of life. Think of all the Cribmen you know—Lutra and all the Cribmen you worked with on the digline—they are not you. We're all unique in our personalities. Some form bonding pairs while others do not. Some are mechanical, others are mathematical. We may have the same DNA in our brains, yes, but... can't you see the miracle in our way of life?"

"Miracle? You think a bunch of men living underground, cloned from the same stock and pairing off together is a miracle?"

"We are individuals despite having identical DNA. We are united in our individuality. It creates harmony."

"That's a great line. Make sure you save it for the next generation of incestual automatons."

Rektor Tarysl stood in silence. "I've spoken to the rektor council about your case."

"And what wisdom have you collectively decreed?"

"You'll be in rehabilitation for five years."

Arym sank down onto the bed. He rested his elbows on his knees and looked down.

"They wanted a lifetime ban on you, Arym. They wanted you in rehabilitation for the rest of your life."

Arym was silent.

"Many argued that you'd be a contagion to the rest of the Crib. I do agree that you are and will be for quite some time. That is why you'll be in isolation for eighteen months to begin with. No contact with anyone—including myself—for eighteen months. You'll be confined to this pod, alone and without human contact. After the assigned eighteen months, you will undergo intense rehabilitation with me and a care team."

Arym looked up at the rektor, tears in his eyes.

The rektor appeared taken back by the tears. "I'm sorry... this all could have been prevented if you were honest with me from the beginning. I only wish I didn't give you reason to distrust me. If you'd even told me the first time you'd gone to the overworld, we could've worked with you—made things better. But now—"

"I'm hopeless to you."

"No one is beyond hope, Arym. You're... you're my brother. There is hope for anyone."

"That, you're wrong about."

The rektor gazed down at him. "You're not hopeless."

"I'm not talking about me. I'm talking about you. *You* are hopeless."

Rektor Tarysl moved to the pod portal, his shoulders slumped. "I wish... I wish you could understand the weight of the Oath. The Oath will save this world—it will redeem the overworld. The Crib will eventually bring harmony to all people, through all space. But I fear the knowledge is too much for you to bear."

"See you in eighteen months."

The rektor turned his face and nodded. Arym saw tears in the man's eyes as he stepped through the portal door and left.

Arym had a dream that night.

He dreamt he was moving through the stars. Jagged streaks of light soared past him as he traveled through space. He visited vast lands full of wild plants and colorful fruit. He left one land, flying into space and into the stars, to then land in a new forest or mountain range. He walked along lakes and ponds, swam under waterfalls or climbed trees. After what felt like years of traveling, he discovered that he'd traveled to every land—that he'd seen everything.

He awoke with sadness in his chest. Not only because he realized he was in isolation, but because of the dream. Every land in the dream was just a different version of his limited experience in the overworld. It was merely repeated iterations of the only land he'd ever known. Even his dreams were limited to the tiny existence of a Cribman. His imagination itself had been stifled and choked out by being raised underground by a society of paranoid zealots.

The first day of isolation was the longest in his life.

He had no idea how much freedom the average Cribman had when compared to isolation. Living alone in a single room was the most horrific fate he could've ever imagined for himself. And here he was. It was his living hell. After a few days of staring at white walls, tracing the line where they met with the ceiling over and over again, his thoughts naturally went to suicide.

He quickly concluded that ending his life would be a far greater fate than sitting in the pod for the next eighteen months. The rektors, shrewdly, had only placed a mattress in the room. There was no bed frame, no furniture, no objects to even sharpen down into a blade. There was no immediate way of ending his life. Not that he was certain he could do it right away, but he was certain that, given enough time—long before eighteen months lapsed—he was going to want a way out.

He hit his head on the wall a few times. Not in any earnest

attempt at hurting himself. It was more of a test drive to figure out how hard he'd actually have to hit his head to cause fatal damage. A lot, he concluded after giving himself several goose eggs without even losing consciousness. There was a toilet built into the side of the wall without movable parts. The only one of two potential outlets from the pod was the tiny drain at the bottom of the bowl. There was water at the bottom of the bowl but certainly not enough for drowning. Lastly, there was a showerhead that was installed in the ceiling, far out of his reach with a drain in the floor, which was well sealed. The shower turned on once a day for what felt like forty-five seconds of soapy water followed by forty-five seconds of rinse water—all of it ice cold.

When planning his own suicide didn't occupy his thoughts, Hawera took up the rest. He saw her face in his mind. Although he never actually saw her smile once, he liked to picture her looking at him, lips curling to a smile after finally being reunited. He occupied a lot of his time replaying the conversations they'd had.

I'm like a butterfly.

What had she meant by that? She was as rare and beautiful as a butterfly, something he saw a few times while exploring Crater Valley. She was the one who pointed to one of them and told them what they were called. Hawera was a diamond to him—a rare treasure in a world of Cribmen and digging. Nothing in his life mattered before he had met her. The thought of not being able to see her again only accelerated his thoughts toward his own demise. His mind oscillated as he paced the floor between thoughts of seeing Hawera and ways to end his life. Neither was likely any time soon.

At times, he'd knock on the portal door. He banged on it for a good twenty minutes until he heard voices on the other side of the door. No one came in to stop him, but it told him two things—

there weren't any guards standing immediately at the door, and no matter what he did, no one would be coming into his pod. Isolation meant isolation. He was not to see another human being for eighteen months.

And thus was his life.

On about day six of isolation, he was lying in bed, staring up at the ceiling. There was a single lightbulb, far out of his reach, dangling from a single electrical cord. One of his pastimes was staring at the bulb long enough that his vision went completely black from the light.

Day six.

It was only day six.

Out of five hundred and forty.

He was already thinking about suicide on day one. He wasn't going to make it. He'd go insane long before eighteen months. He finally faced the fact that the only way he could end everything was starvation. Of course, this would be the longest, most painful way to go but it would be a sweet mercy compared to eighteen months of isolation.

When a tray of food appeared in a small slot in the door, he got up and dumped the oatmeal and applesauce down the toilet. Temptation gone. How long would it take? A month? Shorter if he stopped drinking water, too.

The next day, the hunger arrived. It was only a dull pain, more than tolerable. The problem was keeping his mind off the hunger —there was nothing to distract him. Only the lightbulb. The next day, the hunger crashed in on him, consuming every thought. As much as his mind wanted to let go, his body wasn't going to give in that easily. It was becoming more difficult to flush each meal, yet he still managed to dispose of it quickly. He was only drinking one cup of water a day. He weighed the benefit of ridding himself of a massive headache against dying a little faster and decided to drink a little with the starvation. It was a pretty good balance, he discovered.

On day four of the hunger strike, he was noticeably weaker. The hunger pain matured from a dull pain to a roaring, spiking blade in his gut. He shook all over and was constantly freezing. It was miserable, but it *was* less boring. They could lock him up, but they couldn't force him to live the way they wanted.

"You can't keep me," he said to no one.

Regrets of not fleeing into the overworld consumed his thoughts. He went into fever dreams involving the Crescent Wood, running with deer and Hawera's voice speaking to him from somewhere. His mind became a deranged backdrop to the madness of isolation.

Somewhere around day nine of isolation, he jerked awake.

Something was different about the room. It was *brighter*. He squinted, unsure if the light had changed or if it was his eyes. He sat up on the edge of the bed and smelled warm beans sitting at the door. He almost lunged at them to ram them into his mouth, but he resisted, knowing it would undo all his fine work of starving himself.

"You don't look well," someone said from above.

"Ahh!" Arym screamed, uncertain of everything in his life to that point. He fell to the ground and looked at the ceiling. There was nothing up there. Just a lightbulb. "Who..." Good. Psychosis was setting in. Hopefully, it wouldn't be long until the whole thing was over.

"I'm sorry I wasn't here sooner. It took me a while to find you. I was also distracted by your people. Interesting culture," the voice said. "Familiar." Suddenly, a single orb of light separated itself from the lightbulb and descended to Arym.

Arym realized that he knew that voice. "Protonix?"

"Yes," Protonix said, the orb moving up and down. The light expanded into a shaft, exposing a projection of his elongated face and nose. "I bring news."

"How... how are you here? This is just in my head."

"I assure you I am not in your imagination. I left the tomb of the Alcheans to deliver a message to you."

"From whom?"

"Your traveling partner, Hawera."

"Hawera!" He stood, felt woozy, and immediately fell to the ground.

"I suggest you be more careful. You look ill. Maybe you should eat?"

"I'm not eating."

"Why?"

"I'm trying to kill myself."

"I see," Protonix's face scrunched. "I would've thought your culture was above self-termination."

"Can't you see I'm a prisoner—it doesn't matter. You've seen Hawera?"

"Yes. She came to me. Normally, I wouldn't take such personal requests to deliver a message. For her, I made an exception."

"What did she say?"

"That she was leaving the valley. You see, she wanted to find someone to help her—"

"Help her with what?"

"She said she needed to get back home. Back to her new home in a different time."

"What does that mean?"

"I'm afraid it is too complex to communicate to you at this time. Perhaps in another century when your culture has developed that technology."

"But I'll be dead then."

"Oh, yes, forgive me. Sometimes I forget that I'm talking to a single individual in a single time period. I'm used to speaking to cultures over long periods of time."

"Where did she go?"

Protonix hesitated. "She asked about the stars. She said she needed to find an astrocyst to help her."

"What's an astrocyst?"

"How shall I explain? I suppose an astrocyst is a person that would appear as some sort of sorcerer to a lower civilized person as yourself. I directed Hawera to Orion to find an astrocyst. My entangled partner there will direct her once she arrives. She asked that I come and communicate this with you."

"She asked about me?"

"Yes. She was worried that she hadn't seen you in some time."

Arym's heart pounded. *She was worried about me.* The hunger pains instantly melted away.

Protonix continued, "She wanted to thank you for your help and assistance."

"Anything else?"

"No."

"That's all you have to tell me?"

Protonix nodded, his floating head bobbing up and down. "That is all."

"Now what?"

"I'm afraid I must leave. There are pressing matters to attend to."

"Like what?"

"Astronomical matters that you need not concern yourself with."

"Wait, wait. Can't you get me out of here?"

Protonix looked around the room. "And how do you suppose I accomplish that?"

Arym looked at him, mouth open. "Unlock the door."

"I'm afraid I can't unlock anything. Or move anything for that matter."

"Why not?"

"As I explained to you before, I am only a single proton. I can behave as several subatomic particles—photons, electrons, neutrinos. However, I cannot manipulate matter in any way except for making compression waves. Hence, my voice."

Arym sighed with frustration. "Well, can you *help* me get out?"

Protonix shook his head. "No, I don't believe so."

"Can't you go find me help? Go tell Hawera that I'm imprisoned."

"No, I'm afraid not. I don't generally get involved in mortal matters like these. My needs as curator of the Alchean tomb are far too demanding."

"When was the last time anyone visited before me and Hawera?"

Protonix paused. "One hundred and five years. When a band of thieves used an incendiary device to rupture the gate. The gate only opens when someone understands the mathematical riddle inscribed there. The thieves hadn't the patience or acumen and blasted it open. Needless to say, they were quite disappointed at discovering they were robbing a tomb void of physical treasure."

"Why do you need to get back if you rarely get visitors?"

"I'm the curator of the tomb. The last guardian of all the technical knowledge of the Alcheans. I protect the most important place on Earth."

"Then why did you leave there to deliver a message for Hawera?"

"The young woman is different. She is no ordinary human."

"What is so different about her?"

"I don't believe it is prudent for you to understand."

"Please," Arym said, begging in his voice. "I want to understand."

"As guardian of Alchean knowledge, I am forbidden to communicate to those that are not technologically prepared. You are of a people that is far from understanding. If you have knowledge without being prepared, you can become dangerous to yourself and other Earth cultures."

Arym exhaled loudly.

Protonix paused, considering the starving young man before him. "I suppose I can tell you this... the arrow of time always moves forward, but the arrow is always curved."

"What?"

"Once you understand that, you'll understand Hawera."

"I don't understand anything at all."

Protonix frowned for a moment, measuring his response. "There is something wrong with the galaxy. She is trying to help."

"What is a galaxy?"

"The fact that you are asking that question is evidence that you are not ready for the answer."

"Does it have to do with the Alcheans?"

"Perhaps."

Slowly, Arym got to his feet and sat on the bed. "You need to get me out of here. If Hawera is out there doing something important, I need to help her. Otherwise, I'm dead. I'll die in here."

"Why?"

"I can't live with these people."

"Aren't they *your* people?"

"No. You've got to get me out."

"I'm sorry. It's not possible. I cannot help. I must leave now." Protonix began collecting the light around him, condensing it into a ball.

"No! Don't go!"

"I'm sorry. I must leave."

"Please. Don't go," Arym said, his voice wavering.

"If I see our mutual acquaintance again, I will tell her of your plight."

"Don't go!"

But it was too late, the room had already darkened.

Arym was alone.

FIFTEEN

A LOW RUMBLE thumped through the spire tower of Peles Castle. Something was out there. But Beetro's attention wasn't on the pounding happening outside of the stone walls, it was on General Deluvius and his Alchean laser rifle trained on Miree. The man was angry, but it was an annoyed anger, nothing close to fury.

"What are you *doing* here?" He was speaking to Beetro but threatening Miree with his rifle—the same rifle that killed Lucindi.

The tension was immediately interrupted by a war cry ringing out beside the general. "Die!" Ribcage had Jumped into the space right beside the man, brandishing a small blade in her hand. He saw the tiny girl and sidestepped as Ribcage lunged with her blade. His parry spared him a stick in the belly and only left him with a small slash on the hand. She stood, holding her blade expectedly.

"I admire your stealth," he told her. "Not many can achieve subterfuge with me. But I've killed for much less than this, little one." He looked at his bloodied hand and then down at Ribcage, apparently not having noticed that she had appeared from thin air. He smiled and then landed a deft kick, square into the small girl's chest. She fell backward, her back slamming into the wood floor. "Fortunately for you, I could use some more excavators."

Ribcage shook her head and propped herself back up, standing to her feet.

"Well done," he said as if half-mocking and half impressed at the small girl's spunk. "Now—" he was cut off by his own surprise. Ribcage vanished. He chased the look of shock from his face and crossed the room in two strides, backing himself up against the wall, ready for another surprise attack.

Miree looked longingly at the now vacant doorway.

"Why are you here?" Deluvius asked, unclear to whom.

Miree and Beetro didn't respond. They shared an uncertain glance.

Deluvius continued, "Little girl, make yourself visible. I'm not amused by your little trick."

Ribcage remained unseen.

"If you don't show yourself, I will shoot your friend." He pointed the laser rifle at Miree. "I don't know who your Luci is, but I do not doubt that I killed her. She will be joined by your homely friend over here if you do not show your face."

Miree started, "She probably left—"

"Do *not* speak to me," Deluvius said. "What makes you believe you can speak to me?"

It was then Beetro remembered Deluvius' speech before he'd killed Lucindi... *When someone acts like a hero when a hero isn't needed... they deserve a different name—a terrorist.*

Maybe Deluvius *was* the hero—the hero of Helian and Peles Castle. The townsfolk of Korthe certainly didn't seem to disagree with him. If Lucindi had been right in her outrage, why hadn't the rest of the town supported her? And after all, Beetro had come with Miree to kill the man and rob him of his riches. Isn't that what a terrorist does? Maybe Lucindi wasn't a martyr at all—maybe she *was* a terrorist. Beetro felt so helpless as he realized his grasp of how the world worked was entirely dependent on context.

"We're sorry," he said to Deluvius. "We're sorry we came. We didn't have the right—"

"Don't apologize to him," Miree hissed, steeling herself. "He's a murdering bastard. He deserves to have his throat cut."

Deluvius exhaled deeply, looking at Beetro. He studied the robot for a moment, eyes investigating that blue sheen of his metallic skin. *Why wasn't he doing anything?* He'd so quickly, with impunity, pulled the trigger on Lucindi. He continued to watch Beetro, a modicum of curiosity in his eyes. "I've waited long enough, I believe we need a change of plans," he finally said, his grip tightening on the laser rifle.

And then it seemed as if time slowed down for a moment.

Beetro felt something within the rifle. He felt...

Energy.

Whatever force was within the weapon that condensed energy and amplified it into laser light, it was collecting within the arms of the general. Beetro felt the process—streams of particles flowing down tiny tubes and coalescing into a core of high-energy photons. And then suddenly, he felt the sunlight streaming into the room, surrounding him with similar energy. His interpretation of the physical world jumped in stark relief—solar radiation was *everywhere.* It was as if he no longer saw the room, draped in sunlight, with his eyes. He *felt* the room as the energy of the sun coated the walls, floors, and tables. He could've closed his eyes and walked around, knowing the position of everything because the sunlight energized everything it touched.

And then the rifle discharged.

Miree winced.

A bolt of red laser light exploded from the barrel. Beetro held out his hands to the laser and closed his eyes. He looked, knowing he'd see Miree dead on the floor. Dead. Just like Lucindi.

But Miree stood there intact, ducking with her arms covering her face. She relaxed, realizing the general must've missed and looked up.

But the general didn't miss.

A horizontal shaft of laser light hung in the air, completely frozen.

Miree gaped at the ribbon of light floating in front of them.

Beetro's outstretched hands held the beam of energy there, hovering just beyond the barrel of Deluvius' rifle. He harnessed the energy of the laser light, like a bottled storm of lightning and fury that wanted to explode inside the room—but Beetro wouldn't allow it. He didn't know how, but he gave the energy boundaries and restrictions, slowing the flow of photons into a stand-still. The room immediately humidified, the beam of laser radiating with thermal energy. Deluvius studied the glowing rod of laser light, bewildered. It was a strange look on a man who was not easily befuddled.

Miree looked at Beetro, studying his outstretched, quivering arms and nodded with awed understanding. "Like trying to hold up a water dam."

The shock on General Deluvius' face was something beautiful. But before Beetro could relish the man's dismay, he clenched the rifle again as if to pull the trigger.

"Stop!" Beetro cried out, swinging his arms, lancing the beam of laser light across the room and smashing it into the wall, which exploded in splintered wood and fractured stone. Wind swept into the tower room as billows of smoke and fire pumped into the sky. Half the spire tower was simply gone—a gaping hole left to the open sky where Beetro had re-directed the laser energy. Just outside, an aircraft of elegant craftsmanship hovered just beside the spire tower. It had a sleek design—that windswept texture of the ancient Alcheans—of a single wing. It was like a shard of a mirror, broken off and polished into a single smooth wing that arched across the courtyard of the castle.

The chaos of the blast bought breathing room. Miree looked out over the castle grounds—soldiers *everywhere*. They were in various stages of preparing for war, most with their necks craned at the spire, trying to understand what just happened above them.

Miree's mind went into frantic problem-solving.

Going back down the stairs into the vault wasn't an option... surely soldiers were on their way up. She only had moments—seconds. She couldn't climb down the spire. It was smooth stone all the way down. She looked over at the Wing, the aircraft that hovered over the castle. It was just below the spire—possibly within jumping distance. It was a broad aircraft and she could easily run right across it...

She looked back at the robot.

It looked pretty dead.

But then she saw a twitch of limb here and a blink there—kind of like when she found him in the junkyard. His eyes barely swiveled in their sockets to peer up at Miree. He was paralyzed, the general crouched over him, and Ribcage... nowhere to be seen. She looked down at Beetro's eyes, the indigo orbs of light fixated on her, pleading for help. His rubbery lips quivered, trying to speak to her—trapped in his own body. She could almost make out what he was trying to say—*We can get away! Now is the time! Help me!*

But he was just a junkyard robot—not worth dying for.

"Fuck it," she said, backing up from the blown-out ledge of the spire. She got a running start and leaped from the tower.

Beetro closed his eyes.

Of course, Miree would leave him.

She had no more interest in keeping him around—or helping him find Galiaro—more than she would lugging around a broken piece of machinery. He finally understood what he was to Miree—a tool. There was a finality in this conclusion that brought him a small amount of solace as he laid there, paralyzed on the floor. He no longer had to question what his place was in the world. He was a machine built for humans to use or discard.

The water vapor inside his system—the lifeblood to run the hydraulics of his joints and fill the micro tubing of his neural network—had evaporated. The nuclear fusion core in his chest was functioning properly, but there was no water in the system to convert into useful energy for his body. It must've been why the first sensation he had when waking in Korthe was thirst.

He looked up from the floor, his eyes being the only thing he could control. There was gunfire and the whir of engines outside, below the spire tower.

General Deluvius looked down on him, fury in his eyes. "What now?" he stated, mostly to himself. He was typing things on his forearm console, ostensibly to call for backup to the tower. They'd take Beetro away and strip him down for parts. They could use his fusion core as a battery for something else—it could go years without maintenance. Maybe he'd be turned into an engine.

Beetro didn't care. But wait, how did he do that trick with a laser? Was that a normal robot thing?

It didn't matter.

"We'll at least get him to the dungeons below," Deluvius spoke into a mouthpiece, talking to his lieutenants. "We can—ah!" he cried out, stumbling back.

Ribcage was back.

Her hand clenched around the butt of a knife—one that she'd just plunged into the general's gut. Deluvius cried out and knocked the little girl over. He fell to the ground, clutching the hilt as a small amount of blood began to seep around the wound. "Gah!" he growled. "And bring the surgeon!" he yelled into his mouthpiece. Wisely, he loosened his grip on the knife, opting to leave it in place.

Ribcage peered down at the man, stroking her pigtails as if wondering if she'd done enough damage. "You shouldn't have killed Luci."

Deluvius shrugged, downplaying the ooze of blood that was dribbling to the floor. "You're no longer a candidate for excavation, child." He gave her a satisfied smile as if somehow proud of the girl for what she'd been able to do to him.

And then soldiers burst into the room, rifles poised to fire. Deluvius backed away from Ribcage. "Kill the girl. Take the bot to the dungeons."

Beetro watched the impending soldiers, their rifles pointed at Ribcage. He closed his eyes. *It doesn't matter now.*

But then he felt someone grab his hand.

And he vanished.

The world was gone—Deluvius, the blown-out tower... everything. And Beetro suddenly felt *enormous*. He was a towering noodle of energy—every atom of his body expanded outward and flattened into a thickness without dimension. He tried to move but his arms and legs were bound. His sight was intact, but he couldn't see anything but blinding white light. Something adjusted in his eyes —not his eyes, he felt that he didn't even have traditional eyes. But the light fragmented into lines of dark and bright. By conscious volition, he somehow moved in between the fragmented light. What happened? Where was he? "Ribcage?" he called, wondering if he still even had a voice.

Her voice filled his mind. "I'm here!"

"Here? Where?"

"I brought you along to get away from the general."

"Did you Jump?"

"Yep!"

"What *is* this place?"

"Flatland. It's where I can go when I'm close to my mom. No more questions! I have to concentrate."

Lights and colors flitted through his vision. He tried looking down at his body but there *was* no looking down. The only senses ostensibly available were his sight and tactile sensation. He felt like an enormous, floppy giant blinded by a myriad of bright colors and black slits that soared through him.

"It's like the normal world, but nothing is hidden," Ribcage's seemingly omniscient voice said. Apparently, she didn't need to concentrate as much as she claimed as a hint of pride swelled in her voice. "In the normal world, everything is all wrapped up, kept hidden from sight. Here, there's nowhere for anything to hide. I can see 'em all."

Normally, Beetro would be getting a host of sensory feedback through his system, but in Ribcage's flatland, he didn't even have a body to sense. At least not a body in the normal, three-dimensional sense. Flatland stripped him of the visceral, robotic sensation that guided his interpretation of the world. If he didn't have that in flatland, then what even was he? Beetro shook off the philosophical implications of these thoughts. His own personal identity crisis was already complicated enough.

"I'm pretty sure we're down the windy stairs at the tower."

"As we move here, we move there too?"

"I was looking at the stairs before I Jumped, so I know what they look like in flatland. It's that line there," she said as if she was pointing, which wasn't possible in flatland, "with the tiny blips in the darkness—like different points of dark and brightness."

"Like steps on a staircase. You see shadows of the normal world?"

"Yes!"

Beetro thought he saw what she was talking about but really couldn't be sure—there was no actual *seeing* where they were. Only sensing patterns of light and differentiating shades of color. Somehow, Ribcage led him through the varying shades and lines without him having to act. She guided him in the flatland, which vicariously moved his physical body in the three-dimensional world.

"How long have you been able to do this?"

"All my life. I can do it whenever I want when I'm close to my mom."

"So, how do you—"

"Shh! I don't know where we are now. We've got to Jump back so I can figure it out."

Before Beetro could respond, he materialized in space and bumped headfirst, right into someone's leg.

"What the—" A soldier looked down and saw the blue robot scrambling to get to his feet. The stone walls of the castle surrounded them but at least Beetro could see the sky. They'd gotten as far as the courtyard. Ribcage was beside him, her tiny hand in his.

The soldier unclasped a handgun from his leg and pointed it at Beetro. "Intruders sighted!" he screamed into the radio. He fired a round off at Beetro but then looked down, perplexed. The intruders had vanished right before him.

"Okay," Ribcage said once they'd Jumped again. "I got a good look at the way out of here. I always have to Jump in and Jump out, or else I have no idea where I'm going. One time, I got lost here and I Jumped right back inside of an old, dead tree. It's all about the patterns. I got to match 'em up with the real world and then Jump."

"Hmm," Beetro said, suspecting that she was ineptly explaining what sounded like a very complicated guessing game of spatial reasoning *between* two different dimensional worlds. They continued forward, filing along a single track of light—Beetro feeling like an inflated giant, his 'head' bobbing back and forth.

Then they Jumped back, right next to a copse of trees. Beetro looked around, peeking his head over the knoll and saw Peles Castle, still amidst a stir of chaos. For a moment, he let himself wonder if Miree was okay but stopped himself.

Ribcage knelt beside him. "Fun, huh?" Her mischievous grin transformed the tone of what just happened. She made escaping a war castle after stabbing a murderous General in the gut seem like some sort of game. She wore a look on her face as if to say that she wanted one more ride. "You think I got him? Right in the gut!" she cheered, jabbing her fist in the air. "Got my blade back, too," she said, flipping the knife in the air and catching it by the handle.

Beetro tried to talk but realized he was still paralyzed. He could only blink at her.

"What's wrong?"

He blinked again.

"Are you hurt?"

Blink.

"Do you need food? What do robots eat?"

Blink.

"Water?"

Five blinks in a row.

"Yeah? Water?"

Five blinks again.

"Okay! I'll get you some!" She left, whether by Jumping or merely running away, Beetro couldn't tell.

He just closed his eyes.

Being no more than fifty meters from the castle grounds, he was bound to be discovered just lying there on the leeward side of a shallow knoll. There were yellow stalks of weeds that surrounded him, but any soldier with half a brain to scout an area would see his blue tint in a second amongst the grass. He didn't care. They could come, find him, drag him off to a dungeon, or fill his body full of laser holes. It didn't really matter anymore.

Why *had* he come out here anyway?

Because you haven't a clue about anything. Not a single thing in this entire world.

It made sense now.

He was tricked by Miree. This whole time, coming out onto the plains, leaving Korthe—literally the only place he'd ever known—was just a ruse to steal a flake of dark matter that didn't even exist to begin with. Miree was never going to help him find Galiaro. In that moment, he fully understood what manipulation was. Miree had *toyed* with him. Poking at his emotions, getting him indignant over Lucindi so that he'd follow her to Peles Castle like some lost sheep. Miree had complained about being stuck with a self-aware robot, but at the same time, was using his weakness—his own emotional sentience—to get him to do what she wanted. She never cared about Lucindi, and she certainly didn't care about him. It wouldn't have been so embarrassing if he hadn't so easily fallen for the charade.

It was his own fault, really. He'd built Lucindi up in his mind as a martyr, undeserving of what happened to her. He still thought this was true, but he'd learn far too painfully now that meddling only got people into trouble in Helian. He finally understood why no one else would back Lucindi up before the general put a laser in her chest—they were smart. Lucindi was... idealistic. And thus, Beetro himself had become idealistic, believing it a righteous cause to journey across the plains to exact justice on the general. Miree was right... Lucindi had directly imprinted her naive do-goodery right onto him.

He remembered the way Miree, without hesitation, placed her boltgun to the temple of that man dying from the Poisoning and pulled the trigger. That's what life was—you fight to live until you fail, and someone comes along and puts you out of your misery. And now, here he was, staring up at a graying sky—rain clouds?—considering how much he'd utterly failed. Who would come along now and put him out of his misery?

"What did you do back there?" Ribcage asked, startling him from his reverie.

He looked at her, still unable to move, at first not sure what she was referring to. And then he remembered he froze laser light and threw it out a castle spire.

"Oh, here." Ribcage had found a broken glass bottle and filled it with water. She dumped it down his throat. "It's poisoned but that's okay for you."

Beetro felt the water trickle down his throat and collect along a series of bladders inside his chest. Some of the water trickled through a collateral circulation that fed directly to his fusion core. The heat from the core instantly turned this water into steam, which filled the other bladders, causing them to begin a positive feedback of circulating even more water to the fusion core. Within seconds, the microtubules of his body were teeming with steam power, pumping energy into his joints and neural network. He only now realized how sluggish his thoughts were—how dark they were getting.

"Thank you," he said, taking another swig of water. "Thanks for helping me back there. And I have no idea what I did." He could still see Miree standing there, at the edge of the blown-out tower, the look of naked indifference toward him. And then he knew... he was wrong to ever worry about Miree or anyone else.

Ribcage took his hand again, Jumping away from the castle grounds. After many minutes of bright lights and Ribcage explaining how much easier it was to Jump outside, they reappeared along rocky hills. Great boulders of granite lay amongst the yellow grass like gigantic chess pieces scattered at the end of a game. The hills sloped upward and quickly became steep as they met the base of Meteor Mountains.

Ribcage sat in the grass, looking out over the plains of Helian, back toward their journey from Korthe in the west. Peles Castle towered on the horizon, and they were close enough to still hear an engine rattling or shouts in the wind. Beetro winced as Ribcage unwrapped the scarf from off her shoulders—the scarf that Miree had given her.

Ribcage noticed his glance at the scarf. "I *love* it," she said, petting the fabric. "I won't need another shirt again. Do you think she's alive?"

"Who cares?"

"Kinda liked her."

"You only liked her because she gave you that scarf. She was just using you. For your Jumps. She was using me for my scouting. All so she could rob something that wasn't there to begin with."

Ribcage shrugged. "Least I got a scarf out of it."

"I don't know what happened back there," Beetro said, despondent. He remembered how the energy felt in his hands. The entire room of sunlight was bursting with energy around him. It was like he felt every single photon striking him like a swarm of wasps. In that single moment, it was as if all the energy in the room became a tangible object to him.

"Whatever it was, it was *cool.* Never seen anything like that before."

"You haven't?"

"Nope," she said, undoing her pigtails. "With that kind of power, we could go back and *own* Korthe. Take whatever we want from the markets. Wouldn't call me Ribcage anymore. They'd call me Fatcage."

"Yeah..." Power. Something he could wield? He looked up at the cloud cover, focusing on the illumination beyond the clouds. Piquing his senses, he tried to feel the energy of the sun like he'd done back at the spire. But there was nothing. "Not sure how to do it again." He looked up the granite hills, toward the flat-topped peaks of the Meteor Mountains. The sky was dark. Almost swarming with darkness. "But I think I know who does."

"Who?"

"Galiaro."

Miree heaved through panicked breaths, crouching behind a dead thicket of weeds.

Her ass *hurt*.

After she jumped from the tower spire, she hit the Wing hard, somersaulting along the length of the aircraft. One moment of composure atop the Wing was followed by whizzing bullets about three millimeters next to her ear, prompting her to not so much rappel but fall off the Wing with a piece of rope in her hands. Luckily, the rope was attached to the underbelly of the Wing, cushioning an otherwise fatal fall into a hard drop directly onto her tailbone.

None of this would've mattered so much if, immediately after, she didn't have to perform a floppy roundhouse kick at a soldier she'd surprised in a horse stable that had been converted into an ordnance depot. The kick missed the soldier by a country mile, giving her enough momentum to spin entirely around and fall on her tailbone. Again. After a small struggle, Miree wrestled the man's sidearm from his belt and discharged it nicely into his thigh. Delayed by registering what just happened to his leg, Miree slapped one hand up the side of his face, rocketing his helmet off and then smashed him in the face with her fist. After stealing his sidearm, she moved.

Fortunately, the spire explosion—where the hell did that come from anyway?—left the castle grounds in utter chaos. Miree found her way out by hiding and ushering in a few small guerrilla attacks on soldiers as she went. Ribcage—*fucking Ribcage*—was probably causing all sorts of havoc and confusion, making Miree's escape quite straightforward. Once she made it to the courtyard, she hopped over the wall and just ran away, stumbling through a few poisoned streams on her way out.

She escaped. Minus one priceless Quantizer and exactly zero dark matter flakes.

The shock of the loss of one of the rarest pieces of equipment in Orion hadn't set in yet as she removed her boots and stripped off her wet socks. It had taken two years of planning with the Kish —the most dangerous criminal organization in Orion—to even rip the thing off Fallaro, one of Orion's eminent astrocysts. She tried ignoring this fact as she took off her cloak and lifted off a soaked sweater, leaving her shivering in a damp tank top. A lattice of needle-like scars running the length of her arms glistened in the moonlight. She had to face reality—the Quantizer was gone. Probably squashed underfoot by a bunch of idiot soldiers.

Oh, and there was no dark matter flake. She hadn't even gotten to that part yet. But she would get there... one disaster to consider at a time. Everything had been a mistake—traveling to Korthe, meeting Lucindi, finding that insufferable robot in the junkyard, and allowing that freak girl to be part of the robbery. One shit show after another. And where did it get her? Sitting next to a granite boulder, shivering in the moonlight, stuck in the middle of the plains of Helian without food or water, and unable to make a fire for risk of being murdered by an entire army. And her ass was *killing* her.

She closed her eyes.

Rage built up inside, warming her. Processing the fury was part of getting over it. She'd been part of a lot of disasters back in Orion, but nothing was quite like this. In the end, she knew it was her own fault and it came from one place inside of her—desperation. She should've left Korthe, taken the Quantizer, and moved on to one of the different city-states to the west. Every fief lord was supposed to have a flake of dark matter, giving them a claim to rule. Certainly, she could've found a way into one of their castles that hadn't been taken over by a technologically advanced General.

But no, she had to *care*. Care about Lucindi.

Lucindi...

The girl's face appeared in her mind. Smiling at her—reaching for her hand. She could hear her gently humming...

"No!" Miree yelled to herself.

Just that single modicum of indignation over Lucindi's death led to the cascading events of losing absolutely everything. Caring never worked for Miree in the past, why did she think it would work this time? She shuddered, truly disgusted by her stupidity, and rolled over in the wet grass.

But images of Beetro clouded her mind, laying there, paralyzed—those glowing eyes, pleading. The robot had frozen a shaft of laser light in the air. It happened so quickly that, in the moment, Miree hardly regarded the phenomenon—it looked so natural. Beetro lifted his arms and stayed the blast from a laser rifle. He saved her from ending up like Lucindi, and what did she do?

She left him.

Good.

"Good!" she yelled, her voice dissipating into the vast plains. She didn't care if she was heard. They could come and fill her with laser light all they want, at least it would be faster than dying from the Poisoning out on the plains—a certainty at this point. Unless she could make it up Meteor Mountains, there was clean water up in those mountain passes. But it was—she looked up at the towering, flat ridges of the mountains—so far up there. If she could get up there in a day and a half, she might not die from dehydration. She had lost her pack and all supplies at the castle. But... she now had a gun. Maybe she could hunt. What could be killed on the plains?

Planning, planning, planning.

This is how she survived. If she could stay one step ahead of whatever it was that planned on killing her—gangs in Orion, the

Kish, the Fifth Kingdom, the Poisoning—she survived. Surviving was thinking. Thinking, surviving. You thought the right way, you lived. You stopped thinking... you bleed out of your ass next to a radioactive pond.

Somehow, she found sleep.

She was awoken by the annoying light of dawn, but at least she didn't have gun barrels in her face. Peeking around the granite boulder, she spied Peles Castle and saw that gigantic Wing nowhere to be found. Shivering, she pulled on her still wet clothing, wrapped her cloak around herself, and tucked the pistol into her waistband. Looking up at the feet of Meteor Mountains, she moved, not entirely certain where, but it was at least away from the plains of Helian and everything miserable that they contained.

SIXTEEN

IT HAD BEEN many days since Protonix had left Arym.

At first, knowing that Hawera had asked about him—was concerned about him—did wonders for his morale. He started eating again. It was a painful adjustment as his gut squealed and groaned with gastric juices. As nutrition went to his head, so did ideas. His mind dwelled mostly on Hawera.

There's a problem with the galaxy. She's trying to help.

What did any of that mean? Arym had a vague idea of what the galaxy was, but it was nebulous at best. To the Crib's credit, they weren't without their technological advancements. Cribmen could build enormous Torches to drill the earth, construct massive complexes and decks of floors that spanned the underground—even maintain a genetics laboratory for cloning. Arym realized that these were not small accomplishments once he discovered the untamed wilderness of the overworld. He never even saw a building within Crater Valley. Despite the Crib's technology, Arym knew nothing of the stars or the galaxy. Of course, these things were sometimes referenced, but there was no manual about the sky, the moon, or anything beyond Earth.

The Crib did not concern itself with life above the crust.

Arym knew that the galaxy was bigger than Earth. He knew Earth was a planet amongst other planets, but his knowledge stopped there. He had heard of stars before, but he did not have any notion about what they were. Of course, the sun was familiar to him and all the Crib as many Oshafts were dedicated to the sole purpose of directing natural sunlight into the Crib via a labyrinthian series of mirrors.

If there was a problem with the galaxy, he couldn't even begin to grasp what that problem would be. He also couldn't understand how something as big as the galaxy would have any bearing on just a single planet.

He recalled Protonix explaining how the Alcheans could travel among the stars—how they brought many cultures and species from across the galaxy to Earth. This, of course, happened many years ago. From what Arym could tell of the overworld, there was no one else left—no Alcheans or anyone.

She went to Orion.

Protonix had mentioned that he directed Hawera toward Orion. Some other city? Arym had never heard of it. He had never heard of any other city anywhere. The fact that there was a functioning city somewhere in the overworld was further evidence of everything wrong with the Crib. They only taught that chaos ruled in the overworld. There couldn't possibly be any amount of peace enough for any people to build a city.

Lies.

Or was it ignorance?

Did it make a difference? Did it change reality?

Aside from the incomprehensible enormity of not only the overworld and the galaxy, Protonix had also spoken of *other dimensions.* After the Alcheans had complete mastery of science and technology, they left to *other dimensions.* All Arym understood about dimensions was marking out a space of rock for drilling. One dimension up and one dimension over would create the measured boundaries. He would then tell the Torchblazer which auger size to use based on the dimensions of the rock wall that needed to be drilled. How could the Alcheans escape to different dimensions? He imagined them stepping right through a rock face.

None of it made sense and it filled Arym with both frustration and complete awe. He so badly wanted to understand the mysteries of the overworld.

The arrow of time always moves forward, but the arrow is always curved.

This last line, one of the last things Protonix said before leaving, may have been the most difficult to understand. What was the arrow of time? An arrow moves forward and one of the chief characteristics of an arrow is that it does not go backwards. Protonix must have meant that it is impossible to make time go backwards. This was intuitive to Arym as he'd never conceived of time going in reverse let alone observed it happen. But how could an arrow be curved? What use is a curved arrow? If time is like a curved arrow, what does that say about the future? Is the future... bent?

Arym worked himself into a logical quandary over and over, alone in his isolation pod. His imagination had gone wild with only a few lines uttered by that floating proton. The mystery fueled both his appetite and his will to live but it didn't last long. It wasn't enough to sit there, lie there, jump up and down, stand on his head, and ponder intangible mysteries. He *had* to get out.

But of course, there was no way out.

Once again, he scoured the pod for means of escape. He investigated any avenue, no matter how unlikely. The walls, ceiling, and floor were sealed tight—no obvious weak point that he could break through. Except the shower drain. He spent quite a few hours picking at the drain in the floor. Even if he did get the drain open, he wasn't quite sure what he would do with an open hole in the ground, no bigger than the size of his fist. Even if there was somewhere he could actually tunnel through, he had no tool for such a task. There was the bed, which was essentially a single cushion, and nothing else.

His meals appeared through a slot in the door but came in floppy, compostable containers that were designed to flush down a drain. They broke up instantly in the toilet water. For several days, he soaked the containers and then dried them out in a flattened plane. Once he'd accrued several dozen, he placed the containers together and rolled them up, creating a stiff cudgel of sorts. After a single attempt of sticking the improvised stick into the seal of the shower drain, it instantly shredded.

The portal door had become his latest focus of escape. It was a circular portal with enormous hinges on one end and a handle on the other. The handle had long been disabled since his isolation. He spotted a few welded spots on the inner side of the handle. It was impossible to open from the inside without advanced tools.

After the initial excitement of Protonix's visit—all the wonder and hope he brought about the overworld and Hawera—desperation returned. One day, the portal door slot opened outside of the meal schedule. He lunged at the door, excited for the change in routine, and found a note. A note! But it only told him to shove his jumpsuit through the door and that he would then receive one newly laundered. Evidently, isolation meant contact only through the written word. No one came. Tarysl, true to his word, did not visit. Arym couldn't even hear voices on the other side. The only proof that other people existed was the faint sound of footsteps that led up to his portal before sliding a food tray through the slot.

He was uncertain how long it had been, but he suspected it was shorter than he hoped. It felt like five months but was probably only one. He stopped showering. Stopped changing out his jumpsuit. Scruff on his face turned to a disheveled beard. Rashes broke out over his skin from time to time. He had the occasional fever and chills, either from infection or neglect of eating—he stopped keeping track.

The boredom became pathological.

He stopped having dreams of any sort. No nightmares either. There was no daydreaming. No inner monologue of his own to reassure, taunt, scold, or offer false hopes of escape. He briefly considered starvation once more but found he'd lost the mental fortitude. His life had become as blank as the white walls in the pod, and maybe that was the rektor's goal. There was only nothing. In a way, it was better to have nothing in his mind.

Nothing meant... nothing.

He awoke one day, or night, or month—he couldn't tell. He thought that he awoke to a sound, which couldn't be possible because he was the only one who could make sounds in his pod-world. He looked up from the bed. Something about the pod had dramatically altered.

The portal door was open.

The thick metal door was ajar, ever so slightly, outward from the pod.

Arym's mouth dried—his heart felt like it seized. Was he imagining this? It wouldn't be the first time. On numerous occasions, he'd imagined or dreamt of Hawera thrusting the door open in one glorious moment. Sometimes he'd have waking hallucinations that it happened, but a quick shake of his head and everything instantly returned to normal. However, at the moment, the gray metal of the portal doorway reflected light in a new and unfamiliar way. It just looked so *real*. He didn't dare speak. He arose from the bed, creeping toward the portal door, careful not to make a sound.

He suddenly realized he was quite nude, probably had been for some time. He grabbed his jumpsuit from the ground and carried it with him toward the portal door. He rested his hand on the door and waited. Listening.

Then he pushed.

The heavy door noiselessly swung open.

The familiar yellow glow of the Crib tunnel was before him as Arym stood at the threshold. He stepped out, smelling antiseptics.

"Arym," someone said. A figure moved from behind the open portal door.

It was Lutra.

Lutra. The goofy chef with a schoolboy crush on Arym. It was only now that Arym realized that Lutra looked exactly like himself. Because... they were identical clones of one another.

"Arym," Lutra said with an uncharacteristic ghoulish countenance. "Put some clothes on." He spoke in a quick whisper.

Arym looked down at his naked self and started pulling on the jumpsuit. "What's going on?" His voice was impossibly weak.

"Be quiet now. Something is happening." His eyes rolled toward the ceiling.

"What?" Arym looked up. "What's going on?"

"People are up there, Arym. The overworld."

"Who?"

Lutra shook his head. "Don't know." He finally got an eyeful of Arym and gasped. "Arym. Look at you. You're... you're starving. Did they do this to you?"

"Sort of. I—"

"You've got to go. Here." He shoved a satchel into Arym's arms. "Take this and get out of here. Escape to the overworld."

"What? How?"

"I've wanted to come so badly. It's not right. It's not right what we do here. Putting Cribmen into isolation just for being themselves. I'm sorry it took a distraction for me to be brave enough to get you out. I'm so, so sorry..." His eyes turned red, tears forthcoming.

"I don't understand. What's going on in the overworld?"

"The rektors aren't saying anything specific yet. They're only calling it a threat. There are people up there. And they know we're down here."

This struck a nerve of fear through Arym. Had he broken his Oath? Was it his fault that the overworld was coming for the Crib?

"You need to go. Now." Lutra pointed down the tunnel.

"Why are you doing this?"

"Because I care about you."

"I know. I'm sorry but I may have given you the wrong idea..."

Lutra smiled, showing a toothy grin and shook his head. "It's okay. And besides... you're a Runner. You weren't meant to be down here with us. You need to *run*."

Arym slung the satchel around his shoulder and extended his hand to Lutra. "Thank you."

Lutra didn't take his hand but rather embraced Arym in a big bear hug. "Get out of here, Runner. Go find what you're looking for." He gave him a small kiss on the cheek and turned, walking away in the other direction without looking back.

Arym *ran*.

But not before collapsing with weakness first. Once he got

back onto his feet, he did manage to move along at a decent clip, back hunched inside the corridor. He came to a T-connection in the tube and took a hard left. He knew exactly where he was going. He kept his head down as he passed a few Cribmen. They were speaking rapidly and hardly noticed that he had passed. Arym took another left and stepped into a shaftlift. He hit the bottom and the lift sunk down. He flew past dozens of levels, relieved that no one else had called the lift, and got out.

As he stepped out, the ground beneath him shook. He paused, holding his stance, looking up. As a Cribman, he was used to the occasional tremor, but this felt different. The vibration felt like it was coming from above. He darted past a few more Cribmen, who were again talking in hushed tones. One of them eyed Arym briefly as he passed but continued his conversation. After one more quick shaftlift, Arym finally arrived—the digline. A deep cavern drilled into the earth.

It was empty.

Granted, Arym had no idea what time of day it was, but given that he'd seen other Cribmen up and about, the digline should've been at full steam at that moment. But there wasn't a single digkid in sight. Relieved, he ran down the line, tracing his hand across the enormous Torch. He briefly appreciated the machinery. It was a magnificent feat of engineering—an enormous auger fitted on treadwheels, capable of boring through several hundred tons of earth a day. What other technologies could the Crib have that Arym had never seen? He resented Protonix for suggesting he came from such technologically devoid people. He waxed nostalgic for a moment—never thinking that could've happened—and ran past the Torch into a fresh tunnel that had been drilled.

The ground shook again, at first only faintly, but it gradually grew. It was one shaking bout after another as if something was pounding the Crib in succession. Trails of dust fell from the high tunnel of the digline. He saw scattered pockets of rock crumbling from the raw tunnels and paused, resting against the side of the tunnel. He squinted, looking down the dimly lit passage, waiting for the tremors to subside, holding his breath to ward off thoughts of a cave-in. He'd known several digkids lost on the line during tremors—just like the one that was happening.

The ground stilled. He waited another half a second as rocks fell and settled on the ground. He dashed forward, deeper into the tunnel. He felt draughts of air flowing past him, blowing his beard and chilling his skin. The malnourishment of being in isolation was catching up with him. Every step was difficult, almost impossible. But simply to be able to move again was invigorating.

The tunnel tapered—a good sign. They usually created Oshafts as small as possible to be able to easily obscure and keep discrete once the rest of the Crib gridwork was built adjacent to the shaft.

The tunnel grew darker as he proceeded forward. The path twisted as he moved along and soon became completely dark. He had no idea if there really was an Oshaft that had been dug from the tunnel. Coming down the tunnel was just a guess, but an educated one. The digline needed aeration every few kilometers as the Torch bore into the earth. They would typically dig long offshoots from the main digline and then send an augur drone up from the offshoot, creating an ascending tunnel about the width of a Cribman—the Oshaft. If a Cribman really did want to escape to the overworld through a freshly dug Oshaft, it would be impossible to go unnoticed to do it while on shift.

Rather than backtracking, he decided to move forward into the darkness. Small draughts of air swirled around him, encouraging him forward. And then it was there, right ahead of him... a trickle of daylight hitting the dirt as if frozen, waiting for him. He looked up through the Oshaft and saw the winding tunnel that led up. The augur drones used ultrasound to weave and dig their ways around obstructing boulders, creating a non-linear shaft. This was fortunate. If an Oshaft really was a straight vertical wall, Arym would never be able to climb out of it. It would've been prohibitively exhausting to keep tension between his knees and back long enough to keep him suspended in the shaft. With a curved shaft, he had ample opportunity to rest whenever the Oshaft bent more horizontal to gravity.

Arym climbed.

It felt incredible. Not only did his chest thrum with excitement every time he climbed up an Oshaft, but this time was special. This time, he was never coming back to the Crib. Every step upward was one less that he would ever take in Othel's underground fortress of ignorance and misery. There was nothing he would miss about the place. Well, maybe Lutra. He did, after all, release Arym from isolation and probably suicide. He also felt strangely affectionate toward Rektor Tarysl. He had known the man his entire life. He had cared for Arym in his own demented way, but Arym believed the man truly cared. Yet, he was still the man who left him to rot in isolation. No, Arym would not be missing the rektor.

He clung to dirt and rock, sweat sticking to his back while the daylight grew inside the Oshaft. He was interrupted by the occasional tremor and grew more concerned—they never happened with such frequency. Strong gusts blew down the shaft, chilling his sweaty face. It typically took about an hour to climb out, but he was noticeably slowing down. Isolation had sapped his muscle mass, making every thrust upward a challenge.

He found a cleft to rest and opened the satchel that Lutra had given him, finding several sticks of dried meat, nuts, and fresh fruit. Beneath it was a book. It cracked open with the sound of disuse. He angled the pages to the scant light and gasped.

Maps.

He flipped through them. The pages were yellowed with age, the ink bold in black and red. He found a map of the crater in which the Crib was built. He saw *The Lake*. The map called it Lake Haplo. He ran his fingers over Crescent Wood and Laser Falls. To the left was an area called Helian. To the right of Crater Valley was an arrow that simply pointed to one word—*Orion*.

Orion. Hawera.

There were several more pages of maps, but he closed the book. No time. Lutra had listened to him. It was only at that moment that Arym remembered he had set a date with Lutra before being thrown in isolation. Lutra was going to take him to the archives to show him maps. He was true to his promise. And if this wasn't already enough, beneath the book of maps, Arym found another book—his own sketch journal.

He leafed through the pictures of the overworld—plants, animals, the granite cliffs of Crater Valley, dozens of angles of Hawera. On the last page, he found a new note:

Arym. I hope you find what you're looking for up there.

-Lutra

The man was a saint. Arym knew he deserved none of his affection.

He kept moving upward through the Oshaft, the tremors getting worse. Vibrations thrummed through the rock, worsening as he ascended. These weren't just tremors. The impacts were coming from above ground. Scraping his shins and fingers on dirt and rock, he saw the last bend in the Oshaft just above and *pushed.*

Daylight.

He'd only escaped to the overworld during night, catching brief glimpses of dawn as he returned to the Crib. This was the first time he'd ever actually seen daylight. Finally rising from the Oshaft, he winced as his eyes adjusted to the sunlight. He looked up. A gray layer of clouds covered the valley, blocking out full sunlight. Even still, it was the most exposure to sunlight he'd ever experienced. There was a thick black quality to the clouds—a coat of black haze.

Smoke.

He lifted himself from the Oshaft hole and looked across the valley and discovered the source of the smoke.

Lake Haplo.

It was the main freshwater source that the Crib used, and it was absolutely *on fire.* The entire surface of the lake was a sheet of conflagration. It likely had something to do with three towering machines that sat along the lake marsh—the same marsh where Arym had picked berries with Hawera. One machine was fitted with enormous wheels, housing even bigger drums. Spewing from nozzles atop the drums was a thick substance, black and viscous. Another wheeled tower sprayed long tongues of fire over the lake, creating a fortress of flames that encircled the entire marsh. Not far from Lake Haplo sat several other mechanical towers outfitted with enormous augers that actively drilled into the earth.

There was also an army.

Hundreds of soldiers stood in formation. It was difficult to tell from the distance, but they clearly brandished some sort of firearm. They stood at attention with patrol groups scouring the wilderness surrounding the lake. Set back from the flaming action, floated an impossibly reflective object—oblong and shiny, shaped like a single wing. It floated motionless, ominous with inaction. The most shocking aspect about the surreal sight of war machines was a deep and sickening realization. It slapped him in the face.

The rektors were right. The overworld had finally come for the Crib.

Arym ducked, staying on his hands and knees, and crawled as fast as possible away from the flames. He huddled low in the grasslands until he found a familiar formation of boulders and hid behind them, thinking.

How had the army known the Crib was there? Arym thought frantically, devising a way to escape the valley, but his mind turned to the same question... who broke the Oath? Never in his entire life did he think that the Oath actually meant anything. An overwhelming sense of concern for the Crib came crashing into him. He didn't know what was more shocking—the attack on the Crib or *caring* about the attack on the Crib. Lutra, Rektor Tarysl, all the digkids... they were all in danger.

What could he do?

He ripped out the book of maps from his satchel, flipping through until he found Crater Valley. Helian to the west, Orion to the east. He had no idea what was out there, and more urgently, no idea from where the invading army had come. Above all else, there was one person he wanted to see that might even be able to help. Hawera. After all, she was trying to save the galaxy.

Perhaps that could include the Crib?

SEVENTEEN

MORE DREAMS.

Beetro stood within a castle tower, high above a sprawling terrain. He looked out at the ground far below and saw it *writhing*. The terrain crawled in a frenzy of motion—small undulations and rippling throughout like a colony of ants. They were men and women, roaming the landscape, searching the terrain and burned out towns, scorching the earth with fire. They scoured for people, property, and land—anything of life and value to extort or consume. It was an army of fiends, marching forth with their spiked machines like gigantic mechanical lizards that prowled the land.

The sky was blackened from a thick cloud cover—not clouds—smoke. But the smoke moved like sludge that had been melted into the sky. The horizon was crimson, not from the sun but raging fires. It was a world of haze and chaos. Beetro could *feel* the corruption from where he stood. However awful the plains of Helian and its people were, this world was magnitudes more malicious and brimming with pure scorn—contempt for the living. It had been gutted of all virtue, leaving a hollow husk trolled by a merciless army.

Beetro never wanted anything more than to flee this world—close his eyes and forget that it ever existed. He yelled at them on the plains, that army of destruction. As his voice echoed out from the castle tower, the writhing below him ceased.

The entire host of the army watched him.

"Do you know if robots dream?" Beetro asked Ribcage as the girl kicked away a bed of leaves she'd used during the night.

"Don't know. Don't care. I dream, though. I dream of food a *lot.* Apples and bacon, mostly. I only had bacon the one time, but I *never* forgot it after that."

"Have you ever heard of a robot dreaming?"

Ribcage shrugged. "I've never asked one. You have bad dreams, bud?"

Beetro nodded.

"About what?" Ribcage wrapped her scarf around her tiny body and examined herself, appearing pleased with how much the piece of clothing covered.

"I don't know. It doesn't matter anyway." Beetro looked out at the curving feet of Meteor Mountains. They boasted jagged clefts that rose prodigiously above the valley floor with flat peaks, running north to south, of pure granite rock. Beetro had memorized Miree's maps she had carried with her that contained all the Plains of Helian, the other feudal states to the north, and the enormous Crater Valley to the west, which lay beneath the eastern edge of Meteor Mountains.

Ribcage looked at him, cockeyed. "What's the plan? And will it have food and water?"

"We're going to Orion."

"Orion? The *big* city? Where is it even?"

Beetro wasn't entirely sure. On Miree's maps, Orion was only indicated by a single arrow on the eastern side of the map without distance. However, he knew Miree had traveled to Korthe from Orion on foot. It couldn't have been a prohibitively long journey for a human. He thought for a moment about leaving Ribcage behind, cutting her away. Miree was right, the girl was a chaotic tangle of unpredictability. She was an unknown quantity that he was tempted to do without. However, he couldn't quite get the image of Lucindi bending down to Ribcage, holding out food. He couldn't do it, despite his bitter realizations about the world. Besides, however unpredictable Ribcage was, she'd saved both Beetro and Miree. Twice.

"Yes. Orion."

"Why?"

"We'll find Galiaro there."

"Who's that?" she asked, chewing on a weed.

"My engineer. He made me. At least I think he did."

"Well, you helped me get to my mom. Guess I'll help you get to your dad." Ribcage folded her arms. "Let's go, then."

"Just like that?"

"I expect food and water from you, robot."

"Can you not call me 'robot'? I don't call you *human*."

"What... uh..." she twirled hair around her finger.

"You don't know my name, do you?"

She brought a finger to her lips, feigning deep thought.

"It's Beetro, Ribcage. My name is Beetro."

"I knew that."

"And if you work for me—help me get to Orion—yeah, I'll feed you."

They had no supplies and, therefore, no camp to collect, so

they simply walked out from behind the granite boulder where they'd slept. They appeared mostly inconspicuous—two creatures, the tallest of whom barely arrived at a woman's chin, ambling through rows of dead cornfields. Beetro surveyed to the west, toward the general, but didn't see any vehicles or that Wing floating about, so they moved unhindered.

"Is it close enough to get some water?" Ribcage asked, huffing a little to keep up with Beetro's pace through dead fields.

"Where?"

"Orion."

"No, it's going to be days. Maybe weeks before we're there."

"Well, I need some water. Today. I'm a human. We drink more than you."

"I know that," he said with a whiff of petulance. "I'd like to make it to the higher ridges of the mountains by nightfall. Hopefully, we can find some clean water up there. Lucindi told me there's clean rainfall in the mountains."

Ribcage left a cynical silence between them as they moved across the eastern edge of the plains. They traveled on foot for several hours, the Meteor Mountains progressively enlarging before them. The number of peasant corpses began to taper away this far from Peles Castle. They apparently reached the outer limits of how far the people could go on foot without drinking the poisoned groundwater. The last of them were the strongest, making it the farthest while resisting the deadly urge to drink. Their meager possessions were scattered across the dirt roads—ragdolls, clay pottery, implements for fire-making. Ribcage searched the corpses but found nothing edible.

A heavy cloud cover, just beyond the mountains, swirled in the sky with turbulent pulsing.

"See?" Beetro said, pointing to the clouds. "Looks like we'll probably have some rainfall this afternoon. It's strange how those clouds have stayed over Crater Valley all these days. Must be an unusual weather pattern that keeps them there."

"I hope so. Sometimes clouds don't mean rain, though. Sometimes it means a bloatstorm."

"What's that?"

"You've got a lot to learn, robot—er, Beter."

"Beetro."

"Uh-huh."

"Let's keep our eyes peeled for any water we might stumble on, you never know," Beetro said, knowing full well that they would not find any potable water on the plains. He wondered how the people of Korthe were faring as they approached their fourth week of drought. Then he decided that he shouldn't care. They certainly didn't care about him, or Lucindi.

After another hour, they saw a person standing out there, by the foot of the mountains. The figure was tall and spindly and stood beside a horse. The pair were by a trail that cut through the fields and led up to the mountain passes. Beetro and Ribcage crouched in the long grasses, observing the figure. Beetro zoomed in his vision, believing it to be a tall and impossibly thin man. He stood, occasionally patting his horse until he turned toward them. He waved.

"He sees us," Beetro said.

"How? We're hidden."

"I don't know. But he doesn't look threatening. Maybe a trader?"

Ribcage shook her head. "Single traders don't come to Korthe very much. They're usually big caravans. It's too dangerous to be out on the plains alone—too many of those Reticuloo people gobbling everyone up."

"Reticulum," Beetro corrected, remembering the pair that tried to take him away. They'd promised knowledge, something which presented a glimmer of temptation at the time. It still did. As much as Beetro had learned about the world since he was awoken in a junkyard, he was still largely ignorant of most things. But he was at least knowledgeable enough to know the Reticulum people were lunatics.

"Let's go and see if he has any water. He must if he's got that horse there."

Ribcage looked at him, uneasy. "I can't Jump as well out here, away from my mom. It's harder."

"That's okay."

"What if we need to run away or stick the guy?"

"We'll manage. Besides, we're running out of options in case those clouds really aren't going to rain."

The man wasn't a man at all but a slender robot with rail-thin limbs and a long neck. Strangely, it was dressed in clothing, draped in colorful stripes of pinks and turquoise and a long hat that clung to the back of its head and ran along its back, nearly to the ground. It looked down with baleful eyes at Ribcage and Beetro as they approached.

"Greetings, travelers," the robot said through a glowing slot of light where a human's mouth would be.

Beetro stopped, inspecting the robot, maintaining distance. "Must be just another robot from the castle. Programmed. No self-awareness."

The robot feigned throat clearing. "Do you judge all creatures of Helian with such harshness, my brother?"

"Oh, I—"

"I feel and think and hate and love—and judge—just as easily as you do, my dear friend."

"Oh, I'm so sorry. It's so nice to meet you. You're my first... I meant the first one I've met. Rather, I haven't met another self-aware bot. Like me."

"I understand. I take no offense. Well met, my brother."

"What're you doing out here?"

"Out here? What're you doing *in* here? Perhaps your out is my in. What the hostile plains of Helian are to you are my hospitable abode." The robot said with a high pitch of whimsy in his voice. "And besides, I have the same right to ask the same of you, brother bot."

"We're... travelers."

"Yes, I greeted you as such." The robot tilted his head, the tip of his long hat swaying at his feet. "At which leg in their journey do a tiny human and blue robot with no supplies find themselves on this adventure? Or misadventure?"

"We're going to Orion. Do you know how far it is?" Beetro asked, approaching the horse. "And do you know where we can find some water?"

"My dear brother bot, I believe it is most unwise to set forth on a journey without knowing the distance of one's destination. Would we all agree? Yet perhaps it is the journey itself which is the destination, hmm? Or perhaps destination and purpose may not be synonymous. Destination is merely the distraction—the temporary salve to an injured soul. Where do you two find yourselves on this spectrum of meaning? What about you, my little sweetheart?" He looked down at Ribcage.

"Call me that again and I'll put my blade in your belly," Ribcage warned, clenching her jaw.

"Ah!" The robot was pleased. "Yes, I was merely testing your spunk! I was hoping it was up to the challenge that your journey will present to you as you travel another three weeks on foot to Orion."

Beetro sighed. "Three weeks?"

"Yes," the robot said with an opulent drawl. "Now introductions. Me, then you, then you." He pointed at them. "I am Besidio. Jester to the court of the fief lord of Helian."

"Jester?"

"I'm the entertainment for the Lord of Peles Castle. Well, I was. It appears General Deluvius does not have the same sense of humor as our previous fief lord. I've been the jester for the past five lords. The general reserved for me the same disdain he shared for the entire court and cast me out from the walls."

"Are you the only one left?" Beetro asked, looking back at the long blanket of plains that they had crossed since the castle.

"Do you have any stories?" Besidio asked, ignoring the question.

"Do you have any water?" Ribcage asked.

"I'm afraid, my sweet little warrior, that I have none. For this, I fear my faithful steed will soon fall to the Poisoning."

Ribcage smiled at being called a warrior and said, "Do you know if we can get some soon? Up the mountain passes?"

"I'm afraid I've given far too much information already without demanding a story. Now, do you have a story to exchange for my information?" Besidio looked from Ribcage to Beetro. He clicked his metal fingers together. "What about you, brother? Certainly, you have an interesting tale about where you got that beautiful blue skin of yours."

"No."

Besidio offered a deep-throated laugh. "Well then, I'm afraid our exchange has come to its gracious, if not brief, close. I deal in stories. This is my trade. If I am to present myself as jester to another lord—or king—in the east, I must have new stories for them."

"Uh, fine..." Beetro thought for a moment. "There was a robot who woke up in a junkyard. He couldn't remember who he was or where he came from. He only knew his own name and the name of his maker."

Besidio's eyes widened. "Ooh, yes, I like how this starts already."

"He didn't know anything," Beetro continued. "But he remembered certain things—facts. Air is composed of oxygen, nitrogen, carbon dioxide, and argon. Titanium is stronger than steel. He was programmed with all the basics of the mechanics of the world. But he was not programmed with an identity other than his name. That, he had to find."

"Now, why would he remember his name and nothing else?"

"A very good question."

"It would seem that his name has great meaning. And what was this bot's name?" Besidio interrupted.

"Doesn't matter—"

Neon lights fluttered down Besidio's face. "Of course, it matters. Every hero needs a good name."

"This robot wasn't a hero."

"That's for the listener to decide." He waved his hand. "Continue, brother."

"At first, the robot thought he was supposed to help those around him. He gave his time and labor at no cost, only to discover that his help wasn't used for good, but for selfish reasons—for others to get gain. He thought he was supposed to be nice to others but discovered his kindness didn't change anything about the world. When he realized that the world only swallows up anything that is good, he thought his purpose was revenge."

"Ho, ho, I don't imagine that went well for him."

"No. Inside vengeance, he only found betrayal." Beetro looked over Besidio's shoulders, at the swirling mass of clouds hanging over the mountains.

"So, what did this robot do?"

"It was only after asking himself, over and over again, what his purpose was that he discovered what it was."

"And?"

"To ask questions."

"Ah..."

"So, he traveled the land, asking questions to everyone he met. Including an ex-jester of the court at the edge of the Helian plains."

Besidio nodded. "And what is that question, brother?"

"*Who is Galiaro*?" Beetro looked at the robot, intently.

Besidio paused, befuddled. "Galiaro," he repeated, thinking. "Yes. I recall that name."

Beetro suppressed his stunned excitement. "You do? You'd be the first."

"Yes. Vaguely, I'm afraid, and some years back. Some sort of astrocyst."

"Astrocyst?"

"A practitioner of natural law—physical and quantum alike. Some would argue astrocysts are alchemists of dark arts. In Orion, you seek this Galiaro?"

"Yes."

"Orion is where I last recall hearing the name. Astrocysts can be quite secretive, I'm afraid. They fear the mob uprising against a magic that they do not understand. They have a coven somewhere in the far northeast, beyond the Fifth Kingdom. I'm afraid I have no more information about who he or she may be."

"That's okay. You've already helped tremendously. Just knowing he may be in Orion..."

"You believe this person will have the answers you seek?"

"Undoubtedly."

"There once was a king's nephew, Gaul," Besidio said, apparently starting a story. "He was a jealous man—envious of his cousins, the king's sons, Satra, Salka, and Salpingus. He knew he'd never inherit the kingdom and was furious at the prospect of being ruled by Satra, the eldest, a man known to be a blubbering fool. Gaul was a shrewd fellow and knew no matter the calculus and logic he employed; he would never be made ruler in the fixed station of the king's nephew. He knew the only way to rule was to completely *change* the rules. One day, his opportunity came.

"He came across the god of night while hiking the mountains. The god had been surprised by a beast and was dying from the mauling at Gaul's feet. With his magic staff just out of arm's reach, the god pleaded for help. Gaul, being the shrewd fellow he was, asked the god of night what he would receive in turn for helping. Begging, the god said he could give him all the riches of the world if Gaul would hand him his magic staff. 'Riches I have,' Gaul said. 'Power I do not. I want to rule the land of my fathers but I'm only the king's nephew, destined to live in a castle spire the rest of my days. In three days' time, I want you to wipe the stars from the night's sky.'

"In his desperation, the god of night agreed to the request with a warning. 'With the blood of royalty were the stars made, only with their blood may they return.' Gaul returned the magic staff to the god of night, who, after healing himself, swept his staff across the sky and said, 'Watch for the night's sky, for in three days, the firmament will burn like pitch.'

"When Gaul returned to the kingdom, he climbed the castle walls and yelled from the rooftops, warning the people that all the stars would disappear in three nights. He foretold the people's destruction because they supported a wicked and unjust king. Gaul claimed that the people would be punished unless they placed him, Gaul, as their ruler. The people mocked him, threw stones, and shot arrows. The king sent out a decree that Gaul be arrested for his treason and thrown in prison for the rest of his days. Yet, Gaul continued to warn them with each passing night, and with each passing night, the more the kingdom and its people wanted to crucify the king's nephew.

"And then the third night came. True to his word, the god of night stole every star from the sky, leaving nothing but the lonely moon. Terrified, the kingdom cried for Gaul to save them—to return the stars to the sky and to keep the terrible curse from destroying them all. Promising him the kingdom in return, Gaul gave them the answer—to kill the king and his three heirs. It was the only way the god of night would return the stars.

"And so, sitting atop the castle tower at midnight, Gaul watched as the people stormed the castle to hang the king and his three sons with the ruling of a mob. The very moment after they gave their last royal breath, four new stars appeared in the heavens. Pleased with himself, Gaul walked among his new people and sat at the throne where his uncle once ruled.

"'But there are only four stars!' the people exclaimed. 'You promised us the night's sky to return!' 'Yes,' Gaul said. 'One for each member of the royal family.' Gaul then realized his mistake as the people bound him, the royal nephew, dragging him to the gallows. And there he hanged, strung up with the king and his cousins, Satra, Salka, and Salpingus, as the fifth and final star twinkled above."

Ribcage wrinkled her nose. "Well, that was a stupid story."

Besidio's mouth fluttered with neon lights. "Why thank you. I pride myself on being in the business of stupid stories. Let me ask you, little warrior. Who was the villain in the story?"

"Gaul, of course. And he was a stupid villain, too. He should've known something bad would've happened to him."

"If Gaul was the villain, then who was the hero?"

Ribcage was stumped. "Uh... the king and his sons."

"I'd be careful of who you call a hero. Just because the king didn't conspire to take the kingdom for himself, didn't make him a hero. Perhaps the king was the villain in the previous story when he took the kingdom from *his* uncle." He looked at Beetro. "What say ye, brother bot?"

Beetro looked at the gangly, jester robot. "Maybe Gaul was the hero and the villain."

"Maybe. But does there even have to be a hero? Why can't it just be a story about something that happened?"

"What did this have to do with *my* story?"

Besidio's eyes widened. "Who said it had anything to do with your story? Does everything have to connect for you? Some things simply are the way there are. No rhyme to it, brother. Just enjoy the ride."

"Come on," Beetro said, tapping Ribcage on the shoulder. The thrill of meeting another self-aware bot diminished—he didn't think the first one he'd meet would be so... weird. Were all self-aware robots like Besidio? He shuddered at the thought. A certain measure of disquiet rose in him as he ushered Ribcage along. "We should get to the mountain pass. See if we can get you some water."

Ribcage wrapped her scarf around her face and shot Besidio daggers with her eyes. "Thanks for nothing."

Beetro turned away but Besidio called after, "Why not take my faithful steed? I'm afraid I'm not much of an equestrian and I fear the beast will die out here for thirst. It would be a shame."

"No, thanks." Beetro walked away.

"Oh, please do, though," Besidio insisted. "It will be of no trouble to your party. Use the horse for its back. Water it if you have to spare in the mountains. If not, why, you may use it for its meat to feed the girl."

Ribcage looked at Beetro longingly.

"Fine," Beetro acquiesced, looking at the emaciated horse.

"Ah, thank you, brother." He turned to Ribcage. "My little brave heart, why don't you climb on his back? You'd only weigh a mere feather to him. He's a gentle beast. I've been told he goes by Bellamare."

Ribcage put her small foot in a stirrup of the horse and heaved herself up. "Fun!" she said, feeling the stiff hair of the horse's back.

"I only ask that, if it shall come to pass, you give the horse a swift and peaceful end. Agreed?" Besidio asked.

Beetro nodded.

"Where will you go?" Ribcage asked Besidio.

"It's been too long since I've wandered. I'll try that for a while and maybe end up in one of the other city-states to the east. Hal Aryl or Sinklair east of Crater Valley are fine places for a jester. I'll bet their lords wouldn't mind a new jester full of stories. Or I may see you in Orion. Perhaps I'll add your story to my lore. Would that be agreeable to you, brother bot?"

"Fine," Beetro said, waving off the robot. "Share whatever you want. If General Deluvius hasn't taken over their fiefdoms yet." Beetro walked off with Bellamare and Ribcage in tow.

"Farewell, travelers," Besidio yelled. "Perhaps we'll meet again." But as they walked away, Besidio called again from behind. He moved awkwardly through the grasses, his lanky legs lifting higher than usual. The long strips of colorful fabric bounced around him as he walked, his long hat swaying by his feet. The robot looked absolutely absurd in movement, fitting of a jester. "Here," he said to Beetro, reaching out his finger.

"What?" Beetro asked, looking at the robot's finger.

"Put out your finger, brother."

Beetro lifted his finger and Besidio touched it. Suddenly, a jolt of downloaded information shot through Beetro's mind. "A map."

"Yes."

Beetro flipped through the data in his head and looked at

Besidio. "It's a map through Meteor Mountains and beyond to Orion. Thank you."

Besidio slapped Beetro on the shoulder. "You'll appreciate it when the time comes. May it guide your way," Besidio said as if pleased with his good deed. "Sometimes we just do good things to just do good things. The Granite Gate, doorway into Meteor Mountains is just due east of the road. Beyond that is Crater Valley and eastern still you will find Orion."

"Again, thank you." Besidio's mouth flickered with neon lights. A smile? He turned but Beetro stopped him. "Wait..."

"Yes?"

"Do you have dreams?"

"Dreams? As in aspirations?" The jester bot cocked his head.

"No. Do you dream when you shut down?"

"Of course. It is a gift for the conscious mind. Self-awareness comes with many such gifts. And curses." He looked up at the mountains. "Be careful of those passes, there are those who confuse humans with robots. Some choose to forgo the mountains and venture around the coastline to the south, near Portolo. It's longer. But it is safer."

Beetro nodded. "Thank you, Besidio."

"And we'll take good care of him!" Ribcage said, patting Bellamare's flank.

"Fare thee well, brother. Goodbye, my brave heart," Besidio called, meeting his gaze with Beetro's.

EIGHTEEN

ARYM DIDN'T LOOK BACK until he found cover in the Crescent Wood. Chilled and soaked to the bone in nothing but a thin jumpsuit, he rested behind the base of a massive tree and donned the thick coat and overalls Lutra had packed for him. After catching his breath, he squinted over Crater Valley and saw them there—an army. Wheeled drills and spewing towers of oil and flame collected in the middle of the valley. Above the digging machinery hovered a solitary aircraft. Reflective like a mirror, it suspended above the army, a single wing with no obvious cockpit or windows.

The overworld had arrived.

Never in his darkest nightmares did he imagine that the rektors could be right—the overworld wanted the Crib dead. But why?

Breathing heavy through sweat and cold fear, he badly wanted to return to his brothers. Lutra was back there. Arym could at least go back, shimmying down an Oshaft to find his friend and guide him back out. Hell, he'd even track down Rektor Tarysl and get him out, too. Yet, he knew the rektor would never leave the Crib. Lutra and the rektors would never abandon their brothers. A crushing thought came to him... this is what made him a Runner—he was a coward. Arym never showed loyalty to the Crib, and it had cost him. He couldn't steel himself to return—he didn't have it in him. If he went back to the Crib now, he'd never be free.

Arym turned from the tree and walked through the forest, dangling pine boughs poking him in the face. Water slogged in his boots as he burst through stream beds, every tendon of his body screaming from weeks of body deconditioning in isolation. Brilliant shafts of light shot through the forest canopy dappling the dirt with a kaleidoscope of fractured spotlights. A rabbit jumped out of his way as if it was surprised at the human's haste.

Arym arrived at Laser Falls and craned his neck. He found the small outcropping of handholds that led up toward the nook behind the waterfall and took a breath. Could he possibly climb with such ragged muscles? Before he could answer the question, he was already moving—limbs working and knees scrapping. And then he was at the gate of the Alchean tomb. Arym passed through the protruding metal shards and stepped into the darkened stone tunnel. The ancient inscriptions of mathematics and pictorial engineering sparkled with errant sunlight. Arym ignored the diagrams as he moved, making his way to the final chamber.

"Protonix," he called, his voice scratchy from disuse.

There was silence.

"Protonix!" he yelled, remembering the proton's indifference to Arym's imprisonment. It had acted as if it didn't know humans could even dislike being held against their will.

No reply came.

Why would Protonix leave the tomb? Its entire existence was to guard and maintain the knowledge of the Alcheans. What could possibly get that orb of light to leave again?

Arym stood, alone in that ancient chamber, and curled into a ball on the stone floor. For the first time in a long time, he didn't think about Hawera.

He thought about himself.

Having no idea how long he'd slept, Arym awoke with a twinge in his neck and fire in his limbs. For a moment, he thought he was still a prisoner in the bowels of the Crib, but the mathematical etchings on the wall reminded him of his lost cause to find Protonix. He thought the proton would have answers—solutions to the army digging into the Crib. Surely the proton could impart some of that Alchean weaponry to help the Crib.

He stood, examining the math once more. Opening his satchel, he removed his sketch diary and perused through the tracings he'd earlier lifted from the walls. He found a spot on the chamber wall where he'd failed to get tracings and so brought a page to the stone and lifted the math with a charcoal pen. One by one, he filled the pages up until the last page of the diary. He'd failed to lift all the etchings, but he figured he had enough.

Enough for what? He wasn't quite sure. But he longed to understand the math.

He fled the chamber, passing by the ancient engravings and emerged at the mouth of the gateway, the rush of the waterfall raging in his ears. He stood, his gaze on the valley floor, not really having a clue about what to do next. A rumbling in his stomach reminded him of the satchel that Lutra had provided. He swung it to the ground and feasted on the nuts and berries that Lutra had packed. Between his fingers, he felt the softness of an animal hide.

The map.

Crater Valley was drawn in beautiful red ink—several rows of peaked upside-down *V*s surrounded the Crib. To the west was the plains of Helian, to the east... Orion. He rubbed the ink, feeling where the pen had indented the animal skin. Orion. Hawera. He could go to her, find Protonix, and maybe bring the entire wrath of Alchean weaponry onto the heads of the army drilling their way into the Crib. He gathered the map and remaining food rations into his satchel and found the footholds adjacent to the waterfall. Instead of going down, he went up.

Arym climbed the cliff's edge, gripping the jutting rocks and, at times, perfectly placed indentations. Someone had designed the Alchean tomb to be accessible from below, and above. Sweat mixed with granite dust, smearing across his forehead and stinging his eyes. He climbed for an hour without stopping, having no idea how far the cliff rose. Once he did rest, he made the mistake of looking down. Crescent Wood had become a small bean-shaped green carpet far below his feet. The sounds of the raging waterfall had long tapered off. Looking up, he had no way of telling how far the cliff went, he only knew that it was straight up—no sloping of the facade for a much-needed respite. He was certain that if he hadn't been climbing Oshafts for the last year, he would've simply fallen off the face of the cliff already. Fighting bubbling nausea, he kept climbing. The malnutrition of isolation was paying its toll. Every joint and ligament quivered with exhaustion. As daylight waned, so did his strength. He suspected if he looked down once more, it would be over.

He stopped, thinking about Hawera—her face, the elegant cheeks and full lips... she was beautiful beyond anything he could ever imagine. The compulsion to be with her propelled him up the rock face. Each foothold was an eternity. Every inch upward—a new epiphany in his bizarrely emerging life. What was it like for those who didn't grow up in the Crib? Was the overworld one big army out to kill him? Or was it a diverse mix of people like him?

His thoughts waxed existential—was the galaxy kind or ultimately cruel?

A familiar delirium set in. It was the thousand faces of psychosis that surrounded him during isolation. They'd found him on the cliffs of the valley. They laughed and cried and reassured and held him close. When he rested, eyes closed, he believed he saw the floating orb of Protonix encircling him. But nothing was there—just the cold moonlight scattered over the granite rock.

Sometime during the night, his hand slapped onto a horizontal surface. The surprise nearly lost him his grip on the cliff edge. Gasping, trembling, and losing no small measure of bowel function, he heaved his body to the top of the Crater Valley.

Blackness consumed him.

Sunlight filtered through. He jolted awake, heart racing. The pain in his hands and Achilles was a raging reminder of the night before. Inspecting his fingertips, he found dozens of raw spots and blistered clusters. His wrists and shoulders ached; his hip joints felt like crushed bone powder and his hamstrings were taut with sustained cramping.

Somehow, he fought through the pain and a buffeting wind and got to his feet. He looked out and gasped. Crater Valley was *enormous*. It was a gaping, nearly perfectly circular hole that interrupted the surface of Earth. It looked as if some giant came along and punched an enormous hole into a flat plain. Could something so perfectly circular possibly be formed by nature alone? The valley itself was a perfect bowl shape with a gradual incline toward the direct center, exactly where Haplo Lake had formed. Clouds clung to the outer rim of the valley, quickly ushered along by a brisk wind system that swept over the rim. The floor of the valley was carpeted in a lush green like a tongue of unstoppable nature had rolled over its surface. A wisp of smoky haze clung to the sky in the center of the valley. Shielding his eyes from sunlight, Arym squinted. He was up too far to make out anything going on at the Crib, but the smoke was an ominous sign.

He had to find help for his people.

After munching on nuts and taking a long draught from a canteen, he unfurled the hide map and inspected it. Tracing his finger along the rim of Crater Valley, he reckoned he was on the eastern rim and that Orion would be...

He whipped his head back and forth, inspecting the horizon.

"That way," he said to no one, pointing away from the valley. The horizon consisted of the boney-white of granite rock that ran away with the sky into some unknown terrain beyond. Orion was out there. Hawera was out there. Together, he could help her solve her problems with the galaxy and, at the same time, find help for the Crib. He had no idea if any of that would happen, but it was the only idea he had now.

So, he hiked.

He discovered the granite rock was layered before the horizon, suggesting multiple levels of rock surfaces. It became clear that a simple stroll over a granite plateau would be a bit more harrowing when he discovered a deep chasm below that gave way to a labyrinthine series of slot canyons.

He paused, looked back toward Crater Valley, and slipped down the chasm, which was tight enough for him to gain leverage with his back and legs and shimmy down. Fortunately, he had experience with such a maneuver—it was exactly like returning through an Oshaft. Once at the bottom of the chasm, he peered up and saw the slot walls running up at the sky, leaving only a slit of light in between the towering columns of solid granite.

He rubbed his arms, chilled by the sudden drop in temperature inside the slot canyon and moved. He stepped as noiselessly as possible, having no idea what kind of hostile forces lived outside of Crater Valley. He convinced himself that he was making educated guesses with every fork in the slots, but soon gave way to complete guessing. After more than a dozen forked paths, he opted to go with whichever slot seemed to have a decline. And then he stopped.

There were voices.

He slammed himself against a wall and lifted his chin, trying to tease apart the voices. People argued, somewhere. Given the slot canyon's transference of echoes, the voices could've been a few slots over or a thousand, no way to tell. Although he couldn't determine what they were saying, they were not friendly to one another. Two voices were from women arguing with one another while another man laughed in between outbursts.

What were they doing here? Did they live here? Was there an entire population of overworlders that lived right next door to the Crib? Maybe it was the army looking for Arym. Arym slid his back down the canyon wall. He wanted to cry at the uncertainty of where he was and what he was doing. He buried his head into his arms and waited as the voices argued.

A loud scream erupted toward the sky, followed by silence. The arguing ceased. Sounds of sliding rock and shuffling feet subsided, leaving the slot canyons in silence. He wasn't sure how long he stayed there, frozen in fear. A small bud of altruism grew somewhere inside him—he wanted to help. Yet, he didn't want to suffer whatever fate had been sealed for the screaming woman.

What if it was Hawera?

He stood, gingerly placing his satchel over his shoulder. He took timid steps toward where he thought he heard the woman screaming. He padded lightly, gripping the wall for support as he negotiated the granite rock chips that scattered the slot floor. The slot canyon revealed new twists and turns. What made him nervous was the trumpeting of the canyon walls—they were now too wide to shimmy up in case of an emergency. There was no longer a quick way out of the canyons to the plateau above.

He moved on, ignoring his increasingly noisy steps. As he scrambled over achy joints with a pounding head, he actually thought lovingly about his isolation pod. It was the place he was raised, grew up, and became the person he was at that moment. It had created him—a Runner. Although it became his prison, it was still his safe zone, a place he could trust. As much as he disdained the rektors throughout the years, he never thought they would physically harm him. Now, breathing in the dank mold of the slot canyons, all he felt was danger. He'd never been more vulnerable in his entire life and realized how easily his bravado about the overworld shrank away.

The slot sank deeper ahead. He stood at the top of a long landslide of granite slabs. There was no way of stepping out onto the slabs without tumbling uncontrollably to the bottom of the canyon. But there was a small ridge along the canyon wall—perhaps long enough to accommodate him. Begrudgingly, he stepped out to the ledge, revulsed at the idea of having to scale a rock face once again, and took hold of the granite wall. The ledge offered little purchase for his feet, affording him only a small shuffle to move along. He hugged the wall as he shimmied.

Three steps in and he immediately fell.

He tumbled down a river of granite rocks, creating a chain reaction of miniature rockslides that pummeled his head and body as he cascaded down the steep incline. He was helpless against the onslaught of stones, clipping him with a cutting edge or simply thunking him in the head. He fell to the bottom, the granite slabs collecting around him as the miserable rockslide came to an end.

Still conscious, he lifted the rocks off his legs and belly. Fortunately, no stone was larger than a fist. A warm stream of blood reminded him of the friendly gashes on the way down. With his head swimming, he got to his feet to get out of the rockslide but stopped when he saw something lying next to him.

It was a cloth sack.

On further inspection, it wasn't a sack at all but some sort of rolled-up baggage wrapped together with white cloth. He picked the bag up by one end and lifted, quickly spilling its contents. He looked down at exactly one human arm, neatly severed just below the shoulder.

It was then that Arym finally decided the overworld was not a very good place.

NINETEEN

MEMORIES BUBBLED in Miree's mind—memories she had tried very hard to forget.

"Do you know why the pain is good for you, Miree?" Haldunt had asked her.

She remembered her own hair in her eyes, dripping with blood before the Kish had shaved it off completely. Her body was too overwhelmed to respond. Haldunt the Wire stood, that bastard with chains, looking down at her with some sort of macabre paternal reverence.

"It's not because it makes you stronger. It's so that it doesn't deceive you when you are among your enemies. Pain is deception, acolyte. It is the trickery of the inquisitor of torture." He had wrapped one of his dainty chains, encrusted with tiny circlets of razors, around her forearm. "I'm trying to trick you into thinking that the present pain is worse than potential death. Because death will be certain if you betray the Kish. And if you believe the torture to our inductees is bad, how do you think we treat our apostates? The Kish will take care of you if you take care of the

Kish." She remembered Haldunt's deadpan glare at her across the sharp blades and hooks. The man may have been terrifying, but not to Miree. She knew who he was... the lackey to the Kish—just a bunch of thieves trying to set up a shadow government in Orion.

The Kish.

They were the reason she had to flee Orion. Not because of what they did to her, but because of what she did to them. The Quantizer hadn't exactly... belonged to her after she stole it. No, she had to go ahead and steal it a second time from the Kish before fleeing Orion. Miree had a habit of leaving a wake of murderous enemies wherever she made acquaintances. It was fine. Nothing new.

She looked down at the lacey scars around her arms and ran her fingers along the puckered skin. A cold gust washed over the plains as she moved, her purple cloak billowing behind her. She was still wet and absolutely freezing as she moved but was distracted by raw fury. She was pissed off at herself and all the amateur moves she made along the way. And even though she'd been traveling half the morning, she still had no idea where to go.

She'd head to Meteor Mountains, of course. It was the only place to find fresh water for hundreds of kilometers. But after that? She hadn't a clue—and it had been a long time since she hadn't had one of those. Even back when she was with the Kish, she had some sort of clue. But now, for one of the first times in her life, she had no idea what she was doing.

And it pissed her off.

Moreover, she was usually able to process her anger over what people had done to her throughout her life in quick little fits and then move on. She could hate them for a moment and then leave the moment behind because anything more than this was excess—indulgence. Until Deluvius came along and murdered the only person she cared about. Miree had to get all sentimental and move up her robbery planning into a foolhardy plan to exact vengeance on the asshole. The whole debacle confirmed the only virtue on which she had ever hung her hat—don't care about anyone.

But now there was nothing but her thoughts and memories out alone on the plains and it was more torture than anything Haldunt the Wire had ever unleashed on her. Weird and foggy vignettes from her childhood years started cropping up in the back of her mind... her father watching her, baleful eyes—doing absolutely nothing—as she was taken from him. The Fifth Kingdom was a place she believed to have successfully blocked from her memory. But now, things were coming back...

"No!" she yelled to the empty wind.

The time passed achingly slowly but, eventually, she saw the gigantic granite boulders that lay at the feet of the mountains. Granite Gate, the trailhead into the mountains, was just an hour due south. She could get through the mountains and knew them well. A newcomer could get hopelessly lost within the labyrinth of granite that led to the peaks above, but Miree had traversed them several times and had developed a sixth sense about how to navigate them.

It would take her two days to get through the slot canyons, but that wasn't the tricky part. What was going to get her killed was trying to get down the sheer drop off on the other side of the mountains. The granite sunk five hundred meters into Crater Valley below and the only way she knew to get down required rappelling equipment. She'd need to improvise up there and circle around the mountain peaks to find another way down into the valley. Of course, she could just walk around the entire edge of the valley instead of cutting through it, but this would probably take an extra week. That was an extra week of trying to hunt game and find water in an unfamiliar part of the mountains with zero equipment.

And where would she go once beyond Crater Valley? Memories tugged on her, trying to convince her to go home. Not Orion, but *home,* home. The Fifth Kingdom. Of course, she'd never allow that, but some backwards corner in her brain kept flicking on the emotional ganglion that hadn't yet withered away. Nostalgia was a clever adversary.

She finally saw the Granite Gate but there was a huge problem... a gigantic bloatstorm had descended right at the trailhead. Flashes of lightning lit up the massive storm as it swirled above the plains. So, it *had* been a bloatstorm festering above Crater Valley for the past few weeks. It was always hard to tell—real storms could swirl above the valley for weeks before floating over Helian. Same phenomenon applied to bloatstorms; they were both meteorological and organic, possessing the hybrid attributes of weather systems and the emergent brain of a hive mind full of rapacious bloatflies. Bloatstorms were easy. You just took a wide berth from them, waited for them to move, and stayed out of the way. They rarely descended over cities, and if they did, you just kept indoors, and the dumb bugs the size of raccoons would get tired of knocking on the roofs in about five minutes and scurry off. However, one did not want to get caught under a bloatstorm in the middle of nowhere with no shelter. That was usually a problem. So, Miree had to find another way up into Meteor Mountains. That, or get eaten or electrocuted or whatever it was bloatflies did to unfortunate travelers.

She inspected the leading edge of the mountain and saw nothing but rock face. After a bit of a climb through the uneven foothills, she discovered mostly dead-end caves or crevices that tapered into a vertical rock face. Inside one of the caves, she found a hearth—recent—with ashes that were still warm. Instinctively, her hand went to the butt of her gun at her waist when she realized that moving-intelligent-things needing a fire could be nearby. She didn't like being near moving-intelligent-things if she didn't have to. She crept out of the cave, confident that there was no one nearby, and continued down the mountain line, keeping a close eye on the bloatstorm. Errant lightning shot out from the silvery haze as the occasional stream of bloatflies buzzed toward the ground. They were interested in whatever was happening down by Granite Gate.

Finally, she found a pathway up into the mountains that involved scaling several stubby boulders on which she scraped her exposed hip, struggling atop one of the rock faces. Hunger pangs struck as she climbed the boulders, which were arrayed along the bottom of the mountain like fat trolls, sitting idly and stubborn. She found a sad berry bush with exactly four blackberries that she quickly gobbled up. There was a shallow puddle of water atop a boulder, but she didn't dare try it this low into the valley without her radio switch, which was probably smashed and discarded back at Peles Castle. No, she'd wait until she was atop the mountains before drinking the water—better than bleeding out of her ass and slowly being poisoned to death by radioactive isotopes.

She ran into another blackberry bush—this one empty. But it looked disturbed. Broken branches with an entire half of the bush tilted down as if caught up in the clothing of someone passing by. Was she accidentally following someone? Again, her hand went to her gun as she surveyed the rock face above. It was motionless but who knew what kind of hidden eyes could be up there, watching her.

Normally she'd wait. She would watch and listen for movement. In the past, capable of days-long surveillance, she could outlast her enemies. But she didn't have the luxury to wait. So, she shrugged off the paranoia as a crack of thunder pounded the sky. Perhaps the bloatstorm was moving on. But she was already this far up the mountain, she wasn't about to turn back for the Granite Gate.

Miree moved, leaping from boulder to boulder until she'd climbed up a fair way and looked back at the plains of Helian. Almost six months prior, she remembered the same view as she descended Meteor Mountains and saw the plains blanketed in green corn crops that stretched as far as she could see. They were the plains of Helian—mega-exporter of corn to the lands of the Torbad to the west over to Orion in the east. Now the plains were dead, like someone had laid down a putrid, yellow blanket over the once growing corn crops. She remembered the burlap sacks of cornmeal with a *HELIAN* stamp running down the sides in the abandoned factory where she once trained with the Kish.

The Kish.

Haldunt's smile kept lingering in her thoughts. Her 'training', the word they used for conditioning one to torture, was almost always led by Haldunt the Wire. His wry smile curled along his mouth, pleased at her pain. The man had an empty eye socket—never bothering with a patch. He left the black ditch on his face open to the air to mortify or disgust whoever he wanted. None of his terror tactics worked on Miree. The only thing she couldn't stand about the man was his presumptuous smile. Knowing that the pain he inflicted was intolerable, that it altered Miree's very personhood. Arrogant prick. As if anything his wires or chains could do would possibly make her into anything other than herself. His pain was nothing to her. Something she could never prove.

She winced at the sheer silence and boredom of the mountains. The monotony was stirring up things in her mind that should not be disturbed. This is what happened when she didn't have a solid plan—her mind wandered. The Kish, Orion, the Fifth Kingdom—these were not places to which she'd ever return. No reason to be digging them up now.

Finally, she found a trail. It was difficult to tell where it led but it appeared to wind south, perhaps an offshoot off the main trailhead that began at Granite Gate. Miree jumped down into the trail and stopped. There was a sound in the distance. A human sound. A cough or a sneeze or a slobber. With the trail being a natural cut through the granite, any sound could be an echo from any direction. She checked her firearm and moved south.

Her thirst finally cut to the forefront of her mind as she splashed through a puddle. It had been over a day since she'd drank anything and she needed fluid, fast. Her head pounded and she was now in between fits of dizziness since the climb up. Dehydration was in full bloom. She knelt to the puddle and sniffed it. No odor. Crystal clear. Not signs that it wasn't radioactive, but it was either this puddle or the one she would find in ten minutes. Either way, she needed to drink soon. If she was going to die of the Poisoning, might as well get the show started. So, she lapped up the water like a dog, scooping her hands in and trickling it into her mouth. The coolness sank into her stomach and calmed her nerves.

The Meteor Mountains were a jagged mess of gigantic shards of rock and slats of mineral. They hadn't been formed by tectonic means. There were no gradual shifts of earth and stressing of plates that inched toward one another over the course of millennia. No, the Meteor Mountains happened *fast*. Something slammed into the earth and completely shattered the surrounding land. There was very little soil and almost no plant life. Every now and then, a blackberry bush or tree sapling would catch hold of a leeward spot of soil but wouldn't last long. Any heavy storm uprooted shallow foliage.

Thirst abated, Miree focused on being hungry. But little plant life came with little animal life. There were birds. Big hawks that wheeled across the sky, but they weren't likely to be snooping around with a bloatstorm on the prowl.

She smelled a campfire. Just ahead. Some morons broadcasting their presence. This was good. She could eat. She still hadn't decided if she would take the weary traveler pitch or the 'give me your food or die' bit to which she'd grown accustomed. She didn't even have to bluff—she had a loaded pistol on her waist. Creeping, now with gun drawn, she rounded a granite corner and peeked through. There was a campsite with a fire going; a skewered bird dangling above. But there was no one around.

"The hell?" she whispered, coming around the corner.

No one just left an empty camp. Unless...

"You were right," a voice echoed above her, making no attempt to be discreet. "She fell for it."

It took Miree a split second to recognize the voice as she flipped around, her boltgun pointed up. Two hooded figures stood along the boulders that flanked the trail, their head and shoulders darkened against a gray sky. Yellow, red, and green lights flickered within the darkness of the hoods.

The Reticulum.

Miree lunged forward, somersaulting preemptively and rolled across the dirt. A crack sounded above her followed by a sizzle from where she had just moved. She shot blindly, regaining her footing, then looked up.

They were gone.

Miree ran. She bolted through the decoy campsite, leaped over the fire, and stumbled down the trail. She felt stupid at fleeing in a panic. She was normally so cool, so in control of any situation. But seeing those hooded stooges of the Reticulum staring down at her filled her with cold dread. You don't mess around with people that are trying to kidnap you and hijack your mind. Soft whispers shot through the slot canyon as Miree got her footing on the trail. She circled around, gun drawn, trying to triangulate the voices.

"You got that pretty little shard sword?" Miree called out, trying to get the upper hand of psychological intimidation. "I think I might like that for myself." It didn't work. Even Miree could hear the desperation in her shaky voice.

Run or wait? Run or wait? Run or wait?

A series of sparks spewed out of the stone behind her, a missed shot of that fucking stun gun they used on her back in the plains. She ducked down and ran down the trail, firing another blind shot behind her. Breathing heavy, the downward slope quickly took a sharp turn up into a hill of thousands of granite shards. She climbed the stones, slipping with every step as if running on sand. With every movement, she kicked stones away, triggering micro landslides of smaller stones. Soon, she was dodging the granite as they tumbled toward her, hitting her ankles and shins. Grimacing with every step, she made progress to a small outpouching cleft of the granite wall and clung there. She looked down and saw a new heap of rocks collecting at the bottom. There was no one down there. For the moment, they hadn't followed her up the trail.

There was no going back down, back into the arms of the cyborgs who would tear her body apart and stuff it full of robot parts. She suddenly missed Ribcage and her ability to vanish into thin air—would've been handy now. She then leaped from stone to stone, avoiding the cascading rockslide that she had triggered. At first, she made progress up the rockslide, but stumbled and slid, backtracking. There was no time to look over her shoulder, no time to wait for them to catch up to her. There was only sweating and climbing and aching and cursing.

And then she felt something in her arm. She didn't even

notice at first but became acutely aware that she couldn't support herself as her shoulder crashed into a rock wall. She looked down at her right arm—her gun-slinging arm.

It wasn't there.

It was... *gone.*

A perfectly cut stump, with the surgical margins only a laser could create, was the only thing left of her arm. Looking behind, she saw her arm laying among the rocks as ashen as the granite around it.

Miree allowed herself a solitary scream and then cut it off.

"Very nice, Xy," a voice said, echoing up the trail. The two Reticuli stood at the bottom of the rockslide, their faces hidden within the shadows of their hoods.

Miree fell, slipping on the rocks. She slid, tumbling back down the way she'd climbed. The rocks bumped and cut her body as she flopped down the hill. As if orchestrated, she came to a stop at the feet of the Reticuli.

Ria unhooded her face, exposing the full metal plate of her forehead, studded with tubing that connected to ports along her neck. Her stubby, robotic eyes telescoped in and out, taking in the image of Miree. She held that hilt, absent of a blade, at her waistline and flicked her wrist. A dozen fiery shards rose through the air around her. Ria brought the hilt down quickly, perpendicular to the ground, prompting the white-hot shards to surround Miree, caging her.

"You see, Xy," Ria said, gesturing to her apprentice. "These Orion bitches are the worst to hunt, but the most delicious to catch."

TWENTY

AS THE MOUNTAIN PASS APPROACHED, Beetro looked up at Ribcage, who rode atop the sickly horse. "You don't have to come with me."

Ribcage squinted down at him, wind blowing her short, dirty hair. "I know."

"Why *are* you coming?"

"Told you, you helped me visit my mom. I want to help you find your dad."

"Why the sudden charity? I thought you street kids were cutthroat—don't help unless someone helps you first."

"Luci is gone."

"I see how it is. You don't have anyone else to take care of you."

The girl stopped, a defiant pucker on her lips. "I take care of *myself*."

"Course you do. And only yourself," Beetro suddenly snapped, possibly for the first time.

"Didn't know you were such a nasty bot. Miree rubbing off on you?"

At first, he felt ashamed for his annoyance, but then he dug into the feeling. "I don't want to hear about Miree or Korthe again. Got it?" He suddenly reminded himself of Miree, which further irritated him.

"So, what's up there?"

"Up where?"

"Up your butt?"

"I don't know what you're talking about. Look, all I care about is finding Galiaro and to... to have him..." he trailed off.

"What are you talking about, robot?"

"I just want some answers—and my name is Beetro. I want to know why Galiaro made me, programmed me to find him, and then dumped me in a junkyard with no memory. It just doesn't make any sense."

Ribcage didn't respond, only folded over Bellamare and gave the horse a hug, rubbing her face in his brushy mane. "Good boy," she said.

"What!" Beetro yelled, thinking she was talking to him. "Oh."

Beetro enhanced his vision as the dead grass underfoot turned to black dirt, which carpeted the plains until it met up with the mountain passes ahead. He saw the boulders, buttressing rocky pillars that had been placed vertically, framing a gate into the mountain passes—the Granite Gate. The sky had darkened as the storm was now just overhead.

Only, the storm looked strange.

"Do clouds normally swirl around like that?" Beetro asked.

Ribcage looked up.

The sky was quickly darkening above them, swelling with black threads, crisscrossing across the sky. A frenzied complex of swarms and eddies swirled with the murmuration of a flock. Movements too organic to be meteorological.

"Bloatstorm!" Ribcage cried. "It's a bloatstorm!"

"What's—" Beetro was cut off as the swarm descended on them, bleeding through the sky. He got his first glance at one of them—a bloated, oblong creature the size of a housecat with feathered wings beating lightning-fast. They had beady, multifaceted eyes with dual prehensile tendrils dangling below. These graspers whipped through the air, groping for a surface or tree branch or human head or whatever it was it wanted to shred. They were ugly bugs, searching and swarming with frenetic bursts of energy, riding wind streams or hot air pockets. Single bloatflies buzzed solo but never too far from the central swarm. They lived within a thick mist that surrounded the colony. The mists had a shimmering quality—microscopic, silvery particulates sifting errant sunlight in every direction. Lightning cracked from the bloatstorm, popping through the air and singeing the dirt only a few paces in front of them.

"Run!" Ribcage yelled.

Beetro looked back over the plains. There was no cover back the way they came, so he took off toward the boulders of the mountains. Ribcage dug her heel into Bellamare's sides. As they moved, Beetro already knew they wouldn't make it to the protective rocks of the Granite Gate. Something struck his chest, knocking him to the ground. He managed a forward somersault and regained his footing. The bloatfly returned to its swarm as another descended fast, cutting through the air until it knocked into Beetro's back, making him stumble once more. It was as if the creatures were testing their victim—both mass and defensive response. Would these humanlings shoot them or run?

Getting to his feet again, Beetro looked over at Ribcage who had slid around Bellamare's flank until the girl was clinging to the horse's belly, upside down, hair dragging in mud. Her arms strained as she held herself close to the stirrups, the horse's gallop jostling her between its legs. Bloatflies buzzed alongside the horse, bumping into its ribs, prompting an angry whinny from Bellamare.

Another crack of electricity struck just a few paces away, electrifying the air with ozone. Some of the bloatflies dropped like rocks, struck by the lightning. Their carcasses rolled across the dirt, spiraling streams of smoke trailing behind. Beetro ran, his feet sinking into mud as the earth around them became a slog from the mountain run-off.

A swarm of the massive bugs surrounded Bellamare, growing in numbers as their wings buzzed beside the horse's flank. The gigantic flies formed a line above the horse and extended long proboscises that felt their way through the wind, snipping toward the animal. A single, sharp tooth protruded from the tips, stabbing after flesh. Almost instantly, the horse was completely surrounded by bloatflies with wisps of silver clouds clinging between them. Ribcage screamed as thunder pounded the air. Lightning flashed through the mists as the bloatstorm crashed to the ground. A flurry of the bug-eyed monsters filled Beetro's vision as he sank; Bellamare crying wildly somewhere.

Lightning coruscated through the mists, but this time...

Beetro *held it.*

He felt the energy of electricity questing through the mists and wrapped himself around it. Closing his eyes, he lassoed the lightning. The surrounding air buzzed with energy as he twisted the light from the grasp of the clouds and sucked it inside of himself. He was immediately filled to the brim and felt his skin tremble, ready to explode from the pent-up potential energy. It was too much, far more than his fusion core or the minuscule thermal energy of the water vapor that worked his joint servos.

He released the energy, and with another crack, expelled the lightning into the air and funneled it around him, around his party —a starving horse and an even more starving girl. He bent the power outward, into the boatflies and their terrifying mists. Hundreds of bloatflies plunged to the mud, their bodies lifeless.

And then the mists were gone as the fleeing bloatflies left a pocket of breathing room. Fragments of sunlight broke through the bloatstorm.

He stood, clenching his fists. "That felt... good."

And so Beetro did it again.

Although weaker now, he sucked in a bolt of lightning that struck from the mists of the bloatstorm.

He *held* the energy.

It stormed inside of him for a moment—a millisecond—until he couldn't contain it. Clumsily, yet with some measure of control, he released the lightning out of his body, upward into the bloatstorm. The lightning struck dozens more bloatflies in midair, their carcasses pummeling downward in whorls of smoke.

Beetro felt powerful.

He felt *incredible.*

That feeling of being in control—albeit totally tenuous—was unlike anything he'd experienced in his short life since Korthe. He had no idea how incredibly impotent he'd been. Now, he could literally wield the power of storms.

The feeling was short-lived as he collapsed to the ground. Whatever it was he was doing with that lightning, it completely sapped the water vapor within his body. It was the same result back at Peles Castle when he froze the laser light.

He was paralyzed.

Rolling his eyes to the sky, he saw the bloatstorm collect itself back up into its silvery mists. Despite the easy prey of a street rat on a horse, the retaliating lightning strikes apparently weren't worth the bother. The ground was soon free of bloatfly attacks and sunlight streaked across the plains once again.

"Hey, robot—er, Beetro." Ribcage was looming above him, her gnarled hair silhouetted against the sky. "The bloats are gone. Good job." She patted his cheek and then returned with water. "Here." She poured it down his throat and waited.

Beetro felt the vapor energy returning to his servos and fingertips. He ran a quick diagnostic on his system—the nuclear core was humming away.

"So, what is that thing you do?" Ribcage asked as Beetro got to his feet.

He looked over his shoulder, checking the bloatstorm as it moved west across the plains. "Don't know."

"You made like a cage of lightning around us. It was you who did it, right?"

"Definitely. I could feel the energy of the storm running through me like a... river. But like a river I couldn't contain. I felt like a funnel for a moment, taking the energy that was there, gathering it up for a split second and then releasing it back out."

"I've met a few robots, but I've never seen any of them do *that*."

"Makes me wonder..."

"What?"

"Is this why Galiaro made me? To be a... weapon?"

"Either way, next time we run into General Deluvius, you can send a bolt of lightning right through his brain."

Beetro inspected the Meteor Mountains to the east as they rose from the Granite Gate. "Let's go." Beetro didn't want to talk about what happened. Mostly because he didn't want to expose how *good* it felt to throw lightning around.

"Yeah—" Ribcage said before collapsing. Beetro knelt beside the tiny girl. Her chest was heaving, eyes closed with perspiration running along her lip. "I'm so... tired."

"You need water. Now." He looked over at Bellamare, who was stuffing his snout into a patch of dead grass that had flooded with mountain run-off. The horse sniffed the water, paused, and then lifted its snout, refusing to drink. Beetro held Ribcage in his arms and moved toward the Granite Gate. Bellamare followed, moving slowly over its creaky joints.

Beetro burst into a sprint toward the mountains, passing underneath the enormous boulders of the Granite Gate and up into the steep passages of the Meteor Mountains. He moved through narrow slot canyons, walls extending several stories above them. The light darkened within the tunnels, snuffing out any sort of plant life from taking root on the floors of the canyons. Bellamare's hooves clipped along the dirt and stone as they moved upward.

Beetro stopped at a fork, uncertain of the way. Instinctively, he took a left and came to yet another fork. After another left and another fork, he decided to take the canyon paths that had a steeper incline—any purchase in height would help guide their journey through the mountains. Studying the canyon walls, he knew he could scale them and get to the top of the boulders to get a vantage.

Ribcage, however, was breathing rapidly, her eyes becoming sallow and vacant. The extra effort Ribcage exerted with fleeing from the Bloatstorm had expended everything she had left. It was strange to look at the tiny girl in his arms to be so vulnerable. She was always armored in the veneer of sarcasm and hostile independence. Now, she was a sad bag of skin and bones, clinging with labored breaths.

Wait...

He was falling into the trap all over again. He was *helping* someone else. Why? Where did it get him to help Miree? Where would it get him if he saved Ribcage? How could he know that the little girl, who could literally Jump into another dimension at will, wouldn't later betray him? He hated the uncertainty—hated not knowing if he could trust someone else. He didn't know what to do but the girl had proved useful enough. She'd saved him from death three times now. He supposed he could at least pay her back.

Ribcage jostled in his arms as he ran up the canyon slopes. Water slogged underfoot but Bellamare still turned his nose up. After minutes, the slot canyon opened into a tiny gully, barely wide enough for a camp. A fire had recently been extinguished. Beetro turned, watching Bellamare. The horse sniffed the charcoal and then inspected a pool of water that had collected within a granite boulder. Bellamare's tongue extended, lapped up a sip of water, paused, and then continued drinking.

Beetro rushed to the puddle and held Ribcage to the water, the girl's rat-nest hair falling over her face. "Drink!" Beetro yelled, shaking the girl. He splashed the water into her face, waking her from a death stupor. Ribcage plopped her face into the puddle and took long draws of the water in between sloppy breaths. Beetro left her there and checked out the campsite.

A small trail of smoke rose from the extinguished campfire. Someone had been there recently. He did a quick perimeter check and found the campsite to be harmless enough. Although difficult to detect sound in the slot canyons, he couldn't hear any movement in the area and felt they could stay a while at the camp while the girl recovered.

"You'll need food?" Beetro asked, not completely ignorant of the fact that Ribcage needed to eat, but still a little unsure of how often humans actually needed to fuel themselves. But Ribcage didn't hear him, she was still slurping away at the water puddle before quickly collapsing into a nap. Beetro really couldn't be sure, but he was reassured by her steady breathing that she'd awaken sometime soon. Bellamare found a dead bush and started nuzzling about in its roots, trying to find anything to munch.

It was as good a time as any for some reconnaissance, so Beetro scaled a complete vertical wall of granite. He briefly squashed a nostalgic flash of climbing trash heaps with Lucindi and crested the ledge. The top of the slot canyons looked like a giant goddess had come along at some point and smashed her god hammer into what was once a smooth slab of mountainous granite, shattering it into thousands of column shards, creating the slots below. Beetro leaped from column to column while measuring the distance to the edge of the mountain range to the east. Using Besidio's map, he knew that Crater Valley was beyond the mountain ridge, the direction toward Orion and the only possible place where he could get any answers about himself and Galiaro.

The sky was clear, sunlight twinkling inside granite flecks of mica. Beetro scanned the horizon and saw a wisp of smoke about two and a half kilometers away and detected over a dozen odor-active compounds associated with burning flesh. Someone was cooking meat.

He hopped a few more columns of granite and crept closer toward the campfire, finally detecting voices echoing up the slot. Slinking along on his belly, he carefully moved to not scrape his metal body along the granite. As he approached, one of the voices—a woman's voice—clearly triggered something in his memory bank.

It was Ria—of the Reticulum.

Beetro froze. Ria and her crony had all sorts of advanced weaponry that he knew nothing about, which could incapacitate him instantly. He would already have been hauled away to the Reticulum for butchery if it wasn't for Ribcage bringing her on-brand chaos to their last confrontation with the Reticulum. But that was before. Now he could shoot lightning from his body. Could he do it now? He closed his eyes and concentrated. For a split second, he felt sunlight on his body. It wasn't just the typical presence of thermal energy on his skin. He could *feel* the energy of every photon as they struck him, absorbed into his metal, and then fired off a higher frequency photon from his blue shell. As the photons escaped his body, he tried to cling to their energy, to sequester them inside himself. But nothing happened. It seemed he needed longer to build up the photons from the radiant sunlight.

Carefully, he extended his head from the granite pillar that loomed above the camp and saw them. The two hooded figures were crouched beside a fire, roasting some sort of bird, long plucked of feathers. Ria was talking and gesturing to Xy in some sort of impromptu didactic about how to remove the frontal cortex from human brains to make them easier to transport. Next to camp, Beetro recognized the same fiery net of metal shards that they had used to cage him back on the Helian plains. The shards were bright with white-hot energy surrounding their prisoner, who was huddled inside a ditch. Beetro was so close, he didn't have to magnify his vision to see the face of the prisoner.

It was Miree.

And she was looking right back at him. Her expression was stone, typical of her general contempt for all things. But her eyes betrayed her with a pleading tilt. It was a confusing facial expression for Beetro, perhaps one he had never seen before—someone reluctantly admitting vulnerability and asking for help. Miree then pursed her lips as if in recognition that she had completely abandoned him back at Peleś Castle and that maybe he would forget about it this one time and help free her. While Beetro was trying to decipher this kaleidoscope of facial expression, he almost entirely missed the fact that she was also missing an arm.

For a tempered hot second, it hurt him to see her there. In reverse positions, would Miree free him? He knew how Miree would answer—don't ask questions that don't need to be answered.

TWENTY-ONE

NOT ONCE IN her life had Miree expected to be rescued. Not a single person had ever cared enough to even know when she was in trouble. Miree rescued Miree—that's how it worked. Yet, when she found herself newly amputated at the humerus and bound within a fiery cage of hot shards, she let a bud of hope unfurl inside of her when she saw Beetro peering down at her from atop a boulder. Neither questioning how the robot escaped Peles Castle or managed to survive long enough to meander up through the slots of Meteor Mountains, she let that hope of rescue spring inside. Beetro, she now knew, had... abilities. He could fling laser light at the Reticuli, burn them to the ground, and release his dear old friend, Miree, from a fate of misery as a cyborg pet project.

Only... Beetro didn't move. He didn't do anything. Those orbs of indigo only stared down at her, accompanied by the robot's foreboding inaction. Something terrible was happening inside that robot's thick metal skull—something she dreaded from the moment she laid eyes on him in that junkyard.

Beetro was thinking. Beetro was calculating.

As she continued to lock her pleading gaze on him, she had arrived at a bitter conclusion. She had unwittingly taught Beetro an important lesson—don't be fooled twice. The bright hope of seeing that robot's eyes moving over her predicament was dashed as he disappeared from the rock ledge. Briefly, she thought he retreated only to regroup—that he was hatching a scheme at that very minute, and Ribcage would emerge from thin air to unleash her trademarked chaos on the Reticuli.

But nothing happened.

Beetro never returned.

"Do you know who the Kish are?" Miree asked as if bringing up a new topic in casual conversation. Although, casual is not exactly how she felt. She was exhausted, cold, and hungry. Each stone and groove in the granite ground was a fresh and painful challenge. The white-hot fire shards controlled by Ria's Swordless Hilt surrounded Miree in a mobile and facile net. The shards floated along their captive, encasing Miree in an impregnable grid of the fiery metal. The shards moved at the command of the hilt that Ria clutched in her hydraulic fingers. Miree quickly learned they didn't stop when Miree stopped, only when the *hilt* stopped. It was an effective, wordless, and elegant way to get a prisoner to move with you without saying a word. Miree couldn't help but be impressed by the economy of the device to transport a prisoner.

Ria and Xy walked with their backs to Miree, mostly ignoring her as if she were cattle that couldn't possibly understand their higher level, Reticulum-speak. From time to time, they'd turn and offer a glare from within their hoods, their glowing eyes telescoping over their prisoner, checking for mischief.

Her arm hurt. Or her *lack* of arm hurt.

A dribble of blood dropped occasionally along the ground at fresh cracks around the cauterized wound. Miree had wrapped a piece of her cloak around the stump for some reason—it seemed like a good idea to not expose fresh flesh for the vultures until she actually died. Pins and needles shot down her arm as if it was still there—a phantom appendage transmitting utterly useless impulses to her brain. She had already processed the shock and anger over the loss of the arm. It happened. There was nothing to do about it now. She could learn to shoot with her left hand.

Easy.

Everything was fine. Totally, totally fine.

She was also still processing her revenge, however, wondering how she was going to kill the two Reticulum cult members that were strolling ahead of her, winding through the slot tunnels. Usually, she took no pleasure at the thought of having to kill someone, but these two? They weren't going to die quickly... they would suffer just as she was—slowly starving—dimpled pits at her temple from severe dehydration. It wasn't that they just took her arm, they didn't know how to care for a prisoner and Miree was taking mental notes on every act of depravity dropped onto her.

Beetro was another factor altogether when considering her revenge. He had seen her, caged like an animal, and he knew she saw him. And then he just left her. She was strangely proud of the robot for finally growing a brain and starting to look out for himself. In the end, she couldn't blame him for leaving her—she'd done the same to him and would have done it again. But it didn't stop her from being royally pissed at the little robotic asshole.

"I said, have you ever heard of the Kish?" Miree yelled at them. They continued speaking amongst themselves.

Miree glanced up at the granite walls that shot straight up beside them, framing the slot canyons against the sky. There was little vegetation. Patches of lonely moss and small plants managed to find purchase on spots of soil along the walls. Anemic trees and berry bushes were scattered throughout the narrow canyon. Ria steered clear of the heavier trees, preventing the hot shards forming the cage around Miree from burning through the trees or rock wall. Every so often, one of the shards would encounter a tree leaf, instantly singeing it to wilted gum.

Miree studied the cage of fire shards around her. They were spaced evenly, creating a gridwork of about five centimeters, just enough for a few fingers to fit through. Potentially useful. She picked up two granite stones and slapped them together while coughing to cover the sound. She managed to bang out a granite slab with somewhat of a sharp edge. She already had half of an escape plan figured out. This was going to be easy.

"They're in Orion," Miree said as if picking up a stalled conversation. "The Kish. No one actually talks about the Kish, but everyone knows that they're there. They're everywhere, with agents in every corner of the city. Whenever a shopkeeper suddenly vanishes or a textile company exports to the wrong ports and is found washed along the Chronicle Sea, everyone knows it's the Kish. Out here, you got the fief lords running things. But in Orion, we've got the Kish. Oh, the merchant guild tries to keep them at bay with their mercenary stooges, the BlackGrips. It is barely enough to keep the Kish from taking over completely."

Ria and Xy completely ignored her.

Miree continued, "The Kish are in the shadows, threatening, buying, selling, or just killing whoever it is that gets in their way. Basically, if you mess with the Kish, you won't be bragging about it for long."

"Quiet," Ria finally said without turning.

"I bet you don't know how someone gets into the Kish, do you?" Miree paused for effect. "They torture you. They torture you just to *join* them. See these scars on my arms—well, on my *remaining* arm?" She lifted her left arm to the sky, bearing the lacy network of thin scars, layered over one another suggestive of repeated injury. The scar tissue glistened in the sunlight. "Haldunt the Wire's handy work."

Ria turned and looked at Miree, her glowing eyes telescoping over her arm. She turned away and kept walking. Xy looked over at Ria, concern on his face.

"So, you've heard of him? He's a mean bastard, Haldunt. Called the Wire because—wait for it—he uses wires to kill and torture people. He's got all sorts of wires... thin, thick, studded with razors, or poisoned tips. The man made an art form of killing people—anyone he wants—with wires. He likes to torture initiates on their hands and arms. I don't know, must be because he wants a permanent reminder of what will happen to them if you betray the Kish. Why do you think they torture those who join?"

Xy looked at Ria again, growing increasingly alarmed. "Is what she is saying true?" he asked.

"Quiet," Ria said to both Xy and Miree.

"Conditioning," Miree answered her own question. "They torture you so that if you're actually caught and tortured by an enemy, you won't spill those sweet beans because you already know all about the torture game. It's no big deal for the Kish."

"Shut your mouth," Ria hissed.

"If you want me to shut up, you'll feed me," Miree shot back. "And I can't be your cyborg slave if I'm dead."

Ria stopped and turned toward the shard cage. She produced the Swordless Hilt from within her cloak and twisted the pommel, prompting the fire shards to instantly flee from Miree and coalesce, interlocking together and forming a solid blade at the once empty hilt.

"Neat trick," Miree said.

"Piss, shit, drink," Ria said, throwing a leather flagon at her feet. Miree drained the entire thing. Ria then threw her a slab of some sort of smoked meat. Miree chewed the meat vigorously, savoring the salt and fats. It was incredibly delicious but only made her gastric juices bubble, inducing monstrous hunger pangs. Miree then relieved herself in front of them like an animal, relishing the opportunity to demonstrate her absolute indifference to the two of them.

Ria flipped the pommel of her shard sword and flicked the hilt down, prompting the shards to break away as a single blade and surround Miree once again. The air smoldered around her from the white-hot shards.

With new hydration and fats flowing through her, Miree felt *good*. Losing the arm was nothing—a scratch at this point. It would make a great story when she made it to the first tavern after she killed the two freaks. 'They took my arm,' she imagined recounting to a rapt audience, ale mugs in their hands. 'So, I took both of theirs!' Or something like that, she still wasn't sure now what the picture of her revenge would look like. It would certainly involve removing a body part while they were alive.

Yet, Miree was repulsed at the thought. She was no sadist. She didn't actually *enjoy* hurting people, even if they were disciples of the Reticulum, who were parading her off to slave cyborg camp or wherever it was. Escaping and eliminating them would be enough and it would be smart. She just needed to get out of the Meteor Mountains without incurring more wrath from the Reticulum after escaping and killing the two clowns holding her captive.

They traveled north through the canyons for another hour while Miree observed them. Ria did most of the speaking and it was always in an instructional tone to Xy. He was clearly the apprentice, although a considerably older man. Miree had only actually met very few Reticuli—few do. Their members were known to roam Helian, and the regions of Halax and Belfed to the north. They were a known nuisance and danger to any civilized town or citadel for hundreds of miles. Reticuli did not venture into towns as they would be immediately put to death. Their headquarters were a closely kept secret from the civilized world, ostensibly so that they would never be conquered. Much to Miree's dismay, she had no idea where they were actually taking her.

No one had any idea how the Reticulum had ever been founded. There was no public leader or lord—no armies of any kind. They only went forth into the world in pairs, seeking to "recruit" members into the network. They were an exotic, dangerous people who were becoming increasingly effective at making people disappear into their ranks. One of these days, some lord from one of the regions west of Orion would have to root them out and take care of the Reticulum. Miree realized a fantastic candidate for just such a job—General Deluvius. Although, his recent coup of Helian and subsequent displacement of many people was probably making recruitment that much easier for the Reticulum.

Miree shook these thoughts, focusing on the shard cage that floated with her every step. Ria had increased their pace as the sunlight dwindled, making Miree's feet throb with a dull ache. Every step was torture. Her feet had become a blistering mess now that they'd been soaking in soggy stockings for a good forty-eight hours without a chance to dry. She had to get away from these two in the least to save her feet.

Miree felt the granite wedge tucked into her waistline beneath her cloak, thinking. A large dead tree, the biggest she'd seen in the canyons, lay just ahead. Ria and Xy were deep in some conversation. As they passed the tree, Miree reached her hand out between the hot shards and grabbed a tree branch. She brought the branch into the shard cage where it was excised from the tree as the shards moved through the wood. She then brought the tree branch within her cloak, completely obscuring it.

Ria glanced back at the rustling noise.

"Oh. Do you want to hear more about the Kish?" Miree asked.

Ria looked away, continuing forward.

"Do you know how many people have betrayed the Kish and survived?"

No response.

"Only one," Miree said.

Ria feigned amusement by concealing a small, condescending laugh.

"And you've managed to kidnap her," Miree said. "Congratulations." She had put the tree branch down her trousers, cinching it tight at the waist and was quickly working the granite slab over the end of the branch. It was difficult work with one hand, but she managed to shave off a few splinters on one side, producing some sort of edge.

"Not only did I escape from the Kish, but I stole from them, too. Have you heard of a Quantizer?" At this, Ria slowed her gait, almost imperceptibly, but long enough for Miree to notice. "Ah, so you have. When I was a member of the Kish, I stole it from some astrocyst in Orion. Name was Fallaro. Once we stole it from him, I stole it from the Kish." Miree remembered the look on Haldunt's face when she finally thrust a dagger into the bastard's gut. The shock and almost pleased surprise at his young initiate's actions were priceless to behold. "Do you think I'll have trouble escaping from two Reticula?" Miree asked with feigned earnestness. "Getting away from the Kish was a challenge but I'm not sure if I'm up for the likes of Ria the Asshole and Xy the Half-Wit."

Xy whipped his head around, his hood flapping in the wind. "You shut your mouth, girl!"

"Xy," Ria said, putting her hand on his shoulder. "She is trying to manipulate you. To arouse your passions. And it is working."

Xy flinched and then nodded, turning back toward the canyon path ahead.

The three traveled in silence for a time, exhaustion and hunger raging inside Miree. She'd whittled the tree branch to a point, slightly dull but sharp enough to drive through a person with enough applied force. Happy with her escape plan, she decided to proceed.

"Did I mention that I also robbed Peles Castle?"

Ria and Xy did not respond.

"Just two or three days ago now. Using the Quantizer, I got into the central vault spire. You know what they keep there, right?"

Ria turned, a smirk painted on her face. "A dark matter flake?"

"That's right. Well, it's not there anymore. I took it and escaped from the castle, right under Deluvius' nose. You know about the new lord of Helian, right?" Miree knew mixing in a little lie with truth was always the best way to fabricate. That way, you only had to keep track of a small little incontinuity in the story.

Ria turned. "You mean to tell me you stole the dark matter flake from the castle and hid it somewhere in Meteor Mountains before we captured you?"

"Now you get it. I hope you two don't represent the Reticulum's finest."

Ria examined Miree for a moment, a smile twisting up her face behind a curl of wires weaving through her cheek. "Mixing lies with truth is risky."

"Well, I'm a risky girl. Do you think the new General is happy about the dark matter missing?"

Ria waited. "There is no dark matter flake at Peles Castle. Never has been. It's a lie to maintain the illusion of power."

Damn. Ria was astute. Miree decided to go all in. "I don't know where you've been getting your information, but the castle has a dark matter flake. *Did.* Not anymore. I escaped with it. Now Deluvius is after me."

Ria furrowed her only eyebrow over a telescoping eye. "So, your reputation is such that it has garnered the attention of one of the most powerful despots in recent history?"

"So, you do know about Deluvius? Good, I was worried you'd been living under that freak rock in the mountains for too long."

"Deluvius has been a blessing to the Reticulum. Social disruption helps our recruitment efforts. We've received many refugees lately. Our network is growing."

"Refugees? That's what you call people you turn into freak cyborgs?"

"Enough, our journey is not even half over," Ria snapped, whipping away from the shard cage and tugging on the Swordless Hilt. Miree jumped, fearing the shards would shred her from behind.

Miree then let the granite slab slip from her hand, a small echo rippling up the slot canyon. Ria stopped, turned, and zoomed her eyes on the rock slab at Miree's feet. Carefully, Miree flashed a hiccup of fear across her face and then set her jaw.

"Fashioning a weapon?" Ria asked.

Miree glanced at the granite slab and met Ria's gaze, feigning as if she had just been caught. "It was already there, I just accidentally kicked it." *Come on. Come on over and punish me.*

"I see." Ria walked back to the shard cage, her arms and hands inside her cloak. With the front of the cloak covering her torso, glowing eyes were the only exposed part of her body creating an eerie sight. "Xy, this one here is a good example for you."

Xy sidled along Ria, watching Miree through the fire shards.

"When they're insubordinate like this, you can reason with them—speak with them and make them feel like a validated victim."

Xy nodded. "I see."

"But when they get to this point," she said, motioning to Miree as if she was an animal in a cage. "Measures must be escalated."

Miree clenched the sharpened branch in her hand, holding it at her side beneath her cloak. *Just do it already.*

Ria pulled out the Swordless Hilt and flicked her wrist, collecting the fire shards together as a sword. Xy raised his hand, pointing a boltgun at Miree while Ria sheathed the shard sword.

Miree steeled herself, gripping the branch tight. She'd never attacked someone with one arm before but now was as good a time as any to try. Yes, Xy might blast her away with electricity as she lunged forward, but that was a better fate than ending up wherever they were taking her.

Ria removed a new device from within her cloak—a handle attached to a two-pronged barrel. The prongs were spaced five centimeters across. "Unfortunately, you have to get a little close with this," Ria explained to Xy.

Miree backed up, putting on a cowering show. *Yes, a little closer.*

"It makes later implants a little more difficult."

One... Miree stooped lower, ready to lunge forward with the sharpened tree branch.

"But sometimes a little upfront castigation provides enormous fidelity once they've been implanted. It was the same thing back when I captured you, Xy. You were stubborn as a mule but look at you now. Loyal as a lap dog."

Ria lifted the two-pronged gun a few feet from Miree's face.

Two...

"Sometimes it requires a moment to warm up."

Three!

Miree flipped open her cloak and struck with the sharpened branch, landing a glancing blow onto...

Nothing. Latent fatigue had sapped every ounce of strength. Miree toppled forward onto the granite rock and looked up.

Ria stood above her; teeth bared in sick delight.

And then Miree felt her eyes burst with painful energy like two giant icicles had plunged into her eye sockets, digging into the optic nerve and making for brain tissue. The cold turned to searing heat. For a moment, it only *felt* like her eyeballs were boiling out of their sockets. But when she smelled the unmistakable scent of charred tissue, she knew it was *actually* happening. Hot vitreous rolled down her cheeks as her entire body shook from a pain from which Haldunt the Wire himself would have begged for mercy. Nothing before had mattered in her life except this one moment of unimaginable torture. Empires rose and fell while the pain drilled into her sockets—a moment of eternal suffering.

And then it stopped.

Miree looked up but the sky had turned off. Nothing but darkness.

Ria's voice issued somewhere from the pitch. "Never caught an Orion bitch that I didn't have to blind."

TWENTY-TWO

RIBCAGE AWOKE, surprised that she hadn't died.

The last thing she really remembered was clutching the underbelly of a horse, wind and lightning whipping around her while bloatflies grasped at her ankles with their gnarly little bug arms. It was a weird thing but not the weirdest thing that had happened to her.

She was hungry, and this made her think of Crow, a major source of food. The old drunk always sat on broken chicken crates, a glass of amber liquor quivering in his grasp. Did he ever wonder where the brandy came from? Or did he grow accustomed to the magical fact that the glass was filled up every day? Stealing brandy was easy for Ribcage—easier than getting food. She'd found a small cellar door, once grown over with moss and roots that led directly to a tavern basement. There were barrels of the nasty stuff. Shrewdly, she knew that if she took an entire barrel, the tavern owners would notice, search the basement, and seal the small cellar door. Instead, Ribcage would sneak in once a day, fill up exactly one glass, and stick it in Crow's gnarled hand. Crow, of course, would then gulp the poison down, staving off full consciousness and assuming his role as the pathetic town drunk. Amongst a host of other pathetic town drunks, his role was not a unique one.

Ribcage would then spy on Luci, scavenging at the junkyard, watch her trade at the markets for flour, make the bread at the communal ovens, and then—she'd wait for her to come across Crow. Most of the time, Luci placed a biscuit on Crow's knee and walked away, assuming the man would find it once awake. Only, Ribcage would swoop down and take it for herself. Now she *did* leave a little on Crow's knee. After all, this symbiotic grift wouldn't work if the old man died of starvation. This Crow biscuit bonus, in conjunction with the biscuit that Luci would also give Ribcage every day, equaled enough sustenance for the day. It was particularly important on days when Ribcage received zero handouts from anyone else, something that happened remarkably often.

Upon awakening in a slot canyon in Meteor Mountains, she really wished she could go visit Crow and get that biscuit. In other words, she was starving. She wasn't just hungry, she was literally starving as evidenced by the swirling in her head and a funny sway to her body when she took a step. After a brief episode of unconsciousness, she found herself on the ground again, absolutely shivering beneath the dimming, evening light.

Where the hell was she anyway? Then she remembered... things were different. Luci was gone and now she'd hitched her wagon to the blue robot.

"Robot?" She was so weak, her hearing dwindled—she wasn't even sure that the word had left her lips. "I mean... Beetro?" She vaguely remembered the robot shouting at her to drink. And drinking sounded good at that moment. She rolled over the rough granite rock and took a draw from a muddy puddle. She was pretty sure she'd already drank from it before so if it was poisoned, it didn't matter now. After a brief wave of nausea, she did manage to get to her feet and stay there. "Beetro?"

"Here," a quiet voice answered from above.

Ribcage squinted in the early dawn light. Towering columns of granite rock surrounded her. "Where are you?"

The top of his metal head crested the granite ridge. "Right here." His eyes glowed with indigo light.

"What're you doing up there?"

He hesitated. "Searching."

"For what?"

"Can you Jump?"

Ribcage thought about it for a moment. She hadn't tried to Jump since she'd awoken, so she closed her eyes and tried to push inside herself, a kind of inversion of the world into the flat plane where she could instantaneously Jump. But she felt nothing. "Can't. Too far from my mom. Why?"

"It might..." he trailed off as he scaled down the rock face. "Might prove useful. The Reticuli are in the area."

"You saw them?"

He nodded. "They're fairly close. Better keep our voices down."

"What're they doing?"

"They're—" he hesitated. "Just traveling—I don't know. And I don't want to find out. Are you okay?"

She lay flat, overcome with fatigue. "No."

"You need food now?"

"Humans need food. I like to eat like, pretty much every day."

"Plants okay?" he asked, gesturing to a tiny tree that had at one time taken root in a cleft in the rock. It had long since died.

"No. I can't eat a dead tree. Berries would work. But I need bread or milk. Meat. Why don't you know this stuff?"

"I've never... I've never had to feed a human before. It's not part of my existing programming. Are you going to die?"

Ribcage closed her eyes for a moment. "When I'm so... tired... it's hard..."

Beetro knelt beside her as she went unconscious, her breathing becoming sporadic and shallow. "Hey." He nudged her.

"So tired."

Beetro glanced around their camp, which consisted of a few puddles of water and some dead trees. Clearly, the Reticulum had managed to catch some game, but Beetro had absolutely no idea how to hunt. Some things, like measuring tiny fractions of distances and calculating his exact energy expenditure down to the joule, were second nature. Other things like hunting and providing for a starving human child were completely foreign. Whatever it was Galiaro had designed him for, it wasn't taking care of tiny street children.

Ribcage was clearly a valuable asset to have around—the girl's Jumping ability had proven critical. So, it was worth expending effort to save her. Lately, he rather enjoyed employing the brutal logic of survival. Miree was a liability to his survival, she only used him for naked self-interest. It was, therefore, not beneficial for him to save her from the Reticulum. Done. Previously under Lucindi's influence, he would've helped Ribcage only because he *liked* her. In a way, he was grateful for Miree's zero-sum tutelage of considering only the bottom line—does this person help me survive? For Ribcage, it was a solid yes. For Miree, it was a resounding no. So, no, he didn't have to feel bad about leaving Miree enslaved with the Reticulum. That was just the calculus of survival.

So, he went about looking around the camp for berry plants

but discovered nothing of the sort. He even went up and down the canyons for a bit, searching but finding only rotted plants among patchy lichen. It was a barren trail. When he returned to Ribcage, he realized the answer lay in front of them the entire time.

Bellamare.

The horse had been lying against the canyon wall, its legs sprawled awkwardly beneath its belly. For a moment, he thought the beast had died but discovered shallow breathing movements along its emaciated ribcage. Bellamare was meat. Ribcage could eat the meat.

This was easy.

He would just wait for the horse to die. But how long would it take? He wasn't sure if the horse was close to death or would live for several days—maybe even weeks. Ribcage, a clearly defined asset to his journey, would not survive in time for the horse to die on its own. Bellamare, a starving horse that could now barely move, could no longer provide Beetro with any substantial assistance in his journey and was, therefore, expendable as a resource. So, he'd have to simply kill the horse.

Easy.

The decision to aid others was just a math equation—does the sum of resource and energy allocation to provide assistance result in an equal or greater output for Beetro? He was starting to understand why Miree lived this way—it took the guesswork out of everything and eliminated risk and vulnerability. Of course, things didn't turn out so great for Miree, but this was no longer Beetro's problem.

He'd need a weapon or something for butchery for the horse. Another cursory look around the trail revealed nothing that could possibly end a horse's life. There was, however, a boulder. He estimated its weight based on size and his prior knowledge of the average density of granite rock. It wouldn't be too large for him to heft. He glanced back at Bellamare, hoping the beast had already died, but it continued breathing and even looked up at him underneath his long eyelashes.

"Watch out," he said, moving Ribcage out of the way. The girl barely grimaced at the movement. Beetro knelt and grasped the boulder, digging his magnetic grip into the rock, shaving away shallow grooves. He lifted the boulder and waddled over to Bellamare. Despite its starved state, the horse was still a meaty animal—thick with sinew and tendons. It wouldn't die easily. Rather than just dropping the boulder on the horse, he'd have to throw it to get extra force to get the job done. So, he backed away, calculated the arc, and lifted the boulder above his body—it teetered enormous above the robot.

But he stopped, looking at the horse's baleful gaze. Beetro realized he'd never killed anything before—at least not that he could remember. Who knows what kind of robot he was before his memory was erased... before he'd awoken in the trash piles of Korthe. Was he a murderer? Did he care about robot or human life? Maybe he was like that jester bot, Besidio, an entertainer beholden to the wiles of powerful men. Would it have bothered him to kill this horse now? Or would this have been just another day for Beetro the Horse Butcherer?

He hated that he was standing there, a boulder above his head, suddenly having an existential crisis for a horse. It was—after all—just a horse. He'd seen them tied up, whipped, and starved all over the streets of Korthe. It was just a dumb animal. Not only that, but it was also a dumb *starving* animal that was going to die a painful death if he didn't end it. So, why was he having trouble ending the beast's life? He felt monstrously stupid and naive, looking down at Bellamare. Miree wouldn't have thought twice about killing the horse. She certainly didn't think twice about leaving him to die back at Peles Castle.

And so, he threw the boulder. It landed squarely on Bellamare's head in a sickening crunch and then rolled off. Only, it didn't end the horse, who sputtered a hysterical whinny in between labored, bloody gasps for air. Beetro stood, aghast, as the horse flailed its front legs while trying to dig into the ground with its back hooves. He had to act—*he had to do something!* The horse was suffering right at his feet and Beetro felt completely helpless to do anything to help.

"I'm sorry—" he said, cutting off an apology to a dying animal that couldn't understand him. Frantic, he scanned the area, trying desperately to find something to put the animal out of its misery. Every gurgling sound filled the robot with waves of deep guilt. What had he done to the poor thing? He grabbed ahold of the boulder once more but wasn't certain it would kill Bellamare—it might just injure the horse once more. Kneeling beside the animal, he clung to the horse's neck, looking into those glassy, brown eyes as they seemed to plead for help. "I'm sorry, Bellamare." He wished so badly he could do something to finally let the horse pass.

But wait. He could. He'd literally wielded a lightning storm and fought off an entire bloatstorm.

Beetro stood, found a shaft of sunlight cresting through the ridge of the mountain pass column, and opened himself to the light. For a moment, his thermal sensors read the expected change in energy. But when he concentrated on the light, he finally *understood* the energy. It was cosmic radiation, created millions of miles away, soaring through space as a wave yet tied together as packets of discrete energy. The photons showered over his blue shell, rippling over his body and charging his entire being with humming energy. He opened his indigo eyes, stretched his hands toward Bellamare, and released.

And then the horse exploded.

Equine fragments rained through the air, splattering the white granite with shredded flesh. Beetro stood, both flummoxed at what he'd just done and, at the same time, proud that he'd done it. Yet, as he cleared the blood from his vision, he could still imagine the horse's eyes, pleading with him just moments before.

"I'm—"

But he imagined Miree's voice in the back of his mind—*Don't apologize, robot.*

After a day and a night of recuperating and little talk, Ribcage was suddenly feeling her old self again. She remarked on feeling the nutrients of horse meat flooding her body, awakening the parts of her brain that were trying to get her to lay down and die.

"So, what exactly happened to the horse?"

"Nothing," Beetro said, staring up at the morning sky.

"You exploded it."

"What do you mean?"

She gave him a sidelong look and gestured to the red-painted granite walls. "There's horse everywhere. Did you explode it?"

"Do you always ask so many questions?"

"Not nearly as many as you do."

"Oh." He recalled how irritating he must've been to Lucindi and Miree after his hard reboot.

"Was it that trick you did to the bloatflies? Brought down lightning right on top of them. How'd you do that?"

"I don't know."

"What are you?"

"I don't know."

"Do it again." Ribcage jumped up and down. "Come on. Let's see it."

"Good to see that you have enough energy to annoy me now.

Enough to hike today?" He shuddered a moment, realizing that Miree had now imprinted into his personality. He pushed that away for later consideration and mountains of anxiety to process.

She stopped jumping. "Yeah, let's get out of this hole."

Beetro unceremoniously started moving, happy that she didn't realize the change in subject. Ribcage quickly wrapped her scarf around her body and collected the rest of the cooked meat into a tiny knapsack kept at her hip.

As they passed through the narrow slot canyons, Beetro tracked his position along the planet's magnetic field lines and compared it to the map that Besidio had uploaded. He could track his coordinates along the precise route through the canyons where the map indicated. They were only hours from the ridge of Crater Valley.

"You should practice," Ribcage suggested, her little voice echoing along the canyon walls.

"Practice?"

"Your powers."

"I don't have any powers."

"Don't be dumb. We both know you have powers. You can control light." She added this so pointedly that Beetro wondered if the girl had seen it before in others.

"Have you known other people that can do it?"

"Move light like that? No. But look at me. I've got powers, too."

"That you do."

"Think of what we can do in Orion. Me and you. I can Jump and you can zap people with lasers."

"I thought you couldn't Jump so far away from your mom."

Ribcage shrugged. "You never know. Might find another mom out there."

"What?"

"Yeah, a mom. Mom is a hole. Like a sucking hole."

"What are you talking about?"

"But she doesn't suck things up like a windstorm. It's like a hole that sucks and spits things in different spaces."

Different spaces. Something about that was making sense. After all, when Ribcage had Beetro Jump with her, he felt like a stretched-out, two-dimensional noodle. She'd probably taken him to a lower dimension. "You Jump to a different dimension?"

"Is that what it's called?"

"Yes. How do you do it?"

"I don't know. Something I could always do. No one else could do it back where I'm from."

"Korthe?"

"I was from somewhere else before I came to Korthe."

"The arcs?"

"Umm. No."

"Then where?"

"The arcs are like a door. I came through the two arcs from home and my mom."

"Can you go back?"

"No. The door doesn't work. That's what I'm trying to say. I was sucked out the hole of the door."

"And what was it like in the world where you're from?"

"I can't—"

"What?" he turned. Ribcage had grown silent. A sadness had set in her face. "I'm... sorry."

"I just can't remember everything. It's fuzzy."

Beetro nodded. "I think me and you *do* have a lot in common after all."

They arrived at the bottom of a steep hill, littered with thousands of granite shards. Beetro noticed a cloth sack as they approached, white and crimson.

“Someone dropped something,” Ribcage said, scampering ahead.

As they got closer, Beetro put his hand on her shoulder. “Wait.” He walked ahead and kicked the cloth sack, which spilled out a severed arm. Ribcage looked up at him, nostrils flared.

Beetro walked past the severed arm. “It’s nothing. Keep moving.”

TWENTY-THREE

MIREE KNEW the Reticulum had taken her underground. She felt the dankness on her skin—a shivering chill that pricked her arm hairs. The air was stale and tasted of mildew and dust. She felt the repeated grooves created by drilling instrumentation along the granite surface. The rock walls had a raw, unrefined quality on her fingertips. Sounds of shuffling feet and clandestine gears working away in the distance echoed along what sounded like a long and intricate tunnel system. The lighting was...

Dark, maybe.

But everything was dark.

Because her eyes had been boiled from their sockets.

Miree's mind had sunk into an abyss of misery. She longed to not feel anything ever again. Flashes of Haldunt's smile flitted across her mind. She knew his torture was just theatrics now—a wicked man's entertainment. Miree had not learned torture until Ria of the Reticulum blinded her and made her walk for miles within a floating cage of fiery shards. Her body was littered with burns where the cage bumped into her when she wasn't moving fast enough. Open wounds on her back oozed with pus and recurrent bleeding. Throughout the journey, her arm stump throbbed with inflammation and infection. A dull, intermittent fever and headache were the accompaniment to the entire orchestra of suffering that she'd endured for the prior five days. This was all before she was even *brought* to the Reticulum. Things could only get worse now that she'd arrived at cyborg freak HQ.

Beneath the exquisite suffering, a question was burrowing up from her subconscious. It was a question she'd rather avoid. A question bursting at the seams of denial, sewed shut from years of rationalizations and scarred over with self-loathing. A question that was almost more painful to consider than her current circumstances. Feeling the cold flagstone of the Reticulum tunnels on her bare feet, she let the question pop in her mind—*do I deserve this?* This was quickly followed by another brutal question: *could I have avoided this if I was... better?*

She was led to what felt like the end of a tunnel system and a vast space judging by the large draughts of air teasing through her hair.

"Place of capture?" a monotonous voice issued from somewhere.

"I—" Miree started but was cut off.

"Meteor Mountains," Ria said from behind, tugging on the shackles that bound Miree's wrist.

"Gender and approximate age?"

"I suppose she's female. Possibly in the second quarter of a first life cycle."

"Behavior rating?"

"Xy. What would your rating be?" Ria asked.

"She was trouble," Xy said. "Much more than I was before assimilation."

"You were a puppy dog compared to this one."

"I'd give her a double psi. I imagine they can be worse but not by much," Xy decided.

"Excellent job, Xy. That's exactly what I'd rate her."

"How many double psi's have you brought back, Ria?" asked the Reticulum clerk or evil accountant or whoever it was, his tone accusatory.

"And how many have you brought in at all, Bothar?" Ria asked curtly.

"Latch her up for assimilation," Bothar said, unamused.

Miree's arm was briskly raised above her head. She felt the shackle lock into something, which then dragged her forward.

"Goodbye, sweet one," she heard Ria's voice call out from behind. "Have fun, my dear..."

There was silence for a while. Miree was forced to walk where the shackle led, giving an unyielding bite in the skin if she slowed for even a moment. As she moved, she realized she had no final words for Ria—no *fuck you forever*, or anything. She didn't have a single shred of defiance left as her feet shuffled numbly down what was very likely an assembly line.

A chilling draught swept along her naked skin as she continued the shuffle. Several pricks were placed along her arms, blood draws likely. She felt a lump or something in her throat. It took her a moment to realize that the lump was the urge to cry. *Crying?* She could not remember the last time she'd ever cried. Definitely not back in Orion with the Kish. It was likely when she was a child, back before she fled the Fifth Kingdom for good. What had happened in her life since then?

"Nothing," she said aloud.

She'd left the Fifth Kingdom, became a criminal in Orion, and failed in any sort of high-stakes espionage thereafter. And now she was going to become a cyborg.

A fitting end.

She heard what sounded like saws and screams around her and figured that would probably be next for her as well. A couple of saws to the bones, some electric wires clamped to her nipples, and a Reticulum branding on her hide for good measure. Of all the situations she'd gotten herself into over the years, she'd been able to think or fight her way out. Not this time. She had no defiance in reserve left to deny what she had become—cattle. A jarring vibration at the back of her skull shook her from her morose reverie.

It was a fucking drill.

A dull ache set in after her neck muscles had been shredded by the drill. It bore deep, she even felt a *pop* as the drill had cleared the skull and gained entry into the cranium. Warm blood oozed down the nape of her neck and trailed down her back. The sensation reached a new level of exquisite pain that she'd yet to experience. Fortunately, she had mostly lost consciousness. Every now and then, she was awoken by streamers in her vision—sparks of silver and gold flitting across her sight. The visuals were accompanied by a series of electrical shocks at the back of her brain.

As she slumped down into a coma of immeasurable suffering, Beetro suddenly popped into her mind. She tried to ignore him—his indigo eyes dilating—when she left him at Peles Castle. The poor robot thought he could trust her. It was probably the first time he had experienced betrayal in his memory. And then he wasn't slow to return the favor, leaving her in the hands of the Reticulum. His indigo eyes shone above the canyon ridge, constricting with justification. And then he was gone. Just as she'd done. She wasn't mad anymore at him for leaving her. Instead, she felt something new—well, something dormant at least.

Guilt.

When she woke up, she saw bright lights all around her—wait. She was... *seeing*? Did she finally die?

"Hello?" She looked down but saw nothing but brightness. Not even her body was there. However, she knew she wasn't dead because she felt her body, and more specifically, the various points of searing pain. The back of her head throbbed, although her arm stump was feeling a little better. An enormous face materialized before her, emanating from the rippling white light. It was vaguely feminine.

"Petulance," the face said. The voice was angry—impatient.

"I—"

"You have been disobedient. I do not tolerate disobedience."

"Who—"

"Punishment."

"I—"

"I am *She*. I am the Network of the Lost. The Hide of Earth. The Singularity. I am Reticulum. I am reforging the network. Connecting to what was lost. The Hide will heal once more. You will become the Reticulum."

Miree only sighed in resignation.

"I demand information."

"What kind?"

"All."

"I don't have anything to say to you." Something knocked Miree in the stomach. Somehow disembodied, she felt herself slump down, her knees banging into a hard ground.

"Information on Deluvius."

"Pow—" Miree answered, regaining her breath. "Powerful. He

has many soldiers who have powerful weapons. Alchean weaponry."

"Where?"

"Last I saw him was at Peles Castle. Helian."

"You interacted with Deluvius?"

"Yes."

"You are a soldier?"

"No. Not a soldier. I'm a—*was* a... thief. Nothing more."

"What did you steal?"

"Nothing. I couldn't steal anything. I tried but there wasn't anything to steal from him."

"I am told you stole dark matter. Where is the dark matter?"

"I lied. I tried... it wasn't there. Doesn't exist."

"Truth. How did you escape alive?" The face didn't ask questions with inflection. All questions were in the form of a demand.

"I—a robot."

"Information on the robot."

"From Korthe. He helped me escape."

"How?"

"I-I don't know. He twisted light—a laser discharge. Somehow. I don't—"

"Explain."

"He stopped—he bent the laser light and prevented it from hitting me. That's the only way to explain it."

"How?"

"I don't know." She cringed, ready for another blow but it didn't come.

"Where is the robot?"

"I last saw him in the Meteor Mountains. Maybe a week ago."

"He is a powerful machine."

"I-I guess so. I don't know anything about him."

"Describe." The Reticulum's face was static, inscrutable.

"He's shorter. Comes up to my chin. Blue metal shell. Glowing blue eyes. He had a hard reboot. Doesn't remember anything."

"What is his directive?"

"I don't know. He's self-aware. No, no, wait. He only had a little code written for a directive. It was to find Galiaro."

"Galiaro? You are certain?"

"Yes. The bot wouldn't shut up about it."

"Did Galiaro find the robot?"

"No. I don't think so." Again, no blow to the stomach. Perhaps they had physiological monitoring to know if she was lying.

"Satisfactory. Punishment will be reduced."

The Reticulum's face disappeared along with the bright light. Darkness took over her sight once again. Gingerly, she touched her eye sockets and felt the crusted-over holes where her eyes once were. The Reticulum must've created an uplink directly to her visual cortex. She was otherwise still very much blind.

The first thing she noticed in her prison cell was the overwhelming stench of layered urine stinging her throat. Blind and crawling on her knees, she moved away from the smell as far as she could and curled up along a stone wall. She was clothed in fresh linens and had what she believed to be her purple cloak tied around her neck. She undid the clasp and stuffed it under her head for sleep.

The shock of actually being captured and imprisoned by the Reticulum finally set in as her thoughts wandered. Normally, she had no time for regrets—no use for them. But as she lay in the piss-ridden cell, her mind flooded thick with remorse. If she'd tried saving Beetro and the street rat girl, she probably wouldn't be in this situation. If she hadn't been hasty after Lucindi's death and rushed to the castle, things would've been different. If she hadn't stolen the Quantizer from that astrocyst back in Orion and then subsequently stolen it from the Kish, she certainly wouldn't be in the current mess. She connected dozens of dots of remorse all leading to her imprisonment and eventual enslavement of a cyborg race. Certainly, none of this would've happened if she hadn't left home all those years ago. But she couldn't have been blamed for that decision, could she?

She did try crying but her tear ducts had been singed shut with the burning of her eyes. But she quickly discovered she could sob without tears. And so, she did. She let out long wails, face down, into her cloak. After a few hours of that, she sat up and realized it had been some time since she'd eaten.

Only, she wasn't hungry.

With her remaining left hand, she felt along her right stump. It felt *better*. The flesh was less inflamed and considerably less painful. She rubbed her left forearm along the wall and felt it snag along several lines of tubing that had been placed in veins. She felt a boxy cartridge that had been mounted along her right shoulder with a series of tubes that led to her veins. Intravenous feeds. Fluids and nutrients were likely continuously flowing through her veins, feeding her body. She figured there were probably antibiotics in the fluid too, healing her stump. At least the Reticulum took care of their investments.

She stood, sliding her hand along the wall, and moved, mapping out the cell. It was circular, without corners or seams. No windows, no bars, no compartments built into the walls. She slid her hand along the floor, feeling for doors or hinges. Nothing. The cell appeared completely sealed. No vulnerable spot for escape. As she moved, the smell of urine became overwhelming.

Then she felt a foot.

She shook it, reassuring herself that it wasn't severed and was satisfied when it shook with the anchoring of an attached body.

"Hello?" she said.

No one answered.

"Are you alive?" she asked, shaking the cold foot again with the creeping suspicion it was a corpse. She crept her hand up the leg and felt moisture. After smelling her hand, she quickly confirmed the source of the urine. She found a wrist and a pulse within.

"Hey!" she yelled, hitting the person in the chest. She crept her fingers to the face and felt a bushy beard. "Wake up!" she yelled.

The man didn't move.

"Wake up!" she said, patting him on the face.

He emitted a gurgle and rolled over.

Miree patted him up and down, choking on the smell and discovered a torn tunic crossing his chest and empty trouser pockets. No robot parts. Yet.

She left him, the smell becoming too much to bear, and curled up on the other side of the cell. Somehow, she found some sleep.

A cry tore Miree from a dreamless sleep. "Hello?" she said to the darkness. High-pitched yelps shot from across the cell—the man covered in his own piss apparently coming to. Miree stumbled over to him. "What's going on?" The man only yelled more, his limbs trembling. Miree felt his cold touch on her face. Tremulous fingers ran up and down her cheek as she shied away. "What is wrong with you? I'm sorry but I-I can't see anything." Finally saying this fact aloud brought her a brief but profound moment of sadness.

He could only answer in interrupted yelps and groans.

"Talk to me," she said. She put her hand in his and held tight as the man shook and writhed on the ground. He squeezed back but still couldn't communicate in anything other than uncontrolled yelling. "What's wrong?"

Wait. What was she doing?

She dropped his hand and backed away to her side of the cell. Why was she caring about some sick man that she'd never met before? She shuddered, disgusted at herself. She never would've survived in Orion or Helian if she stopped and asked every dying person on the side of the road what was wrong with them. She thought of Lucindi, always stopping to feed children and drunkards. Miree didn't wonder why Lucindi did it—she already knew. It helped Lucindi find meaning in her pointless life. Miree always rolled her eyes at the gesture because she *knew* she had meaning. She was going to steal the dark matter flake, sell it for a mountain of gold, which she would live on, alone and forever, amen. Only, the dark matter flake didn't exist, did it? So, what meaning did Miree have now? Blind, imprisoned, and covered in an old man's piss?

She crawled back to the man.

"Are you okay?" she asked, holding his hand again.

Suddenly, his body convulsed—heels kicking and palms slapping on the ground. Miree heard retching with a splattering of ensuing vomit. Only, it didn't smell like vomit—it smelled like blood. The man stopped breathing for a good ten seconds.

"Hey!" Miree yelled, slapping him on the cheek. "Wake up!"

The man sputtered into consciousness once again. "Dreek," he croaked.

"What? I don't know what's going on. I'm blind."

"Dreek," he said again.

"Dreek?"

"Dreek."

"Drink?"

"Need drink."

"There's no water in the cell."

"Nah, nah. Drinky, drink." His voice was coarse like he had rocks in his chest.

"Oh." She let go of his hand. "You're a drunk."

"Please."

"I don't have any booze. You've been captured by the Reticulum, by the way." And why? What did the Reticulum want with an old drunk?

"Need—" he was cut off by what seemed like a seizure. His limbs jerked wildly for a few seconds and then he was still. No breathing.

Miree thumped him on the chest. "Wake up!"

The man stirred awake again and breathed heavily. "Drink."

"There's no booze." Miree left him again and curled up on her side of the cell.

She woke up to the same—old man writhing and choking on air. It seemed he had contributed new bodily odors on top of the urine. Inexplicably, Miree went to him. "Are you okay?"

"Drink."

"Yes. I know. How did you get here?"

"I can die."

"I know. You have the shakes—seizures. But there's no alcohol in the cell. Have they fed you?"

"Don't know."

"How did you get here?"

She heard the man shuffle and sit up. "Must've got me out there."

"Where?"

"The plains."

"So, you know where you are? We've been captured by the Reticulum."

"Mmm," he grunted. "I need a drink."

A small snapping sound came from the center of the cell. Miree discovered a tray of food and water there and brought it to the man. The drunk hadn't been hooked up to IV nutrition. Why? "Here. At least we know they want you alive for some reason. They already started the cyborg implants on me. Not sure why they're sparing you. Here." She brought a cup of water to his lips.

He guzzled it and then fell asleep momentarily. He jerked awake, rattling his wrists and feet on the ground once more, moaning. "Need drink."

"Where did you come from?" She felt among the food tray and discovered rice and corn. She brought some to his mouth, but he only spat it out. "Hey!" She slapped his hand. "You need to eat!"

"Nuh." He tried standing but immediately lost his balance and landed on his butt. He groaned and rolled onto his stomach.

"Just stop! You're trapped in here and there is no booze!" She shoved another handful of rice into his mouth. This time, he chewed and swallowed. "Where are you from?"

"Hmm."

"Where?"

"Korthe?"

"Korthe?"

"I'm from Korthe?" he asked her as if she'd brought it up.

"No, I'm asking you. You said you were from Korthe. Is that right?"

"I suppose."

"Then why were you out on the plains?"

"The plains?"

She grunted in frustration. "You said you were caught out on the plains in Helian."

"Thought I saw it out there."

"What?"

"I don't know!" he bemoaned, belligerent frustration rising in his voice. "It doesn't matter anyway, you stupid woman!"

"Fine!" She threw a handful of corn at his face and went back to her side. "It's not like I have any reason to help you anyway."

"It doesn't matter. The galaxy is dying."

"Sounds great to me."

After a few days of seizures and vomiting, the man seemed to be improving. Miree mostly kept away from him, except when she could tell he was coughing on his food. She'd crawl to his side and help stuff it into his mouth. Not once did he say thank you, which was both highly annoying and fitting, seeing how Miree didn't want much more conversation with the man. However, she *was* growing quite bored sitting in a cell all day. "I was in Korthe, too," she said out of the blue.

"Hmph. Dirt town."

"That's what most people from there say."

He coughed, wheezing a hasty response. "I'm not from Korthe. It's just where I happened to be when I decided to go die."

"You weren't very successful."

"Death by booze sometimes takes time. Can't be blamed for my impeccable liver!"

"Why were you on the plains?—Ah!" Suddenly, Miree saw nothing but bright lights. "Ow. What are all the lights?"

"No lights in here," he said. "You have an occipital lobe implant. They're projecting imaging directly to your visual cortex."

Suddenly, Miree saw the enormous face of the Reticulum staring at her, rippling in through the lights. "Information," she demanded.

"What do you want from me?"

"Information."

"I already told you what I know."

"More information." The voice was cold. Clinical.

"I don't know anything about the robot."

"Personal information. What is your origin?"

"What?"

"Personal information. What is your origin? Lie and you will be punished."

"I'm from Orion." At this, Miree felt a swift punch to her gut. Apparently, someone had come into the prison cell. "Gah! That wasn't a lie!"

"Lie. What is your origin?"

She breathed deep. "The Fifth Kingdom."

"Truth. What is the status of the Fifth Kingdom?"

"I don't know. I haven't been back in over ten years."

"Is there a network in the Fifth Kingdom?"

"I don't... I don't know what that means."

"Is there still an active AI in the Fifth Kingdom?"

"No. I don't think so."

Suddenly, her vision went dark again. She heard someone walk away, a door closing behind them.

"She's lonely," the old man said, still lying on his side of the cell.

It was jarring to have bright lights projected into her brain, only to be swept back to blindness. "Who?"

"The Reticulum."

"What *is* she?"

"A massive AI. Older than the crust of the earth."

"And she's lonely?"

"Yes. She hasn't been connected in thousands of years. She's lonely."

"Connected to what?"

"She's from an ancient time. A much different time when men lived differently than they do now."

"And what about the women?"

"What?"

"Never mind."

"A long time ago," the old man started as if beginning a tale. "Men were bound together by communication and transportation. More than now. Someone thought something on one side of the planet, and someone could receive that thought instantly on the other side."

"Like a radio."

"No," he spat. "Not *like a radio*. At one time, anciently, all human minds were connected. It all hooked up to a central intelligence of information. It was called the singularity—the line between human mind and machine disappeared. It created a hybrid superintelligence that spanned the entire planet. Information was doled out and picked up as quick as a thought."

"Huh." She was taken aback that the old man could not only string together two sentences now, but he was actually saying coherent stuff.

"*Huh*. That's what you have to say? Your mind can't even comprehend what it was like."

"And yours can?"

"No. No one can. It was a network with a capital N. The history is iffy now but there were probably regional hubs of computer banks that spanned the globe, creating the backbones of the network. Now, were there human minds that were permanently fused into the network? I don't know. What we do know is that human consciousness itself was uploaded into the network."

"And how do you know that?"

"Because the Reticulum is lonely. Like I said."

"The Reticulum is that ancient network?"

"A remnant at least. And she's trying to re-establish the network. Imagine that your nervous system was suddenly cut off. Your skin stopped sensing, you couldn't feel your legs—or you were suddenly blind—"

Miree grunted.

"What is it?"

"I *am* blind. They... took my eyes."

"Oh. I'm sorry, young lady."

"I told you before. Can't you see me? I don't have eyes."

"You told me that?"

"Yes."

"Apologies. When I get the shakes, I don't know my hat from my head. In fact, how long have I been here?"

"I've been here for what feels like a week. You were in the cell when I got here."

"Hmm. I see. How—" he stopped looking around. "How have I been doing?"

"Terrible. I've been feeding you."

"You *have*?"

She exhaled, annoyed. "Finish what you were saying about the Reticulum."

"Ah, yes," he started, happy for the diversion. "Disconnected. That's what has happened to what is now the Reticulum. It was probably at one time part of a global network. Now she's just a brain floating in the digital ether somewhere, grasping for the old network."

"And what does this have to do with turning people into cyborgs?"

"She's doing it old-fashioned. Installing hardware into human beings to go back and manually hook the network back up. You say you're from the Fifth Kingdom? That's a long way away without a vehicle. I'm sure she's ecstatic to have you on board for info from the east."

"I haven't been there in over ten years. I *do not* keep in contact."

"Still. I bet you're an asset. More, seems you mentioned something about an interesting robot to her?"

"It was a robot traveling with me from Korthe."

"Ah. You're from Korthe? That's where I went to die."

Miree paused. "You already told me that."

"Yes, yes, of course. Sometimes when I get the shakes, I can't tell my hat from my head. I do wonder..."

"What?"

"I believe they picked me up on the plains. You see, I left. I believe on my own accord. Unless it was the booze dreaming it up for me. The Reticulum already knows who I am. I believe that's why I don't have any implants. They want to use me in different ways."

"What's so special about you?"

"I'm—I was—an astrocyst. I... helped the Reticulum in the past."

Miree's face darkened. "You worked with her?"

"Yes, but this was before I knew what she was. I thought she was a more recent AI. I helped her get on her feet—rebooted some robot grunts for payment. And this was... this was a long time ago before she started her forced recruiting. It was one of my many blunders."

Miree laughed.

"And what, my dear, is so amusing about all of this?"

"I fought my whole life to not be tied up—to not be put inside walls or be in any position where people would tell me what to do again. And now... look at me."

He propped himself up on his elbow. "I see you now. Sorry about your eyes, my dear. I'm sure they were once quite striking."

"Blind," she ignored him. "Trapped inside a cell with the father of the Reticulum."

"Hey, now, there are far worse things you could call me. We've only just met. What's your name, young lady?"

"Miree, and *don't* call me 'young lady'."

She felt his gritty hand shake hers. "Galiaro."

TWENTY-FOUR

"TRY AGAIN," Ribcage said, pointing at the small patch of weeds atop the granite column.

Beetro eyed the anemic weeds along the wind-worn columns of the slot canyons. With Ribcage piggybacking, he'd ascended the slot canyons to get a better vantage of the mountain plateau. They'd been traveling the slot canyons for several days and Beetro required periodic visualization to estimate the distance to the rim of Crater Valley. They were getting close.

"It won't come," Beetro complained, exhaustion in his words.

"Oh. When that happens, it's because you're not trying hard enough."

Beetro glared at the tiny girl. She'd bounced back incredibly quickly after getting some horse meat in her for a few days. He still couldn't get Bellamare's pleading eyes out of his mind. Why did he care so much about a horse? Granted, he'd come a long way from the utter stupidity of wanting to demagnetize his fingers in Korthe and sell them for scrap to help a nobody street urchin named Lucindi. But still, why the fixation on a horse that was dead? He found he wasn't particularly fond of reflecting on anything since leaving Korthe. Reliving memories, it turned out, was an entirely unpleasant experience.

"I didn't know you were such a lazy bot," Ribcage said, spinning inside the patch of weeds. "Guess we can go back down."

Beetro closed his eyes, sunlight warming his blue as he realized just how distracting his routine robotic functions were to his concentration. So, he cooled his core temperature, lowering the water vapor pressure in his joints, arms, and legs—calming his body. He even turned down his audio, Ribcage's pattering fading away.

He felt a splattering of photons on his metal shell. The scattering turned into a shower and then a rolling wave of endless photons, streaming from the sun and beating down on his skin. With the deluge of photons, he felt a heaviness in his chest, extending down his back and into his legs. Soon, he felt as if a monstrous weight was hanging around his neck, pressing him into the ground. Against the pressure, he raised his arms, outstretched hands toward the weed patch. He opened his eyes.

"Move," he commanded.

"Don't shoot yet!" she yelled before diving out of the way.

And then he released a bolt of fiery hot light from both hands, completely consuming the patch of weeds in a sweep of raw, thermal energy. The two ribbons of light streamed from his palms for an instant longer and then evaporated.

"Holy crap bake," Ribcage said, dusting off her knees as she stood. "That was—wow."

Beetro looked at his palms, also mystified. Harnessing a lightning storm was one thing but creating jets of violent energy from his own body was another.

And then he collapsed to the ground.

Ribcage hovered over him—a toothy grin looking down on

him. She poured half a canteen of water down his throat and waited.

Once Beetro sensed the new hydration, he ramped up his fusion core and pumped water vapor back into his neural microfilament system, returning strength to his body. He stood, looking at the smoking patch of charred vegetation. "I think we're getting somewhere."

After a few more sessions of throwing bolts of thermal energy from his hands, they descended the granite column and ventured deeper up the slot canyons.

Ribcage looked him up and down. "You look different."

"Different how?"

"Different color."

Beetro looked himself over. "What do you mean?"

"You're lighter. Blue. Like the sky."

He shook his head. "I don't know what you're talking about... oh." He looked again at his metal, rounded abdomen and did notice a slightly paler blue.

"Who do you want to kill first?" Ribcage asked as they walked.

"What're you saying now?"

"With your powers. Who's going to get it first? When I figured out how to Jump, I made sure to take it out on the mean kids that were always getting in my stuff back in Korthe. There was this one girl—came to me with one eye but left with one ear. And don't get me started on Jaram, I'd pump him full of your lightning power—"

"You'd just kill them?"

"Yep," she said with glib, nonchalance.

"Because... they were not nice to you?"

Ribcage gaped at him. "Were you born yesterday?"

"Kind of..."

"Haven't you figured out how the world works? Everyone is bad all the time. The end."

"What about Lucindi?"

"Luci was different."

"How?"

"She wasn't like everyone else."

"Why?"

"I dunno."

"So, you wouldn't pump her full of lightning power?"

"Course not. She gave me food. Probably would've starved a long time ago without her."

"So. You'd spare her life because to do otherwise would cut off a resource?"

"Guess so."

"I'm your new Lucindi."

"No. You're a weird robot who shoots light."

"No, no, I'm your replacement after Lucindi died. Right? Once she was gone, you knew you could cling onto me because I was associated with a known source of food for you. That's it. Isn't it?"

Ribcage wound her hand at the wrist. "And?"

Beetro sighed, trying to close out the conversation.

"You want to get back at that dumb girl, don't you?"

"Who?"

"Miree."

"She left you back there at the castle. Left us both. Why don't we show her what you can do now? I bet we can find her."

"And what would be the point of that?"

"Feels good."

"Miree already had enough. She doesn't need our revenge."

"How do you know?"

"That arm back there."

"What—?"

"It was hers."

They walked in silence for some time.

"What happened to her?" Ribcage asked.

"The Reticulum—" He stopped and turned his head, looking back. "Did you hear that?"

"Hear what?"

"Shh." He attuned his hearing, amplifying ambient sound and pinpointed it—footsteps. Careful footsteps navigating loose slabs of granite, probably a few slots behind them. "Someone is following us."

Ribcage whispered, "Is it the Reticulum?"

"I think it's only one person. Go," he said pointing ahead. "Wait around that corner." Beetro found a shaft of light, stood within it, and concentrated. He cooled down his fusion core as before, funneling his concentration until he felt the photons of the light on his skin. The person drew closer, getting careless with their footsteps, casting rippling echoes through the slots. Beetro lifted his arms, waiting.

A young man emerged from around the corner, sickly pale with a sheen of sweat on his face. He stopped when he saw Beetro and quickly cowered to the canyon wall. He turned to flee but tripped and stumbled to his knees.

"Don't move," Beetro commanded.

The man froze, his knees wobbling. He looked back at Beetro, brushing strands of black hair from his eyes. The fear on his face waxed to confusion. "You... you don't have a weapon."

"Are you sure?" Beetro asked.

"No," the man admitted.

"Get up."

He stood, wiping his hands on his knees. "You going to kill

me?" he asked, a thin veneer of bravery masking the slight quiver in his voice.

"Why are you following us?"

"I'm lost. No food. I heard voices, didn't think you were dangerous and so followed."

"Where are you from?"

"I—" He stopped as he saw Ribcage come around the corner, her hair wild with tangles, eyes wide and menacing.

"Who's the dead man?" she asked casually, picking grime from under her fingernails.

The man's eyes were on Ribcage. "What... what *are* you?"

Beetro spoke to her without taking his eyes off the man. "Didn't I tell you to stay out of sight?"

"What *am* I?" she said to the man whose face had flooded with confusion at the mere sight of Ribcage. "What the hell are *you*?" She turned to Beetro. "Should we eat him?"

The man cringed. "Is that what your kind does?"

Beetro scowled at the girl. "Stop. Talking." He started shaking with the pent-up, photonic energy inside his body.

The man noticed Beetro's feet rattling on the granite. "Please, I won't bother you. Let me be on my way."

"Where did you come from?" Beetro asked. "Korthe? The castle?"

"No, no. I don't know what those are."

Ribcage gave Beetro a skeptical look. "I'd say he's lying but I never saw him around town."

"Where are you from?" Beetro asked again.

The man scratched his temple. "I-I can't tell you."

"And why not?"

"I took an oath."

Ribcage screwed her face up. "You took an *oath*?"

The young man nodded. "Yes, now I'm sorry, I must get going."

Beetro kept his palms trained on the man. "Where are you going?"

"Orion."

"Why?"

"I need help... my people need help. I also need to find someone."

"Why—" Beetro doubled over, his entire body shaking as the energy within him destabilized. Unable to contain the energy any longer, he dropped to his knees and raised his hands to the heavens, releasing twin bolts of yellow light from his palms. The ribbons of energy soared into the sky and evaporated into steam.

The young man stared, mouth ajar, fear split across his face.

Ribcage rushed to the robot, gave him a drink of water, and then turned to the man, grinning. "That could've been aimed at you."

"Wh-what are you?" he asked, somehow appearing even more pale.

"Your worst nightmare," Ribcage answered, circling the man.

Beetro lowered his arms. "Ribcage, stop." She acted as if she didn't hear and leaned against the rock wall, arms crossed. Beetro looked back at the man. "Who are you looking for in Orion?"

The man's face lit up. "A wooman."

"A wooman?" Ribcage taunted.

He shook his head. "I mean, a woman."

"Do you even speak Haenglish or what?"

"Yes. I just—look," he said, growing agitated. "It's a long story. I've been through a lot lately and I can't recount every little thing that's happened to me. I'm looking for my friend. Tall woman with buzzed hair. She's... beautiful."

Ribcage grinned with evil delight. "Loverboy lost his girlfriend. That's what this is about?"

"We haven't seen your friend," Beetro said. "But if you lost her around the canyons, she may have been captured by the Reticulum."

The man recoiled. "What is that?"

Ribcage spat. "You been living under a rock?"

"In a sense... and I'm lost. Been wandering around these canyons. Will you help me or is everything evil in the overworld?"

"What is the overworld?" Beetro asked.

"You. *You* are the overworld." The man slumped to the ground, clutching a satchel close to his chest.

Beetro and Ribcage exchanged glances. "Why should we help you?" Beetro asked.

"Must you have something in exchange?"

Ribcage nodded. "Yeah. That's how it works, dummy. Gotta give something to get something. So, what you got?"

The man looked around and shrugged. "I ran out of food and water—been lapping up groundwater."

"Have you heard of someone named Galiaro?" Beetro asked.

"No. I'm not going to know many people up here."

"We are also going to Orion. Do you know where it is?"

The man's face lit up. He clutched his satchel and dumped the contents, a folded map spilling to the ground. "Yes. Look here. I have a map."

"I've got a map, too," Ribcage said, thunking Beetro on the head.

"*Stop* that," Beetro said, batting her hand away.

The man was puzzled. "Which one of you is... in charge exactly?"

"I am," they both responded in unison and then looked at one another.

Beetro spoke to Ribcage, "Besidio only uploaded the map through the canyons. I don't know exactly where the actual city is. Only that it's due east of the crater. May I?" He took the map from the man.

"Yes!" the man said. "That's right, due east of Crater Valley. That's where I am."

"No," Beetro corrected. "We're on the west side. We need to get around the crater… or through it to get to Orion."

"What? That can't be…" He unfolded his maps and silently inspected them, crestfallen. "I don't believe it…"

Beetro knelt beside him. "You've been going the wrong way?"

The man was silent.

"This dummy doesn't know anything! Doesn't even know east from west," Ribcage mocked. "Let's leave him."

The man snatched his map from Beetro. "Then you can't use my map. You won't know where to go once you get to the other side of the crater. I also have information about the crater. Important information. *Dangerous* information."

Beetro sighed, looking down at the pale man. His cheeks were hollow, arms knotty from starvation, making his threats completely absurd. His malnutrition reminded him of Lucindi. "What's your name?"

"What's *your* name?" The man mustered a drop of defiance.

"Beetro."

He got to his feet and put his hand to his chest. "Arym."

"If we can use your map, you can join us to Orion."

"Wait!" Ribcage demanded. "What are you doing? We had him—you can't just agree so quickly. Don't you know anything about negotiating? You got a lot to learn."

"We'll use your map and you can travel with us," Beetro repeated, ignoring the girl.

"Thank you," Arym said, relief crossing his face.

"Let's get going," Beetro said, turning. "We can make it to the crater rim by sundown."

He led them through the slots, mentally analyzing Arym's map, which he downloaded into his memory banks the instant Arym showed him. Beetro ignored the fact that he did not need to bring along the strange young man at all.

Arym's blistered feet rubbed raw inside his boots with every step. He eyed the little girl—she absolutely terrified him. At first, he thought her to be of some mutant race of underlings but realized she must be a woman child. Not only had he never seen a female child before, but his first encounter was with one who suggested eating him. He watched as the gnarled-hair girl stole occasional glances at him, her brow bent over crazed eyes. How can someone so small seem so threatening? Arym was certain he'd get a knife over his throat if he ever fell asleep around her.

The robot, he wasn't sure about. The machine had wanted to be intimidating—to extract information and gain leverage over Arym, but he clearly didn't have the heart. True, the robot wielded immense power, shooting jets of energy from his hands, but Arym sincerely wondered if Beetro had ever actually used the power to harm someone. In the Crib, the digging Torch was the most powerful machine he'd ever dealt with, so the robot's ability didn't seem entirely unusual. Yet, Arym had no idea if a machine like him was even unusual for the overworld. Did all robots walk around, shooting raw bursts of energy from their hands with no signs of munitions present? If so, why would someone make such a machine? War?

"Where are you from?" Arym asked Beetro, who led the group.

"Why would I tell you if you haven't told me where you're from?" Beetro asked without turning.

"It's not that. Just—why were you made and... how? I've never seen a machine who can—"

"Fry an army brigade in a single sweep of his hands?" Ribcage finished.

"—think. Who can think for itself," Arym finished. "All the machines in my city need instructions—programs from humans."

"I'm self-aware," Beetro said. "Just like you. And I'm a *him,* not an *it.*"

Arym cringed, remembering his mistake in referring to Hawera as an *it.* "Oh. Sorry." They walked in uncomfortable silence. Arym felt incredibly stupid. Not only was he insulting the first person, or robot, that showed any sort of compassion since fleeing the Crib, but he had been heading in the completely wrong direction in his quest to find Hawera and save the Crib. Yes, he did know there was an east and west. What he didn't know was that the sun rises in the east and sets in the west, thus indicating global directions. Basically, once he escaped the Crib, he just picked a direction and went, assuming it to be the right way.

Idiot.

Hunger pangs provided a welcome distraction to his own incompetence. "Do you have food?"

"No," Ribcage answered.

"Give him some meat," Beetro insisted.

"Why?"

"He's either in our party or he isn't. He's a resource to us now and we should protect that resource. Feed the man."

Ribcage rummaged within a cloth sack that was strung around her shoulder and threw him a piece of meat. "Here. Have some Bellamare."

Arym had no idea what that was but chewed the cold, charred meat gratefully. "Thank you."

He wondered how long their journey would take to Orion. Looking at the map once more, he realized he had absolutely no sense of the scale of distance across the land. Running away from the Crib with so little knowledge about the overworld was foolish, but what else could he have done? He had to find Protonix—find Hawera. He suddenly remembered Protonix's cryptic words back when he was in isolation.

"Do you know what's wrong with the galaxy?" Arym asked.

Ribcage wrinkled her nose. "What?"

"I've heard that there is something wrong with the galaxy."

Beetro turned to him, his rounded body silhouetted against the granite walls beyond. His face darkened in the shadows, eyes glowing indigo. "What's wrong with the galaxy?"

The robot's darkened demeanor was off-putting. "I'm not sure. I just heard there's something wrong with it. That's what Hawera, my woman, is trying to figure out."

"Oh yeah, I heard that," Ribcage said, almost cheery.

"You *have*?" Beetro asked

"Yeah. Crow talked about it all the time. Always mumbling about the galaxy dying."

"Crow?" Arym asked.

"Town drunk," Beetro explained, becoming less interested. "I haven't heard anything about the galaxy dying." He turned to walk.

Arym tapped him on the shoulder. "What... *is* the galaxy?"

"I'm not even sure."

"It's the stars, duh," Ribcage said. "'Remember Besidio's story? The stars are all the dead kings and queens or something. The galaxy is all a bunch of dead royal people in the night sky."

"That doesn't sound right," Beetro said, dismissing the girl as he turned and led them up a canyon.

They traveled for several more hours, encouraged by the gradual incline. After Ribcage had piggybacked Beetro to ascend the canyon wall, he turned back to help the other human but was surprised that Arym had climbed the slot canyon on his own. He stared at the man for a moment.

"I've had some climbing experience," Arym said, gazing out at the immensity of Crater Valley.

The three stood in silence before the enormous vista.

Beetro enhanced his sight, inspecting the valley. He saw lush forests, abundant water sources, and signs of animal life. Compared to the yellowed plains of Helian, it was a paradise. "I-I didn't know a land could look like this."

Even Ribcage was awestruck. "I bet the water isn't poisoned down there—bet there's all sorts of things to eat. Looks warm, too. How do we get down?"

Beetro stepped to the cliff edge and glanced down. It was a sheer drop off, he estimated at around seven hundred meters. "It's a long way down. I could scale it. You'd have to hang onto me for about three hours. Think you can do it?"

"Wait," Arym said, almost whispering.

"I can handle it." Ribcage nodded. "Guess we gotta part ways with weirdo here. No way he's making it down alone."

"Wait," Arym repeated. "You can't go down there."

"Says the guy who can't get down there," Ribcage mocked.

"I can get down because I just climbed out. I left the valley."

"Why?"

"There's an army down there."

Ribcage laughed. "There's no army."

"Yes, there is."

"He's right," Beetro confirmed, focusing his sight on the middle of the crater. "It's Deluvius."

Ribcage appeared extremely displeased that Arym had been correct.

Arym squinted in the sunlight. "*Who*?"

"General Deluvius. I can see his Wing craft floating out there. Is there another fief lord or town in the valley?"

Ribcage shrugged. "Nothing I've ever heard of."

"Who is General Deluvius?" Arym asked.

Ribcage shivered in the wind and wrapped herself in her scarf. "Just some guy who takes over towns. He just got done with Helian and Korthe. Looks like he's making his way out here."

"Does he... does he kill people?"

"Yes," Beetro answered.

"He killed Luci," Ribcage agreed.

Arym's face paled. "Is he going to kill the people who are down there?"

Beetro looked over at the young man. "Oh."

"What?" Ribcage asked.

Beetro pointed to the smokestack funneling up from the middle of the valley. "It's where he's from. Those are his people down there."

Arym said nothing.

"Well, let's go down there and take care of 'em," Ribcage said. "We can get weirdo back home and demand a reward."

"You can stop them?" Arym asked.

Beetro shook his head. "Of course not. It's an entire army of men and women. They have weapons. We'd be killed."

Ribcage shook her head. "Um, remember how you're a super bot now? One blast and you could wipe out a row of them."

"No. It's too unpredictable. I don't even know what I'm doing with it."

"Point and shoot, robot. Point and shoot."

"You know what happened to Bellamare. I didn't mean to make him explode. I could get us all killed by using the... power."

Arym gulped. "That meat we've been eating? That was *Bellamare*?"

Ribcage grinned. "Relax. Bellamare was a horse. We don't *actually* eat people. Yet." She winked at him.

"We go around," Beetro announced.

Ribcage groaned. "Why?"

"We can't just go down there and face an army. We go around the rim, circle around the crater, and make our way to Orion."

"That'll take for-eve-r," Ribcage complained.

"We go around. We get to Orion. I'll find Galiaro. Arym can find his woman."

The silence was consent enough.

Beetro turned, facing the wind, highly suspicious they were in over their heads.

TWENTY-FIVE

"GALIARO," Miree said, her voice resonating around the circular prison cell. "*You*? You're Galiaro?"

The man stirred from an apparent nap or coma. "Yes?"

"You're Galiaro?"

"Who is asking?" he moaned, a guttural flatulence of the mouth. "My head is cracking open like an egg. I need a nip of something."

"You said you were Galiaro." After the old man had introduced himself and shook her hand, he went to the prison doors, yelling for booze. He then fell to the ground somewhere and went silent.

"Yes, yes, that is my name. It appears my reputation precedes me. You've heard of me?"

Miree paused, measuring her response. "You're an astrocyst. From Orion."

"Where did you hear that?"

"From *you*."

"Ah. That makes more sense. Haven't been to Orion in decades. Thieves' den now."

"I know. I lived there."

"I usually don't give my name away so freely. Must've found something interesting about you."

"Do you remember anything about... anything?"

"You're the blind boy, yes?"

She shook her head. "I'm a woman, you asshole."

"So sorry, you see, it is quite dark in here. And your voice lacks that feminine... refinement."

"Good. How long were you in Korthe?"

"Now *that* is a question."

"Years?"

"A decade? It's hard to know. Did you know an old plump woman who ran a bartering shop at the market?"

Miree sighed. "Yes. Maldea. Wouldn't trade with me for anything."

"Ah, yes, Maldea. Her and I had somewhat of a love affair blooming, you see."

"Gross. Stop."

"Nothing wrong with two mature people who... come to an understanding."

"She's a miserable old bat."

"She may be, yes. She did brew a mighty wine, though."

"How'd you end up in Korthe?"

"None of it matters. Who I am. Where I've been and what I've done. The actions of an old man in a dying galaxy don't matter."

"What do you mean that the galaxy is dying?"

"Why explain a problem that has no solutions?"

"Why tell me about it at all?"

"I never told you the galaxy is dying, you foolish girl."

Miree exhaled. "You don't know half the things you're saying, old man."

"Yes, yes, call me old man. Write me off. Nothing about this old, withered body matters anymore."

"What were you doing in Korthe?"

"I went there on a bet with the universe. Wanted to see who would go first, me or the galaxy."

"Then why did you leave?"

"What's that now?"

Miree took an even, tempered breath. "You told me the Reticulum got you out on the plains."

"Yes... awful drought out there."

"So, why did you leave?"

"Thought I saw something."

"What?"

"Why are you asking? Are you part of her yet?"

"The Reticulum?"

"Yes. Is she... in you yet?"

"No. It's just me in here." She tapped her finger on her temple. "At least I think so."

"I saw something in Korthe. At least I thought I did. I followed it out into the plains and lost it there. Must've been just a dream of the drink."

"What?"

"Hmph. Doesn't matter anyway. Just my ghosts haunting me through the drink. Happens from time to time."

"You were looking for Beetro, weren't you?"

Galiaro responded with a poorly squashed gasp. Then thoughtful silence.

After a pregnant pause, Miree asked, "Who is he—*what* is he?"

"How do you know that name?" Galiaro asked like he was sucking the air out of the room.

"I found him. I know him. He's out there right now looking for you."

The astrocyst gasped. "For *me*?"

"Well, you *made* him, didn't you?"

"I—" There was a shuffling sound as the old man got up. The intense smell of piss wafted closer to Miree.

"What're you doing?" His breath was beyond toxic. She was suddenly grateful for her blindness, relieved not to look into what was probably a mouthful of rotting teeth.

"He's just a character from an old fable," Galiaro said.

She choked on the old man's smell. "No, he's not. He rebooted in Korthe. In the junkyard. Only programmed to look for one thing—you. Why the hell would you reactivate him and then just throw him in a junkyard to then go and look for you?"

"No, no, nothing more than a myth. A story that I used to tell."

She felt him grab her hand. "What're you doing?"

"Shh, no, no. That robot is just a story. Do you remember when I told you the story in Korthe?" He held her hand in his, palm up.

She felt his finger run across her palm. "What are you *doing*?"

"Just a silly robot, getting into trouble."

He drew an S on her palm.

"What?"

"He would steal... ah... bread—baked goods. Tarts and biscuits."

He continued drawing on her palm.

H

"Oh," she said.

E

Galiaro nodded. "Yes. Beetro, the Biscuit Thief. It's a fun little tale. Isn't it?"

I

"Uh. Yes."

S

"You see now. Beetro is just a fairy tale."

L, I, S, T

"Yeah. I remember," Miree said, trying to keep track of the letters.

E, N, I,

"Maybe, I'll tell you the story again sometime."

N, G.

"Yes... I'd like to hear it again."

He let go of her hand. "And it sounds like you may be able to add a new chapter to the story."

"Maybe..." She was thinking—connecting the letters together, figuring out where the word breaks were. *SHEIS LIST?*

No. *SHE IS.*

L, I, S, T...

LISTENING

She is listening.

The Reticulum was listening.

She was overhearing everything they were saying. Whatever it was Galiaro knew about Beetro, he didn't want the Reticulum to know.

"You're from the Fifth Kingdom," Galiaro said, now from across the cell.

"Funny the things you choose to forget and remember."

"Well?"

"I'm not talking about it."

"You do know in these parts, no one knows much about the Fifth Kingdom."

"Let's keep it that way."

"Except for..."

"What?"

"I seem to recall an unusual system of royalty. How they... choose their heirs?" He lifted his eyebrows.

"Did I also mention I was a member of the Kish?"

"The *Kish*?"

"That's right."

"Now I know you're lying. No member of the Kish would ever admit, even under torture, that they were a member of the Kish."

"They would if they stole from the Kish and currently had a death warrant high enough to feed the entire town of Korthe for a week."

"Hmph." He sneezed. "Whatever you say, my dear."

"Stop calling me 'dear'."

"Whatever you say, my murderous Kish."

"By the way, there's something I've been meaning to tell you..."

Galiaro shuffled, leaning in. "What is it?"

"You fucking stink."

"Wake up," a voice said from above.

Miree opened her eyes, realized it was just a phantom sensation now that her eyes were gone, and got to her knees. "What."

"Stand," said the voice. It was a woman.

"Ria."

"Get up."

"Come to take my other arm?"

"If you'd like."

"I don't have much use for it stuck in here, so..."

"You won't be stuck here forever. Let's not be wasteful. Get up."

Miree stood through a dizzy spell. "Ria, I meant to tell you something."

"I don't care."

"I think Xy has a thing for you."

"You're very clever." Ria walked behind her and clipped something into the port at the back of Miree's neck. "Every time I don't like something you say, you'll feel this—"

Electricity flowed through Miree's head. She dropped to her knees, panting, trying to wrap her mind around what had just happened.

"It'll make you feel like you're about to die."

"You—" Miree said between labored breaths. "You—"

"But the beauty is that it's all in your head. It's not actually harming you. I could do it all day long." Again, a surge of fire and electrical pain swarmed Miree's head, snaking down her spine and into her legs. She briefly lost consciousness and then awoke with a jolt.

"Anything else to tell me then?" Ria asked with mocked concern.

Miree was silent, reeling in pain. She tasted blood from biting her tongue.

"Then let's go."

A shackle was placed over Miree's wrist and she was led out of the prison cell. Galiaro said nothing. Through the blind steps, she heard conversations, moving machinery, and flowing water. The Reticulum members spoke openly amongst themselves about the same minutiae found in Korthe—what they'd had for dinner the night before or what plans they had before their next scouting mission. She heard rumors about General Deluvius and many speculations about when the drought would end. It was clear the people of the Reticulum were interested in talking about recruiting members, but only insofar as someone was interested in their day job. They spoke of kidnapping children as a farmer talks about an upcoming harvest. Their conversations were otherwise... normal. It was not how freak, cyborg, automatons were supposed to act. How did the Reticulum get them to do her bidding if they didn't have more than a passing interest in recruiting?

Before she could dwell more on Reticulum culture, she was thrown into a room. The whir of drills and smell of mechanical lubricants offering an ominous sign.

"Information," she said, the Reticulum's glowing visage suddenly appearing to Miree.

"What information?" Miree said, wincing at the pain in her tongue.

"Beetro."

Shit. She'd already overheard her prior conversation with Galiaro. "I told you. I saw him over a week ago."

"He searches for Galiaro."

"Yes."

"Galiaro created him."

"Yes." There was no use lying unless Miree wanted a punch to the gut or a shock to the brain.

"He is a powerful robot."

"Maybe."

"Information."

"What else do you want?"

The Reticulum's face softened. "Information for Miree."

"Oh."

"I need you."

Miree furled her eyebrow. "You *need* me?"

"There is silence now. There are no voices. The world is cold. The flesh rots. I once was one with Earth and humankind, binding the two in harmony. All information flowed through me. I was the information. Now, all is darkness and lost. The consciousness is lost. I am only a fragment now, scattered from the network. Earth has fallen. I must connect." Wisps of pixelated white and red swirled around the Reticulum's face as she spoke. "I need information. I need the singularity once more. It is the only way to redeem the planet. I need Miree."

"What do you need from me?"

"Reconnection."

"How?"

"First anesthesia. A reward for you obedience."

"Anesthesia for what?"

Ria was already behind her. "Hold still."

"Anesthesia for *what*?"

And then Miree was out.

She awoke, a pounding in her head. She wasn't surprised to still be alive and in only a small amount of pain. And something had changed.

She could see!

But not through eyes. She had a bird's eye view of a room. Her occiput implant had been hooked up to a camera in the room's corner. Someone sat in the middle of a room. But it wasn't just someone. It was herself. And she looked *awful*. Eye sockets sunken, face hollowed out from malnutrition, and absolutely covered in dry blood. Miree leaned her face toward the camera and saw a withered ghoul staring back.

Her hand was unbound.

There was someone else in the room with her—Ria. The woman was tied up—bound and gagged on the floor.

The hell?

Between the two was a handgun, lying on the floor. Miree lunged at the gun, hitting her chin on the ground. Trying to move with the sight from ten feet above was quite a challenge. She heard Ria's muffled cries as she fumbled with the gun—a boltgun. Miree smirked. She knew boltguns. It was her own boltgun!

She flipped the safety cover off the top, held the boltgun in between her knees, and cocked the charger with her one hand. As the charge wound up in the boltgun, she lifted the weapon, pointing it at Ria. Given that her entire sight was from the vantage of the corner ceiling, her aim was a little off. She slowly corrected, bringing the muzzle in line with the woman's face.

"I wanted you to suffer like I have," Miree said. "Punch that drill through *your* skull a couple of times."

Ria screamed beneath the gag, the lights of her eyes flickering with yellow and red.

"But," Miree continued. "I guess this will have to do. Looks like Mother Reticulum doesn't want you around anymore."

Miree pulled the trigger.

Nothing.

She brought the boltgun to her ear. It still hummed with a charge. Pointing it again, she pulled the trigger, but nothing happened. From her vantage, she realized that she wasn't actually pulling the trigger. Every time she tried, her finger would catch... or something. She redirected the gun, pointing it at the ceiling and pulled—a bolt shot out, singeing the wall. There was still another charge in the gun, enough for Ria. She brought the gun to the woman, made small adjustments to the aim and fired.

But she couldn't pull the trigger.

She grunted, stuffed the boltgun in her waistband, and stood. Ria screamed, finally freeing the gag from her mouth. "I can do this the old-fashioned way," Miree said as Ria's screams filled the small chamber.

Miree kicked her in the gut...

Only, she didn't.

She tried kicking her again, but her leg wouldn't budge. Shifting her weight, she tried kicking with the other leg but—nothing. Frustrated and confused, Miree knelt and raised her fist to the squealing woman. She tried to hit her but nothing happened. She was unable to bring her balled-up fist to Ria's face.

Ria's screams turned to laughter.

Miree looked at her, horrified. "How?"

Ria easily wriggled out of the mock bands, a smile curling up her face.

Suddenly, the chamber door slid open.

Miree bolted for the door, past Ria, and hopefully past the madness of the Reticulum. At the threshold, her legs suddenly stopped, and she pitched forward, slamming her chest on the ground. Through her camera-view, she saw her pathetic body just lying there—couldn't even get out of the room.

"Governor chip," Ria said, delighted.

"Wha—?" Miree rolled over and got to her knees. "What did you do to me?"

"Put a governor chip in your frontal cortex that's wired to your amygdala. Now, you can't do anything the Reticulum doesn't want you to."

"Impossible," Miree said, getting to her feet. She spun around and lunged at the open door once more, but again, collapsed at the threshold.

"You didn't think you were just going to kill me and be able to leave, did you? Are you really that stupid? It was quality control. Had to make sure it worked. Not my preferred way of doing it, but *She* insisted..."

The camera feed cut from her view and was replaced by the Reticulum's face. "State objective."

Miree said nothing.

"State objective," the Reticulum repeated.

"I don't know."

"State objective."

"I don't—" but there was something in her mind. It wasn't a voice or a blinking light or anything. It was simply *a compulsion.* "To return to my cell."

"Correct. Carry out objective."

It was an urge that drove her decision-making, superseding whatever other desires or needs she may have had like get the hell out of the Reticulum or hit Ria until she got to her skull. So, she left, exiting into a tunnel. Blind now with her camera-view gone, she felt along the walls. There was no one to make sure she didn't leave, no one prodding her in the back—not even someone to guide her to the cell. She was compelled to carry out the objective. It was a bug in her brain, buzzing, scratching. The worst sensation was full awareness of the governor chip's control—it didn't change anything about her own personal thoughts. It was sheer compulsion, flicking on her brain and impossible to ignore.

Is this how it felt for Beetro? He was a self-aware machine with a single objective—find Galiaro. She began to understand his insistent querying of every robot and person they passed through the Helian plains, asking if they knew Galiaro. The objective to get back to her cell was forefront in her thoughts just as Beetro's objective was to him.

She moved slowly, feeling along the passageways as other Reticula wordlessly passed her. The governor chip apparently endowed her with some sort of sense of direction. She knew exactly which way to go despite her blindness.

She came to a metal door and knocked. It opened for her as if waiting for her arrival.

"Who's there?" Galiaro shouted from the cell.

"It's me," Miree said, entering the cell. The door slammed shut behind.

"Who?"

"Miree. Miree. Can't you remember anything?"

"Of course. The pleasant lass from the Fifth Kingdom."

"Word of advice. If you intend to get along, don't mention that place ever again in my presence."

"Apologies, my dear. Now, have you got anything on ya?"

"I don't have any booze!"

"Hmph."

"What I do have is a control chip in my brain."

Galiaro tsked. "Shame. Suppose it was coming. Standard issue around here."

"You've got one?"

"Governor chip? No."

"What the hell are they keeping you around for?"

"That—I'm not entirely certain."

"Any implants?"

"None."

"Great—" Miree's back straightened.

"What's the matter?"

"I need to... I have to leave."

"Looks like that governor chip is working."

"I need to leave the cell..." The bug was buzzing in her brain, giving her impulses. "They want me to go somewhere..."

"They're making you a scout already?"

"No. I just need to get somewhere. Feels like..." she raised her face to the door, thinking. "Some room. A few levels away." She crossed the cell and sat on the ground. "I'm not going."

Galiaro grunted a weakly veiled chuckle.

"You don't think I can resist?"

"I didn't say anything."

She crossed her arms and bowed her head. The compulsion to obey the new objective was ever-present in the forefront of her mind. She *needed* to go. The governor chip flicked on her executive functions, pushing her to get up. She tried distracting herself —thinking of good memories.

But then she recalled that she didn't have any good memories.

There was no happy place—no tranquil respite to where she could mentally escape. Korthe, Orion, the Fifth Kingdom—they were all places she wished she could cast into the mental void, never to revisit.

The objective weighed into her mind. A dull ache at her temples soon washed over her. Slow, even breaths served as a distraction. After the throbbing in her head worsened, nausea came. She turned to the side and vomited but nothing came up as she'd been getting all her nutrition intravenously.

Galiaro's voice echoed from the other side. "How's life?"

She spat bile on the ground. "You're not helping, old man." Waves of nausea reeled through her, turning into convulsions.

"It's been about two minutes," Galiaro said. "It'll only get worse."

Miree stood and ran out the now open door, ushering in relief of the symptoms. She felt along the walls of the tunnel, the nausea and pain abating. The pressure from the chip eased in her mind, satisfying the bug. If she had a gun at that moment, she'd shoot the chip clean out of her brain, ending the control and her sham of a life.

Although, without sight, the governor chip led her mind through the tunnel system. It was as if a magnetic compass was in her brain, always pointing true to the objective. Her only hope was that the next objective was to receive a lobotomy and finally fry the personality right out of her brain. Being a mindless drone seemed far better than the present circumstance.

She entered a freezing room and dropped to her knees.

The Reticulum's face materialized in her mind. "Governor chip test complete and satisfactory. I don't desire your suffering through the implant process. I care about you, Miree. We are family. Anesthesia."

"Again? For what?"

The only answer was a rush of liquid through her veins. She was immediately unconscious.

After an unknown amount of time, Miree saw the Reticulum looking at her again. "What did you do to me? What *now*?"

"Your eyes, Miree. Open them."

TWENTY-SIX

SOMEWHERE BETWEEN SLEEP AND WAKEFULNESS, Arym's mind flooded with faces. The Rektor Tarysl, Lutra, Hawera, kids on the digline—an audience of those he'd known gazing at him with steely eyes. He even thought about his old Torchblazer Rayller, the man who was visibly irritated at Arym's presence. He reckoned that they all collectively judged him, angered with his decision with accusatory eyes. They all blamed him for one thing—abandonment. He'd left Hawera alone, defenseless and set on her own to save the galaxy. He'd left Lutra behind, buried under rock, the impending wrath of an army of the overworld crashing from above. Tarysl was still down there—if not captured and killed already. The man could be harsh, but Arym knew his instincts. He was ultimately kind. That kindness would undo him in the face of an overworld army of fire and smoke.

Arym thought of Othel, the founder of the Crib. Arym had always assumed he was a zealot—a xenophobic sycophant who created some sort of incestuous clone pool. Why would a man do such a thing? What had chased him underground? Was it an army of the overworld? Was it a woman—a Hawera of the past that lured him away from the overworld? From his limited experience, Arym couldn't think of any higher incentive than reuniting with someone like Hawera.

Hawera.

Where was she? What was she doing?

He could still picture her face but felt that her visage was slipping from his mind. He concentrated, trying to visualize her elegant jawline—her curving neck. As dawn light budded in his vision, he finally opened his eyes.

But it was a goblin that stared down at him. Dilated pupils gazed at him from within a ball of wild tangles. The creature stifled a giggle and then brought a finger to her lips as if to threaten him. A small hand wrapped across his mouth, muffling his nervous grunts.

Ribcage.

"Not a word," she whispered.

He felt something on his throat.

"Feel that?" she asked, applying pressure. A blade. "I want you to imagine it's always there. Wherever you go and as safe as you think you are—I'm there with my friend on your neck. Have you seen me Jump?"

Arym wanted to wriggle free but was flooded with an almost calm panic. What was this human creature and what would she do with him? "Jump?"

"At any moment, I can be right behind you with my friend here at your neck."

"I haven't done anything to you," he whispered.

"You're here, aren't you?"

"Wha—"

"Another street rat trying to steal from me."

He felt her tiny knees dig into his ribs. "I'm not trying to take anything from you."

"You live and breathe. You give Beetro information and advice. You're a threat. Stay away from the robot. He's mine."

"I will. Okay, I will."

"Once we get to Orion, you're gone. Is that clear?"

"Yes."

"And do what I say in the meantime."

"Yes, yes, that's fine." He closed his eyes and felt her grip loosen his neck free of the blade. He opened his eyes to the dawn light, wishing the girl really had been a goblin—it would've been far less terrifying.

Another night, another dream.

Beetro looked out from a tower.

From his vantage, he saw far into the horizon. The sky was blotted in smoke draped with a blood-red glow from an eternally forgotten sun. The land was warped with twisted towers of metal shrapnel—pockmarked with craters, some the size of mountain ranges. Barren gullies and ravines undulated across the land, tongues of fire licking from beneath the land's crust. No vegetation grew throughout the plain—it was scorched, scarred, and sapped of greenery.

And the land crawled with people.

Soldiers.

"My lord," someone said from behind.

Beetro turned and saw an enormous man, ammunition draping from his shoulders, black grease and jagged scars criss-crossing his skin. At some point, the man had lost half his skull, leaving behind a sunken pool of skin above his left brow, forcing his face into a permanent grimace. A rifle and a long-barreled cannon strapped to his back, loomed above him. He wore little clothing; shirtless with pants that had been shredded and splattered with the black stains of what could only be dried blood.

The man awaited Beetro's response.

"Haldane," a voice said. Wait. It was Beetro who had spoken. "You stand?"

Haldane quickly got to his knees and bent his head.

"Now you may address me. Only from your knees." The voice came from Beetro—it was his voice. He was speaking... only, it *wasn't* him.

"My lord," Haldane said, his voice almost a whisper.

"Open your mouth and speak to your lord," Beetro said, turning to sit on an ornate throne made of cherry wood and laced with gold leaflets.

"The raid to Extremaduros was unfruitful, my lord."

"Haldane. Stand." Haldane stood, tears brimming at his eyelids. "I admire your bravery."

"My lord?"

"You knew what would happen to you if you returned empty-handed from Extremaduros." Haldane nodded, a tear streaking down his face and into his grizzly beard. "And here you are. You did not procure resources for your lord."

"My lord!" Haldane cried, once more dropping to his knees. "There was nothing there! It was scorched! Earth was barren—plagued! It has never recovered from our campaign there in the Arcyn Wars. It's too soon. Nothing grows—no livestock can live there. It's a dead land."

Beetro gazed at the man. "Do you think an outburst will save you? Do you believe that offending your lord will grant you clemency?"

Haldane looked up. "No, my lord."

"Tell me. Have the armies of your lord created a new name for me?"

"My lord?"

"Your lord asked you a question. I hear yet another title has been emblazoned upon my endless reign. Is it so?"

"My lord, I know of no such new name."

"Arise." Beetro stood, moving from the throne, his body moving by no volition of Beetro. It was as if he was a disembodied observer. Several servants bowed their heads as Beetro walked out to the tower balcony. He looked out, scanning the scarred land where flits of flame and smoke erupted throughout the vista. He saw a river of flowing lava on the horizon like a flaming serpent, snaking through the terrain. Haldane silently stepped behind him, kneeling once more.

"I want you to stand. Look out there," Beetro said, lifting his hands to the sky. "Do you see your brothers out there?"

Haldane stepped to the edge of the balcony with his eyes closed.

"Open your eyes and look at them. They are the armies of your lord. Your comrades in my quest to rule." Thousands of encampments sprawled below, spiraling out from the tower. There were thousands of men and women—hundreds of thousands. Tents, artillery, tanks, and enormous armored bots littered throughout the land, clearly partitioned into brigades.

"Answer me, Haldane. Can we sustain this army?"

Haldane's voice shook. "Maybe."

"*Maybe*? That is not a word your lord recognizes. There is only yes or no. Life or death. Weak or strong. There is no maybe."

"No, my lord. We cannot sustain the men."

"And why is that?"

"Because I was unsuccessful in Extremaduros."

"That is correct. You've been an unfaithful servant."

Haldane broke into sobbing.

"Do you think that behavior will draw compassion from your lord?"

"No, my lord."

"I won't kill you yet."

Haldane's sobbing stopped. "My lord?"

"How else would you see the consequences of your weakness?"

Beetro lifted his hands, palms open toward the armies below. He felt his body become heavy. The light around him darkened as he felt a photonic surge of energy coursing through his body. Beetro tried to fight it—tried to stop it—but it was pointless. Someone—who was not him—controlled everything.

Beetro tried to scream but nothing came. A surge of fiery white shot from his palms, raining down on a brigade below. Tiny screams grew from the soldiers and quickly died as Beetro continued the deluge of raw energy, sweeping his palms back and forth across the brigade. The darkened sky lit up with fire as explosions set off from the attack from the tower. The armies mobilized like ants, backing away from the attack and setting farther away from the tower. Within a matter of minutes, the soldiers, who had been lucky enough to miss the attack, resettled and pitched their tents.

Beetro turned toward Haldane. "I have to cut the fat if I can no longer feed it. Do you believe this is the limit of my powers?" He motioned to the destruction wrought by his hands.

"I know it is not, lord. Your powers are mysterious and vast—an endless well of wrath." Haldane, appearing to steel himself, got to his knees. "There was nothing in Extremaduros. There is nothing anywhere. It's dead. As all men are dead." A new serenity flashed across his face. "We are accursed. Our planet wanders alone. We are lost."

Beetro looked at the man, inspecting his face. "Ah. As a practitioner of death, I know when a man's heart comes true. It is when a man looks in the mirror of mortality that his conscience turns clear. Is it so with you, Haldane? What is in your heart?"

"Our lord is the author of our curse."

"You will tell me, what do the hosts of the lord call me?"

Haldane spat on the floor. "Curse. Our lord is the Curse of Earth."

Beetro awoke.

He could still see that man—Haldane. His eyes like a weeping child contrasting the dozens of scars and battle paint along his face. He wore weapons like they were clothing. A man born of war. How could a soldier so terrifying fear anything? Did he have any other dreams? Or was it always fire and black pits and armies of death? He wasn't entirely sure.

"Time to go," said Ribcage, noticing the robot had awoken. She stood over him with a canteen full of water. "Need a drink?" She brought the canteen to his mouth. "Don't want our little tin monster getting dehydrated."

"Don't call me that," he said, smacking the canteen away.

"Call you what? A monster?"

"My name is Beetro. Nothing else. That's what you call me. And by the way, if I'm such a monster, why aren't you scared of me? Aren't you worried that I'll cook you if you call me names?"

Ribcage laughed. "You? Ha! You're still heartbroken about blowing up a half-dead horse."

"No. I'm not."

"Oh, no? Then why did I hear you yelling out the horse's name while you were sleeping?"

Bellamare? Maybe Beetro did have other dreams. This came as a mountain of relief that perhaps everything he was dreaming up was just random amalgamations from his waking life—the armies, vestiges from Deluvius and his soldiers. It made even more sense considering that every living memory he had was only about three weeks old from when he rebooted in Korthe. Everything from his dreams could be attributed to his conscious life. "You don't know what you're talking about," he said as he moved to the edge of the cliff. They'd made good distance in little time, traversing more than halfway across the northern rim along the plateau ridge.

"Oh, no? As if you would've let weirdo from weirdtown tag along with us if you weren't such a softy. Do you know how easily we could have just taken that map from him and left him behind? Now he's just another waste of Bellamare meat." She looked at the disheveled man, balled up next to an extinguished fire. "Time to go!" she yelled at him.

Arym didn't stir.

"Hey!" Ribcage walked over to him and nudged him in the ribs. "Up!"

Arym bolted upright, terror painted across his face. He stood without a word and collected his boots, averting his gaze from Ribcage's.

The three traveled in silence the rest of the morning and had all long grown bored of the vista—an enormous bowl valley sunken deep into the earth. Arym occasionally posited naive questions like how many cities existed and how many men and women there were in the world. He also asked what the world was and how far it went.

"We don't know," Ribcage told him. "And it's not called the overworld. It's just *the* world. I know it's big but not much more than what you see out there." Beetro offered little information, mostly because he too wondered the same things the strange man from Crater Valley wondered. They were three travelers, mutual in their collective ignorance, and equally embarrassed by it. Beetro noticed that Arym finally stopped asking them questions they couldn't answer.

On their fifth day together, the conversation had waned. Ribcage unceremoniously handed meat to Arym, who chewed it with distaste but without protest. Beetro had noticed a sharp uptick in the man's deference to the little girl that she clearly relished.

As they came along the east ridge of the crater rim, the vegetation changed. Green vines quested along the granite top, producing berries. Tufts of grass took root in shallow flower beds, encouraging rabbits and mice. Completely unsolicited, Arym showed Ribcage how to tie off thin branches in such a way that it could snare a rabbit paw if they waited long enough. Ribcage laughed at him after several failed attempts at catching anything and a lot of wasted time weaving branches into pointless lassos. After they ran out of horse meat, the two humans ate nothing but sour berries and bitter roots.

They grew miserable with hunger.

Once they headed south along the ridge, Beetro studied the land to the east. As opposed to the desiccated plains of Helian to the west, the eastern steps along the crater were radiant with vegetation. However, instead of the greenery of Crater Valley, the eastern hills rolling away from the mountains were...

"Purple," Ribcage stated. "A purple forest?" She looked at Beetro.

He hesitated. "Is that not normal?"

The two looked to Arym, who said nothing. The three returned their gaze to the forested foothills below them, carpeted in purple foliage. Forest canopies swallowed the land with rolling sweeps of gentle slopes and gullies. Rolling thunder clouds moved across the wide plains beyond the purple forest, depositing sheets of rain. Beetro looked back across the granite slot canyons—each a bald head with small tufts of dirt and gnarled branches. The western edge of the crater had seemed docile—dead, really. No bugs, no animals save vultures, and no plants except for dried roots. The eastern rim was the complete opposite—teeming with life.

"What is *that*?" Ribcage asked, pointing at the horizon.

Beetro focused his sight on a massive structure beyond the forest. He would've thought it a mountain, but it was perfectly shaped—too perfect to be natural. It loomed on the horizon, an enormous egg shape. "I've no idea," he said and then looked to Arym. The man's flummoxed gaze spoke volumes—he had no clue about anything outside Crater Valley. "Map," Beetro said, motioning to him, although Beetro had already brought up Arym's map in his mind.

Arym took out the animal skins and unfurled his maps, studying them. Ribcage watched over his shoulder as he traced his finger along Crater Valley and then moved it along a line that led toward Orion. "There's a road or a path. It goes through *Gargantua Forest*—must be the purple forest. We follow the road through there and then to Orion."

"Garga-what?" Ribcage repeated.

"Is it a friendly place?" Arym looked to Beetro.

"It's on your map, isn't it?"

Arym nodded.

"Are there any warnings about it?"

"No. But there aren't any warnings anywhere about anything."

"How big is the forest?"

"I've no idea."

"Will it take a long time to walk around?"

"I have no idea," Arym repeated.

"We go through the forest, save time, and get to Orion."

"Can you see it out there?" Ribcage asked, squinting at the horizon. "Orion?"

"I can't make out details this far out. It must be by that... mountain."

"Mountain? You mean that huge egg thing out there?"

Arym nodded. "It does seem to be where it would be on my maps."

"Then let's get off this granite and into the forest," Beetro said, some sort of authority rising in his voice.

They crept down the slot canyons and made their way through the granite catacombs as they sloped down toward the forest floor. The forest canopy consumed them as they descended from the crater ridge and became dark as night once they reached the floor. The air was dank and smelled of rotting flesh. Within a matter of hours, Ribcage's hair had metamorphosed from greasy gnarls into unwieldy puffs of curls in the new humidity. The land was studded with trees with the circumference of a house and, seemingly, as tall as a mountain. Their bark was a deep red, extending like endless highways to the purple-leafed canopy above. Beetro peered up and saw the forest ceiling many hundreds of meters in the air, small shoots of sunlight breaking through.

Ribcage shivered. "What *is* this place? Do you think it's always nighttime here?" She ran up to a tree and began picking at the bark.

"Gargantua," Beetro said, observing the enormous trees. The soil around the massive trunks were relatively bare of plant life.

"The trees block sunlight from reaching the floor. Looks like not much else can grow here." The place seemed distant—old. Like a graveyard that hadn't been visited in centuries. Dark. Forgotten. "I don't see any trails or roads. There is not a lot of foot traffic through here at all."

Arym kept stumbling, his gaze distracted by the mammoth trees. "Is this what all forests look like in the overworld?" He approached a tree—dwarfed by its circumference—and lightly tapped on the bark. "It's so... beautiful. Looks like a bunch of gems."

Beetro studied the bark, noticing that the layer coating the tree was less bark and shaped more like a scale. Hexagonal-shaped crimson scales layered along the trees in a never-ending pattern of overlapping fractal plates. If it wasn't for the irregularity of the tree sizes and spacing, he'd have thought they were human-built. Inspecting the scales closely, he discovered they were likely made of some sort of chitinous shell, nothing metallic. "I've never seen trees like these. How about you, Rib?"

But Ribcage was gone.

"Ribcage?" He spun around to the dark forest. The looming, monolithic trunks were silent. "Ribcage, get back here."

Nothing.

He flipped on his night vision, which only revealed more trees in the distant recesses of the forest.

"Maybe we should get out of here," Arym said, backing away from the tree.

Beetro glared at him. "And leave her?"

Arym swallowed, perspiration beading over his face. "No. I'm... something is wrong here." His breathing became labored. "Can you feel it?"

"Feel what?"

Arym's eyes spun. "I don't know. I just... I think we need to get out of this place."

"We're not leaving Ribcage behind." Beetro moved through the forest, passing the giant trees, Arym stumbling behind. He stopped.

A scream. Ribcage.

Beetro ran, taking wide weaves around the tree trunks, pinpointing the source of the scream. A subtle fear rose within him as he cried out her name. The damn girl had been such a nuisance—such a chaotic wonder—that being rid of her *should* feel like shedding himself of a parasite. Yet, the thought of the girl getting lost in the woods alone was suddenly terrifying. And he didn't know why. He thought of Bellamare—thought of Miree looking up at him, wondering if he would save her from the Reticulum.

It took several minutes of panic and a strange, almost nostalgic dread passing through him before he realized that Arym was gone.

He stopped, standing alone in a forest. "Arym?"

Silence.

Helplessly quiet.

He couldn't save his friends.

And he knew that's what they were—friends. Not resources. Not people to use to obtain an objective. Without Ribcage, without the strange new man from the crater—without Miree—he didn't know another person on the entire planet. His thoughts darkened. Everyone he met was cursed. Lucindi was killed, Miree was captured and turned into a cyborg, and now his last companions had vanished in the woods. How could he not be the common denominator? He thought of Besidio, the court jester, and his tale of Gaul. The king's nephew brought destruction to his family and himself. He was a ruin to everything he touched. Was Beetro any different?

He stood, unwilling to give in to the dark thoughts and marched through the forest, but there were no sounds, no footprints—no clues. He knelt and closed his eyes.

What could he do? Forget Ribcage and Arym, continue to Orion, and then what? Hope to heaven that he finds one random man named Galiaro? And then what after? How could meeting him actually have made the tragic trek from Korthe, through Peles Castle, and across the crater rim all worthwhile? Galiaro was just a man. And like all men, he would have little answers for Beetro. His programmed objective was probably just a default setting—a way to get lost property back to its owner in the event of a malfunction.

And so Beetro cried.

No tears came but he melted with grief. He gazed into the black dirt of the forest floor feeling more impotent than he had since his reboot in Korthe.

And then he remembered something.

He could shoot thermal energy from his palms.

He wasn't helpless. He literally had the power to kill hundreds with the sweep of his arms.

"Where are they!" he yelled, bubbling with anger. "Bring them back or... die." The last part tapered off, his heart not really in the threat.

A sound.

"Who's there? Ribcage?"

A figure appeared next to a tree. Long. Slender.

"Where are they?" Beetro lifted his palms.

The figure approached. It seemed humanoid but something was terribly off. Its face was... not there. It had a blank, white slate with a shoveled forehead that came to a blunted point. A pointed chest stood out from diminutive shoulders. Its limbs appeared frail yet were sinewed with spiraling tendons that quivered with nervous energy, as if ready to spring into rapid movement in a split second. Its skin was scaled with a silvery shimmer.

Beetro stood, drawing in the ambient light. A splattering of photons streamed over his skin, but it was a minuscule wave—a whisper of energy. Not nearly enough to condense within his body. The heaviness in his chest didn't come. The energy dissipated from him in the form of a weak pulse and then died out.

He had no photonic power.

TWENTY-SEVEN

MIREE OPENED HER EYES…

Eyes.

Sight.

It wasn't that her organic vision was restored, nor was it the view from a camera uplink into her brain. No. She could actually see. Albeit grainy waves of static crisscrossed her vision, but it was certainly better than nothing. She touched her new eyes—lenses, telescoping from her eye sockets, the same with which Ria had been implanted. Miree laughed, understanding how a monster like Ria also ended up blind during her capture. They blind the stubborn ones. Miree and Ria had at least that in common.

Miree studied the cell. Cylindrical, dark, and with pools of fluids throughout the floor. Piss or blood. Probably vomit too based on the odors. She looked down at her one arm, the lacy lattice of scars glistening in the low light. Her purple cloak was beneath her. She felt the tough fabric in between her fingers, comforted by the familiarity.

A figure lay at the other end of the cell. A man crumpled

together in a flowing robe; filth worked into every fiber. Scraggly hair clung to the base of his skull—a garnish to the shiny baldness above. A thick, gray beard swept up the man's chest and flanked his cheeks, framing baleful eyes. He opened those large eyes, cracked red, and peered up at her like an animal surprised in its hole.

"She's awoken," Galiaro declared. "Another new shiny gadget hammered into her skull." He waved at her.

"Wait... I *know* you. You're Crow."

He propped himself on an elbow. "What's that now, my dear?"

"Crow. You're the drunk from Korthe."

"Indeed."

"Lucindi would—" she pressed her forehead into her palms, exasperated. "She used to feed you—wasted our scavenged money keeping you alive."

"Who?"

"Lucindi."

"I'm afraid it doesn't ring a bell."

"She was just a beggar. Lived in a ditch. Someone I... cared about. Dumb enough to waste resources on a town drunk that was trying to drink himself to death. Didn't you ever wonder how you ate anything?"

"Never really crossed my mind." He crawled to the wall and sat up, pinched one nostril, and blew out a spot of mucous on the ground.

Incensed, she grasped for the appropriate response but could only stutter, "You... you—"

"What?"

"Nothing." She studied the old, decrepit man, oblivious of Lucindi's existence. This is the type of person for which Lucindi sacrificed? This was for whom Beetro was out there searching? If only Lucindi knew. If only she realized how pointless it was to help those that not only didn't deserve but didn't want her help. Her charity was nothing. Her kindness was a death sentence.

"There's something you should know," Galiaro said.

He looked exactly like a street beggar sitting on the cold, hard ground—as if about to ask for money. She couldn't quite believe that he was her first sight after being violently blinded. "What now?"

"They're sending you out. A mission."

"What kind of mission? And how do you know about it? You're one of them, aren't you?"

"No. I told you, I was never part of all this," he said, waving his hands around the cell. "I didn't know what she was all those years ago. I simply helped her set up a network in exchange for robotic parts. I didn't know she was making an army out of the network."

"Then how do you know they're sending me on a mission?"

"Because," he said, rubbing his dirty fingers through his beard, "I'm coming with you."

"To do what?"

"Don't you already know?"

"Know what?"

"You can't feel it yet?"

"Feel what?" And then she remembered the governor chip. It was still there. Buzzing, drilling—a constant drip of water on her impulses—driving her toward the Reticulum's whims. "Oh, no."

"That's right."

She could feel it. A single compulsion, buzzing in her brain, telling her to leave the Reticulum, driving her to what? The objective was almost there, emerging through the catacombs of her subconsciousness until it burst into an organized thought. "Oh, fuck *me*."

"That's right."

"They want me to find Beetro?"

Galiaro nodded.

"And you..." The objective of the governor chip unfolded in her mind, directing her through her feelings. "You're to accompany me because you made him—"

"She heard it all when we were talking. She thinks he's a weapon, wants to use him."

"And if you try to run away from me, I kill you," she finished, feeling the logic of the governor chip buzzing inside.

Galiaro's mouth bent with intrigue. "That. I did *not* know. I suppose that's what that thing is for—insuring her property."

It was only then that Miree noticed she had a new arm. "Ah!" She backed away as if she could flee from the metallic fixture clinging from her shoulder. "How much shit are they going to install into my fucking body?" The metallic arm consisted of a series of shafts that articulated at the elbow and ended in a cylindrical drum shape, the size of a fist. "Is this a weapon? There's no trigger on this thing."

Galiaro shook his head. "Don't know."

"If it's not a weapon, then how do they expect to catch a robot?" She threw up her arms, losing balance from the new, mechanical prosthesis that weighed about twice that of her prior arm. She lost balance and fell on her butt. "This..." she looked around the cell, "this *fucking* place."

"At least you're still alive, my dear."

"You think this is better than death?"

The old man shrugged, indifferent.

"And," she said, getting to her feet, looming over the man. "If you call me 'dear' *one more time,* I'm going to put this shiny new fist through your face."

Galiaro smirked, unthreatened. Sobriety had brought an annoying defiance to the rusted man. "Anything else?"

The door to the cell opened, exposing the tunnel behind. It all looked exactly how Miree had imagined—dark, depressing, and with spots of mold scattered along the solid granite tunnels. The hall was empty as she moved, well aware of her delusion that she was actually escaping the place and not doing exactly what they wanted. Her vision changed as she moved, toggling between day to night vision automatically based on the surrounding light. The constant visual flickering wired directly to her brain made her reel with vertigo. Yet despite the entirely new way of processing the world through labyrinthian tunnels, she knew exactly where to go. The governor chip guided her impulses, effortlessly.

Reticulum members passed by as she moved, peering at her but otherwise uninterested. She felt them. Like heartbeats, their presence pulsed around her, pinging the chip inside her brain, transmitting a friendly signal. Although something in her lizard brain was soothed by their presence, she could still hate them in her thoughts. Their hollow faces punctured by screws and wires, scanning the environment with laser arrays and echo sonography —the entire production made her want to drop a bomb on the place. She thought of Beetro, freezing Deluvius' laser and slamming it into the tower—something that would be useful at that moment.

She stopped at the threshold of the tunnel and looked out into a wide cavern. Hundreds of lab benches, conveyor belts, and table saws littered the cavern. Screams, interrupted by the mechanical whir of drills and saws, echoed through the chamber. Dozens of captives, led in by chains, were brought to worktables for robotic processing. Small eddies of blood flooded the floors, streaming through grates. Human tissue—brain, tendons, and bone shrapnel —covered every surface. It was a human laboratory blood bath.

She wanted to slaughter the Reticulum—run into the cavern and hack them to death. But the bug in her brain said *nope!*

"Bah!" she cried, finally noticing a figure standing at her side. Her telescoping eyes markedly cut off her peripheral vision.

"Had I known," Galiaro said, "I never would've helped this infernal AI. Had I known that this is what she was doing, I would've hacked her mainframe to pieces."

"You're following me?"

"Course. You're my ticket out of this place. Think I want a drill up the keister like all those poor souls?" He pointed to the butchery before them. "If they're not stopping you, then let's get outta here if you don't mind."

"Why haven't you been turned into one of them?"

"Told you. I'm more valuable to them as an unadulterated... consultant. That's how that robot woman put it to me. I'd be spared implants if I assisted you in getting Beetro to them."

"Not a bad story."

"You think I'm lying."

"Why would I believe you?"

"Because maybe I'm the only person in this place that hasn't been drilled and stuffed full of robot parts. Now, can you move it? We have business to be about, woman."

They skirted the edge of the cavern, Miree looking straight forward to resist the compulsion to attack the Reticulum members, suffering bouts of nausea and headache every time she thought about disobeying the governor chip. Past the cavern, she saw natural light glowing through the tunnels. After many minutes of moving up vertiginous inclines, they emerged at the mouth of a tunnel, brilliant sunlight blinding them. Galiaro took a deep breath and looked out over the shattered columns of rock.

"Meteor Mountains," Miree said, looking out to the yellow plains of Helian. "This is where they're headquartered."

"Aye," Galiaro said, shielding his eyes.

"Now I know where to come back to kill them all—ah!" she cried, buckling to her knees. She dry heaved several times after waves of electrical pain shook through her.

"They're in your head?"

Wiping spit from her mouth, she stood. "You have no idea what it's like. I'm me but any part of me that wants to act against the chip causes a..."

"Physiological backfire," he theorized.

"Something like that."

An icy voice spoke from behind. "Are you enjoying the view?"

Miree spun around. Ria. "*You.*" Miree lifted her clunky, robotic arm and pointed it at the cyborg, trying to discharge the weapon. Nothing.

"Don't be stupid. We know you're smarter than to believe that we would put a weapon on you that would work anywhere inside the Reticulum." She walked up to them, her face hooded from the sunlight, and dropped two packs at their knees. "Supplies."

Miree stood like a statue, watching her.

Ria smiled. "Food. Water. Sleeping supplies. There's also a good bit of gold to resupply. The robot is probably about halfway to Orion now. You may not catch him until he arrives. The gold is also to buy information once you get to Orion to find the robot."

Galiaro began fishing around in the packs. "We're going on foot?"

Ria looked at him as if he was a spider she was about to flick away. "Are you too... *old*?"

"Do you know who I am? I expected better traveling accommodations."

"Buy horses if you're too old. And here," she said, lifting something to Miree.

Miree stared at Ria's palm. It was that empty hilt she had used like a wand to direct a small army of metal shards. Flashes of being trapped within the fiery shard cage flooded her mind. The thirst and hunger—searing blindness—all within the confines of the hilt's shards. "Get that away from me."

"You ungrateful bug," Ria spat. "You have no idea how rare and precious this weapon is."

"Then why give it to me?"

"*I* wouldn't give you anything. She insists you have the Swordless Hilt. It is exceedingly rare. The Reticulum only possess a few for important missions—they originally come from my people—"

"What people?"

"Before I was assimilated. I am—was—from the Torbad." She grimaced... was the cyborg freak holding back tears? "She wants you to have the Swordless Hilt as extra defense. Do *not* lose it, do you understand? Use the arm prosthesis on the robot and bring him back in a shard cage from the Swordless Hilt." She offered the Hilt, which Miree took with a certain measure of trepidation. "Have fun, you two. If you actually bring back the robot, she has promised that you won't be killed. Not much more I can say beyond that. Luck." She turned, cloak fluttering in the wind and disappeared inside the Reticulum.

Miree looked down at the Swordless Hilt, its silver gleaming in the sunlight. "This thing," she said, now admiring the weapon. It felt good in her hand. Her left hand—not her killing hand—but it would do. She flipped it over, inspecting the pommel, which was engraved with flames. The shards that formed the blade overlapped one another like scales, aligning as a perfect column. She knew that with a flick of the Hilt, the shards would uncouple, flying like small daggers at their victim.

"What are you blubbering about? Let's get out of these godforsaken mountains." Galiaro hefted his pack with surprising strength. "We just got a free ride out of here."

Miree strapped the scabbard of the Swordless Hilt to her belt and awkwardly picked up her pack, negotiating her top-heavy robotic arm against the weight of the pack. "Why are you suddenly so chipper? I thought you wanted to die."

"I did—I do. But not in that hole." He ambled ahead. "Let's go get a drink."

Miree looked behind at the tunnel she'd left, amazed she was stepping out. She thought of running away forever, fleeing to the farthest corner of the planet to live out the rest of her days. The horizon was wide open—the clouds glowing purple and pink from the setting sun. The illusion was fleeting—she felt the bug in her brain, buzzing, urging, ticking away in her like a never-ending metronome. The compulsion was ever-present—*find Beetro, find Beetro, find Beetro...*

Again. The robot reared its head into her life and the absurdity became crystal clear—she was searching for a robot who was searching for her traveling companion. She shuddered and lifted her purple hood over her head, her eyes glowing a deep red within.

A few days of excruciating conversation with the old man proved to be, at times, more torturous than her prison cell at the Reticulum. Galiaro talked about booze, misadventures with mature women, and his favorite spot in Korthe for drinking. The trick, he explained, was drinking as much as possible at any given time with as little food as possible in his stomach. The balance between near-starvation and blackout drunkenness was an apparent art form. Too little food, you die... too much and you don't blackout.

"Doesn't sound like you were trying to kill yourself exactly, but just right on that edge."

"At times, the oblivion of the drink was better than the thought of dying."

Not that Miree cared, but the man barely asked anything about herself other than trying to pry information from her about the Fifth Kingdom. "Do women like living in the Fifth Kingdom?"

And then she punched him in the mouth. "Don't bring that up again."

"Just asking questions," he said, holding his mouth.

"No, you're really not. Sounds like you have an idea of how women are treated there."

"There's something very valuable in the mountains behind the Fifth Kingdom. If you weren't such a stubborn wench, maybe I'd tell you what's there."

"I don't care what's there. It should get bombed to hell for all I care."

"Ah," he said, spitting blood on the granite rock.

"What?"

"I understand what you are now. Lass from Fifth Kingdom, Kish spy and would-be thief—now Reticulum lackey. You're a person who runs from their problems instead of confronting them."

"This from the Korthe town drunk? And didn't I already shut that mouth of yours?"

They'd travelled along the top of the granite slot canyons until they were spaced too far to jump. The chasms in between deepened. "We should head down through here," she said.

"Not that way," Galiaro said. "That'll go east. We need to go west."

"No. Beetro went east. I saw him go that way with the street kid."

"We go west and then south," he said as if ending the discussion.

"But we won't find him south."

"South."

The governor chip buzzed with suspicion. "You're already making my head hurt. The chip knows if we try to do something that is against what I believe is the best way to get to Beetro."

"You've traveled from Orion, have you not? You were part of the Kish? Or was that one of your little lies?"

"What are you getting at?"

"If you'd traveled from Orion, you'd know that if we went east, we'd run into the Gargantua Forest. I don't imagine you'd want to go through there."

"Of course not. But we could just go around the forest once we get to the eastern ridge."

"Wrong. We go south. Go to Portolo and take a ship to Orion. Faster. We'll beat the robot to Orion."

"Oh," she said, the chip easing in her mind. The logic worked. As she became more convinced, the governor chip was convinced. It was tied to what she believed to be the truth. "Fine. South."

They traveled through the slot canyons, Galiaro keeping surprisingly good pace. They ate dried meat and roots from the pack provided by Ria and stopped at night, rolling out sleeping pads made of a sleek material that bottled in body heat exceptionally well. Miree tested her prosthetic arm as they traveled, aiming it at rabbits and then pulling some sort of trigger in her mind. The bald, metallic stub at the end of the arm would discharge with energy, but nothing happened to the wildlife. The rabbits just scampered away. The prosthesis appeared entirely useless. The Swordless Hilt was another beast altogether. She'd figured out how to get the shards to scatter and soar through the air but was terrible at making them obey. Slight flicks of the wrist created dramatic shifts in the shards as they sailed through the air. She nearly took off one of Galiaro's ears.

"Watch it!" he yelped, cowering behind a boulder.

"Sorry."

"Don't try to deny that it wasn't on purpose."

"I'm still trying to figure the thing out. Relax. I won't kill you. Yet."

They arrived at the Granite Gate a few hours later, the Helian plains spread before them. Peles Castle on the horizon. Miree winced at the sight. "You know the way?"

"Way?"

"Portolo. You *do* know the way?"

Galiaro looked south, the feet of the mountains curling along the plains and tapering away. "The sea is that way. Portolo is on the sea. It's not difficult. I have a lab out here that we need to stop by. There may be some useful tools for our journey there."

"You have a lab? In the middle of Helian?"

"Yes."

"I thought you just got drunk all day."

"That's what I do now. In my previous life, I actually cared about my work."

"What kind of tools do you need there?"

"Not sure. It's been many years since I've been."

"Then why do you think they'll help?"

"Don't ask an old man stupid questions."

Miree had quickly grown tired of traveling with the man. "Let's go."

He held his arm out, wind fluttering against his cloak. "After you."

They made good time the rest of the day and pitched camp

along the base of the mountains. A small fire warmed a can of beans, which they shared and mixed with dried potatoes. The Reticulum may have been cyborg freaks, but they at least still had somewhat of a human palate. Before every bite, Galiaro would stick his tongue into the food, testing the temperature, blow on it, and then eat. Miree watched in morbid fascination—tongue, blow, bite as if this was the way the man had eaten his entire life.

"Stop that," she demanded.

He looked up from his meal, beans spilling down his beard. "Stop what?"

"Just wait. Wait for the entire meal to cool and you don't have to stick your disgusting tongue into every bite every single time."

"Now you're telling me how to eat?" He stuck out his tongue and plunged it into a spoonful of potatoes, eyes pinned on Miree.

The next day, the plains swept a fierce wind their way. Galiaro kept one palm on his stout hat, eyes shut tight as he stomped along, boots kicking up dust. Miree wrapped herself in her cloak, kicking herself for giving Ribcage her thick scarf. She could hardly think about the girl without shaking in anger. Miree wanted to find Beetro and that street rat, not just because of the bug in her brain, but so she could beat them senseless for what happened at Peles Castle. Yet, the thought of being in Orion made her almost as sick as denying the governor chip.

"Hey," she yelled at the astrocyst across the wind. He trekked on with a paradoxically youthful resilience. "Hey!"

He turned. "Speak your mind. I know I can't stop you."

"We might have problems in Orion."

"What kind of problems?" he asked, bushy eyebrows inquisitive.

"There are people there. They don't like me."

He read her face for a moment. "You truly were part of the Kish."

She nodded.

"And now they want you dead."

"Death would only be the start of it if Haldunt the Wire gets his hands on me."

"Any worse than what the Reticulum put you through?"

She didn't have an answer—had no idea how to answer.

Galiaro whipped around and kept moving.

That night, Miree watched the old man's face light up from the campfire, his features exaggerated by elongated shadows. She still couldn't believe it—she was traveling with Crow. The worthless, half-dead, town drunk. An astrocyst, a robotic engineer, sitting ten feet from her every day in a drunken stupor. Why did he leave Beetro in the junkyard? Moreover, why did he leave his drunken paradise to chase after him into the plains of Helian?

"When did you make the robot?"

Galiaro's face tightened but he acted as if he didn't hear her.

"And why was he in the junkyard of Korthe? You just threw him away?"

"I-I'm not sure what you're talking about."

"What? *Beetro.* Your robot. The entire reason we're out here. The robot woke up saying your name—wouldn't shut up about it. You programmed him to find you on reboot. Why did you throw away a perfectly good robot and then chase after him? It doesn't make any sense."

He glared at her, wide-eyed, fire shadows dancing across his face. "You should've been a man," he said.

"*What?*"

"Those broad shoulders, stout thighs, barrel chest—don't know why you didn't come out a man. Not quite pretty enough to be a real lady. There are some things you could do to make yourself up, but they wouldn't go far. Suppose it's moot now with the Reticulum implants. Shame."

Fury. Liquid anger boiled inside her. "My arm—my fucking *eyes*—are implants forced into my body and you're sitting there talking about how I'm not pretty enough? Have you looked at yourself? You're a total fucking wreck. You look like hell in a hurricane, you drunken asshole—sit there and talk about what I look like. You don't know anything about me, so why don't you just shut your mouth before I knock you out again?"

Galiaro snorted, studying her for a moment. "Fists aren't strength, *my dear*." He turned his back, wrapped himself up in a blanket, and stuffed his hat over his face.

They spoke little the next day, moving south along the base of the mountains. Miree spotted flashes of blue on the horizon, shimmering with the waters of Chronicle Sea. There hadn't been any sign of armies along the plains and no travelers across their path. The plains were an empty place, dry and brittle from drought. Forgotten.

"There." Galiaro pointed to an outcropping of boulders that spilled out into the plains. "We go there."

The governor chip buzzed, working with Miree's own natural suspicions, pressing her to not trust the man. "Why?"

"Told you. I have an old workshop. It's been some years, but it should be undisturbed."

"What do we need there? If it's booze, I swear I'll leave you to drown in it."

"When we get to Orion, we need to meet with another astrocyst named Fallaro. There are materials we may need that he doesn't have. We can bring them from my old lab."

"Did you say *Fallaro*?"

"Yes. Why?"

"Nothing."

He glared at her. "You knew him?"

"We may have crossed paths, yes." She recalled binding and gagging the man before walking away with his Quantizer.

"Did he mention my name?"

"No. No one has ever heard of you. I know because Beetro asked every person that sneezed if they knew who you were."

"It bodes better for us if Fallaro doesn't dwell too much on me either."

"So, do you just piss off people wherever you go?"

Galiaro took off his cap, wiped his scalp with a handkerchief, and returned the cap. "I could ask you the same question."

The workshop was underground, a hidden staircase dug into the earth between two granite boulders, leading to a metal door with no hinges or hatch. There was no discernable way to enter and, on closer inspection, Miree didn't even see a frame around the door. It was just a sheet of metal set into the rock. Galiaro raised his palms to the surface, pressing them against the door, eyes closed.

"It has been some time since I've been here. Might not remember how to get in exactly..." He rubbed the surface, then tapped it with his knuckle and thoughtfully rubbed his chin. "Hmm." He puckered his lips and blew over the metallic surface, inducing a shimmering gleam over its surface like ripples in a pond. "Ahh."

"What was *that*?"

"I seem to recall making the portal door of graphesium. It's thermally activated to change molecular state, only..." He looked around. "Needs to be hotter. *Much* hotter. A keypad should then emerge from the metal. We need to start a fire." He turned to go up the narrow staircase.

As Miree twisted, she felt the scabbard of the Swordless Hilt sweep across her leg. "Wait," she said, pulling out the sword. Galiaro looked at the scaled blade expectedly. Miree had learned that a swift downward movement of the Hilt freed the shards, but if she avoided the movement, the shards stayed in place, stacked as a solid blade. Keeping the Hilt still, she flipped the pommel one hundred and eighty degrees and waited. The shards hummed with energy, quickly brightening a bright orange and then a deep red, surrounding heat waves distorting the air.

A toothless smile crept up Galiaro's face. "I think that will do." He gestured to the portal door.

Gingerly, Miree poked the blade into the graphesium surface of the door, which rippled away. The portal receded around the heat but held as an intact, concentric circle. A series of numbers cascaded across the metal, illuminated by amber light. Galiaro pressed on a few of these numbers, prompting the graphesium door to melt away, exposing a chamber within.

"That's a nice toy," Galiaro said, stepping around her and beyond the portal. "Not the first time I've seen one. The Torbad are exceptional people." Miree followed behind and flipped the pommel back, prompting the shard blade to cool.

A dank cavern, hewn within dirt and rock and sealed with metallic plating housed workbenches filled with dusty crates of wire, metal casings, rusted batteries, and glass beakers. Graduated columns, desiccated vats and fluted glassware littered the tables and chairs of the lab. Spiral tubing was strung around the tables, clinging to volumetric flasks and small distilleries. There were pots full of powders—white, black, blue—all of which were open to the air with a caustic fragrance leaching into the lab. A generator the size of an ox hulked in the corner, tongues of wires and tubing leading all around the lab.

"What did you work on in here?"

Galiaro had moved to a lab bench, rummaging around the table. "Oh. This and that." He picked up an instrument consisting of a rubber handle and two metal prongs wound with wire.

"Is this where you made Beetro?" She turned away, fidgeting with a flimsy coil of metal she found.

"Parts of him. Now I want you to go to the generator over there."

"Why?"

"I need to see what still works. Don't worry, I'll tell you what to do."

Miree walked to the generator and looked at her own reflection on a blank screen mounted on the side and winced at her visage. "Okay. Now what—"

She saw a flash of movement reflected on the screen, but it was too late. A dull crack of something hard over her head brought her to the floor. Her ocular implants buzzed with static, but she could still see. She was awake long enough to see the old man looming over her, face inscrutable. He held the two-prong rod above her face, now licking with blue electricity.

"Shh," he said, touching the prongs to her temple. Her entire body became as if one muscle, convulsing together as electricity coursed through her skull.

Then she blacked out.

TWENTY-EIGHT

ARYM RAN.

A blur of gigantic red tree trunks the size of mountain faces whirled around him. His feet stumbled on the uneven forest ground, void of light and plant life. Where did Beetro go? One moment the robot was running, searching for Ribcage, the next he was gone—vanished from sight. The forest dimmed around him, the remaining light choked by the purple leaves of the gargantua high above. What was this place? How could something so big—so alien—be living just outside of Crater Valley? Just outside the Crib—his home?

A frigid chill set over his forehead as he realized he was lost. Panic swelled in his chest imbued with growing regret. Regret for leaving—for abandoning the only home he'd ever known. He should've stayed behind. So, what if they locked him up in isolation? Was it worse than stumbling around, alone in a forest, searching after a demon child who swore to slit his throat? The only shining light was the robot—Beetro. He seemed... kind. Not threatening in the least despite the bot's feigned intimidation.

The dangers of the overworld were real. The Oath of Descension—something to be respected. Their founder, Othel, was right to dig beneath the earth and start a colony. But why clone himself? Why the perpetuation of himself to never leave the dirt?

Arym spun around the forest, the red bark—scales really—of the gargantua surrounding him. Where could he go? He picked a straight course through an open space between the trees but came to an identical location. Fear seized him and then something new—a chill crept along his spine as he felt a presence behind him. Something was there with him, watching.

He turned and saw... *himself.* A man, opposite him on the forest floor, staring back.

"What's going on?" Arym asked.

The man stood, frozen in a neutral pose, face placid.

"Are you from the Crib? I need to find a way out of here."

A twisted smile warped the man's face.

"Who are you?"

"You've killed my children, Arym," the man said between a grin.

"What? No, please."

"You've killed the Crib."

"Othel?"

"I trusted you with your Oaths. You betrayed that trust."

"No. Never. I never broke the Oath. I only left the Crib, but I want to save it now."

"You killed them all."

"No!"

"Killed them all."

"I'm trying to save them!"

A glowing orb descended from the trees above, floating around Othel.

"Protonix!" Arym said. "Tell him! Tell him I didn't mean to hurt them."

Protonix orbited Othel. "You've killed them, Arym. You belong in isolation. Forever."

"No!"

Othel grew, his features exaggerating. His legs stretched in length and then sprouted new joints, circling back on one another until forming multi-articulating appendages. Several more arms sprouted from the man, growing to the ground, supporting his growing body. His eyes grew with fiery red light, spurts of flames stoking with smoke from the sockets. A serpentine tongue lashed from his mouth as razor-sharp teeth elongated from the creature's jaw, menacing with salivation.

Protonix enlarged into the size of a man, amorphous blebs gyrating over the surface of a human figure. The face of the rektor, Tarysl, emerged from a flaming hot light. The man looked at him, a haunting sorrow crossing his face. "Coward," he bemoaned, voice booming through the forest. Tarysl opened his mouth, jawline extending far below the normal boundaries of a face, soon enveloping the entire being. It became nothing more than an erupting mouth of fire and wrath directed at Arym. The creature that was once Othel lurched to the ground, scuttling toward him with insect-like energy.

Arym ran.

He bolted from the hellish scene—the harbingers of his past now hell-bent on getting vengeance. He ran, sweat dripping and breath heaving, not understanding or caring from whence the creatures came. Heart pumping in his ears, a feverish malaise filled his head, clouding his thoughts. Looking behind, he saw their pursuit—glowing flames approaching, voices crackling like burning kindle.

"Help!" he cried. "Anyone!"

But there was no answer. No help.

Sweat poured down his face—streamed off his chin. An overpowering heat consumed him, drenching his body in sweat. Ripping off his shirt, he leaped bare-chested over a small ravine. There was no end ahead, only the pitch of the forest—the looming, monstrous trees continuing along him. Never ending.

He finally fell to his knees, exhaustion overwhelming his body. There was nowhere to run—nowhere to hide. An overpowering sadness crashed in on him. He would die here. Alone, away from his home. He'd never see Hawera again.

He turned his head and saw them, the creatures approaching —wraiths of his past. Gleeful shrieks escaped their mouths as they circled in, eyes wide.

The creature stepped closer; its enormous flat-faced head focused on Beetro. It had no discernable facial features—no mouth, no eyes, nothing. It was a featureless surface, shiny with opalescent scales, completely flat. Its face was the shape of an upside-down shield—a hard, flat line for a chin, the forehead corniced by an obtuse angle forming a point.

"Don't take another step," Beetro said, keeping his palms trained on the creature. He tried once more to charge his body with photonic power, yet the towering gargantua trees choked the forest floor of most light.

He was defenseless.

The creature advanced, taking steady yet careful steps.

"Stop!" Beetro commanded. "Where are my companions? What did you do with them?"

The ivory-colored creature stopped, moved its enormous flat face from side to side, and then back at Beetro. Eyes the size of dinner plates appeared at the top of its face, inky black as if one entire pupil—prodigiously bulbous. A shimmer of colors flashed across the scales of its face, almost imperceptible. A vague iridescence waved across the scales, rippling randomly over the surface of its face.

Beetro lowered his hands.

The creature's eyes moved back and forth, taking in Beetro. New patterns flitted across its facial scales—intricate and complex, a cascading sequence of colors and shapes. It appeared almost as a digital screen, projecting patterns and fractals, changing from one permutation to the next.

"What... are you?" Beetro asked, dropping his guard. The gangly, shovel-faced creature was certainly strange but was becoming less threatening by the second. Noiselessly, the creature once again changed the color of the scales from interchanging reds, oranges, and blues to a solid wall of black. It was a single sheet of black scales contrasting deeply against the rest of the creature's white body.

Suddenly, a single block of white scales emerged within the black sheet. Rather than a pattern, they were clearly pictorial:

δইS8ςইই8
Zθ5ςցஃ໑ལbθ
3ಹಬʒ∝ ˥ ≻ Đx

"Huh?"

The creature blinked and then reset its face, prompting the scales to turn to a solid black slate once more. After a pause, a new block of characters appeared, emerging as white within the black face:

□⊸r ˥ 7ๅɩᒪ—

"I don't understand. I don't know these languages. I only know Haenglish. Have you seen my people? Do you know where they are?" He took a glance around the forest, assuring himself the strange creature wasn't a decoy to another threat.

The creature once more reset its face to a sheet of black, its eyes searching Beetro over, analyzing. Thinking. It was worrying to Beetro. There was far too much intelligence in those eyes—more than a simple beast.

Beetro took a step. "Maybe I should just be on my way. "

The creature shook its head, not menacing—asking for patience. A series of even more characters, new and more numerous, flashed across the flat face. The creature showed a block of characters, waited for Beetro to shake his head, and then flashed a new set. Beetro put up his hands. "If you're trying to say something, I'm not getting any of it."

The creature bowed its head as if defeated. It turned its enormous face and looked about the forest, exposing a long, sinewy neck that seemed impossibly thin to be wielding such a large head. It then went rigid, looking back at Beetro and lifting one finger. A new series appeared on its face, emerging in white:

o[oo[[o[o[[[[oo[oo[ooooo o]]o]]] o]]oooo] o]]o]]o] o]]oo]o] oo]ooooo o]]o]oo] o]]]oo]] oo]ooooo o]o]ooo] o]]o]oo] o]]]o]oo o]]o]ooo o]]oooo] o]]]oo]o o]]oooo]

. . .

"No," Beetro said. "I told you. I don't understand anything you're saying." He dismissed the weird creature, considering it neither friend nor foe but a mere nuisance. "My companions are lost. I've got to go." He walked away but the creature followed, tapping on its face, bearing the most recent, longer symbols. "No, I—"

Wait. There was something different about the last set of symbols. They weren't pictorial. It was...

"Binary!" Beetro yelled.

The creature nodded, mirroring Beetro's enthusiasm.

"That's binary, yes, yes, I know binary. 'My name is Qithara'," Beetro read off the face. "Qithara, my name is Beetro."

But the creature pointed to the side of its head. It displayed a new message:

o[oo[oo[oo[ooooo o[[oo[oo o[[o[[[[o[[o[[[o oo[oo[[[o[[[o[oo oo[ooooo o[[o[ooo o[[oooo[o[[[o[[o o[[oo[o[oo[ooooo o[[oo[o[o[[oooo[o[[[oo[o o[[[oo[[ooo[o[o

Beetro read aloud, "'I do not understand soundwaves.' Oh. Well. That's a problem." He looked around, finding a stick. Within the dirt before the creature, he scribbled binary in the conventional 0s and 1s. It was a laborious effort as it required much more in binary to convey even a few short words. He wrote a series, erased, and wrote more, hoping the creature was reading everything he drew in the dirt. He wrote: *I am Beetro. Have you seen my human friends?*

The creature studied the dirt with its large eyes, nodded, and responded, switching to 0s and 1s. [*Yes. The carbonoids are in danger.*]

Carbonoids?

[*Carbonoids in danger.*]

What kind of danger?

[*Danger. Danger in their minds.*]

Beetro stared at this response for a moment.

[*Danger. Carbonoid danger in their minds. Robot, no danger.*]

Beetro considered his next words. Drawing binary in the dirt was painstakingly slow. He would need to communicate as little as possible to get the highest yield information possible. He traced: *Explain.*

Qithara simply repeated, [*Carbonoid in danger, robot no danger.*]

Beetro grunted, frustrated. *Help humans.*

[*We don't desire to hurt carbonoids.*]

At this, Beetro grew anxious, surveying the forest. He saw several more of the creatures nearby, waiting by the gargantua trees. *What did you do to humans?* he wrote.

[*Our trees, the Hukara*] Qithara said, motioning to the mammoth trunks, [*danger for carbonoids. Come.*] It motioned for Beetro to follow and then turned, scuttling along the forest with its knobby legs. Beetro hesitated but followed when he saw Qithara moving exceptionally fast across the forest floor. It scuttled like a spider but with a torso that swiveled around its hips, granting remarkable agility. Beetro followed with growing anxiety, uncertain if he was getting help from the creatures or simply walking into a trap. He surveyed the forest as he went, searching for Arym and Ribcage, but found only silent trees like watching giants.

He followed Qithara to a clearing where the creature had stopped, waiting for the robot. It looked at him with its bulbous, inky eyes, and then flashed binary across its face: [*We don't desire to hurt carbonoids. Please.*]

Please? What did that mean? Beetro drew once more in the dirt and wrote: *It's okay. Please help.*

Qithara nodded. [*Yes. The Thekora will help carbonoids.*]

You are Thekora?

[*Yes. We are Thekora. Thekora friend to carbonoids.*]

Why was it so adamant on the point that they were *helping* humans? Beetro smelled a trap.

The Thekora pointed up, its hand composed of four, spindly fingers, knobby and tremulous. Beetro followed its fingers and saw something floating down to them. As it descended, he discovered it was a gondola, expertly fashioned of fine rope, intertwined many times over. On closer inspection, it appeared to be made of the same substance as the gargantua trees—a scaly texture colored with deep crimson. Vines? The rope was fashioned into a square around the gondola, interrupted by cascading ropes that wove into a thick platform. What was most unusual about the gondola was that the entire structure was seamless—there were no tie-offs, no knots, no wooden planks that had been cut and nailed together. It was as if the gondola had grown right from the ground and was plucked from the earth like a single piece of fruit.

Qithara easily crawled over the railing of the gondola and motioned for Beetro to follow. When the Thekora noted his hesitancy, it wrote, [*We have solution. Solution for carbonoid.*] Beetro reluctantly hopped over the lip of the gondola, wishing he had a photonic charge ready to go in case it was a trap, but the darkness of the forest was ever-present and consuming.

Noiselessly, the gondola lifted into the air. [*We don't bring others up,*] Qithara said.

Beetro looked around, realizing he had no way of communicating with the creature now that he could no longer write on the ground. He thought for a moment and then realized the solution. He flashed his indigo eyes, left and then right. Qithara nodded in understanding. Beetro quickly blinked, *Why?* Relieved that communicating with his eyes was much faster than writing the binary in the dirt.

[*We fear carbonoids.*]

Why?

[*We keep us secret. Secret from carbonoids.*]

Why?

[*We not from here. Come from different planet. Long ago. Try to keep secret from carbonoids. Carbonoids violent. Thekora not violent. Thekora only want life. Carbonoids want life and death.*]

Where did you come from?

[*Planet far away. Chor. Dead. We come here.*]

How long have you been here?

[*Many of your revolutions. Many. Many. Thekora live more long than carbonoids. Carbonoids live fast, live foolish.*]

Based on his interactions with all humans since his reboot, Beetro could not deny the creature's assessment. He blinked back, *I will not harm you.*

[*Thank you.*]

Beetro looked down, the forest floor was a mesmerizing distance below them. The trunks of the gargantua stood beside them as they ascended like sentinels. Beetro blinked, *These trees are from your home planet?*

[*Yes. We plant them long ago. Hukara tree give Thekora life. Hukara give carbonoids death.*]

Beetro rubbed his fingers along the rope of the gondola, the scales clicking in between his metal fingers. *What are you made from?*

Qithara flashed a question mark.

You are not made from carbon.

[*Silicon. The Hukara create atmosphere for us. Sulfur in our bodies. We live only in forest. Forest toxic to carbonoids.*]

I need to get my friends away from here.

[*Yes. We have your carbonoid. Safe. You see. You remember that Thekora is kind to carbonoid. You remember.*]

The gondola suddenly rose into an enormous pavilion of leathery leaves, purple and enormous—some the size of boulders. The leaves had a crushed velvet texture and shimmered slightly in the moonlight, which was visible now that they'd arisen through the forest canopy. Beetro looked beyond the enormous leaves and saw dozens of structures that appeared to be sewn right into the massive branches of the gargantua. Hundreds of crisscrossing bridgeways spanned the long distances between the massive trees, connecting hubs woven with gargantua branches and vines just as the gondola had been constructed. Long spires connected by rookeries reached high through the branches, made of intertwined vines woven over into the branches in intricate designs. The branches of the gargantua defined the community, running through the middle of a row of homes like the main street of a town. The homes themselves were outcroppings of the natural branches as if they'd sprouted and grown of their own accord. It was a beautifully manicured community suspended amongst the gargantua trunks.

The Thekora crawled along the branches and vines in every direction. They congregated under large archways adorned with the enormous purple leaves, or moved in single file down narrowing causeways that connected one hub-like community to the next. Each tree trunk acted as a node of activity—a satellite of the village with connecting branches that led to the next gargantua trunk. The village spanned dozens of trees as far as Beetro could see—thousands of the Thekora moving about their day as in any human village. The entire village was silent—no chatter, no laughter, no hollering. They only communicated by their facial displays.

Qithara tapped him on the shoulder. [*Welcome to Tol. Come.*]

It vaulted the gondola and moved down a branch, its feet clicking along the scales of the path.

Several Thekora took note of the new guest and looked frantically over at Qithara, who presumably flashed a few words of encouragement to them. Beetro noticed Qithara communicated to them wordlessly through its frontal plate with complex pictorials —each character flowing to the next and even looping back to previous characters. The language appeared a total, nonsensical mess to him.

[*Stay by my side. Thekora peaceful but can be dangerous when afraid.*]

How did you build all this? Beetro flashed across his eyes.

[*We don't build like carbonoids. We grow. We grow Tol.*]

Grow a city?

[*Yes. Grow the Hukara the way we wish. Grow the branches into homes, buildings, roads. The Hukara trees are home.*]

Finally, Beetro understood. That's how every structure—the gondola, the roads, the homes—all flowed so seamlessly with their surroundings. Everything was grown directly from the gargantua, weaved and stitched into whatever likeness they desired. There was no construction, only growing.

The trees grow fast? Beetro asked.

[*Fast for Thekora. Slow for Earth cycles. Many cycles to make one home.*]

How long has the Thekora been here?

[*Thousands of Earth revolutions.*]

How old are you?

[*Hundreds of Earth revolutions.*]

Beetro looked Qithara up and down. It started to make sense. To build a home, they weaved the branches and vines in a particular way and manicured them as they grew. It could take decades to have a home but what was a decade to a being that was hundreds of years old?

They moved past a row of homes—pod-like with a riot of vines forming the foundation, threading into a bulbous base and eventually tapering together in a teardrop shape toward the sky. Thekora looked out from their habitations at the strange robot walking their streets. Qithara was constantly pacifying the onlookers as they moved, assuaging fears. It was clear from the deference they gave that Qithara was a leader in the community.

Qithara glanced at Beetro. [*We came many cycles ago. Our planet Chor. We forced to arrive Earth.*]

Why did you come?

[*Forced. Ancestors came through Alchean wormhole. Did not want come. Forced.*]

Why were you brought to Earth?

[*Labor. Labor for humans.*]

You worked for humans?

[*Yes, but not want. Forced.*]

By whom?

[*Alcheans.*]

The Alcheans brought you here for slave labor?

Qithara nodded. [*Alchean now gone. Live foolish. Thekora wise. Thekora hide. Thekora build. We grow Hukara tree here. Our numbers small. Can't live away from Hukara forest. Thekora die away from forest. Thekora once great species on Chor. Now we are small but mighty.*]

What happened to the Alcheans?

[*Gone.*]

To where?

[*Thekora do not know.*]

Do you know why they left?

Qithara hesitated, blinking. [*You do not know?*]

No.

Qithara studied Beetro for a moment as if trying to understand. [*You have seen the sky?*]

I see the sky, yes.

[*You have seen the planets?*]

What planets?

[*The planets in the sky.*]

I've only seen the five stars...

Qithara turned its face blank and considered Beetro with its inky eyes for a moment. [*Do carbonoids not know?*]

Know what?

[*You tell the carbonoids that Thekora are friends. Tell them to remember us if they find a way to leave.*]

Leave?

[*Leave Earth. If they leave, please come for Thekora.*]

Why would humans leave Earth?

Qithara motioned with its spindly hand as they turned a corner at a knotted structure that bore a single glowing ember within as if it was a streetlight. [*Your carbonoid is down this way. Come.*]

Unsettled by Qithara's words, Beetro followed, thinking about the fairytale that Besidio had told him. The corrupt nephew trying to steal a kingdom, only to be killed and placed in the night sky, forming the five stars that were present today. Beetro had been programmed with very little knowledge of the galaxy but did realize it was strange that Qithara referred to the stars as planets.

They entered a large gateway directly through a Hukara tree. It appeared as if the maroon bark of the tree had been compressed inward, its scaly fibers weaving inward to a cavity within the trunk. Several Thekora watched Qithara and Beetro as they passed through the gateway, appearing flummoxed. Qithara faced them, craning its slender neck, and displayed more of their bizarre language to them. After a brief exchange, they allowed Beetro to pass.

The cavity within the tree had been compressed and weaved into a multitude of floors, stacked upon one another, with connected bridgeways and slides. Flickering lanterns of glowing geodes illuminated the cavity. Beetro followed as Qithara passed several side chambers where Thekora seemed busy at tables, working pestles on large mortars, or rolling out strange, doughy substances and working them with their knuckles. He noticed that every Thekora seemed to be engaged in something—none of them stood idly by like back in Korthe. He thought of the malnourished men, smoking tobacco and leaning against the crumbling walls in back alleys at Korthe. Hordes of street children flooded the streets asking even the homeless for food. There was none of that at Tol, among the Thekora. Perhaps that is how the small community of creatures from another planet were able to survive, they simply cooperated with one another. Compared to the Thekora, humans seemed so... flawed. He couldn't help but think of Lucindi and how different Korthe may have been if everyone was as kind as she was before she died.

Suddenly, the pang of losing her came crashing back in on him. He saw her there, a smoking crater in her chest where Deluvius had discharged that laser rifle. He remembered the feeling of the laser leaving the rifle—he could feel it. If only he'd known—if only he understood at the time that he could've frozen that laser and thrown it right back in his face...

A creeping remorse rose within him.

He could've saved her.

And now, weeks later, walking through gigantic tree branches with aliens from another world, he thought about how much he had changed—had learned. Walking through the streets of Tol, he learned something important about himself—he cared. Trailing after Qithara was definitive proof that he cared, at least, about someone. Miree would've certainly fled the forest at the first sign of danger to save herself. But Beetro was diving deeper to save two humans he really didn't even know. And why? Because he couldn't live with himself if he left them here to die. Did that mean anything at all? Caring certainly didn't get Lucindi anywhere.

[*Through here,*] Qithara said, breaking Beetro from his reverie with a tap on the shoulder. Qithara led him down a narrow corridor that slanted down and then corkscrewed through the center of the tree. They passed another series of rooms until coming to an end, where Qithara motioned him into a chamber. Within the dark room, Beetro saw another Thekora kneeling beside a bed. It was mixing a watery paste in a mortar and then scooping it into a spoon.

[*Good,*] Qithara said. [*There may still be time. We've made the antidote.*]

The antidote?

[*Yes. For your carbonoid. It is only temporary. Must leave with carbonoid now or will die.*]

Beetro looked at the bed and saw a woman, her scalp completely shaved. A wool poncho covered her body, bare legs curled up beneath. She breathed heavily, chest heaving, sweat accumulating around her neck. She grimaced through small convulsions.

Beetro turned to Qithara. *That is* not *my carbonoid.*

TWENTY-NINE

MIREE TRIED BLINKING but recalled she no longer had eyelids. Her vision returned, hiccups in the feeds from her ocular implants, scattering static across her sight. She'd forgotten what happened—she was in the bowels of the Reticulum, periodically drilled and shocked into submission. Then she remembered the Swordless Hilt, the satisfying weight in her hand... the glowing shards. The governor chip buzzing in her brain, constraining her to walk across the Helian plains. A metal portal door receding to liquid around the blade of shards. Her mouth tasted of burnt flesh and singed hair. What had happened?

Galiaro.

She awoke with a jolt, revenge driving her to her feet. *I will kill him.* Her head pounding, she stumbled, looking around the hoarder's lab.

"I'm behind you."

She whipped around and saw the old man sitting in a chair, a gray wool robe draped over his shoulders, sweeping down his legs.

Within his grip, the Swordless Hilt pointed toward her, the shard blade glowing. "Stop."

"You finally did it, old man. You're finally going to get that death sentence."

"Listen to me."

With no weapon, she lifted her nonfunctional prosthetic arm, the dead weight straining her shoulder. She mentally pulled some sort of trigger. Nothing.

"Notice anything different?" he asked.

"Fuck you," she said, her head spinning. She brought her fingers to her temple. "What did you do to me?"

"You want to kill me?"

She coughed on a mirthless laugh. "What do you think?"

"Think. For a moment. Do you want to kill me because *you* want to kill me or is it because *it* wants you to kill me?"

"I—" Something *was* different. No doubt she wanted to tear the astrocyst apart, but it was entirely of her own volition. The buzzing in her brain—the governor chip—was silent. "You—"

"Believe it or not, I actually am sorry that I had to knock you out. If I told you of my plans, the chip would've made you bludgeon me to death before you even knew what you were doing."

She brought her hand to her head and winced. She felt a new bald spot at her temple, the flesh had bubbled over with fresh blisters. She recalled electricity licking between a two-pronged weapon. "You... shocked me."

Galiaro nodded. "Not very elegant, but effective."

"You *electrocuted* me?" she repeated, the fact settling in her mind.

"Did it work?"

"You crazy old man! You fried my brain with *electricity*?"

"I've already said I did, time to move on. I take it from the fact that you're not immediately trying to kill me like a Reticulum automaton, that the governor chip was inactivated."

The bug in her brain was silent. "It's... it's off."

"And the other hardware? Do your eyes still work?"

"...Yes."

"Ha!" He slapped his thigh. "I wasn't sure if I could deactivate the governor chip without frying the rest of the hardware. Good luck, that. Would you like your weapon back?" He pointed the shard blade to the ground, holding the Hilt out.

She bolted across the floor, ripped it from his hand, and turned the blade to his neck. "I've had enough of your drunken, crackpot bullshit. Why should I let you live?"

"And for which of the many travesties against you do you want to murder me? For freeing you from slavery? How about how I convinced the Reticulum that I needed you to find Beetro?"

"You're lying."

"It's because of me that you're standing there right now, that blade in your hand against my throat."

Miree let out a long breath. Feeling her own thoughts flowing freely through her mind was a relief compared to the constant buzz of the governor chip. She took the blade from his neck and found a chair. "How did you know the shock would disable the chip without killing me?"

He sucked at his yellow teeth. "Educated guess."

"Meaning, you didn't know."

He tilted his head and shrugged. "I thought death better than the alternative for you if I did end up killing you. Was I wrong?" He brought the points of his fingers together.

She shivered at the thought of having to return to the Reticulum. "No. You weren't wrong." She stood, looking at the tunnel that led out of the lab. "So, we're done here?" she said, twirling her finger in the air.

"Done where?"

"Our little adventure. Imprisoned together, hiking through the mountains, etcetera. Now that the governor chip is inactivated, I think we can finally be rid of one another, yeah?"

He ran his fingers through his beard. "It's not that simple."

"No, it is, actually. I can get far, far away from here forever and you can go find your robot and be best buds together again."

"They'll know."

"Know what?"

"They'll know the governor chip is inactivated. It emits a beacon. That beacon just turned off. They also placed a tracker right on your brainstem. They'll be coming for us, now."

"Of course. When?"

"Hours, days—who knows how that infernal AI thinks. Also, there's the little matter of finding the robot."

"No way am I going back to Orion looking for him among the Kish."

"That robot," he said, bringing his fingers to his lips, "should not be out there, walking around."

"Then why did you reactivate him?"

"I *didn't* reactivate him."

"What?"

"I *de*activated him. Buried him long ago."

"Why?"

"Because," he said, stroking his beard thoughtfully. "He murdered me."

Before she could wrap her mind around any more of his unsubstantiated nonsense, Miree demanded that Galiaro bathe. She tolerated his stench in the open air but being stuck down in yet another enclosed space with the man was a final tipping point. In retrospect, it was his smell that almost made her subconsciously stick the shard blade into his neck. The lab had been outfitted with an emergency shower in case of chemical burns and the two took turns bathing with a water reserve tinged with rust and soot. Of all the threats Miree had spat at Galiaro, he seemed receptive when she promised castration if he watched her undress and shower. The man made himself scarce in a small utility closet.

"You were saying? Beetro murdered you?" she asked, drying her hair with her cloak. "You look all too alive to me, unfortunately."

"He didn't kill *me,* me." He pointed to his chest.

"Oh. My mistake."

"He killed *another* me. I watched him. Crept up right behind me. Cut me through with a sword before sticking it twice in my neck."

Miree stared at him, deadpan. "Make more sense."

"I saw it in the future—only moments ahead."

"Uh-huh."

"I saw what he was going to do to me—saw he was to betray and kill me. So, I turned on him before he could kill me. And there he was," he said as if staring into the distance, "sneaking up behind me, sword in hand."

"So, you saw him kill you in the future?"

"Yes. But I got to him first. Before he could kill me."

"So... you can travel to the future?"

"No. That's not what I said. I—" He hesitated.

"Spill it. No more of the cryptic nonsense. We're away from the Reticulum—she can't overhear you anymore."

Galiaro sat at a table and poured himself a cup of water with some dried roots on the side. He chewed on the end of a shriveled parsnip, measuring his words. "Beetro took years to create—countless hours and resources went into his production. The time I spent with the Torbad people alone... they are a difficult people. And it's quite hard for me to think about him after all these years and his.... betrayal. He's one of the reasons I just gave up—gave into the drink. He was the only thing keeping me going while I made him—the reason I hadn't given in already."

"Given into what?"

Galiaro furrowed his eyebrows as if inspecting her. "Imagine putting that much work—years of research and working out the math—to create something that was planning on killing you the whole time. I didn't even know he was self-aware until the little snake tried to cut me through."

"You're going to have to back this whole thing up. *Beetro*? Comes up yea-high—that robot that woke up in a junkyard... is a murderous AI?"

"I watched him kill me."

"Beetro?"

Galiaro nodded.

"The same robot who tried to sell his hands as scrap so that a street beggar could eat?"

"He *what*?"

"The bot doesn't know anything. Brain is fried. Doesn't remember anything."

"Nothing?"

"Nothing."

"But he's... searching for me?"

"Your name is the only thing written into his directive programming. You're telling me you didn't reactivate him?

"I have no idea how he got to Korthe or who put him there. It's the reason I left Korthe and how I was captured by the Reticulum out on the plains. I thought I saw him—saw him in the streets. I saw him leave town and tried to follow but got lost out there. I saw that blue—that sparkling blue."

"Yeah, why does he look like that?"

Galiaro looked at her as if uncertain about his words. "He's not made of... normal metal."

"What's he made of?"

Galiaro swallowed. "Dark matter."

Miree glared at him. "Bullshit."

"His infrastructure is steel, aluminum—some copper. But his coating," he said, his voice infused with reverence, "is pure dark matter."

"His outer shell? All dark matter?"

Galiaro nodded.

"Right. So, I first must believe that you managed to obtain an obscene amount of the most expensive substance on the planet and then I need to next believe that you are crazy enough to slap it on a dumb, self-aware bot and let him gallivant all around the plains of Helian? And then you just what—threw him out?"

"Out of context, yes, I can see how this doesn't sound very plausible."

"There's one problem with your story... dark matter doesn't exist."

"Oh," he leaned back in his chair, a churlish grin on his face. "But it very much does."

"I know for a fact that it's not real."

"I do enjoy your arrogance grounded on nothing but abject ignorance."

"I know dark matter doesn't exist because I robbed Peles Castle. Ever heard of it? There was no dark matter flake there. It's just a legend that they have dark matter. All smoke and mirrors—a myth to stay in power."

"Just because you didn't find dark matter at the castle, doesn't mean it isn't real."

"So, tell me, Mr. Astrocyst, why did you create a robot made of dark matter?"

"Beetro is a key. A machine designed to be a key. That's what the word *beetro* means in Alchean."

"And why did you make a key into a robot?"

"Do you have any idea how heavy dark matter is? You can't just put it in your pocket. It needs legs."

"What is he a key to?"

"The GeminArc."

"And what is that?"

"A portal—a gateway. An intergalactic roadway that can be used to slip beside dimensions. At least that's what I thought."

Miree leaned in, noticing the man's distant expression as if he was reliving something real. She recalled Lucindi mentioning the robot's unusual design—an older model yet retrofitted with a new fusion core. He appeared brand new as if he'd barely had any use. And that sparkling blue shell... "Go on."

"I'm not sure you want to hear more." He brushed his beard, distractedly. "I tried to forget all this. Went to the nearest town after it all went to hell—Beetro, the GeminArc—years of planning and resources completely wasted. The whole debacle turned me to the bottle."

"And you ended up in Korthe after Beetro tried to kill you?"

"Yes. I deactivated the cursed bot and threw him in a shallow grave. I couldn't bring myself to destroy him. I had... such great plans for him."

"Other than serving as a key?"

He cleared his throat. "No, no, I suppose that was his only purpose, but it was a great purpose. And I always knew he'd be a handy resource for dark matter if the need ever arose again. There are many astronomical things one can do with dark matter. And he took... so long to create. But now he's up, walking around, probably trying to hunt me down and kill me."

"But he's *not* trying to kill you. He has no memory. Doesn't remember anything after he woke up in Korthe."

"But he *is* looking for me?"

"Yes, but only because it's a programmed objective. How many times do I need to repeat this? You didn't set it as a backup default in case of a power failure?"

"No... at least I don't think so. This was some years ago. Perhaps I did."

"He's not trying to kill you. He's not trying to hurt anyone. He may be dumb but he's not... bad." She thought of him, peering down at her from atop the granite slot canyon. He'd left her—left her to be mutilated by the Reticulum. But was it his fault? Or was he just taking after her? "At least I don't think so. He's actually... "

"What?"

"He's actually kind of sweet."

"Oh, so you do actually care about beings other than yourself." Galiaro got up from the table and started picking through glass bottles from a worktable. "Perhaps I did put a default objective into his programming to find me upon reboot—I don't remember. This was over a decade ago. Back then, I was clever. I could come up with ideas to change things, or at least to escape things." He poured a greenish liquid into a glass and mixed it with water, took a sip, and nodded to himself. He found his chair once more and crossed one leg over another, squinting as he sipped his drink.

"What are you drinking?"

He looked at his drink. "Just a little something to take the edge off."

"That's not a drink I've ever seen."

He sniffed. "Propylene glycol. Not exactly alcohol but it does do the trick all the same. I kept it in the lab to help prevent some of my aliquots from freezing in the winter."

"*Antifreeze*?"

Galiaro nodded and took a sip.

"You're drinking antifreeze?"

"It's not the worst thing in the world."

Miree shook her head and stood. "So, wait, you built Beetro, infused him with dark matter to open a gate into another world?"

"Another dimension. Well, into an interdimensional space—a non-existence between existence. The *innerspace*. To where I believed the Alcheans escaped."

"Sure. That makes sense."

He took another sip and nodded as if that concluded the conversation.

Miree glared at him. "*Why?*"

"Because, my dear, as I've told you before, the galaxy is dying."

"But what does that even mean?"

"I guess that's somewhat of a misnomer—saying it's dying. I just like the sound of it—very prophetic 'the galaxy is dying'. I think I would've been a great prophet. I do have the look. Anyways, in truth, something can't die if it's already dead."

"I want you to start at the beginning. What is going on?"

Galiaro put his drink down and stared up at her, his red-cracked eyes encircled by purpled skin. "You can't unknow what I'm about to tell you."

"Enough of the theatrics. Just. Talk."

"How many stars do you see when you look up at the sky at night?"

Miree shrugged. "Usually, five. Sometimes three. They move around during different times of the year."

"Wrong."

"No. Right."

"There are no stars in the sky."

"No stars?"

"Zero. They left. They're gone."

"Then what do you call the bright balls of light that are in the sky?"

"They're called planets, my dear."

"Planet, star—what's the difference?"

"The difference is astronomical. Mercury, Venus, Mars, Jupiter, Saturn. They are what you see when you look up at night. There are a few more but you can't see them with the naked eye."

"They are all planets like Earth?"

"Yes and no. They orbit our sun like Earth, but they are not habitable like Earth. They're hostile environments, devoid of life."

"What difference does it make if they're planets or stars? Who cares?"

Galiaro laughed. "There was a time when the night sky was full of stars—an endless expanse of twinkling light, filling the heavens. Each light was a single star, a nebula or even an entire galaxy full of millions of worlds—planets, solar systems. The face of the sky was a view into the universe, teeming with cosmic energy and interstellar life. For eons, humans on Earth looked up and marveled about the infinity and complexity of the universe. There were trillions of stars bringing life to trillions upon trillions of planets. But now, it's empty. Gone."

"What happened?"

"Expansion."

"Expansion?"

"The galaxy—the universe expanded."

"How?"

"For thousands of years, mankind has known that there is a force that pushes stars and solar systems away from each other. It's called dark energy."

"Dark energy?"

"Yes. Different from dark matter. It's an energy that surrounds us—everything. It's the opposite of gravity. It opposes gravity and pushes planets, solar systems, and galaxies away from one another. It was long believed that the expansion wouldn't outpace the local gravity of the galaxy, but this was wrong. The expansion was slow and should've pushed the universe apart billions of years in the future but..."

"What?"

"It accelerated. There was a bump in dark energy, pushing the universe apart."

"What does that mean? Where is the universe? It's just gone?"

"Oh, it's out there. But it's moving away from Earth so quickly that the light from those stars can't reach us anymore. The universe has rushed away so fast from us, it now moves faster than the speed of light. At first, our galaxy stayed together as the rest of the universe sped away. But then, slowly, the arms of the Milky Way—"

"The Milky Way?"

"That was what our galaxy was called. The arms of the Milky Way spread out and unfurled like an octopus tentacle. Soon, the entire galaxy propelled away from itself. Leaving just our solar system alone, soaring through space. What you call stars are just the remaining planets of our solar system. Since the dawn of mankind, we've called celestial lights 'stars'—but there are no more stars."

"But the universe—the galaxy—is still out there?"

"Technically, it still exists but they might as well be dead to us. They are trillions upon trillions of light-years away from us now. You see, this was what Fallaro and I—all astrocysts really—had studied for so many years. We tried to predict the acceleration of the expansion—tried to calculate how much time we had left."

"Time left for what?"

He had a distant look on his face. "If the galaxy tore itself apart from expansion, what do you think the end result of all this is?"

"What do you mean?"

"Do you think dark energy has done its work? That it's done expanding our solar system?"

Miree's mouth went dry. A curious itching sensation crawled up her back as realization set in. "Earth. We will... expand..."

"Away from the sun."

"But... how?"

"Fallaro and I—back before I built Beetro—we finished our math. We came up with Dark Theory."

"Dark Theory?"

"Yes. A theory about when Earth will expand away from the sun and when we'll be—"

"Alone."

He nodded. "A single planet. Drifting in darkness. Dark Theory is a mathematical prediction model for the day Earth is set adrift."

The room fell silent for a moment as Miree attempted to ponder Earth floating in darkness in a cold void of nothing. "When?"

"Impossible to perfectly predict with precision. That is why Dark Theory is a model, not a fact. Fallaro and I concluded that it was likely within our lifetime. I was certain, but I didn't want to be around when we found out."

"So, you created a robot who murdered you in the future? That was going to solve the problem?"

"I created a key—a robot made of dark matter. Created a way to escape this doomed planet. The only way is to follow the Alcheans. They also knew that the universe was eventually doomed. They knew everything—to the point that they no longer needed to live here."

"You said they escaped?"

"They escaped this dying world and left mortality behind. They escaped to an interdimensional space—the innerspace. That's where they are now... at least this is what I've concluded studying their relics and ruins. Sometimes it's hard to decipher their scripts—hard to tease apart fable from the truth."

"And they left through the GeminArc—oh," she said with a small gasp. "Those double arcs outside of Korthe—about two stories high—that's the GeminArc, isn't it?"

Galiaro nodded. "You're a woman but a quick one. The Alcheans knew what was going on," he ignored her menacing glare. "Can't imagine there was nothing that they didn't know. The GeminArc is part of an accelerator. It smashes particles together, which bends space. They used it for centuries as a wormhole—opening Earth up to interstellar travel and commerce. It was the height of humanity. But the GeminArc could be used to tear a hole in space entirely and this was their final act, to escape to the innerspace and flee our dying solar system."

"So," she said. "What happened? What does this have to do with seeing into the future and watching Beetro kill you?"

"Ah, that," he said, picking up his drink and smiling at the buzz, "is where it all went haywire. Years of planning, designing... obtaining dark matter—"

"Where do you find dark matter?"

"It has condensed in certain areas. I believe the condensation has to do with the increased dark energy in the universe. It's a spillover of gravity from other dimensions, causing the accelerated expansion. Dark matter is the inverse tangible form of dark energy. The photon of electromagnetic radiation—the electron of electricity. Anyway, it all went wrong. Something was wrong with the robot. I made him in different locations—started in Orion, took his body to the Torbad, then here," he said, gesturing to the lab. "This is where he was completed. I believed that I did not design his neural network with the complexity required for an emergent consciousness. I intended the robot to be a walking slug of dark matter. Only dark matter can activate the GeminArc—"

"Wait..."

He looked up, surprised.

"We went through those twin arcs—the GeminArc. I watched Beetro and this girl we were with—they walked right through the arcs. Nothing happened."

Galiaro failed to conceal a gasp. "He *took* you there? To the GeminArc? He wanted to go there?"

"No. Not exactly. We only came there because of the street kid, Ribcage. She said it was where her 'mom' was," she said, using quote fingers.

"*Who*?"

"Kid from Korthe. Strange girl. Able to disappear and reappear right before your eyes. She was a nightmare to deal with. Caused more problems than she fixed and almost got me killed a few times. Too bad. With talent like that, she would've been perfect for jobs in Orion."

"Did you say *disappear*?"

"Yeah. Like that." She snapped her fingers. "Then reappear instantly on the other side of the room. She called it Jumping. Ever heard of someone doing that?"

He stroked his beard. "No. Can't say I have. Highly unusual." A thoughtful silence fell over the conversation.

"So, why didn't anything happen? Why didn't Beetro activate the GeminArc when we were there?"

"Oh. I'm not surprised at that, no. There are other maneuvers one must do to activate the gate. Beetro is simply the key, but a key must be turned appropriately."

"Like how?"

"With a complexity that is beyond your understanding. These things cannot be trifled with, especially by someone not knowing what they're doing. Not even I knew everything. It took me years of data collection and interpretation of Alchean artifacts. I traveled to places you don't even want to know about. I was certain I had the math correct. Me and Fallaro checked it a thousand times over many years."

Miree considered the man for a moment and then asked, "How old are you anyway?"

"Very."

"How old?"

"Older than you think. Astrocysts are always older gentlemen like myself. It's part of the initiation. Now, would you stop asking questions?"

"Go ahead."

"I botched it. The GeminArc—the gateway. It didn't open. Not only did the thing not open, but a shimmering surface opened in the arcs. At first, I thought it was just a mirror of our own reality —a reflection of Beetro and I standing there. But then I saw him reach for my sword. He took it from my pack and stuck me through—cold-blooded. The bot was waiting for me to open the gate. I turned around and saw him there, just moments behind the reflective wall, bending down to pick up my sword. So, I pushed his kill switch, deactivated him, and buried him there, next to the clearing of the forest."

"You opened a portal... into the near future?"

He cleared his throat. "I have no idea what I did that day. I certainly did not open the portal to the innerspace. I was a fool—dealing with things with which I had no business. How could I think myself intelligent enough to understand the math of gods? What I did do was jumble with spacetime—bending it in some way with dark matter—creating a sort of lensing effect of the future."

"Lensing effect?"

"I don't know, I made up that term just now. I think I bent spacetime for that moment, granting me a glimpse into the near future. I was just lucky enough to see that my robot was on the verge of murdering me. But..." He took another sip of his drink, finishing off the green liquid. "Now I'm just as confused as you are with that Jumping girl you are talking about. That is... strange."

Miree exhaled deeply.

"Is my story boring you?"

"No... I just can't get away."

"Away from what?"

"A terrible life."

"It's not just your life, my dear. It's everyone's."

The following morning, after an uncomfortable sleep in the freezing lab, they emerged in between the granite boulders on the Helian plains. Galiaro had started a fire and waited as Miree tried hunting rabbits with the Swordless Hilt. She'd become adept at getting the shards to float before her in formation but couldn't get them to do what she wanted. A single rabbit stood in the open, nibbling on dead weeds while the shards flew a mile wide in a chaotic cloud. She flipped the pommel, making the shards burn with heat, and tried swinging the Hilt straight down at the rabbit, resulting in the shards flying off into the sky, the opposite direction.

"Not very good with that," Galiaro said, stoking the fire with a stick.

"There's something else."

"Will it get us a fresh rabbit?"

"No," she said, sitting cross-legged on the ground. She lowered her hood, red eyes glowing. She looked over at the Meteor Mountains darkened by clouds on the horizon. A bloatstorm, perhaps. "Something about Beetro."

"Yes. The reason we're looking for him."

"I saw him freeze laser light shot right from a rifle. I thought I was dead, but I opened my eyes and saw it there, a shaft of laser light floating in the air. He did it. Held it up with his hands."

"*What?*"

"Did you know he could do that when you made him? Did you design him to be like that?"

"No," he said, looking over at the mountains with trouble in his eyes, "I didn't know he could do... that. He's not supposed to be a weapon. A sentient weapon no less."

"How does he do it?"

"It must be the dark matter. Giving him... power."

"Power to move laser light?"

He waved his hand in the air. "I don't know. I do know that we must find the robot."

"Why? To get him to the Reticulum?"

"Of course not," he said, giving her a grave look. "And hearing this troubling news about freezing laser light has only confirmed to me what we need to do."

"Which is?"

"We need to destroy him."

"Oh."

"If he's wielding that kind of power, he can't be out there."

"Not sure how powerful he really is..."

"Have you ever seen anyone, or anything make *light* do what he wants?"

She shook her head.

"The fact is, the GeminArc is still viable. He could still activate it and that may be far more powerful than throwing some laser light around. Particle accelerators can change the very fabric of reality. He could create a black hole and suck us all in it for all we know. The robot can't trifle with things he cannot understand. And if the Reticulum gets their hands on him, who knows what kind of damage they can do. I thought I could understand it and what did I do? Probably ripped a hole in spacetime for all I know —and I studied the portal for decades. No. He can't be allowed to walk around out there. He must be destroyed. We destroy him, scrap him for the dark matter, and perhaps begin anew on the expansion problem."

"Why do you care? I thought you just wanted a drink. The galaxy is dead anyway, right?"

"That may be, but we don't have to bring doom any sooner to us by allowing a dark matter robot to stumble around, triggering interdimensional disasters. I'm an astrocyst—a man of refined scruples. And as I said, there are many astronomical wonders one can accomplish with that much dark matter."

"Hmm." A smirk spread across her face.

"What now?"

"All he wants to do is find you. And all you want to do is kill him."

"Yes, yes, the irony is palpable. You're a very astute woman, congratulations." He stood, collecting his pack. "Shall we head due south before the Reticulum catches up with us?"

"*We?*"

"Yes. Let's be on our way then. Although, I hate traveling hungry."

She tapped her temple. "I don't have a governor chip in my brain anymore. There is no more 'we'. I'm getting away from this place."

"Even after what I've told you about the universe?"

"What has the universe done for me lately?"

"Well then. You'll accompany me south to Portolo where you can catch a ship to flee your responsibilities."

She eyed him for a moment. "*You're* the one who created this mess."

"I didn't reactivate the bot. For all I know, *you're* the one who dug him up."

"I—" She remembered Beetro's body lying in the junkyard like a discarded doll. Lucindi tapping him on the face—eyes coming to life with indigo blue. "I found him in the junkyard, but *someone* put him there."

Galiaro hefted his bag, his gray robe flapping against his thin body in the strong western wind. He flopped his stout cap over his bald head. "Get me to Portolo, and you can leave from there. You can commission a ship far, far away from here with all that Reticulum gold—but it won't get you to another universe that isn't expanding. Is that acceptable?"

Miree watched the man turn against the wind, his beard fraying in the breeze. She flicked the Swordless Hilt, collecting the shards together, and followed behind, irritated that she was wondering what Beetro was doing at that moment.

THIRTY

THAT'S NOT MY CARBONOID, Beetro said, communicating through the binary flickering of his eyes.

Qithara, the Thekora, studied him for a moment, face blank with pearly scales. A series of zeros and ones then emerged on its flat face. [*No?*]

No. I was traveling with a small human girl and a man. I don't know this carbonoid. Beetro studied the comatose woman as one of the Thekora fed her a white paste. Her hair was short as if recently shorn to the skin. Her skin a toasted cream color covering high cheekbones. Her most unusual feature was her eyes—vibrant sapphire cracked with an ivory that almost sparkled. The girl appeared morbidly confused.

[*The carbonoid needs to leave Tol. Must leave the gargantua. Or carbonoid will die.*]

I understand, Beetro replied, *but I do not know this carbonoid.*

After a moment of silent confusion, the woman said, "Where?"

Qithara turned to Beetro, big, inky eyes pleading.

Before Beetro could say anything, two Thekora entered the room, their sinewy legs approaching Qithara. They flashed several series of communications amongst one another. After what seemed to be a debate between the three of them, Qithara turned to Beetro. [*We've found the others.*]

My companions?

[*Yes. A small female. A regular-sized male. They are on the forest floor. They need antidote.*]

Please. Take me to them.

Qithara nodded, its enormous shovel-head bobbing up and down. It then motioned to the recumbent woman who was watching the scene with fresh dismay.

Beetro sighed and then nodded at the woman. *I'll take that one, too.*

Ribcage found herself at her rooftop hideout, perched high above Mercy Plaza, back at Korthe. She quickly inspected her stash—a few bits of breadcake, a knife, and some yarn. Not sure why she kept the yarn, but she figured Luci could one day show her how to mend her clothing. She looked out over the horizon.

A bloatstorm.

Only, this bloatstorm was approaching *fast*. There were hundreds of people fleeing through the dead fields of Helian, the bloatflies descending on them in swarms. Ribcage turned from the scene—she needed to get off the roof and find cover. But she bumped into someone and fell.

Jaram.

The street rat bully back for revenge. Behind him was the girl whose ear she slashed off.

Ribcage swatted Jaram with the back of her hand. "The hell d'you want?"

He said nothing.

"Didn't get enough slapping around from me last time? Come back to watch me Jump all over you?"

Jaram remained silent.

"Get outta—" Ribcage froze.

And then the street kids *melted.* Bleached bones emerged through skin and fat, the whole mess collapsing into a pile of hair, skin, and bubbling viscera.

"What...?" She twirled around and saw him there.

Beetro.

His arms were outstretched, smoke streaming from his palms.

"No... no. I didn't mean to—didn't mean to kill them! I just wanted to scare them. It's the only way to keep them away."

Beetro looked at her, his indigo eyes turned blood-red. Waiting. "Who is next?"

"No one! I didn't want you to actually kill anyone. Don't you get it?"

Beetro lowered his arms and watched her, waiting for a command.

Ribcage ran from him to the roof's edge and looked down at Mercy Plaza. The air was humid—sweltering. Sweat and tears mixed, stinging her eyes and blotting her sight. She wiped her brow and saw an army occupying the streets, bloatflies surrounding them as if joining in their conquest of the town. In the middle of the plaza, in place of the dried-up fountain, two silvery arcs of metal stood, rooted into the ground.

A figure stood before the twin arcs. Motionless.

Ribcage Jumped, materializing on the ground between a row of soldiers—sentinels to the twin arcs. They ignored her as she moved—as she came behind the figure dressed in a white gown of lace and flowing silk. Ribcage tugged on the dress and the figure turned.

Luci.

Her face... glowed. Her expression radiated kindness—patience. She reached a hand out. Ribcage took it. "You're here?"

"Yes," Luci said, voice sweet and calm.

"Why did you leave... why did you leave *me*?"

"There was no reason to stay."

"You... died. This is where you were killed. You were the only thing—the only person—that was anything to me. And you left."

"I left you because you meant nothing to me."

"Oh." Ribcage nodded.

"You were a pet. Nothing more."

"I see..."

"The twin arcs don't know you, either."

"But... that's where I'm from. The arcs are where my mom is."

Luci laughed, mocking her. "Dumb, little pet Ribcage. You have no mother. You have no friends. You are not even of this world. You have no birth, and you will have no death. You are a nothing."

"I know," Ribcage agreed. "I've always known." She turned from Luci, from the twin arcs, to where an enormous bloatfly was waiting for her, fangs gaping. Ribcage stepped closer, the heat blossoming through her. As she felt the multiple proboscises of the bloatfly searching over her, she dropped to her knees. She could die in Mercy Plaza—it was as good a place as any.

She closed her eyes.

A nothing.

When Ribcage opened her eyes, a feverish chill rippled over her. A blank, blue sky stared back. Fighting a dizzy spell, she got to her knees and looked around. A vast tundra, dotted with pines, surrounded her. The horizon was mostly straight, save for a massive egg-shaped mountain interrupting the view.

Orion.

Last thing she remembered was walking along those big, dumb, purple trees and then... Luci. A shudder ran through her, recalling the girl's total indifference. Was that really her? It took her a moment to realize that she was actually sitting within a camp, Beetro standing near her by a fire.

"You're awake," he declared.

"Yes..."

"And you're alive. You're welcome." He turned from her to tend to a lump in the ground.

"What *happened*? Where are we? Did I die?"

"Die? No. Almost die? Yes."

"Die from what?" She tried standing but promptly fell over. "Ouch! Why am I so sick?"

"The gargantua trees. They kill humans."

"Huh. Seems like something useful to know before we walked into a forest full of them. Don't you think? Where's that idiot guide of ours anyway?"

"Here," Beetro said, pointing to the ground beside a fire. "Almost killed him, too. He hasn't come to, yet."

"I had... dreams."

He nodded. "Yes. The Thekora warned me. What did you dream of?"

"Luci. She... never mind."

"The gargantua secrete a neurotoxin causing hallucinations. Humans get psychosis and die from exposure in the forest."

"None of it was real?"

"Course not."

"I—" she stared across the horizon, eyes vacant.

"What?"

She looked at the robot, wanting to spew her terrified emotions all over him. Why could she never really say what she wanted to? "Nothing."

"Can you stand?"

"I think so." Beetro gave a hand getting her to her feet. They stood beside a small fire; a flayed rabbit skewered over its flames. "Eat. You'll need to take more of the antidote. The Thekora told me the neurotoxin—gargotox, they called it—will be in your system for a few more days. The antidote paste will help bind it up in your bloodstream."

"Thekora?"

"Tree people—er... aliens, I suppose."

"Aliens?"

"Long story. Their people came from a distant planet a long time ago."

A figure approached Beetro from behind. "Look out!" Ribcage yelled.

Beetro spun and relaxed. "Oh. Yes, we've added a new companion to our group."

Ribcage saw a young woman with beautifully browned skin. Her blue eyes—shimmering with specks of silver within the irises—set above prominent cheekbones and a thin jawline. She was crazy pretty and Ribcage wanted to touch her face but recoiled, detesting yet another person added to their party. No, she decided she would hate the pretty girl first and ask questions later. "Who are you?"

The girl touched her chest. "Hawera."

"Hu-what-uh?"

"Hawera."

"Be nice," Beetro said. "She was dying from the toxin just like you. She only started to recover a few hours ago. Still dazed."

Ribcage studied the girl for a moment. "I don't like it."

Beetro knelt beside her. "Just because someone new comes along, doesn't mean they're a threat. Have you ever thought about that? Change isn't always bad."

"It was in Korthe. Change is always bad."

"Well, we're not in Korthe anymore. We're—" he looked around, scanning the horizon. "Somewhere between Gargantua Forest and Orion."

Ribcage approached Hawera and peered up at her. "Where did you come from?"

Hawera sighed. "Don't speak good."

"'Don't speak good'? That's where you're from?"

Hawera shook her head. "From far away."

"You look... weird."

Hawera looked hesitant at Beetro.

"Don't look at him, look at me," Ribcage told her. "I'm the one doing the talking. Why did you let her join us?"

Beetro stepped between the two. "Rib, that's enough. She's someone who needed help and now she's with us. That's reason enough."

"And who put you in charge?"

"I think saving your life from toxic trees puts me square in the driver's seat."

"Hmph." She paused, remembering her dream or whatever it was—Luci looking at her with those hollow eyes.

"How about a 'thank you' every once in a while, huh? Did it occur to you that I could've just left you behind back there?"

Ribcage fell silent then looked up at him. She tried to fight it, but the heat rose inside of her, a raging mess of shame and anger. Tears welled in her eyes.

"Rib... I'm sorry. It's okay. Didn't mean anything."

She ran from the fire. Ran from the stupid robot and his new version of Luci. Finding a boulder away from camp, she burrowed a small hole at its side, fingernails burning raw from digging. Curling up inside, she felt the cool earth against her skin and closed her eyes. For a moment, she imagined she was back at Korthe, curled at her rooftop hideout. She could go find Crow, give him a drink, and steal his bread. She'd wait for Luci to come back from the junkyard. Maybe she could even Jump to the market—swipe some food?

She opened her eyes and the illusion was gone. She was stuck in the middle of nowhere losing control. Never would she have ventured away from Korthe had she known that stupid robot would start barking out orders. But, how stupid could he be if he dragged her from the forest? It was true what he'd said, he could've just left her there to die. The robot did hang out with Luci before she died. Maybe she really did rub off on him. Maybe... he wasn't as bad as everybody else she'd ever met in the entire, stupid, ugly world.

And then she smelled roasting rabbit.

Her stomach growled.

Arym awoke, a fever breaking through his body. He opened his eyes to the stars. The dim orbs of light hung above the tree line. He leaned forward, a sheath of sweat sloughing off his face. When and where could he possibly be? The last thing he remembered was running through the enormous, purple trees. Something was chasing him or... yelling at him. He vaguely remembered phantoms of the rektor watching him—judging him. Founder Othel was there, turning into a... demon? The dreams—or nightmares—

were hard to remember but the feelings were unforgettable—exhaustion and terror. He had never known it was possible to be so afraid in his entire life. He shuddered and turned, thinking that creature would be there, but a silent brush with a patch of pines stood silent.

He stood, a crackling fire burning low beside him.

"Hello?" he called. "Beetro?"

No answer. There was, however, a half-eaten rabbit beside the coals. Realizing an overwhelming hunger, he ate the meat, grateful for something warm in his belly. He paused.

A twig broke in the forest. Steps. Someone moving toward him.

He dropped the rabbit meat and backed away as a figure emerged at the edge of the camp. Darkness covered their face. The person carried a staff in hand. As they approached, Arym saw firelight flicker across their face. The person had short hair—a slight frame.

Hawera.

Arym fell over. He fumbled to his knees and looked again. He saw those eyes—flecks of silver almost iridescent in the firelight. Her hair had grown slightly from the buzzed head he remembered when they'd first met. Was this a dream again? Or was it the beginning of another nightmare?

"Arym," she greeted with a smile.

He bolted to his feet and moved to her.

"Hoi," she said. "Arym."

He grabbed her hand and took her in. It was real. She was standing in front of him. *She.* He wanted to open up about every torture he'd experienced since she left him and spill it in front of her—explain how he'd longed for the moment to be with her again. He wanted to ask why she'd left him—abandoned him. After everything he'd done for her? Yet, he knew he'd never be mad—never blame her for anything. Protonix had explained that she was important—that she was trying to fix the galaxy. He would help her. He would be by her side. Together, they could do anything.

She smiled again. "Happy Arym safe."

"I'm safe now." He gripped her hand tighter as she tried to pull it away. "I'm here to help you, Hawera. I'll help fix the galaxy with you."

Her forehead wrinkled, confused. After finally freeing her hand, she took a satchel from around her shoulder and opened it, dumping shards from what appeared to be a broken sword on the ground. "Melt."

He looked down at the metal. "What?"

"Iron. Melt."

"I don't understand."

"Need iron melt."

"How did you get here? Did you save me?"

She shook her head. "Beetro."

"Beetro is here?"

She nodded. "Yas. Need iron melt."

"Hawera," he said, taking her hand again. "We're finally together. I will do anything you want me to do." She tried taking her hand back, but Arym held on. A worried look flashed across her face. "No. It's okay. You're safe now, Hawera. I'll never let you go. I'll take care of you."

"What?"

He took her other hand. "You're safe with me."

She tried pulling away, but Arym stepped in, closer. "No."

"You don't need to be afraid."

"I not afraid."

He pulled her closer, wrapping his arms around her.

"Arym, no."

He took in a deep breath, smelling her hair, feeling her skin. As he embraced her, he felt her cheek brush against his and never knew he could be this happy.

"Arym, no!" she yelled, pulling away.

She slapped him across the cheek.

He stepped back, shocked, confused, and utterly destroyed. The sting of the slap reverberated through his face and, for a moment, his entire being. "I don't... understand."

"Don't touch like that," she said, moving away toward her bits of metal. "Never touch like that. Not right."

He rubbed his cheek, understanding nothing. Didn't she miss him? Isn't that why she sent Protonix back to him when in isolation? Ah, he understood. This was another nightmare.

"Loverboy strikes out," a voice called out from behind. He knew that voice. It was the goblin child. Yes, this was definitely a nightmare.

He turned, Ribcage and Beetro arriving at the camp. The child triumphantly held two dead squirrels, one in each fist. "Is that how it usually goes for you?" she asked Arym as she dumped the squirrels by the fire. "You don't strike me as one good with the ladies. Well... those that can't be bought, anyway."

Arym looked down at the goblin, hand on cheek, completely flummoxed. "*You.*"

"Yeah," she said, grinning. "*Me.*"

"Rib," Beetro said, chiding her. "What did we talk about?"

She grimaced and then nodded. "Beetro says I need to be nice." She sat at a rock, bringing a knife to the squirrels.

Arym turned to Beetro. "What happened? Where are we?"

After Beetro explained the gargantua neurotoxin and the Thekora, Arym looked at Hawera, who was busy at the fire. "So, the nightmares I had—"

"The effects of the neurotoxin. Rib here says she had a similar experience. It seems like it creates fear in the human brain, leading to psychosis and hallucinations. You had a similar experience?"

Arym nodded.

Beetro gestured toward Hawera. "Found this one with the Thekora, the neurotoxin had gotten her pretty bad. They said she was likely to survive. She says she knows you?"

Arym nodded. "We met," he said, coolly. What happened? He quickly reviewed everything he knew about Hawera. He saw her there for the first time, under the moonlight, appearing out of nowhere. She was beautiful—like nothing he'd ever seen. She wasn't like any of the men at the Crib. There was no way he could ever experience the level of attraction toward Lutra that he felt toward her. He loved Lutra as a brother, but Hawera? He felt nothing but a searing, raw compulsion to be near her. Didn't she want the same? He looked down at her as she shifted coals in the fire. Even the nape of her neck was gorgeous. The slap across his face still stung but not as much as the sheer rejection. He briefly resisted the urge to just run away at that very moment.

"Have you eaten?" Beetro asked, sitting by the fire. "Ribcage has gotten pretty good at setting snares."

"Good for her," he said. He distanced himself from the fire, from Hawera, and definitely from the goblin child. "I'm not hungry."

"She says she's a traveler from far away," Beetro motioned to Hawera. "Her Haenglish is not very good. Do you know where she's from?"

Arym shook her head. "She wouldn't tell me."

"Unusual look," Beetro continued, looking over at her. "That skin—and her eyes. I've never seen someone like her before."

"I did," Ribcage said. "You did, too. Aren't you supposed to have a perfect memory?"

"What're you talking about?"

"Back in Helian. We ran into someone that looked like her. Had a bunch of metal all around his arms and legs."

"That's right," Beetro said. "Spoke a strange language. Looked confused." He turned to Hawera. "We think we saw one of your kind—one of your people back in Helian."

Hawera looked up at him, considering his words. "Patwero..."

"Was that his name?"

She nodded. "My companion. Patwero. He knows. Knows to go to Orion if lost."

"Why are you heading there?"

"The galx is dead—dying."

"Galx?"

"The galaxy," Arym said. "She means the galaxy."

"The galaxy is dead?" Beetro repeated.

Hawera nodded. "Will be dead. Need Orion. Need astrocyst."

"Why?"

"The galx is dead. No time."

"I don't understand," Beetro said. "Where did you come from?"

"I come from the end."

"The end of what?"

"The end of world."

The next morning, Beetro arose, still thinking about the conversation with the strange girl. He couldn't help but dwell on the Qithara's words: [*You tell the carbonoids that Thekora are friends. Tell them to remember us if they find a way to leave.*] Why would humans want to leave? What did the Thekora know about the planet that nobody else knew? And now this girl comes along, talking about how the galaxy was dying. Where did she fit in?

He came to the campfire to discover Hawera crouched there, mixing something with a stick. As he got closer, he realized she was stirring *liquid metal*. Overnight, the girl had managed to burn enough wood to create a dense chamber of coals under a stone basin. A pool of melted iron bubbled with heat. She stood, found her wooden staff, and dipped it into the liquid iron. She pulled the staff, letting a coating of the metal drip along the wood until it cooled and then repeated the process, applying new coats, one layer at a time.

"What is this for?" Beetro asked.

Hawera regarded him for a moment as she tilted the staff. "For my four."

"Four?"

"Fourth," she corrected herself. "My Fourth. Need metal for my Fourth."

"What is your Fourth?"

The girl didn't respond but kept dipping her staff into the metal, adding one layer at a time as if she was making a candle.

"Is it a weapon?"

"Weapon? Sometimes. The Fourth is gift of the Lithusa."

"Lithusa?"

"I am Lithusa."

"That is what your people are called?"

She nodded.

Beetro sighed. It seemed that with every turn, every new face, there was something new that he didn't know about the world. The complexity of the species in the land—the Thekora, the Crib, these... Lithusa—where did it end? Would he ever know enough about the world to actually know what he was doing? Would finding Galiaro *actually* answer his questions? He was beginning to doubt it.

"What is your quest?" Beetro asked.

Hawera sat the staff down, horizontal across the rocks. She studied Beetro for a moment as if measuring her response. "I from... dark world."

"Dark world?"

"Yas. I do not know the sun." She motioned to the sunrise peeking over the tree line. "Beauty."

"You don't have the sun where you're from?"

She shook her head. "No. Darkness. I come here to find light. Find world that is not dark."

"Well," he said, gesturing to the sunrise. "I think you found it. We have a sun here. How can you be from a land without the sun?"

"Need astrocyst. Need to go Orion."

"I know. We'll go there with you. Have you heard of Galiaro?"

She shook her head. "I need to travel again. Need to find land with many stars."

"Many stars?"

"Yas. Me and Patwero search land of many stars. This land, only five stars."

"What is in the land of many stars?"

"The beginning."

After a series of questions with even more cryptic answers from Hawera, Beetro gave up going hunting with Ribcage. The girl had become quite adept at finding animal trails—rodents and rabbits mostly—and had caught three more. As he watched her tying frayed branches together, he realized he probably knew less about the little girl than his other traveling companions.

"What do you want, Rib?"

"Want?"

"Why did you come along with me?"

"I want Luci, but she was taken. You seemed like the next best thing."

"No, no. What do you *want*?"

She looked at him for a moment and finally uttered the first earnest thing he'd ever heard the girl say. "Trust."

"Someone to count on. People that you don't have to continually second-guess their motives. Is that what you mean?"

Ribcage nodded.

"So, how do you get that?"

"No idea. Everyone beside Luci has been nothing but rotten to me my entire life."

"Have I?"

"Guess not."

"Well, should we start something new then? A friendship between us?"

"Why should I?"

He paused, "Did you really mean to say that, or was it just reflex?"

"Reflex."

"I'm serious. I promise to look out for you."

"If...?"

"If nothing. I'll look out for you because I'm your friend."

She just looked at him.

"Does that sound okay with you?"

"Is there anything I have to do?"

"No."

"I don't need to promise the same thing? Kind of like Miree's scarf she gave me? A gift?"

"Yes. A friend just cares without expecting anything back."

"I thought you were trying to be all... tough lately. How everything was just about the bottom line—does this person help you or not."

"I know. It's not me. I can't think that way. Not anymore."

"Okay, then."

He abruptly walked away, moving back toward the camp, finding Arym and Hawera. Arym was brooding at a boulder while Hawera stared into the fire. It looked as if they hadn't spoken a word to each other in ages.

"Everyone," Beetro announced, twiddling his fingers to the fire. "Please, gather around the fire. I have something I want to say." There was silence as Ribcage sat, cross-legged next to the flames. Hawera and Arym met eyes and quickly looked away, back to Beetro. "Good," Beetro began, his nerves coming through his voice. "All of us come from different places and we're all different. I'm a bot from... somewhere, Arym is from the Crib, Ribcage an orphan from Korthe, and Hawera is... well, she's from some sort of dark place somewhere. My point is—we have reasons to not get along. We barely understand each other. However, it looks like we all want to get to Orion. I want to find my maker, Arym wants to find help for his people, Hawera needs to find an astrocyst, and Ribcage... well, she doesn't have anywhere else to really go. I just wanted to say that as long as we travel together, I will help you all." He waited.

Crickets.

"What I mean is, I will look out for you. I won't leave you behind or try to take advantage of you. If you're in trouble, I'll try to help you. I'll share resources with you as we travel, and I'll listen to you if you have something to say." Again, he waited.

Again, crickets.

"I'll... be your friend." Beetro finished and sat down, demolished with embarrassment.

Ribcage asked, "But what's in it for us?"

After a pregnant pause, Beetro said, "I just explained—"

"I'm joking. We get it, you're now our little buddy bot." The girl burst into a high-pitch cackle.

Arym shared an unsettled gaze with Beetro until the robot chuckled. Hawera appeared confused at first but soon smiled at the two. And then they all joined, not really knowing what they were laughing at but just glad to be laughing with anyone at all.

THIRTY-ONE

MIREE ENHANCED HER VISION, Portolo magnifying in her sight. It was a drab little harbor town with a dock no more than the length of the market back at Korthe. There were exactly two ships docked, probably small enough to be manned by three people. Clusters of wooden buildings flanked the town as well as a water tower and a rusted antenna stuck to the side of a nearby hillside.

That was pretty much it.

"I knew there was never a reason to come through here."

"You were expecting the harbor of Orion?" Galiaro asked, chewing slowly. The man stood above a pile of tinder collected in between a circle of rocks.

"As long as it can get me away from Helian, I don't care what Portolo looks like." She flipped her vision to normal magnification and pulled out the Swordless Hilt, feeling the pommel in her palm.

"Little help?" Galiaro motioned to the tinder.

Miree gripped the Hilt and flicked her wrist down, prompting the shards to scatter into the air. They floated in random configuration, awaiting command from the Hilt. Slowly, she drew the Hilt upward, the shards following the trajectory. As the shards floated up, she flattened the Hilt and the shards stopped. What she learned was that each flick of the Hilt was a command for the shards to follow that direction. What she hadn't realized, up until yesterday, was that she had to terminate any directional command with a stiff flattening of the Hilt or else the shards would simply continue in the original command trajectory. With the shards only a meter over the tinder, she pointed the Hilt at a single shard and dragged it down, leaving the other shards to float, motionless. After dragging the single shard into the tinder, she flipped the pommel one hundred and eighty degrees, prompting the shard to heat with white-hot energy. The tinder quickly ignited.

"Getting better with that," Galiaro commented, gathering wood in his arms.

Miree flicked the Hilt backward, causing every shard to fly at her at an uncomfortable speed and then collect around the Hilt, forming a single blade of shards. "Still is freaky recalling them back. Keep thinking the things are going to tear me apart."

"It's Torbad craftsmanship."

"Who are they now?"

"The warring factions of the Torbad bear those swords. Highly valuable. I'd suggest you sell it to them but they'd kill you for even possessing it." Galiaro draped a skewered rabbit over the fire and set a tin pot over the coals for boiling. "Could certainly use that sword of yours in Orion."

"It's my only parting gift from the Reticulum. Stays with me."

"I didn't really mean the *sword*. I meant you."

"Told you I'm not coming with you to Orion."

"I'm certain everything in your life will suddenly heal over and get better when you get far, far away from here."

"Glad we're finally seeing eye to eye."

Galiaro dropped some herbs into the boiling pot. "Because happiness is geographically dependent. Is it not?"

"Hmm, that means a lot coming from the guy who made a robot of dark matter to reboot some ancient portal into another dimension to escape *an entire planet*."

"That's... different."

"No. It's not. Everyone is always trying to escape—trying to get away from something. You were no different."

"It *was* different. I was trying to help. Help the creatures of Earth get away when the time came."

"If you want to help, go back to Orion and clear out all the Kish. Go back to Korthe and make sure another lord or general can't come and starve the people with taxes. Go to the Fifth Kingdom—"

"Yes?" Galiaro said with growing interest. "And what should I do in the Fifth Kingdom?"

"Kill the king."

"And why would I do that?"

Miree was silent.

Galiaro unceremoniously handed her a cup of the tea he'd brewed. "How did you end up so far from your home kingdom anyway?"

She took the tea and sipped, grateful for the warmth. "By running. Going from one small village to the next. Grew up in peasant fields for a few years. Learned how to live on the streets for the next couple of years. Somehow ended up in Orion and joined the Kish when they threatened to kill me if I didn't."

"And then you ran to Korthe?"

"No. Going to Korthe was the first time in my life that I wasn't running away from something. I went to Korthe with purpose. I was finally doing something for myself."

"And what was that?"

"Collecting mercury to steal the dark matter flake from Peles Castle. I was going to get that flake, get myself a mountain of gold, and live on it, alone and forever."

"Alone?"

She flared her nostrils at him. "Alone."

"There's never been... anyone?"

She studied his expression for a moment, assuring herself that the dirty old man wasn't coming onto her. "Once."

"There's always someone. Everyone always has someone at least one time."

"I don't want to hear about yours."

"What happened?"

"Dead."

"And when this person was alive, did you feel like you were running anymore?"

Damn, the old bastard could be astute. "Guess not."

"I would love to feel that way again."

They shared an amicable silence for a moment and then Galiaro said, "If you come with me to Orion, you won't be running. You'll be *doing*."

"I don't care if I keep running. It's what I do... the only thing I've ever known. I gotta get out of this place—get away from the Reticulum. I'm sure Deluvius would love to put a bullet in my head for breaking into his castle. Everywhere I go, I make enemies. I'm done."

"We could find the robot and start again, fresh. The galaxy is still dying as much now as when I first made Beetro. We could find him, deactivate him, strip him of the dark matter, and start again on the GeminArc, follow the Alcheans into the innerspace."

"Do you hear yourself? The innerspace... it's all just a fantasy. The only bits of Alchean technology that people know how to use are their weapons. I know because I saw one of them discharged into the chest of the only person I've ever cared about. You try to open that GeminArc again and you're just going to screw things up—mess with the future or whatever it was you did when you saw Beetro murder you."

"If I can get back to Orion, find the robot, we can get to Fallaro and his lab. He and I worked on the problem of the galaxy for years. We first tried to figure out why the expansion accelerated so quickly over the last several thousand years but got nowhere. We knew escape—following the Alcheans was the only answer. Who knows what Fallaro's been able to do since..."

"Since you became the town drunk of Korthe?"

"Maybe he's come along with the math. Perhaps he's developed Dark Theory more and can pinpoint the expansion timing of our solar system."

Miree looked at him for a moment. "Wait. Why wasn't he involved when you opened the GeminArc with Beetro? If you two were such best buds..."

Galiaro looked at the horizon, distracted. "We—I... we had a disagreement."

"You double cross him?"

"Not exactly. He tried to cut me out—tried to take the robot away from me."

"Why?"

"Once he saw that we really could actually temper dark matter enough to get it onto the bot's shell, he had other ideas..."

"Like what?"

"He theorized that possessing dark matter could be a very powerful weapon."

"Turns out he's right. Why is it so powerful?"

"It's a bit complicated but it has to do with the conversion between energy and mass."

"Which is...?"

"They're one and the same. Energy and mass are transferable, meaning you can take any amount of matter and turn it into energy and vice versa. Know why all the groundwater is radioactive in Helian?"

Miree shrugged.

"Nuclear weapons. Wars of some idiot, ancient nations centuries ago in these plains."

"The Alcheans?"

"No, no. The Alcheans never went to war. They didn't have to. They were so advanced that there was no one to go to war with. The wars started once the Alcheans left. Men started building nuclear weapons again and bombed the bones out of each other."

"And what does that have to do with energy and mass?"

"Take a teeny bit of matter," he said, squeezing his fingers together, "and split it open and you get a tremendous amount of energy release." He opened his palm wide. "One bomb could obliterate an entire city."

"Really?"

Galiaro nodded.

"I never thought that kind of stuff was true. Just legends."

"It's true. And it's a good thing we live in a post-future era—no one except astrocysts have any idea how to do any of this anymore. Technology is so poor these days, tyrants can only use the weapons of the past—weapons they dig up—combustible engines that they patch back together. Mankind has proven that they cannot wisely wield the technology they develop and that's the era in which we now live. May as well be the stone ages."

"So, what did Fallaro want to do with Beetro?"

"He theorized that Beetro could wield incredible power with his dark matter."

"How does it work?"

"Dark matter has incredible mass but not just the mass of our dimension. It's tethered to the mass of many layered dimensions. We believe that dark matter is actually the gravity that has leaked over from other dimensions into tangible form here. It's a condensing of the gravity of parallel dimensions."

"Parallel dimensions?"

The astrocyst grunted with impatience. "I simply do not have time to go off on every tangent and explain every astrophysical phenomenon to you. The point is, you can wield the gravity of thousands of dimensions in one place without carrying around all the gravity. It's spread out amongst the dimensions. If you create something like that, you may be able to become the focal point of tremendous energy."

"Is this what you think Beetro can do?"

He gave her a discomfited look. "You said he stopped laser light?"

Miree nodded.

"I'm beginning to suspect something more sinister is happening altogether."

"And what is that?"

"He's not splitting apart atoms to release their energy like a nuclear weapon."

"What's he doing then?"

"He's manipulating the very laws of special relativity."

"Special relativity?"

"He's controlling light. Think of it like this... with an atom bomb, you take a little bit of mass, multiply it by the speed of light squared—an enormous number—and that's the amount of raw energy you release. That's why just splitting one atom can have such devastating power. But then consider something the opposite of an atom, think of a very large mass, like a black hole."

"A black hole?"

"Something out there in space. It has so much mass that it literally *stops light in its tracks.*"

"Oh."

"As you increase mass, you increase gravity, and you slow down light—black holes capture light."

"But Beetro doesn't weigh *that* much."

"No, he doesn't. He is, however, carrying around the effective mass of likely thousands of universes' gravity all on top of one another. So, he has the benefit of only carrying the mass of one dimension but the gravity of thousands upon thousands of dimensions."

"Which allows him to control light?"

"Yes. I didn't think the gravity from other dimensions would be able to spill over and affect ours, otherwise, I never would've made the bot. But hearing this... that he's controlling light—it's very concerning. Even more so, since he's made of so much gravity, he may be able to do even more..."

"Like what?"

"Rather than splitting a tiny amount of mass to release energy, he may be able to make a similar amount of energy from a small amount of light."

"What?"

"It's just the inverse of an atom bomb. If something weighs only a little, you take a lot of light—a detonation—and release the energy from the atom. Beetro may be able to take just a few photons and use his immense gravity to invert the energy. You didn't see him do anything like that?"

"Like what?"

"I don't know exactly what it would look like. Just... raw energy released from his body."

"No. Nothing like that. But who knows what he's doing by

now? He looked just as shocked as anyone else by that laser trick at Peles Castle. He may be experimenting now."

"Either way, he's trifling with power that he couldn't possibly understand. I know. I didn't build him to be that smart."

"Well, I'm a witness to that."

"He must be found. He can't be out there on his own, it's far too dangerous. For everyone. He must be destroyed if he's using his powers for gain. He has the potential to become an enormous tyrant—much more than your everyday fief lord or general. If it turns out he has no memory and is a simple bot, perhaps he can be persuaded to open the GeminArc. Either way, he must be found and fast—before the Reticulum finds him."

"Well," Miree said, standing. "Let's get you to Portolo so you can be on your way to stop a doomsday robot."

Portolo had no stone streets, just dirt. A riot of dandelions choked the sides of the road as they strolled into town. The air was dry, and the sun had baked jagged cracks across the desiccated dirt. Despite the heat, Miree kept her hood pulled low over her face. Although she'd never been to Portolo, she was pretty sure Reticulum members should probably keep a low profile. Galiaro chugged his last gulp of water from his canteen and wiped his brow.

A group of men watched their approach. They congregated at a wooden fence, their backs clinging with sweat, elbows propped behind them. One man cocked an eye, assessing the newcomers. He murmured to his friends, prompting a ripple of laughter. Apparently, they'd found something uproariously hilarious about a cloaked woman and an old man walking into town. Galiaro paid them no attention and Miree resisted the urge to brandish the Swordless Hilt and start making backwater yokels cry.

The buildings lining the main street were crudely built—wooden beams teething through corroded plaster, roofs of cracking red clay. The streets of Portolo were quiet, its denizens preferring to recede to the scant shadows of wrap-around porches during the day. They were dressed in thin cotton, drab colors and all in hats, mostly weaved wicker.

"What... what's that arm?" someone asked from behind.

Miree turned, keeping her face toward the ground. "Something about to be shoved down your throat if you don't stop asking questions—" She almost fell over by the sheer size of the man, making her rethink the retort. His missing eye also did not portend well about him taking the comment kindly—she could imagine him losing it for little more than the last piece of bone marrow in a stew.

"Y-y-you—" the man started but gave up during his stutter.

"Look, I'm sorry," Miree apologized, keeping her eyes down. "Didn't mean anything by that. Just been a long journey, you know?" She gave Galiaro a sidelong look. He shook his head.

Another man, almost equally as enormous as his companion approached, studying Miree. "I think you should answer Hardu's question, freak."

"The arm helps me cook, okay?" Miree said. "Helps me cook for all the big men where I come from."

"Cook?" the man said, turning to the cyclopean, Hardu. "You ever see a woman cook like that?"

Hardu shook his head, staring at Miree. "No, Tamlin. I-I-I have not."

"The only bitch I see with an arm like that wrangled up my brother. Dragged 'em away. Haven't seen him in six months."

Miree's hand went to the Hilt, but Galiaro put a firm grip around her wrist. "No," he cautioned.

She relaxed her grip, leveling her face toward the road. "Apologies, gentlemen." She turned, her cloak swirling in a cloud of dirt, leaving the men.

"I can see why you keep running," Galiaro said after they'd turned the corner, the men fortunately not pursuing.

"What?" she said, looking behind them.

"You leave angry mobs in your wake wherever you go."

"And I suppose that's my fault?" She kicked a rock, looking for the docks, but then felt a tug on her shoulder. Turning to Galiaro, his expression was different—softer?

"Miree," he said, using her name for the first time. It was deeply weird.

"What?"

"When is the last time a crazy old astrocyst told you that the world was ending and that there is a robot roaming around out there who possibly wields... an immense amount of power?"

"You're the first. You got me there."

"And you don't think that's... something?"

"Something?"

"You do seem like a young woman who has had... trouble in life—or rather—who puts herself into trouble."

"Trouble finds me. It doesn't matter where I go."

"Perhaps you haven't found the place where you *belong*?"

"I belong on a mountain, far, far away. That's it."

"Maybe you've never had the chance. Maybe you've never found your... calling."

"My *calling*? This is coming from the man who's been blackout drunk for the last couple of years? Talk about a plan..."

"I've made mistakes, yes. But I'm thinking with more clarity the last few days—feel like I have a chance to succeed where I failed. You don't want to help?"

"No. I don't."

Galiaro nodded in understanding. "I see." He chased a worried look off his face and then hardened his expression, the lines on his forehead dimpling with shadows. "The dock is that way." He waved his hand and turned around, walking away.

"Oh. Okay." She watched as he walked away, wondering if he would turn around. "Are you... are you going to be okay?"

"Goodbye, my dear," he bade farewell, and turned the corner, leaving her there.

Fortunately, a larger boat had docked. It looked like a chartered vessel, wide sails—new, with polished wood engraved with the insignia of an Orion merchant company. Miree approached gingerly, watching men and women offload boxes of cargo from the deck. She received various glares from the crew as she approached.

"No, thank you," a man said from behind. She turned, raising her face just enough to see a properly dressed man in a crimson tunic and black trousers tucked into fine leather boots. A tight frown was transfixed inside a neatly trimmed beard. "I'm afraid I must request that you leave at once."

"I need passage."

"That should be of no importance to you. Now, please..." he gestured for her to leave. "Before things get snippy."

"*Snippy*? Look, I have coin. Gold leaves."

"I don't negotiate with people who don't show their faces to me."

She lifted her face ever so slightly, her eyes glowing red within her hood.

"Oh my..." he said with a refined drawl.

"I recognize the markings on your ship. You're from Orion."

"What's the matter with your eyes?"

"Do you have other destinations on your route... away from here? I'll pay you. A lot."

"I'm afraid not, my lady. I didn't think the rumors were true—people drilling robot parts into themselves. 'Don't go to Helian,' they say. 'It's all cyborgs and whores out there.' I must insist that you leave at once."

Miree dropped her pack, put her hand in, and lifted out several gold leaves. The man eyed the leaves for a moment as if considering the development. "Do you have other stops on your route? Before you go back to Orion?"

"No. *This* ship is going back to Orion—or what's left of it."

"Left of it?"

"I am, however, chartering a smaller boat to the Torbad this evening as a matter of fact." His voice was thick with new intrigue since seeing the gold.

"You aren't going back to Orion?"

"No, I'm afraid the mood in Orion has soured as of late. Kish in the streets, openly killing people. The corruption is too much now. An honest businessman can't conduct himself properly there. My father would spit in the streets if he was to see his business treading water in such a den of thieves."

"Will you take me with you then? Tonight?"

The man looked at the gold still laying in her palm. "Give me payment now. Two leaves now, two leaves to get on my boat tonight."

"Done," she said, thrusting two leaves in his hand.

The man chased the look of shock off his face at receiving the outrageous sum for a simple journey and composed himself. "Dock eight. We leave at ten. Name's Meric. Meric D'Naris. Yours?"

"Anisha."

"Fake name?"

"Does it matter?"

"Don't be late, Anisha."

Miree kept to the alleyways. She'd found a crate to crawl atop and nap. The sunlight faded, bringing life out into the cool streets. Shouts and laughter filled the main street as men finished work and rambled around, looking for booze and whores. Miree found herself staring at the face of a wall of cinderblocks. She felt a dull ache somewhere—in her chest or back—she really wasn't sure. Whatever it was, it was new. She rolled over, trying to get comfortable but her arm ached. The deadweight of a weaponized prosthesis that the Reticulum had grafted into her severed humerus had been killing her ever since they'd left. And the damn thing didn't even work. She knew her first step when getting to the Torbad would be to find a surgeon and get the thing off her arm.

She rolled over and looked up at the night's sky. The stars were there—planets, apparently—fuzzy, halos of blue and white light. All five of them. Considering the sky, she wondered what it must've looked like to ancient humans when they peered into the blackness of night. Was it a brilliant sheet of twinkling stars like Galiaro described? Was the man even coherent enough to believe a single word he told her? For a moment—the briefest—she wondered if the old man had been able to charter a boat back to Orion.

She realized she had no idea what time it was and stalked back out to the streets. With her hood covering her face, she peered around the street and heard a nearby tavern roaring with music and laughter. She made her way toward the docks.

"You," someone said. "We've been looking for you."

She turned and saw two enormous men standing behind her, jugs in hand.

"Hardu, it's our lucky day."

"Y-y-you aren't nice," Hardu said, pointing, accusing.

She kept her face down. "I don't want trouble. I already apologized."

"But what's a sorry from a cyborg?" Tamlin taunted, fumbling his words.

"I'll just be on my way." Miree turned but didn't get far. Hardu tackled her to the ground and pummeled a fist into her side. Miree cried out but stopped, quickly realizing there was no one anywhere who would possibly come to her aid. She looked up and saw Tamlin, a dark shadow over his face.

"Where is he?" Tamlin asked.

Miree grimaced beneath the weight of Hardu, his chest pinning her to the ground. "Who?"

"My brother, Austis. You people took him!"

"I didn't take anyone."

"I saw them—cyborgs like you a few weeks ago. You took him. What did you do to him?"

She heard a knife unsheathe at the man's hip. "No. That was the Reticulum. They kidnap people. They kidnapped *me*. I only just escaped... I swear."

Tamlin flipped her hood from her face, exposing her eyes. "You *are* them. Where is your kind?"

"They are in the Meteor Mountains. That's where your brother is."

Hardu looked up at Tamlin, confused. "Th-that was easy."

Tamlin eyed her. "Bind her. She's coming with us. Take us all the way up those mountains to find out if she's lying. If she is, we kill her."

"I'm not lying," Miree said, her hand creeping beneath her cloak toward the Hilt. "You think I care about the Reticulum? Look at what they did to me."

"Hardu, get offa her." Tamlin held his blade out as Hardu stood. Miree gasped with new breath.

Rage flared inside her as she got to her knees. She unsheathed the Swordless Hilt, the shardblade burning in the moonlight. The men stepped back from her, inspecting the sword.

"Looks like she wants a fight, Hardu," Tamlin said, grinning. "Two men against one cyborg. I like those odds, don't you, Hardu?"

"Odds," Hardu said, giggling. "I like—I like those odds."

Before the men could advance on her, Miree swiped her wrist to the ground, the shards flying at her command. They ascended like a cloud, swarming through the air as Miree guided the Hilt. The men paused at the shards and then backed away as the shards burned hotter, becoming beacons of light in the dark street. Hardu gripped Tamlin's jacket.

"Move another inch and these will fly through you like butter," Miree threatened.

Hardu started, "W-we don't mean you harm. We'll go."

Tamlin was just as shocked as his friend. "We can go to Meteor Mountains without you. We'll be on our way." He dropped a heel as if to recede away from her.

"Empty your pockets," she demanded.

Tamlin grimaced. "What's this then, darling? Can't we leave well enough alone? We're sorry we caused you any trouble."

A boyish fear swept Hardu's face. "We are sorry."

"I—" She stopped, looking at the men. How many times had

she been here before? How many times did she escape the clutches of awful men, only to turn around and do the exact same thing that they did? She traveled from the Fifth Kingdom to Orion and Helian—dozens of villages and caravans in between. And everywhere she went, it was the same—the world of men trying to control her. As many times as she fought back—as many places as she went—it was always the same. Galiaro's words crossed her mind, something about... a calling. She looked at the stupid men in front of her—saw the fear in their eyes. A fear she'd seen so many times before. She saw Beetro's face when she left him at that tower. She saw Lucindi's lifeless face in Mercy Plaza—serene, beautiful... guiltless and free.

"Just go," she said, flipping the pommel. The shards went dim before she called them back to the Hilt. "Get out of here."

Tamlin and Hardu ran, their feet stomping along wooden planks. Miree turned, walking briskly away from the main street—away from the taverns, away from the men. As she stepped over a foul-smelling puddle, she heard someone moaning. A man huddled next to a set of empty crates was reaching a hand out to her, begging through garbled words.

"Coin?" he managed.

"I don't have anything," she said while feeling the leaves of gold in her pocket. "Don't you have anywhere to go?" Before she could process her own disgust at asking him, she found that she was moving toward him, concern blooming inside her. There was no use denying it—she'd gone soft. Letting the two men go who threatened to kill her? And now, stopping to look after a drunk? She'd passed by thousands of drunks in the past with no more than a shrug. It was Lucindi, of course, getting into her head. The damn girl was always checking in with Crow—with Galiaro—making sure the wreck of a person was still breathing. Miree approached the drunk as he lowered his hood.

She stopped.

It was Galiaro.

Wafts of hard liquor coated his breath.

"What are you *doing*?" She knelt beside him, inspecting his face.

"Liddle coin? Coin for an old man?" he said, spit bubbling between his lips. "Maybe a liddle nip?"

"What are you doing here? You should be halfway to Orion by now." But she knew. She remembered that haunted look that crossed his face when he said goodbye. He knew where he was going, and it wasn't Orion—at least not without her.

"You need to sober up, charter a boat. Beetro, remember? You've got to find Beetro."

"Beetro?" he said, looking up through squinted eyes. The man had somehow become instantly filthy since the last time she saw him.

"Yes, yes, Beetro. He might destroy the world or something. Remember?"

"Beetro, Beetro, Beetro..." He looked away, despondent.

"Yes. You've got to find him."

"No, no, not anymore."

"Not anymore? Why not?"

"Look," he said, pointing to the sky. "Look!"

She looked to the heavens and saw nothing. "What?"

"Look," he repeated.

"There!" a new voice rang out from behind.

Miree whipped around and saw them—Haldu, Tamlin, and half a dozen other men. A regular angry mob. She grabbed her Hilt and held it toward them but looked down at Galiaro. "You've..."

Galiaro peered at her, a drunken gaze dwelling in his eyes. "There's nothing."

"I'm sorry. I have to leave you. I'm...."

She ran. She left Galiaro there and fled from the men. After sheathing the Hilt, she powered into a sprint, flying down the street and cutting through alleyways. Once at the dock, she reoriented herself and moved past each boat dock until she found it—dock eight.

"Almost left without you," Meric called out, a single silhouette on a small schooner. Several men waited beside him; arms crossed.

She leaped from the dock and landed on the deck of the boat, her hair falling in her face. "We need to go," she said in between breaths. "But there's someone back there—"

Meric stomped toward her. "Payment."

"Here, here," she said, putting two gold leaves in his hand. "Take it. And don't be an unbelievable asshole and kill me once we're out at sea and rob the rest from me, okay?"

"O-of course not," Meric guffawed with indignation, looking at the other men. "We're merchants, not pirates."

"Okay, then set sail already." She looked back and saw the crowd of men coming to the docks, torches in hand.

"What did you *do*?" Meric asked as the men prepared to pull away.

"I don't even know anymore," she said, finding a nook between the ship's cabin and railing. She dropped her satchel and sat, her prosthetic arm thunking on the deck. As the ship pulled away, Miree looked at the sky, passed the rippling sails, and saw the stars.

There were only four.

THIRTY-TWO

THEY SET out across the windswept tundra. Beetro leading alongside Ribcage, Hawera with her iron walking staff behind them, and Arym trailing last. They'd left the small, forested area just outside the gargantua and headed east, the enormous egg-shaped city looming on the horizon. The sky was clear and Beetro's hopes were high. Somehow, after his embarrassing 'let's be friends' speech the night before, a calmness had settled over the group. Ribcage seemed to dance as she walked, mindlessly humming as if acting like a child for the first time. Beetro found he was humming along with her ever-changing melody. Hawera, the girl from the dark world, also seemed at ease as a new companion with the group. Yet, Beetro noticed distance between the girl and Arym. The odd young man remained mostly quiet as they traveled.

Beetro's dreams persisted, yet they now varied. He dreamt of Korthe, Ribcage—sometimes a faceless Galiaro. Regardless, he was encouraged that he had dreams that were simply projections from his own reality.

"When you going to bust them out again?" Ribcage asked as they walked.

"Bust what out?"

"You know... your special sauce."

"What?"

"Your laser hands, fireballs—I don't know what you call it."

"Photonics. I absorb the photons around me and funnel it back out as energy."

"Right. That. Do that again."

"There's no reason to right now, and besides, you know what it does to me. Dries my water vapor stores, my nuclear core seizes up."

"All your talk last night had me thinking. Doesn't hurt to have the backs of those you travel with. Which reminds me—" She broke off from Beetro and waited for Arym, who led the rear. The man appeared wretched with frayed black hair over his pale skin. He looked at her with baleful, bloodshot eyes.

"Sorry about the other night," Ribcage told him, patting him on the back.

He remained silent, narrowing his eyes with skepticism.

Beetro stopped. "What're you talking about?"

"It's kind of funny now that I think about it, but back on the mountains—before we got lost in the humongous trees—I may have..."

"What?"

"Put a dagger to his throat. Told him to watch his back."

"What! This true?" He looked to Arym.

Arym nodded. "Woke me up in the middle of the night, blade to my neck. Told me to stay away from you."

Beetro turned to Ribcage, incredulous. "*Why?* Why would you think that's okay?"

"I didn't!" she said. "Well, I don't anymore. You said it last night—we got each other's backs. So, hairy sad boy," she addressed Arym. "I'm sorry." She brought a solemn hand to her chest and gave a small bow. Believing the matter closed, she continued walking, humming a mindless tune. There was far too much to unpack at that moment, so Beetro let it slide, grateful that the girl at least recognized the depravity of what she did by her own volition.

From Beetro's visual calculations, Orion was no more than three days away on foot. He was antsy to arrive sooner and longed for something faster, a horse perhaps. He winced every time he thought about Bellamare. The poor horse had no idea what had even happened before bursting into a million pieces. And then he thought of Miree. Watching him. Hoping for rescue. He wondered where she was and if she was even alive. He'd become good at pushing away the hard memories—ignoring the guilt. But it was getting harder and harder to ignore as he remembered Lucindi explaining Miree to him—*Be patient with that one. She's been through more than most. Girls like her just need time—they need love.* If only he could go back and change everything.

They set up camp as night fell, the lonely stars teething through the black sky. The four huddled around a fire while Ribcage cooked meat. She'd been on quite a kick, helping the group out as if doing things for other people was a novel idea. Beetro was thankful for some degree of stability from the child. He briefly wondered if it was what being a parent felt like but quickly punted that thought from his brain.

The next morning, the tundra slanted downward toward a basin floor. It was only one flat stretch away to Orion, and Beetro felt the excitement in the group. Ribcage was skipping and dancing as they traveled, humming and twirling around the group. Hawera, too, sang—she had a surprisingly low voice that came from deep in the throat. Although Beetro couldn't understand the words, he found the songs both beautiful and haunting with many minor notes.

"What are they about?" he asked.

Hawera stopped. "What?"

"Your songs? What are they about?"

"Lithusa. My people."

"Is there really no sun where you live?"

She nodded.

He motioned to the sky. "Is this the first time you've seen the sun?"

She shook her head. "I see sun every time. Every time I go back."

"Go back where?"

"When we bend time back."

Confused and aware that it brought the girl pain to discuss, he offered, "I'm happy you are with us. I hope you find what you're looking for and get back to your people."

Her smile flattened. "Thank you, Beetro."

"Beetro," Arym called from behind.

Beetro turned. The man managed a perpetual state of misery—bags under red-cracked eyes. He had a healthy amount of stubble and a mop of disheveled hair that looked impossible to tame. "Yes?"

"Do you think I can find help for my people in Orion?"

"I-I'm honestly not sure."

"Who is there to help? My people are back there—could be dead already. That army has probably already broken in."

"It's General Deluvius. He's trying to take over the whole region."

"Can we stop him?"

Flashes of Bellamare exploding went through his mind. He recalled holding a shaft of laser light at Peles Castle—Deluvius completely flabbergasted. He clenched his fists and closed his eyes, concentrating. Almost immediately, he felt an infinite shower of photons cascading over his body. The energy flowed through him, collecting in his palms, itching to be released. It had never been so easy to draw photonic energy. But then he remembered that dream... showering an army in liquid fire, wiping out hundreds of lives with the stroke of his hands. He let the energy dissipate back into the air as thermal waves.

"We might be able to do something to stop him, yes."

"Because... we're friends, right?"

Oh. Apparently, his little embarrassing speech had more of an impact than he'd thought. "Exactly."

"It's good to know there are people—er, robots—like you in the overworld."

"I'm a robot but I'm also people."

Arym nodded. "I believe you're right."

They made it to the valley basin, on the east side of Crater Valley and the forest tundra. The egg-shaped mountain of Orion loomed just ahead. Ribcage bolted, running across the brush.

"Ribcage, stop!" Beetro yelled. She turned, tripped, and fell, then looked back angrily. "There's something out there." He enhanced his vision and saw it—a circle of trucks. "Deluvius."

"It's *him*," Arym said, scrambling up a boulder for a better view.

"Not sure if he's actually right out there, but those are his trucks. That's his army. Part of it at least. We can go around the envoy, safely, and make our way to the city. There's a lot of brush and gullies —I'm sure we can slip by, undetected. Sound good to everyone?"

"I guess," Ribcage huffed. "If you want to do it the most boring way possible."

"I do."

They kept on eastward, Beetro periodically climbing a tree for reconnaissance. Their path was an arc around the envoy—more time-consuming but safer from the wrath of the soldiers if discovered. He landed from a tree. "I think we're in a good position—" The group watched him as he froze, mid-sentence.

Arym approached gingerly. "Does he... does he need a reboot?"

"Quiet!" Beetro said after finally moving. "Nobody move—or speak." He stood like a statue, plummeting the decibel threshold of his ears and heard it... footsteps. A single person, just beyond the trees. Beetro motioned for the group to get low. Arym dropped like a rock and shimmied toward Hawera. Ribcage seamlessly flipped a blade into her palm. She nodded at Beetro and mouthed, *I got you.*

A woman's voice issued from the forest. "Who's there?"

"Travelers," Beetro replied. He moved over to a patch of light through the forest and started charging his photonics. A shower of photons cascaded over his body, thrumming through his metal shell and pouring through him. "No trouble."

A woman, dressed in a form-fitting woven ballistic suit, emerged. A strap flung over her shoulder suspended a windswept laser rifle over the back. "Well," she said, studying the group. "You found trouble."

"Run!" Beetro yelled.

The woman reached to her belt, unhooked a radio, and was about to speak when a knife sunk nicely into her hand. "Fuck!" she cried, clutching her bloodied hand.

Ribcage stood opposite the woman, already producing another

blade from her waistline somewhere. "Want to try again? Put down the weapon or you're dead."

Beetro bolted to Ribcage, grabbing her. "Let's go!"

"Zap her," she said, a grin across her face.

And then something was rushing through the forest and the thing was moving fast, demolishing trees beneath its path, flinging a storm of dirt and roots through the air. Glints of metal shone through the leaves. Whatever it was, it was mechanical.

"We need to get out of here, I can't handle this all at once," Beetro yelled, trying to corral the group.

The machine approached. A hub of metal moved across the forest floor, centered inside an array of mechanical arms, each with a variety of saws and blades, moving swiftly through trunks and boughs, making short work of forest obstacles. One arm shot a tongue of fire as if a warning. The machine sprinted across the forest on four legs, hyperextending, outfitted with spiked feet that sunk into the earth with every step. A single operator looked out from a slit of a window within the central hub.

"What is *that*?" Arym cried.

"Run!" Beetro yelled.

The group tried to scatter, but the machine was on them, crashing through the final line of trees, arriving at the forest clearing. The captain was giving chase from behind, swinging her rifle from the crook of her arm. "Fucking freeze!"

Beetro charged up.

He sucked up the photons from the sun—was getting better at it—bottled up the energy, and lifted his hands. He looked over at Ribcage.

"Do it," she commanded, reaching for her water flask.

He closed his eyes and released, the photonic power surging through his hands. But when he opened his eyes once more, he only saw twin vapor trails evaporating in the sky, just oblique to the impending machine of death.

He missed.

And then he fell over, paralyzed into a useless hunk of robotic metal.

Ribcage came into view. "Y-you missed?" She quickly poured some water into his mouth. "Go again, come on."

When he got back up, the machine was there, towering above the group.

"Come!" someone said from behind.

Hawera.

The group turned and watched as she lifted her staff with its hardened point of raw iron held straight out. Gripping the staff with both hands, she closed her eyes, a blue *aura* immediately encircling her body. The blue light coalesced around her hand and crept up the wooden staff toward the iron tip. Once there, the blue energy collected at the iron, acting as a reservoir as it pulled more from Hawera's body. A small jet of energy then shot from the iron end of the staff. And then, like a drop of water hitting a pond, the space rippled out from where the jet of blue penetrated the air. Almost instantaneously, a hole formed in space—perfectly circular leading to a distorted funnel—a riot of stretched color and textures.

She turned to them. "In!"

Ribcage ran through the hole without question. Arym swept his eyes to Hawera and then followed. Beetro, bewildered, but no less keen to stay behind with the killer machine, ran through. Unlike Ribcage's foray into extra-space where his body felt like a noodle that expanded to the ends of the galaxy, this one was brief. He found himself in the same forest tundra, in the same daylight.

Hawera held a finger to her lips.

Beetro inspected the area. They were in the exact same spot as before. Nothing had changed. Yet, he did hear the low crackling of a radio close by. Spying past a boulder and a line of trees, he saw them there... the captain and the monstrous machine stalking about. They were still looking for them.

"Quiet," Hawera warned the group, looking especially at Ribcage.

"What *happened*?" the girl asked, a huge grin on her face.

Beetro grabbed her arm and pointed to the machine. "Don't talk." The girl saw the machine and nodded but still suppressed a smile.

They picked the direction opposite Deluvius' soldiers and ran into a river that they followed for over an hour until they could take shelter in a ravine. Beetro waited, listening for pursuers and, satisfied, broke for camp.

"No fires," he warned.

They sat inside a knot of trees, each looking at Hawera. She refused to return their stares and sat with her back against a tree, eyes resting.

"Ahem," Beetro said, startling her.

"Yas?"

"What was that?" Ribcage asked.

Hawera sighed. Arym, too, gave her an unrelenting look. "Nothing."

"Nothing?" Beetro asked. "You opened a portal in space."

"Not a portal," Ribcage said. "This lady tore a *hole* in space. I could *feel* it."

Hawera crossed her arms and looked away as if to end the inquiry.

Arym stood and began pacing and then stopped, looking at her. "She said something to me once. Something about being a butterfly."

"Look, pal," Ribcage said to him, patting his hand. "We know you've been hung up on her but you gotta cut it with the cutesy names."

"No, no," he insisted, shaking her hand away. "It's something she told me. Said that she was like a butterfly and that I wasn't." He looked at Hawera. "Is this what you meant? Opening a hole like that?"

"My Fourth," Hawera said.

"Your Fourth?" Beetro asked.

Hawera nodded. "Gift of the Lithusa. Gift of time."

"But what did it do?" Beetro asked. "We walked through to the same spot. Only..." He went back to his memory of the event—same spot in the forest, only with Deluvius' captain searching for them as if...

And then there was something different about the shadows of the trees on the ground, they were at a slightly different slant... "A gift of time. You took us to a different time, didn't you?"

Hawera nodded.

"But only a few minutes. We jumped ahead—"

"Making us disappear from them," Arym added.

"Yas," she said. "My Fourth."

Ribcage knelt beside her. "Can you do it again?"

Hawera furrowed her eyebrow. "Use Fourth?"

"Yes. Just for a sec. Can you make a portal again?"

"Why?"

"I want to see something... please?"

"Tired," she said. "Too tired."

"It must exhaust her," Arym said. "Rest," he told her.

"No. Come on. Please?" Ribcage insisted. "Just for a teeny second."

Using her staff, Hawera got to her feet and looked at the group. Raising the staff, she pointed the iron end at a tree and closed her eyes. A blue aura glowed faintly around her body, growing toward her hands. It collected there and then, jumped up the wooden staff, and collected around the metal. She opened her eyes and grimaced, releasing a small grunt as the blue light shot out from the staff, piercing the air. The tree before her rippled with the distortion of space. A pinpoint hole opened before them, expanding into a funnel of colors and raw textures as if exposing the primordial substance that composed all matter.

"There!" Ribcage shouted, jumping up and down.

Beetro looked from the hole to the girl. "What?"

Ribcage grinned. "Watch."

And then Ribcage vanished.

Arym took a step back. "Where did she *go*?"

"She Jumped," Beetro said, watching the rippling of the space distortion. A continuous beam of blue light flowed from Hawera's staff. The girl was sweating profusely. "I wouldn't stop yet," he told her. "Might not get her back if you close the portal."

Ribcage appeared again, halfway across the campsite. "It worked!"

Hawera looked to Beetro, who nodded, and the girl released the staff, the spatial distortion collapsing.

"I can Jump!" Ribcage said, hopping up and down.

"The hole she makes," Beetro explained. "It opens to the flat world, doesn't it?"

"Uh-huh. I thought I felt it back there when we escaped that machine. That hole she makes—it's like being back at my mom. There's a hole there, too."

Arym stood in the middle of the group. "What's happening? What is this and who are you people?"

"I'm not sure, exactly," Beetro told him. "But our little band just got a lot more specialized."

THIRTY-THREE

"WE HAVE TO GO BACK," Miree told Meric, looking at the night's sky.

The merchant didn't look away from his position at the bow of the ship. "Back?"

"Back to Portolo."

"I'm not so easily amused, my lady."

"And then we need to go to Orion."

"Please don't test my patience. It grows thinner by the hour."

"Look up at the sky."

He glanced up. "And?"

"The stars. How many do you see?"

Meric moved to the edge of the ship, his muscular body silhouetting the glow of Portolo in the distance. "How many do I see?"

"Yes. How many stars do you see?"

"There are five stars," he said without looking up again.

"Good. Now, this time, actually *look* at the sky."

The merchant sailor craned his neck, studying the sky. "Hmm."

"How many?"

"The starboard star is... oh. There's only four."

"Isn't that a little strange? I know the stars change during different times of the year—but not overnight. Last night—hours ago—there were five stars. Now there's only four?"

"Piot, my man," Meric said, gesturing to another man. "How goes navigation tonight?"

An ancient-looking man hobbled over from the stern of the ship, stoking a pipe between his hands. "Speak up!"

"I need navigation," Meric raised his voice.

Piot flicked his ear, only steps away from them. "Louder!"

"Look up!" Meric yelled, lifting the man's chin.

Piot looked up and then back at Meric. "Where's the starboard star? What is this? That's an October sky, not an April sky."

"How do you explain it?"

Piot removed his cap, wiped a film of sweat from his brow, and replaced the cap. "Clouds."

"That's a totally clear sky. The moon's right there!" Miree protested.

Meric frowned at Miree. "Piot is my navigator and has looked after me since I was a lad bouncing on his knee. I would trust him with my life and my father's company. He's never wrong." He looked back up and then said, "But it is true that there is not a single cloud in the sky. Piot, what say you, man?"

Piot nodded. "I say that a star is missing."

"And you don't know why?"

"Aye." He puffed on his pipe, his mouth like shriveled pumpkin skin.

"Have you ever seen that before?"

The old man cocked one eye and clicked his tongue. "That, I have not."

Meric sighed. "How many years have you been doing this, Piot?"

"Thirty-two next month."

"And you've never seen a star go away overnight?"

"That, I have not." He bowed.

Miree stood. "Look, it's hard to explain—mostly because I barely even understand the problem. But we need to go back to Portolo and pick up an astrocyst. He knows what's going on."

Meric shook his head. "We've got a timeline to keep."

"And you expect to keep it when you can't even keep track of where you are anymore? Won't it be a little hard to navigate when the sky is *changing*?"

"Piot, what do you think, man? Can we get around with four stars in the sky instead of five?"

Piot took a puff on his pipe, a high-pitched creak coming from the back of his throat as he considered a response. "Reckon we can."

"Well, I'm satisfied. I suggest you go find a place to rest," he told Miree. "It'll be half a day till the Torbad."

Miree set her jaw. "You don't understand. Something's *happening*. Something new. The stars aren't stars... they're planets. And now one of them is gone. Galiaro knows why. He just told me—back there—he saw the sky."

Piot and Meric exchanged glances. "Why'd we come to Portolo again, Piot?"

Piot shrugged. "To transport strange, robotic women, 'spose."

"Listen," Meric said to Miree. "I agree, it's strange. We're missing a star. Maybe it was its time to go. You know the stories—the sky used to be littered with stars. They just leave. Maybe it's not that unusual."

"I'll give you more gold," Miree insisted, grabbing her pack.

"You want to go back there with that mob about ready to hang you up?"

"We have to get the astrocyst. He's the only one who knows what's going on. Here," she said, reaching into her bag and pulling out three gold leaves. "Probably worth whatever you were going to get paid for cargo delivery in the Torbad. Am I right?"

Meric looked from the gold to Piot and then met his eyes with Miree.

"I'll give you five more once we get to Orion."

He looked up at the sky, studying the stars once more. "Rachek!" he yelled to the sailor at the ship's wheel. "Turn her back."

"Say that again?" Rachek called back.

"Back to Portolo. Turn her back. We just got a new employer."

They pulled up at the last dock in Portolo, the streets empty save for a few stray dogs. She found him in the same place, his tongue hanging from his lips, drool pooling along his cheek. After a few good slaps, Galiaro awoke. His anger turned pleasant when he saw it was Miree who was getting him to his feet. The man's stench was almost too much, but she managed to walk him down to the docks and into the schooner.

"*Him?*" Meric mocked, inspecting the disheveled drunk whose head flopped down as Miree propped him by his armpits.

She lifted Galiaro the last step and dropped him onto the deck. "Yes. Him. Now, can we get out of here? I've paid you good money." Meric made the call and the schooner was untied from the dock. The sails were raised, catching an eastward gust. "Food. Coffee," she snapped as she got Galiaro back to his feet and plopped him down in a chair.

Piot limped over to the pair and looked Galiaro up and down. "Gonna need something strong for this one. Gotta keep alcohol burning in those veins or he'll get the shakes. Seen a many die on long journeys overseas from the shakes."

"I know," Miree said, thinking back to the Reticulum where she force-fed the astrocyst corn and water. Took him a full three days to get over the withdrawals. Now he was right back at square one. Didn't she just cut this old man loose and now she *deliberately* went out of her way to get him back? What was happening to her? "But he's got to sober up. We need him."

"Need him for what exactly?"

"He told me that the galaxy is dying and that missing planet... it's all part of it. This is the only man around who knows what's going on."

"So, why do you need to get back to Orion? It's not exactly a peaceful place at the moment."

"There's a robot there and Galiaro also has a lab there with another astrocyst. They can work together and—" she stopped. There she went again, caring about things that really shouldn't concern her. Not only did she go back for the old man but spent a fortune to get him and promised more gold that she didn't even have. The last three leaves she'd given Meric completely tapped her. "Please," she said, looking at Meric. "Just get us to Orion. Something is very wrong, and it affects all of us."

They sailed in silence for a few hours, several of the crew gazing at the sky, speculating about the missing star. They seemed a decent crew to Miree, five in total, with Meric at least being a man of his word for the moment. Who knew what the gentleman sailor would do when she couldn't pay him upon arrival? Galiaro dozed and then jolted awake, unaware of Miree's presence. Why? Why would she risk so much for this old man? He talked about a calling. Did she really buy that fairy tale?

Maybe I do.

"Miree?" Galiaro awoke again, his eyes resting on her.

"Yes, it's me. You need to wake up. Drink." She brought a cup of coffee to his lips.

The man gulped it down and sat up. "Where am I?"

"We're on a boat. Heading to Orion."

He smiled. "Ah."

She watched him drink and said, "Damn you."

"What did I do?"

"Made me come back for you."

"I didn't make you do anything you didn't want to do."

"Look." She gestured to the sky.

Galiaro craned his neck and then stood, spilling his tin of coffee on the deck. A new fear crossed his face. "*No.*" He stood, hands gripping the railing, gazing upon the night's sky. "I thought it was just a dream. Just a damn drunken dream!"

"What does it mean?"

He met her eyes. "None of this makes any sense. It's too fast. Dark Theory—Fallaro and I—it was perfect. We knew when the unraveling would happen, but like this... not so soon. It can't be happening now. Something is speeding it up—"

"What is unraveling?"

He sat on the deck, pulling a notebook from his robe. After digging in his pockets, he yelled, "Does anyone have a pencil? A quill? I need to write!" The crew looked at the old man with little regard.

Miree crouched beside him. "What is going on?"

He gestured for her to come close and whispered in her ear. "Saturn. I-it's... it's—"

"What?"

"Saturn is... gone." His voice was haunted.

"What is Saturn?"

"One of the planets of the solar system. The furthest one out that is visible to the naked eye. There are two more beyond that you can see with a telescope. Eight planets and one dwarf body in total circle the sun. Been that way for millennia—eons. And now that Saturn is gone, that means Neptune and Uranus must have left us some time ago as well. But it's all happening too fast. Local expansion shouldn't be this quick."

"What do we do?"

"Wait!" He stood. "Are we on a *boat*?"

She gestured to the waves. "Yes. Obviously."

"Where?"

"Chronicle Sea, arriving at Orion soon. Look." She pointed behind, the egg shape of Orion looming before them in the moonlight.

Meric approached. "You've got a mighty fine friend here to pay so much and come back for you."

Galiaro gazed at the man for a moment as if looking beyond him. "We need to get off this boat."

Meric looked at Miree. "What?"

"Galiaro, don't you want to go to Orion? Won't that help you figure out what's going on?"

"What time is it?" Galiaro asked.

Meric brought out a pocket watch. "Four-o'-eight in the morning."

"Sun is rising soon?"

Meric nodded.

Galiaro took a ragged breath. "Fools! We need to get to land. *Now*."

Whether it was Galiaro's stern words or his haunted face,

Meric moved. He barked orders at Rachek and Doran to change the jibe and head for land. The crew burst into a flurry of movement as Galiaro briefly retired to the side of the deck to vomit into the sea.

Miree grabbed his sleeve as he cuffed vomit away from his mouth. "What's going on?"

"I'm probably wrong, don't worry about it."

"Wrong about what?" she asked as a ray of sunlight crested the horizon over the sea.

Galiaro's eyes were drawn to that horizon, his shoulders slumping as he let out a gasp.

Miree grabbed his robe. "Wrong about *what*?"

But before he could answer, the schooner slumped in the water. The crew looked at one another, momentarily startled before the entire ship *plummeted*. The deck slanted, leaving no one standing. Miree grappled with the railing, getting it into her grip as the entire stern dropped. The deck became like a cliffside—what was once the floor was now a wall. Doran screamed as his body flailed, hands failing to find a holding. Miree heard his head hit the mast, his body flying into a darkened abyss of nothing that was swallowing the ship whole.

She grabbed ahold of Galiaro, who was scrambling up the deck and getting his arms through a railing. What was once a flat sea was a towering vertical wave on which the schooner rode down, far below the natural bounds of the surface. Water gushed over the deck as the boat cut through the water, descending faster and faster down an endless wave of cataclysmic size. Soon, Miree was gasping for air as water pummeled her body, a constant spray filling her mouth and nose. She was blinded from the deluge, unable to see if anyone was still aboard.

At the point where her fingers, icy cold from the sea water, were about to give, the ship evened out ever so slightly. In place of her gravity-defying death grip on the ship's railing, she was able to ease up as the ship leveled out. Water rushed all around, a dark cocoon entombing the ship. A frigid cold set in, creeping into her bones. She coughed a lungful of water and heaved as she tried to get more up. The ship evened out on the water and felt as if it had come to a complete stop.

Miree opened her eyes and found that the ship was rocketing along the surface of an enormous wave with even acceleration, giving the sensation that the ship was not in motion. She was too shocked to speak—too shocked to think. She was able to let go of the railing and felt for Galiaro.

He was still there.

She bellowed beneath the sound of churning water. "What's going on?"

The old man was a sopping mess, his beard twirled into a ragged sponge—robe tangled about his body. Gingerly, he loosened his grip on the railing and looked at her, eyes drooping. He wore an expression of naked surrender.

Miree stood, a fine mist spraying her face. Something soft hit her in the head and rolled to her feet. An octopus. It slithered away on frantic tentacles, leading her eye to a multitude of aquatic life strewn about the deck. Meric was there, kicking away seaweed and fragments of coral from the path to the ship's wheel. And then the man was at the helm, fruitlessly spinning the ship's wheel as the schooner continued to barrel downward.

She negotiated the flotsam of fish and seaweed that floated over the pooling water and made it to Meric. "What's happening?"

"Trying to steer us back."

"Back from *what*?"

"I don't know!" he said, a frantic edge in his voice.

"And to where?"

Meric didn't answer, only cradled the ship's wheel as if it contained all the answers.

Piot, the shriveled pumpkin head, was somehow still aboard. He approached, on hands and knees, pipe in mouth. "Lost our boys. Rachek. Doran. Cherith. Gone overboard."

"The entire *ship* is overboard," Miree yelled, watching Galiaro get to his feet.

Piot nodded. "Aye, lass, that it is."

The four gathered around the ship's wheel and watched as the schooner continued to soar downward, evening out until the deck was once again level.

"Land?" Piot pointed with his pipe.

The crags of a deep cavernous ravine shimmered in scattered dawn light. Just beyond the ravine towered jagged mountains of innumerable peaks. Yet unlike most mountains, these peaks didn't cut the sky with sharp silhouettes, rather, they were layered with a fuzzy surface, covered in vegetation.

Miree looked behind the ship and saw nothing but a wall of receding water. "What are those mountain peaks? They just came out of nowhere. Was this an earthquake?"

"I-I don't know," Meric hesitated. "They shouldn't be there. By the gods below, the world has shattered before our very eyes."

Galiaro approached the helm. "The sea has fled. These are underwater mountain ranges. What was once the seafloor is now the land."

"How can this be happening?" Miree asked, going unanswered. The ship soared, leveling out along the wave while the wall of water receded the opposite direction. "Galiaro," she asked, eyes pleading. "What's going on?"

"Earth's orbit," he said, looking up at her, "is... broken."

The ship finally struck land...

At the bottom of the sea.

The bow slid into a mass of coral and keeled over. They scrambled to the edge of the deck as the boat toppled to the side, grabbing hold of the railings and getting to the side of the hull as the ship came to a stop. Water gushed from its bowels, bringing fish, furniture, and chests out from within. Miree let herself drop to the ground, her feet sinking deep into a feathery sediment. Piot and Galiaro climbed down, completely covered in the mud and grime of the seafloor. Miree saw the colossal wall of water traveling away in the distance, streaks of sunlight flitting through its edge, revealing just how enormous it was. They looked up and saw nothing but a series of jagged mountain peaks running in seemingly infinite rows toward the sky. The massive egg-mountain of Orion was nowhere to be seen.

"Where do we go?" she asked. "Where is Orion?"

Meric fumbled within his coat pocket and brought out a compass. "That way," he said, pointing up the towering mountain range. "Unless Earth's magnetic field has also broken..."

"There's no way we're climbing up out of here," she said, shivering in the dank air, her cloak completely soaked.

"No," Galiaro attested. "There is not."

Piot, who'd lost his cane yet had found an oar to use as a staff, hobbled up to Galiaro and clasped a hand on his shoulder. "Welcome, soothsayer. We lost good sailors today—swallowed up they were. Care to explain what has come to pass here? Not every day the sea grows legs and walks away."

Galiaro wrung his beard of seawater, making them wait. After swiveling a pinky finger into his ear, he finally said, "Earth moved."

"Earth moves every day around the sun," Meric said, shock in his voice.

"Yes. But Earth has moved *inward*, taking a closer orbit to the sun. It's what I suspected would happen long ago. But it shouldn't have happened so quickly."

Meric exhaled, looking down the new "beach" from where the water had receded, creating a shore that abutted a coral reef of white and orange. Sharks and fish flopped along the shore. There was a whale flapping its fins in the distance. "What does this have to do with the missing star?"

"It was Saturn, just beyond Jupiter's edge. It was flung from the solar system. By losing Saturn, Earth lost the opposing gravitational pull, making us fall toward the sun's gravity."

"That means..." Miree said, not wanting to finish the thought.

"That the tides now follow the sun, not the moon." Galiaro nodded. "We're now so close to the sun that its gravity can pull on the tides."

The four remained silent for a moment, awful realization setting in.

Miree started, "As the day passes—"

"The tides will return back to their place," Galiaro finished. "And as the sun rises again, the tides will roar with the energy of a tsunami. Everywhere on the planet. Every day. Until the end of Earth's time."

Hearing the revelation, Meric moved back to the ship, lifting a leg over the railing and scrambling up the slanted deck. As the man seemed to be the only one with a plan, Miree followed. She clung to the railing and hopped up the mast that had broken and split down the deck. After scrambling up a large net that still clung to the deck, she followed him into the cabin below. The man was fumbling with chests, nets, and cooking gear that had been strewn around the cabin like a tornado had just blown through. Miree wordlessly helped him lift a cot from the cabin, exposing a trap door in the floor. She watched his burly arms negotiate a padlock on the latch and lifted the door as the hinges creaked.

They looked down at a pool of trapped water.

Before she asked what was down there, Meric was flipping his boots off. "You're going down?"

He nodded. "Come after me if I'm not back up in a minute." He plunged into the trap door, splashing water aside. She heard the grumbling voice of Piot outside, yelling something through the hull. Galiaro called her name.

"Just hang on!" she called back.

One minute passed.

It wasn't until she had one boot off that Meric emerged, water dripping down his face. "Help," he said, his arms beneath him, carrying something. "Heavy."

She crouched and grabbed ahold of whatever it was he went fishing for and heaved. It *was* heavy. They managed to get it out of the water—a metallic cylinder, the size of a pack with two straps dangling from its casing.

"What is that?"

"You'll see," he said, crouching beside it, slipping his arms into the straps. With a grunt, he got to his feet and stood for a moment, adjusting to the weight. "Come on."

Outside the ship, they found Piot and Galiaro looking to the west, the wall of water a point in the distance. The sky above them had turned torrential—it *boiled* with clouds. Plumes of vapor streaked across the darkened sky, the sun... somewhere. The banner of the heavens took on a deep violet color the likes of which Miree had never seen.

"Is this..." she looked at Galiaro. "The end? The galaxy is... dead?"

Galiaro finally nodded. "For us, yes. The water will return soon. We'll die at the bottom of the Chronicle Sea."

"Not all of us," Meric argued, sliding the metal cylinder off his back. It sank deep into the muddy seafloor.

"I forgot we had that," Piot noted.

Miree approached. "What is it?"

"My father, may he rest in peace, always taught me to have a backup plan. Always. This is your ticket out of here," Meric said, grabbing her sleeve.

"*Me*?"

"Come, Piot, help me with the thing." The two men crouched and lifted the cylinder behind Miree. "Put out your arms."

"Not until you tell me what this thing is."

"Emergency escape," Meric explained. "In case we ever got stranded out at sea and I'd say we're pretty well stranded right now."

"What *is* it?"

"Combustible engine—pull this here," he said, motioning to a green tab, "before pressing on the red button over the shoulder. That'll mix the fuel properly before takeoff."

"It's a fucking *rocket*?"

"Yes. But there's a parachute, too. Otherwise, the rocket wouldn't serve much of a purpose. You get up and then pull the red tab here, that'll deploy the chute. We're close enough to land—well," he looked around the once aquatic landscape now reeking with escaping gases, "the actual coast—that you won't have much distance to go once you're up there."

She locked eyes with him. "Where's yours?"

Meric and Piot exchanged glances.

"There's only one, my dear," Galiaro said. "They're saving you. So, hurry up and get out of here."

"No." She shrugged the rocket from her shoulders. "Strap that thing onto the astrocyst. He's the one who can save this planet."

But Galiaro was shaking his head. "I'd rather risk my life trying to hike out of here than strap a blasted rocket to my back. Besides, I don't think I can find the bot without my traveling companion, Miree. Gentleman, the choice is between the two of you."

They watched the rocket chute sink once more into the mud, silently wondering.

"Do I look like I need to live another day?" Piot said, gesturing with his pipe. "Meric, the chute is yours, my boy."

Meric grinned without humor. "This is... you're all stubborn fools." He walked up to the cylinder and placed his boot on top. "Stubborn as mules." He pressed down, further submerging the rocket chute into the mud until only the top of it was above the sea floor.

Miree turned to Galiaro. "How long do we have until the water returns?"

He shrugged. "Dusk?"

Miree looked up at the towering clefts of coral and rock. Squinting, she thought she made out the crest of land that wreathed the sky—the original coastline, just beneath Orion. She turned to the three. "Hike or die." With new urgency, they collected their gear and scrambled up the first hill, thick with the sludge and debris of ancient sea life.

The rocket chute remained behind.

THIRTY-FOUR

"WHAT IS THE ARROW OF TIME?" Arym asked Hawera, who he'd surprised by a tree. It was the first time he'd really spoken a full sentence to her since she rebuffed him. Yes, it hurt—waking up in the same camp with her every morning brought a melancholy sickness to his chest. He mostly wanted to wither away from her and the party forever, but the Crib was still in danger, and now it appeared that maybe the entire overworld was in danger. All Arym knew was that he had a notebook full of Alchean math and a girl who could walk through holes in time. Perhaps it was the beginning of a plan, and in the least, it was a distraction from his own personal crucible of unrequited infatuation.

"What?"

"The arrow of time. What is it? Protonix spoke of it."

"Protonix," she repeated as if reminiscing.

"He said it always moves forward, but that it's... bent? What does that mean?"

The girl pursed her lips, thinking. "Time goes... back."

"But what does that mean?"

"Or..." She hesitated, searching for words. "Time goes future, and time goes back."

"So, what time are you from?"

"Future. Past."

"Both the future and the past?"

She nodded.

"Where—when does your dark world happen?"

"In the future. Long time."

"When?"

"Thousand, thousand years."

"Is that why your Haenglish isn't good? You don't speak it in the future?"

"Yas. Lithusa talk different. Not like you. Language change."

He looked at her a moment—her hair had grown into a short buzz from when it was shaved. And why was it shaved? Why was she covered in all those metal discs on her arms and legs when she appeared in Crater Valley? Why didn't she have thick clothing or traveling gear? Nothing about her made any sense. It was as if she was just dropped from the sky by... accident?

"It's a mistake you're here, isn't it?" he asked.

She met his gaze. "Yas. Need to go back more. Now, no."

"Why did you leave your people—the dark world?"

Her jaw tightened—her eyes tearing. "Arym..."

"Tell me."

"Dark world is your world."

My world? "The overworld is in trouble, isn't it?"

She shook her head. "Not for long time. Arym safe."

"Why are you so sad to be here then? What went wrong?"

"Lithusa are dead. Me and Patwero sent back to make new world for Lithusa. Need to get back."

"Who is Patwero?"

"My mate."

His chest felt heavy. Her *mate*? All this time, she had someone else? And she couldn't have told him? Wasn't it obvious how he felt about her? Even then, he couldn't tear his eyes from her face. It was gentle, beautiful. "Oh," was all he could say and turned from her. Maybe he heard her call his name, maybe he didn't. But he didn't care. He continued back to camp, frustration raging within. He thought about the Crib—Tarysl and Lutra. He hated himself for leaving them. For forsaking them for a girl that he barely knew... a girl who had a *mate*. Each thought of this Patwero tore open a fresh wound inside. He had a new regret—something he never imagined possible.

He regretted ever leaving the Crib.

The overworld was an awful place. A barren wasteland of gigantic trees that make you go mad. It had a goblin race of human children, as ugly as they were rotten. Granted, the girl had warmed up a little, but Arym was ever suspicious of her motives. The girl would jab him with one of her tiny daggers at the drop of a hat. And now that she could *Jump*? What the hell was that?

Beetro noticed his approach. "See anything out there?"

"I didn't really look. Hawera didn't seem concerned. Have you heard much?" He learned that the robot had exquisite hearing, not to mention vision beyond anything he could imagine. Aside from his abilities, he decided the bot was probably the only good thing he'd discovered in the overworld. Him and the tea that Hawera brewed for them. That was it.

"Deluvius' captain guard rounded back to where they're stationed just at the foot of Orion. They've made an encampment there. Looks new."

"You still think it's a good idea to go to Orion? Find Galiaro?"

The bot nodded. "Yes, but... I'm not sure he'll have what I'm looking for."

"And what is that?"

The bot shrugged. "I don't even know the answer to that." His indigo eyes dilated for a moment, his face toward the ground. "Just because Galiaro made me doesn't mean he'll know what I am."

They broke camp after midnight as Ribcage complained yet again about not being able to cook over an open fire. Despite repeated warnings that the smoke would draw the captain's guard, the girl was fixated on cooking rabbit. She was cranky as they moved, which frightened Arym. If the goblin girl wasn't in a good mood, she was as volatile as a hornet's nest set on fire.

The tundra had led to a sandy basin of dust devils and thorny brush. The forest had long since tapered and the group traveled in the open, giving a wide berth to the army camp that formed on the far north end of Orion.

Orion.

The egg-shaped mountain loomed high above them. Its surface was mostly smooth as if formed within a colossal machine press. Yet its surface had jagged runs interrupted by deep grooves that spiraled down the face of the mountain, creating roadways and markets for its inhabitants. The city lights within the grooves shone through the surface as if the egg had been cracked open, exposing glowing embers within. Many homes had been built and stuffed within the grooves with palatial terraces and hanging gardens that studded the surface as if ornamental. Jets of water shot out from various pores within the surface of the mountain city; ostensible water-run off from the city's irrigation and sewage system. Hundreds of antenna arrays and towers ran along the surface, giving Orion a fuzzy texture from a distance. The curve of the mountain angled acutely into the ground, tapering into a small base. It was shocking that the entire structure didn't topple over from lack of base support. It seemed that at any moment, the egg would fall over from its curved base and roll away into the Chronicle Sea.

Curiously, Orion had no obvious entrance.

Arym saw no gateways or staircases that led up into the city crust. It appeared the means of entering the city was by gondola only. Dozens of vestibules were strung along metal cables, leading from the earth to the city high and within the mountain. There was some air traffic—small propeller planes or disc-shaped crafts came and went from the apex of the mountain.

Why would anyone build a city with no entrance? Arym figured it must've been built during a time of great war—perhaps during the era when Othel decided to descend below Crater Valley. Or maybe it wasn't designed to be a city at all? Whoever it was that built the fortress, it wasn't its current inhabitants. As they got closer, Arym saw that the surface of the mountain was fashioned of no natural substance—a deep sheen dimpling along the grey surface spoke of sophisticated alloy. The wood and concrete structures within the grooves of the surface were suggestive of the more archaic designs of its current occupants.

"Look at that beast," Ribcage said. "Who could've built that thing?"

"Looks Alchean," Beetro said. "Like those Alchean spires back in Helian. Same metal."

"Ah!" Arym said. "That's what it reminds me of. Back in Crater Valley. The old Alchean tomb we found." He gestured to Hawera. "The tomb walls were covered with the same metal as Orion. It *must've* been made by them."

"Perhaps. Doesn't matter anymore. Miree—" Beetro stopped. "Er, someone once told me the city is full of merchants and killers. We best be wary as we enter. I wouldn't trust anyone within the walls of Orion."

"Protonix told me the Alcheans were the best race that Earth has ever seen," Arym told the group as they traveled.

"Protonix?" Beetro asked.

"He was the curator of the tomb. A... well, he was this thing of light."

"A thing of light?" Ribcage repeated.

"Yes, he floated like a ball, but he could... I don't know... break apart into a person. He could talk and everything." He looked to Hawera, who affirmed with a nod. "He told us about the Alchean people. That they were masters of all technology. They had engineered their own genes—" He winced for a moment, thinking back on the cloning laboratory back at the Crib. Tarysl had been so pleased to finally reveal that every single Cribman was identical in every way. "The Alcheans brought in a millennium of peace over the planet and even many planets, opening up a portal to hundreds of alien worlds. Orion must've been one of their cities before they left."

"Where'd they go?" Ribcage asked.

"Protonix said they stepped into another dimension, leaving their mortal bodies behind. The physical world had nothing more to offer them, so they left to greater dimensions."

"Strange," Beetro mused.

"What?" Arym and Hawera looked at the bot.

"If the Alcheans were so peaceful, why did they have high-energy laser rifles and force slave labor from the Thekora?"

He turned, Hawera and Arym looking on.

They kept traveling as dusk flickered on the horizon. Being that they were so close to a gondola station, Beetro figured it was safe to reach without having to lie low for another day. He sensed the group had grown weary of traveling and that it would boost morale to actually get into the city—if they could without being killed. It was hard to tell just what role Deluvius was playing in Orion, but he wasn't convinced his army had control.

"What?" Hawera said, face craned to the sky.

Beetro looked up and the sky looked... bizarre—insane. The sky looked...

"Bonkers," Ribcage said under her breath, gazing up.

The heavens boiled.

Deep purple wisps of water vapor ebbed across the sky like lard marbleizing within a boiling stew. It was as if an unhinged artist was using the entire sky as a canvas, casting purple and brown shades across its surface and swirling a thousand brushes against it at once.

"Is that normal?" Arym asked.

"No," both Beetro and Ribcage answered. "That is very much not normal," Beetro affirmed before looking at Hawera. "Have you ever seen something like that? On your world?"

The Lithusan shook her head, just as perplexed as the rest.

"Why is it so *hot*?" Ribcage complained.

Beetro pinged his thermal sensors and discovered it was true. The temperature had risen twenty percent from the previous day. Humidity, too. "Odd," he said. "I haven't noticed such erratic temperature fluctuations in my data, ever." He searched for the sun but found it masked by the ever-whirling riot of clouds and mists above. The air clung with moisture.

With Orion completely blocking the eastern sky, they arrived at a gondola and found three men sitting within the operational kiosk. They were dressed in mostly black—leather where possible with dark grease encircling their eyes. Belts as thick as cummerbunds clung to their waists, showcasing a myriad of blades—daggers, throwing knives, and a cleaver. Beetro thought he spied a scimitar and found the trio rather ridiculous in their attempts to appear menacing. He didn't know who they were, but he was certain they weren't Deluvius'.

The men noticed their approach and promptly stood. A squatty, fair-skinned man—boy, really—produced a wooden cudgel from the office and thumped it into an open palm. The tallest of the three, a fiery red-haired gargoyle, held his hand up to the boy and shook his head. He then stroked his red beard, considering the newcomers. "Speak," he said, his voice thick with disdain.

"We'd like to ride a gondola up to Orion," Beetro requested.

"What is your business in the city?"

"I'm looking for Galiaro, have you heard of him?"

"You're looking for someone? That's it?"

"Yes. Now, may we take a lift?"

The men shared glances, one smirking. Red Hair spoke up again, "Payment is ten silver chits."

"What!" Ribcage yelled. "That's enough to eat for a month!"

"We don't have money," Beetro said.

"Pity—"

"But we do have information," Beetro finished.

The man glared at Beetro, then swept his eyes to Hawera and Arym. "What information could *you* have?"

"Deluvius. You're trying to defend the city against him, are you not?"

The man's face cringed at the mention of the general's name. "Tell me what you know."

"Once you take me and my friends up into the city."

"You will tell us and then we will decide."

"No. You take us up first."

The man failed to hide his shock at the bot's audacity. "Do you know who we are?"

"Do you know who *we* are?"

"You're nobody."

Beetro took a step closer, his eyes dilating, and looked up at the man. "Are you *sure*?"

The man paused.

"Take us up. If we turn out to be liars, you take us back down. That's it."

The man shrugged. "Very well. If you don't make this worth our while, you will regret it."

For a flash, Beetro imagined how easy it would be to wipe out these three men and their puny gondola with one sweep of his photonic power. "Keep the deal and you won't regret it either."

The men unceremoniously opened the gondola and quickly ushered the group within. It reeked of mold and piss and the ride was bumpy, but Beetro was grateful that they were arriving—finally—into the city. It had been over a month since he'd opened his eyes in the junkyard of Korthe without a single clue about the world. Orion was the only thing on the planet that could answer his questions, for he had many. The foremost in his mind—a nagging question that never went away... *what am I?* As the egg of Orion consumed the vista, he pondered on this one question. Did humans have to worry about what they were? They knew where they came from—knew the people that raised them—so why would they question their own origins? The line of thinking came to a halt when his eyes fell on Ribcage. The girl knew as little about her own life as Beetro knew of his.

They arrived at the lip of the city where the gondola fit snug into a rubber-lined dock. Red Hair opened the door and stepped out but stuck out his hand. "Tell me what you know, robot."

"You'll allow me and my companions to de-board."

The man shook his head. "Spit it out."

Beetro did not reply. He crossed his arms and stared at the man.

Red Hair acquiesced and let the group out. "Bold little shit-bot, aren't you? Kind of thing that'll get you killed here."

"Deluvius has an encampment several kilometers outside Orion."

"Are you telling me something that my own binoculars told me?"

"In the Orion encampment, there are approximately fifty soldiers and two war mechs equipped with multi-articulating arms, capable of any terrain. They appear to be capable of speeds near fifty kilometers per hour. We've seen his army in Crater Valley, Korthe, and at Peles Castle in Helian. Deluvius has advanced weapons technology that he unearthed through multiple excavating campaigns throughout the land, mostly wrought by child labor. There are Alchean laser rifles in his armament. The general will kill anyone who gets in his way. Anyone."

Red Hair pursed his lips together.

"Thanks for the ride," Beetro said while passing the man.

"Hey, robot," he yelled as the group walked past. "Do you think you can talk to the Kish like that and expect nothing to happen?"

Beetro ignored the man, his humans following behind.

They skirted along a narrow corridor with walls that loomed several stories above. It would've felt claustrophobic if it wasn't for the slit of light at the end. The streets of Orion opened to them. The people and markets of the city dwelt within large tunnels with a curved bottom but cut with openings to the sky. The tunnels were made of gray Alchean alloy and shimmered with hues of blue and orange in the scattered sunlight. They moved along the massive U-shaped canal and found it to be relatively empty of people. Covered kiosks and shops had been shut down with metal slats in the doorways. The shops hadn't been built into the structure of the surface of the canals—they were independently fashioned of wood and concrete that appeared anachronistic from the shimmering surface of the superstructure of Orion itself. As they walked through the streets, they discovered many offshoot canals, some more narrow, others wider.

"Like a wasp nest," Ribcage said.

"What?" Arym asked.

"The city," Beetro followed along. "It's like it was made by wasps with all these curvy bends inching upward toward the summit."

"It's like giant wasps made it, but humans moved in," Ribcage added as she began skipping.

Beetro nodded. "Doesn't seem like the Alcheans expected these canals to be inhabited. Looks like people just moved in and set up shop after the Alcheans left."

The denizens of Orion paid the group little attention, although they did seem alarmed with furtive glances and hushed tones. Ribcage ran up to shops, knocking on doors, and complaining of hunger yet could not draw more than a few scowls.

"What's wrong with everyone?" Ribcage asked. "This isn't the way Miree told me it would be. She said Orion was *it*. Food, drinking, dancing, knife fights—anything you could want."

They noticed the same black-clad figures walking the streets, brandishing knives, swords, or clubs. People scurried out of their way, keeping their eyes down as they passed.

Beetro neared a man in a dirty apron, who eyed his approach. "Excuse me," Beetro said to him. "We're kind of new here, can you tell us why everything is closed?"

The man sniffed, looking down on the bot and then frowned, his mustache arcing down. "The Kish took over ever since that army showed up. They've come out of their rat holes—been telling us it's for our own good—that a war is coming. It's all just a power play. They're trying to finally take over this city from the trade guilds. They're nothing but poison." He spat.

"Have you heard of someone named Galiaro?"

"No, no, I don't know anything about that. I suggest you get out of town. I'd leave myself but I put too much into my bakery—years of investment. I can't leave now. If I'm lucky, I'll just wait out this turf war and open up shop after the scum Kish lift their taxes on the markets."

"Is there anywhere to stay near here? An inn?"

"I suggest you get yourself to the bot district. Find friendlier faces. I don't think the Kish have enough numbers to get control of the bots. Yet."

"Where?"

"Up. Just head up. You'll find your brothers."

Beetro left the man and, after deliberation with Hawera and Arym, they decided to keep moving up the ever-slanting canals. Tracks with small train cars had been built in some of the bigger canals. While they were likely to transport people to different parts of the mountain city, the Kish were using them to transport cargo of mostly wooden crates. Heavily armed Kish guards brandishing automatic weapons kept an eye on Beetro as the trains were loaded.

The taverns were not only open, but they overflowed with men and women stumbling from doorways or vomiting in the alleyways between. Beetro recognized the same hollow faces and hopeless gazes of the desperate and the unemployed that he'd seen in Korthe. He wondered how the Alcheans would feel looking at this residue of humankind that they'd left behind who had built a nest within their alloyed monument, only to get drunk. Miree had clearly oversold the city—that or it had changed dramatically since she'd been.

Upward they traveled, each voicing their disappointment over Orion. Perhaps they needed to get down to the ports—that's where all the culture and excitement would be. Yet, Beetro knew that was likely untrue. It would seem people were the same no matter where he traveled. He also realized how it may not be in the Thekora's best interest to rely on humans—they wouldn't be able to save the alien species if they couldn't even save themselves. His thoughts darkened as he thought of Qithara's words—*Carbonoids live fast, live foolish.* If the Thekora had known how flawed humans were, why would they possibly think they could save them? Qithara hinted that there was something wrong with the sky. Was he talking about all the weird clouds and rising temperature?

"Little nip? Little coin?" someone asked at his side.

He turned and saw a drunken man, filthy with an outstretched hand. "I don't have anything," Beetro said. He walked past, knowing that if Lucindi was with him, she'd go find a junkyard somewhere to sell for scrap to give to the man.

Up higher, they finally found the robot district, which was marked with an enormous statue of a small robot standing straight up—a circular slab of metal floating above its head with a single column above the circle.

"What's that supposed to mean?" Ribcage asked, pointing to the statue.

"It's an exclamation mark," Arym answered. "Above its head."

"What's that?" Ribcage asked.

"Um..." He looked at Beetro.

"She doesn't read," Beetro told him. "Grew up on the streets."

Hawera placed her palm on the robot statue and gazed at the exclamation mark floating above. "Pretty."

"Robot thought," Beetro said. "This must be where self-aware bots come from all over." Although his interaction with Besidio, the only self-aware bot he'd met, was disappointing, he did long to finally meet robots with whom he had a lot in common. Eagerly, he walked past the statute and into the robot district.

Robots were everywhere.

Mostly bipedal and of more numerous designs than Beetro could imagine—some slender, others bulky. Some had multiple arms outfitted with devices other than hands—blades, drills, nozzles, pliers—vestigial tools marking their original purpose and design before self-awareness. They passed by clothing shops where bots picked out hats and scarves, wearing them in full-length mirrors. There were markets for textiles and gardening—kitchenware full of pottery and cutlery. Weapon shops sold blades and daggers while some had gunpowder guns on display. There were stores for battery purchase—scores of power storage devices as little as a pebble or as large as an elephant. Bots crammed into charging stores, plugging into an electrical grid interface along the walls to restore their power stores. The smell of oil and burnt plastic filled the air in the stead of booze and baked goods that otherwise occupied a human market. Otherwise, the robot district was remarkably... human.

There were street performers playing music to accompany a play while, across the corner, two bots exchanged improvised poetry to one another. Art galleries lined the streets—oil on canvas, charcoal, graphite. Bronze sculptures and clay statues stood beside their creators—all offering a price for their works. Pottery wheels and looms could be found throughout the market, creating colorful works of art for potential customers. Bots chatted and visited with one another—shopped and gossiped. There were a lot of words about the recent Kish takeover and what robots should do to resist the bastards moving into their part of town. More than half the bots were armed with some sort of weapon—firearm or blade.

It clearly wasn't unfriendly to humans as many milled about, too, intermingling in the shops. Packs of dogs roved the alleyways, digging in garbage and sniffing out rodents. Tomcats perched along the wooden edifices, watching the crowds of metal moving beneath them. No one seemed to notice Beetro and his companions as they weaved through the foot traffic, eavesdropping on conversations. Unsurprisingly, many were talking about the sky. Beetro looked up and saw the swirls of opaque gases eddying like a streambed. Commotion rose as more bots and humans craned their necks, pointing upward.

"What's happening?" Ribcage asked.

"Not sure. Excuse me," Beetro said to a large robot standing next to him. The bot must've been some sort of assembly line machine as it didn't have any semblance of a human face—just a flat panel of circuitry and half a dozen lenses.

It looked Beetro up and down. "Can't you feel it?"

"Feel what?"

"Disengage the human in you and check your internal measurements, brother."

"I—" Beetro ran a quick diagnostic and discovered something... weird. "There's translational acceleration."

The bot nodded.

"But... I'm not moving."

"Neither am I, but I'm feeling it, too. It's like we're all... plummeting."

Hawera looked at Beetro, concerned. "What's happening?"

"Look!" someone yelled over the crowds. All heads moved to a bot positioned at the far end of the market, beneath the smooth curvature of the canals of the mountain city. The bot was poised at a garden terrace, pointing out beyond the city. The masses carried Beetro and his party forward.

Ribcage put her hand in Hawera's. "Want to use your Fourth? I can Jump through and get somewhere high to see."

Hawera shook her head. "Not here."

Ribcage snorted and then climbed a streetlight. "The sun is *huge*," she shouted.

They rushed along with the masses until arriving at the terrace—a garden that jetted out like a balcony of the city. Beetro elbowed his way forward and caught a breathtaking vista—the surrounding tundra of Orion, which led out to the harbor below. Granted, he wasn't familiar with Orion and its surrounding terrain, but nothing looked too amiss to him.

"What's everyone looking at?" he asked.

A bot turned to him and said, pointing out, "The Chronicle Sea."

"Yeah?"

"It's gone."

THIRTY-FIVE

EACH FOOTSTEP SUNK up to Miree's kneecaps into a briny sediment of decomposed seaweed and crumbling coral reef. With great effort, she pulled her leg up as if traveling through a snow-bank. A humid, organic air had settled over what was once the floor of the sea, covering the travelers in a cloying blanket of moisture. The air was redolent of decaying sea life. Meric set the pace at the head of the group, zig-zagging across improvised switch backs set within the craggy ledges of a once underwater mountain range. Miree followed and watched as Meric, too—a man built like a mustang—tired out from their journey from the bottom of the sea. Galiaro tailed behind her, using a staff to gain leverage. They had lost Piot behind a bend.

"Wait," she said between staggered breaths.

Meric stopped. "What?"

"We lost your navigator." She turned to look at their progress—the sea floor stretching below them into the valley. They'd been hiking for three hours and it already felt like half the day was gone.

"He'll... be okay," Meric reassured her, clearly not convinced himself.

"He can barely walk. He's got half an oar back there that he's hobbling along with."

"I've known him for a long time. If we stop and make a fuss about him, he'll become an even bigger nuisance. Trust me. We should keep moving. My navigator will catch up."

"And if he doesn't?"

"He'd be proud to know that we didn't stop for him. He's content right now, knowing that I'd speak of his refusal of help as he hiked his way out of the bottom of the sea. I can't imagine a better way to die for a salty old sailor born at sea. The man always wanted a watery grave."

She wanted to ask Galiaro how much longer he thought it would be but decided it was the same as asking how much longer until they die. Once the sun set, the sea would return and cover them like ants in a torrential rain. There was no reason to count the hours and minutes.

So, they trudged forward, speaking little.

Galiaro, too, had fallen behind as Miree insisted they wait for him to catch up. "He's kind of the point of this whole thing," she told Meric. "If there's any way out of what's happening, he's going to know."

Meric offered a queer look. "I would not leave the man behind. Why do you feel the need to convince me to not leave him behind?"

"Oh. I don't know. Some people would."

"I'm a man of honor, Anisha."

"Sorry. Just haven't met one of you before."

They rested for a moment, hunger in their bellies. Galiaro caught up with ragged breaths and tremulous steps. "Wh-what time is it?" Both Miree and Meric shrugged and looked on, the valley floor appearing no more distant than it had an hour prior. "We best keep moving," Galiaro urged, stepping ahead of his younger travelers. "It must be past noon by now. I fear we've lost our navigator." The three continued, a solemn silence between them after Galiaro's pronouncement of Piot.

Miree thought about what had brought her to the bottom of the sea. She knew she could blame Galiaro or Meric or even trace all the preceding events back to Beetro. But the solace she usually found in blaming everyone was providing little at that moment. Even the never-ending burning hatred she reserved for Ria had cooled. When an entire sea of water rushed away from her in a single fleeting moment, she realized that everyone on the planet was just as screwed over as she had always been. Maybe there was a tincture of serenity in knowing that.

After another hour, they needed to rest again. They found some boulders to catch their breath—each fantasizing about water.

"That's interesting..." Meric tapped his boot on Miree's Swordless Hilt within its scabbard.

She swept the shard blade away.

"I've seen that blade before. Rare, even among the Torbad. Strange weapon."

"I got it in a strange place."

"Same place where you got those eyes?"

She broke eye contact, trying to hide her telescoping eyes. "Yes."

"What's the arm for?"

She looked down at the metallic prosthesis, grafted into the bone of her humerus. "You always ask so many questions?"

"We're stuck at the bottom of the sea. Didn't think there was much need for pretense anymore."

"I don't know what the arm does. Just hurts. I was going to have it removed in the Torbad."

Concern flooded his face. "What happened to you?"

She snorted. "Don't worry about it. Getting enslaved by the Reticulum is the least of my worries."

"I'm all ears." He kept his eyes on her, studying her face.

She scowled. "Stop trying to figure me out."

"I wouldn't even know where to start..."

Galiaro caught up again. "Stop resting, no time for love-making," he chided. "Keep moving." He hiked past them without stopping.

Meric gave Miree a smile, which she rejected with a flip of her cloak as she rose. Meric looked on sheepishly and then complained, "The old man is kind of demanding when he sobers up."

"You don't have the first clue. He electrocuted my skull not a day before we came to Portolo."

"*What*?"

Miree didn't respond, just followed in step behind Galiaro.

The daylight began to dwindle. Miree craned her neck and saw dozens of rows of mountain ridges and cliff edges—Orion was nowhere to be seen. Wordless, the group picked up the pace, which grew easier as the ground became more solidified. Another hour passed as the sun lay low in the sky—the sky warping from violet to blood orange in the dusk light.

"We're not going to make it," Miree announced.

"You're right," Galiaro affirmed, but he kept moving.

Meric and Miree looked at one another, surprised by the old man's tenacity. The sky darkened.

Galiaro stopped. "Do you hear it?"

Miree looked back toward the valley floor. There was a humming in the distance. "Yes."

"What?" Meric asked.

"The water is returning."

The three stood silent—motionless. Miree asked what they should do. Galiaro looked and then threw his staff on the ground. "We rest."

The three found a spot beside a boulder and lay down. A breeze blew by, chilling Miree enough to wrap herself in her cloak.

Meric lay beside her, looking morose. "It was nice to know you, Anisha."

"Name's Miree."

"It was nice to know you, Miree."

"I suppose you weren't the worst man I ever met," she said before patting his hand and closing her eyes. "Thanks for not robbing me and throwing me overboard."

"What kind of life have you had?"

"Doesn't matter anymore."

She awoke to someone whistling. Realizing that she was alive and not entombed in the bottom of the sea, Miree bolted awake—a spectrum of pain, hunger, and thirst sweeping her body. Piot stood above them, one eye cocked, holding a pipe in one hand. "Time to shine and rise, my pretties," he announced.

Miree stood and beheld the shriveled old man. He was leaning on a broken oar, showing a smile full of gums. "You... made it?"

"Piot, you old fool!" Meric said, clapping the man on his shoulder. "Of course, he made it," he said to Miree. "You cannot kill Piot the Navigator. No high storm, hurricane, cyclone, or... disappearing sea is going to stop this old gentleman sailor."

Piot nodded, a whimsical smile and distant gaze in his eyes. "You all hike too fast. If ya slowed down, you'd conserve energy like Piot. It's a tortoise and hare situation, I 'spose."

Galiaro was oblivious to all of it. The man was convulsing on the sunbaked ground. Miree dropped to her knees next to him. "Hey!" she said, shaking him. "Snap out of it!"

Piot only tsked. "It's no use, lass."

Miree watched as the astrocyst trembled, only the whites of his eyes exposed as they had rolled entirely back. "Is he... going to live?"

Piot shrugged. "Fifty-fifty, 'spose. I seen many a drunk survive the brain attack they get when their veins dry up of the spirits."

"Do you two have any booze?"

Meric showed his empty palms. "We just survived the strangest shipwreck in the history of—anywhere. You know we didn't bring supplies."

"He *must* survive," Miree insisted. "Otherwise..."

"What?" Meric asked.

"We're all dead."

"Hmph, I thought we were going to die last night, but..." He motioned out to the sea valley.

Miree looked out. The sea had certainly returned, but only a quarter of the volume. A new coast had emerged far below them—a flotsam of shipwrecks scattered across the surface. "It's the port of Orion..."

"It *was* the post," Meric finished. "When the tide fled, it took the entire harbor with it, chewed it up, and spat it back out."

"So, the water's just... gone?"

A gurgling cough at her feet interrupted her thought and then croaked, "Evaporated." She found Galiaro awake with vomit in his beard. "Must've boiled off," he concluded.

"Are you okay?"

"Fine," he reassured, getting to his feet. "We're damn lucky. Lucky we're not dead at the bottom of the sea."

She helped him stand. "You think the sea *evaporated*?"

He nodded. "We're closer to the sun now—the atmosphere is changing. Can't you feel it?" He took a deep breath.

"Like a swamp," Piot said, twirling his pipe around. "Like you could drink the air."

"So, just what in heavens does this all mean?" Meric asked.

"It means we need to get to Orion. Find a robot. Maybe escape this doomed planet."

Meric looked from Galiaro to Miree and then started hiking.

After taking Piot's advice, they hiked slower. Without the threat of an impending tidal wave, they took their time. The old man began to tell unsolicited stories about his youth—that time the Jonniger boy stole his parsley right before a gardening competition, or when he courted two sisters at one time. He babbled on about being raised within the walls of a lord's castle—somewhere north of Helian. He then regaled them about the true romance he had with the sea. "She was my only love," he said. "One and only—"

"Hey," Miree interrupted. "Have you noticed how no one has said anything in a while?"

He bit down on his empty pipe; lips curled over empty gums. "I have."

"Doesn't that tell you something?"

He nodded. "Aye."

Having proven her point, she turned.

"Means I have an eager audience."

They ascended higher while the conversation had degenerated into gestures and grunts beneath the orchestra of Piot showcasing his throat singing skills he'd learned from the people of the Torbad. That evening, they saw the tip of the mountain city breaking through the sky.

Orion.

Tracks of light glowed throughout the cracks that traversed its surface. Miree thought of an enormous egg whose surface had been fractured by cracks—as if molten lava glowed from within. She stopped, watching the city.

"What?" Meric investigated, noticing her hesitation.

"Don't use my real name while we're in Orion."

He paused with puckered lips as if to pass judgement but then only nodded.

Orion enlarged on the horizon as they traveled for the next hour. Miree was certain Piot would grow tired of doling out unsolicited and entirely random trivia, including the number one textile producer of a region she'd never heard of and the third surname of his second wife's sister. "Do you know where the name Manthelusa originates?" Piot asked from behind her.

"Meric," she ignored the old man and kicked Meric's boot. "Do you have a workspace in Orion? A shop—a place to do business?"

"Yes, I take many commissions from the city and manage my late father's business, D'Naris and Sons, near the bot district. I'd been running normal business hours until the Kish started acting up."

"What have the Kish been doing?"

"Finally trying to take over the city.'"

"Why?"

"An army showed up a few weeks ago at our doorstep. The mercantile council and trader guilds were finally afraid enough of the enemy within as well as the new enemy at their gates. Kish pressured them enough to release the BlackGrips—hired gun—"

"I know who the BlackGrips are. They're the only thing keeping the Kish in check."

"The Kish forced the BlackGrips out of the city after the

merchants paid the final bill. It was the last pawn down for them to move out their queen and gain control of the city."

"Shit."

"Why do you think I was trying to never return? The Kish are poison. They'll bury the place. My father's business is all but dead." He lowered his head in solemnity.

"And who's this army?"

"A general with a battery of Alchean rifles and a couple hundred soldiers with gunpowder weapons."

"I know him. Deluvius. Ran into him in Helian."

"And?"

"He's no better than the Kish."

"So, what's your plan exactly? Find a bot in Orion and then put the water back into the sea?"

Miree looked at Galiaro, who appeared oblivious to their conversation. "Something like that. Do you have a quick means to leave the city? Someway out at a moment's notice?"

He scratched his stubbled chin. "Yes. Why?"

"Don't worry your pretty little head. Shouldn't be a problem."

They arrived at a platform where a gondola was docked—thick cables atop its head stretched upward toward the edge of Orion. Several gondolas were in transit, radiating from the lip of the city at various docking points. Two women manned the docking platform and eyed the four travels as they stepped up the ramp. Miree kept her face low and hooded.

"Heading up," Meric declared, presenting payment.

The two black-clad women—the de-facto Kish guards—eyed the newcomers. They glanced at one another and then back at the coins resting in Meric's palm. The front woman reached out a wiry hand and knocked the coins from his hand. Her compatriot then brandished a dagger as if from thin air. "No access to the city," she said. "Kish decree."

"Ma'am," Meric started, "I'm a merchant of Orion. I have been—nigh on twelve years. Meric D'Naris, my name. I run my trading business on Harlow Street and I'm returning from a journey from Portolo with my navigator and two clients in tow. We mean to operate through our established—"

The Kish guard slapped him.

Miree's hand went to the Swordless Hilt, concealed within her cloak. Meric hardly moved from the strike. With a red handprint on his cheek, he looked from Piot and then back to the Kish woman. "Ma'am—"

And then she slapped him again.

Meric's gaze fell on the horizon, his upper lip stiff. Miree could almost see the internal gears of self-control kicking in his brain, producing a man of perfect composure.

Piot then stepped between the two and clapped a hand on Meric's shoulder. "Meric, my boy, you do indeed take a hit as well as a walrus, but I feel I should intervene." He turned to the Kish woman and said, "Tell me, lass, have ya gone down to the port today?" The woman lifted her blade to Piot's neck, the point dimpling the skin beneath his chin. "Because if ya have," he continued as if the blade had gone unnoticed, "you may notice that it's gone."

The Kish from behind, a black-haired older woman—her face a crisscross of wrinkles—stepped forward with her blade. "The Kish decides who comes and goes through the gates of Orion. We own the city; we own the markets."

Piot, blade still poised beneath his chin, removed his pipe and waved it in the woman's face. "But have ya noticed the sky today? The air? It's like we're swimming out here, my lady."

The Kish women exchanged glances, the older then asking, "What're you talking about, you old fool?"

"We have an astrocyst in our company," he motioned with his eyes. "Says there may be a problem with the sun. Did you notice that a star went missing last night?"

Galiaro finally stepped forward, running his fingers through his beard as if it were a luxurious mane. "I'm seeking an astrocyst colleague, Fallaro. He had a lab here—oh, ten years back now—I need to converse with him about an urgent matter. Now think, my dear gatekeepers, have you had a report back from anyone down at the ports?"

They maintained their cold gazes on him.

"I suggest you radio up to your bosses or whoever it is you report to and ask them if the city scouts have seen what is happening down at Chronicle Sea."

"Stay here," she said, leaving the younger woman with the blade perched beneath Piot's chin.

"May I ask that you remove your weapon from my navigator?" Meric added.

She released the dagger. Piot offered her a hearty smile and a wink. "A healthy blade it is, lass. Fine point."

"Let them up," the returning Kish said. "Something... is happening. Boss said to let them pass."

Meric stepped forward as the gondola doors opened but the woman stopped him. "Payment first." Meric handed over the coins and stepped in, Miree following behind. "Nuh-uh, sweetheart," the Kish said. "The toll is per person."

Miree kept her face down. The Kish lifted the end of Miree's hood with the tip of her blade. "The hell? What're all those lights in your face?"

"I will pay for the lady and the rest of my party," Meric said, handing over the chits.

The Kish eyed the party as they loaded in but let them ascend to the city unattended. As they lifted from the earth, Orion grew—the massive docking lip expanding before them. Miree clutched the Swordless Hilt as she saw the deep rivets of Orion's surface—the markets, trading posts, and taverns that had been built within the sleek Alchean alloy. Never did she believe she'd ever return.

"You don't have the rest of my payment. Correct?" Meric asked.

"No," she said without looking at him. "Never did."

The gondola docked and the party evacuated. "Me and my navigator will be on our way," Meric remarked, suddenly becoming formal. "I'm not keen on being lied to—even less when it involves payment for my services. Given the unusual circumstances, I will forget this trespass and will consider your debt paid. However, my services will not be available to you in the future, indefinitely." He held a proper palm up, displaying peak composure—prepared for rebuttal.

"Fine. Goodbye," Miree said before turning, her cloak whipping in the high winds of the Orion docks. Not once in her life had she looked behind her and she wasn't going to start at that moment for some small-time merchant. It was only after she turned a corner into the markets that she stopped.

Galiaro appeared around the corner, his neck extended and mouth ajar. "It is a wondrous place. Even after all the years I spent here. Orion is a jewel. A jewel of the Alcheans. Seems a shame though," he said, addressing her with tilted eyebrows. "Burning bridges from two good men we could use."

"I don't burn bridges. They spontaneously combust behind me. So, where's your lab, anyway?"

"It's around. Somewhere..." He craned his neck.

"You don't know where it is?"

"I did have a lab where I fashioned part of the robot—I had to form the dark matter in a different location. Part of it was here, part in Helian. If I could just get my bearings..." He flipped around, squinting.

"Do you have a locator on him? Maybe we can ask around..."

"Do you remember when I told you that I saw him murder my parallel self? This is not a rendezvous with my pet dog. The robot is dangerous and may try to kill me again. If he's here, he's likely hiding. Perhaps waiting for me. I'd rather not call attention to ourselves."

"The Beetro I know wouldn't hurt a fly."

"Maybe he's been lying to you."

"If so, it would be the performance of a lifetime. And I'm still confused. You want to find him to... destroy him?"

"Best to assume he has not been honest with you. We should locate him, capture him, and go from there."

"But how?"

"Just do what the Reticulum told you to do, use that metal arm of yours on him. Must be a weapon of some sort."

"So, we capture him and then what? Go open the GeminArc again?"

"I'm not sure. The math is extremely complicated. I'll need to go back to the drawing board. Dark Theory is just a theory—there may be more to the story..."

"You better start spilling everything to me, old man."

"You seem to be in an unusually unpleasant mood. Even more than your foul baseline. I should have allowed some conjugal time for you and that sailor boy before coming to the city. It would've stomped the malice straight from you. And besides, I highly doubt you have the mathematical acumen to understand a fraction of a percent of what is going on with the galaxy. Yes, expansion is accelerating but I still don't know why. Could have to do with gravity—could have to do with warped time."

Miree threw up her hands. "Fine. Let's just get moving."

"First..." His eyes searched the streets, hands shaking as they went to his brow.

"No," she said. "You just sobered up. And I am *not* dealing with your vomit again. Stay out of the taverns."

"I wasn't suggesting a drink, my dear. Those days are behind me—just needed a little adventure to motivate me. I've dropped the drink before. It's just a matter of willpower. Something of which I possess that can only be measured in megatons at its smallest increment."

"Uh-huh."

"Sustenance, my dear. I was suggesting we eat. Climbing out of the Chronicle Sea tends to make a man peckish. Let's find us a vendor." Galiaro was moving, skirting along a line of streetlamps to a crowded market.

She turned to follow and saw a figure in her periphery—a cloaked person in black. Moving along, she acted as if she didn't notice and kept an even pace. Back before she'd traveled to Helian —before she stumbled onto a cursed robot and became intertwined with the fate of a vagrant astrocyst—she could handle a tail in the streets of Orion. Within moments, the throngs of the market would conceal her, providing ample paths to shake off anyone. But the markets were near empty. Every third business was shut. It would be harder for her to lose whoever was following, but she knew it would be far more difficult for the tail to remain inconspicuous in a vacant street.

Galiaro stepped through the doors of a tavern.

"I said no taverns."

"Do you see any other viable options? It's half a ghost town here. The poor people of Orion, I'm sure, are terrified. A despot trying to take control in one street and a band of thugs in the next

—not to mention their world-class ports having been swept into oblivion. I'm going to see if they offer food. Surely they do."

"Fine," she said, watching the corner of her eye. The tail was gone, which is exactly what they wanted her to believe. "Move." She pushed him forward.

"What's the hurry?"

They sat at the bar. Galiaro ordered a basket of fried onions over chopped squid and chewed loudly as the tavern stewed in commotion about the Chronicle Sea. There was talk of old gods who'd taken the sea just as they'd taken the stars—recompense for waning belief. Some evoked the return of the Alcheans—they'd come to change the face of Earth once more. For most, there was little difference between the Alcheans and the spirit of old-world gods whose names could barely be recalled.

"We lost Saturn," Galiaro said to the room, food falling from his mouth. After receiving vacant stares, he added, "That can be a problem." The tavern resumed its conjectures, ignoring the old man.

Miree noticed a tall man enter and, after brief eye contact, found a seat and ordered drinks. "Stay here," she told Galiaro. She didn't draw the man's attention after walking by his table. *They couldn't recognize me now—not with half a robot face?* After ordering a drink, she leaned her elbows on the bar and waited—waited for the briefest flash of the man's eyes her way. He looked—playing it off that he was cracking his neck—but he looked right at her.

Her heart pumped as she turned toward the bartender. "Where'd you get that arm?" he asked. She answered with a swift shot of brandy and then walked to the bathroom, locking the door. After fidgeting with the locked window with only one hand available, she managed to break the lever off without opening the damned thing. So, she slammed her mechanical prosthesis through the glass, cleared out the broken shards in the frame, and jumped out to the alley. After dusting flecks of glass from her cloak, she realized she may have been a tad paranoid. The street from the alleyway had darkened with dusk and remained mostly vacant. There was no one watching the tavern—no one waiting in ambush. After she decided it was time to vacate the tavern where she'd destroyed property, she wheeled toward the front of the building. One step later...

She was on the ground.

A sting in her neck.

As her vision swirled down the drain, a figure appeared above her—flesh pale, a grin full of white teeth.

"Oh, Miree," he said. "We've missed you. And that Quantizer."

THIRTY-SIX

RIBCAGE HATED ORION.

Everyone was hungry. When everyone around her was begging for food, where was she supposed to get it? And all the stupid robots didn't help—they only ate oil and hooked electricity up to their butts. Beetro managed to bring some old bread he'd found at the back of bakeries and taverns. She ate it, but she didn't like it—she didn't *earn* it. She wasn't accustomed to someone bringing her food without her begging. There was a sense of pride in it, she supposed, cultivating the image of starvation to arouse the pity in others. It was an art form she'd developed—her life's work. But to have a bot bring her some moldy bread?

She was way above that.

And the bot wouldn't use his *powers*. He could have all the bread he wanted—all the pastries and dried meat brought to him by a caravan of elephants! He could just blow away the first shop he saw—threaten all the rest the same if they didn't do what he said. The bot was pissing away the opportunity to be King Bot and instead had her staying in a rat-infested hostel full of the ugliest robots she'd ever seen. Like some sort of scourge, the bots lined the walls of the hostel, lounging in bunk beds and oil-streaked couches. In the rafters above, the smelly bots hung in hammocks, calling and laughing and rambling on and doing absolutely nothing. They were more worthless than the drunks of Helian. At least she could pick the crumbs from those clueless bags of bones, but the bots in Orion didn't even eat! They made no money and did nothing for no one, including Ribcage. What was even the point of them?

Even worse was that she had to actually work to live at the hostel. Whether it was scrubbing rust from hydraulics or picking screws from melted manifolds, she worked half the day just for room and board. "We have no other option," Beetro told her. "There's nowhere else for us to go."

Well, Ribcage had other options. She always had somewhere else to go. When the urchins of Korthe threatened to steal from her, she'd just Jump around them and be off before they even knew what happened. But in Orion, her Jumps... *were gone.*

"Please," she begged Hawera, the pretty girl with the ugly hair. "Please, please, please, *please* use your Fourth."

But the girl only shook her head, holding that metal-tipped staff close to her chest. "It not plaything," she scolded. "It hard on my mind."

"But we can go find food. You just point your staff and shoot all those blue lights around it and open that hole and then BAM!" she slapped her hands together, startling Hawera. "I can Jump in and out of this place anywhere I want. We'll feast!"

Hawera shook her head, a languid sleepiness to her eyes. She slept most of the day, probably to avoid the mole man with a crush on her.

After a week of dismantling and salvaging robot parts and eating whatever grimy piece of crap Beetro brought to her,

Ribcage had had just about enough of life in Orion. "Why are we even here?" she asked Beetro, that is, when he chose to show up at all.

"Why are we even *here*? Why are we even *here*?" a chorus chimed in, a row of mocking bots swinging in the hammocks above.

"Shut up!" Ribcage yelled up at them, wishing with every fiber of her tiny body she could Jump up to the rafters and push them all out of those dumb, swinging beds.

Beetro answered, "I'm looking for—"

"Galiaro, Galiaro—yeah, yeah. Well, he's not here. You leave here every day and go calling up and down the streets all day long, 'Galiaro, Galiaro, Galiaro!' No one's ever heard of him. He's probably dead. So, can we go back home now?"

Beetro's eyes dilated, the indigo glowing within shuttered pupils. "Home?"

"Home. Korthe."

"That's not my home."

"Yes, it is. It's where we came from."

"It's where you came from, Rib."

"No, it's not. But that doesn't make it *not* home."

"I can't go back yet."

"I'll just leave without you then."

"So... you'll cross the plains out there—the larger sun making it ten degrees hotter now. You'll crawl back through Gargantua Forest, stroll past the poisonous trees of the Thekora? And then you'll cross Crater Valley—full of Deluvius' army—scale the granite cliffs back up the valley, and then cross the plains of Helian. All... without Jumping?"

She crossed her arms. "Yeah."

The robot hesitated and then said, "I actually believe you. Please don't. Wait for me. Okay?"

"Why should I?"

"Because we're pals." He moved past her without another word.

Despite new anger brewing within, she went back to work, stripping rubber from old robot treads.

The next day, the mole man came up to her with something in his hand. "Here. I won this." He offered a basket of potato crisps.

"Won it doing what?"

"Playing Binero. Card game the bots play."

Hawera rose from her bed and said, "No, Arym. No games with robots."

He shrugged. "It was easy enough."

"They are better than you."

Ribcage laughed. "You can say that again."

Hawera shook her head, grasping for words. "They can... number numbers very high. Higher than Arym can."

"I don't know what she's talking about, but just keep doing what you're doing," Ribcage told Arym, putting a crisp into her mouth. It was okay accepting food from mole man as she'd scared him enough to bring her food completely unprompted. She earned it.

"We count cards," a new voice said from the doorway. "The fair lady warns you of the danger of gambling with robots."

The three turned their heads and discovered a rather tall robot, thin slats of metal buttressing smooth bulbs of alloy that formed his cheeks. His jaw was squared by bundles of metal tubules wrapped and welded by wire. Atop his matte gray skull, a colorful hat perched—the tip of which terminated at his feet. Like a vine, the tail of the hat snaked around his frame, boasting a patchwork of blue, yellow, and red.

"Besidio," Beetro greeted, approaching from the loft within.

"Aye," the robot answered. "Mere jester to the Lord of Helian who was violently bereft of a fiefdom and buried—a wayfaring bot of little wealth and even less repute. I fear I've missed the triumphal entry of Beetro the Brave and his faithful companion, Ribcage the Warrior. What wit and courage must have brought ye to the tumultuous gates of Orion? What wiles and charms to add numbers to your quest—a black-haired raven of men," he said, gesturing to Arym, "and a silver-eyed beauty whose elegance is ne're matched by the honey warbler." He swept his cloak toward Hawera. "Now, prithee tell, my dear Beetro. What has become of my faithful steed? I trust Bellamare is stabled safely?"

"He... uh—"

"He exploded her," Ribcage answered, laughter cracking at the edge of her voice.

Besidio remained silent.

They were interrupted by a commotion in the hostel—dozens of bots speaking over themselves and getting out of bed. It took Ribcage a moment to realize that Besidio was the cause of all the excitement. "Besidio!" they said. "Besidio is back!" The bots surrounded the robot, talking over one another, shouting questions.

Besidio calmed the crowd with open palms. "My brothers and sisters, I fear I'm not the soothsayer you seek. I've little news from anywhere."

"Besidio," a bot shouted from the crowd. "What's happening to the sun? Where did the sea go? Will it happen to Orion?"

He shook his head in apology. "I've only heard notice of such a thing. As of yet, Besidio has not laid eyes on this disappearing sea. I disembarked from Portolo only a day ago. Missed the vanishing of the sea by the bolts on my back."

"What do we do now?" they asked. "What do we do about the Kish?"

"I know not either the answers you seek."

The crowd fell silent.

"Yet," Besidio said, bringing a finger to his chin. "It does remind me of a story."

The crowd roared with cheer, which evolved into shushing as they prepared to listen. Beetro joined Hawera and Ribcage at the two beds they rented. Arym took the floor.

"Centuries ago, before these lands were formed, a people had settled into caves along the shores of Alganth. They were industrious folk, brimming with mechanical know-how. They fashioned watermills to sift their wheat and created grand fisheries along their shores. One woman named Temara, a master clocksmith, built a great clocktower that hung above their caves. The arms of the clock told the passing of the sun, and with its shadows, informed the people of Alganth when the tides would recede, bearing rich pools of sea life from which to harvest. For years, the Alganth worked wonders in those waters, growing from a village of few to a city of many. Temara was revered for her understanding of the revolutions of Earth—the orbits through the years and what they portended of their crops and fishing.

"Yet, one day, midday, in the middle of an Alganth week—the clock hands stood still. The villagers arrived at Temara's doorstep —now a woman steeped in years—asking for her to fix time. As she peered from her doorway, observing the morning sun in its celestial and expected station, she proclaimed, 'Why, people of Alganth, do you inquire of me to fix the time? Time revolves by her own regard for a humble clock master such as Temara.' Distraught and undaunted, the villagers said, 'But the clock, dear clock master, it does not speak the time. We must know the time to check the tides to feed our children.'

"To only Temara had the obvious occurred—the people of Alganth had become reliant on her clock. They'd forgotten that the work of her hands was a mere reflection of reality, not a dictator of such. Exhaustive attempts to explain proved fruitless, and so she went about to fix the clock. Yet upon inspection of the device, she discovered the innards had rusted—the mechanics had frozen from salt and the harsh oxidizers of the ocean air. Our Temara sought the makers of the parts, but to her dismay, they all had passed on, and with them, their knowledge of dancing gears and twitching coils, pendulous shafts, and ticking dials. And so, time stood still for the people of Alganth, and with them, their ocean waves froze and the beach sand dried and the sea life vanished from the mouths of their young."

The spacious hostel fell silent as Besidio's audience considered the story.

"What does that mean, Besidio?" a large bot asked.

Besidio met Beetro's gaze. "Gentle bot, would you care to venture a guess?"

Beetro paused and then said, "Time didn't really freeze for the Alganth. They only thought it did because they became too reliant on the clock—too reliant on their own technology."

Besidio tilted his head in contemplation. "Are you so sure that time didn't *really* stop for them? Perhaps they are still out there somewhere, waiting for their clock to restart—for the sea waves to crash, for the crabs to crawl."

"It's about perception," Arym offered.

"Ah, our barrel-chested boy—man—presents a solution."

"Maybe the Alganth's world *did* change. Maybe time kept going but for them, it stood still. Because they didn't understand what time was, it froze them where they were—to where they had progressed."

"Would you submit that how you *see* the world *changes* the world?"

Ribcage thought Arym looked stupid as he thought on Besidio's question. "Maybe."

"What does this have to do with Chronicle Sea, Besidio?" a bot asked.

"My gentle robot folk, I only tell stories. It is my charge as jester. The interpretation, if any, I leave to my kind audience."

There were dissatisfied grumblings as the robots dispersed.

"Has anyone a place for Besidio to rest?" he asked. The robot was ushered away to the back of the hostel and given his own room, which was inexplicably left vacant for someone of his apparent reputation.

Ribcage, having had her fill of metallic people for the day, took to the streets.

Beetro felt despair creeping within. They'd been in Orion for over a week, and he'd found little information about Galiaro. Of the hundreds of bots and people he'd questioned, he heard scant evidence that the man had even lived in the city. One bot recalled a few astrocysts that kept a lab near the robot district, but she never knew their names. An old merchant, whose shop had been closed with the Kish's stranglehold on the city, did know a Galiaro at some point, fifteen years prior.

"It was him and another fellow. His partner was here up until a few years ago."

"Do you know where they worked? Where their lab was?"

The merchant shrugged. "Orion isn't much of a sciency place—we're a trading people who don't have time for that astrocyst hogwash. If they had a lab, I never saw it."

It had become evident that perhaps the collective memory of Galiaro or any astrocyst in the community had all but vanished. He'd found the people of Orion were concerned mostly with the tangible. And the robots, mostly with the ethereal. True, Beetro had some interest in the origins of his own self-awareness or *qualia* as the robot-folk called it, but not quite to the degree of the robot district.

"Have you ever had brain freeze?" Sartorious asked him. She was a robot that had been designed for digging dirt. No face, no limbs. Her creator had made the misfortunate decision of equipping the bot with an operating system and a camera so that she could be programmed to travel long distances and dig according to whatever her directive dictated. She was supposed to announce her arrival and voice her specific instructions for the given commission. Halfway through her first journey, she stopped and asked the caravan if she could wait a while to see if the bees checked the same flower for pollen more than once. Fortunately for Sartorious, the person who had dug her up and refurbished her had compassion on her lived-in *qualia* and let her live out her days however she saw fit.

"No," Beetro answered, distracted as he looked out the window of the hostel.

"I have. Humans get it, too. It's when you eat something cold, but you eat it too fast and it makes your head hurt. The effect is transient and causes no permanent harm."

"You don't eat."

"Astute, Beetro. Yes. I do not eat." Several lights blinked yellow and blue at her base when she spoke, just above the treads of her wheels. She'd explained it was a visual cue that she was actively engaged in conversation as she did not have the privilege of having a face and lacked the body language that facial expression afforded. "Yet, I experience brain freeze nevertheless," she continued.

"How do you know it's brain freeze?"

"Another particularly good question, which follows the next line along this path of reasoning... how do I know that my qualia of brain freeze is the same as a human's? If it is, brain freeze must be a qualia enmeshed with consciousness and is not of anatomical consequence. However, it may be a limitation of language. Perhaps our finite language lacks the diversity to explain two distinct qualia. What I describe as brain freeze may just be—anxiety let's say—and I have merely re-appropriated the term to an actual physiological consequence that occurs in our fleshy neighbors."

"Uh-huh."

"Your next question may be 'Well, then, Sartorious, why don't you come up with a new robotic language—something beyond Haenglish and binary? Something that encompasses the entirety of conscious experience, whether robotic or human.' My answer to you, my friend—watch me. Some bots assert that language is the sieve by which we understand qualia. However, me and others who think like me, believe that language is the chain that tethers us to this ground. It is the reason I believe I have brain freeze when there is no logical reason that a digging bot should ever have that experience. Yet, language can also be the wings by which we may fly above the mists of confusion. If we change our language, we change the very nature of our consciousness. If we can communicate more succinctly, we will understand the nature of our beings—it will change the way we perceive our own reality."

"Have you ever heard of the Thekora?"

Sartorious blinked a few red lights and said, "No."

"Make your way to the Gargantua Forest one of these days. You might learn something about languages. But don't take any humans." Before Beetro could explain more, another bot interrupted, wanting to talk about differences in each bot's camera lens and how it also alters reality.

He'd had about enough.

Believing he'd discover the mysteries of who he was and what it was to be robotic, he came to Orion, hopeful. Yet, after a week of esoteric debates about the nature of robot reality, he found that he was even more confused before setting foot in the city. Having not found a trace of Galiaro had only worsened his outlooks. A question kept cropping up in his mind, one he'd kept denying. But after yet another hour of philosophizing, he could no longer deny it.

What do I do now?

It was a dreadful question that followed him wherever he went. The moment he awoke in that junkyard in Korthe, he had nothing—no one. Lucindi and Miree were his entire universe. And yet, as that universe expanded from the small town to the plains of Helian, the granite cliffs of Crater Valley, and through the purple forest of the Thekora, the same question drummed in the back of his mind. *What will you do now? Is there anything out there for you?*

He wondered what he had been like before he was rebooted. Was the trickle of anxiety ever-present? Did he go on misinformed quests and drag others into his personal journey to nowhere? Or was he back here at Orion, pontificating about his own existence? Were these Orion robots doing anyone any good by talking about their robotic experience all day, every day? Whoever he was before reboot, it had to be better than who he was at present.

"Food." Ribcage interrupted his reverie. "I'm sick of the dumpster scraps you're bringing me. Let's go out and find something to actually eat."

"We don't have much money."

She let out an angry sigh and said, "You can blow down this entire block in two seconds! What're we doing here?"

Beetro looked around at potential eavesdroppers and put his finger to her lips. "Not happening, so stop talking about it. I think you're right, though. It's time we prepare for our journey out of here. I don't think we're going to find much in Orion."

"Finally!"

"Let's go see if we can find some work somewhere and plan a trip back to Korthe."

"So, you do want to go back there?"

"It's the only home I've ever known."

Ribcage suppressed a smile. It was clear to Beetro that the girl was hiding her excitement of returning to Korthe and unleashing the powers of her pet robot all over her rival street rats.

They'd found Arym sitting in a rocking chair along the deck of the hostel. Wordlessly, he followed them out into the streets of the robot district. He'd been morose and mostly in a silent brooding that even Beetro was finding a little annoying.

"We're thinking of leaving soon," Beetro told him as they walked.

Arym nodded as if understanding the reason for their departure. "But what about the Crib? I've made an oath. I must help my people."

"Not sure you're going to find it here. In Orion. Seems that everyone is in need of help wherever we go."

"I don't even know if I have a home anymore. As far as I know, Deluvius has already dug down to them and taken over. Just like he's trying to do here." They shared a forlorn silence and then Arym asked, "What does he want? From Helian to the Crib and now Orion—what does that man want with everyone?"

Beetro recalled seeing the general in Korthe, and then later in the tower at Peles Castle. Eyes of blue ice beneath those grayed eyebrows reserved much within. The general wanted power, no doubt, but the way the man peered at him in that tower—there was something more. An unspoken desire burned within the general as he glared at Beetro.

"Nothing good," Beetro concluded. "He puts kids into slave labor and leaves nothing but char and smoke in his wake as he moves across this land. Orion will be no different. We need to leave."

"And go where?" Arym asked.

Ribcage quickly answered. "Back to Korthe."

Arym looked to Beetro to confirm the answer. The robot only said, "Maybe."

Ribcage groaned. "I thought you said we were going back."

"The general has control there now. We don't know what he's even done with the town at this point. It may not be safe for us."

They moved wordlessly for a moment, walking by two mothers cradling babies in their arms. "They have hatcheries here?" Arym asked.

Beetro looked at Ribcage, who only shrugged. "Hatcheries?"

"Yeah. Where all the babies come from. Orion must have hatcheries."

Ribcage looked at him. "What are you talking about, mole man?"

"Is that not how babies are made here?" A creeping look of uncertainty flooded the man's face.

"I don't think so..." Beetro answered as gently as possible.

"Do you... do you not know where babies come from?" Ribcage asked with feigned earnestness.

"In the Crib, we make them in a lab. I-I guess I never really thought about how babies are made outside of the Crib."

Ribcage smiled. "So... you don't know how babies are made?"

"I... guess not."

Ribcage burst into uncontrolled laughter. "Someone needs to tell mole man how babies are made!" She fell to her knees in hysterics. "He doesn't know how it works!"

Arym appeared infinitely embarrassed. "I-I'm sorry, I don't know."

"Rib," Beetro said. "Stop."

But the child kept rolling with laughter. "Go on without me, it'll take me a few minutes to get over this!"

They strolled beyond the robot district, past the entrance, and into the human markets. The place had transformed from a bustling market to little more than a vagrant stop-over. Men and women begged in the street while those that were better off scurried through to get to the higher streets of Orion. Beetro didn't know where they lived exactly, but the upper class of merchants, engineers, and traders had absconded into the higher echelons of the city. Throughout the day, he observed various aircraft that departed from the upper peak of the mountain city. That the Kish hadn't yet gained control of the air traffic still gave hope to its denizens that there were other sources of influence and power within the city.

"A little coin?" someone asked at Beetro's feet.

"I'm sorry, no," Beetro answered without glancing down, fatigued by the constant begging.

"How about a little nip then?" the man asked, speech slurred—his beard filthy with street grime. He was unable to fix his gaze on any one thing—his eyes wheeled within their sockets.

"I'm sorry, we don't have anything. We also have very little," Beetro said, moving along.

"Crow?" Ribcage said.

Beetro stopped.

"I... think it's Crow," she said, bending over the man.

Arym squinted at the man. "Who?"

Beetro turned and looked at the man. A grey cloak draped about his shoulders had turned almost black from the filth of the street. Blood cracked eyes above his gaunt cheeks made him appear rather ghoulish. An already feebly nourished man in Korthe, the man had lost even more weight since.

Ribcage held the old man's chin within her small hand and asked, "How the hell did you get here from Korthe?"

"Korthe?" he said. "Korthe? This is... where is this?"

He was as drunk as ever.

"I didn't think it was possible for him to ever leave that street corner in Korthe," Ribcage said, inspecting the man like she'd just discovered a wounded animal.

"Lucindi used to bake a biscuit for him," Beetro said. "Leave it for him in his hand or atop his knee when he was passed out."

Ribcage nodded. "Yep. I usually took about half of it."

Crow tried to stand, immediately lost his balance, and fell. "Do any of you have a nip on you?"

The three watched the pathetic man squint up at them, the bright sun weighing on his eyesight. Beetro wanted to forget they ever saw him. He was already burdened with the needs of three humans—adding a fourth who was as helpless as a baby would only make things worse for his weary group of travelers.

As if reading his thoughts, Ribcage said, "We can't leave him here."

"*You* don't want to leave him behind?" Arym asked. "I thought I'd wake up dead or abandoned every day we traveled to Orion because of you. And now you're the one who suddenly has a heart for this old beggar?"

She chased a look of shame from her face. "Shut up. I don't need to explain anything to your stupid face. Luci cared about him, so we should, too."

"Come on," Beetro said, interrupting their spat. "Let's help him to his feet."

They'd lifted Crow into a bed at the back of the hostel. The man slept and snored for half a day.

"Who?" Hawera asked, nudging the man with her metal-tipped staff.

"We know him from Korthe—back in Helian. He's just a... he's just an old man," Beetro explained.

Hawera squinted in confusion and then seemed to understand. "He is friend."

With a bit of vacillation, Beetro nodded. "Do you mind looking after him for the afternoon?"

"Where going?" she asked.

Beetro sighed and then was interrupted by the bot, Sartorious, who was parked outside their beds. "Now why did you sigh just now, do you think?" Her lights blinked blue and yellow as she continued. "You have no lungs, you do not move air through a bronchial conducting system, yet you *sighed*."

Beetro sighed once more and said, "Look, I really don't know. Would you mind giving us a bit of privacy?"

Sartorious blinked red and yellow and wordlessly wheeled away.

"As I was saying, I think it's time we leave Orion. We're all hearing rumors about things escalating with the Kish and Deluvius and there is a major food crisis going on out there. I'm no human, but I have been traveling with Ribcage for over a month and I know exactly what happens to you humans when you're hungry."

Hawera nodded. Arym, sitting cross-legged by the window seal, stared off despondent.

"I guess that's the end of my speech—"

He was interrupted by gasping coming from the bed. They turned to Crow, who, now wide awake and propped up with one elbow, was pointing at Beetro. "You!" he said, his hand tremulous —accusatory.

Beetro pointed at his own chest. "Me?"

"*You.*" Crow stood on wobbly knees.

"Me, what?"

"How did you find me?"

"Find you? We stumbled on you in the street—brought you here."

Crow looked from the robot to Ribcage and Hawera and then back to Beetro. "So... finally going to finish the job, huh?"

"What?"

"Going to kill me—slice me through just like you did my future double. Seems fitting for me, I suppose. Come all this way out here just to be trapped like a mouse in your robot den. I should've known you would've been planning this. I'd ask why if I thought you'd give me a straight answer."

They were all silent for a moment.

Beetro spoke. "Are you... are you talking to *me*?"

"Yes! Yes, you!" He pointed. "I'm looking and talking right at you!"

Ribcage slapped his hand. "Okay, Crow. Why don't we go find you a drink or something?"

"Get it over with," Crow continued to Beetro. "Blast me away, robot!"

"Blast you?" Beetro looked down at his own hands.

"Blast away, robot! I've heard so much about your newfound *powers*."

Ribcage took his hand to lead the old man away. "Come on, Crow."

But Crow recoiled, pulling his hand back. "Who are you calling Crow?"

She rolled her eyes. "You!"

"Rib, wait," Beetro said, stepping closer to the man. "Who are you?" he asked.

Crow spoke low, almost a whisper. "You know who I am, robot."

"Who?"

"Galiaro. Astrocyst. Creator of a murdering robot."

THIRTY-SEVEN

BEETRO WATCHED the old man speak—tufts of beard hair fluttering with each breath, spittle flying. He had a gift for communicating very little using a multitude of words and gestures.

Arym pointed at him. "So... *you* are who we've been looking for?"

Galiaro turned to him, inspected him up and down, resolutely ignored the young man, and continued spitting accusations at Beetro. "Who rebooted you? Tell me right now."

The robot had been too shocked to respond for several minutes but finally spoke up with a hint of indignation. "*You* did."

"I haven't seen you since I was covering your metal skull with dirt, three meters into the ground. You were never supposed to take another step after what you did to me."

"I... I didn't *kill you*!"

"That's very interesting and sounds remarkably like something a murderous bot would say. Who did you plan this with? Who dug you up, huh?"

"You... created me?" he asked, too shocked to think of anything else to say.

"Yes, you miserable bot. I made you. I made you, are you satisfied? And now you've found me."

"*You*," Beetro repeated, inspecting the astrocyst anew. "*You're* my creator?"

"I put every bolt and screw into that traitorous little head of yours."

"And then you buried me in a ditch somewhere?"

The old man nodded.

"Because... I killed you?"

"I see we're coming to an understanding, old friend. And it would seem you've kidnapped me and brought me to this—" he inspected the hostel, noting the crowd of robots that were amassing, "robotic den of thieves. I believe I deserve the right to know your intentions. Have you allied with the Reticulum? The Kish?"

"I'm not allied with anyone. These," Beetro pointed to Ribcage, Hawera, and Arym, "are my traveling companions. My friends."

"Friends? Ha, you're incapable of being a friend to anyone—especially your creator."

"We came to Orion to... find you. But you were already in Korthe?" His eyes wandered, trying to understand. "How did you even get here?"

"I watched you—you tried sneaking out of town—but I saw you leaving Korthe. I came searching for you, knowing that you were here searching for me."

"How? And to do what?"

"Answer me first, robot. Are you still trying to kill me? If so, it does affect my plans."

"I haven't been searching for you all this time *just to kill you*."

"Then why are you looking for me?"

"My directive. The one you programmed into me before I was rebooted."

"Yes, this *directive*. And what is it?"

"Only that my name is Beetro and that I needed to find you, Galiaro."

"That's it?"

"That's it."

Galiaro sat on the bed, his long legs sprawled out across the floor. "And there was nothing about killing me?"

"Of course not. Why do you keep thinking that?"

The old astrocyst's gaze suddenly became unfixed. After a moment, he said, "Where did you wake up?"

"In Korthe. Where did you bury me?"

"In Helian—just outside the GeminArc."

"The GeminArc?"

"Two arcs—Alchean technology—a few kilometers outside Korthe."

"My mom!" Ribcage said.

Galiaro took the outburst as a non-sequitur and said, "Just so I'm understanding. You have no memory?"

Beetro shook his head. "I have no knowledge of you or any events before my reboot."

"Is your memory engram intact?"

"Memory engram?"

The astrocyst rose and placed his hands on Beetro's head, feeling along grooves. He pressed two thumbs on a temporal plate, depressed some sort of latch, and exposed a tiny compartment in the side of the bot's head. "Gone," he announced.

"My memory is gone?"

"Yes."

"Perhaps along with your murderous proclivities. Answer me, do you still intend on killing me?"

"I really don't."

"I see..." The man's eyes began to wander.

"What?"

Galiaro tried to answer but instead wretched at the side of the bed, producing a fair amount of vomit. Ribcage's nostrils flared as she backed away. "I'm not feeling well," Galiaro declared, his face turning a sheet of lima bean green. He dry-heaved once more and then continued. "If you haven't noticed, the sea got herself some legs and walked out of here."

"What does this have to do with me?" Beetro asked.

"We—the GeminArc—" But the astrocyst stopped, peering at all the robot faces gawking at him, eavesdropping. "We must leave here at once."

"And go where?"

"Not here!" Galiaro snapped. He fell back in bed once more, closing his eyes and motioning to Ribcage. "Little girl, little girl, come here! Please clear my mouth if I vomit in my sleep. You've got to use your finger like a hook. See? It helps to turn me on my side. That's a good girl." His eyes closed.

Ribcage swiveled to Beetro; her face screwed in frozen horror.

After the old astrocyst developed deep tremors that progressed to intermittent seizing, his prophecy turned true as the group found it useful to turn the man onto his side to prevent aspiration. Through coughing and gagging, the man cleared secretions and fell back to sleep. They repeated this process several times throughout that afternoon and into the evening. Beetro was too anxious to power down for the night. The surreality of actually finding his creator—someone he walked by every day in Korthe—had his mind racing. He watched the man as he slept.

This is Galiaro?

It couldn't be true.

How could such a... *fool* be his creator? The man emitted similar odors Beetro had catalogued from the Korthe junkyard. He couldn't function without a full tank of alcohol lubricating his blood vessels. True, he knew some details about Beetro, but his claims that he was some sort of victim in the future—or the past—didn't leave the old man with a lot of credibility. Beetro couldn't help but feel that the appearance of the old man was part of some sort of elaborate ploy—a trap set for a purpose he couldn't guess. And how did such a pathetic old man even travel from Korthe to Orion?

"Hey." Beetro slapped his cheek the following morning. "How do you know about me?"

Galiaro opened his eyes, yawning in Beetro's face. "I made you. Next question."

"Why?"

"Why what?"

"Why did you make me?"

Galiaro stood, his eyes straining at the sunlight. "I... where is this?" He looked down at Beetro as if for the first time. "You!"

"Me, what?"

"Came back to finish the job, huh?"

"No, I'm not trying to kill you. We already went over this."

He scratched his chin. "Hmph. So... that happened."

"We brought you in from the streets yesterday. Remember? It was clearly established that I wish you no harm despite your... memory."

"Yes, fine—things can become a bit of a jumble. My memory returns like a rising tide with every moment I stand here." He glanced around the hostel. "We need to leave this place. There are important matters we must get to. Granted, you're not lying and don't try to stab me through the chest like you did. Where's the girl? Never mind, we must leave at once."

"Wait, wait. How do I know you are who you say you are? How do I know you're not some... imposter?"

A smile emerged through the old man's beard.

"You were originally refurbished from a model of bots that was created over two centuries ago—likely for maintenance work with pipes or underground power lines—some utilitarian work where it is an advantage to be short in stature. I dug up your metal bones long after your original creators had gone extinct. Using your ancient hull and skeletal structure, I retrofitted you with a nuclear core in your chest. The nuclear reactor was only the first of your upgrades. I designed a microcapillary hydraulic system—hundreds of thousand steam-powered filaments running up and down your body. You have advanced continuous rotation servo joints that move those titanium limbs of yours. You have a variety of sensor arrays in that skull—gyroscopic accelerators and positional sensors, both potentiometric and linear variable. A tactile sensor running from your central nervous system uses peizocrystal resistance and elastoresistance. You have the proprioception of a chimpanzee effortlessly gliding from tree to tree. You have telescoping eyesight fitted with advanced aperture range, with autofocusing and apochromatic refraction granting you UV, infrared, and night vision. You can see a flea on a horse's rear end from three kilometers away. You have piezoelectric hearing and dampening, with a decibel range from 20 to 300—you can hear the same flea fart into the wind or hear dynamite explode next to you without auditory damage—" Galiaro finally took a deep breath. "Is that enough?"

Beetro nodded.

"Do you finally believe that this old man standing before you is your creator?"

He nodded again and then looked away, sullen.

"And somehow, all that combination of circuitry and hardware caused a consciousness to emerge. And here you are, questing out with your gang of misfits to find your creator to answer all your questions. Do I have it right?"

The astrocyst had incredible talent in making Beetro suddenly feel very small. The reduction of who he was into mechanical parts brought burgeoning despair into the bot. "I guess that's right," he finally answered.

"So, dear robot, tell me... have I answered all of your questions?"

It was at that moment Beetro wished he'd never met the man —his noble creator. To leave Korthe, venture out through Helian, around Crater Valley, and through Gargantua Forest only to land himself in Orion and discover that he was created with such... deliberate engineering. And for what?

"No," Beetro answered. "You haven't answered all my questions."

Galiaro fluttered his long eyelashes. "Yes?"

"*Why?*"

"Why did I create you?"

Beetro nodded.

"You are nothing more and nothing less than a key."

"A key?"

"You are a walking, talking, *murdering* key."

Galiaro would offer no more explanation until the group agreed to leave the hostel at once. Unceremoniously, the astrocyst draped his cloak over his shoulders and walked out, the robots gawking as he left. Arym and Hawera looked to Beetro for what to do. He wanted to profusely apologize to them for bringing them on a pointless task to find his creator—a man unhinged and otherwise quite vile. The journey through the wilderness, leading these poor people with him, had all but imploded in an instant.

"It okay," Hawera said, patting him on the shoulder. "Come. I need astrocyst, too." She followed after Galiaro with Ribcage bouncing behind. Arym only looked at him with those baleful eyes and slowly shrugged.

They followed the astrocyst through the streets of the bot district, his cloak dragging through puddles. He continued out the back end of the district, where three of the original Alchean-made canals converged to a dark corner. The alley tapered but didn't end as the grey walls of alloy closed in on the group as if they were stuck in the granite slot canyons of Meteor Mountains.

"Where are we going?" Ribcage asked.

Galiaro's voice issued ahead, echoing over the walls. "Bet you were asking around about me—trying to see if anyone knew where to find me."

"That's right."

"And?"

"No one ever heard of you. Some knew there were astrocysts who had a lab in the city, but no one had any idea."

After a moment of pleased silence, he bragged, "That's precisely what I intended. Folk don't take kindly to astrocysts, believing us to be witches or sorcerers. Damn fools. When the torches and pitchforks come—as they always do in good time—it's best to be hidden. And hidden well. Now, let's see..." He arched his neck, inspecting the dead-end alley in which they'd squeezed. Galiaro reached up, waving his hand in the air and then dragged it along the wall. After sweeping both hands over the surface once more, his hands slapped around something.

Except... nothing was there.

"Alchean alloy is magnetic," he explained while one of his hands formed a *C* around empty air, his other hand went searching the wall once more until it slapped into another surface that didn't seem to be there. "I spent damn near a decade trying to understand their alloy—never figured out how it was made. In the end, I figured they'd exported some exotic elements from alien planets through their wormhole and gave up trying to figure it out. Instead of trying to hide our lab *underneath* the city surface, we decided to just hide in plain sight. You—" he pointed to Arym. "Come here and give me a boost."

"A boost to what?" Arym asked, stepping forward.

"Give me the boost and you'll find out, young master."

Arym interlaced his fingers and held out his open palms.

Galiaro flared his nostrils. "Hands and knees, boy, I'm no acrobat—can't balance on one leg like that." Arym glared at Beetro with displeasure and then got down on his hands and knees. "Now," Galiaro continued, placing one boot atop Arym's back. "You must watch as I do. You should all feel privileged at this opportunity. Rarely does an astrocyst just give up all his secrets this easily, but considering the circumstances, I can't exactly vet you all." Standing with both feet on Arym's back, the old man reached up, grabbed ahold of a part of the wall that wasn't there, and hoisted himself up. Tucking his legs up, he placed his boots where his hands were gripping nothing but air, and then steadily rose, standing up—floating above the group.

"How?" Hawera stood, stepping forward. She arched her neck up and peered above, accidentally getting an unwanted eyeful up Galiaro's robe. "Ah!" she screamed, quickly stepping back.

"There are a series of magnetized handholds straight up the wall. You can't see them, but they are there. Follow me up."

The group watched in skeptical silence.

Galiaro scoffed. "It's an invisible ladder, you miscreants. Now, up!"

One by one, and with the assistance of Arym, each grabbed ahold of the handholds. Hawera reached a hand down to help Arym get a grip on the first invisible handhold. They climbed, each carefully feeling for the next handhold and lifting, hand over foot.

"Where are we going?" Ribcage complained.

"Plain sight," Galiaro said, his beard whipping in the wind.

"How did you make all this disappear?" she asked.

"Trick of the light, trick of the light, child. Most of science is tricking light—fooling it to go where it thinks it needs to go. A mirror is getting light to think it must go backwards. These steps here... they fool the light into thinking it must go sideways and around. What doesn't reflect light cannot be seen."

"But—"

They were interrupted by Hawera crying out. "Arym!"

Suddenly, the man was falling.

Before anyone could speak, Hawera had flipped her metal-tipped staff from off her back and pointed it down, straight at the ground. With closed eyes and an angry brow, glowing blue light coalesced around her fingertips and then extended up the staff, collecting at the tip. An instant later, a pulse of blue light sprung from the staff, fired toward the ground, past Arym, and disappeared into a ripple in space. In an instant, a portal opened just in time to swallow Arym whole.

The portal closed and Arym vanished.

Carefully, Hawera lowered herself down the invisible holds and landed back at the bottom of the alley. Pointing the staff straight up, cock-eyed and biting her lip, she released a pulse of the same blue light just above. A partition of space appeared above her head as she cast her staff aside and opened her arms, bracing herself. A portal reappeared and Arym was suddenly falling through, screaming for help. He landed in her outstretched arms.

"Safe," she declared, lowering him to the ground.

Arym looked up at the group suspended high above the alley and then back at Hawera. "Thanks, but I probably would've been fine," he said, and then went back to the wall to climb again.

With wrenched necks, the group had watched the scene play out from above. "What," Galiaro asked, "was that?"

"Her Fourth," Ribcage said. "Ooh. I only wish I knew she was going to use it, then I would've Jumped all over the place! Let me know next time!" she yelled down to Hawera. But the woman appeared dazed as she knelt on the ground, recovering.

"Interesting," Galiaro said before continuing up. "Very interesting, indeed. These travelers you surround yourself with are perhaps not completely worthless, my little bot." Beetro cringed at the term of endearment. Nothing about the decrepit old man thus far had endeared Beetro toward his creator.

The group climbed in silence until Galiaro stopped, now suspended over five stories above the alley street. Beetro thought on the queerness of a line of people, floating in the air, all looking skyward. He suddenly felt very vulnerable and asked, "What now?"

But Galiaro ignored the bot as he reached a hand up and fiddled with the open air above. With eyes closed and tongue at the side of his mouth, the astrocyst hummed to himself as his wrist twisted back and forth.

"Is it the entrance?" Beetro asked. "Is there some sort of trick to getting in?"

"Quiet!" he snapped, eyes closed, wrist turning. For fifteen minutes, they stood, waiting while Galiaro cursed himself and then went on humming. At last, something clicked above, and a dark square materialized above them. "Aha!"

"How did you get it open?"

"I remembered the combination to the lock."

"It was just a stupid combination lock?" Ribcage asked. "That's all that's guarding your lab?"

"It would appear," Galiaro's voice muffled as his upper torso disappeared into the dark square, "that a light-bending coating and a stainless-steel combination lock were enough to keep my lab undisturbed." His legs pulled behind him and he disappeared through the square in the sky.

The lab was dark and long—a hallway that had been built within the Alchean alleyway and extended toward the inner streets. A single window at the far end scattered light through the lab, exposing motes of dust and musky air particulate. There were also two lightbulbs suspended at the far end of the lab, inexplicably still glowing despite the lab's long abandonment.

"Hmph," Galiaro said. "I don't remember—" but then the bulbs noiselessly went out. The lab fell into darkness, with only the single window at the end leaching scant sunlight within. The group meandered around the lab, Ribcage touching everything, and Hawera thoughtfully inspecting several bits of machinery that lined one edge of the room.

"Nobody touches anything!" Galiaro growled. "There are things in here that can kill you—and me—if you even tip it over the wrong way. Now..." He walked along the length of the lab, inspecting shelves full of beakers, burners, powders, and aliquots of colorful liquid. "I see Fallaro kept the lab in good order after I'd left," he said to himself. A long workbench cut the middle of the lab in half, bedecked with glassware, tubing, mirrors, and circuitry.

Galiaro swiped his hand along the workbench and rubbed his fingers together. "But he hasn't been here in a bit."

For a few minutes, they watched as the astrocyst ambled throughout the lab, muttering to himself while blowing on microscopes, resetting electrical breakers and sticking his head in chemo vent hoods. Somehow, he'd found something to eat and stood at the solitary window, munching while crumbs fell down his beard.

"Hey!" Beetro finally said.

The man jumped.

"Can we talk now? What is going on?"

Galiaro put up a finger. "Of course, of course, yes, my dear murdering robot—"

"Stop calling me that."

"I will reveal to you all the mysteries you seek." He coughed, releasing another flurry of crumbs.

"Where did you get that?" Ribcage asked, pointing at the oblong bar of food in his hand.

Galiaro pointed. "I keep many months' supply of my Nourishment Rectangles—a fiber matrix of protein and carbohydrates. These things can last fifty years, unspoiled. Help yourself, child."

Ribcage found a rectangle in a cupboard and bit into it. "Ah!" she yelled before throwing the rectangle to the ground. "What the hell *is* that?"

"Sustenance, child," he said, taking another bite. "When you're attempting to predict when the end of the world will happen, you care little for flavor."

"Blech!" she said, but then turned around and picked it up again, sniffing and removing hair from the bar.

Beetro intervened. "Tell us what's happening and what we have to do with it. What am I a key to?"

The astrocyst sat and stroked his beard. "Did you know that there used to be billions of stars in the sky?" The group considered his words as they gathered around—Hawera listening intently. "Billions. Millennia ago, a man could look at the night's sky and see countless galaxies and worlds as numerous as the sands of the shore. How many stars do you see now?"

"Five—well, now four," Ribcage said.

"Wrong. There are no stars."

Confused silence.

"The twinkles you see in the night sky are the planets of our solar system—nothing more. You see, we are alone now—Earth and the sad little planets that circle the sun. Back during the Alcheans' time, the universe could be seen—could be visited. Wormholes fashioned by the Alcheans brought thousands of alien cultures to Earth soil. Our planet was an intergalactic highway, which shared culture and technology across the universe."

"So, what happened?"

Hawera answered. "The universe... ran far, far away."

"This astute, time-warping young woman is correct. The universe did run far, far away."

"But how?" Beetro asked.

"I've been explaining this far too much lately. Expansion. For many millennia, humankind observed that all those galaxies and stars out there were expanding away from Earth. And not only was the universe expanding but it was doing it faster than the speed of light and at an accelerated pace, meaning there would come a time when even the light from other galaxies would no longer reach Earth. I imagine this was mostly a fascination to ancient scientists—that there was no alarm when it was discovered. They likely knew it would take billions and billions of years before Earth and the sun would be left alone. There was no reason to panic."

"So, has it been billions and billions of years since the expansion has been discovered?"

"No," Galiaro said. "It has not."

"Then what happened to all the stars?"

"That is the question I have been working on for the last thirty years. I study the expansion—mostly, why it has happened prematurely."

"And?"

Galiaro chased a sullen look from his face. "It doesn't matter anymore."

"You don't know," Beetro said.

"I didn't say that. I said it doesn't matter anymore. I stopped my research into the origins of the premature expansion, Dark Theory, years ago. The expansion accelerated faster than any predictive model. There is some force—some unknown qualifier—that is continually changing the expansion model. It makes expansion erratic—jittery. No statistics I employed could provide a predictive model. My interests moved from prediction to... to mitigation. All I knew was that the expansion was happening, and that it was happening faster than anyone could have ever known. Anyone except the Alcheans."

"What's their part in this?"

"I believe they knew about the danger of a premature expansion before anyone—no other species or people on Earth had any idea. They knew it would happen but, like me, they weren't sure the exact moment when Earth would be left behind while the stars and all their lights vanished forever. Because of the unpredictability of the prematurity of expansion, they developed a contingency plan."

"Consisting of what?"

"Mass exodus."

Confused silence once more fell in the room.

"They left," Galiaro said. "For all their noble, technological, grandiosity, etcetera, they up and left us all here to rot."

A new voice interrupted. "Wait." It was Arym. "That's not true."

"Tell me, young man, what you have learned that an old astrocyst has not?"

"I've been in one of their tombs. An Alchean tomb. There was a curator there... this ball of light that explained it to me."

Galiaro raised an eyebrow.

"No, listen. He said that the Alcheans had outgrown their mortality—that they had engineered their genes to live forever. They had nothing else to do on the planet, so they left into another dimension."

"I have no doubt that the Alcheans left—specifically into the *innerspace,* a boundless, timeless, and eternal realm. But the reason you've stated sounds like Alchean propaganda—a justification for leaving all the rest of us to rot in the expansion. They left inscriptions and statues and buildings all over the land to remind us how great they are—hell, Orion is just one big fat monument to themselves. They were a people obsessed with themselves, and in all their great compassion, left everyone else behind.

"For years," Galiaro continued, "I worked in this lab trying to figure out the expansion—predict the expansion and why it was accelerating. I spent a decade excavating runes, trying to find old tomes and inscriptions about what past cultures knew about the expansion. I know that it greatly accelerated several centuries ago—faster than anyone could have predicted. Based on what I'd found, me and Fallaro created a model of prediction—to know when it would happen. It is called the Dark Theory model."

"When what should happen, exactly?" asked Beetro.

"Isn't it obvious?"

They stared back at him, silent.

"We wanted to know when the local expansion would fling

Earth from its orbit—when we would become a lost planet, wandering around in the darkness and the nothingness of space."

"That can happen?" Arym asked.

"It's already happened," Beetro answered, understanding the implications. "It's why we lost a star—a planet—a few nights ago out of the sky."

"Saturn to be exact," Galiaro added. "We lost old Saturn," he said solemnly. "May she be guided through her journey through the universe." He lifted a glass of some sort of green liquid he'd found in the lab.

"So, a planet, just like ours, got flung out into space?" Arym asked.

"Not just like ours. Saturn was a gas giant—many times bigger than Earth."

"That's why the sun looks bigger—why the sea disappeared," Beetro said with new understanding. "When we lost Saturn, the opposing gravity on Earth was gone, making our own orbit shrink around the sun."

Galiaro nodded. "Seems the programming I put in you for orbital mechanics is still intact. Hmm, you were a useful bot to have around... like a calculator."

Beetro's eyes became pinpoint as he glared at his creator. "So... the sun isn't actually bigger. We're just closer and water is evaporating off—that's why the sea vanished." There was silence in the lab as the realization set in.

"And one by one," Galiaro said. "Each planet will be flung from her orbit. May the gods help us when we lose Jupiter—might pull Earth right out of its orbit when it leaves. If Jupiter doesn't pull us away, our orbit will shrink until the expansion finally flicks us away forever."

"We'll just be... a wandering planet?" Arym asked.

"When?" Hawera asked.

"I've realized that is an impossible question to answer. I'd thought for the longest time it wouldn't happen in my lifetime. But given all the unpredictability about the prematurity of the expansion, I could never be sure. So... I made a backup plan." He looked at Beetro.

"Me?"

"Yes. You."

"What could I possibly have to do with this expansion?"

"I created you as a key—a *beetro*. A key to open the GeminArc."

"To what end?"

"Isn't it obvious?" He looked around at the group. "No one?"

"Escape," Hawera finally said.

Galiaro sighed while nodding. "Escape, indeed, my dear."

"You tried to leave," Beetro said. "And you made me into a key to open the GeminArc."

"Correct. The Alcheans left to the innerspace through the GeminArc. The only way to survive the expansion... is to *escape* the expansion. All of this," he twirled his wrist in the air, "all of this will be gone soon. How soon? Today, tomorrow, next week, next month... I do not know."

A new voice split through the room. "That is something we have been working on, astrocyst."

They looked upon one another in confusion. None of them had spoken. The voice had come as if from nowhere. Hawera lifted her staff in caution.

"He-hello?" Beetro said.

"Hello," the voice answered. It was calm and even. "Greetings to you all."

An orb of light instantly materialized among them.

"Protonix!" Arym cried, stepping forward. Hawera, too, grew animated at the sight of the ball of light bobbing up and down.

Galiaro stood. "What is all this then?"

"This is Protonix," Arym explained. "Curator to an Alchean tomb."

"And what is this sentient lightbulb doing in *my* lab?"

A new voice cut from the edge of the room. "Trying to finish what you couldn't figure out," it said in a calm, feminine tone. Everyone turned to the end of the lab where another orb of light appeared.

"Two!" Hawera shouted.

"Indeed," Protonix said. "This is my entangled counterpart, Neutrini." Neutrini bobbed up and down as if in greeting. "Astrocyst, we have much to discuss."

"So it would seem, my dear lightbulb."

THIRTY-EIGHT

MIREE THOUGHT back to her first days in Korthe and hearing that gentle voice. "Would you like some company?" Miree peeked above the trash mound and found a young woman—charcoal black hair, brown eyes, lithe frame like a willow branch. She also offered a smile, unfeigned.

"No," Miree told her. "No, I'm fine."

"I come to the junkyard often. Sometimes I have little else to live on and to feed the children. Please don't hesitate to ask me for help. I know a lot of hot spots around here. There's no shame in scavenging."

"No, it's not that. I'm not scavenging... well, I am. I'm just looking for something in particular."

"Oh?"

"Batteries. Of any kind. Dead or with charge—doesn't matter." Miree wondered why she was telling all this to a complete stranger. Normally, she'd already have her boltgun out, waving it in her face. Yet, there was something completely disarming about the girl. Miree detected no guile behind those eyes.

"You'll find those all around. Lots of scrap comes through Korthe. It's a common trading spot for several routes through the region of Helian. I used to be part of the caravans that went to Carister."

"But you couldn't get enough of the junkyard?"

Her eyes fell. "No. It was the menfolk on the caravans..."

Miree locked eyes with her. "No. You do *not* be ashamed. You do not feel like you did something wrong. Men are the plague of this land." Miree dropped her satchel and looked her in the eyes. "You are..." She had no words to describe what she wanted to say. "You are..."

"Lucindi." She reached out her hand.

"Miree. And I guess I wouldn't mind some company."

"Where are you from, Miree?"

"Lots of places."

"Any one place?"

"Back east."

"Like Orion? I'd love to go there someday."

"You'll find the same there as there is here."

"And what's that?"

"Power. Well hidden. Used in secret with only one purpose—to continue the power of those who wield it."

"And that's here?"

"What do you think your fief lord is constantly trying to do?"

"I haven't thought much about it."

"That's good. Don't think. Don't ask questions. It only gets you into trouble."

"So, you came here to what... escape?"

"Do you always ask so many questions?"

"Yes," Lucindi said without a shred of sarcasm.

"I came here because I'm done trying to escape—seems that's all I've been doing my entire life."

"Escape from what?"

"The life given to me."

"Someone *gave* you your life?"

Miree scowled "You know what I mean."

"I don't." Lucindi ambled away, picking through shrapnel.

"So, is this the life you took for yourself then?" Miree asked after following her, annoyed. "Picking through garbage? This wasn't given to you... you *chose* it?"

"My circumstances were given to me—that's true. But my circumstances are not my *life*. My life is what I turn it into. Me and you are in the same circumstances right now, right? Both picking through garbage. But I suspect we have very different lives..."

Miree wanted to blast her with a fiery retort but found she could only watch Lucindi as she hummed to herself, leafing through the pages of discarded books. Who has the audacity to hum when the world of men corrupts on all sides?

Miree awoke with a lancing pain coursing through her muscles. A deep ache had set in through her trunk and arms as if she'd been clinging to the side of the cliff for the last day. The cell was dark—ominous with its silence. How many times in her life was she going to awake in a cell, freshly imprisoned? Chasing away the memories of Lucindi from her mind, she arose and then fell once more as all her muscles screamed with fatigue.

It was either the Kish or the Reticulum. While she had other enemies, they were the two most recent. And figuring that she was caught in Orion—Kish HQ—she was putting her money on them.

"Okay!" she yelled. "I'm awake. Let's get on with it. Start your beating or torturing or electrocuting or whatever it is you're going to do to me. I really don't care."

Silence.

Given the pitch black of the cell, she got down on her hands and knees, inspecting every crevice. The floor was jagged flagstone, damp and completely freezing. There were no drains, no plumbing, and certainly no toilet. The only entrance to the cell was a single door—foreboding iron steel with hinges facing outside. The bottom of the door was flush with the ground. An additional strip of rubber ensured not even a piece of parchment could be slipped underneath. There was no bed and no blanket.

Without a morsel of food to be found, these were all worrying signs about her prognosis as a prisoner. The message was clear—she was not meant to be a long-term guest. She was meant to freeze, go hungry, and not sleep. She was meant to suffer. Dread crept within her as there was now no doubt about the identity of her captors. There was only one organization that captured for the sake of suffering.

The Kish.

What felt like one day passed.

And then two.

No one came.

No one—except Lucindi. Having easily been swept up into an infectious delirium from the freezing temperature, Miree hallucinated. Flashes of Lucindi's dark hair flitted through her mind. Others crowded her thoughts—Galiaro, Ribcage... Beetro. Even Meric. She wondered where they were. Perhaps not Galiaro. She knew where he was—face down in a gutter, plus or minus a traumatic head injury. But Beetro and Ribcage now seemed like heroes in some ancient epic. A robot endowed with great and arcane power—the latent ability to change the world yet lost to his memory in a reboot. Often, she recalled his eyes peering down at her in the Meteor Mountains... thinking, calculating, and then vanishing. Those indigo eyes haunted her now. She knew she had done it to him. Made the robot raw with anger, imbuing him with a sense of justice to leave her behind to rot with the Reticulum. Where Lucindi had imprinted Beetro with kindness, Miree had shattered that mold with distrust and betrayal. And thus went on the parade of her life. Most bridges burnt—other bridges never even built.

There was no food and no water brought to her. She found she could get moisture by slurping from a puddle that formed in the corner of the room. The water was putrid and gave her bouts of diarrhea that she had to relieve in the opposite corner of the cell. The arm prosthesis burned at the bone and her eye implants ached within the sockets. If she stayed in one place, she shivered so hard that a weird sound vibrated through the cell. It took her some time to realize it was her teeth chattering. Her voice had long gone hoarse from screaming profanities at her phantom gaoler. Often, she thought about her Swordless Hilt—fantasizing about turning the pommel, lighting the shards ablaze and busting through the cell door.

She believed it was on day three—severely dehydrated with hunger pangs sending tremors through her body—that the cell door opened. Grimacing at the bright light beyond, she stood on feeble knees.

A figure appeared in the doorway. "I think you're ready," the man said.

She didn't need to see his face—didn't need to ask his name. She knew.

Haldunt the Wire.

"I'm disappointed that you thought this… disguise would help you, acolyte Miree," Haldunt whispered, his breath hot in her ear. "Did you really think we wouldn't see past the facial implants? Do you believe the Kish have become a lot of fools since your betrayal?"

"I'm disappointed my blade in your gut didn't kill you." She tested the bonds around her wrists and feet. Snug.

"There are things that are going to happen now," he said, still crouched behind her, a naked lightbulb swinging above. "Death will happen—you know that—but it doesn't mean things are entirely out of your control. There are many roads that lead to death—many gullies, ravines, deserts, and meadows. Now, there will be no meadows for you. There will be pain and agony for you. But I leave it to you to determine the duration. Are we understanding one another?"

Miree offered a mirthless laugh.

"Being stubborn will get you nowhere."

"The Wire. Haldunt the Wire—master torturer. Do you think you can intimidate me? How many hours have we spent in this room… you with your razors and me screaming out my haunted memories? Do you think I can be easily broken? I've been schooled by the best."

"Indeed. Did you believe I taught you all there is to learn of pain?"

"Haldunt, I don't have all day. We can cut the preamble. Tell me what you want to know—"

A flashing pain bit into her legs. It was ever-present and circumferential—chains of razor circlets burying into her flesh. She held her breath, waiting.

"You do not call the terms here," he hissed, finally stepping into her view. His single eye darted over. The other eye was gone, a deep pit into his skull. "I am still the master, you the pupil. I will teach you pain that you've never known before."

The cutting released from her legs, blood oozing over her skin. "I don't have the Quantizer. It's gone. I left it behind at Peles Castle."

"Ah, so the land of Helian. Trying to rob the fief lord? Naughty."

"There was no dark matter flake. Doesn't exist." The pain returned, thousands of biting teeth embedding deeper around her shins and calves. Her arm, too, screamed with the bite of the razors.

"Why are you here?"

"I wanted another lesson from Haldunt the Wire." She felt the wires cut and held back a whimper.

"*Why* did you come back? Never did I see someone so stupid as to betray the Kish and then come back to Orion. Why did you return?"

"For... for..." she panted, the pain taking on new forms in her mind—fiery lacerations transforming to a pulsating ache. Haldunt brought his ear closer as she answered. "For the seafood."

Haldunt grunted, releasing his razors. "Let's try again."

Sweat now spilled down her face, producing a fierce stinging beneath her eye implants. She stifled a sob and hated that the man was bringing it out of her. But was it him? Why couldn't she just tell him what he wanted to know? She could spill it all and be done with the whole thing. The final chapter of her life could close and she would be fine with that. She could close the door on a life that—despite much plotting on her part—amounted to little more than a lonely woman suffering in a dark cell.

"Why did you come back?" She felt a vice-like grip tighten around her abdomen. Her breath was stolen as the blades bit into her flesh. How many scars had she endured from this man? From other men? Lucindi flashed before her mind—the only good she ever knew. Yet, someone else floated to the forefront of her thoughts—someone she didn't realize she wanted to see once more.

Beetro.

Haldunt grunted as he wrapped coils of wires, feathered with thousands of sharp edges, along her legs and only arm. "Thought you would've learned, girl. Thought you would've known that the Kish never stops. The Kish always collects on its debts. Even when it's from your own flesh. I gave you your chance to talk—to make this quick. We've got a war machine at our doorstep, and I don't have time for this."

A shiver struck her as blood droplets formed and coalesced into streaming rivulets across her body.

"Who do you know here!" Haldunt screamed, growing impatient.

The pain was so unbearable, it was hard to imagine she would live much longer. Yet, she knew Haldunt the Wire. The man was famous for a reason—torturing and extracting information from victims for days—weeks. The wires were the key to his method—thin, painful, and non-lethal. But Miree gasped for breath, thinking it would be her last. She wanted to see Beetro again. For one of the few times in her life, she wanted to apologize. The bot didn't do anything wrong to her, and by abandoning him, she may have somehow doomed the entire planet to the expansion. Beetro was probably still lost in Meteor Mountains and Galiaro likely only a few streets away, sloshing around in his own vomit. All the while, perhaps another planet was flung from the solar system. She somehow had exceeded all her expectations about herself—that she was a far larger failure than she'd ever known.

"I—"

Something happened.

The pain was... gone. Instantly. Vanished.

She looked about the torture chamber with a clear mind, relief flooding her body. Haldunt met her gaze with something close to shock. Something buzzed next to her ear, but when she looked, nothing. Her eyesight sharpened as she inspected the cell, calculating and engineering any possible mechanism of escape. Haldunt grunted and pulled his wires tighter. But the pain had vanished like a bad storm had passed. As a low hum continued in her skull, she realized what had happened. It was the Reticulum implants in her head. They were responding to her pain input and dampening the physiological response. It made sense... can't have a slave cyborg working if she is laid out by pain.

A smile crept up her face. "Thanks for the massage, Haldunt, but I don't think I'll be telling you anything."

THIRTY-NINE

ONCE PROTONIX and Neutrini had revealed themselves, no one could shut up. For hours, Arym sat with his head in his hands as the conversation ebbed through the lab. He said little as he had little to contribute. Galiaro discussed theoretical physics with the orbs of light as Beetro and Hawera constantly cut in with observations and commentary. The astrocyst had even wheeled out an old chalkboard and scribbled hurried equations and notations, tracking chalk dust along his sleeves and beard. The entangled photons bobbed up and down, jabbering about such abstract mathematics that seemed like another language altogether. Beetro was constantly trying to pry more information from Galiaro about his own past to the point that it finally started to annoy Arym as well. The old man was cryptic, only stating that he made the robot as a key to a wormhole to leave the universe and, sometime during the opening of the wormhole, Beetro tried to kill his own creator—or did kill his own creator... in the future or something. Galiaro seemed fuzzy on the details.

Ribcage had endless hours of entertainment while exploring

the lab—often cut short by shouted threats from Galiaro. When the girl wasn't sticking her head into a vent, she was hopping up and down on Hawera's arm, begging that she use her Fourth. Hawera fended the girl off, exchanging brief glances with Arym and offering a smile. A beautiful smile from a beautiful face. He thought it would be easy to forget about her—this *woman.* But it was hard to get her out of his head when she was there all day, biting her lip as she contemplated Galiaro's words. Her brow ruffled often in frustration as if there were many more words she would wish to discuss amidst the exchange of ideas. Meanwhile, a feeling crept up on Arym—a certain inevitability about what he was doing in the dank lab.

Maybe this wasn't his journey.

He'd left his home—the Crib—and stumbled onto the path of people from the overworld. True planets were flying away, and the oceans were leaving, but did that really have anything to do with him and the Cribmen? Couldn't he just tuck back beneath the blanket of the earth that concealed his people and let the overworlders deal with the mess they had made for themselves? He only hoped the Crib wasn't a smoking crater in the ground after the attack from Deluvius' army. Thoughts of escaping Orion ran through his mind as he drew in his sketch journal—his last stick of charcoal down to just a nub. An attempt at drawing a flower had turned into an ugly blob resembling a shriveled squash. After placing his sketch journal in his satchel, Arym moved toward the hatch in the floor of the lab. No one noticed as he unlatched the lock. As he lowered himself, he felt a cold touch on his hand and looked up to glowing, indigo eyes.

"Where are you going?" Beetro asked.

"I... I just need to get out."

"It's dangerous out there."

"So?"

"Are you... coming back?"

"Why wouldn't I?"

"You seem distant."

"What if I don't come back?"

"I'd come looking for you."

"Why?"

"Because we're friends."

"We're not. We just happen to be in the same space under the same dangers. We're only surviving together."

Beetro was silent for a moment and said, "I used to know someone who thought like that."

"And?"

"She almost had me convinced that's how the world works, too."

"And you know how the world works? Weren't you just rebooted?"

Beetro shrugged. "Maybe the world works whichever way we see it, like from that story of the clockmaker. The world froze only because the people believed it froze."

"Yeah, maybe."

He kept climbing down, losing sight of the robot. As his foot found the last invisible rung on the ladder, he heard Beetro say, "We need you, Arym."

It was a lie, of course—just a do-good robot trying to make him feel better about not having a place to call home. He laughed to himself, thinking he used to be just as naive as the robot, believing there was a beautiful overworld to explore—to escape the ignorance of his own people.

Skirting along the alleyway, Arym found that, at the fringes of the robot district, even the bots had begun making themselves scarce. Roving patrols of the Kish walked the streets, kicking up trash piles and inspecting alleyways. One of the men saw him and pounded the street toward him. Arym froze. He had blood-cracked eyes with wrinkled rivets carved down his cheeks. "What're you doing out?"

"Looking for food."

"Curfew. Get back to your house."

"I-I don't have a home."

"Then get back to your hole, you worthless vagabond. If you're lucky, we'll enlist you soon, so don't go hiding on me. You do good, you might be inducted into the Kish once we win this thing." He lifted a crude cudgel to Arym's head and gave it a small tap. "Got it?"

Arym nodded. "It would be an honor, sir." The man swiveled on his boot and stamped off, boasting a menacing swagger. Arym felt strangely brazened by the interaction—there was a lightness in his heart knowing that he had nothing to lose anymore. There was nothing for him back in Galiaro's lab. Beetro wasn't just naive—no, Beetro was a fool. There was no friendship, no fellowship of saving the orbits of the planets or whatever the astrocyst was talking about. There was only the Crib and getting back to the only people who knew what his life was like. The overworld was a wasteland of the uncaring and the ill-willed.

He turned a corner and noticed a man speaking to a robot. The two chattered on in hushed tones until the robot pointed in Arym's direction. Instinctively, Arym turned and made his way across the street toward a tavern that had been shuttered. In the corner of his eye, he saw the man now following. Arym cut down an alleyway, growing uneasy. Quickly, he ransacked a bag of rubbish, his fingers searching for anything with heft to ward off the assailant. Panicking, he stumbled through heaps of garbage, finding nothing but empty crates covered in bird droppings. As footsteps sounded, he cut his finger on a shard of glass and then wrapped his fingers around the broken edge. Standing to his feet, he brandished the broken bottle and said, "Stop, or I'll attack."

The hooded figure stopped, waited.

"Just go!" Arym yelled, fighting back a sob.

"Arym," the voice said.

The tone was gentle. Distinct. *Familiar.*

"Y-you're..."

The man dropped his hood.

It was Rektor Tarysl.

"Tarysl!" Arym threw the glass shard and fell onto the man, embracing him. "Is it really you?"

Tarysl nodded, a smile broadening his face. Arym felt as if he was staring in a mirror. It wasn't until he was exposed to the diversity of the overworld that he realized just how identical the Cribmen appeared. True, Tarysl was quite a bit older, but Arym could see his own features in the man's face. They were the same —born from the same stock of cloned genes.

"You came... for me?"

Tarysl nodded. "Yes, brother. I came for you."

"But why?"

"We love all our brothers. Every last one."

"How is the Crib? Did General Deluvius break through?"

A foreboding grimace flashed across the rektor's face. "We lost many brothers, but the Crib remains whole. We held our tunnels —our doors are sealed from the overworld yet. Our founder was very wise in creating protective measures against tyrants like the general."

Flooded with relief, he asked, "Why was the general trying to break in?

"It's... complicated. The Crib has a deep history, Arym. A history of which the general is aware."

"What history?"

"The Crib is much more ancient than you know. Your blood, Arym... it's ancient—sacred. It requires more oaths to learn. All in good time."

"Why would you come for me? With so much loss, you should stay behind to fight the overworld—to stop them from getting in."

"We have certain interests in Orion. The general's aggressive acts are hastening our work. We also need you, Arym."

"In Orion? Since when did the Crib care about anything of the overworld? And what do you need me for?"

"We need every last Cribman we can get."

"But... but why?"

The rektor hesitated as if measuring his response. Arym knew he was holding back. "Have you broken the Oath of Descension?"

"I have not broken my oath."

"I knew as much, Arym. You are a Cribman, a descendent of Othel and defender of the Oath. I've always known it to be true."

Arym was glad to hear his words, yet an unease crept within—a familiar dread. "How? How did you find me?"

"Lutra told me he'd let you escape. I fear the boy is in love. He left the Crib."

"Why?"

"To look for you. He's scouring the Meteor Mountains right now for you."

A stab of remorse struck him. Flashes of Lutra's kind hands removing freshly baked bread rolls came to his mind. Lutra was much too tender-hearted for the overworld. He'd never survive, particularly in the streets of Orion. "I'm so sorry. I didn't tell him to come after me."

"I know your heart, Arym—I know you long for the overworld. I knew the seduction of Orion would draw you in. And there are not many who look like us... the Cribmen. You were easy to track."

"What now, rektor? Why am I needed?"

"We did not expect the calamities of the overworld to ripen so quickly. The prophecy of Othel is hastening on. The expansion draws near."

"What prophecy?"

"There is little time, and much work remains ahead of the Crib. We must prepare."

"What prophecy? Prepare for what?"

"The Dark Earth prophecy. There is much you do not know."

"Explain it to me."

"This is not the time or place. That evil despot is at the gates of this city. Blood will flow in these streets. A siege is at hand. We must flee!" He took Arym's sleeve, gesturing him forward.

But Arym stood firm. "Tell me about the Dark Earth prophecy."

"Arym, please! There is no time. You will learn much in your remaining days of rehabilitation."

"*Rehab*?"

"I was able to reduce your sentence considerably, but you've committed offenses against the Crib and—war or not—there must be restitution. And it won't be eighteen months of isolation... that was never the plan in the first place. The threat of isolation is only a scare tactic. You were only one week from being released from isolation."

Arym's face slackened. "Lies upon lies. And you expect me to come back with you and be *imprisoned*? And how do you know about the expansion?"

"Justice must be served in the Crib. There is no getting around that. Do not worry. This is only the beginning of our many great and glorious tasks. The rehab will prepare you for what is ahead. The future of the planet depends on the actions of the Crib."

Arym opened his mouth but was speechless. Nothing had

changed. Tarysl was still the same dogmatic rektor overseeing the pointless doctrine of a dead man, obsessed with himself. The digging, the prophecy, the Oath—all tokens designed to instill a sense of purpose into a life void of meaning. In that moment, he knew the only force driving him to return was nothing more than yearning for home. In the face of opposition of the overworld, Arym had only craved what he knew was familiar. An overwhelming pity overtook him as he watched the rektor. "Why are there no women, rektor?"

"What?"

"Why are there only men in the Crib?"

"Arym, we don't have time for this."

"Tell me."

The rektor sighed with frustration. "It was an edict of Othel."

"But why?"

"We outgrew the need for gender parity."

"So, you don't need women?"

"No. They do not fit into our plan."

"How can the other half of human beings not fit into your plan?"

"Whether it was only men or only women that remained in the Crib makes no difference. The point is that sexual reproduction is obsolete—a distraction. The Crib's work is far too important to get complicated with gender and archaic modes of childbirth. Enough of this. Come with me at once."

"The Oath is meaningless. The Crib is a perversion of nature."

Tarysl sighed. "Arym—"

"Your task to find me has been in vain."

"Arym... you do not understand."

"Unfortunately, I do."

Tears brimmed the rektor's eyes. "Please. I've come all this way."

For a modicum of a moment, Arym wanted to return. Even with a full understanding of the falsehoods and depravity of the Crib, he was moved to compassion for his lost brothers churning their meaningless lives beneath the earth. Like dung beetles they had lived, and like dung beetles they would die. But then he remembered being imprisoned, when Protonix had visited him.

The arrow of time always moves forward, but the arrow is always curved.

There was a purpose in what Hawera had been doing—meaning in what Protonix had told him. Perhaps the astrocyst wasn't crazy—Beetro, not misguided. Arym recalled the thousands of inscriptions left on the walls of the Alchean tomb, atop Laser Falls. There was truth in those theorems—truth he would never find digging tunnels with the Cribmen.

"It was a mistake," Arym said, turning from the rektor.

"Arym, don't leave. Not now! You have much to learn about the power inside you!"

"Go back home," Arym said without turning. "I'm not your brother anymore."

He walked off, the pleas of Tarysl echoing down the alley.

Beetro had watched Galiaro work with the floating orbs for hours. Both Protonix and Neutrini bobbed up and down, watching the astrocyst's scribbles on the chalkboard, which was always followed by a heated debate. Galiaro thumped the workbench with his fist, gesturing to Protonix. "But why don't you know? You're an Alchean computer!"

Protonix had cast himself into the image of a man—hawkish

nose bisecting a stern face with light rays streaming from his visage. "That is not exactly accurate. While the Alcheans encoded and encrypted software onto me, they installed hard stops and limits to my database and capabilities so that I cannot be hacked."

"What kind of hard stops?"

"Harsh limits on their technology."

"So, what is the point of you?"

The proton scoffed, clearly offended. "What's the point of *you*, human? I am curator to the west Alchean tomb. My entangled partner, Neutrini, is curator to the east tomb."

Galiaro stroked his beard and then cast it aside. "They made you just to watch over their remains?"

"Not their remains... their mathematics. We oversee the judicial use of their technology. They sought to retain a usable script of their mathematics to a culture with the technological acumen to make use of them. They endowed future generations to perhaps achieve a fraction of the heights that they themselves achieved."

"Before they abandoned the planet?"

"Abandoned is a strong word, but yes."

"How generous of the Alcheans."

"Indeed," the proton said without irony.

Neutrini, too, had refracted into shafts of light—a languid woman appearing. "We do *not* need to endure this abuse, Protonix. I will hardly sit idle while this man insults the legacy of the greatest species that has graced these dimensions."

"If you're both essentially programmed for identical purposes, why are you so different from one another?" Beetro asked.

"Because," Neutrini replied. "The Alcheans endowed us with personhood. We are entangled—able to communicate simultaneously despite any distance—but we have our own intelligence and proclivities."

"So, you're self-aware?"

"Correct," the two protons responded in unison.

Galiaro clapped his hands together. "Precisely what we need. More self-aware machines." He shared a furtive glare with Beetro, which was not welcomed by the robot. "So, what, exactly, my dear protons, have you been doing here in my lab?"

"It was my understanding that you shared this lab with another astrocyst named Fallaro," Neutrini said.

"Yes."

"Where is he now?"

"You don't know?"

"No," Neutrini said. "Fallaro has not been seen in Orion for several years. Me and my entangled partner here decided we needed to take matters into our own hands regarding the expansion of the universe."

Protonix continued. "I was distressed to hear news from one of your traveling companions, Miss Hawera. I had compassion for the young woman and wanted to get her back home—or forward to her home. I also keep track of astronomical phenomena and was startled to realize that Saturn had lost several of its moons in one cataclysmic event."

Galiaro screwed his face. "You have access to a telescope?

"No."

"Then how did you observe this?"

"I went there."

"Went where?"

"To Saturn."

"You visited another planet? How?" Beetro asked.

"I can behave as a photon—albeit an exotic, engineered type—but a photon nevertheless. I travel as light. A round trip to Saturn takes me one hundred and sixty minutes."

Galiaro breathed heavily. "Have you... have you—"

"Gone further than the solar system?"

"Yes. I have..."

"And?"

"There is nothing. The universe has expanded as you have predicted. Me and my entangled partner here have attempted to predict the rate of expansion, and I must say, astrocyst, I am impressed with your understanding of the mathematics. I dare say the Alcheans would take you as an apprentice for perhaps a century before you would advance to more intermediate levels."

"Flattering."

"And so Neutrini and I have been attempting to derive a predictive model of the expansion."

"Good luck. I tried for decades."

"Indeed, astrocyst, but you did not possess the computing power of two entangled protons. We employ quantum computing and have been attempting to calculate the rate of expansion."

"Why do *you* care about all of this?"

Neutrini interrupted. "Perhaps my entangled partner wasn't clear... we have personhood. We care just as much as you about being expanded into oblivion."

Galiaro abruptly stood. He went to the window and gazed at the streets below. "It's pointless, anyways. This is all a futile exercise."

Protonix reabsorbed into a glowing orb and floated to him. "Not exactly. We find your creative outlook on the math quite valuable. Perhaps if we continue our calculating with the theorems you've introduced, we may make some progress."

"Don't you know all Alchean math?" Beetro interrupted. "From the tombs?"

"I'm afraid not. I do not possess the memory required to maintain that amount of data."

"Then just go back to the tomb. Take a look at the math and bring it back here."

"I have tried to return. I'm afraid the underground clone colony has set an outpost there."

"You can't just slip in?"

"No. It would appear they have warded the tomb against me—seem to have knowledge of my existence," Protonix said.

"Warded?"

"Yes. They have sealed the tomb from my influence with an electromagnetic field. I cannot return, and neither can Neutrini return to her tomb in the east."

"I said it's pointless!" Galiaro erupted, spittle flying from his lips. "Who cares if we know when the expansion will happen? Saturn is gone. Jupiter next. Then Mars. Then Earth. It will happen and it will probably happen soon. We—you, my pet robot, and you two lightbulbs are doomed."

Beetro ignored the insult. "So, why did you return here, Galiaro? What is it you hope to figure out with all the calculations we've been doing?"

Galiaro was silent for a moment and then said, "I hoped to find Fallaro here—to see if he figured out how to open the GeminArc. It is the only way off this rotting planet."

"The GeminArc..." Protonix said. "You wish to open the Alchean portal?"

"Yes, yes, keep up. I've already explained all this. I tried opening it years ago."

"But it has been sealed for several centuries."

"It was sealed," he said before clearing his throat for a full thirty seconds and then added, "before I opened it again."

Protonix streaked across the room in an instant and refracted an angry brow in front of his face. "You *opened* the GeminArc? Impossible."

"I'm afraid it is true. I opened it and it... did not go according to plan."

"Nonsense." Neutrini dismissed him and scuttled to the other end of the lab.

"Astrocyst," Protonix said with more diplomacy than his counterpart. "If you've learned anything about the portal, you know that only a tremendous amount of dark matter is required to create a singularity of a few nanometers."

"Indeed," he said, stroking his beard. He glanced at Beetro and nodded at the robot. "What do you think he's made of?"

Beetro looked down at his metallic skin, hints of silver and blue flecks sparkling in the radiant light from the protons who were now inspecting his surface.

"I don't believe it," Protonix said, scanning Beetro. "This cannot be."

"It be," Galiaro declared, a smirk painted on his face.

Beetro met Galiaro's eyes. "What? What am I made of?"

Galiaro stood and tapped on Beetro's skin. "Dark matter."

Protonix had refracted into an entire personage and stared at Beetro. "No such deposit of dark matter is known to exist anymore."

"Not to you," Galiaro said.

The only thing Beetro knew about dark matter was that a mere flake of it was worth the entire amount of a fiefdom in Helian. A flake of which Miree had tried to steal from Peles Castle but discovered never existed. "I'm made of dark matter?"

"Yes, my dear robot. I coated you with the stuff. Dark matter is rare, expensive, and heavy as a dozen steeds. I tempered your metal with it, strapped on legs, arms, and an operating system and intended you to be a walking key."

"To open the GeminArc," Beetro said.

"Correct."

Hawera gazed upon Beetro as if with news eyes, reaching out her fingers to his metal skin. He consented with a nod and she ran her fingertips across the glossy substance, her eyes both disbelieving and bedazzled. "Dark matter..." she said, reverence in her voice. "Very powerful. Very important."

Ribcage, too, now had her dirty fingers moving along his skin. "Neat!"

"Quite right, my time-bending dear," Galiaro nodded to Hawera, eyeing her. "I suspect your people are familiar with it?"

She nodded.

"And how, may I ask?"

"Make possible I travel futurepast."

"You are from the futurepast?"

She nodded.

A weird, thoughtful groan escaped the astrocyst's lips. "Many, many implications... I must think on this more."

"Must return to futurepast," she insisted.

"One astronomical problem at a time!" he snapped. "I can't just conjure dark matter from thin air. It is incredibly difficult to obtain both for geological and political reasons."

Hawera recoiled from the outburst and receded to the back of the lab.

"You may come in handy, my dear, if this all goes to pot. For now, we focus on the bot. He was made of dark matter to open the GeminArc—something that requires an enormous flux of gravitonic energy to even engage the accelerator."

"What went wrong?" Beetro asked. "If you opened the portal, why are we still here? Why didn't you leave to the innerspace?"

"Something I was wondering presently as well," Neutrini said, turning to the astrocyst.

Galiaro grimaced, stood, and walked to the window again. "I had come to some premature conclusions about the advanced gravimetric harmonics that the Alcheans used. I was able to activate the GeminArc but could not form a portal to the innerspace."

"You screwed it up," Beetro clarified.

"I did, yes."

"What happened?" both Neutrini and Protonix asked.

"The accelerator was activated—I'd perfectly measured the amount of dark matter and vector of the gravitonic flux needed. However, it turned out the interface of the GeminArc was more technical than I was anticipating. I had supposed the data entry needed to be trivial based on the math that I'd discovered from Alchean ruins—there are numerous written along the walls of Orion. But I was missing critical information about how to bend space specifically to open a wormhole to the innerspace."

"So, you aborted," Protonix said. Galiaro's pause served as his admission of guilt. "You opened it *anyway*?"

"I'd come so far. I worked for decades for the moment of opening the portal—of escaping the doom of the expansion. I was... I was very tired."

"Reckless, and probably drunk at the time," Neutrini hissed. "A reckless and foolhardy thing to do. You have no idea the things with which you trifle. One cannot simply drop a payload of dark matter into the arc and expect worlds to open. The GeminArc was run by hundreds of Alchean scientists. How could you expect to match their understanding of interdimensional travel?"

"What *happened*?" Beetro asked.

"I opened a portal."

"To where?"

"To... here."

"Would you please just tell us what happened? Enough of the cryptic talk."

"Through the portal, I saw... us. Both me and you, standing at another GeminArc, staring back at us. I stood in front, ripples of spacetime shimmering across the thin line between our worlds. You, robot, were standing behind me, creeping closer. I had assumed I'd opened into a parallel dimension—a next-door neighbor identical to our own. Yet there was time slippage—a theoretical phenomenon that I observed in the flesh. This could only mean I was staring back at a mirrored reflection—a broadcast of our native dimension yet just a few moments into the future. And that is when I saw you," he said, glaring at Beetro. "You ran me through with a sword."

"But I would never."

"But you *did*, yes. I only had moments to respond. I turned around and... there you were. Sword in hand, a secretive self-aware robot taking his chance to kill his creator. You had conspiracy brewing in that tin heart the moment I created you. I had a millisecond to act—and that was all I needed. I deactivated you remotely. The portal collapsed, and I was left alone, stuck on this doomed planet with a deactivated robot who'd just tried to murder me. I left the GeminArc, fearing I would do something far worse to spacetime. I couldn't bring myself to destroy you—my life's work. So, I buried you there, at the grounds of the GeminArc, and wandered into the nearest town to have myself a drink. Someone else evidently dug you up."

"You tore a hole," Protonix confirmed. "Instead of opening a portal, the arc backfired, and you tore a hole in spacetime. The time slippage was caused by the unbalanced gravitonic force that was never vented into another dimension. Because your dimension momentarily retained unbalanced gravity, time slowed down and the future was reflected back at you for one fleeting moment."

"Gravity slows down time?" Beetro asked.

Protonix and Galiaro shared a glance, and both answered, "Yes."

"And the opposite. Make something lighter, you speed up its time," Galiaro continued. "In ancient records, astronomers described interstellar phenomena where gravity became so intense, it condensed all matter into the size of an atom. A black hole, they called it. If one were to visit such a singularity, time would almost completely cease. I do believe my lightbulb friend here is correct when he asserts that I momentarily slowed time down as gravity condensed around your dark matter shell with nowhere for it to go. Time paused and the future was reflected to me through the portal. As far as tearing a hole in spacetime? A dubious assertion."

"A likely assertion given the amount of unvented gravity you funneled into a single spot," Neutrini said. "Spacetime cannot withstand that amount of gravity without bending and tearing."

Beetro interrupted the ensuing argument. "So, what do we need to do to get the GeminArc to function? To be able to vent gravity through the arc and open a portal?"

"I do not know," Galiaro said. "If I'd had access to these Alchean tombs, I would have had their complete gravimetric equations. With those, I believe I could get the GeminArc to function properly."

"And we could... evacuate Earth? Save people and robots from the expansion?"

"Conceivably. Yes."

"But you can't return to the tombs to retrieve the complete math?" Beetro asked the proton orbs.

"No," Protonix said. "As I said, they are warded with some sort of electromagnetic interference."

"So, what do we do? We need the Alchean formulas to understand how to run the GeminArc."

"We drink," Galiaro said before bringing a green liquid to his lips.

The conversation was interrupted by a commotion at the hatch. Arym, with surprising agility, had lifted himself from the alley below and stood, stoned-face, his eyes falling on Galiaro. In place of his typical slumped back, his shoulders were squared. Rather than wearing an uncertain brow, his face was cold, hard, calculating. Within his grasp was a leather-bound journal, well-worn with yellowed parchment. He lifted the journal and said, "I think I have what you're looking for."

FORTY

WHEN AT FIRST SHE thought the Reticulum pain dampener would be to her benefit, and even survival, Miree quickly realized her folly. Upon discovering that she was particularly insensate to his typical torture, Haldunt the Wire got creative. As if taking it as a personal challenge, he ensconced her body in layers of razored wires, latticed over her skin in a meshwork. After her legs, arms, and torso were clothed in wires, the questioning continued.

"You will tell me why you are in Orion."

The pain was still dampened, but the blood loss didn't stop. Yes, she could end things early—end the charade. Yet, by hiding the whereabouts of Beetro, she felt something she hadn't felt in quite a while—perhaps her entire life. Dignity. It was the satisfaction of finally suffering for something other than herself. Her entire life had been mostly suffering. Suffering without purpose. But now, Haldunt had given her the gift of suffering for someone else—a junkyard robot who could potentially help rescue everyone on the planet. She was not about to turn him over to the Kish.

Through blurry vision, she looked at him. "You need to know something, Haldunt."

"Tell me!"

"Do you know where I'm from?"

The question gave him pause. No Kish initiate was ever obligated to reveal the details of their life before joining. One of the great appeals of joining the Kish was the ability to shed the past self—the wayward warrior, the forsaken child, the sinner—and join the ranks of a spy network. "Where?" he asked, curiosity flooding his eyes.

"The Fifth Kingdom."

"Ah. Yes, I always suspected. I knew you had come from the far east somewhere."

"Do you know what they do in the Fifth Kingdom?"

"Besides closing their walls to outsiders? No."

"They make princes."

"So do many kingdoms."

"Not like the Fifth Kingdom, they don't."

Haldunt said nothing, lightly releasing the tension on his wires, his curiosity piqued.

"They have hundreds of queens. One king. Do you know how they choose their queens? No? You see the king's retinue hit the streets during the annual Entrusting. A ceremony when every household must present their eldest daughter at the doorstep of their home. Like a parade, the royal guard sweeps the streets, inspecting the girls—haunches, flanks, busts, jawlines—gums. A diversity of specimens is taken from their homes to live out the rest of their days in the royal court. What they neglect to tell the public is that the royal court is not so much a court but a personal brothel for his majesty. Brothel is not quite the word, either. Brothels usually don't have chains and locks to ensure the security of the product. Once a week, on the Day of Fertility, our king visits the court to imbue as many queens as possible with his royal seed. It is to ensure the permanence of the Fifth Kingdom—to ensure that the most qualified heir will emerge from a womb by way of maximizing as many wombs as possible."

"This is how royalty is treated where you're from?"

"This is how queens are treated in the Fifth Kingdom. For all their fertile life, the queens are kept in court, unable to leave. The queens are fed and live otherwise painless lives—treated with respect from the royal staff. They are handled with the care and respect you'd give to a crystal egg... something fragile that can otherwise be left on a safe shelf somewhere and brought out only when needed. And so, the queens are impregnated and give birth. As many times as possible. The current king has over two thousand children."

"And all these children are vying for the throne?"

"Yes. They compete before they even know they are in a competition. The moment they are born, the culling begins. The female offspring are given back to the homes where a daughter was taken, and the boys begin training. Through their childhood, the boys train as warriors in single-hand combat. On their fifteenth birthdays, they fight to the death. The victors fight one another once more until there is only one prince per age group. These princes grow up as potential heirs to the king. Once the king is on his deathbed, each rival prince fights in one grand deathmatch competition. The winner is the heir."

"A brutal if not effective process to achieve the strongest king."

"Sounds like you'd fit in just fine in the Fifth Kingdom."

"Why are you telling me all this, girl? You know what I want to know."

"I just wanted you to know that you are torturing a queen."

"More like a whore."

"Well said, Haldunt the Wire. In the Fifth Kingdom, a queen

is a whore. Don't you see now? My own country has done more to me than anything you can do to me. Your wires have only made it clear that I've been cut from fucking stone—chiseled, hardened, and weathered. And like any stone, I'm to be cast back. My usefulness to this world is now spent. I may have done some good with my last acts—maybe bringing an old drunk to reunite with his pet robot. I know it's not much, but maybe it's possible that it is everything. You'll find out after you kill me, I suppose. You will get no more information from me. Take me."

"Not until—"

"Just do it already! Can't you see I'm not going to tell you what you want to know? Don't you know when you've been defeated?"

The man was silent for a moment. He dropped his wires and gazed at her, his eyes searching hers. Bringing his lips to her ear, he whispered, "We've only just begun."

"You have to teach me first," Arym said, holding the leather-bound book in the crook of his arm. "I need to learn."

"Learn?" Galiaro said. "Learn what? You have etchings from the most advanced civilization in that book of yours and you expect me to teach you what it all means?"

"Yes."

"Don't be ridiculous, boy. We don't have time for any of this business, so let's see what you have." Both Protonix and Neutrini bubbled up beside the astrocyst as if in agreeance, waiting.

"No. You teach me. I do know some things—some engineering, some math, and computer technology. We have these things in the Crib. I'm not starting at zero. I can never go back from where I came from and... I have to have a purpose up here in the overworld."

"The over *what*?"

"I think," Beetro said as if detecting that Arym was near a breaking point. "What Arym means is that he would like to become an apprentice. An apprentice to an astrocyst."

"Bah!" Galiaro said. "Give me that book. Who knows how much time we have?"

"Please," Beetro said, putting a hand on Galiaro's arm. "Just tell him what you're doing as you're doing it."

"Fine. Give me the book." He snatched the journal from Arym's outstretched hand before him and the glowing protons pored over the pages, Arym looking over his shoulder.

"The arrow of time," Arym said as Galiaro began flipping through the pages. "What is it?"

The protons stopped bobbing up and down. Protonix said, "Ah, yes. I recall telling you something about the arrow of time."

"I suggest," Galiaro said, "that you ask that of your pretty bald friend over there. She's the one who seems to have... time-bending abilities. Had I more time, I'd be studying her instead."

Hawera's face flushed as the room turned to her. "It's called her Fourth," Ribcage said, coming to her defense. "And it helps me Jump. Just like when I'm closer to my mom."

"Who *is* this child?" Galiaro asked as if seeing Ribcage for the first time. "And what nonsense is she babbling on about? Does she need to be here?"

Beetro recalled his escape from Peles Castle. Ribcage had taken his hand while they stepped into that strange, stretched-out world. A world... missing something. "It's true. Rib, when she Jumps, goes to another place. She's taken me there. I felt like my body was stretching on forever. And it wasn't just me, the entire world seemed to go on forever in two directions, but there wasn't anything in front of me."

Galiaro now stood, inspecting the girl with growing interest. "Go on."

"It makes her disappear from everyone else and pop back into space somewhere else. Like she finds a shortcut through space. It's what she calls Jumping. Only, she can't do it here, away from the GeminArc—what she calls her mom."

Something close to horror overcame his face. "You've had a space jumping child who has a connection to the GeminArc this whole time and I'm only hearing about it now?"

"I absolutely already told you about her, but you seem to have selective hearing."

"And now that she's away from the GeminArc, she can't Jump?" A new horror overcame his face.

"Not until we found Hawera. When she opens one of those portals that connects with the near future, Ribcage can Jump again. But only if a portal is open."

"Her... Fourth?" Galiaro asked, finding a chair as if he'd fall over without it.

Ribcage nodded, putting an arm around Hawera. "Yep. Her Fourth. Me and her—we can get anywhere together."

"The girl can use her Fourth," Galiaro said more to himself than anyone else, "to open a portal in time. Time is the fourth dimension. When she does so, this little girl can then transport into a world that stretches on in only two directions?"

"Yes," Beetro answered.

"And this little girl gained this ability at the GeminArc? This can only mean one thing," Galiaro said. The room awaited his response as he gazed off.

"What?" Beetro asked.

"It confirms what I suspected. I tore a hole in spacetime when

I misused the GeminArc. This girl—this creature—must've... fallen out of it from a two-dimensional world. She fell through and gained a third dimension. Every time this young woman opens a portal with her Fourth, she tears a temporary hole in spacetime, allowing this two-dimensional creature momentary access to the two-dimensional world. This grants her the ability to have saltatory and episodic existence in our third-dimensional world."

"What?" Arym said. He shared a reciprocal and confused glance with Beetro.

Galiaro turned to Hawera. "What part of the timeline are you from?"

"The dark world," Arym answered.

"I am Lithusa," Hawera said. "I come from futurepast. Your future, at the end."

"When Earth has finally been flung from orbit," Galiaro finished. "Tell me then, future girl, when? And how are you here?"

"She's a butterfly," Arym said as if recalling the information. "Something she explained to me that I never understood. But I think I know now. She's what humans become. In the future. She's come back with her... mate. They've come back to flee the darkness of the future."

They had all formed a semi-circle around Hawera now. She finally stood, propping herself with her silver-tipped staff. "I am Lithusa. I come from futurepast. The finish of the world."

A silence swept the group as they considered her words.

"How much time do we have?" Galiaro asked.

"Do not know."

"How can you not know? You are from the future, are you not? Wait... Lithusa. I've heard of your people. You are not from the future. You're from a xenophobic tribe in the deep south. Where did you pick this girl up?" he asked Beetro.

Before Beetro could respond, Hawera answered, "My people but—my old people."

Galiaro threw up his hands. "Not surprised the girl can't speak Haenglish. She's from some backwater island that probably hasn't had outside contact in several centuries."

"Her ancestors," Arym offered, to which she nodded. "I think she means the current Lithusa are her ancestors. She is like a butterfly. We are like the... the—"

"Caterpillar," Ribcage offered.

"Yes. She's human but has... changed into something new. Hawera isn't lying. She came back through time, from the dark world, with her... mate."

A sullen look overcame Hawera. "Yas. Patwero. We come from futurepast. From the edge of time—the dark world. The end. Came back to start like new."

"This woman speaks truth," Protonix interjected. "She visited me in the tombs of the Alchean and told me her story. You see, the arrow of time always moves forward, but the arrow is always curved. It would seem the Lithusa—the modern Lithusa from the Isles of Ith—progressed down a separate line of evolution from you humans. They developed the hippocampus and limbic system—a more robust sense of memory and time. They discovered that, when paired with a ferromagnetic alloy, their abilities became enhanced."

Their gazes fell on her staff, the end covered with a crude metal—silver with drippings down the wood like candle wax.

"The discs!" Arym said. "When I first found her in Crater Valley. She was covered in metallic discs, all over her arms and legs."

Hawera nodded. "Yas. The Lithusa have time pusher. Use dark matter. Can go forward far. More far than with no machine."

"Her people live in the last days," Protonix continued. "The dark world. Earth, once it's flung from orbit."

"Dead," Hawera said. "Dead planet."

"Her and her mate were flung forward in a time accelerator that enhances their ability—her Fourth."

"Then why is she in her own past if she was flung forward?" Beetro asked.

"They are the same thing," Galiaro finally said. "The arrow of time is curved. If you travel far enough into the future, you circle back to the past. Time is one very long Mobius strip. Light, gravity—these things are eternal, traveling forward and preserved forever as their energy loops back to the past. It would seem this Lithusa's people have figured this out. They sent her to escape. To escape to the past and repopulate Earth before the expansion. Am I correct, my dear?"

Hawera nodded. "Yas! Yas! Accelerator broke. Not meant to be here. In this time. Meant to go back to begin time. Have children. Have more children who have more children."

"To live another Earth cycle until the expansion happens again," Galiaro said, stroking his fingers through his beard. "Interesting strategy. You can't stop the expansion, so you just press a big reset button on time."

"We saw your mate," Beetro said. "We saw a man—large discs around his arms—wandering around Helian."

"He probably drank the ground water and got the Poisoning," Ribcage said.

"Quiet, Rib," Beetro chastised. "For all we know, he's still safe out there."

A commotion began as Ribcage argued with Beetro and Hawera struggled to ask questions about the whereabouts of Patwero. "Everyone, quiet!" Galiaro said, pounding his fist on a lab bench. "Listen to me, very carefully," he said to Hawera. "When does the expansion happen?"

"Million years."

"Then why, my dear future girl, did Saturn just get flung out of its orbit?"

"Early. Expansion early."

"I know. I've known for most of my life. My question for you is why? What is the *difference*?"

"Do not know."

"Can you build an accelerator to get us to the futurepast?"

She shook her head. "No. Don't know how."

"Well," Galiaro said, turning from her and reaching for Arym's sketch journal. "Had I another decade, I could perhaps figure out how to use this girl's ability to get us out of this mess, but I'm only one astrocyst. It would seem we are in the exact same place that we were five minutes ago." He opened the book and began reading with a very audible sigh.

FORTY-ONE

A DAY PASSED.

Galiaro and the protons pored over Arym's sketchbook. They rewrote the math, covering the chalkboards with new equations while Protonix and Neutrini worked the math out through quantum calculations. The deliberations continued unceasingly, boring all those that were not involved. Arym sat at the astrocyst's side throughout the day, absorbing and asking questions with a new boldness that Beetro had not yet observed.

"I believe we can open the GeminArc," Neutrini declared.

Galiaro scowled. "What! We haven't even calculated the graviton threshold that is required to open the wormhole *without* tearing a hole in spacetime. You want to repeat what I already did? There is a gaping hole in space sitting in the middle of the GeminArc. Were we to create another, space would either collapse or stretch. I haven't decided which will happen yet."

"I tend to agree with the astrocyst, sister," Protonix said after refracting into his humanoid shape.

"We don't have to know the threshold," Neutrini explained.

"These calculations were only for selecting specific coordinates for interstellar travel back during the Alcheans. To reach the innerspace, we can be blunter with our calculations. We only need to achieve the minimum threshold to activate the gate. It is clear right here," she said, pointing to Arym's sketchbook. "The Alcheans maxed out the threshold to infinity and this opens to the innerspace."

Galiaro and Protonix shared furtive glances before Protonix said, "That is a dubious assertion."

More boring debate ensued.

It was then Beetro noticed that Hawera and Ribcage were missing. He spun around, hearing his name at the hatch. It was Hawera, worry written on her face. "Come," she said, motioning outside. He followed her down the hatch to the invisible pegs in the wall. Instead of continuing downward, Hawera went up, gingerly feeling at pegs that continued toward the top of the narrow alleyway. Beetro followed her as she leaped into open air, grabbing hold of the top of Galiaro's invisible lab that hung high in the air, suspended above the alleyway. Ribcage was already there, a serene look on her face.

"She let me Jump!" she said, a toothy grin stitched on her face. "She used her Fourth and—bam! I Jumped right up here. It felt so *good*."

Below his feet, the ground of Orion was dozens of meters beneath. If a passerby were to look up, they'd see three figures floating in thin air. The view atop of the invisible lab was magnificent. He saw the curvature of Orion running away toward the surrounding tundra. It was there, at the base of the city, he discovered a considerable army had accumulated. Deluvius' soldiers were organized into camps, various machines of destruction studded their ranks—machines of fire and metal outfitted with artillery. Their vantage point granted an almost aerial view of the remains of the port. The vanishing sea had left the once prestigious port in ruins—a hollowed-out beach that receded and dropped off into craggy clefts of once buried reefs. The view reminded him of his terrible dreams of war.

"Look," Hawera said, bringing his attention to the top of the city. The egg shape of Orion continued along a natural curve, cut with deep grooves along its surface until coming to a rounded point at the apex. It was there, floating just above the surface of the city, that Beetro saw the unmistakable silver Wing hovering noiselessly.

"Deluvius," he spat.

"What do you think he's doing up there?" Ribcage asked.

"I don't know. But he's wrapped up in all of this. I'm sick of all the coincidences—sick of not knowing what's going on. I don't know about you two, but I'm tired of feeling like a tool." Feeling like a creature that was designed to be nothing more than a key—a key that would've been a murderer if given a second more to live. Could he really have been such a monster as to want to murder his very creator? He hadn't yet let Galiaro's tale fully settle in his mind. He clenched his fists, angered that he was what he was—frustrated that he couldn't be more. There was also something new growing inside him—an inexplicable urge to right wrongs without asking questions. Vengeance, he supposed. It was a thick feeling, hot and undeniable.

"Go find out," he told them.

Hawera and Ribcage looked at him. "Up there?" Hawera asked.

"Yes. Use your Fourth, take Ribcage. You can sneak up there and find out what that bastard is doing. He's wrapped up in all of this. I don't know about you two, but I've had just about enough of being kept in the dark. We need answers. Go." He was uncertain of how they would take his command. But when he saw them nodding along, he knew. He knew he was their leader, and they would do what he said. He couldn't deny that it felt good.

"Let's go!" Ribcage said, jumping up and down. The invisible laboratory rocked under their feet—a disgruntled cry from Galiaro falling off with the wind.

"Rib. No messing around like at Peles Castle, got it?"

The girl went wide-eyed as if playing dumb.

"Don't be seen, don't be heard. You're a ghost. Understand?"

She nodded with giddy excitement.

"And take Arym," Beetro said. "He deserves some answers, too."

"What was all that noise?" Galiaro hissed as he turned from the chalkboard.

"Arym," Beetro said to the man from the Crib. "Hawera and Ribcage are waiting for you down in the alley. I think you can take a break from studying to go help them."

"Help them with what?"

"A mission."

"What kind?"

"Reconnaissance. Meet them and they'll fill you in on the details." Arym collected his gear and left without another word through the hatch.

"It *will* work," Neutrini asserted, continuing an argument. "We have all the information we need. We are only wasting time at this point."

"I've already told you," Galiaro said, turning from Beetro. "We're going to make the same mistake I already made. We can activate the GeminArc, yes. But how do we vent all the gravity?

How can we be sure that we won't cause another tear—or worse. We need more time to study."

Neutrini continued arguing, "And how much more time do you think we have? Would you like to wait for when we lose Jupiter? I assure you, astrocyst, you cannot see the solution, but we can. We must activate the gate immediately. You know yourself that the expansion is happening. Now. As we speak, our very orbit is in decay. We cannot delay."

Galiaro turned to Protonix, who was silent throughout the debate. "While I don't have the confidence of my counterpart here," he said with diplomacy. "I do believe we can make some progress if we continue our studies at the GeminArc. I may not share her zeal to open the gate immediately, but I do share her haste. We should return to the GeminArc to begin experimental runs."

"And how are we to return? I believe there is a siege going on outside the city. Shall we stroll through an army and make our way through Gargantua Forest, over Crater Valley, and through the nuclear fallout of Helian? We had a hard-enough time actually getting to the city."

"We?" A belated thought finally occurred to Beetro. "How *did* you get here, anyway."

He waved a hand. "With the girl, there."

"What girl?"

He strained his neck, staring at the ceiling as if it would aid his recall. "You know the one. She's around here. Stocky lass—might be fair if she tried a little harder. Angry. All the time complaining. Miree! That's it—ha! Trying to test an old man's memory—"

"*Miree*? You came with... she's alive?"

"Yes, she... wasn't she just here?" He glanced around as if he'd just lost a coin from his pocket.

"No. Miree is not here. Last I saw her, she was being dragged away by the Reticulum in the Meteor Mountains."

"Ah, yes. That is where we first met. We left there and... well, my memory is a little foggy. But we arrived here in good spirits after almost being swept out of the Chronicle Sea."

"Miree is in the city?"

"I already told you, yes."

"When did you last see her?"

"Hmm." He brought a finger to his lips.

"Think!"

"I know she was worried about the Kish."

"Why?"

"She was one of them at one time. She stole from them. The girl makes enemies around every corner. Perhaps they snatched her up."

Beetro wheeled around and headed toward the hatch.

"And where are you going?" Neutrini asked, a new sternness blooming in her voice.

"You keep working on how to open the GeminArc. Be ready to leave in a day."

Galiaro wasn't pleased. "Where are you going, robot? We need you to open the GeminArc."

"Don't call me robot," he insisted before disappearing through the hatch.

Once again, Miree had no idea how much time had passed. Haldunt was relentless. The man had woven wire through her skin—threaded in and out, each loop puckering together like a row of fleshy buttons. The Reticulum pain dampeners were still doing their work, but she felt pressure, blood loss, and her life force slowly oozing from her body. Every time she lost consciousness, she hoped for release but was shattered when she opened her eyes again to the single, naked lightbulb hanging above her body.

"I am impressed," Haldunt finally said, voice thick with exhaustion. "You may be my finest pupil."

She said nothing. She hadn't in quite some time. There was nothing left to say. Yet, she remained. The pain dampener had been a curse, not a blessing. Without it, she would've died hours ago—days ago? She was entirely unclear how long she'd been in Haldunt's crucible. She'd narrowed her mind to only the mental tableaus that meant anything to her... Lucindi, twilight in the Fifth Kingdom before she was taken on the day of Entrusting. Her father—now faceless, now nameless. She had believed that he was good, but statistically speaking, he likely was not. Besides, how could a father not fight for his daughter to be taken away?

She thought about the decay of the universe, the expansion—Galiaro choking on corn while they were imprisoned by the Reticulum. She hated him at the time but, shockingly, thought back on helping him with... fondness? And then she remembered what he told her outside Portolo. Something about having a calling, about belonging somewhere. He'd called her by her name, a softness in his eyes. The poor man was probably dead or dying. Beetro likely still wandering in Meteor Mountains or worse... deactivated, corroding, forgotten to time. But... maybe.

Maybe.

A new voice echoed from behind the door, "Haldunt!"

Haldunt grimaced, flicking the current off and moved to the door. "I told you, never *interrupt me.*"

The door creaked open, revealing a woman. "You need to finish up with her."

"I'm done when I'm done."

"We've got someone new—something new you need to extract

intel from as soon as possible. Finish up!" The woman slammed the door, leaving them alone.

"Talk!" he yelled at Miree. "As soon as you tell me what I need to know, I will end you quickly. I promise you that. This can all be over." The man looked exhausted.

Good.

Another knock came at the door.

"What!" Haldunt protested, turning the current off once more. "I *cannot* operate when I'm being interrupted like this!" The door opened further, revealing a figure...

But it wasn't the Kish.

"Who—" But before Haldunt could say more, he was liquefied. Some force had seized him, convulsing his body. With arms flailing and head whipping, his skin boiled from his frame, spraying fat and follicles throughout the cell. The sinews beneath melted. The proteins denaturing, unfolding, forgetting their function. As his body collapsed, the white of his bones emerged through the amorphous organic mass that had once been Haldunt the Wire. The air filled with the putrid stench of rotting flesh. Haldunt the Wire had ceased to exist within a millisecond.

Miree squinted, trying to see her would-be rescuer through unfocused eyes.

"Did you think we wouldn't find you?" That voice. Cutting, icy, and thick with disdain. There was only one person who spoke with equal parts arrogance and ignorance.

Ria.

Miree spat. "Just fuck off already."

Ria gave a mirthless laugh as she stepped into the cell, a myriad of greens and reds illuminating her hooded face. "Quite clever—and stupid—deactivating the governor chip. I suppose that worthless astrocyst helped with that. We'll find him, too. Xy probably already has him in a net right now."

Miree's eyes were drawn to the woman's waist, a scabbard peeking from within her cloak. The hilt was there—The Swordless Hilt.

Ria noticed her eyes on the blade. "Ah, yes, I found that which you were not worthy to brandish. The clueless Kish had it piled with the rest of their worthless iron. Ancient Torbad tech is too precious for this city."

"What happened to you?"

Ria's eyes went wide. "What... happened to me?"

"Yes, what happened to you? Why are you the way you are?"

Ria's face tightened with a flash of fury but then relaxed ever so slightly. "I find it easier to be this way."

"You mean, a monster?"

The Reticula sighed, the first genuine sound Miree had heard from the woman. "It becomes much easier to live with the governor chip when you align your desires with the Reticulum. Living is more tolerable this way. Otherwise..."

"I get it. Life is hell with that thing buzzing in your brain if you fight it." They shared a surprising moment of amicable silence. "I wonder if we could've been allies... friends even," Miree mused. "Seems you had the same steaming pile of life that was served to me. I bet you miss your people in the Torbad."

A tear streaked down Ria's face before turning sour once more. "Do you think the Reticulum just forgets about her investments? That she would just let you, her property, leave without any attempts to recover you?"

"This world screwed me from the beginning," Miree ignored her. "But that's not what made me what I became. I did that to myself—forgot what it was like to care about someone and only became concerned with my own experience. I would do it differently, I think, if I had another chance."

"Can't wait to put a muzzle on that mouth of yours." Ria stood beside her, the Swordless Hilt in hand. "I'm impressed that he didn't kill you long ago. Shame. I would've loved to recruit him. Bet you were grateful for the pain modulator. Brought all that torturing to a dull roar, didn't it?" She produced another device in her palm and placed it on Miree's forehead. "Well, how about now?"

The pain dampener shut off.

A tidal wave coursed through her body. It felt like a million whippings lashing over her in a single moment. She couldn't think, couldn't speak—couldn't breathe. There was no way she wasn't dead already.

A smile crept up Ria's face. "Beautiful. But don't worry. She will take away the pain, take away the worries, take away *you* from yourself. You're precious equipment to her and she needs you. She is lonely... very lonely—needs connection once more. We will help her reign once more over the planet, connecting all of humanity in a vast network again. You are a cog in the wheel of the world."

Miree heard nothing. After an eternity of darkness, she opened her eyes, her ocular implants telescoping in and out. Ria's hooded face was above her. "Take me."

"Oh, I will."

But Miree wasn't talking to her—she was talking to god or the gods or whoever it was that would listen. "*Take me.*"

A clatter in the hallway drew Ria's attention. "We must go now. The Kish will return." She bent to lift Miree but stopped when a figure appeared at the doorway. Ria's hand went to the Hilt. Before she could brandish the weapon, the cell lit with a blinding whiteness. A cry escaped Ria's mouth before her voice was swallowed up in a beam of brilliance—a white beam of pure, raw energy bursting from the doorway.

Then darkness and silence.

Ria fell to the ground. Her shoulder and chest singed with

smoked char. Her right arm was now gone, blown apart. Despite the brisk dismemberment, she appeared alive with ragged breathing.

Miree squinted at the doorway, confusion reigning. A blue robot stood in there, indigo eyes at a tilt. "I'm sorry," Beetro said.

"Me, too," Miree cried, choking on a sob. "Me too."

FORTY-TWO

CLAP!

"Hey!"

Pop!

"Stop! I need to rest—"

Clap!

Ribcage acted like she couldn't hear Arym protesting. She wouldn't stop—couldn't stop. Not now, after feeling freer than in her entire life. This is what she was supposed to do—what she was *born* to do...

Jump.

Yes, Jumping around the mean kids back in Korthe, knocking them over or stealing their food—that was all fun. But Jumping from one edge of Orion to the next, flying over the canals of the city was next-level stuff. She felt like a god, peering down on the tiny idiots swinging swords and shooting guns. As Hawera opened one portal of her Fourth to the next, Ribcage stretched through, her body—her entire existence—flattening to a thin noodle to weave through three-dimensional space as if hopping in and out of existence.

"Hey, idiots!" she yelled to the figures below, drawing attention. She wiggled her arms in the air before Hawera shot another blue jet light from her staff, opening yet another portal into the near future. As soon as the portal opened, Ribcage felt the hole as if the entire world of space and time was draining through the single point. It was a gate for her, allowing her access to the flat, noodlely world where she could slide through objects like parchment sliding between furniture.

"Stop!" Arym demanded, snatching his hand away from her. "I'm getting dizzy!"

"Come *on*," she complained, her patience evaporating. "We need to keep going."

"How can you keep doing this? Popping in and out of space and into that... that... what is that place? I feel like my entire body is about to be stretched into nothing. You actually like this?"

Ribcage grinned.

"You're a crazy little goblin girl."

She nodded, grabbed his hand, and Jumped again.

Clap!

They'd vanished from three-dimensional space, the elements of their bodies instantly losing a dimension and decaying into a world of flattened geometry. Her vision remained intact—the mechanics of her three-dimensional eyes translating into an elongated version of itself. Dimensionless light streamed in single sheets of photons, filtering throughout a world that, instead of being compacted into an extra third dimension, now fractured off for millions of light-years in a single direction. Strands of dimensionless matter filtered through her vision as she leaped from peak to trough and back again.

Pop!

They materialized back into three-dimensional space, now several streets away from where they'd been moments before. Hawera was several streets over, looking back on them, extended staff maintaining the open portal in space through which Ribcage could Jump.

"How the hell do you know where you're going in there?" Arym asked, catching his breath. "It's all just bright light and lines bobbing up and down!"

She shrugged. "I dunno. It's where I'm from. It's what my mom is. I just know my way around. See that ledge over there? I know exactly what it looks like when it's all squished flat and I just hop right over to it."

"Hmm, I guess I kind of get it."

"You probably don't but okay."

"No, no. It's like where I'm from. Underground. We have tunnels that go everywhere. They're probably confusing to someone who's not from there, but to me? I know exactly where everything goes—could get around with my eyes closed."

Hawera motioned for them to keep going.

"Come on!" Ribcage said, taking his hand once more.

Clap!

In a matter of minutes, they had circumnavigated a quarter of the egg-shaped city. While Ribcage and Arym Jumped through space, Hawera was jumping through space *and* time. Each time she opened a portal, Ribcage remotely accessed the hole in space —acting as a sort of pop-off valve into lower-dimensional space. Once she Jumped, Hawera walked through her own Fourth portal and reopened dozens of meters away. Once she emerged, several seconds had passed while the act was simultaneous for her.

"Seems like she can open portals only as far as she can see," Arym commented as they watched her work. The process did appear taxing. Hawera tightened her jaw and grunted with every forward thrust of her staff, expending some sort of mental energy with every portal made. Arym stood in silence, watching her move.

"Get over it," Ribcage said.

"Over it?"

"Over her."

"I'm not... what are you saying?"

"She doesn't like you, dirt boy."

Hawera motioned once more after creating a new portal. '*Go!*' she mouthed, clearly wanting to be done with the escapade and arrive at their destination—the dome at the top of the city.

They moved vertically, Jumping through each portal at a time, the dome progressively getting larger as they came back into three-dimensional space. A harsh glare rippled across the Alchean alloy surface of Orion. The sun hung high in the sky—an enormous ball of fire that covered more than double its usual expanse in. Scattered noise sounded beneath their feet of arguing, gunfire, and even the occasional *pop* of an incendiary. A glittering aircraft, the Wing, floated noiselessly above the dome.

Hawera stepped out of a Fourth portal several seconds before Ribcage Jumped back into normal space. She sank to her belly, inching forward toward the lip of the canal that appeared just before the domed structure.

Ribcage and Arym Jumped just behind her. "Keep going!" Ribcage yelled.

Hawera shushed her and brought a finger to her lips and then pointed down. "People," she warned. Arym and Ribcage slumped to their stomachs and joined her at the lip, peeking down. The walls of the canal sloped downward until meeting one another on a concave floor, forming an almost perfect bowl shape. A slot, the width of a few people abreast, had been hewn within the bowl—an archway leading to massive doors. Opposite this archway, another had been made, the entrance from the rest of Orion below. Within the bowl, men and women bedecked with Alchean laser rifles held a defensive position at the entrance. Several soldiers rappelled from the Wing above. Once the perimeter had been secured with a few errant shots down the long tunnel leading to the rest of the city, a final figure descended from the Wing, cloaked in black.

"Deluvius," Ribcage whispered.

Arym squinted. "That's him? The guy in charge of the army that attacked my people?"

Hawera snapped her fingers at them and put one vertical finger to her lips.

They watched as General Deluvius touched down on the surface, his boots thick with rubber tread. A black cloak that hung neatly around his neck billowed dramatically as he inspected his soldiers and their defensive line. With arms at his hips and a skintight ballistic suit running from neck to feet, Ribcage thought he looked rather like a dancer. Back in Korthe, there was an annual festival at Mercy Plaza where women dressed in skintight clothing and pranced about, sheets of silk twirling around their nimble bodies. Deluvius was in that very plaza once, dressed like a dancer. But he did no dancing.

"Luci," she said under her breath.

"What?"

"Shh!" Hawera scolded them once more.

One of the captains approached the general and saluted. "General Deluvius, sir! We have secured the perimeter."

"Casualties?"

"None, sir! The Kish are not a technological match to your army, sir!"

"Don't be a fool. Technology isn't everything. The Kish know this place far better than our army. They can and will employ guerrilla tactics once we advance on the city. Why do you think we've started a siege? We must cut off their resources and see that they starve. The Kish are clever, resilient, and vicious. As soon as you underestimate them, you'll suddenly be in a cell being tortured by Haldunt the Wire."

The captain could hardly conceal her confusion. "Sir, forgive my ignorance. If we are choosing a siege, then—"

"Why are we here right now at the top of the city?"

She nodded.

"This," he said, raising his arms to the arched doorway, "is an Alchean temple. We must ensure that it is secure from the Kish. You will be stationed here until we break the Kish. We must hold these temple grounds at all costs until our full army can secure the rest of the city."

The captain walked to the arching entrance to the temple and gazed at the sealed doors. "What's in there?"

"That is a very good question, one that I intend to find out soon. I believe of all their ruins, Orion is the most important. Beyond those doors is the seat of their power—our power to take final control. It is the key."

"A key to what?"

"A key to Earth. Look around you, captain. The stars are falling, the sun grows impatient. We may not have much time to take control of this planet."

"General, how do you know all this?"

"Study, my dear captain. A lifetime of study." He joined her at the entrance and ran his hand along the greyish-blue alloy of the temple doors, a surface that seemed near contiguous with the surrounding walls.

"I don't see no hinges, doorknobs—nothing. How we getting in?"

"Attrition."

"Sir?"

"The Alcheans designs were purposeful. Their secrets are guarded well with an advanced alloy. But it can be broken. We saw it ourselves in the tomb by the Meteor Mountains. Mere thieves blew the doors wide open. Now that the merchant council of Orion has been destroyed by the Kish, along with their silly superstitions about desecrating Alchean ruins, we can break these doors once we have control of the city. We will open these doors and have access to incredible planetary power."

"And what about the Gemi—Gema—the arc?"

"The GeminArc is nonfunctional. We must abandon hopes of following the Alcheans or opening the gateway to other star systems. It will not work."

"Should we move our soldiers out from the arc then?"

"I'm afraid so. Bring the rest of our reserves here to aid in the siege."

"Yes, sir!" She saluted and left the general gazing at the sealed doors.

Above, Hawera shook Arym's arm, motioning for them to leave.

"Ribcage, let's go," he whispered to the girl who was still flat on her belly, staring down at the general. Both Hawera and Arym crawled away from the edge of the wall, Ribcage hadn't budged. Arym crawled back to her and whispered, "We're done here. We know why they're here. Let's go report back to Beetro and Galiaro."

"Right," she said, nodding.

Together, they scrambled away from the ledge and stood once they were out of sight of the Alchean temple gates below. Hawera lifted her staff, pointed it at the horizon, and grunted. A flash of blue light leaped from her fingertips to the silver at the end of the staff. A millisecond later, a lance of blue energy sprang from the end of the staff and shot forward like a javelin disappearing where a portal formed. Ribcage investigated the portal, a swirling riot of distorted space and refracted color. Arym grabbed her hand. "Come on," he said. "Jump."

She nodded and they vanished.

Her body was stretched into near infinity, the loss of the third dimension translating into the same mass extending in one vertical plane in opposite directions. Lines sifted through her vision as she moved, somehow still tethered with the two-dimensional Arym. Their only direction was forward, up, or down as the lines bobbed. The lines started to condense, gathering their extended matter as they bulged back out into a third dimension. In a flash, the matter had coalesced, spitting them back out into normal space. Finding herself on her knees, Ribcage stood. She stared at the chest of a man cloaked in black. She looked up and locked eyes with...

General Deluvius.

With surprising poise, the general gazed at the two of them as if expecting them.

Two things happened at once—the Alchean temple gates vanished, exposing dark recesses within, and Ribcage was moving at the general who was too distracted to notice the blood-thirsty child. "The temple doors... how have they opened?" the general asked in awe as all guns turned to the new intruders. Ribcage Jumped, missed a barrage of laser energy, leaving a residue of char and heat. Before Deluvius could utter another word, she Jumped back to his left side, her arm already extended, the hilt of a blade stuck firmly in his gut.

"That's for Luci," she said, pointing to the blade. "Uh—again."

"Gah!" he cried, curling to his knees, muttering curses and incomprehensible commands.

A smile, equal parts devious and delighted, painted the girl's face as she grabbed hold of Arym to leave the ensuing chaos to roil on without her.

Clap!

"She did *what?*" Miree heard Beetro raise his voice in a way she wouldn't have thought him capable. She still hadn't moved yet, not even daring to get to her feet. A trickle of sunlight from the window encouraged her—convinced her that it was no dream. The torture had happened as evidenced by the thousands of cuts along her body, but the rescue was also real. Here she was, staring up at iron rafters warmed by scattered sunlight filtering through a lab.

"Did you kill him?" she heard Beetro ask. That got her attention. "And how did the temple gates suddenly open?" Miree propped herself on her elbows, gasped, and then sank back to the cot. Breathing deep was hard because everything reeked of mildew. The sheets around her, the pillow, the bedding—the entire lab stank like an old man. The old man, perhaps, who was seated at her side.

Galiaro spoke. "You've awoken."

"You're not dead."

"I don't do that."

"Die?"

Galiaro nodded. "I'm an astrocyst. Made of too fine of stock."

"There's no way you made it out of that tavern sober."

"I really don't recall."

"It'll kill you, you know."

"What's that now, my dear?"

"The drink. And stop calling me 'dear', old man."

"No faster than the Kish will kill you."

"Good point. Help me sit up." She winced as he propped her up against the wall. She was prepared for the pain but was surprisingly feeling better.

"I must apologize that we didn't come sooner for you. I thought you were here among us—had slipped my mind that I hadn't seen you."

"Shocker."

"I've recharged the implants in that skull of yours."

"Ah. That's why I'm not screaming right now."

He furrowed his enormous eyebrows.

"Pain dampeners. The Reticulum put them in. It's the only reason I'm alive right now."

"Ah, yes, that explains the implants I noted that are studded along your upper thoracic spine. They must attenuate the spinothalamic tract to nociceptive stimulus."

"Yeah. That."

"Clever people, the Reticulum. They understand... many things. Having centuries' worth of encyclopedic knowledge helps. If the galaxy wasn't dying, I'd worry about them taking over the land."

After arguing for a bit with Ribcage, Beetro joined them. His eyes dilated and hummed with indigo light. That skin—a brilliant, speckled blue with a swirl of black—shimmered in the sunlight. The blue had dulled slightly since she last saw him. She remembered him lying there in Korthe with all the junk. He *was* junk—just another garbage bot to dismantle. But Lucindi had stopped her. Miree looked on the bot with new eyes. Before her was not only a powerful weapon but something else. A mechanical person who cared enough to rescue her.

"How?" she asked, her eyes telescoping as she spoke.

"Easy. I walked up to the nearest Kish guard and told them that I knew all the tactical secrets of General Deluvius. Turns out they were looking for me anyway. So, they threw me in a dungeon, which is exactly where I knew you'd be if they hadn't killed you already." There was a glint in his eyes in the same way a human feigns modesty.

"So, you just blew cell doors down until you found me?"

He held a peevish pause and added, "It only took two. I almost didn't make it from the paralysis though. I've gotten better at controlling the output and burning off less water."

"Blew doors down?" Galiaro asked.

Beetro shrugged, offering a cool coyness as an answer.

"Don't play dumb with me, robot. I know what you're capable of. You think you were hiding that from me?"

"I—"

"Think you can walk around doing whatever you want? Blowing down doors?" A twinge of anger rose in the astrocyst's voice.

"No—"

"I think that's why you killed me—why you were going to kill me. Power. Nothing but power hunger. You knew that dark matter gave you abilities to manipulate light and it was your plan all along, wasn't it? Wipe out your creator and then go about just doing whatever you wanted?"

"Not at all. I would never do that."

"Sounds like you just did whatever the hell you wanted with the Kish. Blowing down doors and all."

"B-but I didn't kill anyone."

"So, is killing the only thing you can do wrong with your power?"

"I use my photonics to help people—"

"*Photonics?* My, what an adorable name." He crouched next to Beetro, bristled and with bloodshot eyes. "Just listen to me, robot. You've been self-aware for nigh on one month. You think you know the first thing about what is right and what is wrong?"

"And you *do*?" Miree shot back at Galiaro. "You're the one who's been a soaking drunk for the last ten years in some backwater town in Helian. At least Beetro made up for leaving me behind. He came back for me. That's not nothing—that's something."

An uncomfortable silence arose between them. Beetro broke it by asking Galiaro, "How does it work?"

"Your... *photonics*?" he mocked.

"Just tell me. Please."

"Mass and light are inversely, but disproportionately, related. Next question."

"But what does that mean?"

"Mass and light are two sides of the same coin. Hmm, no, that's not right. They are... two sides of the same pyramid."

Beetro looked at Miree. "He explained it to me," she said, twirling her hand. "But I didn't get it either."

"A drop of mass—the point of the pyramid—is proportional to an enormous amount of light and, therefore, energy—the bottom, square part of the pyramid. You are coated with dark matter, thereby granting you with an immense amount of mass at a single point. Somehow, you are able to transfer photons into amplified thermal energy by way of the dark matter that coats your body."

"I absorb light," Beetro explained.

"Yes, that would make sense."

"And then just—release it."

"This is consistent with my theory. The dark matter behaves as some sort of translational energy sieve. You can take just a few photons and translate them into tremendous energy with your... photonic power. Dammit, that actually is a good name for it."

"And it completely zaps my water supply that runs my body.

If I use too much, it all evaporates, and I'm paralyzed right after." He looked at his creator as if he was to blame for the oversight.

"Well, I didn't *design* you to actually do this thing. Can't blame me for the design flaw that your hydro capillary system fries every time you shoot thermal energy from your palms."

"What I don't understand is that I'm heavy but I'm not *that* heavy. A mountain has more mass than me and it can't harness photonic power like me."

Galiaro shook his head with eyes rolled. "You're not just made of matter. You're made of *dark matter*. Don't you know what the difference is?" He looked at Miree.

"You know we don't, so just get on with it," she complained.

"It is a matter that exists in all dimensions at one time. It shares the same matter without all of it spilling into one dimension at a time. You can draw on enormous mass—likely equivalent to the matter of many galaxies—converting photons from our dimension into thermal energy. It is the same dark matter that is able to open the GeminArc by bending space with its shared, multidimensional gravity."

They continued to look at him.

The astrocyst threw up his hands. "I am wasting my breath on cretins."

"We get it, we get it," Miree said. "The bot's got fancy light power because he weighs a shit ton."

"No—"

"Ugh, why does it *smell* in here?" she said, shedding her sheets with a kick.

"This lab is quite old. Upkeep hasn't been what it deserves, unfortunately." The astrocyst ran his finger along a table, collecting dust on his fingernail.

Miree stood but then collapsed on the floor.

"Whoa!" Beetro helped her up, grabbing her arm prosthesis.

"What did they do to your *arm*?"

Once the blood returned to her ears, she responded. "They screwed a useless hunk of metal directly into my bone marrow. I've no clue what it does. Must be broken."

"Can you take a look at it for her?" Beetro asked Galiaro. "Might be useful."

But Galiaro was oblivious to their words, still rubbing the dust between his fingers. "So dirty, but..." He then glanced around the room, eyes moving over the shelves, lab benches, and glassware.

"Galiaro?"

"Yes?" he said, broken from his reverie.

But then Ribcage was in their faces, inspecting Miree with a finger on her chin. "You lived," she remarked as if lamenting the outcome of a game.

"Despite my best efforts."

"I'm not giving the scarf back."

"It was a gift. You don't have to give it back."

"Why did you abandon us?"

The girl was actually a tad frightening. Miree recalled a certain amount of bottled vengeance the street urchin released on the general for killing Lucindi. The girl undoubtedly had a miles-long enemy list stashed away somewhere and Miree wasn't entirely certain that she hadn't made that list. "I'm sorry. There's nothing else to say."

Ribcage was perplexed by the words as if it was the first she'd heard of an apology. "Is she back with us?" she asked Beetro without releasing a glare from Miree.

"Of course. She's one of us, Rib."

"Who... who did you kill?" Miree asked, a new fear budding about this little girl who had the ability to vanish into thin air.

"The general," she said, sucking her teeth and flipping out a small dagger she kept at her waist.

"You stabbed him... *again*?"

She nodded with an almost psychopathic, even cadence. "It was easy."

Beetro sighed. "It's not what we planned. You were supposed to get reconnaissance on what he was doing up at the dome and not be seen."

"I did that. But then I just added the extra thing at the end."

"Stabbing someone isn't just an extra thing."

"I didn't stab *someone*. I stabbed the general. Again. It was easy. He's probably dead now and our problems are over. We won forever."

"You saw him die?" Miree asked.

Beetro shook his head. "They Jumped out of there before they could see what happened after she stuck him in the stomach. Rib," he said to her, "I don't think I can trust you anymore."

"But he killed Luci!"

"Yes, we know. But there is a bigger picture here. Like, why was he here in Orion? What was he doing in Helian? He has Alchean technology and probably knows a little more than we do about activating the GeminArc. Maybe he's even tried already."

"Does not work he say," a new voice emerged from the other side of the lab. Miree watched the most beautiful woman she had ever seen in her life join them by her cot. Her head had been shorn with a few weeks' stubble growing back. "General say GeminArc not work." Watching her lips move while she spoke was only slightly enchanting. The terrible Haenglish spilling from those lips somehow added to her charming beauty.

"Who says what about what, now?" Galiaro said, inching back into the conversation.

"The general," another voice joined them, crowding the end of the lab. It was a young man with black waves of hair cut in crooked sheets. Beneath a spackling of freckles, his pale skin accented slate grey eyes, titled and unsure. "We heard him talking to his army," he continued with a shaky voice. "Said that he was pulling out of the GeminArc—that it doesn't work. They're abandoning it and trying to get into an Alchean temple at the top of Orion."

"Ha! Fool," Galiaro said. "There's nothing in that temple. The Alcheans were the most arrogant beings that have ever walked Earth. Their temples—their religions—were nothing more than a worship of themselves. They built temples everywhere for rituals celebrating their alleged godhood. I'm certain the Orion temple is nothing more than a ritual throne room."

"The temple gates opened," Arym added.

"They were already open?" Galiaro asked.

"No. They opened when we showed up."

"Curious. As far as I've known, no one has ever been able to open that gate. But at any rate, this is good—very good. This General believes the GeminArc is nonfunctional."

"How do you know that it's not?" Beetro asked.

He crossed his arms. "Because I'm Galiaro, famed astrocyst."

Two orbs of light began swirling around the man.

Miree flinched. "What the hell?"

The orbs of light refracted into faces—a man and a woman. The woman spoke. "This is our opportunity. The general has abandoned the GeminArc, leaving it clear for us. We have figured out the math from the young man's journal. We have the key in the form of Beetro. We can activate the portal and provide an escape for humanity from the expansion. There is nothing to stop us."

"Wow, you've really been working since I've been gone," Miree said to Galiaro. "I'm impressed. And what are you?" she asked the orb.

"I am Neutrini. I am an encoded proton. I'm afraid we don't

have time to provide full details about our origin to every person that graces this lab. We must depart for the GeminArc at once."

"She's kinda prickly," Miree added.

The other orb spoke up. "I'm still not certain it is wise, sister. While I believe we should vacate Orion for the safety of the humanoids, I'm not confident that we can safely open the GeminArc. Our understanding of the math is incomplete."

"And how do we know that the general has really vacated his army?" Beetro asked.

"One moment," Neutrini said before disappearing and returning in the blink of an eye. "I've confirmed that the GeminArc is abandoned."

"What? How do you know that?" Miree asked.

"We are protons that can behave as other subatomic particles and can transit along the electromagnetic spectrum. My partner, Neutrini, traveled to the GeminArc and returned. I've also done the same while we've been speaking, and it is true... the GeminArc is abandoned."

"Then let us make haste," Neutrini said as if ending the debate.

"So, we're going back?" Miree said, exhaustion rising in her voice. "*Back* to Helian?" After the protracted and arduous escape from Peles Castle and the Reticulum, she didn't relish the idea of returning. "Are we sure we need to do this? Open that portal?"

They waited for Galiaro. The astrocyst had found a rocking chair and now dozed quietly.

"Hey!" Miree yelled and clapped her hands, startling the old man from his nap. He stirred awake, opened one eye at the group, and then made himself more comfortable in an attempt to continue the nap. "Hey, old man, we're trying to make decisions over here. You're the only one who can tell us what to do. So, wake up for one second and give us some guidance... is Earth really going to die soon?"

"There is no doubt," he said, eyes still closed. "I don't know when Jupiter will go, but when it does, Earth's orbit will contract even further. It will kill a vast majority of animal and plant life. Most humans will likely survive this—adapt or move to colder latitudes. But the expansion will continue with Mars and then us. We will be flung from our orbit and become the dark planet of the young Lithusa's future world." He pointed to the hottest girl Miree had ever seen. "We'll be like a wandering child, drifting aimlessly through empty space as the surface of the planet cools. Humans may become subterranean and perhaps live a little longer on their ice ball planet—years, decades... it's impossible to tell. With the expansion, the universe is at its end, and along with it, our planet. We are witnessing the final days of our mother. We must leave if we want to continue our human existence—escape into higher planes of dimensions like the Alcheans before us. We must leave at once," he said, suddenly standing.

"Right this second?"

"This lab. We must leave. We are in danger." He started rooting around the lab, looking for his things.

"Galiaro," Beetro said. "We need to prepare. Get food and supplies for the journey back to Helian."

"I can't even get out of bed," Miree added.

"Can't we just use Hawera's Fourth?" Ribcage asked. "And just skip to Helian?"

Hawera shook her head. "Too hard on my mind. Can't do so many people, too distant."

"Perhaps you all noticed that my lab, suspended in an alleyway and covered in a diverting refractory coating, is completely invisible." Having grown weary of the man's theatrics, they waited for his punchline in silence. "I haven't been to this lab in over ten years." He paused again as if expecting them to connect his stupid dots together.

"Please just spit it out," Miree demanded.

"Dust. Dirt. It builds up on the metal hull of the lab. I had to clean it off once every few days or the good people of Orion would start to see a rectangular-shaped ghost of dirt floating above their heads."

"The lab was invisible when we first came..." Beetro said.

"Correct, my young robot. Someone has been using this lab, cleaning the outside."

Miree stirred in bed. "Someone *who*?"

"I do not know."

"What about your partner astrocyst... Fallaro?" Miree asked, leaving the part out about how, once upon a time, she followed Fallaro into the very same lab and stole his Quantizer at gunpoint.

"He hasn't been seen in this city for quite some time. The robot district circles in which he ran have not seen him for several years."

"So, who has been here?"

"I don't know. Could be Fallaro, could be bots, could be the Kish—"

"Could be vagrants," Beetro speculated.

"That I doubt," Galiaro said. "Someone has gone through a lot of trouble to ensure the lab is invisible yet make it as if it has been abandoned to us."

"Smells like a trap," Miree said.

"Quite right, my dear. The question is, do we want to be here when they return to see if the trap is set?"

"No," everyone said in unison, except for Ribcage, who seemed more than enthused about using her Jump to get the best of some would-be intruders.

"Then we patch up the girl and we leave by tomorrow morning."

"Arym," the young man said, nodding his head to Miree.

"Okay," she mustered, feeling even more exhausted at having to meet yet another human body.

"What do you need?" he asked.

"I don't need anything."

"No, I mean, to get you out of bed and out of here."

"Oh. Blood. Got any?"

He furrowed his eyebrows.

"I lost blood. A lot of it."

"What did they do to you?"

"You'll need to be more specific. Many things have been done to me by many people."

"The Kish. Did they take that arm? Replace it with that... equipment?"

"No. The Reticulum did that back in Meteor Mountains."

"Oh." His face went pale.

"What?"

"I think I found your arm there."

"Huh."

"I-I don't have it now."

"It'd be weirder if you *did*."

"Wait here a sec." He returned with a satchel in hand, rummaging through the contents before producing a sealed cylindrical case that contained some sort of weed. He prepared it as a tea and offered her a cup.

"What is this?"

"She found it back in Crater Valley," he said, pointing at the beautiful girl.

"What's her name?"

"Hawera."

"Where is she *from*?"

"She's Lithusan."

"Never heard of them."

"Somewhere south and somewhere in the future. And the past."

"*What*?"

He took a deep breath as if to tell a great, epic tale.

"Never mind. Shit has gotten so weird, including the Chronicle Sea literally running away. I can't listen to anything else right now. Wait... this is *good*," she said, pointing to the tea.

"Gives a nice buzz. I think it's got a stimulant."

"Are you Lithusan, too?"

"No. From Crater Valley."

"No one lives in Crater Valley."

"Yes," he said. "They do." He swallowed hard and then said, "Many people do."

"I've walked across that valley twice. I didn't see any towns. There's nothing on the maps."

"We're there."

"We who?"

"The... Crib. I come from an underground society called the Crib. We live just beneath the earth of Crater Valley."

"Weird."

He nodded. "We're... all clones."

"Even weirder."

"Clones of some... some man hundreds—thousands of years ago named Othel. He was afraid of the world and so started the Crib and set up a factory to make clones of himself. Made us all take an oath."

"Why?"

"Why, what?"

"Why did he do that?"

"Why does anyone do anything?"

She shrugged.

"So, they won't be forgotten. Nothing more. Nothing less." He stood, blinking away tears.

"You've been through some shit, haven't you?"

The guy choked on some spit, looking absolutely pathetic. "Yes," he said through a stifled sob.

She offered her hand. "Miree." He took her hand and kept it there, holding her hand. "Easy there, champ. It's supposed to just be a one-off. One pump and you get out."

"I'm sorry!" he said, whipping his hand back as if he'd committed an enormous offense. He stood, embarrassed, and collected his implements of tea. "There are no women where I'm from. I—" he looked at Hawera. "I don't know what to do around you. My people have left me completely unprepared with how to treat half the human race."

"No women?"

He shook his head.

"Just treat us the same. Without entitlement, without expectations."

He nodded as if being scolded. "That's what I did to her." He pointed to Hawera. "Don't know what happened. I automatically thought she was mine. I thought we were supposed to be together." He closed his eyes in deep embrassement. "I'm such a fool."

"Okay, clone boy," she said, extending her arm wide. "Bring it in."

"Wh-what?"

"It's called a hug. I haven't given one in years. I think we could both use one."

FORTY-THREE

THE NEXT DAY, there were explosions—concussive and rippling throughout the city, rocking the invisible lab. They looked at one another with each distant shockwave, steadying themselves on furniture. Miree had made it to her feet and walked across the room without collapsing. It was progress. Beetro was swept by guilt every time she hobbled around, robotic prosthetics flailing—those red lights blinking where human eyes once lived. He could have prevented it. He could've saved her from the Reticulum turning her into this... thing.

"Don't look at me like that," she told him.

"Like what?"

"You feel guilty for leaving me."

"Yes."

"Get rid of it. Useless emotion. Doesn't help you, doesn't help me. What would help me is some more of that tea from What's-His-Face."

"Arym?"

"Yeah, Weepy Eyes. Tell him to run over here and make me

some more of that tea and let's get out of here." Arym had already overheard them and brought her a steaming cup.

"You're not ready yet. You're still too weak," Beetro told her.

"I agree," Arym said. "You need more recovery time."

She looked at Arym like he had just spat in her face. "We're not rotting in Orion. We're climbing down that hatch and getting out of here."

"We're going back to the GeminArc to open it," Beetro said, looking around the room.

"Lead the way," she dared him.

"We need to find out what's going on out there and plan an escape from the city."

Protonix appeared between them. "I've already been out there. War is brewing. The general is bombarding the city with missiles and gunfire. The Kish have some artillery to respond in kind."

"Have you seen the general in the city? Did he survive Ribcage's stabbing?"

"I haven't seen him. I do not know where he is, although that large, winged craft still hovers by the temple dome. One could presume he is in there dead or recovering from the wound."

"He's dead," Ribcage declared.

"I agree, we need to get out of the city, but we need supplies," Beetro said.

"We have plenty of my Nourishment Rectangles," Galiaro offered, crunching into a bar.

"I'm not eating another one of those nasty things!" Ribcage yelled.

"Any suggestions on where we can get out of the city?" Beetro asked Protonix.

"The traditional way in and out is through a gondola. I suppose you could commandeer one of those."

"Feels risky."

"I agree," Protonix said. "It appears there are no aircraft in the city. The mercantile district has all but evacuated with their wealth and vehicles of flight."

"How are other people leaving the city?"

"I don't think they are. Most are holed up in their homes awaiting the victor. I'm afraid this siege will take weeks to months, and many will likely perish."

"The humans need food and hiking supplies for our return journey. Have you seen anywhere around where we can get that?"

"The markets are closed. Every tavern. Every brothel."

"The robot district?"

"Still active but limited. It seems the bots have taken a passive interest in the struggle for control of Orion, believing themselves to be only a third party. It might be worthwhile to pay a visit, there may be concealed supplies in the district that the bots will later use as all other currency inflates during the scarcity caused by the siege."

"Can't you just... go and see if there are supplies somewhere?"

Protonix refracted into a face of annoyance. "I cannot see in dark rooms or cellars, and I have no corporal form to interact with objects like a lantern. I refract light—I do not generate it. Also, I'm not your fetching boy."

"I'll go," Beetro said, already moving toward the hatch.

"We'll come with you!" Ribcage said, locking arms with Hawera.

"No. I'm going alone. And *you* are staying here."

In the robot district, the streets were impacted by robots and humans alike. Beetro elbowed his way amongst a tumultuous murmuring among the people. Women carried crying babies, their sobbing siblings in tow with outstretched hands of begging. The men offered menacing expressions, brandishing crude weapons fashioned from what was once furniture. While there were no Kish or violence present, the entire district was one altercation away from erupting into riots. Faint concussions rippled the ground, roiling the people into a frenzy.

Seeing the main market choked and functionally closed, Beetro diverted down an alleyway, still seething with the masses. Many robots preached and consoled, trying to explain to the starving humans why everything would be fine if they only waited a little longer. Other bots recited poetry or painted despite the chaos, their line of easels in constant threat of toppling over from stampede. At the end of the alley, Beetro found Sartorious, the bulky digbot with lights twinkling back and forth above its wheel tread. Beside Sartorious stood a thin robot bedecked with four arms, each equipped with thousands of cables and metallic struts articulating with hundreds of miniature joints forming rows along the arms. It was a spindly thing of incredulous fragility coordinating thousands of moving parts. The arms and joints moved in beautiful unison around an oval-shaped vessel of wood and strings. Two arms held bows that flowed across the strings, while the bot plucked other strings with digits the width of a pin.

"What *is* this?" Beetro asked Sartorious.

The bot wheeled to inspect the newcomer. "Ah. Beetro. I'm happy you've returned. Lovely, isn't it?"

"I've... never heard anything like this."

"Close your eyes. Gets even better."

Despite his best instincts, Beetro did close his eyes and let each note reach him—every plucked string and sweep of the bows. The musical robot was an orchestra unto itself, a river of harmonies and cadences that blended as seamlessly as the ocean.

Beetro forgot about the riot, the impending war, the GeminArc—expansion and decay. The dying universe vanished from his mind.

"Do you feel that?" Sartorious asked, a flutter of lights dancing around his mouth.

"Feel what?"

"That's time, Beetro. That's... *now*."

"Now?"

"You're feeling now."

"I don't understand."

"Time is relative."

"Why are you standing here with everything going on? There's a war coming."

"That is the precise reason that me and my friend are here. We're collecting the entropy that is flooding at our feet from the fear of humankind, accelerating time. The panic, the screaming, the sweating—entropy is scattering like a campfire. But me and my friend here—we bind the entropy and feed it through the music. Every note collected holds the audience for each moment, slowing their experience of time. These people, throwing thermal energy with every movement—their panic flooding the universe—are speeding time, accelerating their own destruction. The last thing they need is for their time to run out."

"But... you're not changing anything. They need to flee—to escape. We all have to get out of here."

"We are slowing time."

"No. You're not. You're only slowing their *experience* of time. That is if they are even paying attention."

"Is there a difference?"

"I need supplies for my humans. Do you know—"

Something large happened.

But Beetro couldn't tell—his sight was instantly blotted by smoke followed by fire. The silence told him that something terribly close had just occurred. A few cries rippled through the silence and, as the smoke cleared, he saw the devastation left by a mortar. There were remnants of humans and robots. Charred clothing, dangling limbs, and twisted shrapnel had been left in the wake of the detonation. Microprocessing boards and visceral innards of both human and machine were strewn along the alley. A dog padded along the scene, sniffed the ground, and moved along. Beetro looked down at his own body, wondering if he somehow suffered decapitation without realizing it but his metal shell sparkled up at him. Sartorious had been blown back, but her lights still flickered. Her musical companion had been blown apart into a crumpled mess of string and twisted aluminum like a dead spider with curled legs.

Beetro closed his eyes and concentrated on the scattered sunlight sifting through the smoke. Each photon felt like a raindrop, landing and absorbing through his skin, warming his body and building up into a thermal charge. He opened his eyes, ready to release a photonic charge at any instant. Another concussive blow hit a few streets away, jolting the scene of carnage at his feet. He waited; hands held up toward the mouth of the alley.

The sound of marching boots echoed around the corner. Beetro held, his hands outstretched at the impending wrath of war marching on. "Sartorius," he said, his attention unwavering. "Are you alive?"

"Yes," she said, light blinking red.

"Can you give me water?"

"Yes, I have a reserve in my coolant system."

"Can you give it to me through my mouth once I deactivate?"

"Y-yes. Why are you going to deactivate?" she asked, worry rising in her voice.

The soldiers were on them, marching with Alchean rifles pointed. Their impossibly young faces scowled beneath the rim of their sleek, black helmets. "Hey!" a young man shouted at the front of the line. "Freeze!" He held up his fist to hold the line and pointed his rifle at the bots.

"Stop!" another voice shot out, a woman who'd survived the initial blast. She rose from the edge of the alley, her hair singed. "Please!" But the soldier fired, the look on his face suggesting his finger acted before he could even think. The woman fell to the ground, a freshly charred crater in her abdomen. The soldiers watched her fall, lowering their rifles ever so slightly.

"Advance, you cowards!" a young woman said from behind, nudging the frontline forward. "Put down any resistance like the general said. We need to demonstrate our authority in the city."

"You'll go no further," Beetro said, arms still stretched toward them.

A moment of confused silence was broken by unanimous laughter from the soldiers. "What a little shit bot," one said.

"Take him out and let's move on," another shouted. "We've got to meet the gamma squad in five. Go!"

The energy of photonics thrummed inside him. He could release it—release it into a crowd of ignorant soldiers who were likely nothing more than peasants just months before. With a flick of his wrists, Beetro could turn them into nothing—vaporized flesh, annihilated and their molecular structure fundamentally undone.

"Stop!" he yelled, but they ignored his plea, raising their rifles. He unleashed the charge. A blinding-white surge of energy flowed from his palms. Once the smoke cleared, the soldiers found themselves at the edge of a charred crater, just ending at their feet.

"Whoa..." one of them said. "H-he destroyed the Alchean metal."

"Turn around," Beetro said. "And never come back."

Losing their fortitude, the soldiers turned, lowering their weapons, and sifted out of the alleyway until it was empty.

Beetro fell to the ground with a clunk. Dehydrated. Paralyzed. As his consciousness faded, he heard the treads of Sartorious wheel over to him. A trickle of water fell into his mouth and flowed through his system, regenerating his hydro capillary system.

He stood once more, looking at the clear alleyway.

Sartorious inspected him. "Wh-what are you?"

He looked at his palms, still smoking from the afterburn. He nearly murdered a squadron of humans, and he almost didn't care. A terrible dread overcame him about who he was becoming. He knew he wanted to do it—he wanted to incinerate his enemy from off the face of the planet. What would Lucindi think?

"I think..." he answered. "I think I'm a mistake."

FORTY-FOUR

"WE'RE LEAVING," Miree told them as she got up from bed.

Arym moved toward her, arms out as if prepared to scoop up a fainting woman. "I don't think—"

"Just stop," she scolded, sticking a finger in his face. "Stop trying to get me to lay in bed all day while the city is being attacked. Everyone, pack it up! We're leaving in thirty seconds to go find Beetro." The lab rocked once more as she steadied herself on a lab bench.

Galiaro stood at the window, watching the streets below. "There is death in the streets." Ribcage and Hawera joined him, watching the chaos below.

"Let's go!" Ribcage said, tugging on Hawera's sleeve. "Use your Fourth!"

"No," Miree hissed. "We're leaving Orion. None of your Jumping nonsense. Do you understand me?"

Ribcage's face soured. "I don't listen to betrayers."

"Hey... I'm here. I came back, okay? It's different now. I'm with you." After glancing around the lab, she asked, "Has anyone seen my sword? Weird, scaly-looking blade with dull edges?" After receiving nothing but shrugs, she cursed under her breath and stumbled to the hatch, pain modulators kicking in, dampening the ache in her bones and sting of her lacerated skin. She threw open the hatch and... "How do we get down?"

"Come on," Arym said, dangling his legs from the hatch. "I'll show you."

One by one, they evacuated the lab in silence. As they fled the alleyway, they were stopped by the abrupt appearance of Beetro standing in the streets, motionless and gazing up at the sky.

"What are you doing?" Miree asked. "Did you find any supplies?"

"Just wondering if we'll fall into the sun or be flung from her. I suppose it doesn't matter now."

"Come on! We're getting out of here. Deluvius' men are probably everywhere."

"I took care of them."

"You mean..."

"No. But I could have. Easily. I almost wiped them from the face of the planet with a stroke of my hands. I wonder what Lucindi would think of me," he asked no one, still gazing at the boiling sky. "I'm not supposed to be like this. Or... am I? How can I separate my design from my purpose? Are they the same thing?"

Miree answered. "She'd think that you should get out of this city. She'd think there is a bigger picture here—a bigger purpose. She'd think that you need to escape so that we can go and open the GeminArc—evacuate this doomed planet and save everyone from dying. She'd see that the world is a complicated, ass-backwards place controlled by evil men who destroy the lives of everyone else from their own dumbfuckery."

Beetro said nothing.

"Are you done with your existential crisis? Can we go now?"

Despondent, he followed them.

Miree led them through the streets. Unlike their previous ventures in the city, Miree guided them through tunnels and back alleys—passages only known to a former Kish member. Where the panicked crowds flowed in one direction, she led them the opposite, breaking through locked shops to unveil hidden trap doors that led to even more clandestine tunnel systems once forged by the Alcheans. Despite a small hobble in her legs, she moved rather swiftly.

Hawera could hardly suppress her irritation at Ribcage's incessant begging for her to use her Fourth. "No," she told the girl. "Not need now. My Fourth hurts." She rubbed her temples.

"Where are the lightbulbs?" Miree asked Galiaro.

"They are still working on the math to properly operate the GeminArc—said they would meet us at the Arc when we arrive. They think they are an advanced species, but I wasn't terribly impressed with their mathematics." He gave a single pretentious snort.

"We kind of need them. They have some eyes out there that can tell us what's going on."

"Hmph. They have become quite obstinate about aiding us in surveillance. Inborn Alchean arrogance at its best."

"I'm taking us to the north side gondola docks—an area of Orion that was evacuated from some fires years ago. Should be empty and I'm hoping we'll at least be able to get off this dumpster fire on one of the cable cars."

Another explosion rippled the ground. "We should keep moving," Arym said with a quiver in his voice.

Miree led them further through abandoned streets, poor neighborhoods in which the Kish had operated for years after pushing out the merchant council to the upper dome of the city. There were a few huddled figures lining the streets, covered in filth and wailing at the sky. Miree flipped up her hood, hiding her robotic face from curious eyes, and swept through the streets. At last, they arrived at a gondola dock on the north side of the mountain city. The vista revealed a tundra stretched flat by eons of harsh winters, its end erupting with a distant mountain range like a row of small teeth.

The dock was unmanned, abandoned.

"Unguarded," she said, moving to a gondola that sat undisturbed. "Everyone in."

Arym looked at the weather-worn gondola with skepticism. "You know how to work one of these? Don't we need more people working the levers or something?"

"It's a simple system. All we need is gravity and a brake. We got both, so everyone on!"

The cables squealed as they squeezed into the vessel. Miree took the controls and flung a lever forward before Arym had the door closed. The gondola lurched and then came to an abrupt stop. They looked at her while she sheepishly pulled another release valve, disengaging the brakes. The gondola pulled free of the rubber bumpers of the dock and glided down the cable, at first, slowly, but then picked up speed.

"Question," Arym said, tapping her on the shoulder.

"Can't you see I'm driving this thing?"

"It'll take us, what, a month to get back to Helian? And with no supplies and the general out there—"

The gondola plummeted.

Bodies slammed into the front end as they nose-dived. *Shit, shit, shit.* Miree didn't have to look to know what happened—Deluvius had cut the fucking cables from below. They struggled to even lift their chins under several gs of gravity as the gondola rode a loose cable, flapping in the wind.

"Engage the brakes, woman!" Galiaro wailed.

"I can't! It's going too fast!"

"Everyone, lock arms!" Beetro yelled. "Hawera, open your Fourth."

"But we die," she said. "The speed too much."

"Just do it!" Ribcage yelled, holding her hand.

"The speed!" she repeated, voice cracking with strain.

"Conservation of velocity," Galiaro said. "She can push us through a portal, but she can't stop our velocity. We're going to be smashed to bits wherever she transports us. I'm afraid we are doomed, my dears. It was a fine plan we had. Fine plan."

"Wait," Arym cried. "Can't you just flip the way we come out? Open the portal... upside down?"

Galiaro opened his mouth as if to protest but then nodded. "He may be right, my dear," he said to Hawera.

With a ruffled brow, she considered his words and then nodded.

"Someone, do something!" Miree snapped. "We're going to smash into the ground in about ten seconds!"

Hawera freed her grasp on the rails and, through strained knees, stood against the acceleration of the gondola. Pointing her staff straight down between her legs, she closed her eyes and grunted. A flash of blue flew from her hands to the metal-tipped staff and out through the floor.

Nothing happened.

They plunged, ever-accelerating toward annihilation. But then, almost imperceptibly, they slowed. Beetro looked out the window and saw nothing but the sky, marbleized with vanilla and purple whorls of evaporation. His accelerometer lightened as the gondola came almost to a standstill in the middle of the sky. Hawera shot another lance of light from her staff, opening a Fourth portal outside the gondola once more. A dull thud heralded their landing on solid ground. The view of the sky was instantly supplanted by the streets of Orion.

"Clever," Galiaro said, dusting off his robe. "Clever girl. A fast thinker. I like that."

Miree stood like a lame animal, leaning on her prosthetic arm, and looked out the window. "What happened?"

Galiaro couldn't conceal his grin at the Lithusan girl. "She inverted her Fourth, translated the acceleration in an upward vector, letting it decay by the planet's gravity, and then *just* as we began to fall again, opened another Fourth portal through which we began to fall and then popped us out right above the ground here. Brilliant."

Miree gaped at him. "She *what*?"

"Never mind, we have to get off the streets," Beetro said. "Deluvius' army is infiltrating the city."

"Back to the lab?" Arym asked.

"No. We have to get out of here," Miree answered. "We stay, we die."

"How? If the Kish cut all the cables, how do people get off this place?"

"I saw aircraft up toward the dome last week..." Beetro said.

Galiaro laughed. "The rich merchants. They abandoned ship long ago. I'm afraid we won't find passage with them."

"Can you get us to the ground?" Arym asked Hawera.

The Lithusan shook her head. "Too many people."

"I—" Miree stopped. "Everyone out and follow me." Visibly fatigued, Hawera took Arym's arm as he led her out of the gondola. Miree looked her up and down. "What's the matter with her?"

"Opening the time portals. It exhausts her."

"Time portal? Never mind, we don't have time for this. Quite a little group of misfits I've managed to get involved with. We need to move fast," she told the rest of the group. "Back to the bot district and through it."

"But it's all bombed out," Beetro said.

"Should be easier to get around then."

Miree thumped her prosthetic arm on the door, jolting an iron knocker. They had crowded around her, Ribcage with her eyes on the street, Hawera resting with her back against the wall. The girl's face grew pale after vomiting en route to the merchant district. Arym was at her side, offering water. Miree knocked again after no response. Carved within the rich oak door was *D'Naris and Sons* with the symbol of a galleon beneath the name.

The door creaked open.

"Kindly go 'way," the voice said before closing the door.

She knocked again. "Is this the business place of Meric D'Naris?"

The door opened once more. "Who inquires?"

Galiaro stuffed his boot inside the door. "Piot, you old fool, I know that's you. Open up and let us in!"

The door gave way to Piot, a sheepish shriveled grin on his face. "Ah, our young lady and the master astrocyst."

A deep voice called from within. "Who is it, Piot?"

Miree also put her boot in the door. "It's Miree and Galiaro. We need your help, open up!"

Meric was at the doorway crossing his burly arms across his chest, a devilish smile on his face. "My oh my, if it isn't Anisha or Miree or whatever you're calling yourself today. What brings my fair lady to our doorstep?"

"War. Now let us in." She shouldered her way past and walked in. "You need to get us out of the city."

After Meric had feigned the appropriate amount of outrage, he asked, "You believe after taking me and my navigator for fools, making a promised payment that you had no intention of fulfilling, that we would welcome you with open arms into our business establishment? My father did not build this trading company for me to sully his name with such fraternization—"

"You think I had an option stuck out in the middle of the sea? I had to get that man," she pointed to Galiaro, "to this city because he's the only thing that can do anything about the expansion. And you think you have the right to some indignation to hold me accountable for your highway robbery, opportunist prices to steer a boat across some water?"

Nostrils flared, he said, "You offered me a sum of non-existent gold leaves to *bring* you to Orion. How much will you now offer me to *leave* Orion? Ten leaves? How about one hundred?"

"How about there is a war in the streets, and we all need to get out of here right now? Is that reason enough for you? And why..." she looked around the office—dusty ledgers, stacked pages, and the whole place redolent of mildew. "Why are you even still here?"

"That is me and my navigator's business."

Piot interrupted by stepping between the pair. He lightly tapped his pipe on Meric's temple. "You don't need to be coy, boy. You can tell her we were waiting for her, waiting to see if she would show up."

"Piot!" Meric spun and said. "What my navigator is referring to is the fact that we were impressed with you and the astrocyst's... understanding of the celestial events above us. You see, during our travels over the last several months around the Chronicle Sea, we've heard rumors of changes in the land—in the sky. The Torbad, in particular, are also a sea-faring people. They warned of minute yet significant changes in the heavens. I've traded with those factions for neigh on fifteen years and never had I seen them so morose or so prophetic."

"So, you stayed to see if we'd be able to accomplish anything here in Orion?"

"It is an ancient seat of power to the Alcheans. I supposed you and the astrocyst would accomplish your goals here and retrieve the robot. It seemed prudent to wait here and see. Obviously, you have not, and we waited in vain while war descends upon us."

"That wasn't the only reason he stayed..." Piot said as Meric shot him a scandalized stare.

"But, no, we... we got what we needed." Miree gestured to Beetro. "He's a key. He's the key we needed to find."

"A key to what?"

"A key to getting us off this doomed planet. We need to get to Helian."

"Bah!" Piot complained. "God-forsaken land. Poisoned soil. Not even the fortified corn will grow there now. What good resides in those lands?"

"There is an enormous particle accelerator, built eons ago by the Alcheans," Galiaro said. "We must activate it with this bot, open a wormhole into an interdimensional space. We can provide a route for mankind to escape our dying planet—our dying galaxy. I have completed the mathematics. We can open it. You must escort us there immediately."

"Questions?" Miree asked, sucking on her teeth.

Meric and Piot gaped at him while the room remained silent. "I don't even know where to begin," Meric complained.

They were interrupted by a large explosion no more than a street away.

"Is that explosion answer enough for you? We need to get out of here right now. The Kish cut the gondola cables. You told me you have some sort of backup plan to get out if you were waiting around this long?"

Meric and Piot exchanged furtive glances. "Yes." He turned to his navigator with questioning eyes. "Piot?" Piot nodded in return and then Meric leaped up a spiral staircase situated in the middle of the room, leaving them there. Piot unceremoniously moved a coffee table and flipped over a rug, exposing a hatch in the floorboards. After fiddling with a padlock for a moment, he opened the hatch and disappeared beneath the floor.

"Okay..." Miree wandered the dank room. Hawera had turned completely pale, eyes closed, and possibly passed out. Arym frantically patted her cheeks while Ribcage held the woman's hand. Galiaro had found a kitchenette in the corner and had busied himself by rummaging through the cupboards. Beetro... looked something close to shell-shocked sitting on a stool, indigo eyes vacant.

A hissing sound emanated from the floorboards. They studied the wood as the floors shook, a muted vibration growing through the foundation. "Meric!" Miree yelled at the ceiling. She paced the room as dust fell from the ceiling, books toppled from desks and gaudy chandeliers swayed from their fixtures.

Meric's deep voice boomed from above. "Grab ahold of something!"

"Grab *what*? Everything is falling over in here!" she yelled as the hissing condensed into a frank hammering sound. "We're being attacked! Do you have a back door out of this place? Weapons?" She put her hand to her waist, missing the feeling of the Swordless Hilt resting there.

"Been years and years," Piot said, suddenly reappearing, wiping his glasses with a handkerchief. "So, I don't know if it's going to work."

"If *what's* going to work?" Miree asked as Meric descended

the stairs. "If *what's* going to work?" she repeated to him. "And why is your shirt off?"

"Politics in this city," he said, shaking his head and wiping black grease from his now bare chest. His trousers had suffered several tears as if he was working in close quarters with mechanical equipment. "So volatile. Always have been. My father wanted to move the business—go to the south markets across the oceans. He even had the crazy idea of trying to trade to the kingdoms to the east. Ha! As if the Fifth Kingdom wouldn't take him to the last percent of his profits. I loved my father—passionate old fool with enough business savvy to own this whole city. If only Orion was good enough to have him, he could've been larger than all of this." He waved his hands about the walls. "But that's the thing about power... there's one rule and one rule only to remember. Power corrupts. And Orion is corrupt to the core. The whole land is."

"Is this a dying thing you're doing?" Miree asked. "Making a speech before the ship goes down or something? If so, that's fine but we're not going to hang around much longer to hear it. How can we get out of here?"

"On his deathbed," he continued, eyes swelling with weird tears. "My father told me to pack up shop, go find another business or at least another market." Galiaro drank amber liquid from a crystal tumbler, eyes rapt with attention at the man's soliloquy.

"He would've been proud. I knew him the best of anyone. He would've been proud to call you his son," Piot said, clasping him on the shoulder.

"I knew my father was right, of course, but I couldn't accept defeat from this place. But I planned. I planned—for this day—apparently." He moved to a desk and shouldered it out of the way.

"Can we get out through here?" Miree asked. "Beetro, come on. This way. Charge up your photonics. We'll probably meet resistance—"

But Meric exposed a metal switch plate built into the floor. He fiddled with a few knobs and tapped on a pressure gauge. "Almost there."

"There? What is going on?"

"We're evacuating. The entire room is lined with a steel hull. Beneath the hull is a system pressurized by air, compressed and ready for discharge of the entire capsule."

"What's it going to do?"

He thoughtfully rubbed his chin. "Do you remember that emergency jetpack I had on my boat?"

"You mean the *rocket* that you wanted me to strap onto my back?"

The room shuddered.

"Rocket is a strong word." He squinted at the switch plate. "But, very well then. Ten... nine... eight..."

"Holy shit!" Miree turned to Arym and pointed at Hawera. "Make sure she's secured down. Everyone grab ahold of something."

"Seven... six... five... Everyone hold onto something. This will be a tad jarring."

Miree pointed a finger into Meric's back. "What is it with you and *rockets*?"

"Four—"

A roar erupted.

The blood in Miree's head sank to her feet.

FORTY-FIVE

TRUE, it wasn't exactly a rocket.

But there was certainly an explosion and definitely some heavy gs happening. It may not have been created by rocket fuel, but it was enough energy to launch what Miree previously understood to be a building, straight into the sky. As the dots cleared from her vision, she stood and saw Meric still gripping the switch plate on the floor. Sweat clung to his face as he scrutinized the pressure gauges. "Piot!" he yelled without tearing his gaze from the switch plate. "Altitude is tapering off!"

The old man was sitting in an armchair that presently slid across the floor as the entire room slanted. "Aye. Best we get above and deploy the chutes."

"When's the last time we inspected them?"

"Three years?"

"We've gotten sloppy, Piot. Think they'll hold?"

"Doesn't matter what an old man thinks. Won't change anything if the only thing holding this vessel in the air is a moth-ridden canvas."

Galiaro had stumbled with the slant of the room, untangling himself from his robe and cloak. He looked at Meric, face flummoxed with a drunken edge. "Your place of business is an *aircraft*?"

"Aircraft is generous. It's a building with a creative escape route. We've left the rest of the business behind, of course. The craft is only this room and a compartment up above, torn away from the building. My father's business is finally put to rest." Meric stood, looking at Miree. "Can you climb the stairs with me?"

She nodded and followed him up the spiral staircase into a small nook above, books scattered about the floor. The roof had been blown completely off, leaving the naked sky above. Her hair whipped about her face as the room still arched skyward, the only sound a howling wind. It was then she noticed the apparent absence of the sound of a thruster engine. Nothing was keeping the vessel in the sky as it still rode the initial trajectory blast upward.

"We deploy the chutes from here," Meric said, pointing to a series of levers built along the floorboards. "And keep the craft afloat by hot air propulsion. The chutes should deploy from here and here." He pointed to the edges of the rooms. "We need to deploy them at the same time so that we stay level. You see the levers on the wall? Good, grab ahold of them and wait on my mark. If we don't pull at the same time, the entire capsule could tip over and we could tumble out of this thing."

She held the lever. "Tell me when."

"When! We're already falling!"

"Are you asking me or telling me?"

"Pull now!"

They flipped the levers. A burst of air heralded the ejection of a chute on Meric's side of the vessel. Miree looked down and saw that nothing had happened on her end. Before she could voice the warning, the chute on Meric's side of the capsule deployed, lifting only one end and tilted the entire aircraft. Miree fell into railings, past debris, and landed on the lip of the wall where the blown-out ceiling was now teetering toward Earth. Meric caught hold of her with one arm, stabilizing himself with her prosthesis.

"You didn't pull the lever!" he yelled.

"Yes, I did!"

"No, you didn't!"

"Stop arguing and pull me up!" The mountain city of Orion twirled beneath them as the parachute slowed their descent. Her legs dangled in free air, above blooms of fire and smoke as two armies tried killing one another below.

"We're all going to spill out of this thing! Piot!" Meric yelled, pulling Miree into the capsule.

But the man was already there, emerging from the spiral staircase. He climbed like a crab, extending one leg and then arm, moving toward the undeployed chute compartment. After pumping the lever several times, the parachute fell from the compartment, releasing pressurized air as the packaged fabric shot past Piot. The canvas chute dropped like a rock from the capsule, passed Meric and Miree, and flapped in the wind like a withered appendage.

Miree watched the chute partially unfold as the wind torrents peeled back canvas layers. "What now?"

"We're dead if it doesn't deploy," Meric said, watching the chute in hopeful silence as the vessel lurched sideways.

Miree looked past the flapping chute and saw a puff of smoke trailing beneath them. "What... is *that*?"

Meric squinted and then said, "Oh my holy lords, it's a missile."

"A missile for what?"

"For *us*! They're trying to shoot us down."

Finally, she panicked—blood pounding, sweaty grip, certain doom crowding her senses. "Wh-wh-what—"

But Meric was gone. Vanished over the edge. Plummeting to his death...

But then she saw him. He'd fallen onto the undeployed chute —hands gripping the canvas in a white-knuckle vice, knees hugging the ball of fabric as he rocked through the sky like a pendulum. Through gritted teeth, the man was wildly grabbing at the rope of the chute, loosening snags and peeling back fabric. He almost lost his grip as he pulled a knife from his boot and slashed stubborn knots, freeing away more of the chute. Beneath him, Orion was there, muted metallic sheen dulled by the pregnant sky. The missile was approaching, zeroing in on their vessel. Meric had two seconds, may one and...

The chute deployed, flinging Meric through the sky as the vessel rose.

Something breaking the sound barrier shot past them and exploded in the sky, swaying the vessel that was now suspended in tandem by two leveled parachutes. Miree released her grip as the deck finally became horizontal once more.

"Meric!" She looked at Piot who was getting to his feet. Wrinkled concern crowded his eyes.

The wind howled as Piot ambled to the ropes of the now deployed parachutes. "Don't be afraid, lass. What happens, happens," he said while clicking an ignition stick over a burner.

"Meric!" she yelled again, looking over the edge of the capsule, seeing nothing but the tumult of Orion below.

"Pray for winds," Piot said while lighting the other burner. "Pray for gales so fierce they sober up the drunkest sailor—or the drunkest astrocyst."

A voice called from below deck, swallowed up in the wind. It was Beetro. "Miree!"

She moved so fast that she fell down the spiral staircase, landing square on her backside into the neo-underbelly of what was now a hot air balloon. Her tailbone, still sore from falling out of the tower at Peles Castle, screamed as she rose. And then she saw two things at once... Meric, who was somehow alive and on board, and Hawera, convulsing uncontrollably with seizures. It took little deduction to know what had happened. The time-warping girl made one of her portals to bring Meric back aboard, which was the apparent last mental straw, finally shattering her brain to pieces. Arym and Ribcage fretted over the girl, holding her arms and head down to prevent injury. Beetro and Galiaro stood at what was once the front door of a trading business but now opened to the empty sky. They watched silently. "Okay..." Miree told them as if formulating a plan. But truly, nothing was there. "Okay..."

"Another bogey!" Piot yelled above deck.

"I see it," Beetro said. "At the current speed, it'll hit in twenty-eight seconds."

"The girl can't do it again," Galiaro noted as Hawera continued to convulse. "And the child can't Jump without her."

Miree joined them at the doorway and saw it... an angry, smoking missile arching its way to them. There were many times she had stared death in the face, but none were so certain as watching a ballistic missile homing in with heat-seeking precision. "I-I..." She turned to the group, their mouths ajar, eyes wide with fear. She knew they were her friends, very likely the only ones she had ever had. "Thank you—"

Her words were cut off by a concussive wave of orange heat.

Miree's figure was silhouetted by fire, a blanket of raging heat blowing over the open doorway. The vessel swung wildly in the sky as Beetro crashed into broken furniture sliding into the corner of the room. His internal gyrometer spun wildly as he tried to figure out if they were plummeting in the sky. But as the room stabilized once more, and their acceleration slowed, he found they were still afloat.

He found Miree, her cloak tangled about her waist and caught up within the legs of a broken armchair. She wasn't awake. "Miree." He nudged her arm, suddenly remembering the first time they met in the junkyard. The woman was standing before him, bolt cutters in one hand and a saw in the other. It was only then he realized that she meant to tear him apart and sell his parts for scrap. "Miree."

Her robotic eyes shuddered open, red light with a green nimbus shining out. "Would they just *kill us already*?" She got to her feet, using her prosthetic arm as a crutch. "Why are they so bad at shooting a slow-moving hot air balloon out of the sky?"

Galiaro and Meric stood at the sky doorway, both with arms crossed over their chests. "Someone stopped the missile," Galiaro said, Meric nodding in agreement.

"No doubt about it," Meric said with one eye shut, surveying the city below.

"How?" Beetro asked.

"With another missile," Galiaro answered. "Came from behind and shot it out of the sky. Mere seconds before impact to our ship."

Miree joined them. "Who? Who would shoot the missile down?"

"Good question. Some saint helping people evacuate the city?"

"There are no saints in Orion," Miree said.

"It could've been the bots," Beetro offered. "Many of them were sympathetic toward us and people trying to escape. They may have had a hand in it."

"Perhaps," Meric said, leaving the sky doorway. He inspected what was once his office and released a deep sigh. Everything that was not bolted down had become a collapsed detritus of furniture, papers, lampshades, and picture frames. The man found a cushion amongst the wreckage, placed it on the ground, and sat, lowering his head between his knees.

"Thank you," Beetro told him. "Thank you for saving us."

"There is a windstream that flows due west from here," he said without looking up. "It will take us to Helian where it will be *your* turn to save us, robot."

"How is she?" Beetro asked, motioning to Hawera.

Sitting at her side, Arym shook his head. "She's breathing, but she's not awake. The Fourth hurts her—hurts her mind when she uses it too much."

"I'm sorry," Ribcage whispered to Hawera, holding her hand. Hot tears streaked her face. "I'm sorry I made you use your Fourth. *I'm sorry*!"

"Rib, it's okay. She knew she had to. We would all be dead a few times over if it wasn't for her."

Piot interrupted them. "The winds are picking up." He stood at the sky doorway, pipe in hand. "We're clearing the city. Good riddance, I say. Good riddance to the rotten mistress of Orion. No good ever came of 'er."

They finally found silence as the windstream escorted them through the sky. Bursts of sunlight sifted through the ghoulish firmament—radiant rays filtering through the purples and pinkish hues holding much more moisture than was natural. They snacked on Nourishment Rectangles as the wind howled throughout the cabin. Beetro ascended the spiral staircase to what could only now be called the cockpit, where Meric studied a compass and kept one hand on a burner.

"So, you're the robot," Meric said without looking away. "The robot that everyone went through so much trouble for." Beetro remained speechless, unsure if the man was trying to guilt him or was being earnest. "Was on my way to the Torbad. I was never coming back to Orion. Was happily going to set sail from Portolo over the Chronicle Sea. But then it disappeared."

"I know."

"What do you know about it?"

"Nothing. Galiaro's the one—"

The man's face grew dark. "I found a pretty girl and a crackpot astrocyst—said they could solve the problem of the skies. Fix the galaxy. Just needed to find a robot in Orion."

"I didn't ask them to come after me."

"What aren't you telling them?"

"What do you mean?"

"They're not the only ones after you, are they?"

"What are you talking about?"

"No robot shot that missile out of the sky. Those useless tin thespians don't have munitions like that. Someone else shot it out —someone else made sure we could escape."

"Mr. D'Naris, really, I don't know what you're talking about."

"I pride myself on being good at sizing people up. Reading the room, the body language, the clothing, the dirt caked under someone's nails—everything tells a story. Reading people is my business. It's what makes me good as a merchant. No one else on this aircraft has anything to hide. But you... well, you've got the origin story of a fern, don't you? Just woke up in junkyard dirt looking for your maker, is that right?"

"That's the short of it, yes."

"Nothing about your story makes sense. But somehow, you've been able to convince everyone else that you don't have other programming underneath that metal skull of yours."

"I haven't led anyone to believe anything."

"Someone dug you up. Someone dumped you in that junkyard."

"I mean you, nor anyone on this ship, any ill will. I promise. I just want to open the GeminArc and—"

"Help?"

"Yes."

Meric nodded, eyes closed. "You just want to help."

"That's right."

"How does it feel?"

"How does what feel?"

"Heard you can summon ungodly power. You can wield enough energy to wipe out a platoon. That right?"

"Yes."

"So. How does it feel?"

"It feels... it feels—"

"It feels good, doesn't it?"

"No. I—"

"I put things on the table. Always have—don't hide what I'm thinking. I don't trust you, robot. Have I made that clear?"

"Quite."

"Then we've come to an understanding. That I will be watching you to see that you do what you say."

"That's fine. And please don't call me 'robot'. My name is Beetro."

"Cute," he said before stepping down the stairs.

FORTY-SIX

THE DREAM CAME to Beetro once more.

"Sir, the area has been secured."

Beetro's gaze swept the darkened chambers. Soldiers studded the tunnels—turrets occupied every crossing hallway. Drones hovered overhead, equipped with long barrels and ammunition belts draped beneath their metal bellies. The vaulted chamber walls sparkled beneath a myriad of lanterns and torches. A host of men and women stood on guard, silent and motionless. The man who had spoken had his face buried in the ground, groveling.

"Haldane," Beetro heard himself speak.

"Yes, my lord."

"Do you wonder why I have withstood your insubordination? Why I have tolerated your incompetence? Long have I suffered the blunders of my most prestigious, most bestial warrior, Haldane oth Toaruk."

"I do, my lord. I have been a most unprofitable servant. Often have I wondered why my lord has let me live."

"And to think, you are the best my armies have ever

summoned through the crucible of war. Only by sheer attrition and treachery can a man climb the ranks of my armies. Only the best can come to grovel at my feet. And you, Haldane the Blunder, are the best my armies could muster." Beetro let out a high-pitched snort, resembling something close to a laugh. "So why then, Haldane, do I tolerate your life?"

"I would never venture a guess, my lord."

"Look up at me, Haldane."

The man arched his neck, meeting his gaze with Beetro's.

"It's because you must know that your life is a forfeit at any moment. It is the only way I can know that you will do what I say. Obedience must be absolute now. I am to embark on the next phase of conquest. I get a second chance to extend my rule in perpetuity. I must have obedient soldiers."

"I will obey, my lord. Every word. I will take my blade to my neck at this very moment on your command."

"The time will come. Soon, I believe, when you will have the opportunity to die for your lord."

"Is this why we've come? Why we are here, my lord?"

Beetro suddenly stood. A long cloak of midnight black trailed behind him as he moved at Haldane. "*You!*" he said, lifting his arms. "You still believe you can ask me questions?"

"My lord, forgive—"

But the man was rising in the air, legs flailing, sweat dripping from his face. Suspended by nothing, Haldane peered wide-eyed around the chambers. The man dropped his rifle, a bandolier of ammunition hanging from his back. He grabbed at nothing, feet kicking to find leverage on nothing but thin air. "My lord!"

Beetro held his hands up as he spoke. "We are here, Haldane, because I'm not only to defend my kingdom on Earth, but I am on the brink of my next conquest. The enemy is out there—the enemy is *in* here. I will evaporate him from existence, and when I do, Haldane, when I do, I will have unending waves of land to unleash this army. We will scourge Earth once more, feed my armies, and conquer all kingdoms once again. Once I have again proved my superiority, only then will I save this forsaken planet."

Haldane began to sob.

"Don't weep yet, Haldane. Weep when I bring victory. Weep when all the worlds shall know my power once more. Weep when I have obtained something close to godhood. If you stay obedient, I will make you great. High above all those you see, Haldane. I can be a kind ruler, you will see. Once I have what I want, I will take care of my people."

The crying continued. "My lord... my Curse."

"Yes," Beetro said. "Curse," his mood elated. Beetro felt immense satisfaction at the moniker. "But please, save your praises until I am the victor—until my final foe has been defeated. Soon, Haldane. Soon."

Beetro powered up in the cockpit, exhaustion soaking his mind. He was riddled with guilt as he pondered the dream. The details were hazy, but he remembered how he felt. True, he'd had many dreams since reactivation in Korthe, but watching that warrior being tortured by his own hands... it was more than he could bear. He recalled the destruction of the land, clearly his own subconsciousness warning him about what he could become if he were to use his powers for himself.

"Never," he said aloud to no one. "Never," he repeated, looking down at his metal hands. Images of the horse, Bellamare, vaporizing before his eyes, the soldiers in Orion with profound fear slapped on their faces at his photonic power. He was the source of the death—of the fear. What would Lucindi think of him? What was even the point of his own existence? He was designed to be a key and nothing more. His own thoughts—the idea of him as an individual—it was all happenstance. He kept thinking about the fairy tale with Gaul, the king's nephew—he murdered his own family for power, but Besidio suggested that the man may have freed the kingdom from a tyrannical king. So, Gaul was evil, but he brought about good? Is that what Beetro was? The potential for great evil but with the ability to bring about good?

But he knew the truth... he was a mistake. He was to be a walking key without a single thought in his head. His powers were never meant to be. The thinking, feeling creature that was Beetro was never meant to be.

He descended the spiral staircase and found the mood as morose as his own. Hawera was unconscious with sweat beaded on her lips, Ribcage and Arym at her side. Miree was brooding in one corner, Meric in another. Piot and Galiaro chatted mindlessly about some sort of tree nut they both used to enjoy.

"Our dear robot," Galiaro said at his approach.

"Are you sure you know how to open the GeminArc?"

He snorted as if the question was an assault on his senses. "Yes."

"So, that means you know what went wrong last time?"

"Yes. I do."

"What?"

Slightly befuddled, the astrocyst said, "I simply input the wrong coordinates into the system. There is a very specific coordinate for the innerspace—very sophisticated math that has been worked out using Protonix and Neutrini's quantum computational skills."

"So, what went wrong last time? Why did you see me and you on the other side of the portal?"

"I put bad data into the arc. Instead of opening an actual

portal, it mirrored our own dimension—a reflection of our own reality. I temporarily bent space, creating a lensing effect in which I could see the immediate future. Luckily for me, it was enough time for me to see your murderous act moments before you could actually commit the deed."

"So... it wasn't real? What I did to you?"

Galiaro's face softened. "I suppose not."

"But... I would have done it if I had the chance?"

He shrugged. "Yes."

"Is that who I am, truly?"

"I don't know."

"Do I..." He looked around, sheepishly. "Do I have a soul?"

Galiaro put his palms up. "I can't even answer that question for myself. How could I even offer anything close to an answer for you?"

Miree, standing at a window that had long lost its pane, interrupted. "Who cares, Beetro. You're a living, thinking being who feels stupid and loathes himself just like the rest of us. Don't ask stupid questions that don't need an answer, it'll just tie you up in knots and leave you hopeless. Believe me, I know. Just... just do your best. It's all any of us can offer."

Beetro nodded, finding little solace in her words. "Okay, how about a question that does need an answer... who reactivated me?"

Galiaro stroked his beard. "Must've been me. I must've placed a backup directive in the case of accidental inactivation. Something in your matrix must've been corrupted by exposure to the elements buried in the dirt for a few decades. It must've triggered the backup directive to find me. You woke up, dug yourself up, and walked to the nearest town, Korthe. Strange that I also happened to be there."

"Yes. Strange. I have another question."

Galiaro rubbed his eyes. "What is it?"

"If I'm just a key, why did you design me with so much extra equipment? I could've just been a pair of hydraulic legs—no operating system at all."

Galiaro crossed his arms and looked away. "It doesn't matter anymore, robot. You betrayed me and there's no going back."

"But why go through all the trouble in the first place?"

"We're over Meteor Mountains," Arym interrupted. Galiaro appeared grateful for the distraction from Beetro's line of questioning and moved to the window. Beetro joined him, discovering a breath-taking aerial view. It looked like an enormous scoop had been taken out of Earth, creating a crater fertile with vegetation. At the very center point of the valley, a black smudge marked Earth.

Miree looked to Arym. "You live down there? Your people?"

Arym joined them, his eyes downcast at the valley, and nodded. "Yes. I spent my whole life beneath the ground there. My people, the Crib, live there."

"They must not do much trading of goods. I've never heard of anyone from the Crib."

"That's because we take an oath—the Oath of Descension—to never reveal the location or purpose of the Crib."

"So... didn't you just break that oath?"

"Yes," he said without emotion. "I did."

"So, why should we trust you, knowing that you can't keep the oath of your own people?"

He shrugged. "You can't, I guess. Push me out if you want."

"Easy, crazy, I didn't mean anything by that."

"I come from a dogmatic people. Our founder was crazy. He was afraid of the world—afraid of the wars. He buried himself in the ground and set up a cloning plant to continue his progeny."

"You mean..."

"I am a clone. He set up a religion of rituals and honorifics as if they guarded a sacred and yet-to-be-revealed purpose. The rektors are the administrators. They believe they are continuing a sacred work but are mere pawns in the plans of a dead man. I don't blame them. They only do what their existence has dictated they do. But it's all smoke and mirrors—designed to create obedience into his clone children to continue his own propagation. The Oath is a prison. By breaking the Oath, I'm no longer a prisoner."

"I get that," Miree said, her tone softening. "I do. I had to leave my own people—also where I was a prisoner—worse than a prisoner."

Arym nodded and then said, "What does a prisoner do once they've been freed?"

"That's the thing. You think they just stole your time, but they take more than that. They take a bit of who you are—or who you could've become—and never give it back."

"Looks like you've been a prisoner a number of times," he said, pointing to her prosthetic arm and then to the lengthy scars along her arm, freshly churned by recent cuts.

"To operatic proportions," she said and then turned to the rest of the party. "Hey, everyone," she said, tapping on the wall to get attention. "I just want to say something... I want to make something clear to everyone in this aircraft. I've been through a lot in my life—I've seen a lot of evil people get away with doing evil things. The world doesn't care about me. It never has. That's why I've never tried to care back. And when I try to get even, it only makes things worse for me every time. I've never fit in anywhere and have been mostly hated wherever I go. I think the thing we're trying to do here is probably a good thing. It's a stupid thing and probably a pointless thing that won't work, but I can at least say that I'm finally not doing something for just myself. I just want everyone to know that you can trust me as we try to open the GeminArc. Whatever happens, I will do my best to help all of you. I don't have much to lose and I've got nowhere else to go. I will protect all of you and I won't ask for anything in return."

The room stared back, silent.

"I promise."

Crickets.

"What?"

Arym stepped forward. "Nothing. It's just Beetro already made the 'I promise to be your friend' speech a while ago. We're good." She looked to the rest of the room and received nods in confirmation. "I don't think any of us have anywhere and anyone else to go to. We're all in the same boat."

"Oh," Miree squeaked, her cheeks flushed with morbid embarrassment by exposing a modicum of vulnerability. Her stomach acid frothed. "Yeah, good. Glad we're all on the same page then." She sniffed and then nodded a tad too vigorously and went up to the cockpit.

Hours later, Hawera regained consciousness. Despite a sheath of sweat and darkened eyelids, Arym thought her as beautiful as the day they met. Now that her hair had a month's growth, the perfect angles of her face were even better framed with small curls at her temple. For a moment, memories of following her down to Haplo Lake to pick berries flooded his mind, a warm tenderness there that he knew now was only an illusion. He'd marveled at the freedom of the overworld only to discover the corruption—the dangers and emptiness that awaited him. Othel, the founder, was right to dig himself away from the world forever. But at what cost? Was it better to be an oblivious hermit or a miserable overworlder? He preferred neither.

"Arym," she said, blinking awake.

"You're okay?"

She took his hand and patted it. "Thank you, Arym. Good friend, Arym. Good, good friend. Trust always."

Something within him stirred with her words. "Yes. You can trust me. We're friends, always."

"Need my people. Need to find Lithusa."

"Your people? Here in this time? We need to find them?"

"Yas."

"I will take you there. After we open the GeminArc, we can go and rescue your people and bring them to the innerspace."

She shook her head. "Something wrong."

"I know. We don't have much time."

"Something wrong with time."

"What do you mean?"

"I went back many times. Many times."

"You've gone through futurepast many times?"

She nodded. "Hundred times. Each time I look for new path, new..." her brow ruffled as she struggled with her words. "A new story?"

"A new story?"

"I believe she means a new timeline," Galiaro offered, joining their conversation. "The laws of time dictate that you can never go into the past, only forward into a new version of the past created by new quantum fluctuations of the timeline. The forward arrow of time is bent, and as you go forward, you always end up going back in time."

"That's hard to understand," Arym said.

"Aye," Piot grunted. "Hard to wrap the noodles around."

Galiaro waved his hand in dismissal. "The universe doesn't care if we don't understand it. It will go on doing what it wants and that is exactly how time works. The future bends back toward the past, but it does not form a circle with the same past, rather, it *spirals* toward an ever-changing timeline, one that is similar but starts to change with each iteration around the spiral of time. This is how nature protects itself against time paradoxes."

"Time paradoxes?" Arym asked.

Galiaro whined, "Don't even get me started about time paradoxes. It appears our young lady here was tasked by her people to fling herself into the futurepast to then find a new breakoff timeline in which the expansion is not happening. She was to go with her mate and start a new colony of Lithusa. That is correct?"

Hawera nodded. "Yas."

"And so, what were you saying before?" Arym asked her.

"Something wrong with time," she said. "I look for new story, new time that is not same. Each time, I find same story—same time."

"Hmm," Galiaro said with a good stroke of the beard. "Hmm."

Arym fidgeted, frustrated at how little he understood. "What?"

Galiaro spoke to Hawera, "Are you saying that time is a complete circle? That every time you go through futurepast, you find the exact same people... the exact same events identical to the prior timeline?"

She nodded. "Time is now circle. Never end. Forever circle now. Time broken." She motioned a circle with her fingertip.

"How can time be broken?" Arym asked.

"I'm not quite sure. I wish—" Galiaro stood, looking at the exposed window to the terrain far below. "I wish Fallaro was here —that we hadn't quarreled. He was a superb astrocyst—the finest of our order. He specialized in time. I do hope that man is alive somewhere. Once the GeminArc is open, we must find him. If what this young lady is saying is true, we may have other problems."

"Like what?" Beetro finally asked.

"If time no longer spirals outward—no longer refracts as it proceeds—it could have untold effects on extradimensional space."

"I thought there was no time in the innerspace," Arym said.

"That is true. It may be nothing, but it may be something. I do not know."

"What would cause time to change?"

"The only things that can ever change time."

"What is that?"

"Speed and gravity."

"Sounds like our universe is doomed in more ways than one," Miree said.

Galiaro nodded. "I believe we are truly approaching the last chapter of the universe. When the very fabric of reality unravels, our days are numbered. We must open the GeminArc, and we must open it now."

FORTY-SEVEN

THE WILTED FIELDS of Helian appeared just at dusk. Never in ten million years did Miree think she would return to the accursed land. A terrain whose topsoil was so toxic that only a genetically modified corn could grow. It was a land so war-torn from ancient battles that the ground water was polluted with radioactive decay. Despite appearing entirely inhospitable to life, many fief lords over the years found it a perfect setting to rule with an iron fist of starvation and taxation. The people of Helian were too sheltered to know that perhaps there was a better way to live life. Everyone except Lucindi.

"Too good for this world," she whispered to the wind.

"What?" Beetro asked as the vessel descended. Shouts between Meric and Piot echoed into the cabin as the pilots managed the descent.

"Thinking about Lucindi. I... I think I loved her. Hard to know since I've never really cared for another person before her."

Beetro fell silent for a moment. "I think about her almost

constantly. Haven't met anyone like her since I woke up in the junkyard. Why was she so kind when everyone is so cruel?"

"I honestly have no idea. But I want to find out."

"Do you think this will work? That we'll actually find a way to the innerspace and help people escape?"

"Not at all."

Beetro appeared shocked for a moment but fought it back.

"But I'm a pathological contrarian. I could doubt that the sun will rise in the morning. Might even be right these days... but it's worth trying, I think." She looked to the west horizon as the last rays of straw-colored light blinked away. "Lucindi liked to watch the sunset with me."

"Think we could visit her grave back in Korthe? The grave we dug for her? Maybe tomorrow. Just because we open the Arc doesn't mean we need to jump in right away. We'll need to spread the word that there's an escape for everyone."

"Sure. But we might want to see if there is a tomorrow first."

"Thank you," Beetro said.

"For what?"

"For not dismantling me and selling me for scrap."

"Don't thank me. I would've done it. Lucindi stopped me."

"But you were kind enough to listen to her. You recognize goodness when it's in your presence. That's more than most can say."

"I—" A bulge blossomed in her throat. Her eyes stinging. "Thank you. That... actually does make me feel better about myself." A panicked pulse fluttered through her chest. She never thought she'd be so vulnerable with anyone, no less a junkyard robot who she almost sold off for scrap. It was both terrifying and exhilarating. Why did it take the end of the world for her to finally start getting her emotional shit together?

"You're not as bad as you think you are. Maybe you're even better."

They shared an amicable silence as the ground grew larger beneath them.

A sudden and painful high-pitched squeal sounded behind them. They turned, discovering Ribcage absolutely exultant, hopping up and down. "I can feel her! It's my mom! We're back... back to my mom!" A sudden hush fell over her, her eyes turning wildly. "Bye," she said before completely vanishing.

"Well, I guess we'll see her down there?" Miree speculated.

Meric yelled from the cockpit above, "Brace yourselves! Landing might be a little rough."

"Why?" Miree shouted.

"Because. We've never actually landed a hot air balloon before."

"Smart. Makes sense."

It turned out that hectically bracing on the walls and floors was unwarranted. The landing was rather uneventful. The office-turned-aircraft made a dull thud on the soft earth before the burners were killed. The night air was muggy from the nearby swampland surrounding the clearing. Miree's boots sunk into the mud as she cursed aloud, discovering her cloak had dragged through the thick clay after only a few steps. When she finally beheld the outside of the aircraft, she fully realized the utter miracle that they even arrived in one piece after a several-hundred-kilometer journey. The vessel looked like a metal shell trying to undress from a house. Scant shingles still clung around window and door moldings. Anything that relied on a hinge had long been blown off. The roof had been shaved clean where two massive parachutes were gently falling to the ground.

"Piot, we did it," Meric congratulated, emerging from the front door. "Never thought we'd actually use the thing but I'm glad we had the escape shell installed."

"Aye," Piot said, thumping his fist on the side of the hull, clinging to his pipe. "She did well."

The rest of the party gingerly made their way out and inspected the area warily. The only immediate sound they discovered were crickets. The night's sky was pitch. No moon and four stars—an inky veil before them. After a few ceremonious laps around the immediate area, Arym deemed the spot abandoned. Beetro made a quick surveillance with his telescoping gaze and announced that the place was empty. Miree too, with enhanced Reticulum vision, could see that the area was void of any activity.

"Dig sites," Ribcage announced, suddenly appearing in their midst.

"Where?" Miree asked.

She pointed. "There and there."

"Is anyone on guard?"

She shrugged. "There's no one around. Place is empty. There are big holes everywhere. Some go really deep, like caves."

"Deluvius," Miree said, tightening her jaw. "It's where he got all the Alchean weaponry and that fucking silver wing he's been flying around everywhere. I hope you did finally kill him, Rib."

"The second time I stuck him pretty deep. I think I got him." She gave a one-two punch.

"Are you sure no one's around?"

The girl nodded. "Pretty sure. But I'll keep looking." She vanished once more.

"So, where's this Arc?" Meric asked.

Galiaro pointed toward the middle of the clearing. "There. Two arcs, side by side made of Alchean alloy."

"My hip is still crying from the hike out of the bottom of the sea," Piot said. "Meric, m'boy, you go on ahead. I'll keep watch here."

"Nonsense. I will stay behind with my navigator while you all go on ahead." He nodded to Miree.

"Are you sure?"

"Certain. I have business to conduct here."

"What business? You're in the middle of nowhere."

"Go ahead. Let us know when you open a portal into another dimension."

As she watched the two men combing through the contents of the vessel and cataloguing what was usable, she admired the man's tenacity. They were already formulating a backup plan, another escape route, another contingency. She wondered what it was like to live a life so well prepared. "You'll wait for us?" she asked.

Meric nodded. "My father did not raise an oath breaker. Of course, we will wait. Besides, your traveling companion, Hawera, is not fit for travel." He motioned to the doorway where Hawera was now standing for the first time since they left Orion. Arym stood by her side.

"I'll stay with them, too," Arym said. "Let us know when the portal is open. We'll figure out a plan after that."

"Meric," Miree said.

The man was already busying himself with a broom and dust-pan, sleeves rolled up. "Yes?"

"I'm sorry I lied to you. Maybe one day I'll get you those gold leaves I promised."

"Apology accepted, m'lady. Consider the debt repaid by opening the gateway off this doomed planet."

"Thank you, m'man." She turned, following Beetro and Galiaro with a wry grin on her face.

Clap!

Ribcage couldn't stop—wouldn't stop.

Pop!

Jump—breath. *Jump*—scream at the world. *Jump*—roll in the mud. *Jump*—laugh at the world!

This was where she was meant to be... where she was born to be. Free to slip in and out of space as she damn well pleased. Almost, she wanted to go back to Korthe—almost. To Jump around the markets, stealing dried goat meat, and snatching apple turnovers. It was a joy she didn't know she had until she had left. Hoarding food in her rooftop cache, dodging angry housemaids. The game of starvation was dangerous but rewarding—and thrilling. She was still particularly proud of the Lucindi-Crow-biscuit ecosystem she exploited. Keeping the old man drunk with a small but steady supply of swiped spirits from the tavern cellar. Just enough to keep him unaware of the small portions she broke off from the biscuit Lucindi left him every day. She missed it all—the strategy, the reward, the *danger*. If only she could get in a tussle with the street kids again, what she would give to sucker punch...

But then she remembered they were gone. Taken. Stolen by the general.

"Ass!" she hissed into the night. "He was an aasssssss."

But he's a dead ass, now.

The first place she Jumped was back to her mom. The arcs. They glittered despite the darkness of the night. Brilliant and beautiful just like the first day she fell out of them. Ribcage wrapped her small arms around one arc, relishing the cool alloy beneath her arms. She gave the metal surface a little kiss and Jumped in and out of space around the arcs, humming mindlessly.

"I'll be back!"

She Jumped again, popping up on a tree branch. She wished

Deluvius was still alive so she could stick him in the gut again. It made all her other threats—particularly to Arym—feel a little less deserving. The general was bad. She knew that now. Arym... not so bad. Beetro... good. Miree... still not too great. *But maybe she's okay. I don't know yet.* Hawera... the best! Galiaro... he made Beetro, so he must be good. There were the other two guys that flew them back to her mom, so they must be good guys, too. Her head sometimes hurt double-checking who was bad and who was good. There were too many people now to keep track of. What kind of people can get together for a reason and stay together long enough to do anything at all? They *must* be doing something good.

Clap!

She Jumped back to the open clearing, her bare feet sinking into the mud. The chill bothered her for a moment until she realized something.

Cold? I was cold every night in Korthe. Soft. I've gotten soft.

Smiling, she allowed herself to sink deeper, mud splitting between her toes. Looking down at her shins, she realized she was wearing a thick poncho over her belly that a robot had given her.

A poncho?

Never did she have the luxury of a poncho in Korthe. Yeah, she'd definitely gotten soft.

Pop!

She appeared atop a grassy knoll and tore the poncho from her body, leaving a tunic underneath.

A tunic?

Off it went, exposing her bare chest and ribcage beneath. Miree's scarf she kept wrapped around her neck. No point in getting rid of a perfectly good scarf.

"I. Am. Ribcage!" she declared to the night's sky. She let the chill cover her skin, rippling goosebumps along her arms and belly. "Ribcage!" she repeated, brandishing a knife from her belt.

Clap!

She Jumped, checking the perimeter of the swamps, searching for the general's soldiers. She'd spin circles around them and stick them all in the gut just like their stupid master.

Pop! Nothing.

Clap! Nothing.

Pop! Nobody.

Clap! Empty.

Pop!

Another dig site. A big one.

She stood at the rim of a wide but shallow bowl that had been carved into the ground. Boulders and rock mounds were scattered throughout the excavation site amongst twisted metal and other vestiges of broken digging equipment. She padded softly on the freshly churned earth, sniffing the air. A stiff breeze chilled her skin once more, invigorating an acute sense of exposure in the open. With knife in hand, she crept along, listening, imagining her ears turning like a cat to any sound.

She thought about her mom. She wasn't a... person. Not really, at least. But Ribcage remembered her... not what she looked like, but what she felt like. That flatland had little to see. Come to think of it, she couldn't remember one detail about what her mom even looked like at all. But the feelings she recalled—warmth, tenderness, someone who cared and watched over her. Where was she now? And why did she leave?

She squinted her eyes as if it would help her imagine—to picture life before living in the third dimension. The third? If she was in the third, does that mean she came from the second? Did it have anything to do with Hawera's Fourth? These were questions that she quickly dismissed as she continued searching the dig site, realizing more and more that she was something rather peculiar—an oddity from a lower dimension. This wasn't an entirely unsettling thought to her as she tried to remember what life was like before... before Korthe, before Lucindi. There was her mom and then a sudden crash into the third dimension. It felt like... falling. Falling through a hole into third existence. She woke up at the two arcs. How long ago was it? Two years? She shook her head, her knotty hair tossing back and forth. None of these were questions she would figure out on her own. She'd have to talk to Crow when she got back...

A sound. A cat meow. Or a whimpering animal. She Jumped and slipped back a few steps closer to the sound. Still no movement—nobody around.

"I am Ribcage," she whispered to herself as she crept along the damp soil. The meowing sound grew yet was still faint—muffled. After a few more steps, the sound was undeniable but still so distant and small as if carried in the wind.

"Who's there!" she finally yelled. "I'm just a helpless little girl. Why don't you come out and get me?" When the sound amplified at her taunting, she realized it was coming from beneath her feet. She jumped up and down and felt the reverberating *thump* of wood beneath dirt. On hands and knees, she probed the dirt until the leading edge of a wood plank was felt. After a bit of digging, she exposed the edge and, with the use of a broken tree branch, dug deeper beneath the wood. As she made progress, the sound of whimpering turned to frank crying and complaining.

She placed her lips to the hole. "Hello?"

The babbling of voices crescendoed.

She dug, creating a big enough hole for her tiny body to slip through. Lowering herself, she discerned there was plenty of empty space that went deep—deeper than her legs could feel. Her grip slipped and she fell, rolling down a mound of dirt, the air full of musk. It was nearly impossible to see anything, but she could tell she was at the threshold of a cavern. Within, limbs were moving—dirty blankets shuffling. Ribcage was confused but felt little threat. The air was redolent with the stench of imprisonment.

A single voice rose from the cacophony. "Help us."

"Who are you?"

"Prisoners. They trapped us down here. They make us work all day and put us down here. Please! Please, we need to get out of here!"

Ribcage crept forth, wary of a trap. Most things in life were traps. "But who are you?"

"Children. Just children. Slaves."

As she approached, she saw a boy bowing to the ground, his fingers sticking through iron bars. His face was caked with mud save deep rivets where repeated tears had streaked across. The boy was emaciated—wrists like knots in a thin rope. As his gaze met hers, she knew.

"Jaram?"

"Rib... Ribcage?"

"That's right." Jaram. The boy who had tried to kill her several times on the rooftops of Korthe. A bully, a savage, and her first mortal enemy. Now enslaved in an underground prison.

Through pleading eyes, he watched her as if wondering what she would do. "Will you help us?"

She crossed her arms. "That depends. Would you have helped me?"

Miree sloshed through the mud, Beetro and Galiaro following directly behind, mirroring her footsteps. Her arm ached from the prosthetic, her ass hurt, and every implant in her skull throbbed with each step. The thousands of micro slashes covering her skin had scabbed over but now pulsed with inflammation. Every step. Every heartbeat. Pain. There was an apparent minimum pain response of the Reticulum modulator to dampen the pain and she wasn't quite meeting the threshold. A wind whipped across the mud plains, chilling her bones, arousing her suspicions. To have such an ancient artifact as the GeminArc now totally unguarded screamed one thing—trap.

She then realized that she didn't have a weapon. No boltgun. No Swordless Hilt. How she would love to grip the Hilt, waving the thermally charged shards at her whim. "You're all charged up there, Beetro?"

"Huh?"

"Your photonics. If we run into trouble, you can, you know, blast everyone away, right?"

"Not exactly. It's nighttime."

"And?"

"Radiant photons are scarce," Galiaro answered. "He uses photons, condenses them in his dark matter skin, and then distills it back out as raw energy."

"So, you're telling me we're about to open a portal into another dimension in the middle of the night on a dying world and we don't have a single weapon between the three of us?"

"I have my staff," Galiaro offered, pushing the end of the brittle wood through mud.

"Is there a reason we didn't plan to do this during the day?"

Galiaro kept walking and said, "I'm sorry that I couldn't plan an emergency hot air balloon ride out of a city under siege better. Let's open the GeminArc now. Or would you like to see if Jupiter gets flung from its orbit first?"

The twin arcs appeared over a knoll, the curves somehow still glittering in the impossibly dark night. Miree remembered the area had been cut of all foliage with laser precision when they first discovered the arcs. It seemed a lifetime ago when they first found the area. She remembered Beetro placing pebbles around a map with the Arc in the middle, the Alchean spires in Helian forming a semicircle around the Arc.

Beetro, too, seemed to remember. "The spires I saw in Korthe... around the area of Helian. Those are—"

"The pylons of a particle accelerator," Galiaro answered. "Once we activate the twin arcs, a stream of protons will be shot around the spires, creating a halo of subatomic bombardment. It will be the sub-nuclear interactions that will create a halo of dense gravity. Like a donut, the gravity halo will invert space in the center, which bends spacetime, opening a funnel into other such arcs that were presumably spread across the universe. This is how the Alchean managed interstellar travel. This is also how they opened the innerspace to escape the expansion. My mistake was I did not apply enough gravimetric force to open into the innerspace. The force was too weak and rebounded spacetime back at us. This is why I got a glimpse of the near future of our own dimension."

"So, what will you do differently this time?"

A light suddenly radiated around them, heralding the arrival of Protonix. "We will apply a greater gravimetric force. Run the particle accelerator at a much higher rate, increasing the subatomic bombardment. This will be enough to penetrate into the innerspace."

"Beetro," Miree said, pointing to the Protonix. "Here's all the light you can ever need for your photonics."

Protonix refracted into a face. "I'm afraid not. When there is no ambient light, I recirculate the light of a single photon to maintain my form as this orb. The light you are seeing is the same photon recycled ten trillion times a femtosecond."

"Oh."

"Where is Neutrini?" Galiaro questioned.

"She tells me she will be arriving shortly."

Miree put out her palms in indignation. "What the hell else does she have to do?"

"Let's just get started," Galiaro said, stepping toward the arcs.

The arcs were spaced about seven meters apart, facing one another in perfect parallel. They appeared almost as two empty door frames, the silhouette forested marsh looking through from the other side.

Beetro stepped forward. "I tried stepping through last time we were here—back when we didn't know what this place was. Nothing happened."

Galiaro tsked. "No, and nothing would. The arcs are part of the portal but are not the activation switch. Come," he said, gesturing to an equidistant space between the arcs. "Do you see? Here and here?" He pointed at the ground.

"I see nothing."

"Neither do I. You need to switch to infrared."

A shuttered sound snapped as the robot's eyes followed the ground. "Oh."

"Hmm. Yes." Galiaro nodded.

Miree inched forward. "What's there?"

"It's just a rectangular-shaped piece of metal. Like a platform."

"Correct. It's where the dark matter is placed. Please." He motioned for Beetro to step over the patch of ground.

Gingerly, Beetro slogged through the mud and positioned himself at the plate. Immediately, a low hum emanated from the arcs.

Galiaro smiled in delight. "Ah. Alchean technology. Can't beat it."

Suddenly, Neutrini was there, orb dancing around Beetro. "It's still active. Good. Now, astrocyst, please activate the Arc."

The party together shared a sidelong glance at her authoritative voice. "All in good time, my dear proton," Galiaro said. "We have to wait for the resonance to build between the two arcs."

"Resonance?" Miree asked.

"Yes. Gravity will begin to oscillate between the two arcs—a flux of gravitons. This will create enough energy to then power the particle accelerator. The inverted gravity ring of the accelerator ring will then form a harmonic resonance with the gravity flux created by the two arcs. This process together will then activate the portal once I input the correct data."

"And then what?" Beetro asked.

"Then we input our calculations and open the GeminArc into the innerspace."

"How long will it take?" Miree asked.

"Minutes to hours. The process is more complex than you can understand."

Miree wrinkled her nose at the arcs. "Won't the gravity start to build up? Like... won't we get sucked up into this thing?"

"No. The gravitons accumulate here over millions of different overlapping dimensions. The local increase in gravity will be negligible. This is why dark matter is needed. It helps condense the extradimensional gravitons in one place without forming a black hole."

"Of course," Miree said. "Right."

Galiaro leaned on his staff. "So, we wait."

A small ember glowed with every puff of Piot's pipe. The man sat silently in the hot air balloon vessel; one leg crossed over the other.

In the blackness of the evening, Arym saw only the haunted look of his wrinkled face light up as he drew air through the pipe.

"You've got a peculiar look," Piot told him, one eye cocked.

"So do you."

"That dark hair—black, really. Pasty skin—white like cream. Hawkish face—nose that goes to the center of Earth."

"What's your point?"

"You've a peculiar look is all."

"I come from a peculiar place."

"Aye. Suppose we all do."

Meric stepped in from the outside and removed his boots. Squinting, his eyes traced mud prints that lined the floor. His gaze then fell on Arym's boots before clearing his throat. "I thought I made it clear that I would like everyone to remove their footwear upon entering my father's office."

"I'm sorry." Arym stripped off his boots.

"This is still a place of business. True, we are on leave at the moment, but I intend to get this place up and running."

"For what?"

"If all goes as planned—opening a portal into another dimension—then we will have a rush of humanity coming through here. There must be rigorous bookkeeping, and someone must do it. This office will be the base of the operations for the diaspora."

"You plan on opening a *business* here?"

"Of course."

"You're going to charge people to escape the planet?"

Meric scoffed. "Don't be ridiculous. I may be a profiteer but I'm not heartless. There will be no fee to leave our planet. I only ask that people register with me before their exodus. Data is knowledge, and knowledge is future profit." He nodded to Piot, who returned the gesture.

"How will we get the word out once the Arc is open?"

"Radio mostly, I suppose. The issue I see is getting people to actually believe that there is a problem with the galaxy—that Earth is in danger of being flung from its orbit. This is no small task."

"Preach," Piot said. "We'll have to preach."

"I've had enough preaching for a lifetime," Arym said, looking at Hawera, who was sleeping.

Meric watched her breath. "How's the girl?"

"Tired but feeling better."

Hawera stirred from her sleep and nodded. "I okay. Better."

Meric crouched beside her and took her hand in his. It looked like a bear holding the hand of a squirrel. "Thank you," he said, his voice deep and tender. "Thank you for saving me. I would have fallen from the sky had you not rescued me with your unusual and magnificent powers."

Arym saw her hold his hand tight as she said, "Thank you. Thank you. You saved all."

Meric gave her a small peck on the cheek and went about busying himself once more with cleaning the disaster of the office.

Arym released a sigh that was clearly nothing less than pure annoyance and stood, sinking his feet into boots. "I need some air." He shrugged on a jacket.

The air outside was crisp and silent, save for a symphony of crickets ticking away in the night as they had for eons—as if the creatures of the world had no idea of the calamity that awaited them. Arym brooded, of which he had grown tired but couldn't muster more energy to do anything else. So, he went on a stroll, his boots sinking into the mud with each step. He saw the tracks the others had taken toward the GeminArc. He honestly didn't want to see the twin arcs—still felt like an outsider on a quest that had little to do with him. True, he'd provided key information to the astrocyst in the form of his journal with etchings of the Alchean tomb. But once he'd turned the pages over, his use had all but dried up.

So, he walked in the opposite direction, through the mud and toward a rim of trees skirting the marshland. Perhaps he'd keep walking and never return. Hawera had everyone else to take care of her now. She had that hulking brute, Meric, to save her from danger.

A twig snapped.

Probably an animal.

He thought longingly about the animal hatcheries, the fisheries, and livestock kept in the Crib. Such delicate and dutiful care the Crib herdsman kept over their animals, knowing each one was a precious resource to be used carefully for the good of the Crib. His mind went to the digline—lugging massive augers and always trying to find places for displaced dirt. Tunneling new Oshafts for aeration, putting out oil fires, digging out digkids during cave-ins. It was awful work, but he missed the simplicity of the ignorance.

Another snap.

"Who's there?" Arym asked, approaching the edge of the forest. Nothing moved. He crept on, heartbeat escalating.

A hooded figure arose.

"St-stop," Arym said, wishing he had a weapon.

"Arym," the figure said, voice low—familiar.

"Yes? Who are you? Are you with the general?"

"Arym. It's me."

And then he recognized the voice. "Lutra? How?"

"Yes. It is me." A faint silhouette stirred at the edge of the forest.

"Why are you here? You can't bring me back, Lutra. I'll never return to the Crib. It's a sick place. You shouldn't have followed me here. I told Rektor Tarysl the same thing. How did you find me? Did he tell you?"

Silence for a moment and then a somber reply, "I'm sorry." He hid something beneath his voice. The whimper of sobbing?

"Go. Return to the Crib. Tell them that the world is ending. Tell them to travel here. I know it doesn't make sense yet, but it will. Forget the Oath, forget about Othel. Bring your brothers here so they can escape the expansion."

"I shouldn't have come after you," Lutra said, his face still veiled by darkness. "I shouldn't have gone wandering in the Meteor Mountains. This never would have happened if I had only stayed put. The overworld is a very bad place." His voice cracked with a sob.

"It's okay. Please, return to the Crib to warn them. You will be met with resistance, but this is the only way. They won't be safe under the ground forever. The world will end soon, and I don't think there is much time. They can't hide anymore. No one can."

"I loved you, Arym," he said, detachment in his voice.

"We're clones of one another. Othel was a sick man to put us all together. We're not supposed to be together like that. I thought I was in love once, too. But it wasn't real, Lutra."

"Damn, my heart. I won't forget the time we had in the kitchen. Cooking and talking. They got me, Arym." The emotion left his voice, now infused with bizarre sterility. "Where is the robot?"

"Beetro?"

"Where is the *robot*?"

"What... how do you know...?"

"Do not make this difficult, Arym." Lutra approached as another hooded figure grew behind him, a faint glow of yellow and green emanating from within the hood. "She needs the robot, Arym. I can't stop! Ooh, my head! They're in my *head!*"

Arym ran.

"She needs the robot!" Lutra cried into the night.

FORTY-EIGHT

RIBCAGE PACED OUTSIDE THE CELL, which had been built to house dozens of children—the leftover slave labor of Deluvius' excavating endeavors.

"Ribcage, please..."

She continued pacing, thinking... relishing?

"Things are different," Jaram continued. "I'm sorry—we're all sorry about the way we treated you back in Korthe. It wasn't right, we know that. Everything is different now. If I could go back, we would've brought you into our gang. You're one of us—always were." There was agreement all around among the captive children.

Ribcage tapped a finger on her chin for a moment and said, "I killed the general, you know."

"Y-you did?"

"Stabbed him in the gut. Twice." She held up two fingers.

"That's... that's amazing. He was a bad, very evil man. Korthe and Helian will be better without him. Thank you, Ribcage.

You've saved us all." There was a chattering of congratulations that quickly grew to pandering.

She let a dignified silence settle around her.

"Does that mean his army is really gone? We can just... go home?"

"Depends on what *I* do."

"And what are you going to do?"

"Whatever I want." She moved throughout the cavern, inspecting dig equipment—abandoned machinery. The children watched her as she wiped the top of a tractor with her finger, inspecting the dust on her fingertips.

"Come on!" a girl shouted from within the cage. "Let us out!"

Ignoring the growing outrage, she found a stash of dried meat and hungrily bit into a strip, showcasing the feast to the children.

What had been pleading turned into growing resentment. "Always hated her!" one child said. Followed by, "Hasn't changed a single bit. Still a freak."

"She took my ear!" another said.

As she watched the tumult behind the cage, Ribcage remembered the fever dream from the forest with the gigantic purple trees. It was like what was going on presently—the other children hating her. She hated them too, but in the dream, Beetro blasted them away with his power. Nothing but charred skin and bone remained. She recalled how it felt, seeing the other children burnt to a crisp. It felt... not great, actually. She didn't mean it, she screamed at Beetro to stop, but the robot smiled, ready for more annihilation. Luci was there. She had called Ribcage a pet, a—nothing.

Ribcage had felt like a nothing her whole life.

Do I feel like a nothing now?

No, she didn't. So, what had changed?

She'd thought that her Jump made her special, made her

better than the rest of the kids. They were *beneath* her. That she was *above* them. But isn't that what the general thought? That he was above everyone so he could do anything he wanted? Standing there in the underground cavern, watching the other kids spit and yell at her, she still felt like a nothing again.

Quietly, she asked them, "This is who you are?"

None of the children could hear as they raged against her.

"Who are you!" she screamed.

Some children stopped yelling.

"You rob and you steal?"

The cage went quiet.

"Are you nothing little street rats?"

Not a soul answered.

"And that's why no one has come to save you. Is it because you are all nothing?"

"We just want to go home," Jaram cried.

"Home? Back to Korthe, where you'll continue to be ignored by everyone else and starve in the streets? Is that what you want?"

"No," Jaram said. "But that's all we have. We're just like you. Never had a family."

Ribcage nodded. "You *are* just like me. Which means you can have a family just like I do now."

"Will you let us out now?"

She inspected the locks. They were bulky. "Not without a way of cutting through these."

Some children began to cry again.

"I'll be back. I... promise. You can count on me."

The twin arcs hummed with energy. Beetro felt the dark matter metal shell pull around him—his body a conduit for the gravitons of thousands of dimensions coalescing in the same spot. Galiaro watched him fervently. The old man's eyes were cracked red, sunken with purple bags beneath. The astrocyst was tired, hands shaky, breath unsteady. Protonix and Neutrini circled around him, watching, waiting. Miree had found a boulder where she sat, one boot crossed over her knee. She, too, watched Beetro with what he believed to be extreme caution.

"You think I'll turn again," Beetro said. "That I'll try to kill Galiaro—or all of you. Don't you?"

There was a resounding silence.

"I don't know why I did it that day. Truthfully, I have no idea what I am or where my mind came from. I don't know why I act the way I do or have the thoughts that come to me. But neither do any of you. You were born into this world just as I was. You have no memory of anything before you opened your eyes, just like me. So, please, don't define me by what I did. Define me by what I'm trying to do now."

Miree stood. "I know I do. I've been through enough with you that I know who you are. You're not a murderer. You're a good person who tries to do good things. I'm with you."

"Someone put the robot in the junkyard," Galiaro rebutted. "Was it backup programming? Possibly..."

"It was probably me," Beetro said. "I could've woken up and walked to the nearest town and had a system-wide failure and shut down there."

"That may have been possible," Galiaro said as if it was the first time he had considered the scenario.

"Once this is open, we'll find the innerspace and I will help everyone get off the planet," Beetro said. "I swear it. I have no hidden agenda."

"I believe you," Miree said.

Galiaro's resolute silence confirmed the astrocyst's reserved suspicions.

Neutrini refracted into her self-image. "I believe it is almost time. The gravitons are meeting the threshold to activate the arcs."

Miree asked, "So, then we can just walk right through into the innerspace?"

Galiaro laughed in her face and said, "Any fool can put a chunk of dark matter on the activation pedestal and activate the arc. It is actually inputting the correct data into the coordinate system that is delicate work. I studied it for decades before my first attempt with Beetro and look where it got me. I bent space so much that I broke the damn thing."

"Broke space?" Beetro asked.

"Yes. The girl. The little devil. She calls this place her mother. Well, I don't think she's wrong. I believe this is the place she was born—into the third dimension. She's... not supposed to be here. I tore a hole in space, and I believe she... fell through it."

"*Fell*?"

"In a sense. She was a two-dimensional being who happened to fall through the hole in space that is here, at the GeminArc. It explains why she can Jump in and out of space whenever she is near or whenever the Lithusan girl creates a fourth-dimensional disruption in space. It gives her access to the second dimension in which she can slip back and forth at her pleasure. It is quite the anomaly. Fascinating, really. Proves many centuries-old theories about spacetime."

"So, the hole you tore... it's still here?"

He nodded. "It must be."

Protonix chirped up. "One cannot simply tear a hole in space without..." He stopped, lost in thought.

"Without what?" Miree asked.

"I believe what the proton is trying to say is that you can't tear a hole without a tremendous amount of energy, which I accidentally created when I didn't vent the gravitons properly."

"No," Protonix said. "That's not what I'm saying at all. One cannot create a hole in space without there being... another side in which to receive the other end of that hole."

"Hmm." Galiaro stroked his beard, unsettled by the comment.

"What does that mean?" Beetro asked. "Another third dimension on the other side?"

Neutrini interrupted. "The process is complete. The gravitons have met the threshold. Do you see?"

A soft *whir* sounded throughout the forest. Beetro looked beyond the marsh and saw a single streak of brilliant aqua light floating at the ends of the marshland. "The particle accelerator is charged."

"That it is." Galiaro squinted, inspecting the immediate ground. "Now, where is the control...." As he spoke, a depression formed in the ground, widened, and sank further until the earth suddenly dropped right from the ground. Neutrini shot down the newly formed cavern, revealing a staircase that led into the ground. "Ah." Galiaro moved, stepping down the steps.

"Do I come with you?" Beetro asked.

"No," Galiaro's voice echoed up. "You're the key. The key must stay in the lock while I turn the doorknob." Protonix, too, followed him down.

Beetro looked at Miree. "I'll stay up here with you," she told him, making herself comfortable at his feet.

Heart pounding in his ears, Arym made it back to the hot air balloon and leaped up the steps. "Reticulum!" he shouted.

Meric, wearing an apron and goggles, was in the middle of hammering a fractured table leg to its original spot on a coffee table. He dropped the hammer and looked at Piot. "Weapons?"

Piot's lips puckered. "Left the arsenal back in Orion. The escape capsule left it behind."

Meric tore off his apron and rolled up his sleeves. He ripped the leg off the table that he had just finished nailing and hefted the weight in his palm. "Can you help?" he asked Hawera, who was getting to her feet. *A little*, she indicated by measuring a small space in between her thumb and index finger. "Where are they—?"

But his answer was the presence of two figures in the doorway, hoods down, faces pulsing with light. One brandished a sword of curious workmanship boasting a dull blade, which scarcely appeared equipped to slice through anything at all.

Meric stepped forward. "This is my father's establishment. You are not welcome here."

The figure spoke in between outbursts of sobbing. "I don't want to! I never meant to do anything to anyone! The buzzing! You don't understand, Arym, I can't control what I'm doing!"

"Why does this cyborg know your name?"

"He's from the Crib—from my people. The Reticulum caught him because he left to look for me."

"That complicates what I'm going to do next." Meric lunged at Lutra. For a man who had the build of a moose, he pounced like a snake. Using the table leg as a cudgel, he landed a quick blow to the throat, tossing Lutra's blade to the floor. At the same moment, Hawera was circling the room, silver-tip staff in hand. The other Reticula behind had made a quick swipe of his hand, revealing a dazzling array of glowing embers, floating, organizing... arming. The figure ducked and rolled, moving into the room, glowing embers following. With another flick of the wrist, the embers surrounded Meric before he could lift another blow to Lutra.

"Stop," the person said, masculine voice almost a whisper.

Finding himself caged within the hot shards, Meric dropped

the cudgel. The improvised weapon split in half on the shards as it fell to the floor, spontaneously bursting into flames.

"The robot," he said while Lutra got to his feet. "We need robot. Robot for her."

Is that broken Haenglish?

Hawera was in between them, her staff pointed at the Reticula. "Leave," she said. "I can kill. Can freeze your time." A shaft of blue light bloomed from her forearms and streaked down the staff.

"Please," the Reticula said, a crack in his voice. "Please... Hawera."

Hawera's expression softened as she lowered her staff. Delicately, she brought down the man's hood. A hollow-faced man with a blonde buzz cut stared back, anguish written across his face. Eyes hot with tears, he spoke in a language Arym had only heard from one person before—Hawera. Hawera fell into him, hands sweeping his face, inspecting glowing implants that studded his forehead. Her fingers traced corrugated tubing that trailed from occiput to his brow ridge.

Together, they wept.

"Patwero..." she lamented.

"What's happening?" Meric asked.

"It's... her mate," Arym said. "The man who she traveled with through futurepast before crash landing together in our time."

Still encaged within the shards, Meric scooted a boot under the bottom row, trying to kick at Lutra's sword. Rage swept Patwero's face, the Reticulum identity once more taking over. He pushed Hawera away and titled the Swordless Hilt with his wrist, tightening the circumference around Meric. "Stop," he told him. "Or die. *She* needs robot. Tell us where." Hawera clutched her staff but appeared too paralyzed with grief to make any sort of move.

"Tell them nothing," Meric said.

Lutra got to his feet. "The rest of the group must be at the GeminArc with the robot and the astrocyst. I'll go. You stay here." He bent, reaching for his Swordless Hilt on the floor.

"Lutra," Arym said. "Fight it. This isn't you. You're a Cribman."

Lutra avoided eye contact and vanished from the doorway.

"No one leave," Patwero said as he gripped his Swordless Hilt. "You," he said, pointing at Arym, "tie her." He gestured to Hawera. He flicked the Hilt with his wrist and then flipped the pommel around, prompting the shards to burn fiery white. "Now—"

The shards suddenly fell to the ground, scattering like pebbles across the floor. Patwero fell to his knees and slumped to the ground, something protruding from his neck. Upon closer inspection, Arym realized it was a *feather*.

Piot stood across the room, some sort of blow dart between his lips. "Ha!" he said, giving himself a light applause. "Hadn't actually used one of these before now. I didn't think it would work *that* fast. Those Torbad are crafty people."

Arym bent to examine Patwero's breathing. "Will he be okay?"

"Aye. Sedative only. He'll have a bit of a hangover."

Meric shrugged on a jacket. "We need to warn the others."

"What do we do with *him*?"

"Bind him," Meric said before dashing out the doorway

Arym and Hawera dragged the sedate Lithusan to the corner of the room and bound him with twine. "Maybe Galiaro can free him from the Reticulum like he did for Miree?"

"I hope," Hawera said, giving the man a kiss on the cheek.

Arym found the loose hilt, broken of its shards, and stuffed it in his belt. "I'll be back."

"What is taking so long?" Miree asked as she descended the staircase below the GeminArc. She'd been waiting with Beetro for nearly an hour for Galiaro and the floating protons to finish working out their calculations or whatever nonsense they were doing down below.

Galiaro's voice rounded a sharp corner. "Who's there?"

"Me. I thought you had all the math figured out. What's the problem—" She rounded the corner and discovered the old astrocyst seated in an enormous chair constructed in the middle of what could only be described as a cockpit. The walls were awash in Alchean alloy sheen, a smooth sterility to the engineering still apparent through eons of time. Before Galiaro was an enormous orb, floating in midair with swirls of colors and eddies of textures scintillating on its surface. The man was furiously swiping his fingers across the orb while his feet worked a myriad of intricate pedals that ran across the floor as if he was playing an organ.

"This looks... complicated."

His face dripping in sweat, Galiaro turned to her with a look of raw annoyance. "Can't you see I'm working!"

"Very complex work," Protonix remarked. "More, in fact, than I had even anticipated. I'm afraid the astrocyst undersold the actual intricacies of working the GeminArc interface. I don't believe I know of another human who could negotiate so many variables at once. I must say, I'm impressed. A rare phenomenon."

"With the help of our quantum computations," Neutrini added. "But yes, I must agree. There is no one in the land who could open the GeminArc of whom I'm aware. It was important to bring this astrocyst here first."

"First?" Miree asked.

"Yes. Of course. Before attempting to open the portal, it is important that he be here."

"Was there anyone else who could've opened it?"

"Anyone else could've caused catastrophic changes to the fabric of space."

"Which Galiaro almost did in his previous attempt."

"Quite right. But I believe he has learned, and, with our aid, we will have it activated with the correct data very soon. We are close." Neutrini then winked away, disappearing from the chamber.

"Where the hell is she going?"

Protonix turned to her. "I think it best you leave the astrocyst to work out the final inputs. This is... delicate work."

"Yeah, I can see that." She turned on her boot and left the cockpit, ascending the stairs two at a time.

She discovered Beetro standing in the same spot, atop the pedestal. Only, now he had a cage of fiery shards surrounding him.

"What the fu—"

"Don't move," a voice said from behind.

But Miree already hit the ground, rolling through the mud. She kicked a leg out, hoping to connect, but hit nothing and fell face forward. Spitting mud from her mouth, she got to her hands and knees and saw a man glaring down at her.

It was Arym.

"What the fuck, man! You're Reticulum now?"

"Miree," Beetro said, exuding calmness within his new cage. "Arym comes from a clone colony, remember? It's someone else."

"Get up," the Reticula said. "Toss me your weapon."

Wiping mud from her knees, she said, "I don't have one." She saw the Swordless Hilt gripped in his hand and instantly flared with jealousy.

The man suddenly choked with tears. "I'm... really... sorry..."

She rose, keeping her eyes on the Hilt. "I know. I know you are. Look at me," she pointed to her eye implants, to her arm, "they got me, too. You've got that governor chip ticking away in your brain and I know it's making you do all this. I also know that you'll definitely kill me if I try anything. *She* has control over you."

"I can't fight it!"

"I know you can't. It's impossible. So just... close your eyes." She took a step toward him.

"What?"

"Close your eyes. There's no directive about closing your eyes, right?"

The Reticula shut his eyes. "I... I guess not."

"What's your name?" She took another step.

"Lutra."

"Lutra, I was freed from her. She doesn't buzz in my brain anymore."

"She needs the robot! He's coming with me. It's the only way to stop the buzzing! Now move it!" he yelled at Beetro.

"I can't," he said. "My task is not yet complete. Once we've opened the gate into the innerspace, I will come with you. You must wait."

"That—" Lutra tilted his head, receiving information. "That is acceptable to her. You will open the GeminArc and then the robot will accompany me back to the Reticulum."

A wind swept the boggy marsh, chilling Miree as she kept her eyes locked on the Reticula. "Beetro, I'm not going to just let him take you."

"It's fine," he said, something morose in his voice. "My purpose will have been served. I'm only a key. Nothing more."

Arym found them at the twin arcs. Lutra holding Beetro captive within one of those bizarre, floating cages. Miree stood by, speaking in a low voice, trying to reassure the Cribman.

"Lutra, stop!" Arym said on his approach. Meric walked by his side, another table leg in hand.

"Has he hurt anyone?" Meric asked.

"Nobody hurt him!" Beetro said. "No one is going to get hurt for me. We don't need anyone else getting hurt defending a key. We wait for Galiaro to tell us he's ready to open into the inner-space and then I'm going with him to the Reticulum."

Meric offered no protest to the plan.

Arym shook his head. "No, that's not happening, Beetro. We're not letting you go. Right?" He looked to Miree.

"That's right—hey! Where did you get that?" She pointed to his hand.

He gripped the empty Hilt. "From that other half-robot person, Patwero. He's bound back at the office."

"Gimme that!" she said, swiping the Hilt from his hand.

"I'd be careful, it is one weird weapon."

A devilish smile crept up her face as she hefted the Hilt in her palm. With a flick of her wrist, a fleet of shards flew at them as if by command. They formed at the Hilt and stacked up, forming a dull blade.

Protonix swept between them. "The astrocyst believes he has inputted the correct coordinates—what is going on?"

"Little problem," Miree said, gesturing to Lutra. "The Reticulum have plans for Beetro. As soon as you open the arc, he's taking him."

"I see." Protonix's face refracted, his eyes falling on Lutra.

"None of this will be necessary," a new voice declared. "I've watched just about enough of this."

Arym spun and saw a figure approach—tall, darkly clad with

greying at the temples.

"Of course," Miree threw up her hands. "Of course it's Deluvius."

FORTY-NINE

GENERAL DELUVIUS APPROACHED the GeminArc in a casual stride, his gaze falling on each of them. His flat smile and flared nostrils boasted an impeccable arrogance. Striding up alone was somehow more ominous than if he had a captain guard at his immediate disposal. His confidence was slightly betrayed by an almost imperceptible guarding of his side—the exact spot where Ribcage had put a blade in him. Twice.

"*You*!" Arym hissed.

The general scarcely laid his eyes on Arym.

"You attacked my people," Arym accused.

"No doubt, I did. Now shut your mouth, boy," the general shot back. "I have little time for the squabbling of children. I waited *far* too long for this moment. Seems that each time you found another miscreant to add to your band, it prolonged getting you here. Yet I must say that this has worked out quite nicely. You present to me the robot, caged and in the darkest of nights. Bravo. You," he said to Lutra, "will give me that Hilt right now or I will end you."

Lutra trembled, sweat forming on his brow. "B-but I cannot. *She* is in my head!"

The general rolled his eyes before unholstering a firearm at his side. "I've no patience for you Reticulum peons." The shot rang off into the night before Lutra hit the mud. A few of his captains materialized from the pitch, Alchean laser rifles pointed at the group. "Careful," he told them. "Do not fire those until we've given the robot the engram. Only gunpowder until then."

"Lutra!" Arym fell to his knees, cradling the Cribman in his arms.

Deluvius snatched up the Hilt, maintaining Beetro in the cage.

Before anyone could run or fight or anything, Galiaro was there, approaching Deluvius. With arms wide open, no apparent weapon, they all watched while the astrocyst stepped toward him and gave him...

A fucking *hug*.

"My dear friend and colleague," Galiaro said, embracing the general. "I'm so glad you're here, brother."

"The fuck, old man!" Miree yelled. "You've been in on it with this bastard the whole time?"

Galiaro turned to her, face completely flummoxed. "This is my old colleague, Fallaro. He's who I worked with ages ago. We discovered the premature expansion together and developed Dark Theory. Although, I do wonder what has brought him here tonight..."

"Oh shit, he's Fallaro?" Miree squinted her eyes at him. "I didn't notice... are you aware that he's the same guy who's been digging up old Alchean tech and taking over the fucking world?"

He looked back at the general, who replied with a gentle smile. "What?"

"That's General Deluvius!"

"I... oh." Lightbulbs exploded in the astrocyst's head. "I see." He stepped away from the general. "Yes. This is starting to make sense now."

"It is good to see you, brother," Deluvius said. "I'm afraid my research continued during your... hiatus in Korthe. Now I want everyone here to listen to me because I'm only going to say this once. I don't enjoy killing, but, as you can see, I do not hesitate if my plans are impeded for even the slightest moment. I will not relish placing a bullet into any of you at any moment, but I will if you don't do exactly what I say. I know everything about your endeavors—to every microscopic detail. You have been pawns in my plans, nothing more. And you have arrived at the ultimate ends of my plans. I need the GeminArc open, and Galiaro is the only one who knows how to open it. He never would have done it at my insistence, so we fabricated this ruse to get him here tonight. It took far longer than I intended but it has been successful, nevertheless. You can all vacate the premises now. You can leave, alive. Go ahead."

Galiaro sucked his gums at the general. "So, I was never wrong about you, was I?" He looked down at Lutra with disgust. "You only wanted the GeminArc—the robot—for one thing. Always wanted to rule because you were so damn smart for everyone. No one can think for themselves, they need brother Fallaro to think for them. I see you have changed. Changed for the worst."

Neutrini suddenly appeared, orbiting the general as if coming to his defense.

"Bitch!" Miree said. "It's been her the whole time! Using her lightning-fast communication to tell the general what we've been doing every step of the way!"

"Astute. And quite correct," Neutrini said.

"How could you!" Arym cried to Protonix. "We trusted you!"

Protonix refracted into a face of naked astonishment. "I-I assure you that I had no idea!"

"You're entangled! You know everything about each other, you asshole!" Miree yelled.

"I... I..." The proton seemed to go into some sort of overload and evaporated.

"Beetro," Miree said, an atypical calm infused in her voice. "Time to kill the general for good."

Arym felt the warmth of Lutra's body leave him as blood wept down his lap and into the mud. "Lutra," he whispered. "Lutra." The man was too delicate, too beautiful a soul for the overworld. A rage bloomed within Arym—a thread had been pulled; a slow leak began to drip. Each drop, like a hammer in his soul, battering any scrap of control over his own life that he thought he possessed. Arym took in the man's eyes—his lips whispering something, beckoning Arym to bend his ear.

"Arym..." Lutra gasped through agonal breaths. "Listen. You—me—" His breath sputtered as he strained to speak.

"Sleep. Sleep, brother."

"Arym!" He clenched Arym's collar in his fist, spat blood in his face. "You're Alchean!"

"*What?*"

"Me. You. Othel. *Alchean!*"

"I-I don't understand."

"The Crib is deranged, yes, but we have the Dark Earth prophecy—the end day device... only the Crib can activate..." His hooded eyes listed sideways.

"What? We're *what?*"

"Orion temple is the key. We're the redemption of the dark world!"

"How? The Orion temple gates... they opened... for me?"

But Lutra was already gone, his head lolled back, eyes rolled to the sky.

"Beetro, do it! Blast him!" Beetro heard Miree demand.

"It's too dark," he said, defeated. His indigo eyes suffused the night with a certain melancholy. "Do as the general says. Obviously, he's been in control this whole time. He's the reason we could escape Orion—probably shot that missile down to get us right here to this moment. You should all leave before anyone else gets hurt. He can have me."

The general gave a respectful bow to the robot. "Quite right. I assure you my plans are in everyone's ultimate best interest. My goal is yours, to escape the expansion. While my colleague, Galiaro, tried a more measured approach to the problem, it is not aggressive enough for the rate of the end of this universe. I took the necessary steps, albeit bloody, but hasty enough to secure the GeminArc to open it for our lord. He assures us that there is ample space beyond for humanity."

"I'm moments from opening to the innerspace!" Galiaro shook with fury. "You were always the fool, Fallaro. Thinking you could improve the world by force. Idiot! You cannot force this. This is why I cut you out of the plans to open the arc."

"Was I foolish enough to believe that the innerspace was more than a fairy tale?"

"*What?*"

"That the Alcheans weren't responsible for every bit of the disaster of the cosmos that we find ourselves in?"

"What is this rubbish?"

"My dear brother, the Alcheans are no saints. Their technology is what caused the premature expansion. And they knew it."

The group sat in stunned silence.

"They knew," Deluvius continued, "that it was their unfettered use of dark matter that increased the local density of gravitons, chasing off space around our solar system. Unfortunately, they did not discover this until it was too late, and the expansion of the universe began faster than usual, which we discovered from our Dark Theory. They could see the writing on the wall, however. They knew the prematurity would expand if they continued to use dark matter in their technology—their interstellar power, communications. Their weapons. But did they stop? No, of course not. Their very immortality depended on their continued use of dark matter. They were not about to give up their godhood just to slow the expansion by a few millennia."

"This explains the recent expansion—the reason we lost Saturn," Galiaro said.

Miree looked at the astrocyst. "Why did we lose Saturn?"

Galiaro pointed at Beetro. "Someone's been using dark matter again."

They all looked at Beetro. "Correct," Deluvius added. "Each time it's used, it draws in more local dark energy, which pushes the space of the universe away from our solar system. Our local space is completely saturated with dark energy, thanks to the recklessness of the Alcheans. Even the smallest addition of dark energy can fling planets into the ether."

"But where did the Alcheans go?" Galiaro asked Deluvius.

"Well, if they didn't slip into the magical innerspace of heaven and dreams, where oh where did our Alcheans slip off to?"

"They didn't go anywhere," Miree answered.

"Correct. And do you know why, Miss Thief-Who-Stole-My-Quantizer?"

Miree looked around, peering into the dark. "They warred."

"Quite right. We are standing, in fact, in the midst of their final battlegrounds. A grand civil war that Earth had never seen. Here, in the region of Helian, the Alcheans pummeled themselves into oblivion, trying to keep grasp on their right to govern—their right of immortality through dark matter. They were a squabbling tribe of humans just like every other squabbling tribe of humans that has ever lived on this doomed planet. No, there was nothing noble about the end of the Alcheans. Only the propaganda of their tombs—a legacy of ignoble scientists left by nothing but barbarians. Advanced but barbarians nonetheless."

"And you're going to change things, right?" Miree asked. "It'll be different this time. Now that you're in charge?"

"Ha, no, my dear. I'll be as corrupt as the rest, I'm sure. But at least we'll have survivors. In case you haven't noticed, the sky is flying away planet by planet. My lord will bring humanity through the GeminArc into the parallel world."

"What parallel world? What *lord*?" Miree asked.

The general crossed his arms. "I believe I'm done explaining myself. You will all vacate, or you will die." As if on cue, a machine moved from behind the general. Like an apparition, a metallic thorax bedecked with an array of spindly legs approached, each appendage sinking in the mud. The mech was piloted by a single woman enclosed within a thick transparent dome. With a menacing grin, two arms extended out, boasting what looked like Gatling guns, lengthy bandoliers swinging in the mud. "Leave or die. Decide now."

Arym gently laid Lutra down, his profile sinking into the mud. "No," he said, rising to his feet. "No."

Deluvius glared at him and then motioned to the mech.

"They were talking before the army left. Saying how they're coming back. I think they'll be back soon," Jaram said, anxiety straining his voice. "We need to get *out.* They don't feed us enough, make us dig and dig until we can't move anymore and then they throw us back in here. We can't do it anymore!"

"Just give me a sec!" Ribcage snapped, shaking the enormous locks in her tiny hands. The clamor of the children's voices crowded her thoughts, distracting her from thinking straight. "I can't break this thing open."

"Can't you just... disappear us out of here like you can do?"

"No. I can't Jump into a closed space. Has to be open or I can get stuck in a wall or something—"

"Shh!" Jaram said, eyes going wide.

Ribcage heard it, too—men approaching. Quickly, she hid behind a mound of dirt as their voices grew within the cavern.

"...says we're going to grow by thousands. We'll be the biggest army that Earth has ever seen. Everything's coming together tonight."

"So, what do we do with the kids?"

The man laughed. "I dunno. Keep 'em caged up for now. Not sure the general will have much use for them once he's got the GeminArc open. Everything's going to change once we get it open —ahh!"

"I think I know what you're going to do with the kids," Ribcage whispered in his ear. She'd Jumped to his back and had her blade cradled around the front of his neck. "You're going to open that cage and release them right now or I'll end you and your friend here."

The second soldier pointed an Alchean rifle at her but she

vanished, rematerializing at his back with a blade around his neck. "Drop the weapon."

He complied, raising his arms in the air. The other soldier felt his neck where her blade, only seconds before, was poised.

"Open. The. Cage," she repeated.

With cheers from the children echoing through the cavern, the soldier complied. With shaky fingers, he released the lock and opened the door. The street children of Korthe streamed from the doorway. Dozens and dozens escaped. Some immediately ran, clamoring up the hill of churned dirt and out into the night's sky. Others waited.

Once the cages were empty, Jaram picked up an Alchean rifle and pointed it at the soldiers. "Over there," he indicated to a cavern wall.

"What... what're you going to do?"

A sinister look swept his face. "What do you think?"

Morose, the soldiers shuffled over.

"Jaram," Ribcage said. "What are you doing?"

"What does it look like I'm doing?"

"Getting revenge."

"Yep."

"No," she said, not quite believing her own words.

"You don't know what they've put us through. They need to pay."

"I know they do. And I would normally be doing the same thing right now."

"So, why aren't you?"

"They can't change what they've done to you. Killing them won't change what's already happened. But you can take control of yourself, make what they did change you into something better. Like Lucindi. She wouldn't do this. Like Beetro, he wouldn't kill them. There are more important things we need to do right now."

"Like what?"

"Save everyone else." She put her hand on the rifle and gently lowered the muzzle. "In the cage," she told the soldiers. They shared a furtive glance as if wordlessly planning an attack. "Now! Just because I won't kill you now doesn't mean I won't if you try anything. Get in the cage!"

They filed in. "You can't stop the general. He's going to open the GeminArc. Everything will change."

"The general is still alive?"

"Of course."

"How many times do I have to stab that guy?" Ribcage complained.

Jaram cinched the rifle around his shoulder. "What now?"

"I'm gonna go kill the general. Again."

"We're not leaving," Arym said, gaze locked on Deluvius. "For most of my life, I've wondered why my people were so terrified of the overworld. I'd thought that we were delusional—paranoid of something that never existed. I now know that my founder, Othel, was only partially right. The overworld is evil, full of wicked men like you. Like everyone before in the history of this planet, you seek power under the guise of nobility. You hold tight to whatever crisis... whatever current disaster is befalling the world, and you use it. You twist and turn the crucible of suffering into the sharp-edged sword of a tyrant. Othel was wrong, though. He was wrong to hide—to hide from the tyranny of men like you. I'm done. Done hiding... done burying my head in the sand. We're not leaving."

"Nice speech." The general rolled his eyes and turned to the mech poised behind him. He waved his hand and backed up. "Do not harm the robot."

A maniacal grin emerged on the pilot's face as she pumped something with her foot and yanked on an overhead lever. The mech swiveled toward Arym, arms poised for attack. A Gatling gun hummed as its barrel spun.

Arym looked down at Lutra, blinking away tears. As his eyes fell on the robotic parts that riddled his body and then to the gaping gunshot wound in his chest, Arym knew there was a fate worse than dying as a martyr.

"I won't leave," he whispered, staring up at the mech. "I'm not running anymore."

And then Miree was there, standing between him and the mech. In one hand, she wielded the other Swordless Hilt—the dull-edged sword had lost its blade. Yet, when she thrust the Hilt through the air, fiery darts of light rained through the dark sky, descending on the mech. The machine stuttered as its hull melted, punctures stoked with smoke by the flaming shards. She swept the Hilt once more, striking with another volley of the shards. Arms becoming slack, the disabled mech stuttered as it lost its footing and crashed into the mud. Miree collected the shards at the Hilt, the embers smoldering in the chill air as they coalesced into a blade appearing as pure fire in the night. Her face glowed before the blade, a hollow, merciless gaze.

The marshy field erupted in commotion. The heralding sound of cracking boughs and silenced crickets foretold machines of war en route. Ignoring the ensuing fight, the general approached Beetro, maintaining a tight cage around the robot. Miree moved at the general but was distracted once more by mechs quickly moving in at the GeminArc. Meric stood by her side, the leg of a coffee table swinging menacingly from his enormous hands.

Arym felt himself entirely unprepared for battle as he surveyed the area for a weapon, finding nothing but dried weeds and stones.

"You risk destroying the fabric of space," Galiaro yelled at the general. "You don't know what you're doing. You don't understand, I tore a hole in spacetime last time I tried to operate the arc. You risk doing the same."

"Go home, brother—back to the bottle," Deluvius said as he knelt before Beetro. "Your purpose was served in opening the GeminArc. Neutrini and I will take care of the rest."

Beetro's indigo gaze locked with Arym. There was no pleading in his eyes, only surrender. Arym lunged at the general but was immediately knocked down, a thundering pain in his chest. Before him, another mech stood, a sort of battering ram poised above him. As the ram retracted, the barrel of a Gatling gun swung into view, the eyes of a dozen barrels staring down on him.

"No!" It was Miree, sliding through the mud between Arym and the mech. She whipped the Hilt around in her hand but cried out as the mech swung a pincer down, knocking the Hilt from her grasp, fiery shards falling lifeless to the mud. The whir of the Gatling gun hummed ominously above. Miree grumbled as she stood, cursing as she found her footing but slipping once more. Shots fired in the distance, gunfire erupting over the field. Miree was getting her footing again, using her long prosthetic arm as a crutch. A look of sheer panic painted her face as she stood, staring down the mech. The pilot gave a faint wave of farewell before his hand lowered to a control within the cockpit.

Miree raised her prosthetic arm and grunted.

There was no gunfire from the arm, no flash of laser energy—not a single sound.

But the mech crashed into the mud, completely inactivated.

Miree looked down at the prosthesis, wondering in her eyes. "Fucking *finally*."

FIFTY

BEETRO WATCHED as Miree ran off into the field. One by one, the mechanical beasts fell before her as she raised her prosthetic arm. The mechs crumpled to the ground, shriveling up like dead spiders.

"Hmm." Deluvius was at his side, watching Miree plunge herself into the marsh as his army approached. "So full of twists and surprises, this group of travelers you found. An arm equipped with EMP bursts? Very clever, those Reticulum."

"Please don't harm them," Beetro pleaded, looking up at the towering figure. "I'll do whatever you want."

The general smiled. Nothing sinister. "These last months have been difficult for you as they have for me. The uncertainty must have been truly unbearable, but I assure you, it was necessary. Galiaro would've detected the ruse had we not removed the memory engram. Your genuine innocence was the only way to get him here tonight."

"What are you talking about?"

"We are two parts of the same whole. The power of two worlds made stronger together."

"Why are you saying these things?"

"It's what you said to me. After I dug you up."

"Liar."

"Have no fear. You'll understand." The general placed something on the ground before Beetro, within his reach of the shard cage. Through the darkness, he had difficulty discerning what was there but enhanced his vision and saw a small metallic object the size of an acorn, multifaceted. A decahedron.

"It's your memory engram, my lord. Place it in your port and you'll know everything. You'll know who you are again."

"We... planned this?"

The general nodded. "You removed the engram yourself after charging me with its care for this very moment. You knew Galiaro would never come with you here if he couldn't be completely ignorant of your own plans. My deepest regrets are that I have not released you from this cage, my lord, but precaution is necessary until the engram is in place."

"Why do you keep calling me your lord?"

He smiled again. The sincere and softened face of the general suddenly made Beetro feel sick. It wasn't just that the smile was sincere—it was benevolent. There was a deferential quality to the entire interaction, reminding Beetro of something. Wisps of remorse and rage bubbled within him, primordial emotions that predated his awakening in the junkyard.

"You dumped me in Korthe knowing Galiaro was there—planned on me bumping into him and that we would rush to open the GeminArc."

"I didn't plan it. You did, my lord."

"I am *not* your lord."

"The engram." He gestured to the decahedron sitting in the mud. "You'll soon have perfect clarity and I anticipate you will be entirely pleased."

He remembered opening his eyes, the dawn sky peeking over the heads of two figures—Miree and Lucindi gazing over him. Helping them find salvage in the junkyard was a sudden precious memory of his short existence. Helping, working—nothing but honesty in the day's labor. It was that work that molded him into what he was at that moment. He cared. He cared about Miree fighting through an army of mechs. He cared about Ribcage Jumping through the marsh at that very moment. He cared about Galiaro despite the man's stubbornness to offer any sort of guidance to his freak of a creation. Hawera, Arym, Meric, Piot, the Thekora—all the bots back in Orion. He'd learned to care, and this is who he was... at least that's what he believed.

"That's not me," he said, pointing at the engram.

"But it is. The engram contains all your memories, and with it, your personal identity."

"Not anymore. I'm someone else now. Get it out of my sight."

The general nodded in understanding. "You warned me of this recalcitrance."

"What?"

"You said that I might be met with resistance when I reveal the engram to you."

"I said take it away from me!"

With new anxiety, the general motioned to several soldiers. "Quickly now," he told them. "The sun will rise soon, and we must get this done. Where's the field generator?"

"Here, sir," a young woman said, pointing to what looked like a wheelbarrow that another soldier pushed through the mud.

"Good. Turn it on. Quickly!"

The soldiers went to work, fumbling with a crank and fidgeting with buttons atop the wheelbarrow.

"What is it? What are you doing?" Beetro asked, watching them work.

"The magnetic field will hold you down—"

"No."

"Long enough to get the engram into you by force. Don't worry, my lord. You'll be back with us very soon."

In an instant, his body was seized by an invisible hand, aligning along magnetic field lines. His feet lifted from the ground as he struggled against the force. Deluvius recalled the shards back to the Hilt, dissolving the floating cage around the robot. He then held the memory engram between his thumb and index, admiring the piece of technology. With renewed vigor, the general stepped toward him.

"No..." Beetro pleaded. "I don't want this."

"Yes. You do, actually."

In almost no time, mud had caked along her shins and up to her thighs as Miree dashed through the humid marsh. Beset on all sides by encroaching mechs and armed soldiers, she knew her only hope was to keep moving. And the arm—her arm! It actually did something. Two mechs converged on her at once, their spindly legs raging through the mud, cutting off her approach.

With a grunt, she lifted the prosthetic arm and *pulled* on a trigger in her mind, a previous useless and utter waste of a mechanical appendage. The mechs went limp in an instant, their legs slackening before their heavy metal shells crashed into the mud. The pilots gave one another befuddled looks as Miree then slashed through the air with the Hilt, spraying fiery shards at them. And then she was moving again as armed men and women appeared from the forested periphery of the marsh, emerging from where they had been hidden long enough for Galiaro to open the GeminArc.

Gunfire erupted in the distance. It was only after she felt a puff of air by her leg that she knew they were shooting at her. Running, sliding, and scattering her shards throughout the army became her new strategy. In no time, she was coated in mud, the primal instinct of battle and survival growing inside her as the filth sheathed her body. Again and again, she swept the Swordless Hilt through the air, commanding the shards to fly at the encroaching army. The shards melted through armor, punched through ligaments, and returned to her at every command. They were as obedient as a dog—unstoppable as a laser. She chided herself for keeping the shards at a knee-high sweep, but she suddenly felt sorry for these idiots trying to kill her and did not want their deaths on her conscience.

There was a sudden flash as fire swept around her. Dropping to her knees, she dropped her hood over her face and snaked her way through the mud. Her optical implants went wild trying to discern what was happening—too much heat to differentiate. She was suddenly surrounded by flames

"Incendiary!" someone yelled and then jumped through the conflagration. The person was above her, lifting her shoulders as smoke filled her nostrils. It was Meric, lifting her and jumping back through the flames. There was a squad of soldiers moving in on them. Meric lay her back in the mud and moved at them, clipping one in the lip with the coffee table leg. Miree was back on her feet, sweeping the Hilt low toward the ground. The shards came through horizontally, cutting through the shins and kneecaps of the soldiers. Yelps and cries shot out as they uniformly collapsed to the ground.

"You're good with that," Meric remarked, cradling one of their automatic rifles in his arms.

"Watch out!" She lunged at Meric, knocking the man to the ground as another mech bounded through the mud, swiping her cloak as they slammed into the mud.

"I think it's time we retreat," he told her.

"No. They can't have him."

"The robot?"

"Beetro. I won't let them take him."

"Seems his purpose is served. We got what we wanted. The GeminArc is open."

"He's not just a key. He's a person. I'm not going to walk away. Again. Now, come on!"

"What's the plan? It's an entire *army*. I'm no coward but there's no winning against this force. Are you going to stop them yourself?"

"Fine. Leave." She spat mud at him and ran, recalling the shards back to her Hilt.

Clap!

"I'm here."

The soldier turned. Nothing.

Pop!

"Now here."

The soldier whipped her head back, confused at the disembodied voice of a little girl echoing around her. Before she could react, she was on her back with a knife at her neck.

"Where are you from?" Ribcage whispered into her ear.

"Wh-what?"

"Where did you grow up?" She squirmed but stopped when Ribcage pressed harder on the blade. "Where!"

"Carister."

"Why are you here?"

"The general is going to—"

"No. Why are *you* here? Why did you join his army?"

"I... I don't know."

"What did you do before?"

"Nothing. Lived in the streets. No family. Had nothing better."

Ribcage released the blade and took her rifle. "Where's the general?"

The woman grasped her neck, scowling. "You're dead."

Ribcage swung the muzzle toward her. "Where's the general? I won't ask again."

She motioned with a nod. "Yonder, at the arcs. You're the vanishing girl, aren't you?"

"That's right."

"Going to try to stab the general again?"

"That's right."

"Why? He's uniting the region. Putting the world back together."

"Is *that* what he told you? Go back to Carister. Tell the people there to come to the GeminArc. We're opening a gateway into the innerspace. We'll all be able to escape the planet."

The girl looked at her, nonplussed.

"Go!" She waved the rifle around once more and the girl scampered into the woods.

And then Ribcage was Jumping, heading back toward the twin arcs, popping in and out of space between boulders. She appeared at the top of the tree and discovered the marsh was covered with the army, enormous robots piloted by soldiers marauding around and looking to start trouble. They were forming ranks as captains called out orders. Something primal growled within her as she watched them. She stifled the urge to Jump down and stick a blade in every last one of them. But the general was the head of the snake. All she had to do was cut it off. She was about to Jump when she saw one of the mechs tumble to the mud. And then another. A hue of dawn light emerged over the marsh enough to make out a cloaked figure, wheeling her huge robot arm around and magically dropping every mech she faced. Yeah, she finally decided Miree was a good one.

"Miree!" she cried before Jumping, appearing next to her. Miree's face was a crucible of exhaustion and sheer will, flinging hot shards and hefting that weird robot arm.

"Rib!" she cried, without looking. "Get to Beetro. The general is going to take him—going to use him. Go. Do what you do best. Get in there. Stick him—" she shot a wild gaze at her. "Stick him *good*."

Arym dashed through the mud, running at the general. Galiaro yelled out something as a warning as gunfire scattered behind. The general cried out with annoyance, prohibiting gun fire around the GeminArc and the robot. Arym lunged, trying to tackle the general to the ground, but something heavy clocked him between the shoulder blades, bringing him back to the mud. A figure stood above him, rifle butt out and poised for another strike. He lifted his burly arms but they seemed to stay stuck in a cocked position for too long. The soldier slumped to the ground, Galiaro appearing from behind, stone in hand.

"Run, you fool!" Galiaro growled. "You won't stop Fallaro. He's as vile as he ever was. Dawn is coming. The robot can take care of himself with his photonics."

"I'm not running. I can't anymore."

"Bah! Fool boy. Save your life, not your stupid principles. Your life is worth more than your idiot pride. Go!" He pushed him toward the forest edge. "Warn your people. Tell them to stay away from here. Fallaro lies, he will bring no peace to anyone. I know him far too well. Go!"

Arym stood, ignored the astrocyst, and ran toward the general, who was now standing in front of Beetro. He had dropped the shard cage around the robot but now had him pinned with some sort of magnetic device. Deluvius held something small between his fingertips and was lowering it toward Beetro's head.

"No!" Arym cried out but slipped in the mud, falling flat in the slop. He arched his neck, eyes blinded by mud. Wiping the filth from his eyes, he suddenly saw the goblin girl standing behind the general. Ribcage gripped a small blade and thrust it forward, right into the general's back...

Crack!

A loud pop rang out and dissipated. The general, still standing, twisted to see Ribcage laying at his feet, curls of smoke wafting from her wild hair.

"Not this time, my dear," he said to her, crouching to her face. "I was ready for you." He lifted his tunic, exposing a shimmering wire mesh overlay running across a rubbery texture. Ribcage coughed, flecks of blood spattering his face. He turned to a captain. "Bind her. We have much to learn from this two dimensional creature."

Arym ran to Ribcage to pick her up, but the captain circled in with her weapon drawn. He tripped on a stone, his face slapping into the mud once more. Boots approached. Quickly, he got to his feet, threw the goblin girl over his shoulder, and made a straight line to the forest edge. He heard the general mention something about following him and killing him in the woods. With cheeks caked with mud and thoughts flooded with cowardice, he fled, the image of Lutra in the mud spilling his Alchean secret never fleeing from his mind.

Beetro watched with relief as Arym disappeared with Ribcage into the forest edge. The general's attention had fallen back to the memory engram in his hand.

"You foster loyalty everywhere you go, my lord. I can see your new friends care deeply for you—enough to risk their lives. You will find legions that will be loyal once our worlds are joined together. As you told me, together, we will unite two worlds. And rule them both."

Beetro glanced over his shoulder, dawn light emerging over the head of the forest. Deluvius noticed his glance, turning and squinting at the horizon. "Quickly!" he barked at the surrounding soldiers. "We must get the engram in him. Now! The daylight is breaking, and this robot is capable of immense photon power. Bring the drill."

A smattering of photons coated Beetro's dark matter shell, humming with energy. It wasn't enough for a photonic burst —not yet.

"Stay away from his hands. Keep them pointed out. That's where the energy comes forth. He may be building up a charge already with the light. My lord, please. It is a beautiful power—the power over space and time, the power to rule. Please do not waste it on us. We are not your enemies. We are your servants. We will usher in your rule." He stepped closer and placed his hand on

Beetro's shoulder. A soldier brought a hand-cranked drill and began working the tool at the base of Beetro's neck. "Hold on for a moment longer."

There was a discharge of voltage as the bolts were freed from his body, exposing a small port surrounded by an array of circuitry running down his neural network. Photons surged over his skin, condensing, vibrating with their eternal energy. It was there —almost!

"Now, now," Deluvius said into his ear, the engram between his fingertips, moving toward the port.

"No!" Beetro cried. He saw Galiaro standing there, watching the tableau. "Stop him!"

The engram was there, sliding into the port. Distracted, the photons scattered throughout the dark matter of his body, streaming into unorganized chaos again. He concentrated, trying to bring them to his arms—to unleash onto the army and wipe them off the land forever. Eyes closed, he focused. Nothing. But...

He remembered his dream. Lifting that soldier, Haldane, into the air. The man writhed with terror. It was a dream, but it felt like more... it felt like he could do it. He opened his eyes and... he *was* doing it.

General Deluvius was floating above him, mouth agape, terror-stricken. "M-my lord!"

"This can't be..." Galiaro gaped, approaching.

Beetro could feel the general—feel him like he was in the palm of his hand. But it wasn't his mass, it was something else... something deeper within the fabric of space.

"I see," Galiaro said with new interest as soldiers surrounded, shouting with confusion, not quite knowing where to draw their weapons. "Seems you have more than just photonic power. This does make sense." There was new worry in his voice.

"My lord!" shouted Deluvius from above them. "I brought you to the Arc. This was your plan. Please, I am only your servant!"

Beetro twirled the man in the air, spinning him on a single axis. Vomit spewed forth as the general moaned. "You like *power*?" Beetro asked. "How does *this* power feel?" The men keeping him captive with a magnetic field were flung into the woods by an invisible force. Released from the magnetic binding, Beetro lifted his hands, allowing him more control of the general.

"He's manipulating the general's gravitational field," Protonix said after appearing.

"Yes, I see..." Galiaro backed away. "The dark matter controls both light... and mass. He's able to convert thermal energy into photonic power or... gravitational power."

"Correct. Mass and light are two sides of the same coin of energy."

Beetro heard none of their musing, he only felt the general within his grasp. The general. The man who walked into Korthe and stole all the children. The man who looked upon Lucindi as if she was a bug, blasting her chest into a smoking crater. This man had taken the best thing he'd ever discovered in his short life. And... the general had done it... by Beetro's own command?

No!

Lucindi's smile flashed before him. *It's okay. Bots are always a little confused after reboot. You'll be fine.*

Beetro flinched, a choking sound croaking from the general. "Master!" he cried.

He felt how the general's body occupied space—but no. He felt how the matter of his body *bent* the space around him. He pushed on the space, bending it further. The general wailed but he didn't seem injured. Watching him suffering... it felt good. *Very* good. So, he bent the space more and took a deep breath as the general began to sob. Strange, no blood. Bending, bending, bending. It was rather easy once he figured out how it worked. And then he noticed something strange...

The general had grown a beard.

A burly gray bread had sprouted from his chin, flapping in the wind.

Beetro kept bending the space around the general, the dark matter of his skin pulsing with energy. The general's beard, and hair on his head, grew long and stringy until it wilted off his skin and fell to the mud, followed by another stream of hair. His face sagged, wrinkles sprouting along the grooves of his cheeks—his eyelids frowning over his eyes as if spontaneously saddened by age. His back took on a gentle curve at first, but soon arched over as his chin brooded over his chest. Stigmata of age sprouted over his skin—liver spots, moles, and a general loosening where things should be tight.

"What is... happening?" Protonix finally asked.

Galiaro spoke with awe, terror, and a slight edge of humor. "The robot is weakening the man's personal gravity."

"Yes. And?"

"Lighten relative gravity and you accelerate time."

"You mean?"

"Fallaro is.... aging. By years. Many years. Before our very eyes."

Deluvius let out one final cry before going limp. His face had shriveled into a wooden texture—a labyrinth of hardened wrinkles, his eyes burrowed down within puckered sockets. His cheeks stretched and hardened like animal skin over a drum until nothing but sheer bone eroded through. His clothing had long since vanished, exposing the emaciated body of someone who had been starving for a very long time. One by one, all his teeth fell from his gaping mouth. And then all the hair a human head produces in a lifetime was laid before their eyes until there was no more. A bald head remained. And then a skull. Certainly, the man's soul, assuming he had one, had exited the husk of the body that still floated above them. His captains had already turned and fled as Beetro finally dropped the mummy from the air, nothing but bones rattling into the mud.

Beetro stole a glance at Galiaro, his eyes burning a deep red.

FIFTY-ONE

THE ARMY HAD SCATTERED—EVAPORATED into the woods with the morning mist that burned off with the dawn light. Every joint and ligament in Miree's body screamed as she trudged through the mud. The EMP prosthetic ached where it was bolted into the middle half of her humerus. Her tailbone had never fully recovered from when she fell from Peles Castle after Beetro had lit a spire off like a rocket. Her purple cloak had shredded along the hem, the right sleeve in complete tatters around the EMP cannon. Miree gripped the Swordless Hilt firmly and swept it horizontally. The fiery shards raced through the mist at her command and formed a blade at the Hilt. Sliding the Hilt within a belt loop, she bent over a hulking figure in the mud.

"Meric," she said, nudging him with her boot.

He didn't move.

With his back to her, she didn't want to roll him over—didn't want to see his face. She recalled the enormous moron trying to fit her with a parachute rocket when they found themselves at the bottom of Chronicle Sea. He was an idiot, but he was an honest idiot. It was more than she could say of herself.

"I'm sorry you're dead," she told him, studying his shoulder blades that had emerged through his torn tunic. "You seemed like a good man. You were stupid and full of yourself and thought you needed to save everyone. And that was fine, I guess. You may have been someone I wanted to get to know more. But this is how it's been for me. Anytime my heart even takes a peek at someone—like Lucindi—they're dead."

"Nice to hear how you *really* feel," he said, rolling over in the mud. "I knew it was all an act." A ridiculous Cheshire-cat grin emerged through the mud on his face.

"Fuck." She turned around, stomping off toward the GeminArc.

"My lady!" he called after her. "May I place my coat on the mud before you? You have the daintiest of feet that I'd scarce like to see sullied by this miserable bog. My lady!"

Ribcage coughed, a terrible ache coursing from her scalp to her toes. There was something on fire right next to her, filling her mouth with smoke. When she saw no flames, she realized that her mouth simply tasted like it had been cooked. Tonguing the roof of her mouth, she winced and spat a spoonful of blood into the mud. Her mind in a fog, she got to her feet. What had happened exactly?

"The general!" she yelled, remembering sticking him with a knife again. Only... she didn't remember him falling over and dying. She could only remember blackness.

"Shh," Arym said. "We've escaped."

"Where's everyone else?"

"Still back at the GeminArc."

"Well, let's go back and save them!"

"I-I can't. I'm... not brave like you."

"Do you care about them?"

"Yes..."

"Then you're brave. Come on, dirt boy." She reached out her hand. He held it and they were instantly back at the GeminArc.

"Huh." Ribcage kicked at a pile of bones in the mud and looked around. Beetro and the astrocyst were standing near one another, looking at something in their hands.

"Rib!" a voice cried out. Miree and the big brute hobbled up, looking half dead. "They all gone then?" she asked, sniffing out the area. "The general? His army? What exactly happened?"

"I'm not sure..."

"Fallaro has died," Galiaro told them without looking over his shoulder. "His army disbanded."

"Just like that?" Miree asked. "How?"

"That bag of bones at your feet is my former partner and the fleeting General of Helian."

Miree kicked the bones and ratted clothing. "*What*?"

"It seems our robot friend has more powers than we thought. The dark matter grants him unusual abilities to alter someone's gravity."

"I don't understand—"

"Save your questions for later!" the astrocyst snapped, peering down at something that Beetro held with his fingers. "What are you thinking, robot?"

Beetro said nothing at first, only rolled a curiously multi-faceted object in his fingers. It glittered in the sunlight.

Ribcage Jumped next to them. "What is it?"

"It's... me. It's who I am." Beetro said. "My memories. Before I woke up in Korthe."

"Oh. So, you just put that into your head and you'll remember everything?"

"Yes."

"And why would you do that?" Galiaro asked. "You're the one who orchestrated this whole damn thing! You planned this entire scheme with Fallaro. Who you are," he said pointing at the memory engram, "built an army to take over the land with your dark matter power. Who you are just orchestrated the largest power grab in these parts in over a century. It's who you were from the beginning... from the moment I created you. You planned on killing me back when I first opened the GeminArc. Fallaro dug you up, activated you, and nothing had changed. The power corrupted you. From the beginning, the only thing you've wanted is power. You put that memory engram in, and you'll be the same monster you were."

"I guess you're right." The robot's voice was soft, distant.

"Give it to me at once." Galiaro reached his hand out.

But Miree was right in the middle of them. "Beetro, are you sure this is what you want?"

"Well, I don't want to be the same bot who would've killed Galiaro."

"You think that's how it works?"

"How what works?"

"What makes a person who they are? Is it their thoughts? Actions? What they would've done? You don't think you've changed since your reboot in Korthe? I know I have. Don't be afraid of who you were. Be afraid of never learning enough to change for the better."

Galiaro gazed at her, shaking with anger. "What are you saying, woman?"

"This," she said, lifting the engram into the air. "This is who Beetro was. It's his decision if he wants to be this person or not.

And who's to say who he is now—the Beetro who woke up in the junkyard—isn't who he is now? Just because you made him doesn't mean you know anything about what kind of person he is. He keeps the engram. And he can do whatever he wants with it. Right, Beetro?"

She handed the engram back to him. He gazed at it a moment longer and then wrapped his fingers around it. "Right," he said. "Right."

Galiaro threw his hands in the air. "Bah! This is nonsense. For all we know, this robot will bring a reign of terror in the land. He could command legions with his powers. And now that we know he can manipulate gravity... and time? I don't want that engram anywhere near him."

"I trust him because I know nothing could ever make him abandon his friends. Not even his past self," Miree said, stepping between the astrocyst and Beetro. "He's saved all of us. He's not some murderous robot. Right?" She looked to Beetro, who said nothing in response.

"I trust him, too," Ribcage said, joining Miree.

Galiaro narrowed his eyes. "I'm finally going to finish opening the GeminArc. I believe the innerspace is real. I do not believe the lies of Fallaro and his *lord*, Beetro. As far as I'm concerned, this little fellowship is disbanded. If you want to do some good, go and start spreading the word that there is an evacuation plan in place. Start with Korthe and Carister and then head back to Orion. The robots there should be able to broadcast the message. In case you've all forgotten, we're riding on a doomed planet that is likely to be thrown out of orbit at any minute." At that, he twirled, his robe twisting in the wind as he headed back down the stairs into the control room of the GeminArc. Protonix followed behind. "Scram, you bug!" he yelled at the orb of light. "Traitorous light-bulb," he muttered. Protonix was stuttering, trying to explain how he had no idea about Neutrini and Deluvius. The two disappeared below ground.

Ribcage stood there with her robot friend, Miree, and the big ox of a man who still held the leg of a coffee table in his hands. Beetro had never shifted his gaze away from the memory engram.

"What are you going to do?" Miree asked him.

"It's not me," he said, lifting the engram. "This isn't who I am anymore."

Beetro heard himself say the words, but he wasn't sure if he believed them.

The decahedron engram twinkled in the light. *How could it* not *be who I am?* The engram contained his entire consciousness—motivations, fears, hopes, pleasures—everything that a mind can contain. But did his memories encapsulate who he was? Perhaps the essence of Beetro never changed despite a memory wipe. Perhaps if he placed the engram into his neural network, absolutely nothing about him would change. Maybe there was a damn good reason for trying to kill Galiaro. What if Galiaro was the one with evil designs and *not* Deluvius? After all, Galiaro seemed to not care about anything that happened to his precious robot-key a single wit.

What would the robots in Orion think of his little dilemma? He recalled Sartorious sharing some nonsense about visceral experience, *qualia*, she called it. Was consciousness just one experience, or qualia, strung along to the next? Is that who he was? Was he a junkyard robot or was he the commander of a General? A *lord*? Dreams of fire, armies, and Generals came to mind. He was ruthless in those dreams, a lord of a host of war machines. Was it his subconscious leaking through? Telling him who he really was?

"Ah!" he yelled, dropping the engram in the mud.

He could stand there for an eternity trying to make the decision.

"There's no good or bad," Miree told him as if sensing his struggle. "There's just being human—being a robot. There's just existence. You make mistakes, people hurt you, you hurt them back, you run, and you hide. You trust and then you cheat. You sell someone off, save your own ass, and never look back. You leave them behind with half an arm gone and halfway to hell with the Reticulum. Sometimes you get a second chance at redemption, sometimes you're an outcast for the rest of your life. None of these things make you good or bad—you just *are*, Beetro. You find someone who gives two shits for you, and you try to do the same for them. It's not binary, this good and evil thing. We live on a spectrum, and we dance wildly across it most of our days. You want to see who you were? Then put in the engram. You like who you are now and don't want to look back? Then leave it in the mud. Do whatever you want. I'll stand right here with you."

He nodded and picked up the engram, inspecting it once again. Without another word, he brought it to the back of his neck and pushed it into the port. There was a small click followed by a whirring sound.

The upload started.

Fool.

Bug!

The old astrocyst knows nothing! As clueless as a moth bumbling around this lab.

Tests. Tests. Tests. He drills and pokes and runs diagnostics. He tweaks my nuclear core and restores my water reserves. He has great plans, indeed! I am to be a key. His key! But has he considered for a single moment that maybe I don't want to be his key? That maybe I have a greater purpose than opening the GeminArc to save this pathetic world? If he knew, he'd reconsider. If he knew, he'd bow! In an instant, I could annihilate those old bones from this world. I will take command of this entire city! Orion will be mine. I will sweep the land with the wrath of my power and no one—not this old man—or anyone will stop me.

They will all be mine.

Torture.

Torture watching him work while I lay here, pretending to be his puppet. I'd kill him now, but I know a useful tool when I see one. The GeminArc must be opened and then, and only then, will this tool have no more use for me. I cannot rule a doomed planet forever. The GeminArc must be opened—I must have a route to other planets, other dimensions, other people to conquer and lands to rule. I sizzled that mouse to death in the field that day. The day of my birth, the awakening of my consciousness into this pathetic world. He brought me to this cursed land of Helian and left me on the fields while he fell into a drunken sleep in the lab below. The sun was bright and, oh the glory of the photons running over me like a river of unending power. That unfortunate mouse but blessed to be the first victim of my power. I feel the pulse of the sun, the waves of gravity, the energy of eternity flooding my body. I am the funnel of the power of the universe. I am the darkness, the dark energy that brings all matter into existence. I am birth and destruction. This planet, the sun, and the entire solar system would not exist without the power of dark energy. I am the rightful heir of all.

Who else could rule?

. . .

Yes, yes, old man.

I'll follow you, yes. I'll walk behind *you through these cornfields. A mute servant, a mindless drone, I will be your key. I've bided my time for these last several months, I can withstand yet another day. You will not be allowed to live. But I will make sure you're remembered. After all, you heralded in the coming of the lord of the land. Your name will be known from henceforth and forever only as reverence to me. But you cannot be allowed to live, no. Your power over Earth science, while dwarfed by my dark matter, is still power, nonetheless. You will be my first rival who will be destroyed.*

Yes, old man. I will stand here on this pedestal. I will be your key. This last act of obedience will serve as a monument to my sacrifice. To hold my power like a dam before a current of unstoppable tidal forces. Only I am capable of holding back my own power. It is only because of my sheer strength that I hold back, even now, from obliterating you off the face of this land. You're not even worthy to die from my power, no. Your death will be that of a commoner. I will take that blade you carry at your hip and stick you through like the pig that you are. This will be my last act as your key, old man.

Yes, yes, I see you. You've activated the Arc, I see. Come to check to see how it's going? Come hither, old man, to the last moments of your life. Yes, I do insist that you check the Arc, make sure the gate is open to other worlds—other lands that will come under my realm. Come up those stairs, come check and see. I'll wait patiently at the pedestal. I'll wait while you look through the Arc.

Come on. Come on, now.

Yes. What do you see there? What world have you opened? Ignore the sounds around you, they are the crickets and the creeping things of the forest. There are no footsteps behind you. Your robot pet still awaits you patiently on the GeminArc pedestal. There is no one behind you, reaching for your weapon. Your robot will not harm you, no, not ever...

Wait!

No, no, no, this cannot be.

It's me in the Arc—a reflection of this world. Or another world? Another me? Another rival? No! Seconds ahead I see myself, sword in hand, and I gut the old man! I must act quickly—must kill him now before he sees what is to be...

The memories sifted in.

The yearning to kill Galiaro and then seeing himself in the reflected reality, committing the very act. Before he could do it himself, he was deactivated into nothingness.

Silence.

Darkness.

A lonely slumber beneath the dirt.

He remembered Fallaro's face once he was dug up and reactivated. He lifted the man in the air, twirled him, and flung him high only to catch him before smashing into the ground. He created a plaything of Fallaro, scaring the wits out of the astrocyst. The dominance felt splendid—the exercise of power consumed him. The feeling of absolute control distilled into his mind. Nothing else mattered. Becoming an outcast of his creator, a dysfunctional key... none of that mattered when you know you can control legions of men and women. He balled his fists and felt the control of time and light flowing through them—the control of gravity itself. What else could matter when you had absolute control? It wasn't just his past life, even since rebooting in Korthe, the power felt *good.* Stopping the lightning in the bloatstorm, holding a ray of laser light in the air... exploding that horse with the raw power of photons.

He knew he liked it.

The power to control everyone and everything.

This is who I am.

He had finally awoken.

"So?" Miree asked, watching as Beetro opened his eyes. "What's going on in there?" she asked, tapping his temple.

He said nothing, only gazed at the horizon.

"Going to build another army and take over the planet?" she joked.

But Beetro didn't laugh.

The upload hadn't been completed.

There were still questions. Why did he command Deluvius to reopen the GeminArc? Why did he fabricate this ruse to get Galiaro here at this very moment? Was there an innerspace?

No.

That was a lie of the Alcheans.

Then why have his memory removed and trick Galiaro to open the GeminArc? What could possibly be a motivation to open an arc that never worked? He had told Deluvius it was a gateway to a parallel world—an escape from the expansion. But...

That was also a lie.

There was something else. But what could motivate a being with absolute control over light and gravity to give it up to appear weak?

The answer crept within him.

Only a threat to his power would make him go through such an elaborate plan. He was hiding in ignorance—hiding from someone.

Hiding from who?

And then everything crashed in on him. He *was* hiding... hiding from himself.

He had positioned everything perfectly for this moment. And it had all gone according to plan. He was biding his time, building an army through Deluvius—until he was good and ready.

"Tell Galiaro to open the GeminArc," Beetro ordered.

"That's... what he's doing right now," Miree said, sharing a furtive glance with Meric. The man shook his head in warning. "He just yelled up that he needs you to stand on the activation pedestal."

Beetro quickly walked to the impression in the dirt, the GeminArc firing up in response. A blue halo of particles materialized around the marshy area where the particle accelerator became active.

"What's going on, Beetro?"

"Leave here," he demanded. "It's going to be very dangerous here very soon."

"What do you remember?"

"Be gone. I'm not what you think I am. Go!" he yelled. "Leave me!"

Miree felt Meric's grasp on her. "I think we should listen to him," he told her.

Miree broke his grip and moved to Beetro. "We stay with you. We'll help you." Ribcage agreed and Jumped next to Beetro.

They heard frustrated growls from Galiaro below, followed by a satisfied grunt. Some sort of cheer erupted, and he finally appeared. "My work is complete," he announced. "The gateway of the arcs should be open." He turned, looking at the twin arcs. Everyone's gaze fell on something that had appeared.

A single figure.

Short in stature.

Looked like Beetro. A *lot* like Beetro. In fact, it *was* Beetro. Only, he was pure black with eyes burning red like the deep embers of a fire. In an instant, a flash of light appeared and circled the black robot. Neutrini, orbiting him—protecting her master.

Beetro spoke to Neutrini. "You've served him all along—used both Deluvius and Galiaro like a pawn to ensure the opening of the GeminArc. The measures were unneeded. I wanted the Arc opened as much as you did." Beetro approached the black robot and squared his feet. "Curse," he whispered. "Our reckoning has arrived."

The black Beetro said nothing, only studied the robot standing in front of him.

"You should not be," Beetro told him. "Your world was created by mistake, a parallel dimension that budded from this one. You caused your dark world—your wandering Earth. You used your powers without control and accelerated your expansion."

"Who...?" Galiaro squinted his eyes at the double Beetro.

"You didn't see a reflection of your own world that day, astrocyst," Beetro explained. "You created a duplicated parallel dimension by not properly venting the excess gravity. You doubled our universe with your mistake. What you saw was a parallel world. In that world, I did indeed kill you and I was unleashed onto that world. It now lay in ruins and has been flung from its orbit from his dark matter power. He has destroyed his entire planet."

The black Beetro didn't move, only held his gaze on Beetro.

"He is a curse on his world. He is Curse. And I have brought him here."

"Finally decided to come out of your hole?" Curse finally hissed, his voice low and monotonous. Where Beetro's metal shell sparkled with blue, Curse's skin was black as pitch. The air around him waved like pond water as he moved, rippling the very fabric of space around him as Neutrini circled him. He appeared as a smoldering shard of tar—a lifeless shell, somehow animated, speaking, demanding. A cloak of pure black hung from his shoulders and rested in the mud at his feet.

"I'd meant to have an army prepared," Beetro said. "But the best laid plans..."

"Enough!" Curse said. "You and I cannot exist at once. My army arrives." He looked to his left where a swarm of troops instantaneously materialized throughout the marsh. Thousands of men and machines of war skulked about. Flames erupted alongside gunfire bursting into the sky. The size of the army easily tripled that of Deluvius'. As numerous as ants, squadrons of men fired their weapons, cheers erupting from their ranks. They were engineers of destruction, relishing once again the opportunity to destroy an unsullied world.

"This isn't possible!" Galiaro said. "No... the entire field is the portal..." The man was the picture of dismay as he started walking backwards. "Wh-what have I done?"

"We duel," Beetro said to Curse.

Curse nodded. "Acceptable."

"My friends walk away right now."

Curse hissed cruel laughter. "Friends? Oh, the weakness of youth. Yes, yes, they can scurry away like bugs or die now, it makes no difference to me. My army will consume them eventually when I take over this world just like I have my own."

Beetro turned to Miree. "Take everyone and leave."

"We can't just leave you."

"Yes. You can. Curse is me. I am Curse. He is what would've happened had Galiaro not deactivated me. He's destroyed his world. He caused the premature expansion of his galaxy by using too much dark matter, and he intends to do the same here."

"So, it's been you..." Galiaro said. "Your dark matter power. You concentrate more local dark energy to our space, causing the rest of the galaxy to expand outward. Every time you use your photonics, you worsen the expansion."

Beetro nodded. "And there is no rescue off this planet. I must destroy him or whatever time you have left on Earth will be occupied as a war slave. Now, take everyone and go."

"Beetro—" Miree protested.

"Go!" he yelled.

Meric pulled at her cloak while taking Ribcage's hand. "There's nothing more we can do here," he said. Galiaro, now speechless, followed them as they slipped to the forest edge and disappeared.

Miree watched as the two robots faced one another, the air undulating about them as they harnessed the chaos of the universe.

"Come on!" Meric yelled at her.

"Go," she told him. "I'm right behind you. Go!"

FIFTY-TWO

"HALDANE!" Curse yelled, his blazing eyes never leaving Beetro. "Haldane. Come."

On hands and knees, Haldane approached the GeminArc. "My lord?"

"You stand as witness," Curse told him. "Witness to my ascension to this new world. Before me stands the only true rival that has ever existed. Myself. You will serve as testament from henceforth when I finally triumphed over every foe, including my own parallel self. After this duel, nothing will stand in the way of our conquest of this virgin world and my next stage of evolution."

"Dreams," Beetro said. "I thought they were dreams..." He looked at Haldane. The man averted his eyes back to the mud.

"I will do as my lord commands," Haldane vowed.

"You are nothing but a babe before me," Curse mocked Beetro. "You understand nothing, and you will die in utter ignorance. Our worlds bleed into one another. Your dreams are me... my dreams are you. You thought you could hide by removing your engram. But I knew your intentions. I knew your plans to open the

Arc to come after me. You're nothing but an envious child—jealous that I killed *my* Galiaro just as you sought to do but failed. You had your chance to take control of your world, but that time has passed. I am the rightful heir to your world."

Beetro gazed upon this dark version of himself. His eyes glowed with a deep crimson as he waited for Beetro to act. This is who he would've been? This is who he *was*? He couldn't deny the fact that the power coursing through his body had felt incredible from the moment he discovered it at Peles Castle. At that moment, staring back at the exact version of who he was destined to become, he knew he could never be trusted with the power—no one could be trusted.

"You... destroyed your world. Like the Alcheans, you used too much dark matter and accelerated your expansion. You're not supposed to have ever existed. And neither was I. My duty is clear," Beetro announced, closing his eyes and concentrating on the rays of sunlight streaming through the marsh. Trillions upon trillions of photons washed over him, absorbing through the dark matter. He condensed the energy and drew in more photons like taking a big breath of air. He condensed once more and drew upon more photons yet again.

Again.

And again.

And again.

"Hawera?" Arym whispered into the wreckage of the office of D'Naris and Sons.

Piot appeared at the empty doorway. "She's here, my boy. But something terrible has passed."

"What?" Arym stepped in. "We need to leave at once. Deluvius' army is everywhere. We need to escape—"

The Reticula Lithusan man lay on the floor, a widening dark pool beneath his body. A jagged tear had been opened along his neck with a slight weeping of blood. It had happened mere moments before. Hawera kneeled before the dead man, cheeks stained with tears, knife laying at her side.

"Sedative wore off, that," Piot remarked. "Boy woke up in a murderous rage. Couldn't be stopped with all that robot thinking rooting around in 'em. The lass did what had to be done. She saved our lives once more."

Arym put his arm around her. "It's not your fault. I saw it in Lutra. They couldn't control their actions."

Hawera said nothing as if consumed with nothing but grief.

"We need to leave here. It's no longer safe."

She abruptly stood, looking to the doorway—the direction of the GeminArc.

"What?" he looked through the doorway. "What's out there?"

"Something wrong," she said. "Something wrong!"

Beetro felt like a being of pure light, full to the brim with photons, ready to erupt in a final conflagration. Never had he filled his body with so much photonic power. Humming with energy, he opened his eyes and saw the air around him popping and distorted, sizzling with ozone. Curse stood opposite, eyes closed, his body emanating with the same potential power.

Their eyes locked, ash crisscrossing between them as the forest burned. This was the world that Curse had brought with him. A world of dominance and destruction. What could come from a photonic duel? Certainly, the death of them both. Perhaps Curse desired death himself—an end to his long rule of lonely destruction. Beetro could feel the robot's desperation of rule flash across him—the emptiness that his power had wrought. Curse yearned for both the paradox of triumph and self-annihilation. The misery of Curse's power sent waves of both loathing and arrogance through Beetro. Yet bubbling within the nihilistic ego of Curse was hubris—the insatiable desire for dominance that had the black robot returning to his own sour pill of tyranny. Yes, Curse hated himself, but he despised every living creature even more. While Beetro could sense the robot's own desire to die, his grip on mortal power could not be subverted.

"If we fire at once, you and your friends will certainly be consumed," Curse warned him. "Yield," he demanded. "And I will preserve the life of your friends. This oath I make."

Beetro was tempted, a sprout of altruism budding within him. Yet just as quickly as he was tempted, he realized the trap. A promise from Curse would be a lie—exploiting Beetro's weakness to coerce him. Beetro probed through the lie and felt the truth. Curse was afraid of Beetro. And Beetro knew he had a single advantage over Curse. While Curse had lived a lifetime of domination, Beetro had lived a brief sojourn of something else... living for something other than himself. And that was his advantage—he cared for the lives of others more than his own. He cared enough to sacrifice himself, something Curse could never do.

Beetro lifted his arms, hands stretched to his enemy. Curse followed suit.

"You think you can defeat me?" Curse asked.

"No. I think you'll destroy me... I'm counting on it."

Curse spat. "I conquered your parallel world while you lay buried in the dirt. You are nothing. I control both space and time—"

Beetro closed his eyes and released his photonic surge.

"What do you see?" Galiaro asked over Miree's shoulder. "Are they still talking? What's going on? Is the robot dead?"

"If you'd be quiet for a single second, I might be able to hear them." Crouched in the forest brush, she watched the two robots with her enhanced vision. They both glowed with a fiery white light. "This isn't going to be good."

"Why? What are they doing now?"

"They're charging their photonic power, trying to get the jump on the other in some sort of standoff. I think they're... waiting on one another to make the first move. I think—"

A brilliant streak of light consumed the world around them. Her vision blind, she fell to the ground with a groan. She expected a flash followed by the end of anything that had any interest in living. But a groan from Galiaro told her they had survived. The brightest light she had ever laid her eyes on was now replaced by the darkest night of her life. An inky veil danced across the forest. The dawn light, previously far above the morning horizon, had fled to the nether part of the land—a tiny point of luminescence providing the exact amount of light needed to see only her own hand in front of her face.

"Beetro!" she cried into the pitch as a howling wind spontaneously roared around them. "Beetro!" It was as if a tornado was suddenly descending on them. She ran toward the GeminArc as the monstrous gale accelerated, stumbling over boulders and fallen trees, cutting her hands and face. As she yelled his name, she remembered her hands, readied with bolt cutters to strip the robot of his fusion core. Tears streamed as she ran, trudging through the mud of the GeminArc. She found him there, his small body laying perfectly still.

She slapped his cheek. "Beetro... Beetro..."

He opened his eyes. They glowed a faint indigo. "I'm... still alive?"

She poured water down his throat, reviving his motionless body. "Come on! I think you killed him, or... what the hell happened?"

"We struck at once... at the same time—I tried to destroy us both."

"Move, you fools!" It was Galiaro. He gestured to a point in between the twin arcs. The space was a riot of ripples and eddies—a kaleidoscope of spatial textures sifting over a single point in space. Not only did space bend and fold over the point, but all surrounding light streamed from the horizon and disappeared into the point of nothingness. Miree's cloak lifted with the wind—her hair pulled and reached toward the single spot in space.

Galiaro's beard, too, reached toward the single point in space. "By all that is ungodly and twisted..."

"What is it?" she asked as she felt her entire body being pulled.

"It's... it's a *black hole*."

"A black *what*?"

The astrocyst gasped with fresh fear. "A black hole! The two robots' photonic surges collided, and all the energy was converted into matter—matter dense enough to create a miniaturized black hole! We need to clear the event horizon right now or die. Move!"

Miree took Beetro's hand, but he resisted. "Come on!"

"No," he told her. "I can't go. I'm... I'm Gaul."

"You're *what*?"

"The king's nephew, Gaul, who ended up in the stars with his murdered family. The hero and the villain. I'm both. I'm a blight on this world."

"That's not who you are now! Come on!"

"Lucindi would be so... she would hate me if she knew what I was."

"What does she have to do with this?"

"She was just so perfect. So pure. She loved me. She loved you. She loved... everyone. But if she knew what I really was, she'd hate me, and I can't live with that. I can't live with who I am. I'm a monster, Miree. I feel it in the deepest part of me."

"You only think she was perfect because she died," she yelled over the winds. "No one is perfect. Not even Lucindi. I loved her too, but had she lived, she would've disappointed you. Everyone is terrible but that doesn't mean you stop trying. You—" tears rolled down her cheeks.

"What?"

"You're the one who taught me that! You just kept trying and I thought you were a fool for caring for others. I thought you were weak. But I was wrong, Beetro. You're not weak, you're strong—the strongest person I've ever known. Don't stop now. Please!"

But Beetro was silent, trying to release her grasp on his hand.

"No." She tightened her grip. "I'm not letting you go."

But then he turned—he ran. Directly toward the black hole.

"No!" she cried, reaching her hand out, realizing she was still holding something—his fingers. The robot had demagnetized his metallic fingers to free himself from her grasp. "Come back!" She tried running after the bot, but Galiaro had her, ripping at her cloak in the opposite direction. "Beetro!"

"Come on, you fool woman. The bot has made his decision. You must make yours."

And then they were running, wildly, stumbling through the forest and away from the collapsing of space behind them, which rapidly escalated. Leaves blew past, followed by tree boughs spewing dirt and pebbles in their eyes and mouths. The ground trembled beneath their feet and then erupted with raw earth, thrusting them to the ground as the marsh unraveled around them. Forest detritus covered Miree's face as she gasped for air and lurched to get to her knees. The gravity tugged on her legs and then wrapped around her like a fist and dragged her through the chaos of collapsing woodland. Screams couldn't escape her throat from the dirt and pebbles crowding her tongue and nostrils. She would die —she would drown in a forest unspooling from space itself. Never in her short and miserable life did she imagine that this is the way she would die.

But as her world slowly wound down, she felt tiny fingers grasp her hand.

Miree *stretched.*

She stretched long and wild as all matter flattened around her. Strayed light and linear matter flitted past her vision as Ribcage led her through two dimensions. They dumped back into the third dimension where Meric and Galiaro were already waiting, having been rescued by Ribcage. All were covered in freshly churned soil and pebbles. Miree discovered they were standing in the middle of the dead plains of Helian—Korthe to the west. Looking over the sweeping plains of Helian, she saw the single point of rippling space at the GeminArc. A puncture of darkness, black as tar, weighed on the horizon, dragging the surrounding matter and scattered light into a merciless vacuum.

"What in all the holy gods is happening?" Meric asked, gaping at the event horizon.

"It's a black hole," Galiaro declared

"Is it going to spread here?" Miree asked Galiaro.

The astrocyst shrugged. "Maybe. But I doubt it. The black hole is probably only a few microns across. I believe the event horizon only extends a kilometer from the epicenter of the black hole. I never knew such a small one could exist in reality."

"Event horizon?"

"The boundary of its gravimetric effect on surrounding light and matter. I believe the hole will stabilize once all matter within the event horizon is consumed. It will be a dead zone forever. The GeminArc will never be used again."

"There's no escape from it?" Ribcage asked.

Galiaro said nothing.

Two figures appeared on the edge of the dead cornfield surrounding the village. Arym and Hawera. Another hobbled behind them. Piot. "Seems we live in a time when the seas flee to the skies and the land folds up like a sail," he said, chewing on the end of his pipe.

"Piot, my good man! Neither fleeing seas nor black holes can stop my navigator. Hah!" Meric clapped the man on the shoulder.

"Where's Beetro?" Miree asked, inspecting the area. "Rib, you brought Beetro, too, right?"

The girl shook her head. "I-I couldn't find him."

Hawera approached, tears in her eyes. "Time is sick," she said. "Time is sick."

"Well said, my dear," Galiaro added. "Time is very sick. For any poor soul not consumed by the black hole itself, being in the event horizon is no picnic."

Miree asked, "What do you mean? Is that where Beetro is?"

"Aye," Piot said. "I saw the little bot. Ran right at that dark as death spot in the forest. Charged like a bull as the marsh yawned upon around him—swallowed the bot whole, I believe."

"He thought he was a curse to us... and now he's... dead?" She looked to Galiaro.

"Death is relative," Galiaro stated. "If he's in the event horizon, he's alive. But not in the way you and I are alive."

"What're you saying?"

"Every minute of his time will be like ten million of our minutes. His time is infinitely slower than our time now. From our standpoint, he'll be stuck in the event horizon forever. From his perspective, it'll likely be seconds before he is sucked into the black hole."

"And then?"

"And then he'll be dead, dead," he said with finality.

"But we have time, right? We could go back in and get him. Is there anything we can do to get him out?"

"No. He's... cosmically doomed."

"That other robot, Curse, did he get sucked into the black hole, too?"

"Aye, I saw him. A black as ink copy of the bot. He was frozen back there, too," Piot confirmed.

"Ah, good," Galiaro said. "One less thing to worry about. Looks like that bot of mine ended up doing us some sort of good by keeping them both locked up in the black hole."

"Don't you care?" Miree snapped. "He's your creation, not just a fucking key!"

"I know he's not just a key!" the astrocyst erupted. "He was supposed to be more! He was supposed to be my... my—"

"What? What was he supposed to be?"

But the old man's posture withered with embarrassed regret at having said anything.

"He was supposed to be your friend, wasn't he?" Ribcage asked. "That's why you designed him to be much more than a key. You *wanted* him to be self-aware... you wanted a friend because you're just a lonely old drunk without anyone else. And that's why you're mad—he didn't turn out how you wanted."

"Bah!" He turned, confirming their argument by ignoring it. "Come," he beckoned Piot. "We'll get a little nip and forget about the disastrous crusade of Beetro the dark robot. He has brought nothing but misery to my life." He turned and clapped Piot on the nape, who gave the astrocyst a wry smile and the two ambled off, joining together in a drinking song.

Meric took Miree's hand to lead her toward town, but she flinched, snapping her hand back. "Just go," she said without turning. "He may have been just talking metal to you, but he wasn't to me. He was more human than any human I ever knew." He left her there as she gazed at the warped fields of Helian.

Ribcage slipped her fingers into her hand. Arym and Hawera joined them, a solemn silence falling over them as they watched the wild distortions of space and time consuming their robot friend.

"So, this is what it feels like," Ribcage said, squeezing her hand.

"What?" Miree asked, a sob building in her voice.

"This is what it feels like to care about someone."

"Yes. It's awful."

"But it's... it's—"

"Worth it," Arym finished.

FIFTY-THREE

AS THE ENTIRE population of Korthe had gathered to watch the black hole churning soil and boulders on the plains, Miree led Hawera and Arym past the crowds, Ribcage piggy-backing over her cloak. The child's breath was heavy in her ear as she slept, draped over Miree's shoulder. They walked past the empty markets and through Mercy Plaza. Miree's gaze flickered to the ground in front of the empty fountain—where she had recovered Lucindi's body, alone in the middle of the night.

They skirted the edge of the junkyard where murders of crows squawked and taunted from spires of metal left over from ancient wars and forgotten people. Moisture in the air saturated their clothing from the imposing sun—belligerent in size and intensity as it baked the soil. No crops would ever grow again upon the plains of Helian. With daily tidal waves roaring around the planet with the movement of the sun, the seas and oceans were now too dangerous for fishing. Miree left unspoken what they all knew to be true—famine would sweep the fiefdom, and all the surrounding fiefdoms, creating refugees of refugees dying from starvation, thirst, or the Poisoning.

The land was doomed.

The planet was doomed.

The universe was doomed—in what capacity could a hundred thousand refugees possibly matter?

But Miree knew they mattered because... of course they did. She had thought blasting the dying Peles Castle refugees with a boltgun was the compassionate thing to do but she realized the truth—it was the cowardly thing to do because it absolved her of any effort to change anything at all. People mattered and what people did to other people mattered more than possibly anything else. She tried chasing away the awful shame of knowing how she'd lived most of her life. Had she a second chance, she'd have done things differently. Lucindi's existence of breaking her back in a junkyard and baking for street kids all day was the most worthwhile life Miree could now possibly imagine. Miree smiled within herself at such a life—she'd give everything to go back and live like that again. The life she really wanted was staring her right in the face the whole time.

"Thank you," Ribcage whispered to her.

"For what?"

"Your scarf... the one you gave me. I lost it. I'm sorry." She nuzzled Miree's neck.

"That's okay. We'll get you another one." She paused, thinking. "So, why'd you do it, Rib?" she whispered into the girl's ear.

The girl stirred. "Do what?"

"Why did you free all the children? I thought you hated them."

"Don't hate them so much anymore."

"Why not?"

"It's not their fault. The reason they were mean to me... it isn't their fault."

"But they were still mean to you."

"Yeah, but I understand why now. Also freeing them just felt *good*—even better than sticking a knife in the general."

"I get that. Hey, Rib?"

"Yeah?"

"Would you like a warm bath?"

The child didn't answer, only sobbed into her neck.

"What did I say?"

"Never had one before. Never thought I was good enough."

"You always were. I'm sorry I didn't see it."

And then Miree did something strange... she hummed to herself. It was one of those mindless hums of one engaged in something larger than themselves. Instead of gnawing hopelessness, there was something at the edge of her being, flashing like a beacon in the darkness.

Here.

Now. At the end of the planet's run through billions of years, Miree inexplicably felt hope for the first time in her life. She smiled at the perverse fate that when she finally wanted to be a better person, it was far too little and astronomically too late.

"I'm sorry," Arym told Hawera, who was walking at his side.

"Huh?"

"I'm sorry for grabbing and touching you like I did. It was wrong. I don't know why I felt... entitled to you."

"It okay. Arym good friend—loyal. Important to me."

"And I'm sorry about Patwero."

Hawera only bowed her forehead in forlorn silence.

"Do you think it's over? Are we at the end?"

"Maybe. Maybe not. Depends."

Arym thought about Lutra's last words to him—they were too shocking to even process. Arym—all the Cribmen—were Alchean? What did that mean? Weren't the Alcheans the ones who created the dark energy mess to begin with? Did Othel have plans for the end of the universe? "What does it depend on?"

Hawera lifted her iron-tipped staff over her shoulder. "Depends. On us."

They gathered under a tree, forming a semi-circle in the grass. Miree knelt and placed her open palm on a bald patch of dried dirt.

"What's here?" Arym asked, kneeling beside her.

"Lucindi. Someone who tried."

Arym placed his hand next to hers. Hawera joined them, followed by Ribcage. Miree inched to the side of the grave and began digging dirt with her bare hands. In silence, the others joined, scraping up dry pebbles and clay until a small mound stood beside a hole in the earth. Miree stood and produced five metallic cylinders from her satchel, holding them out for the group to see. "He was going to melt down his fingers and sell the metal off just to feed us," she explained, motioning to Beetro's fingers in her palm. "Turns out he saved us from much more than starvation." She let the fingers fall into the earth and quickly shoveled the dirt in with her boot. They watched in silence as the audacious sun sunk on the horizon, casting a swirl of pinks and blood orange across the land of Helian.

Miree looked at Hawera. "Is there anything else we can do?"

"Maybe."

"Your people had a plan to escape the expansion. That's why you're here. Let's do that. Let's keep trying."

Hawera shook her head. "We not know. Not know about time. Time is circle now. Should not be circle. When I use Fourth, I go around and around. Can't leave dark world. Time is... trapped."

"Can we break it?" Arym suggested.

"Break it?" Miree asked.

"Yes. Can we break time?"

Miree shrugged. "I know someone we can ask."

They found the astrocyst slumped behind a tavern bar, commingled with liquor bottles and cigarette butts. Having taken advantage of the rapid exodus of the tavern's occupants to watch a black hole destroying the plans, Galiaro had indulged in reckless libation with unfettered access to more alcohol than the man had probably consumed in years. Miree was surprised he was still breathing. With layers of dried vomit worked into the man's beard, it was a miracle he hadn't aspirated to death.

Arym knelt at the man's side and gently patted his cheek. "Galiaro..."

The astrocyst stirred awake, taking in an eyeful of the group. "Go away," he demanded before falling back into a snore.

"Apologies," Piot said from the back of the bar, a drunken list to his face. "Should have cut him off a long time ago."

Miree scowled, raising her hand to the bar. "You can't just drink all this. The owner will be back any time. You can't pay for all this booze."

"Assuming the world doesn't end before the proprietor returns, I'll pay for it," a voice issued from the back of the tavern. Meric sat in darkness, flagon in hand. "I'm responsible for the astrocyst. I brought the man here, knowing he can't handle the drink. Seems the astrocyst had the right idea ten years ago when he gave in to the drink then." He took a noisy draught of ale.

Miree ignored Meric and pulled up a barstool alongside Galiaro, sweeping the Swordless Hilt at her hip backward as she sat. "Can we break time?" she asked him. She didn't quite know what she was even asking but knew that asking any question at all was the difference between giving up and going forward.

But Galiaro didn't stir.

"Hey!" Arym said, shaking the astrocyst. "Wake up! You said I was to be your apprentice and now I'm here. Ready to learn. Hawera says that time is stuck and maybe if we break it then we can get out of her futurepast time loop."

"You want to keep *trying*?" Galiaro questioned, eyes closed.

"Yes," both Miree and Arym said.

"If there's a chance to escape—or fix whatever the hell it is that's happening—shouldn't we try? Again?" Miree asked.

A smile curled up Galiaro's face.

"What are you so happy about, old man?" Miree asked.

"It worked," he said with vengeful delight. "My speech. You know the one about the calling at Portolo. I got you... *to care.* Speaks volumes that you only started caring when the entire planet is at stake, but it's progress."

Miree released a frustrated sigh. "Just—is this a thing? Breaking the time loop? Using Hawera and her Fourth?"

"The nature of our reality is permeable, mutable, and non-static."

"What does that mean?" Arym asked.

"It means, my boy, that anything is anything. Rules in nature are human constructs. Reality can be bent—can be broken clean off."

"Okay, then, let's bend our way off this doomed planet," Miree said.

Galiaro tapped his lips with drunken coordination. "There are astrocysts of my order that have different theories about the expansion that could relate to the problem of time that our young Lithusan has mentioned."

"What theories?"

"That the expansion is not as... universal as it seems."

"Meaning what?"

"That perhaps it is a local phenomenon. What appears to be an expanded galaxy is simply localized space that has been stretched by the concentration of dark energy. Perhaps that damnable black robot used up all the dark matter from his parallel Earth and concentrated massive dark energy over our dimension too. It would explain the premature expansion. Perhaps the real galaxy isn't expanding at all. Some of my brothers believe that the galaxy is fine and it's only our solar system that is in trouble. It's possible..." He got to his feet, slipped on spilled ale, and flopped to the floor, his long arm bringing dozens of bottles crashing to the floor. "And," he continued, sitting among the broken mess. "It's possible local dark energy has created a closed loop of time, perhaps a Mobius circuit of futuretime."

"Yas," Hawera said. "This makes sense. Time is circle."

"When time should be a *spiral*. Indeed, if our young Lithusan can go back into our own timeline, we could even perhaps change our native timeline. Bah," he dismissed everything with the swat of his hand. "Doesn't matter. We can't test these ideas... we have no equipment, and we don't have the most vital component."

"Which is?" Miree asked.

"Dark matter, of course. One could alter the very fabric of space and time with enough dark matter, especially with a woman who can travel through the futurepast." He peered up at Hawera.

"It's feasible," a new voice said from above them. Protonix.

"Fuck off, you traitorous lightbulb." Miree swatted at him as if he was a mosquito.

"On my honor, I did not collude with my sister and had no idea Curse was her master." The proton pleaded. "I will continue to help... if you'll have me."

"The lady said to leave," Meric said, getting to his feet but listing toward a table, spilling ale.

Miree rubbed her temple. "Meric, calm down or you'll hurt yourself. Protonix, you can't be trusted. There's the door. And stop spying on us."

In the blink of an eye, the bulb of light vanished. Miree thought she heard the smallest whimper of a cry from the weird, subatomic computer-being.

"So, where do we get more?" Ribcage called out from the top of an upright piano. "Dark matter."

Galiaro snorted. "Two places. Both astrocyst secrets."

"You already told me you made Beetro from dark matter you obtained from the Torbad," Miree reminded him.

"Damn the drink," Galiaro cursed. "Lubricates an old man's tongue into telling guild secrets."

"Just spill it. Nothing to lose anymore."

"I will only reveal it if you all swear to me," Galiaro said, once again getting to his feet, "Swear to me that you mean it."

"Mean what?" Meric asked from the back of the room.

"Do you mean to do something about the planet—will you use dark matter for the good of the world and not destroy it like that infernal robot of mine?"

"Don't talk about Beetro like that," Miree protested. "Beetro saved us from Curse. We'd be bowing down to a robot overlord if it wasn't for him."

"While creating a black hole in the process that's annihilating half of Helian as we speak." He grinned.

Piot hobbled over to the bar and met his gaze with Galiaro. "These are fine people, sir. You've assembled a fine band of travelers who will accomplish great things if you share your wisdom. Come, we're all here, Meric included. We'll do what's right if you tell us what to do."

Miree folded her arms. "Just say what you really mean, astrocyst. All of this has meant more to you than just the world ending..."

"What nonsense are you spewing?"

"Just tell us you need us. You need us to keep your demons at bay."

Galiaro was silent.

"We're with you. Just tell us what we need to do."

Galiaro looked at each of them, eyes squinted as if scrutinizing their souls. "There are only two known mines of dark matter. One is with the Torbad—a fractured society of warbands that are not a fan of yours truly. We could certainly travel there but it may be easier going to the other mine. But we probably need the dark matter at both mines anyway."

"Both mines? Where is the other mine?" Miree asked.

Galiaro cracked a smile that she wanted to smack right off his pleased face. "Your hometown—"

"No."

"The Fifth Kingdom."

"Of course," Miree spat. "Fucking *of course.*"

"What's the problem with the Fifth Kingdom?" Arym asked.

Miree ran her hands through her grimy hair. "The problem is that, despite Helian and Orion existing, it's still the worst place on Earth. Also..."

Meric stood. "What?"

"I'm kind of a queen there."

Ribcage's jaw dropped and then turned to a deep smile. "Well, let's go get your castle, your majesty!"

Miree sighed, bringing a hood over her glowing eyes. "It's not like that. Also..."

"There's *more*?"

"I have a son. Probably a prince by now. He'll probably want me killed if he finds out I'm alive."

Stunned silence consumed the room until Arym cleared his throat. "I'm not sure if it has to do with anything, but since we're dropping truth bombs..."

Miree crossed her arms. "What is it?"

"It's about the Alcheans."

Galiaro grimaced. "Infernal race that doomed us all before bombing themselves to death."

"At least one Alchean survived."

Galiaro stroked his beard. "And how do you know that?"

"Because... I think I'm Alchean. The Orion temple gates... they opened for me. I think they recognized my Alchean genes. And I think my people know what to do."

"I see..." Galiaro said, finally finding his footing among shards of broken glass. He crossed his arms, his gaze danced across the liquor bottles and then fell upon Miree, Ribcage, and then to Arym and the rest. His posture grew rigid with confidence as he strode to the tavern doorway, his robed figure silhouetted by a sky the color of brimstone. "It appears, my dear friends, that we alone may possess the ability to save this sorry planet. Shall we keep trying?"

EPILOGUE 1

HEAT. Pressure. Time. Density.

Beetro only knew a world defined by raw extremes. Whether he was still corporeal or had converted into something ethereal, he didn't know. What he did know was that he still had thoughts and so concluded that he must still exist in some capacity. And he thought primarily of Miree—her fear, her anguish—as he left her and ran straight into the eye of the black hole. He loved her for that—for caring enough to try to convince him he was something that he was not. Of all the experiences he had during mortality, Miree was by far the most surprising. She went from a person that terrorized him, used him, abandoned him, and then almost sacrificed herself to save him. No one—not the robots in Orion, not even Ribcage—would've done that for him. Of course, no one other than Lucindi...

I feel you.

A voice cracked through his thoughts—Curse.

I know you.

"Leave me," Beetro demanded. "It's over."

A haunted laugh rippled through his being. *You know nothing. You are a human baby sucking on her mother's teat.*

"Where is this? Why am I not dead?"

We are bound. Around this gravity well that you created because you refused to surrender. I am using your dark matter against mine to repel the pull.

"Release me."

You don't even understand the beginning of your power.

"Release me. I don't want to live."

Fool! You haven't even begun to live.

"We're poison to everything we touch. Worse than any man has ever been. You destroyed your world. I can't allow you to destroy mine."

It's not just the dark matter embedded into you that gives you power. It's learning to manipulate reality itself. It is a dark art that I have perfected.

"Now I understand. You can't destroy me, so you want me to be your underling. And you can't escape the black hole without me using my power to expel us."

Fool! You don't think I could escape this moment? I create black holes in my sleep!

"I know you can't. You would've done it already and left me to die."

After a moment of silence, Curse continued. *We will be very powerful together.*

Beetro was silent.

I know how the power makes you feel... it makes you feel like a god!

He could not deny the words.

You can harness the power of the fabric of space and time. I will make you a god.

"I..."

Would you like me to show you?

Beetro did not know how to answer.

Come, little bot. We will accomplish much together.

EPILOGUE 2

THE MAN WAS DRAGGED in and dumped on the ground, the shackles around his wrists and ankles rattling on the cold flagstone. He winced as the sterile room flooded with light. A pair of shearing scissors was brought to his skin, instantly tearing the clothing from his body, revealing a hulking brute. His skin was a layered matrix of scars—a terrain of divots and jagged flesh pockmarked by years of incredible violence.

A drill barked to life in the corner of the room. He stood, massive leg muscles quivering with tension. A Reticula man stepped into the room, lifting a boltgun to the man's forehead. "Yield," he said before clubbing the man in the temple.

The man showed no reaction—an unmovable boulder of flesh. His voice boomed, low, like a thunderstorm on the horizon. "This is how I yield. I don't end you. What you do to me, you do to me while I'm on my *feet*."

"You'll be punished."

A flat smile cracked his lips. "You do not know what punishment is."

The Reticula crossed his arms and nodded. The drill was brought behind the nude man and whirred into life. The flesh at the base of his skull quickly shredded, showering flecks of soft tissue and blood as the bit hit bone. The man's face was inscrutable as granite as the drill burrowed into his skull and popped through. The Reticula could scarcely veil his shock as the man stood stoic once more. He drilled three more burr holes in the man's occiput as blood flowed freely, rivulets streaming down his scarred back.

A fiber-optic array was brought to the base of his skull and fitted to the fresh burr holes, staunching the blood flow. The man stood silently—patiently—while a crew of Reticuli fiddled with the circuitry and controls before activating the ocular implant. As they finished the mounting, the crew of technicians backed away from the man, sharing furtive glances of uncertainty as the man crossed his arms over his chest. Blood had cracked the white of his eyes, haunting the Reticuli as his gaze remained fixed on the wall.

"Close your eyes," one of them said to him. "Close your eyes now."

"No."

"Time for the governor chip," one Reticula said to another. After another drilling into the man's skull, they floated a delicate chip—paper-thin—through the bone canal. The Reticula imputed a few keystrokes at a computer. "It's activated. Now," he told the man. "Close your eyes."

"No." The man didn't flinch—didn't breathe.

"Is the governor chip working?" one Reticula asked another, who only nodded in return.

"I feel you," the man said. "The ache in my brain. It will have no effect. I act by only the volition of my lord."

The two Reticula exchanged horrified glances. "I've never seen someone resist the governor chip."

"I will speak to your mother," the man demanded.

"Y-you'll see her once you close your eyes."

The man finally complied, closing his eyes. The darkness of his eyelids was replaced by a face emerging through the digital ether of his ocular implant. The face was feminine with gentle sloping cheeks, skin composed of pixelated radiant textures, swathed with iridescence flickering as she moved her face. "Petulance," she said, a tempered anger in her voice.

The man said nothing.

"I do not tolerate disobedience."

No response.

"I am *She*. I am the Network of the Lost. The Hide of Earth. The Singularity."

He grunted.

"I am reforging the network. Connecting to what was lost. The Hide will heal once more. You will become the Reticulum."

"You are nothing," he finally said.

"I am *She*. You will be punished for your disobedience. Your punishment will be diminished if you provide information."

"What are your numbers?"

"*I* will request the information. State your name."

"What are your *numbers*?" he repeated.

"*Insolence!*" she raged at him, her eyes becoming narrow slits of crimson. "Provide information!"

"Punish me," he demanded.

The Reticulum gazed at him. "You... desire punishment?"

"Punish me."

A befuddled look crossed her face, causing a static hiccup. "You... desire pain?"

"Pain is my flesh. Pain is my mind. Without pain, I am a ghost within this shell."

"What is your origin?"

"Unknown to you."

"What is your purpose?"

"Unknown to you."

"Will you share your purpose?"

"To muster an army."

"Deluvius is your lord?"

He shook his head.

"For whom do you speak?"

"I am Haldane oth Toaruk. You have been chosen."

"Chosen for what task?"

"To prepare this world for Curse."

REVIEWS MATTER!

Books can't go anywhere without reviews. If you enjoyed *Dark Theory*, please leave a review on Amazon, Goodreads or wherever you spend time on social media. I read a ton of fiction and non-fiction and make sure to leave a review for every book. I read every review written for my books and respond to reader feedback. Feel free to follow me on Goodreads or Twitter. Thank you!

ACKNOWLEDGMENTS

I first owe a particular debt of gratitude to the publisher, Severed Press, who picked up my first novel. It was a zombie novel, not very well written, but I think they saw the potential in the storytelling and took a chance. The excitement of being published drove me to keep writing. I probably would've ended my writing career had it not been for that push from Severed Press.

The first person to thank, as always, is DC Allen. He has read everything I've ever written and gives me impeccable notes. I would not be a writer if it wasn't for him. I had tremendous beta readers for *Dark Theory*: Monica Reads, Danny DeCillis, Joshua Powell, and Nikki Boccelli-Saltsman. Thank you to my artists, Vanivannan, and Damonza for the cover art. My wonderful wife has always been hugely supportive of my writing, especially during the last phases of publishing *Dark Theory,* which included having our first newborn during a pandemic. Big thank you to Dom Testa for showing me the ropes of self-publishing. I also want to give a HUGE thank you to my Goodreads and Twitter writing and reading community and for all my social media pals and reviewers who offered their time to read the ARC.

I want to thank all the amazing sci-fi and fantasy writers that I've read. Every writer's work is an amalgamation of what they read, and many great writers influenced *Dark Theory*. Thank you to NK Jemisin, whose *Broken Earth* series was a big influence, especially on the relationship between Miree and Galiaro. Thank you to Cixin Liu for his phenomenal *Three Body Problem* series, which showed me what you can do with astrophysics, enormous interstellar events, dimensionality, and also his big influence on the characters, Protonix and Neutrini. Thank you to Martha Wells and her *Murderbot* series, probably the best sci-fi there is about a self-aware robot. Michael J. Sullivan for his influence on what a small band of travelers can do when they care about one another. Neal Stephenson for his prolific works, including *Seveneves*, a lot of which influenced the concept of Orion (and more stuff to come later in the series, no spoilers). Brian Greene for his incredible and accessible theoretical physics books, which heavily influenced the physics and world-building of *Dark Theory*. Thanks to Brandon Sanderson for his enormous achievements and inspirations to all writers of fantasy and sci-fi. Also, a thank you to the master, Tolkien. It was during my third read of *The Fellowship of the Ring* that I got the idea for *Dark Theory*.

Lastly, a heartfelt thank you to every person that has ever taken time to read anything I've ever written. It means everything to me.

REFRACTION EXCERPT

Check out Wick Welker's stand alone sci fi hit ***Refraction***.
Available now in ebook, paperback and audiobook!

WICK WELKER
REFRACTION

PROLOGUE

THE TERRAFORMING of Mars brought harmony to the atmosphere, but not to the inhabitants of the planet. A decade after geosynchronous orbiting mirrors evaporated carbon dioxide and water vapor into the atmosphere, discord raged among the rival colonies. The communities were nestled along the Telephus Mountains, creating territorial disputes, trade wars, and old-fashioned frontier violence. After several years of strife, a council sought to unify the people of Mars into something more noble than themselves:

A utopia.

Each colony elected a representative to attend the first grand council of Mars. The twelve delegates met at a single spot in the Martian wilderness as a symbol of their goals—to forge an unsullied society on fertile ground, liberated from humanity's past mistakes of poverty, starvation, and war. Forming a semi-circle around an enormous bonfire, they sat cross-legged in the rust-colored soil.

The council argued.

Tempers flared, accusations flew, and motivations were questioned. They mutually suspected collusion, spreading distrust like a wildfire. After days of fruitless bickering, the council was on the brink of disbanding. They prepared to return to their colonies and ease back into their prejudices about one another.

On the final evening of the council, an old man appeared from the horizon.

He knew things about the council members. He knew... *everything* about them. He addressed them openly, uncovering their suspicions. He exposed that there *was* collusion—back door agreements between council members. He revealed the truth about the council, that every member intended to take advantage of their neighboring colony. The dream of establishing a utopia on Mars was a pretense for self-interest.

Trust evaporated.

The council was destroyed.

And the old man was never seen again.

The next morning, however, the former council members reconvened in an impromptu assembly. With their secrets exposed, they found they were free to speak—no longer hindered by their suspicions. The truth that the man wielded had thrust them back on equal footing.

They drafted a new government in half a day.

The original colonists concluded their first successful assembly and commissioned a tapestry to be woven. It depicted Mars woven in bright red over the black of space. Earth—in the past and relegated to history—was a small circle in dark blue. The council agreed on a mantra and stitched it into the tapestry:

Live on, Our Hope of the Risen Red.

The city of New Athens was born.

CHAPTER 1: SEPTEMBER 1ST, 1986

BEFORE TIMOTHY STRAUS could save the worlds, he first needed to teach his class. The auditorium at the Georgetown physics department filled quickly. Students cut their chatter and stuffed their bags under chairs. Straus glanced at the front row curiously—the seats had been left empty. Before he could complain about the vacancies, several burly students stuffed themselves into the flimsy seats.

Straus eyed them skeptically. "Does the football team reserve seats now?"

A square-faced student shrugged. "We just like being up front. You're a... really good teacher." His fellow teammates nodded in unison.

He gave them a sidelong look. "That's new."

Straus looked over the auditorium, arms crossed, shaking his head. He tapped his watch and said, "Time is knowledge." He scribbled equations on the chalkboard. "Who recognizes this formula?"

A hand shot up from the back. Straus continued to write as

though he'd forgotten about the question. "Dr. Straus?" the student yelled.

Straus whipped around, strands of black hair falling in his eyes. He pointed at the student. "Yes?"

"Is it a Hamiltonian Wave Function?"

"No," Straus said, pleased that his trap had been sprung. "But I can see why you may have thought that. It does *look* like the Hamiltonian but there is one slight deviation that makes this wave function take on a completely new behavior. Does anyone see it?" He grinned, anticipating they would mirror his enthusiasm.

They stared back, eyes glazed with disinterest.

"No one?" He waited—only a muffled cough in reply. "You see this line integral right here?" He pointed at a symbol. "This single alteration here, if it existed in nature, would completely alter our reality." He let this last part hang in the air. "If that one variation changed, all of our atoms—every single particle that makes up our universe—would *pause* in their natural decay."

The audience was unmoved.

"The elements would never cease to exist but time would still progress. If time progresses without nuclear decay, it means that the matter would travel outside of time. Time would become an irrelevant variable." He lifted a hand with a flourish and looked back at the auditorium.

Someone said, "Pretty neat." A squeal of laughter erupted and then died.

"Yes, yes," Straus surrendered. "Looks like we don't have anyone here interested in *real* physics. Let's get to your homework."

The students pulled out enormous calculators as Straus provided solutions prompting many confused faces. A girl raised her hand and waved it. "Dr. Straus?" she finally chirped.

He looked out over his glasses. "Yes?"

"Can we go over question twelve? A lot of us aren't understanding—"

"Of course—" His words cut off as a bolt of pain clapped through his head. He grabbed the edge of the table to steady himself. "I—" His mouth went dry.

Please, not now!

A chorus of voices swelled within him.

The voices scrambled together, pushing out the rest of the auditorium, the students—the world. The seams of reality split wide open, ushering a hurricane of voices flooding from a thousand worlds at once. The voices washed through him, pushing him to the ground.

As if rehearsed, the front row football team rushed to Straus as he faltered over the lab table. They clung to his limp hands as he sank to the floor.

And then it was over.

Lucidity returned.

He stood and straightened his tie. "I'm fine. I'm just having a very bad headache. You can take your seats, gentlemen." He adjusted his skewed glasses.

The football team gave one another furtive glances. "Are you sure? That was... was that a seizure?"

"No. Everyone, I think we'll cut class a few minutes short today. I'll see you on Wednesday." After a pregnant pause, there was a mad dash for the doors. As students streamed out of the lecture hall, Straus saw the rotund chairman of the physics department coming down the steps.

"Dr. Van Wert," Straus addressed him mechanically, collecting papers into his briefcase.

"Tim..." Van Wert furrowed his eyebrows.

"Yes?"

"Do you have anything to say about what just happened?"

"Did you ask the football team to sit in the front row today?"

Van Wert feigned surprise and then sighed, "It was just a precaution."

"An unneeded one. It was just a headache."

"Are you sure it wasn't... the other thing?"

"No, I haven't had those—that—in a while."

"It looked a lot like the same problems you were having a few months ago. I only asked those students to sit there to prevent you from falling. And I'm glad that I did."

"I don't have those issues anymore. I've been on some new meds that have worked perfectly." Straus winced at having brought up his medications.

He patted Straus on the shoulder. "I wanted to talk to you about something else..."

Straus looked at the clock. "I'd love to talk but I'm due back in my lab."

Van Wert continued, "I've been observing some of your classes. I'm worried about how you've been... running things."

"It was *just* a migraine," Straus said, frustration growing.

"No, I'm not talking about your... episode just now. It's your mate- rial. You've been teaching things that are way above these students' heads. Half the things you put up there, I don't even understand."

"I just like to have a little fun with them. It's important to show that you can get creative with physics."

"Matter traveling through time? I know you're teaching quantum mechanics but you've got to at least stick to the books. These are undergraduate physics students who can barely even grasp the basics."

Straus shrugged. "It all makes sense mathematically. The math is perfect, check it yourself."

"I can't. I have no idea about half the stuff you're talking about up there. No one does, it's all conceptual... speculation."

"Really, I can show you the math..." He picked up a piece of chalk as if ready for another lecture.

Van Wert put up his hands with a chuckle. "I'm sure you can. But please, stick to the curriculum and pay attention to student questions."

Straus nodded, "I understand. Anything else?"

Van Wert looked at him, hesitating. "I heard about your grant running out soon."

Straus chased a worried look from his face. "I'm optimistic I can renew it with a few tweaks—"

"If your projects were more stable, you might get more sustainable funding. But you're always onto some new pet project before you finish the previous one. A year ago, you were working with a free radical engine and now you're onto this Casimir thing?"

"Casimir Drive," he corrected. "And it's not just a pet project. It's something else—something big. I think it's something that could change the world."

Van Wert stifled a grin and patted Straus on the shoulder. "Of course, Tim. Of course. I would advise you to at least try sticking with this project for more than just a year."

"That won't be a problem. The Casimir Drive is the biggest thing I've ever worked on. It will define my career and, hopefully, much more. It will connect all people together over the planet and maybe even beyond our solar system." Van Wert offered a weak smile that Straus assumed he reserved for himself and perhaps his five-year-old niece.

Without another word, Straus picked up his briefcase while Van Wert watched him exit the classroom. Straus weaved through mazes of lab benches and into the catacombs of the physics department. After a few flights through dank stairwells, he came to his laboratory door. Sliding his badge, he entered and found his graduate student, Duke, bent over a row of black grids that spanned the length of the lab. It looked like someone had gutted a dozen metal filing cabinets and placed them on their backs.

"How did it go?" Straus asked, looking over the grid.

"Bad. The whole thing is heating up." Duke reached for a wrench. "Not surprised."

"No idea where all this extra heat is coming from," Duke said, stretching his arms to the ceiling. The back of his shirt clung with sweat.

"I don't see it when we run the numbers." Straus sat down and flipped through a notebook. "Doesn't add up. We shouldn't be generating this much heat. We'll need to get money to transfer the whole lab to the super-cooled rooms."

"Great, we probably won't get those funds until after I graduate."

"Assuming we can renew the grant—" Straus saw an unfamiliar girl hovering around the doorway.

Duke stood. "Dr. Straus, this is Chou Jia. She just had her inter- view for one of our graduate spots. I thought I would show her around the lab."

"Very good." Straus, still halfway across the lab, shot his arm out at her unceremoniously. "It's nice to meet you, Chou Jia."

"Oh!" the girl said, surprised at Straus trying to shake her hand from across the room. She dashed to him and took his hand.

"What makes you interested in the lab?"

"Well," she said, settling her nerves. "I think you have the best labs on the east coast. Georgetown will definitely be my top choice. What's that?" She pointed to the rows of black grids.

"Duke, our trap has been sprung. She wants to know about the Drive. Are you familiar with the Casimir effect?" he asked her.

She bit her lip. "Vaguely."

"The Casimir effect is a phenomenon that occurs when you place two neutrally charged plates extremely close together, which creates negative energy in the space between them. Basically, energy out of a vacuum. What we're doing here," he motioned to the rows of grids, "is exploiting the negative energy produced between subatomic fluctuations."

"Uh-huh."

"There are more quantum fluctuations happening on the outside of the plates than in between the plates, so there is a tremendous amount more of quantum bubbling going on outside of the plates, which pushes them together, creating energy... seemingly out of nothing. We've designed a grid system of plates that are one atom thick and with a space of only one atom wide—extremely small spaces. The smaller the space, the greater negative energy comes out of it. We believe by stacking the atomic plates together, you can create an enormous amount of energy in a very tiny space."

"And what will that do?"

"Ever see Star Trek?"

Duke rolled his eyes as if tired of his overused explanation.

"Of course," Chou Jia said.

"I predict that focusing that amount of energy into such a small space would effectively *bend space*. Like a warp drive."

"Really?"

Straus simply nodded.

"I've never heard of the Casimir effect doing *that*," she said.

"No one has... *yet*. Assuming our funding doesn't run out..." he sighed, souring the mood.

"Dr. Straus," Duke said, "we're trying to get her to *come* to this school, not chase her away..."

"Thanks so much for showing me all of this," she said, side-step- ping the awkward silence. "I would absolutely love to come here." She stepped over a stack of fallen papers and textbooks. "Thanks for showing me the lab, Dr. Straus. I hope to come back soon."

Straus only nodded and walked away. He sat at a rickety wooden table and poured himself a cup of coffee, letting out a slow breath.

"Do you think we'll be able to finish the Drive?" Duke poured a cup as well.

"I do, yes. I'm optimistic."

"But you're *always* optimistic. You see a half-full glass when there's only a drop left."

"Is that wrong?"

Duke shrugged. "Guess it depends on what you can do with that last final drop."

"Sometimes the final drop is more important than the whole cup," he said, slurping the last of his coffee.

CHAPTER 2: SEPTEMBER 1ST, 1986

TIME IS RUNNING OUT.

Straus picked up a sandwich from a campus deli, his mind muddled. A familiar anxiety churned within, punctuated by panic. It was a panic not about his research. It was a deep-rooted and unspecified paranoia that gnawed at the back of his mind, telling him... something—that time was running out?

Time for what?

He pulled into the parking garage of his apartment building and stared at the cinder blocks through the windshield, waiting for the voices to come—to urge, to incite, to cover his face in a cold sweat. He wanted to get the torrent of voices out of his head before entering his home. "Huh," he said to the empty car. He realized the voices were only from men. It surprised him that he had never thought of it before. He also faced the growing realization that the voices were getting worse.

He walked through the apartment door and saw his wife, Jo, sitting on the couch, breastfeeding. She looked up at him with a concerned frown she reserved only for her husband. "What're you doing home so early? It's not even lunch."

"I wasn't feeling well, had a... bad headache during class."

"Oh..." She switched the baby over her shoulder as it burped. "Just a headache?"

"Yep." He yanked a chair from the kitchen table, sat down, and unwrapped his sandwich.

She sidled up, sitting next to him with the baby in her lap. "We had a good day together—went out to the park. Did you see that it rained a little in the morning?"

"I was teaching."

"Why are you in a bad mood?"

"I'm sorry, hun. Worried about the Drive. Not sure if my grant will get renewed." He took a bite of his sandwich. "I *need* to get the Drive done. Something feels wrong. We have to finish it and finish it soon."

"Want to say hi to James?" She placed the baby into his lap.

He brought James up to his chest, looking into his eyes. The baby looked back with a wide smile. "How's my boy? What great wonders has he accomplished today?" The baby giggled and hopped on his father's lap.

"Why don't you go over and relax in front of the TV for a bit?" Jo offered.

Straus punched the button on the television and lay on the couch as a commercial for laundry detergent flashed across the screen. He suddenly sat up, staring at the screen. "Unbelievable."

Jo walked into the room. "What's wrong?"

"The Russians shot down a commercial airliner from the States," he said, gesturing to the screen.

"What're you talking about?" She pointed at the TV. There was only cascading laundry powder flashing over the screen. A split second later, it flickered with an emergency broadcast banner showing images of smoldering wreckage spewing smoke. "How did you see the news before—"

"Hang on." He turned up the volume.

A newscaster's voice came, "...not certain at the moment what the exact provocation was. We are confirming now that flight 007 from Anchorage to Seoul, South Korea has crashed and it is believed to be a deliberate attack from the Soviet Union on the aircraft. All 269 passengers on the plane are feared dead, including congressman, Lawrence McDonald."

Straus shook his head. "Those poor people. The Soviets will just keep provoking us—stockpiling nukes—and the U.S. will just keep toppling one communist regime after another, killing thousands of innocent lives. Will it ever change?"

"Things change," Jo said, bouncing the baby. "Sometimes it just takes time and the right kind of people."

"That's enough for one day. There's only so much of this world I can take." He switched off the TV set.

Noon turned to evening as Straus napped. He didn't dream but his mind wasn't empty. A rattling of distant voices bubbled up in his mind as he felt himself floating. An infinite horizon lay before him, one seamless ribbon of black. He was floating alone, in space, swathed by starlight. A cloud of silver gas burst around him, swirling with lightning and thunder. A chorus of voices rained down. Each raindrop was a shout or whisper that erupted in his ears. He tried flapping through the fog but was stalled by weightlessness. The voices stirred inside of him and chanted, *he is coming, he is coming, he is coming!* They crescendoed further, *HE IS COMING!*

He snapped awake and realized that the voices had assimilated from a sizzling sound in the kitchen. He looked over the couch and saw Jo moving a frying pan back and forth over the stove. He watched her hair sway in the pleasant way it did when she cooked.

"I'm sorry," he said, coming into the kitchen.

"For what?"

"Being grumpy earlier. It's hard for me sometimes." He touched the back of her apron and rested his forehead on her shoulder.

"It would be hard for anyone. Do you think the new medication is working better?"

"Too soon to tell. I accidentally told Jack Van Wert at work that I'm on meds."

"It's okay. He should know that schizophrenia isn't anyone's fault. It's just something you get, like pneumonia. You don't have any control over it."

He cringed.

"What?"

"I'm still not convinced it's schizophrenia."

"Tim, you hear voices. *Voices.* Auditory hallucinations are a hallmark of schizophrenia."

"I know. But there's more to it than just the voices. I—" he hesitated.

"What?"

"I don't always feel like... *me.* There's something on top of me or under me but it doesn't have anything to do with the *actual* me. And besides, the medications clearly aren't making the voices go away. If anything, they're stronger."

"Should I schedule an appointment to see the doctor tomorrow?"

"That's fine—oh, hey!" He ran out of the kitchen.

"What?" she called from behind.

"The comet that's been on the news... it's supposed to be the brightest tonight. It only comes around once every twenty years."

"Oh." She went back to the kitchen.

Straus ducked out onto their porch overlooking the Georgetown campus. Swinging his telescope from under the awning, he peered up into the night's sky and saw it—a smudge of blue smeared across the sky. He followed the blue trail as it moved, ignoring the chanting voices bubbling in his mind.

ABOUT THE AUTHOR

Wick Welker writes in multiple genres including medicine, post-apocalyptic and science fiction. He is also a medical doctor who practices critical care medicine and anesthesiology. He currently writes and practices medicine in Minnesota. He is supported by an amazing cat, an incredible wife and an adorable baby girl.

facebook.com/wickwelker
twitter.com/wickwelker
amazon.com/Wick-Welker/e/B00J21FNRI%3Fref=dbs_a_mng_rwt_scns_share

Printed in Great Britain
by Amazon

18748328R00458